THE MAGICAL MATCHMAKER'S LEGACY: BOOKS 1-4

COLLECTION OF SWEET SCOTTISH TIME TRAVEL ROMANCES

BETHANY CLAIRE

Editor: J.J. Archer
Cover Designed by Sarah Hansen, Okay Creations

Available In eBook, Paperback, & Hardback

eBook ISBN: 978-1-947731-54-7
Paperback ISBN: 978-1-947731-65-3
Hardback ISBN: 978-1-947731-66-0

http://www.bethanyclaire.com

AUTHOR NOTE

"Morna's Spell" is the SWEET/CLEAN version of "Love Beyond Time," originally published in 2013 by Bethany Claire.

"Morna's Secret" is the SWEET/CLEAN version of "Love Beyond Reason," originally published in 2013 by Bethany Claire.

"The Conalls' Magical Yuletide" is the SWEET/CLEAN version of "A Conall Christmas," originally published in 2013 by Bethany Claire.

"Morna's Magic" is the SWEET/CLEAN version of "Love Beyond Hope," originally published in 2014 by Bethany Claire.

MORNA'S SPELL

CHAPTER 1

ustin, TX - Present Day

Sun beamed against the windows as I walked down the line of tiny faces peering up at me. I knelt before each one, holding up a number between one and ten on my fingers, looking over each little body to ensure that laces were tied, backpacks on, and lunch boxes were in hand as I waited for their answer. As each called out the right number with a prideful smile, I gave them their daily sticker and moved on to the next student.

I could see Anthony three students down, pestering the unfortunate Harrison, who was standing in front of him and blowing in his ears every time he turned around to face the front of the line. As Grace called out number seven and asked for help with her laces, I threw my most stern *cut it out* look in Anthony's direction. The ornery-but-exceedingly-bright child caught my meaning and returned the look with a sheepish grin as he stepped away from Harrison and stood still as a statue.

Two students later, I stood in front of Anthony. He rattled off the number nine that I was holding up in front of him before I even had a chance to look him over. Both laces were undone, and he had split his zipper so that only the middle of his jacket was actually closed.

"Good job, Anthony! Here's your sticker. Still haven't mastered the old shoelaces yet, I see?"

"No, Ms. Mothgomfrey. I been working and working at it, but I just can't seem to get that rabbit to go around the hole."

I repressed an eye roll as I bent to tie his shoes. Anthony's speech was better than all of the other kindergarteners in his class, and I knew he could say my name, Ms. Montgomery, without problem, but he just lived for the giggles of all the other students every time he said my name that way.

"Well, those rabbits can be tricky, but you just keep working at it. You'll get it soon."

"I sure will! I promise! I sure am tired of watching you tie my shoes every day. Ya know, I'm five years old, it's humilly-aten."

"Well, Anthony. That's sure a big word. Where'd you hear that?"

"That's what my Mama said to Daddy the other day. She said it was humilly-aten to be married to a man that thought it was okay to watch television all day long on Sundays while she cleaned and cooked and did laundry and that he needed to get his fat, lazy a . . ."

The bell rang, interrupting his speech and saving the day as far as I was concerned. I should've seen that coming. I knew better than to ask Anthony an open-ended question.

I quickly checked the last few in line and went to the front of the classroom, motioning for the day's leader, Izzy, to hold open the door while everyone walked outside. Once everyone was out of the classroom and Izzy had returned to her place in the front of the line, I led them down the hallway, smiling at the sound of their tiny, squeaky shoes as they pitter-pattered single-file behind me.

---

*T*wenty minutes later, when the last child had been picked up, I shut the door to my classroom and plopped ungracefully down at my desk. I gently pressed my fingertips against my eyelids in an effort to push away the day's stress. It seemed to help a little, so I stood up, stretching mildly before I tucked my long, dark hair, which was now frizzing after being out in the wind, behind my ears.

I pushed my chair in and circled the room for a quick sweep before I headed home. I bent over every few feet to pick up the various crayons, chunks of Play-Doh, and construction paper scattered across the carpet. I knew the custodian would come along behind me shortly, but I just couldn't bear for her to see the classroom in this state of dishevelment. As I looked over the mess that scattered from one work center to another, I thought to myself, not for the first time today, how glad I was that I had decided against adding finger-painting to the day's lesson plans.

With my arms filled to capacity with various craft litter, I deposited the load into the trash can next to my desk. With a glance around the room, I decided I was satisfied enough to call it a day.

I stacked the handwriting exercises for the letter "G" on top of my desk to grade first thing Monday morning, and I was buttoning my jacket when my classroom aide, Mitsy, opened the door and stepped inside.

"Are you ready for your big date tonight? I talked to Brian and he said Daniel is super-excited!"

I spun quickly to face her, panic settling in my gut. "What? Oh, Mitsy, I totally forgot! Look. Maybe you could just call him and see if we could do it next Friday? You know, I'm really swamped right now. We'd both have more fun if we did it when I wasn't so distracted."

Mitsy placed her hands on both hips and narrowed her eyes as she spoke to me again. "I will do no such thing! And if you think you are going to get out of yet one more date, well, let me tell you, Miss I-have-no-problem-dying-alone, I am not going to let you weasel out of this one! He's a great guy, Bri. I haven't actually met him, but Brian's known him all of his life. His wife died two years ago, and he needs to get out of the house just about as badly as you need to. Just look at it as something that will benefit you both."

I turned away from her as I closed the coat closet and walked back over to my desk to get my purse. "I'm not trying to weasel out of it. I just really need to work on lesson plans for next week, and I think I'm catching a cold."

Mitsy blocked the door to the classroom and caught my wrist as she dragged me back over to the filing cabinet beside my desk. I knew what she was about to grab before she opened the cabinet.

"You are not catching a cold, and don't you dare try to tell me that you have lesson plans to work on." I watched as she paused briefly to yank open the first drawer. "Let's see. What do we have here? All of Monday's lesson plans in this folder? Check. Tuesday? Check. Wednesday? Check. Do I really need to go on, Bri? You should just make it easier on yourself and tell me you're going, because you are, either way. All there's left for you to decide is how soon you want me to get out of your hair." She smiled sweetly and placed my folders back into the cabinet, slamming the drawer shut with immense satisfaction.

Reluctantly, I grinned and held my hands up in surrender. "Fine. Fine. I'll go. But you're going to let me pick out my own bridesmaid's dress for your wedding, right?

Mitsy thrust her hand in my direction. "Deal."

<hr>

I'd just zipped up the back of my dress when the doorbell rang at 7:30. *At least he's punctual,* I thought as I tried to put an earring on with one hand while attempting to slip into my heels with the other.

Taking a quick glance in the mirror, I slathered on some lip gloss, held my hand in front of my face to check my breath, and headed to answer the front door.

Daniel held a bouquet of flowers so that they covered his face, and as he slowly lowered them I had to swallow the audible gasp that crept up my throat. I was able to manage a polite, "Hello. Please come in," as my eyes looked over the thick, gray hair that covered his head.

As he made his way through the doorway, I spotted a few wiry hairs sticking out from the opening in his ear, and the abnormally large nose that some men get when they age was evident from his profile.

He was handsome . . . for a man in his sixties. As I shut the front door, I found myself wishing I'd had that glass of wine I'd thought about when I got home from work.

Steeling myself, I turned to face him. "It's nice to meet you. The flowers are lovely. Thank you. Why don't I go put them in some water, and then we can leave?"

He extended them to me and as he grinned slightly, I could see that his eyes looked exceedingly kind. "I can tell I wasn't exactly what you were expecting. I guess Brian and Mitsy didn't tell you much."

I walked quickly into the kitchen, keeping my back to him so that he couldn't see my face as I spoke. "No, not too much. I know that you're a dentist and are related to Brian. I assumed you were a cousin."

The old man chuckled slightly, and his cheeks reddened as I walked back toward him. "My sons are his cousins. I'm his uncle."

"Oh." I stared down at my purse awkwardly, wishing I actually had something to look for inside it.

"Look. I don't want to make you uncomfortable, but we've both gotten all dressed up. Why don't we go ahead and go out to eat and visit with each other a little bit, then I'll bring you back here and we'll forget this whole thing ever happened. No harm, no foul. What do you say?"

He extended a hand in my direction, and sympathy washed through me as I reached to take it. He obviously had no more idea of what he was getting himself into than I did. "Good food, nice company. What could it hurt? Let's get out of here."

As he held the front door open, I walked straight into the person walking rather purposefully toward my front door.

"Mom?" I said.

I repeated myself for good measure as the uncomfortable feeling of shock ran down my spine for the second time. "Mom? What are you doing here? You're supposed to be in D.C., aren't you?"

She stepped back so that we could look at each other from a more appropriate distance, "Well, I'm happy to see you too, Bri. I'm glad I caught you before you left. I don't have a key to your new place. We need to talk right away. I have some very exciting news!"

I watched as she bounced up and down, the same thirteen-year-old trapped in a fifty-year-old's body that she'd always been. I knew the exact instant she spotted Daniel, still holding the door wide open, watching the spectacle.

As her eyes widened, she stopped bouncing and immediately went into flirt mode—another one of my mother's classic qualities. "Well, hello sir. And who might you be?" She slowly stretched a hand in his direction.

"Name's Daniel. I was just leaving." He paused to pat me on the back and then walked through the door. "It was nice to meet you, Bri. I'll see you at the wedding."

I waved politely in his direction and ushered my mother inside, shutting the door behind me. She spun on me just as I'd latched the door.

"Who was that? Very handsome, but a little old for you, don't you think, dear?"

I leaned against the back of the door and exhaled loudly. "Very long story, Mom. But remind me that I need to have a conversation with Mitsy about what exactly it is that she thinks my standards are."

She laughed, obviously understanding the situation. "Well, seems like she gets my standards just fine. Do you have his phone number?"

I rolled my eyes and made my way into the living room. "No, Mom, I don't, but I'm sure Mitsy will give it to you if you want. Now, what's going on? Is everything okay?"

We sat down on the couch facing each other, and Mom excitedly reached for my hand as she told me her news.

"I got the grant!"

I couldn't help but smile at the excited expression on her face. "The grant to resume your work on Conall Castle? That's great, Mom!"

She squealed as she continued, "Yes, Bri, that grant. It's been nearly twenty years, but I'm finally going to get to go back and figure out what really happened."

My mother, Adelle Montgomery as most people knew her, was a world-renowned archaeologist. Her big break had come while working on an excavating project near the remains of Conall Castle in Scotland.

The tragedy of Conall Castle was one of the most well-known legends in Scottish history, and the mystery behind the destruction of the Conall clan had remained unsolvable for over four hundred years.

Within weeks of beginning her first lead dig at the ruins, Mom had discovered an underground library that, due to the strong stone base of the castle, had survived the infamous fire. It took weeks for Mom and her team to dig their way into the library, but once inside, they found countless archaeological treasures that had brought Adelle into the forefront of archaeology. Dozens of journals, hundreds of letters, and countless documents detailing family lineage with birth, death, and marriage certificates were all found within the library.

The find had propelled her career into overdrive. While the documents found in the basement shed a great light on the mysterious clan, none of the documents had solved the mystery of who had murdered the Conalls, afterwards burning the ancient castle to the ground.

After years of no success in solving the mystery, she moved on from her work on the Conall dig to other projects that sent her all over the world during the past twenty years; all the while, she had been hoping for a reason to resume her work on Conall Castle.

"And I haven't told you the best part!" She squeezed my hand and bounced up and down like my kindergarteners before recess.

I sat quietly, waiting for her to tell me, knowing it would drive her crazy.

She stopped bouncing. "Aren't you going to say, 'what'?"

I laughed and indulged her. "What's the best part?"

"You're going to Scotland with me! I've already registered you as my assistant on the dig."

I jerked up off the couch, hitting the coffee table and sloshing water out of the cup that sat in front of me. "What? You know I can't. I have school. I teach kindergarteners. That's like asking a substitute to walk straight through the gates of Hell!"

"Oh, hush! You exaggerate. You haven't taken a personal day since you started teaching six years ago. I know you have a ton of days built up. Besides, we'll only be gone a couple of weeks. And you have Mitsy. Your students will be fine. You know you've always wanted to go to Scotland."

I reached up and squeezed the bridge of my nose with my fingers. Last minute travel plans did not appeal to me at all, but she was right about one thing. "I have always wanted to go to Scotland."

"Great! I'm going to go book our flights now. We leave Sunday."

Before I could put up a fight, she was on her way back to her car to grab her computer. Recognizing I'd been beaten, I walked back into the entryway and sank down beside the front door next to my school bag. Reaching inside, I grabbed my planner and tried to figure out what I was going to tell my principal.

CHAPTER 2

*S*cotland—1645

*T*he eldest Conall brother paced back and forth outside his father's chambers, reluctant to leave his father's side but understanding the laird's desire to speak to his youngest son alone. After what seemed like hours, Eoin heard the door begin to creak, and Arran Conall emerged from their father's room.

Standing at over six foot four, Arran was at least two inches shorter than Eoin. With blond hair that fell to his shoulders and vibrant blue eyes, Arran was very popular with the lasses of Conall Keep.

Although Eoin knew his own good looks were a fair rival to his brother's, he was careful not to earn a reputation for frivolous dalliances. His younger brother, however, embraced his reputation as a rake; it was a rare evening that Arran spent alone, and even rarer that the same woman was found twice in his company.

Arran's carefree nature and love of life were contagious, and there were few times when Eoin had seen his brother without a smile. But this time, when he exited their father's room, Arran's smile was gone. The red tip of his nose and the strain in his eyes revealed that Arran was too proud to let the flood of tears flow.

Knowing any attempt to comfort would only embarrass him further, Eoin looked at the ground as he entered their father's chamber. Eoin had been only five when his mother passed away while giving birth to Arran, and all

Eoin remembered about her was spending afternoons in her beloved garden, watching her tend the plants with exquisite care.

His father, on the other hand, had been his constant companion. Eoin was the spitting image of his father—same long, dark hair and ebony eyes; same quiet-yet-confident demeanor, so different from his brother's loud and boisterous way of life. As children, Eoin and Arran depended on their father for everything, and although his father had spent the past thirty years preparing him, Eoin had never expected to be laird of Conall Castle so soon.

He would have done anything to prevent his father's fate, but as his gaze fell upon the laird, Eoin knew there was nothing to be done. While the elder Conall had been thrown from horses many times in his life, the fall Eoin's father had taken that morning tossed his aging body onto a rocky hillside. The damage inflicted was too much for his body to heal. His father was dying, and all Eoin could do now was sit at his bedside and comfort him during his last minutes.

*A*lasdair prepared to impart his final wish upon his eldest son as he watched him enter the room. He tried to sit up as Eoin approached his bedside. The thought of his heir seeing him in such a weakened state pained him almost as much as the crushed ribs and deflated lung that forced his breath to come in short rasps. He was a warrior, built strong like both his sons. He found it difficult to believe that it would be a creature as gentle as a horse that would send him to his deathbed, but he supposed that was just another sign that while the body and mind age, the soul often remains oblivious to fragile bones, creaking joints, and moments of forgetfulness.

Despite grayed hair and failing body, Alasdair knew in his heart he was still the youthful, handsome lad who wanted nothing more than to steal another kiss from his beloved wife. It had been twenty-five years since Elspeth passed away, and he still couldn't think of her without tears springing up in his dark eyes.

He pushed thoughts of her away, for he knew he would see his beloved soon enough. As his son sat down beside him, Alasdair allowed his thoughts to drift to the burden he knew he must place upon Eoin's shoulders.

Alasdair would not tell his son the true reason for his insistence upon a marriage between Eoin and Blaire MacChristy. For while he knew the true nature of Morna's predictions, Eoin had never known the witch. Alasdair knew if his dying wish for his son was based on some crazed long-dead aunt's predictions, it would only make Eoin even more resistant to the marriage.

It had long been believed that his son's betrothal to Blaire was to ensure the protection of the MacChristy territory. Donal MacChristy was laird over the smallest castle and territory in Scotland. With poor people and few provisions for safety, the MacChristy clan was ever in need of help from neighboring allies. It had been great fortune that Alasdair had always been good friends with Donal as it had made arranging the betrothal that much easier and more believable.

Alasdair knew that if Morna's predictions and spell came true, Blaire MacChristy would soon be replaced with a lass from the twenty-first century, and he was certain Eoin would not remain oblivious to the strange happenings. To help ease his son's shock, Alasdair had ensured that all of Morna's journals detailing her prediction, spell, and wish could be found in the witch's beloved secret room in the castle's basement, along with the spelled plaque showing Blaire's picture. He had also told the prediction and story to his faithful housemaid, Mary, but he wasn't sure if she'd believed his outrageous tale.

After Morna's death, Alasdair had discovered her journals detailing the enchanted plaque and how she planned for the swap to take place. The identity spell had already been set before Morna passed. Regardless of what happened, there would be a girl born many years from now, identical in appearance to Blaire MacChristy. The exchange of the two girls hinged upon the plaque Morna placed in the center of her sanctuary. If both Blaire and the identical girl were to see and read the words on the plaque out loud during some point in their lives, their paths would combine, and they would switch places in time. This part of Morna's plan was entirely dependent upon fate, and Alasdair strongly doubted if any such fantastic occurrence would ever take place. Regardless of his misgivings, he refused to betray his sister's memory.

"Son." Alasdair's chest began to weigh down on itself, begging him not to say anymore, but he refused to let his body fail before he said his peace. "I doona want ye and Arran to mourn me for long. I have had a full life. Everything I ever wanted, I have possessed."

"I don't want to hear ye say another word about that, Father. Just get some rest, and ye will feel much better come morning."

"Ye can hold your lies, son. My body may be weak, but my mind is sharp. Ye know as well as I do that I am dying. I need ye to make peace with that as well. For I expect ye to continue with the wedding plans as if nothing has happened. Ye will be laird of Conall Castle within the hour. It falls to ye to watch over not only our territory but the MacChristy's, as well, by marrying Blaire."

*D*read crept up Eoin's spine at the thought of going through with his marriage to Blaire, but he refused to dwell on such things right now. He had never argued or denied his father anything, and he certainly wasn't going to start tonight.

"I want ye to send word to Laird MacChristy come sunup. Suggest that Blaire come to reside here at once, so that ye can make yer preparations together. I believe the wedding should be set for three weeks' time. I know she tries yer patience, but I expect ye to treat and cherish her as I did yer mother."

Eoin didn't believe himself capable of showing anyone the kind of adoration that his father had shown his mother. He didn't really think anyone other than his father was capable of loving that deeply, especially not himself. Despite having pursued significantly fewer lasses than Arran, he was no less talented at courtship. But he had never met a lass who made him, even for a moment, dread spending the rest of his life without her.

He would not tell his father that, so instead, just as Alasdair Conall took his last breath and left this world to meet his beloved Elspeth once more, Eoin vowed, "I promise, Father. I promise to marry Blaire, and I promise to try."

CHAPTER 3

ver the Atlantic Ocean—Present Day

"*B*ri, they're about to serve breakfast. Why don't you wake up and we'll talk about our plans for after we land?"

I started at the sound of my mother's voice beside me. I was in a deep sleep, and—as I tended to do when I slept sitting up—I snorted slightly as I came awake and threw my arms up to stretch, smacking the man sitting beside me as I did so. Only semi-conscious, I didn't take notice of my mistake until I caught the man's glare out of the corner of my eye.

"I'm so sorry." By reflex, I reached over and touched the man's arm as if he were one of my students who had fallen down on the playground. "Are you okay? I was still half . . ." I trailed off when I saw the man's glare transform into a lingering smile, urging me to snatch my hand away with a little more force than was probably necessary.

"That's alright, sweetheart." The man's eyes roamed over me as his grin spread.

I quickly faced my mother and scooted away from the man as much as was possible in the few inches that lay on either side of me.

"I was having the most horrible dream. I dreamed that Anthony, my ornery one, led a class revolt against the substitute. They had her tied to a chair and there was finger paint everywhere." I cringed at the images of sticky, wet fingers smearing themselves across the classroom rug and bookshelves.

Mom laughed as she took a cup of coffee for each of us from the flight attendant. "Honey, they're five years old. They can't even tie their own shoes. They won't be taking the substitute hostage."

"I know, but the finger paint is certainly a possibility. I really should've locked that up in the cabinet. I'm just exhausted. I was up at the school until one this morning planning lessons and getting materials organized and making sure Mitsy had a handle on all of the plans."

"It's all going to be fine, Bri. What did your principal say when you asked for time off?"

"He wasn't thrilled, but I think more than anything he was shocked. The only personal days I've taken since I started were when I came down with pneumonia last winter, and then it was only because I truly thought I was going to die. He knew it must be important. He just asked that I try to be back by the Monday after Thanksgiving and to make sure that the substitute had adequate plans."

"Well, that's great. See? You have nothing to worry about. Just try and put all that out of your mind, dear. I really do need your help. I can't let this grant money go to waste."

"You're right. I won't mention it again. I'm here to help in any way I can." I smiled when I saw my mother's eyes lock on the food cart that was headed our way, and I knew our conversation was over. Mom was one of those few blessed people who could eat all she wanted and never gain a pound.

I watched as she inhaled the powdered eggs and cold croissant that sat untouched on my own tray and tried to focus my mind on something other than the pity I felt for the courageous substitute that was filling my shoes.

As I tried to rack my brain for something to ponder, I realized the sad truth: I had little in my life that was out of the norm to focus on. My drastic social decline since moving to Austin had me well on my way to becoming the Miss Havisham of the Lone Star State. I spent every spare second either working on my home or working on my classroom. While I loved the kiddos in my class, I was ashamed that I'd let my life get so unexciting.

I was at a point where many of the goals I'd set for myself had been met. I'd worked my way through college. I was happy with my job, happy with myself, and I owned my own home. But I was ready for my life to encompass more than just myself.

I wanted a friend, a husband, a partner to spend my life with. I wanted children who'd call me "mom" rather than "teacher" or "Ms. Mothgomfrey." But with my social circle filled with PTA moms rather than eligible bachelors, my chances of finding anyone were pretty dismal.

Maybe a handsome Scot will sweep me off my feet? Because that happens to teachers from Austin every day, and there's sure to be a lot of eligible bachelors at the castle ruins . . . where no one has lived in four hundred years.

I shook my head, embarrassed at my little daydream, and tried to pull myself back to reality. "Okay, Mom. What's the plan?"

"Well . . ." I watched as she spoke in between mouthfuls of food. "When we land in Edinburgh, we'll pick up our rental car and drive to the National Museum of Scotland. They've been keeping all of the documents we found at the site. I already have clearance, so I should be able to take a lot of things with us. We'll start there by combing through the documents we already have and see if that brings to light anything we might have missed during the first dig."

"Ok, sounds good to me. Did you make any hotel reservations when you booked our flight?"

"No. I don't want to stay in Edinburgh. I think we should go ahead and try to get into the Highlands, closer to the ruins. I remember a little bed and breakfast we used to pass that was on the side of the road leading to the site. It was so charming on the outside. I always wanted to stay there, but never got the chance. We always just camped out on the grounds. I have no idea whether it's still there or not, but I'd like to take a chance and see."

"Alright. Anything else I need to know?" My blood pressure rose slightly when I learned that our night's accommodations were anything but certain, but I swallowed my panic and set my mind to go with the flow.

"Yes . . . you're going to need to drive. The rental's a standard." The corner of Mom's mouth pulled upward as she suppressed a grin.

"Okay, no problem." I chuckled slightly. Mom was an infamously bad driver even with an automatic transmission. I had never intended to let her drive in the first place.

A chime overhead warned us we were beginning our descent into Edinburgh, and the captain came over the speaker system to ask everyone to return to their seats.

"Are you ready for this, sweetheart? I've always wanted to take you to Scotland, but you were always either in school or teaching school when I was here. I just know you are going to love it." She stood and motioned for me to switch seats with her. "Here. I want you to look out the window. It's beautiful."

I obediently scooted over by the window and raised the plastic shade to look outside. I stared out over the lush landscape and immediately understood Mom's love for this country. It was where she belonged. I knew if I didn't live in the United States, she would have moved here permanently after her divorce.

The ground slowly came closer, and as the wheels touched down on the runway I felt a small tug deep inside. Maybe this was where I belonged as well. Excitement built as we taxied to the gate.

Scotland was going to be good to us. I could tell.

S cotland – 1645

E oin heard his brother's footsteps before he saw Arran plop down next to him and swing his feet over the side of the stone wall that surrounded the castle's exterior. The rocky coast that encircled their home calmed him, and Eoin often escaped here when something troubled him.

"Cheer up, brother. We haven't seen Blaire in over ten years. Just because the two of ye were determined to make each other miserable back then, doesn't mean ye will now. After all, ye certainly aren't the foolish lad ye were a decade ago."

Eoin turned to look at his brother. "Perhaps, but I canna stop thinking about the young lass who shot me in the arse with an arrow because I refused to let her have my horse. I still bear the scar! I canna imagine that she could have changed enough for me to feel anything for her."

Placing his arm around his brother's shoulder, Arran smiled as he spoke. "Who said ye have to feel anything for her? All ye have to do is marry the lass. Perhaps with time, you'll grow to love her. Blaire was quite the beauty and, from what I've heard, she has only gotten prettier since we last saw her. I feel sure a number o' lads would gladly take yer place. Consider yerself lucky, brother. Ye could be betrothed to Laird Kinnaird's eldest daughter. Ye would be, if the old toad had anything to say about it. If I remember correctly, she was just as disagreeable as Blaire but not nearly as comely."

"You're right, o' course," Eoin admitted. "It's just that I'd rather not attach myself to someone I barely know. And as for growing to love her with time, if she is even remotely as difficult as she was as a young lass, I doona think her beauty will be enough to stir my emotions."

As Eoin listened to Arran's laughter at his own disdain for his fiancée, the sound of footsteps made both men turn their heads to the trail leading to the castle.

"Here she comes. Let us go find out if your betrothed is apt to be as difficult to live with as ye seem to think she will be. I, for one, look forward to having a lass about." Arran stood and waited for Eoin to lead the way.

"As if you lack the company of lasses." Eoin placed his hand on Arran's shoulder. "Let me make one thing clear to ye, brother. Regardless of how I may feel for her, Blaire will be my wife. Ye are not to flirt with her, understood?"

"I would never! I may love the company of women, but I am quite looking forward to ye having a lass of yer own. Come. Ye best get that look off of yer face before we greet her, or I predict that ye will start things off with yer bride on a bad foot, no? I doona think most lasses enjoy being greeted with a look o' pure dread and disdain."

"Right." Eoin plastered on the largest grin he could manage as he stepped back through the side window from which he had climbed out onto the wall and made his way to the castle's entrance. He had just stepped into the hallway in front of the grand staircase when he heard Blaire's voice echoing through the hallways.

"There is no use in standing here staring at me all day. Unless ye expect me to carry all my things to my room myself, and surely the laird has more manners than that. But then again, I'm having a hard time remembering very many good qualities about him. He couldn't even be bothered to greet me upon my arrival. I doona know what he has instructed ye, but I demand to be placed in whatever room is farthest from the laird's. We are not married yet. I will only share a room after the wedding, and even then, only if he insists."

Eoin stepped onto the staircase where Blaire could see him and interrupted her before she could berate the old stable master further. "Hello, Blaire. Welcome to Conall Castle. I apologize for not being here when ye arrived. I was sitting out on the wall when I saw ye headed this way." Reaching the bottom of the staircase, Eoin stood before Blaire and placed her hand in his. Flashing a smile that would make the most beautiful of women melt, he gently kissed the top of her hand, his black eyes piercing her own.

"I'm not interested in yer charms, Laird Conall." Jerking her hand away, Blaire bent and began piling her belongings into the stable master's arms. "Believe me, this will be a marriage in contract and nothing more. Any man who would agree to such an arrangement is obviously deranged. If it were up to me, I would be laird of the MacChristy keep after my father's passing. I would do a fine job, most likely better than him, but everyone seems to think women are only capable of running a household, so I'm being married off.

Do ye not think ye and my father could have made an alliance of safety without me being part o' the bargain?"

Blaire stopped fooling with her things, apparently just noticing that the old stable master was already holding more than he could carry. Eoin didn't move as she walked right up to him and jabbed two of her fingers into the center of his chest, her eyes flaring with anger.

"But no. The great Eoin is too small a man to find a woman of his own. He is happy to wed someone who does not love him, care for him, or like him."

Eoin's temper rose as Blaire's fingers continued to jab into his ribs. Seething, he grabbed both of her wrists. "Ye can set the lass's belongings down, Kip," he said, meeting Blaire's defiant gaze. "Go see that her horse is tied safely in the stables, and show her escorts to the dining hall so that they can have a good meal after their journey."

"Right away, sir." The old man struggled to set the large pile down neatly, then took off as quickly as he could out the grand doors.

"As for ye," Eoin released Blaire's wrists but continued to stand within inches of her and hold her gaze. "Has it ever occurred to ye that I may be as reluctant toward this marriage as yerself?"

"Not possible," Blaire muttered, lifting her chin.

"Aye, tis very possible. This betrothal was arranged between my father and yers. I was informed of it as a young lad and was as helpless in the matter as ye. As for yer other demands . . ." He stood straighter, looking down at her, unflinching. "Yer belongings are to be brought to the room directly across from mine. It has already been prepared for your arrival. And while I won't *insist*, upon our wedding night I would ask that ye move into my chambers immediately, Lady Blaire. It is my intention that this be a real marriage in every sense o' the word."

"Ahem . . ." Arran cleared his throat as he walked into the room. "Well hello, Blaire. Had I known the two of ye were going to get along so quickly, I would have given ye some privacy and welcomed ye in the morning. I apologize for the intrusion."

"Do not make the mistake of assuming this is how it appears, brother." Eoin stepped back from Blaire and faced his brother. "Please help me take Lady MacChristy's belongings to the Lavender Room."

"But I have not yet had the chance to properly greet yer fiancée." Arran stepped to take Blaire's hand, but she quickly jerked it away.

"Doona bother. I'm sure beneath yer welcoming façade ye are equally as lacking in manners as yer brother." She snarled her upper lip. "I have often heard it said that ye were the fairer of the two Conall brothers, but I would have to disagree." She quickly whirled to face Eoin again, "Now. I have had enough of both of the legendary Conall brothers for one evening. If ye can simply point me in the direction of food, I can assure ye that I can find the way myself."

Beyond stunned, both brothers pointed to the double doors to her right, staring wide-eyed as she stormed out of the entranceway and through the doors to which they'd pointed. Arran was the first to speak. "By all the saints, brother! I do believe ye were right about the lass. She is quite the beauty, but I'd be wary of a marriage to her, as well."

"Aye. I told ye so." Bending, Eoin began lifting Blaire's belongings, leaving half for his brother, and nodded his head toward the staircase so that Arran would follow.

"I know just what ye need, brother," said Arran. "Let us ride out in the morning and spend the fortnight before yer wedding enjoying yer last few days of freedom! It would do ye good to visit a pub or two with your brother before ye're strapped down to the wench who's soon to be sleeping across the hall from ye. Mary would be more than happy to help with the wedding preparations, and if what I have seen tonight of yer future bride is any indication, she willna be wanting yer help even if ye are here."

"Nothing sounds better, but I doubt my absence would do anything to improve the lass's mood." Before Eoin could speak another word, the doors out of which Blaire had gone burst open once more and she stepped back into the grand entranceway.

"If ye call that slop that was waiting in the dining hall 'food,' I shall starve to death during my imprisonment here! I refuse to eat one bite of it. I expect much better out of the morning's meal. Now if ye don't mind, I will follow the two of ye to my chambers, where I will spend the rest of my night."

As they trudged up the staircase, balancing the loads of her belongings, Eoin leaned over to catch his brother's ear. "Ye're right. Time away from here is just what I need. We will ride out at first light."

---

*M*iles away, Ramsay Kinnaird stood before his large stone fireplace, downing yet another goblet of whisky, when his personal messenger entered the room.

"I'm afraid tis true, sir. Blaire MacChristy moved into Conall Castle this very evening, and she and Eoin Conall are to be married within a fortnight. It was arranged between the laird's father and Donal MacChristy himself. From what I hear, neither Eoin nor Blaire are looking forward to the marriage."

"I doona care one whit about their feelings toward their marriage!" roared Ramsay, slurring his words. "How dare Alasdair make such an arrangement? Donal MacChristy is laird over the smallest keep in all of Scotland, while my territory is by far the largest. With both Donal and myself having daughters of the same age, it is an insult of the deepest accord that Alasdair would pass over arranging a marriage with my daughter for Blaire MacChristy."

"I . . . I believe, sir, that the arrangement was made so that Alasdair could ensure protection for his good friend. As ye know, the MacChristys have been facing difficult times for years. Their land is too scarce and their people too poor to provide adequate protection should their territory be in danger. I do not believe Alasdair meant any disrespect to ye, sir."

"I know perfectly well what Alasdair's intentions were when he made the arrangement, you fool!" He threw the metal goblet into the flames, sloshing the contents of his cup, forcing the flames to heighten and roar at the alcohol's touch.

"I . . . my apologies, sir." The man backed up a few steps, fearing that the laird's temper was about to surge completely out of control. Far too many servants had disappeared simply because they had been in the wrong place at the wrong time when the laird flew into one of his violent rages.

"This will not stand, I can promise ye that. This marriage will provide no protection for the MacChristy clan, for I will wipe out all of the Conalls. Afterward, it will only be a matter of time before the MacChristys wither and die of their own accord. Once his precious Blaire is murdered before she is comfortably settled in her new home, the old laird will be so heartbroken, he will care for his territory even less than he does now." Storming from the room, Ramsay paused briefly, grabbing his messenger by the throat. "If ye so much as breathe a word of my intentions to anyone, I will wipe ye and yer entire family from the face of this earth."

Shoving the servant to the ground, Ramsay Kinnaird flew out of the room, his murderous plan taking shape as he went.

CHAPTER 5

S *cotland – Present Day*

A s usual, everything took twice as long as planned. Despite the fact that our plane had landed early that morning, it was close to six p.m. Dusk was beginning to set in as we loaded the documents from the museum into the small compact rental and headed out of the city.

Several hours later, hungry and exhausted, we finally spotted the small inn that Mom had remembered. I parked in front of the charming two-story home and flipped on the interior lights of the cramped car as I pulled out a map.

"What do you think? Are we close enough to the ruins to stop for the night?"

Yawning, Mom stretched and nodded.

"Yes. We're only about thirty minutes away, and I've always wanted to try this place out. It looks great, doesn't it?"

"Yes, it does. Let's go. I'm totally exhausted."

We unloaded our suitcases and made our way to the inn's entrance. Stepping inside the old wooden door, I smiled as the warmth of the fireplace to the left washed over me, melting away the icy feeling in my fingers and face.

I was loosening my scarf and unbuttoning my jacket when I heard a voice coming from the top of the stairs.

"Jerry! I think there's someone here. Go see if they will be wanting a room and, for God's sake, ask them if they want something to eat."

My stomach growled immediately at the mention of food. I hadn't eaten anything since the plane, and the one bite I'd had of the soggy powdered eggs hadn't held me for long. I reached down to pat my stomach, hoping it would stop growling at my request, just as the most miserable-looking man I'd ever seen walked our way from what appeared to be the kitchen.

Hunkered over, with a head covered in gray hair, he was far too skinny. He had the most severe-looking face, with a long, pointed nose and a chin that jutted far outward. I couldn't help but think that he more than slightly resembled Ebenezer Scrooge.

"Well, hello lassies," the man said with a large smile. "The two of ye look like ye're about to freeze to death, shivering in the doorway. Please, come in and I'll get ye something warm to eat, as I assume ye'll be staying the night." He quickly patted me on the shoulder and then walked back toward the kitchen, waving his hand so that we would follow.

I was certain my jaw visibly dropped, and it took me a few good seconds before I could follow. I glanced at my mother, who was staring back at me with a look of pure satisfaction.

"Never judge a book by its cover, Bri." She smiled and finally followed me.

Once inside the room, we were quickly whisked to a small table in the corner. Two steaming bowls of soup were placed in front of us, then the man's questions began.

"We're so glad to see the both of ye. First guests we've had here in a long while. Out o' the way as I'm sure ye know. Where are ye from? And what brings ye to this part o' the world?"

Mom spoke up first. "We're from the States—I live all over. Bri's my daughter, and she's a teacher from Austin, Texas. I'm here to do some archaeological work on the ruins of Conall Castle. I convinced Bri to come along and help."

"Ahh . . . Texas ye say?" The man turned and looked in my direction. "I know the whereabouts. My wife Gwendolyn grew up in San Antonio. She came here to visit her uncle as a young lass, about eighteen I think she was. I worked for the old man; from the second I saw her running through the field, trying to catch one of his sheep . . ."

He started laughing a deep, belly laugh that shook his whole body. I couldn't help but smile as well, the man's love for his wife evident with each heave of his shoulders.

"Well . . . I fell in love with her right then, and I knew that she wasn't going back to the United States."

"What's that, Jerry? What lies are you telling these poor women?" A petite woman with striking green eyes entered the kitchen, and after planting a kiss on her husband's cheek, came in our direction to greet us.

"I hope he's not boring you two to death with his tall tales. Let me guess, he was telling you about how he swept me off my feet and rendered me so senseless that I never went home. Well, he knows good and well it was this scenery I fell in love with, not this blithering old fool."

She winked over her shoulder at him, and I could tell by the twinkle in his eye he didn't believe a word of her teasing.

The rest of the evening flew by in a blur for the both of us. The old couple talked for hours, and I found myself captivated by the stories of their years spent together.

Finally, at half past eleven, we carried the last load of documents to a small room at the top of the stairs. Gwendolyn had attempted to give us each our own room, but Mom asked that we share, insisting that it would be easier to do research if we were in the same room.

As I listened to Mom mess up the covers while she tossed and turned in the antique bed, I washed my face, brushed my teeth, and pulled on my favorite flannel pajamas. Exhausted, I crawled into the bed and stuck my icy cold feet up against the warmth of my mother's sock-warmed toes.

I sighed and rolled over in an effort to claim back some of the covers that were disproportionately on the other side of bed.

"I know what you're thinking, darling. You'll get it someday."

"What's that?" I rolled over once more to face her.

"You want a relationship like Jerry and Gwendolyn have. I could see it in the way you looked at them the whole evening. You'll get it someday. Not every relationship is like mine was with your father."

"I know. You're right. I just worry sometimes that it isn't ever going to happen for me."

"It will. But, sweetheart, you might want to ditch the retainer and buy some sexier PJs first."

***

Three days later, I sat surrounded by piles of yellowing parchment and dust.

I blew a rogue strand of hair out of my face that had slipped free from its binding. So far, we'd spent our days in Scotland poring over the boxes of documents without luck.

I glanced at my mother, who with each passing day grew more restless. "I think we should take a break," I said. "Let's drive to the ruins and poke around there. Just start digging. Perhaps, we'll have more luck that way."

I was certain she hadn't heard a word. Her brow was creased in concentration, and her mind was clearly elsewhere as her eyes frantically searched the document in front of her. "Mom. Are you . . . ?"

"Oh my God! Sweet Mary, Moses, and Joseph! I cannot believe it!" She jumped up, screaming and dancing awkwardly around the room.

"What?" I stared at her, startled and slightly worried by her strange outburst.

"Bri! Come and look at this. I'm so tired, I wouldn't put it past myself to be imagining it. Quick. Come and see!"

"Everything all right in there?" Gwendolyn's voice called to us from the other side of the doorway, concern clear in her voice.

Mom ran to the door, and swinging it open, threw her arms around the innkeeper. "Oh, yes. Everything is fantastic!"

"Okay, then. Good. Umm . . . there's some lunch for you both on the stove. But, please, take your time. It will be there when you're ready." Gwendolyn slowly backed out of the room, shutting the door behind her, obviously confused.

"Mom. What's the matter with you? You scared her to death!" I chuckled as I reached for the thick, yellowed piece of parchment she was extending in my direction.

"I don't know how I never noticed it before. It must've fallen out of one of Alasdair's journals. I'm certain it's in his hand."

I scanned the crumbling paper, struggling to make out some of the faded lettering. "Do you think it's true? Could there really be another room, a secret room in the basement that was never found in a previous dig? I thought you all had cleaned everything out of that basement."

"I don't know. I would be surprised, simply because we spent so much time excavating the basement, but it's the most promising thing we've found so far. We have to go and check it out."

"Absolutely, we do. Let's get cleaned up, go eat lunch, and hit the road."

"Yes. Let's! You take the shower. I'll take one when we get back here tonight. I'm just going to splash some water on my face."

I turned on the shower and stepped away to grab a towel and a change of clothes while I allowed the water to heat up. As I turned from the tub, I caught a glimpse of Mom's smiling reflection in the mirror and thought for a moment it was myself. All my life, people had told me how much we resembled one another, but I'd never been able to see it until that very moment.

Her eyes were glowing with excitement and, with her grinning broadly, I could see the young woman my mother once was, and the resemblance between us was undeniable.

I hurried in the shower, knowing my mother was anxious to get to the site, but I still felt warm and refreshed when I turned off the steamy spray. I reached around the curtain to grab a towel and saw my mother sitting on the edge of the bed twiddling her thumbs and tapping her feet.

She's always been good at subtlety, I thought to myself as I rushed to get ready as quickly as possible. Her jittering reminded me of my kindergarteners when they've waited too long to go to the restroom.

I pulled out my favorite pair of jeans and a v-cut blue t-shirt that matched the color of my eyes, donning them as I went back into the bathroom to throw on some makeup.

Quickly glancing at myself in the mirror, I pulled the hair away from my eyes with a clip, and walked back to the suitcase to retrieve my tennis shoes. I hadn't even bothered to pack any other pair. I knew that for the work we'd be doing, practicality was key.

I motioned in Mom's direction, waving her to the door so she would know I was ready. Together we made our way down the stairs. As we entered the kitchen, I saw my mother's eyes widen as she noticed the steaming pan of lasagna on the stove and Jerry and Gwendolyn sitting at the table.

"I decided to pull out one of my mother's recipes from the States for our American guests. Hope you enjoy. Come and sit down with us." Gwendolyn scooted over next to her husband and motioned to the two seats on the other side of the table. "I also packed you both a bag of sandwiches. From the commotion earlier, I figured you ladies might be out the rest of the day."

"Thank you." I filled my own plate and sat down across from Jerry. "You really don't have to cook for us every meal."

"Oh, doona worry, lass. We're charging ye for every bit of it." Jerry chuckled as Gwendolyn smacked his arm.

"Oh, you hush. It's really no problem. You wouldn't be able to find any other food, anyhow. We're pretty much in the middle of nowhere."

"Well, thank you. This lasagna is delicious." I shoveled the steamy goodness into my mouth, grateful it hadn't been haggis awaiting us.

"Well, good. I'm glad you like it. I haven't made it in a very long time. Not Jerry's favorite, but it sure brings back a lot of memories of my mother's home cooking."

"Bri doesn't have very many memories of that, I'm afraid. Not much of a cook, myself. Bri's very good, though. Guess she learned to fend for herself once she got tired of boxed macaroni and cheese every night." Mom laughed as she got up to get her second serving of lasagna.

"It wasn't all that bad, Mom. You were a whiz at navigating take-out menus."

Gwendolyn laughed and got up to clear her and Jerry's plates. "Well, you ladies have a good rest of the day. Jerry and I are off to town to pick up a few groceries. We'll see you two in the morning. I'll leave the key by the front door if you don't mind locking it and placing it under the mat on your way out."

"Sure thing. Thanks again!" Mom shouted as we watched the couple leave. "Okay, sweetheart. You ready? I want us to have plenty of time to search around before nightfall."

Mom pulled my plate away from me and placed it in the sink, not waiting for my reply. Obviously, I was through whether I wanted to be or not. "Sure, Mom. Let's get out of here."

I could feel the excitement emanating from my mother as I locked the front door to the inn and climbed into the rental. Together, we mapped out the route to the castle and set off toward the ruins.

CHAPTER 6

S *cotland—1645*

*B*laire yawned and stretched generously over the luscious feather bed that was covered in a color of lavender that matched almost everything else in the room. She had never seen a room more delicately decorated for a woman's tastes, and she suspected that it had once been Elspeth Conall's place of refuge. It certainly had been hers since she'd arrived at the castle. Upon learning of the brothers' quick departure after her arrival, she'd been so furious Blaire had decided not to leave the room until they were back at the castle.

This morning, they'd arrived.

And the end of her life, otherwise known as her wedding day, was set for three days' time.

Eoin was certainly handsome enough, but even as he'd pinned her with his gaze, standing so close to her in the entranceway she could almost feel the heat of his body, not even a hint of a tingle had rushed down her spine.

Different from most women she'd grown up with, Blaire's life did not revolve around men, and her biggest worry was not finding a suitable husband. Blaire MacChristy dreamed of independence, of living on her own, of making her own way in life. As a result, Blaire had been endlessly chided anytime she voiced her desires, and her father made it very clear from an early age that her wishes mattered not. Blaire didn't want to get married, and she had decided the first time she'd heard a crying child that she would always prefer a good lap dog to a suckling babe at her breast.

She never particularly liked Eoin, but the moment she found out she was going to be married to him, she decided to put all of her effort into resenting his very being.

Arran, on the other hand, she wanted to make amends with. She needed a friend in the castle and one with enough power to sway things in her favor if she was going to reside here for the rest of her miserable life.

With winning Arran's friendship set as her number one task for the day, she quickly dressed and pinned up her hair so that loose curls fell around her face. Wearing a light blue gown that beautifully framed her full breasts and trim waistline, she glanced in the mirror and decided that she was satisfied enough to exit her chambers.

As she wandered the many halls and corridors that wound through the castle, she couldn't help but be struck by the structure's great beauty. It had obviously been built by someone with close attention to detail and lived in by people who held great pride for their property and land.

Absentmindedly rounding a corner, she ran into a friendly-faced, plump, elderly woman carrying fresh lavender linens, apparently on her way to freshen up Blaire's bed. She hit the woman with such impact that the servant dropped the pile she was carrying and immediately flew into a string of apologies.

"Beggin' yer pardon, Miss. The bedding was blocking my view, or I would have seen ye coming around the corner. I should not have been so careless. Are ye alright, Miss?"

Struck by the woman's apology, Blaire immediately bent and began to help her gather the load. "Doona apologize. I was the one who was too busy looking up. I should have been paying closer attention. What is yer name?"

"My name is Mary, Miss. I am pleased to make yer acquaintance. In person, that is. I've been talkin' to ye through the door for a number o' days now."

"Oh! Thank ye for bringing all of my meals. I wasn't quite feeling myself. Do ye know where Arran is? I was hoping to apologize for the way I treated him the night I arrived. Also, I believe there is a stable master that I should apologize to, as well. I doona believe I made the best impression."

"Oh . . . the stable master is my husband, and his name is Kip. But doona worry about him, Miss. He needs someone to give him a hard time every now and then. Lord knows he does the same to all of us most of the time."

The woman's belly jiggled as she chuckled, and the corners of her eyes crinkled with her smile. Blaire could see her kindness.

"As for Arran, I expect ye'll find him in his chambers, Miss. I saw him leaving the stables a few moments ago. Just so ye know, Miss, I told them it wasn't a good idea for them to be running off like they did, but they never seem to listen to anyone but themselves. Stubborn, thick-skulled boys, the both o' them. But don't ye worry, Miss. Mary's given them a lecture like they've likely never had in their lives before. They're awfully sorry for the way they've treated ye, and they willna be doin it again, I can promise ye that."

"Well, thank ye, Mary, but I suppose I'm to blame, as well. Now, which room is Arran's?"

"Just on the opposite wall, one door down from yer own, Miss. Right next to the laird's."

<hr>

*B*laire paced back and forth in front of the door, waiting for Arran to answer. When she received no response, she knocked more loudly and resumed her pacing.

Knocking a third time, she decided to try the bolt. It was unlocked, and she slipped inside the door, slamming it loudly behind her in an effort to draw attention to herself. Before she could even look around the room, her back was rammed into the door behind her, and she screamed as the knob jammed into her lower back.

Immediately, the hand gripping her arms relaxed as she slumped to the floor, landing on her bottom. She peered up at Arran, watching as recognition flittered across his face.

"Ach, lass! I'm verra sorry. I thought ye were Eoin, coming to give me hard time for sleeping in the middle of the day. But I expect he's having as difficult a time staying on his feet as I am." He swayed slightly and, hovering over her, propped both hands against the doorframe. "But why would ye walk into my bedchamber?"

"I . . . I'm sorry," she managed. Her back throbbed from the impact of the knob on her spine and the pain had her on the verge of tears. But she never cried in front of others, and she certainly was not going to start now. "I was just coming to apologize."

Arran chuckled slightly. "Why would ye be doing a thing like that? I was quite certain ye'd be ready to tan both of us when ye saw us next."

"It's not ye that I'm upset with. I'm sure ye felt obligated to accompany Eoin when he decided to philander around the countryside. But as to my behavior the night I arrived here, I had no reason to speak to ye so. I hope ye can forgive me."

"Lass . . ." He reached down to grab her shoulders and helped her to her feet. Once she was standing, he resumed his position, both hands propped against the doorway, leaving her trapped between his arms. "Ye shouldn't be so hard on Eoin. It was my idea for us to leave. I talked him into it."

She interrupted him, shocking herself at the pitch of her voice. "I'd just arrived! I didn't even know my way around here! Not that yer confession in any way excuses Eoin, but I canna believe both of ye could be so thoughtless."

*A*rran stared down at her as she continued screaming. She was even more beautiful when she was angry, with her face flushing pink and her eyes a vibrant blue. In that moment, all he could think about was touching her, drawing her to him and silencing her admonitions with a kiss. What would she taste like? Feel like beneath his fingertips? Her hair looked so soft, her skin as smooth as silk, her lips even softer. Yet, there was fire within her; he saw it burning brightly in her eyes. He had never wanted anything more than to merge with that heat, to be consumed by it.

*S*he knew she was making a fool of herself. She didn't even know what she was screaming about anymore. It wasn't until Arran's lips touched hers that she was shocked into silence.

All of her anger melted away, along with every other sensible thought in her head. She knew she should stop him, but when his hands lifted to cup either side of her face, she found herself leaning into him, desperate to get closer. The feeling of his velvety lips undid her completely. Surrendering, she wove her fingers into his hair.

It wasn't until he groaned into her mouth that Blaire returned to her senses. *Oh, God. This must stop.* Doing the only thing she could think of to break his kiss, she lowered her hands from his hair, and with her palms pressed against his firm chest, shoved him away with every ounce of strength she could muster. Caught off guard, Arran stumbled backward as she ran out of the door and back to her bedchamber without stopping to look back.

Once safely inside the room, Blaire sank onto the edge of the bed and stared blankly at the wall until her breathing returned to normal. Reaching up, she brushed her fingers over her lips, the rush of emotions she'd felt only seconds ago coming back to her.

Blaire had always prided herself on not being driven by the mindless need for men most women seemed to possess, but perhaps she'd just been kissing the wrong men.

Before her engagement to Eoin had been announced, she'd entertained her fair share of suitors at her father's home. Many of them had even kissed her, but she had always found the kisses to be only tolerable, if not mildly pleasant. Arran's kiss was far more than tolerable, and it ignited the first glimmer of hope she'd had since arriving at the castle.

rran couldn't begin to imagine how he could have been so daft. Blaire was engaged to his brother. She was the one person forbidden to him, and he had kissed her with such passion he still couldn't catch his breath. Most stunning of all was that, for a few moments, Blaire had kissed him back with equal passion.

If it hadn't been for her shoving him away, he might have done something far more insane than kissing her, not to mention deplorable. He might've taken her to his bed—or tried to. He couldn't remember the last time he'd experienced such longing for a woman. He could blame it on the ale, but he knew that drink was not what had instigated the kiss.

He had been captivated from the moment he first saw her standing in the castle's entranceway. Arran's suggestion to Eoin that they leave town had been as much for his own benefit as his brother's. By escaping his attraction to her, Arran had hoped he could process it, find a safe place within himself to tuck it away forever. Unfortunately, that had not been the case.

The heat between the two of them only moments ago had been indisputable. The moment their lips touched, she had melted into him. Again, he briefly allowed himself to imagine where that kiss might've lead before shaking himself out of his reverie. She was Eoin's. Arran would never tell his brother what had occurred between them, and he would make sure Blaire didn't, either.

He couldn't bear the thought of hurting his brother, and although he couldn't fathom how he would ever find the strength to resist her, Arran swore to himself that he would. Even if it meant avoiding Blaire MacChristy altogether.

CHAPTER 7

*J*ust one more drink and Arran thought he'd be brave enough to have the conversation with Blaire he'd been putting off for three days. He couldn't figure out what it was about this lass, but his whiskey consumption had leaned on the side of excess ever since her reentry into his life. Arran's plans to avoid Blaire had gone about as well as his plan to take Eoin away until the wedding.

It didn't matter how many excuses he made to avoid Blaire, they seemed to continually run into each other, and without fail, he ended up with her wrapped tightly in his arms. He could be working with Kip in the stables, shooting arrows in the field, or helping Mary in the kitchen, and if their paths crossed, moments later Arran would find himself alone with her in some shadowed alcove, holding her, stealing kisses and whispering his deepest longings into her ear.

Each time, she returned his passion, begging him to put a stop to her upcoming marriage to Eoin so that he could marry her instead. Arran couldn't believe how much he wished he could do just that. Marry her, have children with her, wake with her beside him every day for the rest of his life. He loved her fiery spirit, the way she said what she thought without hesitation; he'd never met a lass so forceful with her words.

Her beauty was another matter entirely. The very sight of her caused his heart to race so fast that he could hardly breathe. But it was her wild spirit that he knew could tame his wandering ways. She fit perfectly in his arms, in his heart.

The knowledge that he had to find the strength to deny her for the sake of his brother caused him to reach for yet another glass. Arran downed the ale quickly before standing to make his way to Blaire's room, just down the hall.

He was surprised at how quickly she answered the door, or perhaps it just seemed as such with the way his head was swimming. His lips were warmed by the touch of Blaire's lips, and as she melted against him, Arran had to force himself to push her away. He held her arms gently, but firmly, so that she couldn't come closer to him. The cruelty of what he was about to do almost killed him, but he could think of no other way than to reject her that would convince her to accept her fate and marry his brother willingly.

"Blaire, ye know we canna do this, lass. Ye're marrying Eoin tonight. I canna be the one to marry ye. The contract was drawn between my father and yer own. It isn't for us to be changing it, lass, as much as ye'd like me to." He released his grip on her arms as she ceased trying to move closer. Stepping away, Arran watched her slowly hide any emotion her expression might reveal. He'd expected no less from the fiery, wild lass. He knew she'd rather die than show him a weakness.

"But ye canna tell me ye wouldna like to," she said. "Perhaps, the knowledge of that will be enough to keep me content in between our days together."

"Lass, I can tell ye I wouldna want to marry ye. That's what I've come to say. Ye are beautiful, Blaire, and I've enjoyed my time with ye as much as I have any lass. But once ye've married my brother, I'll not be wanting ye anymore. There'll be another lass in my arms tonight. It's the way I am." His heart pounded off rhythm in his chest, painfully denying his lies. He expected her to match his hurtful words with some of her own, but as he watched her silently turn and walk out the door, he knew just how deeply he'd wounded her.

He gripped the bedpost of Blaire's bed and slid his body down to the floor. Pressing a hand to his chest, he tried to stop the pain that built there with each sob he held back as the scars of his loss carved their way into his heart.

It had been all Blaire could do not to burst into tears. Never in her life had speech so utterly escaped her. With each additional word that Arran spoke, an icy winter spread through her core, making her completely defenseless against him.

She hated it. Hated how much she cared for him. How quickly her feelings had built and made her doubt everything she thought she'd known about herself.

Eoin had been nothing but kind and attentive since he'd returned from his trip. But he would never make her feel the way Arran did. She'd known, deep down, that it was Eoin she would have to marry, but she'd held on to the hope that she'd have Arran's affection as well. That even after her marriage to his brother, they could continue what they'd started – an emotional bonding, if not a physical one. A few stolen kisses now and then, and whispered admissions of their feelings for one another.

With that gone, she didn't think herself capable of going through with her marriage to Eoin. It would be torture to be locked in a loveless marriage. To be so close to Arran, watching him with other girls, would be like throwing her heart onto a pile of burning coals.

If only convention allowed it, Blaire knew she would be happiest making her own way in the world, dependent on no one but herself. If it were acceptable, she would be pleased with taking lovers, remaining single, and taking in stray dogs instead of raising children. But things weren't different, and her marriage to Eoin would be a prison. One filled with the expectations and ritualistic to-dos that would be required of the castle's new mistress.

The idea suffocated her. Each minute marked a minute closer to her wedding, and she could feel her spirit retreating farther and farther into itself. Her heart was breaking.

Stopping long enough to wipe the tears from her eyes, Blaire looked up and realized she had wandered into a part of the castle she'd never before seen. She knew she was lost, but didn't care, and continued to flee down the dark steps, choosing her path at random.

When the stairs downward came to an abrupt stop, she lost her footing and stumbled through the castle's main basement and into the wall on the opposite side. When the wall gave way, she landed on her face with a thud on the cold stone floor.

The fall didn't hurt, but it was the pain in her heart that kept her from pushing herself up off the ground. She lay there crying until her eyes ran dry and her nose was sore, all the while wishing she could just disappear. She would rather be dead, would rather evaporate into nothing, than live her life trapped like a bird in a cage, forced to sing whenever called upon.

She had no idea how long she lay there, but when she had cried all the tears she had to cry, she decided it was time to get up and face the miserable life before her.

Standing, she brushed the dirt off the side of her face and turned her head in the direction of the sunlight streaming in from the small window in the far corner. As she waited for her eyes to adjust to the lighting, she scanned the room and felt herself becoming light-headed. Confused and frightened as she tried to make sense of all that occupied the chamber, she wondered if she had hit her head harder than she'd originally thought.

Hundreds of dusty old books, all circling a large oval desk in the center of the room, surrounded her. Books lay scattered and open on the desk, and as she lifted a page in one of them, a chill moved down her spine. She began to read the words.

Spells. Some to bless, some to curse, some claiming the ability to move time itself. Fascinated, she flipped through the pages, finding instructions on how to cast spells and cure various ailments.

Who could this belong to? Not Arran or Eoin. She glanced up from the dusty, yellowed page. Light reflecting off of something at the back of the table caught her attention, and her blood ran cold.

There, propped up against the back wall, sat a shiny, round plaque with her likeness painted on the face of it.

Underneath were words scribbled in an unfamiliar language. With shaky fingers, Blaire reached forward to touch the plaque. As she brushed her fingers over the surface, some of the paint flaked off on her fingertips.

It was too old, she realized, to have been painted by Arran or Eoin. *Who could have done this then? Not Alasdair. This portrait resembles me now, and I was a small child the last time he saw me. Not my father. Who?*

Trying to form some sense, she sounded out the words written below her portrait, and as she worked through the syllables, a strange energy began to build in the room. She could almost hear the walls humming, and despite something pulling at the edge of her brain, telling her to stop, curiosity piqued her interest and she continued to recite the inscription.

Just as she finished sounding out the last syllable, an unbearable pain shot through her head. Gripping the edge of the table, she screamed out in agony. The entire world felt as if it were shaking, but when she looked around the room nothing seemed to be moving but her.

She spun around to the sound of someone's voice and found old Mary standing in the doorway, a horrified expression on her face.

"Miss! Miss! What's the matter? We've been looking everywhere for ye ..." She stopped speaking as Blaire cried out once more.

Blaire tried to focus on Mary, but the edges around the woman were blurring, and she saw the servant's face swirl in on itself.

It was the most excruciating pain, and she couldn't stop the agonizing screams escaping her lips. She was certain she was shattering into a million pieces.

When she looked down, she could no longer see the end of her dress, and she knew she was dying.

Her last conscious thought as she disappeared into the dust was that maybe she would get her wish, after all.

CHAPTER 8

S *cotland—Present Day*

I t took less time than we had expected to reach the castle ruins, and as I rounded the last corner, I could see my mother fidgeting with anticipation. She started giving instructions the second I turned the compact rental onto the rocky road leading to the site.

"Okay. Just pull over here. We'll walk the rest of the way. I'm going to go ahead and scan the area so I can decide how I want us to maneuver this. Meet me up there after you unload everything."

I pulled over to the side of the road and watched as mom jumped out of the car to make her way to the base of the ruins.

Okay. Sure thing, Mom. You go on ahead. I got it. Really. I'll have no problem carrying both of these backpacks. They're only filled with enough supplies to last us a week or two. I rolled my eyes and continued my mental, one-way conversation with her as I stepped out of the car and walked around to the trunk.

I heaved the two backpacks out and, balancing as best I could, I hung one around my right shoulder and one around my left, wobbling to the top of the hill to meet up with Mom.

Looking out over the expansive area, I couldn't imagine how anyone could tell one area of the ruins from the next, but as I walked up behind Mom, I noticed she was already mapping out the site.

She pointed to the far right corner of the ruins. "See over there, honey? That was the laird's chambers, overlooking the sea. To the right was the grand dining hall, and where we are standing right now would have been the main entrance. Can't you see how beautiful it was?"

"I'm sure it was, but I have no idea how you are able to tell what room was what from staring at these piles of rocks."

"I've been studying this for years. I'm as familiar with these rocks as you are with your classroom, but I'm hoping I'm not quite as familiar as I think, otherwise there's no way another room actually exists in the basement. I think we should go straight down there and start poking around."

"I'm following your lead. But first, you have to take your backpack." I shrugged the heavy pack off my shoulder and dropped it at her feet.

"Let's get started." She quickly picked up the pack and, swinging it onto her back, took off toward the ruins, motioning for me to follow.

I stayed close behind as I followed her to a spot on the left-hand side of the ruins.

"Is this where the basement is?"

"Yes, it's right up here. It's been locked up to keep visitors out. Not completely safe, you see, but I have the key."

"It doesn't look as if it has been opened in a long time." I stared down at the metal door on the ground, closed with a lock that was covered in rust.

"I don't imagine anyone has been in since we stopped our excavation on the site. No other archaeologists have worked here, and now it's mainly tourists that come to look at the ruins."

In unison, we dropped to our knees. I grabbed the side of the heavy lock, holding it up in Mom's direction, so that she could insert the key.

"It's really stiff. I hope the key doesn't break off when I turn it." She paused nervously before turning the key to the left.

Luckily, it popped open with ease. Lifting the metal door open was another matter entirely.

Grass had grown up around the edges of the door, nearly burying it in the ground. Mom was already ahead of me, slipping on her yellow gloves and grabbing her shovel before I had a chance to swing my backpack off of my shoulders.

Half an hour later, with enough dirt dug up around the edges of the door, we were able to grab the large handle and pull it out of place, flipping it onto its other side on the ground.

I wrinkled my nose at the musty smell that rose out of the hole and motioned for Mom to lead the way.

When we reached the bottom of the stairwell, I watched as Mom pushed open the creaky, wooden door that must have originally been the entrance into the basement. Its hinges were worn and decaying, but as it opened, we made our way inside.

The first room was empty, all contents cleared out during the original excavation of the site. At first glance, it seemed impossible that there would be any sort of secret room. How could they have missed it when such an extensive search and clean out of the space had been conducted the first time around? But upon entering, both of our flashlights caught a glimmer of the same crack running down the back right corner of the space.

Mom hesitantly crept forward, obviously trying her best not to get her hopes up. As she approached the crack, she reached behind to grab a chisel and hammer out of the side of her backpack. Cautiously, she placed the thin edge up against the crack and tapped the end with the hammer. Dust and small pieces of debris floated into the air. Gaining confidence at her suspicions, she worked her way down the crack, tapping every few inches. About halfway down the wall, she hit a latch, and with one hard smack the door came swinging open.

Mom took off exploring the room with her flashlight, and I stood back to scan it with my own. Stacks of books surrounded us, and one half of the room had collapsed in on itself, blocking any source of natural light. I slowly ventured further into the room, pulling up the V-neck of my shirt until it covered my mouth to block the dust that was invading my lungs.

I shined the light up and down, almost dropping my flashlight when the light beam reflected off a metal object sitting in the middle of the room and into my eyes. I blinked to adjust to the sudden flash of light and stepped forward to get a better look. When I caught sight of what was propped on the center of the table I actually did drop the flashlight, and I screamed as it bounced off the floor.

It hit the hard stone with a smash, and I was immediately engulfed in darkness until Mom shined her own light in my direction.

"What on earth's the matter? You scared me to death! Did you see a rat?"

My knees were shaking, and I couldn't seem to respond as thoughts raced through my mind. *Surely I saw that wrong. There was not a painting of me on that plaque!*

I reached to place my hands on the desk in front of me, and my hands landed in a pile of dust and cobwebs that painted every surface.

"Can you hand me my flashlight, Mom? I think it rolled over near your feet."

As soon as Mom located it and it was back in my hands, I banged on the end where the batteries were connected and managed to get the light to come back on. Slowly standing, I shined the light onto the center of the table again, and a chill ran down my spine as I looked at my own image peering back at me.

My fingers shook as I reached to grab the item. *How? Why? When?* A million questions swarmed through my mind as I tried to comprehend what I was seeing. The plaque was obviously centuries old. The metal was tarnished, the picture faded, and part of it had been chipped off, as if someone had inadvertently flaked part of it off many years after it had been painted.

Fear gripped my belly as I faced my mother.

"What is this? Is this some kind of joke, Mom? Have you been down here before?"

"What are you talking about?" She reached forward and grabbed the plaque out of my hands, letting out a low yelp as she looked down at the image.

"What's going on, Mom?"

"Umm . . . this is just a coincidence, darling. No, I haven't been down here before. I think it's been a very long time since anyone's been here. We do have Scottish ancestors, you know? You just look a lot like the woman in the painting."

She continued to mumble comforting words, but I could see fear spread across her face. I tugged the plaque out of her hands and blew the dust off the top, revealing etchings underneath the painting of my picture.

I didn't recognize the language, but slowly I began to sound out the words. From the moment I began to utter the strange syllables, I felt the room change.

The fear that had started in my belly moved up until it paralyzed me entirely. Small hairs on the back of my neck stood up on end.

Something pulled me toward the words, forcing me to utter them even as I tried to swallow the sounds coming from my mouth.

As I finished, I felt my body pull apart at the seams, spiraling me into agonizing pain. I cried out at the same time I heard my mother's horrified scream in front of me.

I dropped to my knees as the room trembled around me. My skin was on fire, and I felt as if someone was stabbing me repeatedly.

"Bri! Bri! Oh my God, Bri!"

I wished I could see my mom. I could hear her terrified screams not far from me, but my vision blurred as pain continued to course through my body.

Just when I thought I could bear it no more, I heard what I thought was my spine snapping, and I gladly embraced unconsciousness.

CHAPTER 9

*S*cotland—1645

*V*ision slowly made its way back to me as I waited for the blurry images to clear. I reached to grip the edge of the table and struggled to pull myself to my feet. I moved my hands to press at the sides of my head, only briefly registering that my fingers didn't come away from the table's surface covered in dust. I could hear the blood pounding in my head, and I couldn't catch my breath. A voice from behind me started to penetrate my foggy brain.

On unsteady feet, I spun toward the doorway, struggling to make out the form standing in front of me. I knew it had to be my mother, but it didn't look like her. This was a short, plump woman, while my mother was tall and slim.

I closed my eyes briefly and opened them once more, hoping it would help me clear my sight. It did nothing to increase my vision, but I could now make out the woman's words.

Why is Mom talking like that? I don't understand what she's saying. Am I injured? My head certainly feels like it. Did part of the ceiling collapse? What's happening? Thoughts coursed through my mind as I listened to the woman's ramblings.

"Oh, God! Oh dear, sweet Mother o'God! The old laird was right. What is old Mary going to do now? And with the lass just hours away from her wedding! Lassies picked a grand time to be messing with magic, they did!"

That's definitely not Mom. Am I in the hospital or something? Wait! Wedding? What is going on?

I struggled to process my surroundings as I felt the woman's hands grip my shoulders and shake them.

"Lass! Are ye all right? Old Mary needs ye to speak."

"Please, stop shaking me! It's killing my head!" I gasped and reached to grab my head once more, although I could finally see the woman clearly. The pain that had nearly ripped me in half only moments ago had slowly eased into a migraine.

"Oh, dear heavens, lass! Where'd ye learn to speak in such a manner? Ye must be from far away, dearie. Old Mary's never heard any such speech in her life."

I felt the shaking stop and looked into the gray eyes that were studying me fiercely.

"Oh, by the Saints, lass! I never believed his stories, but ye do look remarkably similar; except Lady Blaire would never dress in such inappropriate attire. Why, ye look like the worse kind of tavern wench! I can see the shape of yer legs, lass! Not to mention . . ."

My head was throbbing too incessantly to concentrate. I scanned the room, while silently willing the woman to stop speaking.

I knew I wasn't in a hospital. The space looked old and somehow familiar. Slowly, I turned my head back to the table I was leaning against now and saw the portrait of myself.

Memories of what I'd been doing only moments before came rushing back, and panic burst forth as I shot out of the woman's reach.

"Where's my mother? What happened? What? What is that?" My voice and fingers were shaking as I pointed to the portrait and stared back at the old woman.

"Oh, ye poor thing. Ye look quite frightened to death."

The woman moved toward me once more and pulled me toward a stool in the corner of the room.

She was right. I was scared. Attempting to stifle my panic, I followed her urging and collapsed onto the smooth, wooden seat.

"Are ye all right now, lass? Allow me to explain to ye, Dearie."

I simply nodded as numbness replaced the sense of panic, and turned to the woman as she spoke.

"I'll not be sure about the where and when ye came from, dearie, but I can tell by yer manner of speech and dress, it is nowhere I've ever seen or heard about. Not that I've been or seen very many places."

The woman paused and chuckled slightly. Then, seeing my confusion, she stopped laughing and pulled her face into a look of seriousness once again.

"But I can tell ye that today is the third day of November in the year sixteen hundred and forty-five. And it is yer wedding day."

I started to refute the woman's claims, only to find that my mouth was dry and my knees were shaking. I sat quietly instead.

"Ye are in Conall Castle, lass, and while I know ye won't be the Lady Blaire, the rest of the castle won't be able to tell the difference, and unless ye want to be locked up, I suggest ye doona let them find out the truth."

As I listened to the woman speak about my upcoming marriage to the castle laird, laughter threatened to bubble up out of my throat.

I definitely hit my head. The room collapsed, and I am in a coma. I'm in a coma, and I'm dreaming that I went back in time to marry a Scottish laird. That's what you get for daydreaming nonsense, Bri.

"And what was yer name before ye arrived here, lass? Ye canna be known by it from now on, but I'd like to know yer true name, all the same."

The woman's question seemed to throw me out of my thoughts, and I found myself answering automatically.

"I'm Brielle Montgomery. But call me Bri for short."

"Well, Briforshort, Old Mary's never heard of a name like that before. I'm pleased to meet ye, lass, but from now on, ye'll need to answer to the name Blaire, do ye understand?"

"Yes."

"Good. Now, I'm Mary, and ye'll be spending a lot of time with me. I'm the one to know around here, believe me. Now what's yer name again?"

I relaxed a little as I noticed that my knees were no longer shaking, and my breathing had returned to normal. I smiled at Mary as I replied, "Blaire."

"Verra good, lass! I could tell ye would be a quick learner by the looks of ye. Now, let's get ye up to yer room before anyone else sees ye dressed in such a manner."

Mary stood beside me and dusted off the bottom of her plain gray dress.

If I'm in a coma, I might as well try and have a little fun. It's probably a good sign that I'm dreaming. I'm assuming that means I'm not brain dead. Maybe this dream will allow my brain time to heal. In the meantime, I guess I'll just marry the Scottish laird I wished for.

I giggled inwardly at myself, deciding to enjoy the dream while it lasted. As I stood to follow Mary, I had to stop and steady myself on the wall to keep my head from spinning.

If only my head weren't hurting so much. But, I guess it probably should be hurting, since a 400-year-old solid stone ceiling collapsed on it. Wait! Oh, my God! The ceiling collapsed! What about Mom? Is she injured?

I tried to calm my breathing once again and sat back down on the wooden stool. *No. I saw her when everything started to shake. The ceiling above her wasn't moving at all, and she was standing close to the entrance. She's fine. She's fine. She has to be fine.*

I continued to reassure myself until Mary's hands touched my shoulders once again.

"Come on, lass. We must start preparing ye for the wedding. I'll try and explain some more while we are getting ye washed up. Follow me."

The old woman took off toward a castle corridor, leaving me with little option other than to follow.

As I walked behind Mary, I rationalized my worries away by concentrating on two pieces of information that stuck out in my mind.

One, if both my mother and I had been hurt in the collapse, I figured there would have been no one there to get help. If Mom hadn't been able to get help, I would be dead rather than sitting in a hospital bed in the dreamlike coma I was in now. Mom was most likely fine. I just hadn't elected to let her into my dream yet, I supposed.

Two, regardless of what had happened, there was nothing that I could do about it now.

Unnecessary stress wasn't good for the healing process, so until I woke up and knew with certainty what had occurred, I was going to enjoy the surreal experience I was having now.

I looked up as Mary came to a halt in front of me and realized instantly that I had been paying little attention to the route we had taken to the door in front of which I was now standing.

It was a magnificent door. Strong yet feminine, the door was carved with precise detail that swirled in and around the wood with great craftsmanship. I thought it odd that I would be dreaming in such detail, but Mary interrupted me before I could explore the thought further.

"This is yer bedchamber, lass. Well, at least for a few hours, anyway. After the wedding, ye will move to the laird's bedchamber for the wedding night." She paused to push the door open and gestured, nudging me inside. "I think ye'll find the room quite nice. The laird's mother used this as her own special sanctuary while she was living. Go on, dearie. Old Mary will be back shortly. I'll have a hot bath brought up for ye."

Before I could utter a reply, Mary was gone.

Alone, I stepped inside the doorway. My first thought was that it was far too large. My entire living room and kitchen could easily fit within this one room. Why did anyone need so much room to sleep? But as I continued to make my way through the space I realized the excess room made it easy to breathe.

The room exuded calm, and I allowed myself to fall onto the bed in the center of it. The bed was covered in the same shades of purple that were mirrored throughout the rest of the room. I was just snuggling deep down into the lush fabrics when the chamber door flew open and Mary rushed in.

"Come on, lass. Up ye go and into the tub." She grabbed me by the arm, hauling me up out of the bed.

My head swam once again as I stood, and I gripped the wooden bedpost to hold myself up as I watched several young men carry a large oval-shaped basin past the doorway. Several steaming buckets of water were poured into the tub, and the servants retreated, closing the door behind them.

As soon as everyone was gone, Mary reached forward, fumbling with my clothes.

"What are you doing?" I pushed the old woman's hands away from me.

"What does it look like I'm doing, lass? We doona have much time. Ye are to be at yer wedding promptly! Get yerself in that tub, dearie." Mary's voice was shrill and demanding as she placed her hands on her hips and glared straight at me.

"Okay. Alright." I held up a hand to Mary and self-consciously stripped down, hopping in the water as fast as I could. The heat certainly felt real and it briefly crossed my mind that I couldn't remember ever having such a sense-filled dream before.

Mary's face seemed to soften as she watched me hiss at the touch of the steaming water. "Lass, I'm sorry everything is happening so fast for ye. I was hoping I would have time to explain, but I'm afraid that will have to wait."

I wondered what there was to explain in a dream. Dreams often made no sense. But as was becoming habit, I had no time to respond before Mary continued talking.

"Here's what ye will be needing to know today." Mary sank down onto the edge of the bed and crossed her arms with a look of exasperation. "Yer name is Blaire MacChristy. Yer father's name is Donal, and it is yer duty to marry the laird, Eoin Conall, to help provide protection for yer father's territory."

I splashed water on my face, scrubbing my body with my hands as I listened to Mary's instructions. Yes, the water was definitely hot. My skin turned pink as I lifted my arm out of it to scrub myself clean.

"Ye look just like Blaire, so once we get ye in yer dress and pull yer hair up, there's not a soul in all of Scotland who would be able to say otherwise. That is, until ye speak, dearie. I've never heard anyone talk so plain. Old Mary's not so sure what to do about that."

Mary stood and paced back and forth around the room. The water seemed to help my aching head, and as I reached over the edge of the tub to grab a cloth and dry myself, I noticed my head didn't spin with the effort.

"Perhaps, I can try to mimic your accent." I began to dry off, feeling refreshed and much more like myself.

"Accent? What do ye mean, lass?" Mary stopped pacing and pivoted to face me.

"I mean, that ye doona have to worry so much. I can try to mimic the way ye speak." I smiled as I tried to tilt my words into the best Scottish accent I could muster. Thank goodness for all the books I'd read aloud to my kindergarteners. They always loved it when I used voices, so over the years I'd developed quite the repertoire of accents.

"Ah! That's not bad, lass! Perhaps, ye can do it after all. That's always what the late Laird Alasdair said—that ye'd be a blessing to us all. But I never believed his stories until this day."

"What stories?" With my head no longer hurting, I found myself quite interested in what Mary was saying.

"Oh, I doona have time to talk to ye about that today, dear. Excuse me. I should have said, I doona have time to talk to ye about that today, miss. Old Mary has to start calling ye miss, if yer going to be lady of the castle." Mary paused and chuckled. "I never woulda believed that today would turn out as it has, lass. Oh my, it's been one turnip of a day for Mary. Not to mention yerself, dear. Ugh. I mean, miss. It's been a trying day for ye, as well."

I laughed and listened to Mary ramble as I shrugged into the pale blue gown that she was holding out to me.

"Oh, Mary, it's stunning!" I looked down at the bodice, quite taken with the image below me. It was the most elegant piece of clothing I had ever worn, and I wondered why women didn't wear dresses more often. I couldn't even see myself yet, with the way Mary had me turned away from the mirror, but I felt beautiful inside the flowing fabric.

"Yes it is, lass. But ye canna look yet. Ye may only look when I've finished yer hair, and ye are all ready for yer wedding."

I smiled, deciding to enjoy my coma. "What does the laird look like, Mary?"

Mary chuckled, "Well, that's a fine question, miss. Look, I said it! I called ye 'miss,' miss!" She paused to laugh. "I doona believe ye could be more fortunate in a husband, miss. I love those two boys as if they are my own bairns, ornery as they are."

"Two?" I interrupted on reflex, and glanced backward at Mary, who was pinning pieces of my hair into place.

"Oh, yes. There are two Conall brothers. But ye are marrying the elder brother, Eoin. The younger brother is Arran. Most lasses would agree that there aren't two more handsome lads anywhere in Scotland. Even I would have to agree, and I'm far too old to unlace my corset over such things."

I let out a small yelp as Mary tugged especially hard on a tendril of my hair.

"Oh sorry, dearie. I mean, miss. Oh! Old Mary will fix her mind on it eventually. Doona be worried." She continued to arrange my hair as she spoke. "Both lads are handsome, but in my humble opinion, I believe ye will be finding yerself spending your life with the finer brother."

I should hope so. It is my coma, after all. Why would I decide to dream up a marriage with some ugly old gnome?

"Wonderful!" I replied and was rewarded with a smack on the head.

"Ye keep slipping into yer strange way of speaking, lass. It's mighty important that ye doona do that anymore. If I can remember to call ye 'miss,' a young lass like yerself can remember to speak proper." Mary turned me around so that I was facing the mirror. "There. All done, miss."

I stared back at my reflection, unable to recall a time when I'd felt more radiant. The blue in the dress made my blue eyes sparkle, and the cut of the fabric fit perfectly. "Thank you, Mary. I love it."

"I'm pleased to hear it, miss. Ye seem to be a smidge more accepting of the wedding than Blaire, so I'm glad ye're here. I can only hope Blaire is fairing well in . . . wherever ye came from."

"What do you mean?"

"Oh. I need to stop speaking of it. I already told ye, I canna explain it to ye today. I'll be speaking to ye in a few days, after the laird and ye have had some time alone together."

"I see." I didn't see at all, but I decided to let it go. Whatever it was couldn't be that important. This was all just a dream, after all.

"Now." Mary gently pushed me toward the door. "It's time for yer wedding."

I smiled excitedly and followed Mary out the door, hoping that I wouldn't wake up before I got a chance to see my future husband and discover why I needed to change my name to someone else's to marry the man I'd dreamed up.

CHAPTER 10

*P**resent Day*

*A*delle Montgomery screamed and reached behind her, grabbing for any sturdy surface to remind her of reality as the contents of the room swirled around her daughter, one minute picking her up into the chaos, the next minute sweeping her away into nothing. Her legs shook, and her ears ached at the sound of her own terrified screams. She reached up and smacked herself hard across the cheek, trying to wake herself from the twisted nightmare. When nothing changed, she forced her eyes to close and shook her head violently, hoping that the motion would clear the insanity from her head.

When she gathered the courage to open her eyes again, she instantly relaxed against the back wall and breathed in deep, savoring the dusty, wet smell that filled her lungs. Bri was there, safe, and just where she'd been moments ago. It was her own head she was worried about. She'd make an appointment with a doctor as soon as she got home.

"Bri. Did I pass out? Fall and hit my head coming through the doorway? I was so sure . . ." She trailed off as she took in the horrified look on her daughter's face. Pins prickled down her back as her eyes took in the floor-length gown covering her daughter's body. "What? What's going on, Bri? I . . . I'm not feeling very well."

Her daughter quickly turned, scanning the room back and forth.

"Where am I? And my name is not Bri? Who do ye think ye are?"

"Bri. What do you think you're doing? Seriously. Your accent is remarkable, but where did you get that dress? Is this some sort of weird joke I'm not getting? Do you think that lasagna was bad?" Adelle pushed herself off the wall and moved over to her daughter, grabbing the skirt of her dress to examine the gown more closely. "It's really remarkable, actually. It doesn't look like a costume, but it's not an antique either. I think it's time you filled me in, sweetheart."

"Sweetheart? Why would ye address a stranger so? And why do ye keep calling me 'Bri'? My name is Blaire, and I doona understand why ye seem so fascinated with my dress. Have ye seen what ye are wearing? Do ye work for Mary? Did she send ye down here to get me?"

Adelle reached up to grab her forehead, her frustration growing at her lack of understanding. "Bri, what in the world are you talking about? It's really not funny. I seriously think I've lost my mind. We need to go back to the inn, maybe drive back to Edinburgh and check me into the hospital. Quit talking like that and let's go. Grab your real clothes on the way." She reached out to grab Bri by the arm, but the hold was broken as her daughter quickly jerked out of her grasp.

"Please, do not lay yer hands on me. I'll not marry Eoin. Ye'll have to send me back home."

"Bri." She reached out to grab her daughter once more. "We still have twelve days before we leave. Surely you're not ready to go back to Texas?"

"Texas?" The woman's brows came together so quickly they almost bumped in between her eyes.

"Yes, Bri. Texas. Where you live and teach. I think we both need to have our heads examined. Maybe we breathed in some sort of hallucinogenic drug when we opened that doorway."

"I'm unfamiliar with this 'Texas' that ye speak of, miss. I live in the MacChristy keep, with my father, Donal. It's a three-day journey from here."

Adelle stopped trying to pull at her daughter's arm and turned to face her straight on. She *had* to be Bri. There was absolutely no question this was her daughter. But the accent? And the clothes? And she knew she'd tried to teach Bri some about the castle's history, but she found herself surprised that Bri was able to remember such names. Adelle stood there, unmoving, trying to think of some sure way to confirm she was looking at her daughter, and that they were both on the receiving end of some powerful mind-altering drug. Whatever was going on, something was very wrong.

A sudden itch in her lower back caused her to jerk her arm around and scratch, and instantly she knew what she needed to look for.

Instinctively, she crouched down low and began to lift up the young woman's dress, digging her way through the layers of fabric until she grabbed the bottom layer. The girl squirmed and protested, but Adelle kept her grip and, giving a hard tug, spun Bri around so that her back was facing her and she could lift the dress above her bottom.

"What do ye think ye are doing? Let go of me. I can undress myself if ye insist that I change my clothes."

"Just hold still. I need to check something." She hiked the bottom of the dress up until the skin of her lower back was clearly visible. "Sweet Mary, Moses, and Joseph! You don't have the tattoo. You're not Bri, are you?"

The girl stepped away so that the fabric fell loose from Adelle's grip and in frustration faced her. "That's what I've been tryin to tell ye. No, I'm not this Bri. And what is a 'tattoo'?"

"It's this." Adelle turned halfway and hiked up the back of her own shirt where the words *we shall never part* were delicately tattooed across her lower back. "Bri has one as well. We got them shortly after her eighteenth birthday."

Adelle watched as the stranger, whose face was so much like her daughter's, slowly turned ashen, obviously remembering something she hadn't thought of before.

"What's yer name, miss?"

"Adelle Montgomery. I'm an archaeologist working on the ruins of Conall Castle. What did you say your name was, since although I have no idea what is going on, I know that you aren't Bri?"

"Ye may call me Blaire. The ruins of Conall Castle? What year is this?"

"What year is it? You really don't know the answer to that? Why, it's 2013."

Blaire slowly backed away until she steadied herself against the wall behind her. "I canna believe it. I knew they'd said she'd been a witch, but I never believed it was true. She left the portrait. It was her words I read."

At Blaire's mention of a witch, an inkling of her prior research on the Conalls nudged at the edge of Adelle's brain, but it stayed just out of reach as fear coursed through her.

"Slow down, sugar. I think it would be best if we made our way outside. Get some fresh air, maybe? I think we both need to figure out what's going on."

Color filled Blaire's face as the pitch of her voice rose. "I already know. It was the Conalls' aunt, Morna. She was a witch, and I stumbled upon her spell room by chance. I found it just moments ago, although I dinna understand what I was seeing. I read the words on the plaque, and then I ended up in front of ye."

"Okay." Adelle nodded obligingly. It was best to agree if she wanted the woman to help her find Bri, until she could remember what she needed so desperately to recall. "Well, why don't you tell me about where you were before you ended up here?"

"I was in this same room. But it was different, ye see? I was supposed to marry the laird of Conall Castle, Eoin, and I fled down here. I could not marry him. I'd only just been wishing I could disappear when I saw the portrait and sounded out the words."

Disbelieving but fascinated, Adelle widened her eyes. "Eoin. As in Eoin Conall, son of Alasdair Conall? Laird after his father died in 1645, for only a few short months until the infamous massacre?" The research came back to her in snippets. Her mind started to grasp the facts one-by-one as they presented themselves.

Blaire's face drained of color once again. "Massacre?"

"Yes. The entire Conall clan was murdered in late December of 1645. As to why, or who was responsible, no one has ever been able to find out. That's why my daughter and I were here, actually. We were searching for documents or evidence that could help solve the mystery."

"That's why she did it, doona ye see?" Blaire moved forward suddenly, grabbing Adelle's arms and shaking them.

"Who? Did what?"

"Morna. Alasdair and Father told stories about her when I was growing up. She could see things that were yet to happen. She must've known I would stumble into her spell room. She did her best to save them before her death. I'm meant to stop it, and ye can help me."

Something clicked in Adelle's brain, and the icy pinpricks rushed down her spine once more. "Are you telling me that this is for real? The old legend about the witch was true? You expect me to believe that you really came here from 1645?"

"Aye. I expect that's where yer daughter is now. Ye said that we look alike, did ye not? And where else do ye expect she'd be? We've switched places, we have. Did she read the words below the portrait, as well?"

"Holy mother of Freddie! You're right. She did. Oh, my God! We have to get Bri back before the massacre . . ." Adelle's stomach turned over as the same icy grasp that had made its way down her spine gripped her around the middle. She wanted nothing more than to jump through whatever invisible void had taken her daughter and be there by her side.

Her logical brain had no advice on what steps she should take next, but she knew she'd be damned before she left her daughter to die, as she knew the Conalls would in just a few short months. Adrenaline kicked in, pushing away all doubt and logic, replacing it with an eerily calm sense of determination. "Blaire. I know you are probably as scared as Bri is—*wherever* she is—but we have to help each other if we're going to get you two back where you belong. Let's go to the car and get the boxes and dollies. We need to gather up every book and piece of parchment in this place, and then get you back to the inn while Jerry and Gwendolyn are gone and get you changed into some of Bri's clothes."

Adelle turned, not waiting for a response, and only briefly registering Blaire's question as she made her way out of the basement room.

"Aye, but might I ask ye a question? What is a 'car'?"

CHAPTER 11

*S*cotland—1645

*E*oin stood at the edge of the rocky hillside that overlooked the ocean at the backside of the castle, waiting for his future bride. He scanned the crowd of townspeople, all dressed in their finest, excitedly waiting for the wedding to begin.

He would gladly trade places with any one of them.

At any moment, Blaire would arrive at the end of the aisle, dread simmering in her eyes as she glared up at him during her long march.

He would take her hand in marriage as his father bid, but he would live each day guilt-ridden for being the source of such great unhappiness for any lass, even one as miserable as Blaire.

He glanced toward his brother, who stood on his left-hand side. Arran looked as if he were having a hard time standing. His face was flushed and his eyes were bloodshot.

He'd been drinking again.

It hadn't escaped Eoin's attention that Arran hadn't stopped drinking since their return to the castle. What was bothering him? Had Arran taken their father's death harder than he'd realized? Whatever it was, he vowed that he would talk to his brother as soon as this wedding was behind them.

A sharp intake of breath from Arran caused Eoin to jerk his head in the direction of his brother's stare.

His heart hammered wildly inside his chest, and his breath lodged in his throat as he locked eyes with Blaire.

Standing at the end of the aisle, she was beaming back at him with a smile so wide and bright he couldn't help but smile in return. It was the first genuine smile he'd seen from her, and it made him uneasy.

Has the lass been drinking also? She looks pleased. He wouldn't have blamed her if she had been. But no, the lass was too certain in her steps to be drunk, and her eyes shimmered with clarity as she neared him.

He stepped forward to take her hands in his as the ceremony began.

The entire ceremony had been a blur. Now, I sat next to my new husband, watching the hordes of merry villagers dancing around the grassy expanse behind the castle. I knew I was dreaming; there was simply no other explanation for the whirlwind of confusion that had been the last two hours of my life.

The swirls of color and boisterous laughter—combined with music that I was vastly impressed with myself for dreaming up—had my head spinning yet again. I tried to stop the pounding in my temples by thinking back on what I could remember.

Meeting Mary. Having not one, but two full-blown panic attacks. Being tossed into a tub and dressed up like a Thanksgiving turkey. Walking down the sloping landscape at the backside of the castle. Laying eyes on the hunk now sitting beside me. Walking up the aisle, grinning like an idiot. It seemed to me that I could recall everything that had happened since I woke up inside my coma. That is, until the point that I reached the end of the aisle. That's when Coma Husband had taken it upon himself to grab my hands, and my brain short-circuited.

No surprise, really. My brain was obviously working overtime just to dream up Laird Eoin, not to mention that it was trying to heal itself out of a coma.

After he had taken my hands in his own, I could recall only two other things about the ceremony.

The first was his eyes. They had immediately hypnotized me. They reminded me of a black stone that used to sit in a bowl at my grandmother's house. When I was younger, I loved to hold it up to the light and examine all the different flecks of brown and gold that danced between the swirls of darkness. His eyes were like that stone. I wanted to examine every speckle of color that stared back at me throughout the ceremony.

The second thing I recalled was the kiss at the end of the wedding. You would think that since I was staring at his eyes so intently, I would've seen it coming. I didn't.

The impact of his lips on mine startled me so much that I tried to jerk away from him on instinct, but I was prevented by his hand, which touched the smallest part of my back and pulled me close to his chest. His right hand cupped the left side of my face as he moved his lips confidently against my own.

Part of me felt I should have stopped the kiss; I was kissing a total stranger, after all. But this was *my* stranger, whom I'd created, and my body betrayed me as fire coursed through my core, sending heat down to the farthest ends of my fingertips and toes.

I couldn't breathe, and I parted my mouth to try and take in some air, but instead of oxygen, I breathed *him* in.

Had it not been for the roar of the guests, I think the kiss would have gone on much longer, but the crowd's cheering caused the laird to jerk away. As he did so, a look of utter frustration, almost anger, crossed his face, adding to my confusion. His expression seemed at odds with the kiss he'd just given me.

Thinking back on the kiss caused my temperature to rise, and my cheeks flushed as the sudden warmth of the memory washed over my body. I reached to lay my fingers against my cheek, hoping to cool them, when Eoin's voice to my left caused me to jump.

"Ye look beautiful, Blaire."

I started to correct him, but quickly remembered that my name while I was in a coma was Blaire, not Bri. Instead I turned to him as he gently lay his hand upon my thigh, and smiled as sweetly as I could.

I expected a smile in return, but instead I was rewarded with the same irritated expression I had seen on his face right after the wedding. He stared at me briefly, ice shooting from his eyes, and then stood abruptly, pulling me up with him.

"Are ye ready to retire, lass? I know ye must be tired."

I nodded as he quickly led me away from the dancing crowd.

I tried to keep pace with his stride, but the bottom of my dress kept getting in the way, and instead I stumbled along, tripping with every other step. Each time I almost hit the ground, I found myself yanked up by Eoin's quick hands. *Couldn't a girl make herself graceful in her own coma?* Not that it was surprising; I didn't have much real-life experience when it came to grace, so I was certain my brain found it hard to dream up.

I sensed anger in Eoin. Anger at me, which I couldn't understand. What could I have possibly done to upset him? This was surely not the best way to start out a marriage. Perhaps this Blaire had done something before I arrived for which I was about to receive the punishment.

He continued his relentless pace, and as I blundered along behind him I realized that this didn't seem like something I would dream. Scottish castle, yes. Scottish wedding, yes. Gorgeous husband, yes. Angry, Scottish brute . . . not so much.

The realization frightened me, and once I knew we were far enough away from the crowd to no longer be noticed, I jerked my hand away with all the force I could muster, causing him to release his grip.

"What are you doing?" I stopped walking and shook out my hand as I glared back at him, completely forgetting to speak in a Scottish accent. I didn't care. My wrist was hurting, and I was frightened by the look in his eyes.

I backed away from him until I felt my back press into the stone wall of the castle behind me. But there was no escaping him; Eoin was in my face before I had a chance to protest. His hands held my shoulders, effectively pinning me to the wall, and his nose was but a hair's width from my own as he spoke.

"What am I doing? What about ye, Blaire? Ye have been moping about this castle since ye arrived, making no secret about how much ye detest me, and now ye show up at our wedding, smiling like a wee fool! Do ye think that ye can act as if ye love me when we're with others, and then reject me when we're alone? I'll do right by ye, Blaire, but I won't be toyed with. Do ye understand, lass?"

My head pounded. He was angry, but there was more than just anger in his eyes. Confusion? Frustration? I couldn't tell.

I didn't understand much of what he was saying, and Mary's story, the little she had explained, wasn't coming to mind as I stood there with the muscles beneath his clothes pressed against my chest. His breath was sweet and warm against my face, and when he stopped talking, I leaned forward without forethought and pressed my lips to his.

After only a moment, he leaned back, breaking the kiss, and met my gaze. His expression had softened, although his eyes remained confused. Confused, beautiful, and intense. So much so, I couldn't look away. When his hands moved from my shoulders to the sides of my face, cupping my cheeks, my heart thumped wildly in anticipation. Every thought in my brain dissolved, leaving only the memory of his mouth on mine, the sweet taste of his breath. I had never wanted anything more than to relive that memory right this second. Only, this time, I wanted more, a longer kiss than the two we'd already shared in the short time since I first saw him, standing at the end of the aisle, waiting for me.

But instead of giving me my wish, Eoin abruptly pulled away, leaving me wanting and baffled. Stepping back from me, he broke our gaze and said, "Doona do that again, lass." He ran a hand through his hair as he paused to catch his breath. "Ye have made it clear ye want nothing to do with me. And though I'm your husband, I'm also an honorable man who intends to abide by your wish that I leave ye be. I'll ask that ye not tempt me to do otherwise. I canna promise I'd be able to resist that temptation."

"Don't then." The words escaped my mouth before I had time to rein them in. It was my dream, after all. I could do what I wanted.

His gaze locked with mine again. "What did ye just say, lass?"

Blood ran to my cheeks as embarrassment set in. I looked down and tried to remember the accent before I continued. It was too late to back down now. "Doona stop yourself. Or me." The words came out breathlessly, and in an uncharacteristic show of courage I reached for his hand and entwined my fingers with his. I shyly glanced up at him, "Please."

I heard his sharp intake of breath, and my own breathing became quick and shallow as his dark eyes searched mine. When I didn't look away, Eoin started off again, still holding my hand as he pulled me swiftly along behind him. I didn't try to stop him.

<hr>

The stranger slowly set down his goblet, made his excuses to the villagers surrounding him, and walked to the side of the castle, watching until he was sure the laird and his new wife had made their way up to their bedchamber.

He'd been given only two orders as he'd left Ramsay's quarters—not be found out as a stranger at the wedding, and to wait until the appropriate time to set the fire.

Pivoting his head, the stranger made sure all eyes around him were diverted elsewhere as he worked one of the flaming rods from its post and turned the flame so that it lay on the ground, slowly scorching and taking root over the grass that sat underneath its light.

Once the ground slowly caught flame, the stranger turned and walked off. Soon he was mounting the horse he'd previously tied to the branch of a tree, far from everyone's sight. The stranger rode as quickly as he could away from Conall Castle.

CHAPTER 12

I stumbled along as we entered the castle's main doors, inwardly cursing the length of my dress as I went. Eoin was moving just as quickly as he had before, and taking the stairs at this pace proved impossible. I slipped, almost busting my lip against the cold stone steps.

I yelped, but before the impact, his hands were around my waist, lifting me off the floor.

"Sorry, lass." Even through my dress, his fingertips warmed my flesh as he held me.

Blushing once again, I allowed my head to fall against his chest. *God, he smells good. I have to remember to write every second of this down as soon as I wake up. I could live off of this dream for years.*

"Doona fall asleep on me yet, lass."

My eyes flew open at the playful, teasing sound of his voice. This man was impossible to keep up with. His moods changed rapidly, and this Blaire person had obviously done something to displease him greatly.

"We're here, lass." He carried me into the bedchamber, and I couldn't help but inwardly chuckle at the fact that I was now living a scene from one of the covers of the various romance novels sitting on my shelves back home. My subconscious was clearly pulling at things from previous fantasies.

Coma Husband set me gently on my feet as he turned to close the chamber door.

I turned away from him to take in the room. Wood, stone, and furs surrounded me, all melding together to create the most masculine room I'd ever seen. I closed my eyes to breathe in the delicious scent of the room's luscious materials just as Eoin wrapped his arms around my waist from behind.

I felt his hot breath on the exposed skin at the top of my dress. My heart raced with anticipation as he touched his lips to my neck, trailing kisses from my collarbone up to my ear. He nibbled it gently, and I reached my hand up behind me so that I could run my fingers into his hair.

His hands left my waist, and he followed the length of my arms with tender, light touches that sent tremors down my spine.

He must have known the effect it would have, for he repeated the action a second time. The sensation drew a sigh of satisfaction from me. Dizzy with anticipation and need, I let my head fall back against his chest, relishing the magic his skilled fingers created. My skin felt so hot wherever he touched me. Hot and sensitive and alive. *I* felt alive, more so in the dreamscape of this coma than I ever had in real life.

He pulled the top lace at the back of my gown, then the second lace, and as my gown began to slip, exposing my bare shoulders, a sudden wave of nervousness swept over me. How could something so impossible feel so real? *What's happening to me? If this is reality, I don't even know this man. And he was somewhat of an angry brute only moments ago. What is he capable of? Am I safe with him?* I silently laughed at myself. *Get a grip. You know he's only a figment of your imagination. This entire scenario is.* But it didn't feel that way.

I turned then, facing him while avoiding looking into his eyes, flattening my palms against his chest.

"What's wrong, lass?" he murmured. "Have ye changed your mind about this?"

"No – I mean yes. I mean…I don't know." I squeezed my eyes shut. "Oh, God. I feel like such an idiot. This isn't happening."

"Ye're beautiful, Blaire, and I apologize for leaving after ye arrived, if that's what this is all about. Yer hesitation, I mean."

"Leaving?" I opened my eyes. "I'm not sure what you're—"

"Shhh . . ." He pressed a fingertip to my lips to silence me. "Ye don't need to make light of it. I know I was wrong to leave, but by God, Blaire, ye have given me grief since ye arrived, and even before, when we were only children." He chuckled quietly. "I have no idea what's caused such a change in ye, but I intend to make certain ye doona again decide I'm so displeasing. If you'll allow it, I intend to show you I'm not the ogre you've thought me to be."

Who could possibly find this man displeasing? I tried to make sense of his words, but couldn't. "It's just . . ." I bowed my head, looked down at the floor. "I guess I'm a little bit afraid."

"Afraid? Of me, lass?" He ran his hands up and down my waist, his cool touch sending hot shocks through my body. "I will never hurt you, Blaire, no matter how much grief ye might give me." He smiled. "I cannot deny I want to know ye as my wife, but not until ye're ready. From this day forward, I'll be the only man to touch ye, lass, but when I do take ye as my own, it will be because ye ask me again to do so, and I see in yer eyes that you mean it."

I'd ask you again right now, if I thought I could form a coherent sentence. And if I knew—

Before I could finish the thought, he hooked his thumb beneath my chin and lifted my face. "Look at me, lass. Tell me what ye want."

I took a breath and met his gaze. His eyes were dark and slightly bemused, but filled with promise. They were also unbelievably beautiful. "I want to know if this – if you – are real," I said in just above a whisper.

He leaned forward then, lowered his mouth to mine, surprising me with his gentle kiss, the sweetness of it. "Did that feel real to ye, lass?" He ran his palms across my shoulders, now bare since he'd undone the top two laces of my gown. Goosebumps scattered across my skin beneath his touch. "Does this?" he asked, his voice low and mesmerizing. "Ye have the softest, smoothest skin, Blaire. I want to explore every inch of it, but not until yer need for me is greater than yer fear."

He stared at me, a look of teasing amusement playing in his eyes.

Still incapable of forming an intelligible response, I simply managed a small smile as I struggled to regulate my breathing.

"Come on, lass, let's go to bed. Ye look as if ye might fall over."

I followed as he gently tugged on my hands, leading me to the bed across the chamber.

"Come, Blaire. I want to hold my new bride in my arms, satisfied that I know she doesna find me as abhorrent as she tried to make it seem."

He crawled into bed beneath the covers, and I looked down at him as he smiled. *That smile has probably found dozens of other women exactly where I am right now.* It both surprised and displeased me, so that the thought sent an unpleasant surge into my stomach. This man didn't actually exist, after all.

He gestured for me to join him, and when I hesitated, he said, "I'll only hold ye, lass. On my word of honor."

A nightgown was spread across the foot of the bed, put there by Mary most likely. Turning my back to Eoin, I slipped out of my dress and into the nightgown. Then I slowly crawled on top of the bed beside him, feeling awkward and hesitant.

He must've sensed my uncertainty. Reaching for me, Eoin said, "We've no rush, lass. Don't worry. I'll see to it that I woo ye properly first."

I stopped my senseless internal struggle as his words sank in. Laughing silently at myself yet again, I joined Eoin beneath the covers and rolled into his arms, wondering if he'd still be there when I woke up in the morning, or if I'd find myself, instead, in a hospital bed all alone.

*M*oments later, a fierce knock at the door caused us both to jerk upward in the bed. Just on the cusp of sleep, I found myself disoriented as I looked around the room to take in my surroundings, trying to remember where I was and what I was doing.

A hand on my back caused me to turn to my left, and the sight of Eoin beside me reminded me that I was still in a coma. I couldn't quite make sense of why I seemed to fall asleep while sleeping. The only answer that came to mind was different medications must be causing the strange reaction. *At least my dream seems to be the same.*

"Who's there?" Eoin yelled toward the door, causing me to jump. He gently rubbed my back in response. "Ye better have a damned good reason for waking my wife."

"Me lord! Ye must come quickly. There has been a fire set outside. It's small, but we must contain it before it reaches the stables."

"What? I'm coming, Kip. Get on with ye, and help the efforts."

I watched as Eoin, cursing, quickly dressed and headed for the door.

"I'm sorry to leave ye, lass, but I must see to the fire. Just go back to sleep, and I'll return soon. I'm sure tis nothing to worry yerself over."

With that, he was gone. I stood and made my way to the window to watch the scene below. The fire was small. Surely there'd been no injuries, but it would take the men awhile to properly put it out and clean up the mess. It seemed silly that I should stay and not offer help, but something told me that the offer wouldn't be appreciated. I didn't worry about Eoin. It was my dream. Surely, I wouldn't let anything like a fire take my Coma Husband from me.

I pulled one of the blankets from the top of the bed and wrapped it around myself as I curled up into the stone window seat that looked out over the back of the castle grounds and out to the sea.

CHAPTER 13

’d just begun to drift, and I could feel my eyelids drooping further with each passing second, when the door handle started moving clumsily. Startled, I jerked upward and wrapped the blanket around my shoulders more tightly.

I glanced toward the bolt, which rattled noisily as the person opposite the door struggled to get into the room. At first I assumed it must be Eoin, but a quick glance out the window showed him still working away at the small remains of the fire. I scanned the room for my dress and spotted it still lying across the foot of the bed where I’d left it.

I scooted off of the window seat and, leaving the blanket behind, watched my skin turn to goose flesh as my toes touched the cold stone below. The nightgown I wore did little to warm me, or to hide my body beneath it. A sheer wisp of a garment, it was obviously made more to accentuate than to cover the figure of any woman who wore it. I tiptoed as quickly as I could over to the bed, and then slipped out of the gown and into my dress. I didn’t attempt to tie up the back; the intricacy of the laces was impossible for me to maneuver on my own.

Twisting and turning, I worked the gown into place so that it fit snugly across the front. Perhaps now, at least, it wouldn’t be quite so obvious that it was completely open in the back. As long as I kept my arms to my sides, I thought it would stay in place while I saw to whoever needed my attention.

The noise at the door had stopped by the time I went to open it, but I still made an effort to smush my hair into some semblance of order before I reached for the handle and opened it.

In a series of movements that came too quickly for me to process, I found myself knocked onto my bottom with a man lying in between my legs.

"Ooomph!" I shoved a foot into the ribs of my lap partner and pushed him away as I struggled to stand and keep my dress in place. "And you are?"

"God, lass! What are ye doing in my bedchamber? Eoin would be none too pleased to find ye here." The man stood with great effort, and I could tell from the glazed expression in his eyes that he'd been either unconscious or close to it when I opened the door.

"I know that I haven't been here long, but you are the one in the wrong room. You must be Eoin's brother?" I started to offer my hand, but changed my mind as I felt the shoulder of my dress begin to slip.

"What the hell are ye talking about, Blaire? Ye know I'm his brother. Ye know me as well as ye know anyone else around here! God, Blaire. I knew ye could be cruel, but I doona see why ye would punish me so! Ye have to know how hard it was for me to watch ye marry him! And why in the name o' God are ye talking like that? I know I've had too much to drink, but ye sound nothing like yerself!"

He swayed slightly and leaned back against the wall. His eyes were red, and I could tell it was more pain than drink that made them so. The hurt behind his reddened eyes went beyond his being drunk.

Something I'd said had upset him. This Blaire had hurt him, and once again I'd forgotten all about her. I'd also forgotten the accent Mary had been so insistent I use. No wonder he thought Blaire sounded odd. I was making all of this up as I went along. It couldn't be good for my brain to be dreaming up something this complicated.

As my current coma state crossed my mind, an uncomfortable flicker of a thought tugged at me, but I was too occupied with the situation in front of me to give it much thought.

I walked toward him and tried to remember the accent once again. "I'm sorry. I dinna mean to upset ye. Ye look as if ye are about to collapse. Let's get ye to yer room. Aye?"

He nodded somberly before responding. "Aye. That's where I thought I was when I fell over outside the door. I'm a fair mess, no? I'm sorry, lass. I doona like for ye to see me so."

"Oh, shhh. I'll help ye down the hall, and we'll forget all about it."

"Thank ye, Blaire, but I can make it on my own. I just missed by one door. I'm a bigger sot than I thought if I canna make it that far."

He pushed away from the wall and tripped with his first step but caught himself by placing his hand on my shoulder.

I snickered and placed my arm around his back, using his side to hold my dress in place as he wrapped his arm around my shoulder. I didn't see how I was going to get him to his room without my dress falling to my feet, but it was clear he wouldn't make it through the door without my assistance.

"Well, looks like ye are a bigger sot than ye thought, no? Let's go. Ye can use me for balance. But doona fall on me, or I'll be trapped under ye for a week."

"There's an idea, lass, and the kind I should keep to myself now that ye've married my brother."

He threw his arm sloppily around me as I started toward the door.

"Come on."

We waddled down the hallway, doing our best to help one another. He leaned on me to stay upright, and I leaned into him to keep from exposing myself in the hallway. This act was exactly the sort of self-deprecating comedy that I could see myself dreaming, and whatever unconscious thought had been nagging at me seemed to recede.

With each step, my dress slipped farther and farther off the shoulder that was underneath his hand, and I increased the pressure of my right side into his ribs.

It was a short distance to his room, but it seemed a mile, each of us struggling with every step. As we made it to his door, he removed his arm from around my shoulder and stepped away from my side.

I quickly made to squeeze my arms back against my own sides, but not before his first step away landed on the bottom of my dress, starting its descent.

Catching the gown just before it slipped off my shoulders, I threw myself against him to keep my chest from being exposed. One more false move, however slight, and the dress would fall to the floor.

I glanced up at Arran to try and explain myself, but stopped as he backed me into the wall next to his chamber door.

"What do ye think ye are doing, Blaire? We canna do this! We shouldna have in the first place, but ye have married him now! We must stop."

"I . . . I..." I had no idea how to respond. Obviously, Blaire had been involved with both brothers. Not that I could blame her. Arran was just as handsome as his brother. I couldn't imagine what their parents must have looked like to have two boys who appeared so different, but were both equally breathtaking. He interrupted my thoughts before I could respond.

"God help me, Blaire! I've tried to stay away from ye. It felt like ye were ripping my heart out watching ye wed Eoin. I thought at the very least ye wouldna seem so pleased to be doing so. Ye have to know I dinna mean a word I spoke to ye this morning."

I clutched the dress between my breasts to hold it in place as Arran lowered his face to mine, his hands on my hips to steady himself. With his cheek pressed flush to my cheek, he continued his plea.

"If I'm being a fool, Blaire, put me out o' my misery and tell me so. If I'm not, I doona think I can stay away from ye anymore."

I scrambled for a response. I didn't want to hurt him any more than he obviously was already, but I was afraid that in his state of intoxication whatever I said would do little to discourage him.

Part of me hoped that if I waited to answer he would simply pass out on my shoulder, and I could leave him snoring in the hallway and make a quick escape back down the hall.

Instead, he seemed to take my silence as surrender.

"God, Blaire! I knew it was not only me. I want ye so badly. I'll regret it, I know, but I canna help myself."

His mouth met mine with a heartbreaking sense of desperation. There was such an ardent sense of longing in the way his lips moved against mine, I couldn't bring myself to stop him. It seemed too cruel to push him away. He wasn't assaulting me. He thought I was someone else, someone he loved. And he obviously believed Blaire would have matched his fervor with her own, but that is where I drew the line. In this dream, I was a married woman, after all. Just as I was about to end his kiss, a roar to my right made me gasp, and before I could blink, someone jerked Arran away from me and flung him to the floor, where he splayed out, unconscious.

Stunned, I felt my dress slip below my breasts before I scrambled to pull it back up.

Eoin whirled on me, grabbing me around the middle, throwing me over his shoulder with far too little effort.

I assumed he was returning me to his bedchamber, but he took off in the opposite direction. He didn't say a word as my head jostled up and down against his back, and as he descended two different sets of stairs, dread settled in my gut.

I could tell he was angry. His face had been blood red when he'd spun on me, and I could feel his anger rising in the form of heat off his back.

I couldn't imagine what he would say or do. I'd seen hints of his hot temper before and that had been over nothing compared to this. But what could I say in defense of myself? *It wasn't me Arran was kissing. It was Blaire. Or so he thought. You see, I'm not her.* I was sure that wouldn't cut it. Not with Eoin. Not on our wedding night. Not ever. It was simply too unbelievable.

Dread turned to fear as the dank and dirty smell of some place far below ground reached my nostrils. I turned my head to see a row of dark cells, as empty and foreboding as the look on my husband's face. He carried me down to the last cell in the farthest corner of the room, which could only be described as a dungeon, and roughly threw me onto a stone seat that was part of the back wall. My back hit with a force that sent pain shooting up through my head, and tears unwillingly filled my eyes.

"Don't ye dare cry! Ye have no one to blame but yerself," Eoin roared. "What do ye expect me to do? Ye slept in my bed tonight and allowed me to hold ye in my arms as ye did so. And then I have to leave for a bit, only to return to find ye in my *brother's* arms! Ye are a liar and a loose woman, Blaire!

I'll continue to protect yer father's territory to honor my own father's memory, but I will never lay eyes on ye again. I will not have a wretch like ye as lady of my keep!"

His hands were trembling and his face was deep red as he took in a deep, shaky breath and turned away. He threw the door shut and locked it in place, leaving me shaking and gasping as I tried to stop sobbing.

---

*H*ours turned into days, and I started to fear that my placement here was not a temporary arrangement made out of Eoin's initial anger at finding me in Arran's embrace. By my count, at least four days had passed. A total of eight meals, two a day, had been brought, as well as plenty of blankets. Someone had come to empty my chamber pot three times daily, and I always had plenty of water to drink.

It could have been much worse, and I was certain that for anyone else who had ever been placed here, it had been. Still, I was accustomed to central heating and air, at least three meals a day, and regular showers. Not to mention a daily dose of television . . . and toilet paper. As far as I was concerned, my pleasant, fantastical coma dream had turned into the worst kind of nightmare. A nightmare that I now firmly believed was not a dream at all, but a state of reality I couldn't begin to understand.

Always an over-thinker, I had learned through the years that it was best if I kept busy. Limiting my time analyzing and thinking about things too much helped me to stay content with work and a home life spent entirely alone.

However, once the initial shock of being tossed into the dungeon had worn off, and I realized that Eoin wasn't coming back to get me, I was left with nothing else to do but think. The dizzying emotional highs and lows, the elusive mentions of Blaire that I didn't understand—everything was far too complicated for me to dream up on my own.

These oddities alone should have been sufficient to convince me, but it was the events leading to my imprisonment that finally forced me to face the truth. More than once, I had been awakened from a light sleep, which means I had been sleeping. The first time, I'd put it off to medication, but it seemed impossible that I would enter some sort of coma dream, dreaming the same thing over and over again.

I truly was in 1645 Scotland. Truly in the castle and surrounded by the people my mother had spent her entire life studying. Every time panic began to take over, every time some unpleasant thought tugged at the back of my brain, it was this realization trying to break through, despite my greatest effort to push it away. Even the wildest imaginary scenarios seemed more favorable than this startling reality.

When I believed I was in a coma, there was hope of escape. Hope of returning to my life, my home, my students. Hope of seeing my mother again. Without that hope, I couldn't begin to comprehend what was happening, how I had ended up here, and what the rest of my life would look like.

However irrational, I was completely unwilling to give up that hope. Coma or no coma, I would escape from this prison and find a way to return home. I knew my being here had something to do with the portrait I'd found when Mom and I were excavating the secret basement room. The words inscribed below my image must have been some sort of spell. If the contents of that room were powerful enough to pull me backward through time, surely there was something that could send me forward.

But first, I had to find a way out of this cell.

"Leave it at the door, Mary. The same as I've been asking ye to do for days, now."

The knocking stopped, but the voice that came through the doorway had Eoin on his feet in an instant, fists trembling with the anger he'd been struggling to contain for days.

"Eoin! Ye know we must talk," Arran demanded. "What are ye doing to her? Ye canna keep her captive in yer bedchamber forever, and ye can not continue to ignore me, either."

"Go away. I've no more use for either one of ye. Unless ye want me to beat yer head in, ye best get away from the door."

"What have ye done to her, Eoin? I swear if ye hurt her I'll kill ye myself, even if ye are my brother! Open the door!"

It had been four days. Four days locked up in his bedchamber, stewing over his anger and disappointment, trying to make everyone in the castle believe he was honeymooning with his new bride. Four days of imagining his brother touching and kissing Blaire, while she kissed him back.

The knocking turned to pounding as a large object made contact with the other side of the door. If Eoin didn't stop him, Arran was sure to draw attention from other parts of the castle, which was the last thing he wanted while his new bride was locked away.

"Stop it, ye fool!" He yanked the door open and stepped away as the post Arran was holding zoomed past his head.

Arran pushed his way into the room. "Where is she, Eoin? No one has seen either one of ye since the wedding, which would be fine if I dinna know how angry ye are." He walked quickly through the room, looking behind curtains, turning over tables, looking for Blaire. "What have ye done with her?"

"She's not here, Arran." Eoin stood still in the doorway, watching as his brother tore through his room. "What do ye think ye are doing? She's my wife, and unfaithful, and ye dare ask me what I've done with her?"

"Where is she?" Arran pounded his fist against the wall and whirled toward Eoin. "It was my fault. I was drunk, Eoin. I thought that I was coming into my own room, and it turned out to be yers. She heard me outside the door and helped me back to my room. I could hardly stand up."

"I doona care whose fault it is. I'll have nothing to do with the both of ye. Now get out of my chamber!" Eoin moved to place his hands on Arran's shoulders, but Arran quickly darted out of his way.

"I'm not going anywhere until ye tell me where she's gone. Did ye send her back home, Eoin? To disgrace her father and territory? Surely, ye could not be so cruel. Ye have already wed her."

"That didn't stop the two of ye from betraying me, did it? I willna listen to this. Grow up, Arran, and stop taking everything ye want!"

"It was a mistake, and I'm sorry for it. She had little say in what happened."

"I don't care," Eoin huffed. "She is staying where I put her, and ye won't be seeing her again."

"She's yer wife, and I'm sorry for what happened. But I will see her and make sure she's unharmed."

"Do ye really think I'd harm her? I've left you unhurt and ye deserve a beating far more than she. How could ye do it? The one person that was forbidden to ye!"

"It was an accident. She was kind enough to help me to my room, and I took advantage of her. If ye dinna harm her or send her away, then where is she?" Arran stepped forward and hesitantly placed a hand on his brother's shoulder.

Eoin flinched at the touch and tightened his fists to keep from striking Arran. "She's down below, where she belongs. Where ye belong, too!" He stepped away so that he could better see Arran's face and gauge his reaction. He was looking for an excuse to hit him, and he hoped that his brother would give him one.

"Down below? Tell me ye dinna put her in the dungeon! No one has been kept there since before we were born."

"That's where I put her, and that's where she'll stay. Ye are more than welcome to join her."

In a flash, Arran's fist hit the side of his face, pushing his body sideways. Eoin quickly recovered, charging toward his brother as Arran screamed at him between blows.

"What is wrong with ye? I would not leave a dog down there. I will not let ye leave her down there to rot."

Pent-up rage erupted as Eoin slammed into his brother, sending them both to the floor in a whirl of kicking legs and surging fists.

"I doona think ye have much say in the matter, brother. Ye may be sleeping with her, but I'm laird. She's my wife. I'll do with the lass as I please."

The sudden sound of Mary's voice in the doorway caused both men to freeze in the midst of their entanglement.

"Oh my God! What is the matter with the two of ye? Two grown men acting like a couple of bairns, and in front of the new lady, too! Why, I'm ashamed of the both of ye! And yer father would be, too!"

Both men untangled themselves and guiltily faced Mary where she stood in the doorway with both hands on her hips, no less formidable to them than she'd been when they were children.

Silence hung in the air, and both brothers knew Mary wouldn't budge until an explanation was given.

Arran broke the silence first. "We were not fighting in front of Blaire. She's not here. Eoin has her locked away in the dungeon."

Mary's face turned ghostly white, only to be followed by a shade of scarlet rushing up into her cheeks.

"Forgive me? I know old Mary's hearing things now. Where did ye say the lass is?"

Arran turned to Eoin who continued to stare blankly ahead at Mary, anger flaring in his eyes.

"No, Mary. Ye heard me right. The brute's locked her away. That's where she's been since the night of the wedding."

Mary leaned back against the doorway, fanning herself dramatically. "Oh, my God. Ye boys are going to be the death o' me! What is he talking about, Eoin?"

"I caught the two of them kissing only hours after the wedding. I could not be near her, and I dinna want the entire castle learning what she'd done."

"Ach Eoin, if ye dinna stand several feet over me, I'd be knocking that pretty nose of yers back up into yer skull."

Eoin raised his eyebrows, and Arran grinned slightly as Mary continued,

"I doona care if ye walked in on the lass lifting her skirts for the entire village. It is unacceptable for ye to leave her down there." She squinted her eyes at Eoin, each circle of gray saying more than her tongue ever could, and stepped to the right so that she was in front of Arran.

"And as for ye, boy! Ye better explain this situation to Mary right fast before I keel over at the stupidity of ye both!"

Arran cleared his throat and shifted uncomfortably on his feet before answering, "Well, truthfully, I canna say for sure what happened. I'm ashamed to say I was too drunk to properly tell which way was up or down, and I wound up at Eoin's bedchamber door, thinking it was my own."

"Eck hmm . . ." Mary cleared her throat disapprovingly and motioned with her hand for him to continue.

"Blaire must have heard me outside the door. She opened it, and I fell in on top of her. She could see I needed assistance walking to my room. She helped me and I kissed her; I'm not too sure about the details."

Mary briefly rolled her eyes before shooting Arran another disapproving look, then slid back over to stand in front of Eoin once more.

"I'll not be letting that poor girl stay down there, Eoin. I doona care if ye never sleep in the same room, or if ye are never seen together except in public for the rest of yer life. Ye have to know she canna stay there!"

Properly beaten and ashamed, Eoin slowly nodded, trying to swallow his anger at the situation.

"I'll not be letting ye retrieve her from the dungeon either, Eoin. I'm sure the poor lass is scared to death of ye after being down there for days." She pointed at the door. "Leave. Right now. Go for a ride, clear yer head, and only come back when ye are ready to apologize and make peace with the lass. But there will be peace. Do ye understand? I'll not have shouting day in and day out just because yer father is not here to keep the two of ye in line." She quickly marched around Eoin and gave him a hard shove in the back. "Get on with ye. Now. Ye can find the lass in the lavender room later."

"What about him?" Eoin jerked his head in Arran's direction, suddenly feeling as if he was eight years old once again, and not understanding why his punishment differed from his brother's.

Mary shifted her gaze back and forth between both men before continuing, "I doona see why it's any concern of yers, but just so ye will both be satisfied, Arran is going to leave for a few days. Ride out with Kip to pick up a few more horses for the stables. He's leaving now, aren't ye, Arran?"

Arran lowered his head and made his way to the door, only pausing to address both Mary and Eoin. "Aye, Mary. I'll go. And Eoin, I am sorry, brother. Doona take it out on Blaire. The blame is mine."

Eoin turned, intent on making it to the stables before his brother left to meet Kip. "Aye. I'm sure ye put the lass in a difficult position, but she should not have behaved as she did. I'll speak to ye upon yer return, Arran. Safe travels."

With that, he turned and was gone, Arran and Mary following silently behind him.

A familiar voice caused me to stir from the restless and—thankfully—dreamless sleep I'd fallen into after hours of unsuccessfully trying to figure a way out of this living nightmare.

Exhausted, filthy, and most of all frightened, it took me a moment to realize that the voice belonged to Mary. I swallowed a hard lump that rose in the back of my throat, bringing with it tears of joy, which came from the almost certain knowledge that she would not let them leave me down here.

"Ach, lassie! Ye sure have managed to upset the men around here. One's yearning for ye so much he has not stayed sober in days, and the other's calling ye unspeakable names. Now, stand up! I've sent both boys away for a bit. I'll place ye in their late mother's chambers, and ye can get yerself cleaned up. Expect some time alone. It will take the lads a while to calm down and realize how foolish they've both been."

I stood a little more shakily than was warranted. Physically, I was fine. Mentally, I was so confused and upset that the effort it took to stand seemed almost too much. My voice cracked when I spoke. "Mary, I need to know exactly what's going on here. You have to tell me what you know."

"What did ye say, dearie? Wait until we get ye settled, and the two of us will have a nice, long talk." Mary motioned to the guard standing at the end of the passageway, who obviously knew better than to question her. He retrieved the cell key from his belt before he made his way to the door and obediently opened the lock.

Now released from my cell, I gladly followed her into a beautiful bedroom directly across from Eoin's. Mary left after depositing me there, but within minutes she returned with a trail of servants carrying steaming pitchers of water to fill the tub. After laying out some fresh clothes, she sat down on the edge of the bed and crossed her arms, resting them on the fullness of her stomach. She waited until the tub was filled with steaming water and the servants had retreated before she spoke.

"Alright, dearie. I know ye must be scared to death after the last few days ye've had here. I apologize for not explaining what I knew before the wedding, but there just was no time. And believe me, dear, I dinna know where Eoin had placed ye. If I had, I would've retrieved ye immediately."

I smiled gently and stood, watching her intently. "I know, Mary. Thank you. But, please, tell me what's going on. How did I end up here?"

Mary crossed her arms, only to cross them once again as I watched her struggle to find the right words.

"Well, the truth of it is, dearie, that I doona know all that much. Before Alasdair's death, he told me a long story. At the time, I put most of it up to his injuries. But then I saw ye, strange as ye could be, and as ignorant as a wee lamb, and I knew everything he'd said was true."

"What did he say?"

"He said that his sister—she was a witch, ye see—placed a spell, and someday soon a young lass in the likeness of Blaire would be brought into our lives. He begged me to watch over ye and to help ye in any way that I could. He said that ye would save us all from something horrible. What he meant by that, I'll never know. I expect more answers could be found in Morna's basement, but I canna read myself and never thought to look."

"Morna's basement? Where is that, Mary? I need to go and look immediately. I have to find a way home."

"Ach, dearie. I doona expect ye'd find anything to help ye do that. There was a reason Morna wanted ye here. I doubt she would make it easy for ye to leave. If ye want to look, I'll help ye anyway I can. But not tonight, lass. Right now, ye are to get yerself into that tub immediately and relax until Old Mary brings ye something to eat, do ye understand? Come morning, I'll show ye to Morna's room."

She gave me no opportunity to argue, and as I watched the steam rise from the tub I found myself less anxious to explore Morna's spell room. I could smell myself, even standing still, and knew I was in desperate need of a bath.

Mary left the room, and once stripped, I sunk gratefully into the tub, bending my knees so that the water came up to my chin and only my head and kneecaps breached the surface. The water had clearly just been taken off the fire. It was almost too hot, but I was too tired and dirty to care.

It seemed odd to go from watched prisoner to complete solitude so quickly. It occurred to me briefly that I should jump out of the tub and flee the castle immediately, but I knew there was nowhere better for me to go. I wasn't likely to find any answers outside of these walls, and at least Mary seemed to know where I might find them, even if she did a lousy job of explaining it.

I hadn't realized how tense I was until the heat from the water slowly worked its way over my body, forcing my muscles to relinquish their tight grip. I breathed deeply, relishing the feeling of my nails against my skin as I scrubbed away the dirt on my ankles and arms.

With the tips of my fingers and toes wrinkled to prunes and my skin red from both the heat of the water and the thorough scrub-down I'd just given myself, I lay my head against the back of the tub and threw my hair over the side, allowing it to dry.

The steam from the water quickly receded, and as my skin tightened in response to the cooling water, I turned my head toward the fireplace and stared into the flames. The brilliant amber beams danced over the wood, and as I followed their movement the cooling water seemed warm once more.

The tub was close enough to the fireplace that some of the heat from the flames warmed my left arm, which hung over the side of the tub. The light emitting from the fireplace mixed with the darkness, which had slowly flooded the room as the sun dropped lower into the horizon. The combination of light and dark was soothing, and my mind drifted closer to sleep with each flicker of the flames.

Just as I was at the edge of slumber, the bedroom door opened and closed, causing me to nearly jump out of the water. Jarred from my daze, I realized how cold I had actually become. My entire body was wrinkled from being in the water too long. I assumed it was Mary who'd come through the door with my food. But when I heard a deep voice, I moved quickly to cross my legs and cover my chest with my arms, knowing they were Eoin's footsteps sounding behind me.

"I'm not sure what to say to ye, lass. I behaved badly by locking ye away, but I was so angry it was all that came to mind," he said quietly.

He stopped next to the tub, but his head and eyes were turned away from my body as he bent and touched the surface of the water with his fingertips, quickly jerking them away.

"Ach, lass! Ye'll get yerself sick sitting in water that cold. How long have ye been in there?"

"I . . . I don't know. Since Mary brought me up here. I might have fallen asleep." I pulled my knees up toward my chest and wrapped my arms around my legs. The position was warmer, and covered a little more of my intimate parts.

Eoin reached toward the bed to grab a blanket off the top. He stretched it out and held it open for me, still looking away. "Here, lass, stand up and go sit by the fire."

I knew he sensed my hesitation when the corner of his left brow creased in frustration. "I'm not looking at ye, lass. I just want to talk to ye, but if ye doona get yerself out of that tub I'll lift ye out of it myself."

Despite the brief time I'd spent with him, I knew he wouldn't make an idle threat. I reached out and snatched the blanket, wrapping it around myself as I stepped out of the large basin.

Silently, I walked closer to the fire, sitting as close to the flames as I could on the stone floor. Keeping my hands, arms, and legs inside the blanket, I hugged myself, enjoying the feeling of hiding every part except my head underneath the blanket, which concealed the fact that my legs were shaking. I was so nervous to hear what he was going to say, I felt like I could vomit. Thankfully, Eoin didn't force me to wait too long before he spoke.

"Blaire. I canna pretend that I'm any less angry than I was before. I know that Arran puts the blame on himself, but from what I saw, ye are guilty as well. I know I must allow ye to live in the castle and act as my wife on certain occasions, but as far as I'm concerned, our marriage is invalid. I'll not be unkind to ye, but I'll not treat ye as I would a loving companion, either."

He paused, obviously waiting for a response, which I didn't have. After a few moments, he gave up and continued talking.

"No one outside of the castle will know the truth about our marriage, but we will live for the most part separately, only joining when it is time to produce an heir. Regardless, ye are never to be alone with Arran again. And we will be spending quite a lot of time together for the sake of appearances, aye? It is my hope that we can both learn to live in peace with one another."

He stared intently, his dark eyes blacker than usual, as he awaited my response. I was so filled with relief at learning that I would be sleeping and living separately from him that I was unsure of what to say. As far as producing an heir, I had no intention of hanging around long enough for that to be an issue.

I could tell Eoin was still furious and it was all he could do to speak to me politely. If I showed him just how glad I was to hear every word he'd just said, I knew it might crack his calm façade. Remorse was the best way to soothe a man's wounded ego.

"I am sorry for what happened, Eoin. I have no good explanation. I understand the reasons for yer requests and, aye, I accept them. Ye have my word that I will not make the same mistake again. Thank ye for not leaving me in that prison." I tried to look as apologetic as I could. I truly was sorry for upsetting him, but I knew the situation was really caused by someone other than myself.

Eoin's eyes softened at my words, and he walked toward me, gently placing a hand on the top of my head. "Aye. I know ye are, lass. I'm sorry that it must be this way, too. I'll leave ye to rest now. We all gather for breakfast in the grand dining hall every morning. Ye will be expected at my side."

I glanced up at him, and he jerked his hand away, his eyes hardening as he turned and left, leaving me alone in the room once more.

CHAPTER 15

"Doona worry so much, dearie. Ye've done fine so far, and it's unlikely that Eoin would press ye with such a question, but it's important that ye know it if ye are here long enough to have to meet Blaire's father. Now, which ear is it that he canna hear from?"

"It's his left ear. He was born that way and can't hear anything unless you speak loudly or into his right ear."

"Yes, dear. So doona be alarmed if he screams at ye. It's only that he canna know how loud he is sometimes."

Mary laughed, her entire belly moving with each chuckle, causing me to smile in return.

It had been two weeks since I'd been released from the dungeon and, while the first few days after my imprisonment found me under Eoin's constant watch, Mary quickly picked up on the problem and suggested that I ask Eoin if I could spend my afternoons with her so that she could teach me how to cook. While it was highly unusual for the laird's wife to spend her time in the kitchen, I knew he was tired of babysitting me, and he consented easily. Since then, I'd spent a large portion of every day either training with Mary so that I could learn family history and cultural customs, or digging through the mountains of books in Morna's spell room.

While I was enjoying my lessons with Mary immensely, the search to find a spell that would get me home was an entirely different story. The small room was crowded with books, journals, and records, most of which had absolutely nothing to do with spells. Morna's records and diaries I could read, but the majority of her spell books were in Gaelic, a language that I did not know. I was slowly having to search through everything written in

English first, all while sorting through the things in Gaelic that looked relevant and setting them aside to deal with later.

I was busy thinking of my game plan for the next few hours, which I would spend sifting through the rooms' contents, when Mary stopped chuckling and spoke once more.

"Ye may have noticed that he doesna seem as angry anymore. He's slowly warming to ye, a little more each day."

Her words surprised me. Sure, Eoin no longer seemed angry in the way in which he carried himself when he was around me, and his eyes didn't look as dark, but 'warming'? I hadn't seen anything to make me think that. "What do you mean, 'warming'? I wouldn't say that, exactly."

"Oh, that's because ye doona know him the way I do, dearie. He doesna warm to people as easily as his brother does. He guards himself closely. He knows that ye have the power to break his heart. Old Mary's known him his entire life, though, and I see the way he looks at ye. He cares for ye, even if he willna let himself know it."

"I think you're wrong, Mary. He's never done a thing to make me think he's anything but repulsed by me. But even if you're right, it's best that he doesn't let himself start to care. I'll be gone from here before too long."

Knowing that today's family history lesson was at an end, I stepped inside the doorway and made my way over to the pile of my modern clothes, which I'd hidden away to put on only while I worked in the spell room. I looked forward to those hours every day, so that I could put on a bra to strap the girls in place and put on my favorite pair of jeans. It was heaven, or as close as I was going to get to it here.

Seeing that I was preparing to work on the books, Mary stood to leave. "Well, dearie, I see that ye are about to slip on those awful shreds of cloth ye seem to care so much about, so I'll leave ye to yer work. I'll come back before the evening meal. But, I'll not lie to ye. Eoin's already allowed himself to care. Open yer eyes up and ye will see it, as well."

With that she turned and left the basement, and I sat down to get to work.

---

*E*oin made his way down to the dining hall for the evening meal and stopped abruptly when he caught a glimpse of his reflection in a piece of armory which hung on the wall. He was surprised to see that the corners of his mouth were pulled up, resembling something of a smile. He tried to relax his face so that his mouth fell back into its usual position, but he found that his lips didn't want to stay put.

Confused, he turned away from the reflection and continued to make his way down the hall, all the while wondering why he was so pleased and excited at the idea of eating. It hit him when he walked into the dining hall to see Blaire seated in her usual place.

It wasn't the prospect of food that excited him. After spending the entire afternoon alone, he was going to get to see Blaire.

He'd done his best to stay angry with her and resolve himself to the fact that their marriage was always going to be one of convenience, but he knew he wouldn't be able to maintain his anger forever. It was getting harder each day for him to ignore his feelings.

When he'd walked in on Arran kissing her in the hallway, he thought he'd seen two lovers stealing a precious moment alone when he wasn't around. But after spending a fortnight watching the two of them around each other, he thought that perhaps Arran had been telling him the truth. Every meal, he watched as the two of them sat across from each other, but there were no knowing glances, no palpable tension that he could pick up on. In fact, they never spoke to each other. All conversations took place entirely between Blaire and himself.

And what great conversations they were! He'd never been around a lass that seemed so interested in his stories. She asked questions and listened eagerly, as if savoring everything new she learned about him. Oftentimes, he would say something and a look of pure surprise or slight confusion would cross her face, and he immediately glimpsed the ornery child he'd known growing up.

But, she was no longer that child. She was a woman, no denying that, and looked to him more beautiful each time he saw her.

He loved the odd way in which she spoke. Sometimes she said strange words, and her accent often slipped into an odd mixture of Scottish and something he'd never heard. He wondered if she'd spent a lot of time around a foreign nurse growing up, whose influence had shaped the way she pronounced her words. He loved the disjointed sound of it and found himself wanting to listen all day.

As he sat down diagonally from her at the large table and looked up at her bright, dimpled smile, he decided it was pointless to remain angry for the sake of his wounded pride. Tonight, he would take the lass somewhere special. Mayhap they both could take a step toward shaping their marriage into what a marriage should be.

*M*aybe Mary was right. The thought crossed my mind several times throughout the evening meal. Halfway through whatever strange meat sat before me—I'd stopped asking after about three days—I'd glanced up to see Eoin staring at me in a way that sent an unfamiliar shiver down the back of my neck. At one point, he even reached over and squeezed my hand in the middle of one of his stories. The touch was so unexpected, I nearly spit up my food.

He seemed to be in an especially good mood, and it wasn't until he stopped talking, as if waiting for me to answer a question, that I realized I hadn't been listening at all.

"I'm sorry. What did ye ask me?" My cheeks suddenly warmed.

"Would ye allow me to take ye somewhere this evening? I'd like to show ye something." He smiled kindly, and it was shocking to me how his eyes changed depending on his mood. I smiled, unable to hide my flattery at the question. Regardless of how much I wanted to get home, I loved talking to him, and I couldn't repress the pleasant hum that settled in my stomach at the thought of being alone with him. "I would love to."

"Aye?" He asked the question as if surprised by my response, but smiled as he stood.

"Aye." As I took the hand he offered, Arran rose from the other side of the table and quickly left the room.

*I*t didn't matter that he was drunk. Arran had stayed that way for weeks. He still knew something odd was happening with Blaire. Something had changed between them, and it had nothing to do with the fact that Eoin had caught them in the hallway.

Arran knew she wasn't avoiding him out of guilt or remorse. In fact, it seemed as if she wasn't intentionally avoiding him at all. She was behaving as if nothing had ever happened between them, that no love had been shared, no kind words exchanged.

He could tell that Eoin was starting to fall for Blaire, and he couldn't blame him. She was his wife, after all, and ever since the night he'd released her from the dungeon, she'd been nothing less than kind, enthusiastic, and alive around him.

If Arran wasn't completely sure that he knew who Blaire really was at her core, he would have found himself charmed by this new side of her, too, and happy that his brother had found himself such a wonderful wife. But, what Eoin failed to see was just how different this Blaire was from the one he'd married only a few short weeks ago.

Blaire's personality seemed to have changed overnight. She was quieter, less feisty, and entirely likable. One of the things Arran loved most about Blaire was that not everyone found her pleasant to be around. As for himself, he couldn't like her more than when she was being her typically stubborn, haughty self.

Even her voice was different now. She said words that had no meaning and mispronounced others that he'd heard her say correctly many times before. She looked at every meal as if she was afraid to eat it, as if she'd never seen such fare in her life.

But all of those things were nothing compared to what really bothered him about her behavior of late. He knew he'd broken her heart the morning of the wedding. He saw it in her eyes the moment it happened, and he'd felt her pain through every inch of his own being.

Her behavior was not that of someone who'd just suffered heartbreak. It was the opposite entirely. She smiled and laughed and asked questions like someone in the midst of the thrilling beginning of newfound love.

Perhaps it was all an act. It must be. Arran was sure of it. For, how could she have healed so quickly from the pain that still rendered him senseless? Perhaps she thought to build Eoin's hopes, only to hurt him as some form of revenge for the hurt that he himself had caused her.

If that were the case, Arran would not allow her to destroy his brother to get her vengeance. Whatever was going on with Blaire, he intended to find out as quickly as possible and put a stop to it.

e made our way to a corner of the castle I'd yet to see in my few weeks here. Eoin reached for a lantern before opening the small door in front of us. Then we moved into a small winding stairwell.

It was totally dark except for the flame that flickered each time we moved up the steps together. Eoin didn't let go of my hand, and with each step upward, our bodies touched, spreading delicious shocks over my skin.

I couldn't see the top landing, so when Eoin stopped and faced me, I continued to try and walk up the next step. Our chests bumped together and I whacked the top of my head hard against the bottom of his chin. Yelping at the impact, I nearly teetered off the top landing, but was gathered in close by Eoin's quick hands.

"Ach, lass. Ye've got a hard head. Do ye see any of my teeth lying around? I think ye might have rattled some loose."

He removed his left hand from my lower back and reached up to rub his chin. I laughed and looked down in shame, my forehead delicately touching his chest. He surprised me by pulling me closer to him and wrapping both arms around me. He gently kissed the top of my head, right on the spot I'd whacked against his chin.

"But, I'm sure my chin wasna so pleasant a feeling on the top of yer head, now was it? Come, lass. Crawl out onto the wall with me."

He raised a wooden panel at the top of the landing, revealing a small window-like space through which he crawled. Once on the other side, he reached his hand through the opening to assist me. I grabbed his hand and, with my free one, hiked up the back of my dress and rather ungracefully made my way out onto the wall.

"Come and sit out on the ledge, I willna let ye fall." He made his way over to the edge of the wall that surrounded the back side of the castle. Deftly, he jumped up onto the stone wall and sat, letting his legs hang freely off the edge.

Seeing that his eyes were turned away as he stared out at the ocean, I quickly hiked up the bottom of my dress and leaped up onto the edge. I sat beside him before he could turn back and witness my unladylike movements.

"Well, I'd meant for ye to see the stars, lass, but there's little to look at tonight. It appears that a storm's headed this way."

The sky was black, and there were dark clouds rolling, as if following the waves that crashed up onto the shore below us.

The wind blew hard, and the sound of it mixing with the harsh crash of waves against the rocks below was oddly beautiful.

We sat silently for some time. The wind chilled me so that I shivered beneath the thick dress that covered all of my body, but I was unwilling to say anything, not wanting to shatter the moment. A closeness between us hung heavy as we shared the long silence, listening to the water crash on the rocks and the distant sound of thunder over the horizon. I felt as if I'd known Eoin for a long time, rather than the few short weeks I'd spent at the castle.

The touch of his fingers as he laced them with mine caused me to cautiously glance toward him out of the corner of my eye. He held my hand gently, drawing small circles along the base of my thumb with his, but he didn't look in my direction, keeping his gaze straight ahead, seemingly distracted by the water below.

I closed my eyes and inhaled the cold wet air, savoring the sensation of his rough fingers against my hand. A loud boom of thunder brought large drops of water down from the sky, soaking us both in seconds.

I cringed inwardly as the rain hit my hair. I was having enough trouble keeping my mane tamed without the use of a straightener.

Eoin swung off the ledge, extending both hands out to me. "Come, lass. Ye will catch a cold standing out in this rain. Let's go inside."

He stood back, allowing me to crawl through the window-space first. As I stood in the dark stairwell once more, I brushed the wet strands of hair out of my face, slinging drops of water in every direction.

I knew Eoin had made his way back into the stairwell, but the candle in our lantern had burned out while we'd been on the ledge. Once he closed the hatch that covered the window, the stairwell descended into pitch darkness.

"Doona worry, lass. I know every inch of this castle, even in the dark. We will make our way down these stairs together, aye?"

Blindly I reached forward, palming the air, expecting to make contact with his hand. Instead, my palm rested on his chest as he stepped closer. Slowly, he backed me into the wall and my breathing accelerated as the evening whiskers on his cheek scratched against the side of my face.

His hands moved so that he held onto both of mine as he gently placed his lips against my own.

The kiss was surprisingly gentle and sweet, but was over far too quickly. Eoin moved his lips right next to my ear and whispered, "Ach, lass, if tis alright with ye, I doona think I can stay angry at ye any longer."

And with that, he turned and led me down the dark stairwell, the heavy thumping of my heart beating in my ears.

$\mathcal{E}$oin stroked the mare's mane as he worked to prepare her for their ride into the village. His own horse sat ready, tied at the end of the stables, glancing impatiently in Eoin's direction.

He smiled at the old, gray stallion, his trusted horse and companion since childhood. "Ah, Griffin, doona look at me so. We will be leaving soon enough. But ye see, Sheila will be joining us today. Blaire will be riding her, and I expect ye to be on yer very best behavior. Do ye understand?"

The old horse neighed as Eoin walked toward him, offering him an apple to placate him until they rode out for the village.

Footsteps from behind caused Eoin to spin around toward the west entrance of the stables. Expecting to see Blaire, he couldn't repress the look of disappointment on his face at seeing Kip make his way over to Sheila.

"Looks like ye did a fine job with Sheila. Her coat hasna shined so brightly in years. But I still doona understand why ye won't let Blaire ride Angus. She's good with horses. She will think that Sheila is too tame." The old man shook his head as he loosened Sheila's reins and went to tie her up by Griffin.

"Angus is only fit for racing through the countryside, not a trip to the village, and ye know it, Kip. Now, I know Blaire dinna treat ye well her first night here, but I wish ye'd ease up on the lass."

"I'll not be having ye tell me what I should do, laddie, laird of this keep, or not. But it doesna matter, my thoughts on her. She's yer wife. Ye are the one that has to bed the ungrateful . . ." He was cut off by a cheery 'hello' at the end of the stables.

Eoin turned to see Blaire making her way toward him. She looked beautiful with her bright eyes and smile and her hair pulled up in a delicate knot at the base of her neck.

He watched as she bid Kip a good morning and was rewarded with a huff from the old man as he retreated from the stables.

"Doona let him bother ye, lass. He's only hard on the outside."

"Oh, it's alright. Where are ye taking me?" She reached up and touched his shoulder, and he had to restrain himself from pulling her against him.

"To the village. There's just a few things that need attending." He walked over to where both horses were tied and gestured toward Sheila with his head. "Ye can take the brown one. Her name's Sheila. Ye will have no problems with her, I'm sure."

Blaire cautiously approached the mare, hesitantly reaching out her hand to touch the horse's throat. Eoin watched, curious as to why she seemed so unsure. He'd always known her to be a fine rider.

"What's wrong, lass? She's got more fire in her than she looks. She'll be a fine ride for ye."

"How do I get on her?"

The question surprised him, but he ignored it as he bent to offer her his assistance in mounting the horse. No sooner had Blaire situated herself than the mare started whining and trying to pull at the reins that kept her fastened to the edge of the stables.

"What do I do with her, Eoin?"

"Just stroke her, lean forward and whisper in her ear, calm her as ye would yer own horse." He turned and climbed onto Griffin, leaning forward to untie the reins of both horses so that they could set off toward the village.

He rode ahead a short distance, waiting for Blaire and the mare to join him, but when he heard no hooves he turned to see Blaire and the mare sitting at the side of the stables where he'd left them.

Clicking, he steered Griffin back toward the stables. "What's the matter with ye, lass? Do ye no longer want to go?"

"No, I do want to. I just don't know how to do this."

Eoin frowned as he pulled back on Griffin's reins, stopping him next to Sheila. He knew Blaire could ride. He'd seen her do it many times, with many different horses. Why was she feigning ignorance now? Perhaps, she was afraid that he'd be angry with her for not wanting to accompany him. Or mayhap she wanted a reason to ride with him on the same horse.

While he wasn't sure of the reason, he enjoyed the second possibility much more. "Would ye like to ride with me, lass? Griffin may be old, but he can carry ye and me together, easily."

"Aye, I think that would be best."

Ah, so she did want to ride next to him. He smiled inwardly, pleased at the notion as he lifted her from Sheila's back and placed her snugly in between his legs astride Griffin.

J rode pressed closely to Eoin as we made our way down into the village. That had almost been an unimaginable disaster. I'd never ridden a horse in my life, and I had no idea what I'd been thinking when Eoin asked if I would like to go with him and to meet him in the stables.

I'd ignorantly pictured some fancy horse-drawn coach taking us into town, like a scene out of *Pride and Prejudice*; I was obviously not taking into account that things of that nature were from an entirely different century that was yet to come.

Still, I much preferred this method of transportation to any sort of pulled wagon, and I relished the feeling of Eoin's chiseled muscles pressing against my back. He rode with his hands around my waist, and the strength in his legs and arms as they surrounded me made me hope it was hours until we reached the village.

Instead, it took us less than an hour before Eoin stopped the horse and dismounted, quickly reaching his arms toward me to help me down. He smiled at me as I reached behind to rub my sore bottom, then gestured for me to follow him as he made his way to a small cluster of cottages in front of us.

Eoin turned his head to tell me something, but he was interrupted by a loud voice coming from one of the doorways.

"Well, if it isn't Laird Conall! Why, it's been too long since we have seen ye here, son!"

Eoin's face lit up as he moved away from me and embraced the large, red-faced man. "Aye, it has, Bran! How's yer wife and children?"

"Fine. Fine. Dona is in bed, nursing our sixth bairn. She gave birth only two nights ago." The man's eyes gleamed with pride as he spoke of his family.

"Six! My God, man! Do ye not ever let the lass rest? How have ye been managing the others on yer own the last few days?"

"I havena." The man let out a loud, deep chuckle before continuing. "They've had free run o' the place while their mother has been in bed. I'm sure she'll be no too pleased with me once she's up. Come inside. Let us have a drink for old time's sake, aye?"

Eoin reached his hand behind him, and I instinctively took hold.

"Let me introduce ye to my wife, Bran. This is Blaire."

I smiled as the man quickly looked me up and down. "How did this old sot get such a beautiful lass like ye to marry him? Oh, never mind. What's done is done, aye? I shouldna try to talk ye out of it now. Come. Ye shall have a drink with us, as well."

I followed the two men through the small entranceway into a one-roomed first floor where five children, minus the newborn, were running around, creating chaos. All were under the age of seven, and a few days without strict structure from their mother had put them in a tailspin.

I knew that the noise level in the home could in no way be conducive to their mother's rest, and my teacher drive immediately kicked in.

"Alright, stop where ye are!" I quickly held my hands up as I stared them down. "My name is Blaire, and ye are all going to follow me outside so that we can allow yer mother some rest time. Aye?"

The three oldest children glanced up to take in the shocked look on their father's face. When he stood silently, they looked up at me and seemed to consent, slowly marching out the front door together. I yanked up the two youngest—year-and-a-half-old twin boys—and placed one on each hip.

Turning to address the two men before following the children outside, I said, "Go ahead and enjoy a drink. I'll keep the children busy so that the two of ye can visit and yer wife can rest with the baby."

Leaving them both open-mouthed, I made my way outside with the two squirming toddlers.

CHAPTER 18

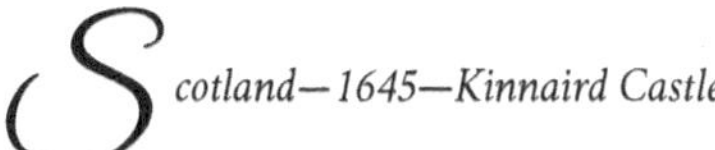

cotland—1645—Kinnaird Castle

"The fire served no purpose! The lad is too foolish to see when he's been warned and to be afraid. He thinks the fire happened by chance, set by a drunkard at the wedding." Ramsay Kinnaird sat at the end of a long table, staring down the two servants unfortunate enough to be called to his service.

"What will ye do, sire? Attack them at once?"

The servant's words were rewarded with a large bang as Ramsay threw his fist down on the table hard. "No, ye fool! To attack by surprise would be too easy! I want Eoin and his brother Arran to sense the darkness coming for them. I want them to feel afraid for their home and their loved ones and know that there is nothing they can do to stop them from losing everything." He stood from the table and walked toward the servants until his own face was but inches from theirs. "The first attack was too simple. We must take something that is precious to them."

"What would be best to take?"

Ramsay contemplated the servant's question. A wicked grin contorted his face as his next plan came into full view in his mind. "The Conalls have always loved their horses. Conall Castle is known for them, and the family boasts of their fine quality. The beasts are all cared for by that pathetic old man they call a stable master." He nodded, approving more and more of the plan. "Yes, the fear of losing their horses will hurt them. Send the two lads that work our stables out tomorrow midday. Take their mother, should they need motivation." He gave one of the servants instructions to pass on to the lads, adding, "Tell them no Conall horse is to be left unscathed."

"No, Arran. I'm telling ye the truth. I dinna ask her to take the children out of the house. She offered to do it all on her own. I was surprised as well, and ye should've seen Bran's face."

Arran ran his hands through his hair as he paced back and forth in front of his brother. He'd spent days trying to make some sense of Blaire's strange behavior, and the only thing he could come up with was that this lass wasn't actually Blaire. That conclusion seemed impossible to him, yet he felt the truth of it all the way to his core.

"There's no logic to it, Eoin. Blaire has no fondness for children. If ye left her alone in a room with them, she'd be more likely to eat them than offer to care for them."

"Aye, I know the Blaire we knew as children was that way, but perhaps she's changed."

"She hasna. Because the lass ye have married isn't Blaire." Arran could sense Eoin's temper flaring as he finished his sentence, and he marched over in front of his brother to stop him from pacing back and forth.

"What are ye talking about, Arran? Ye sound like a crazy man, and ye have for some time. I know that ye are still grieving for our father, but ye have to stop drinking so much. It's beginning to addle yer thoughts."

"I've not been drinking today, Eoin. I know what I'm saying sounds foolish, and I canna make sense of it myself, but this lass is not Blaire."

"Just because she spent part of a day around children doesna mean a stranger has replaced Blaire. God, listen to what ye are saying, Arran. Ye've gone and lost yer mind."

"I havena. Kip also told me that ye dinna even end up taking Sheila to the village because Blaire could not ride her. Ye know Blaire can ride well, Eoin."

"Aye, we left Sheila at the stables, but only because Blaire wanted to share a horse with me."

Arran rolled his eyes, crossed his arms, and leaned back against the wall behind him. "Did she tell ye that?"

"No, but ye are not the only one who can sense what a lass wants, Arran. Doona mention this conversation to me again, aye? I'm worried for ye, brother. Perhaps ye need to go away for a few days. I believe Kip is about to make another trip to bring back another horse or two for the stables. Go with him, and doona drink while ye are gone."

"Aye, I'll go. I canna stand to be around ye when ye refuse to see what's right in front of ye. All I ask is that ye watch her. She doesna talk like Blaire, either. Test her. Take her to do something ye know Blaire was good at as a child, and see if she succeeds."

With that, he turned and left, leaving Eoin to think about all that he'd said.

93

CHAPTER 19

I was going to throw up. There was no doubt about it whatsoever. I was about to be expected to string a bow and arrow and shoot the silly thing right in the middle of the target.

When Eoin knocked on my door this morning shortly after breakfast, I'd been excited. It was unusual for me to see him after breakfast, and with progress moving so slowly in the spell room, I was happy for any excuse to keep me from my work. That is, until he asked me to go shooting with him and proceeded to tell me over and over again how wonderful I'd been at it as a child, and how he and Arran never wanted to go shooting with me because they knew I would beat them ruthlessly.

The gig was definitely up. By tonight, I would undoubtedly be locked away again in the dungeon, where I'd been a few weeks ago.

It's not that I was in bad shape. I did try to drag myself to the gym at least once, and sometimes twice a week. But jogging a mile had nothing to do with maneuvering this huge wooden contraption in such a way that it would send an arrow soaring through the air. I seriously doubted I could even pick the thing up off of the ground.

"Well, that was a fairly good shot, but I have no doubt ye can beat it."

He flashed one of those smiles that made my muscles feel weak—exactly what I didn't need at the moment—as he stepped out of the way to let me take my place in front of the target. "Here ye go, Blaire."

I gripped the bow unsurely, sighing with relief when I found it wasn't as heavy as I'd first expected. My hands shook as I fumbled with the arrow, trying my best to mimic Eoin's movements exactly.

Pulling back, I released the arrow high into the air. Two seconds later, it unceremoniously landed three feet in front of me. I shut my eyes in defeat, only to hear Eoin's laughter from behind me.

"Ach, lass. Has it been a long while then since ye went shooting?" He came up behind me and gave my shoulders a gentle squeeze. "Perhaps my memories are wrong about how good ye used to be at this."

"I suppose they probably were. Best if I just watch ye shoot." I tried to back away, but his hands on my shoulders held me in place.

"Nay, lass, I wasna wrong. It's just nerves, is all. Give it another go, aye?"

Reluctantly, and with the most unpleasant look on my face that I could manage, I reached for another arrow and went about shooting it off once more.

It hit the target right in the middle.

"What? Yes! No freakin way!" I jumped, tossing the bow to the side as I shot my hands up in the air, realizing too late that I'd let my language slip and that I must have looked like a buffoon as I leapt gleefully up in the air.

Eoin cocked his head and looked at me with a confused expression. "What did ye just say lass? 'Freakin'?"

I fumbled for an explanation. "No, I just made a noise, a happy noise for hitting the target. I'm surprised, is all."

"Why would ye be surprised, lass? Ye have always been good at this. Here, let's take turns shooting a few more. Aye?"

They continued to take turns shooting arrows until all that they'd brought stuck out of the target. After the first one, Blaire had hit every single one right in the center.

Eoin had expected her to excel. That's why he'd asked her to go shooting, so that he could prove Arran's ridiculous theory wrong. But why did he feel so surprised?

He knew all that Arran had suggested was impossible, but just to humor his brother, shouldn't he test Blaire in some other way, as well? A fair number of lasses in the Highlands could shoot a bow and arrow decently, and he knew there were always a few people who could succeed at anything upon their first try. Perhaps Blaire was one of those naturally gifted people?

As they gathered up their mess and began the half-mile trek back to the castle grounds, Eoin thought of a few questions that he knew would help put his own mind at ease, and hopefully put an end to his brother's ridiculous notions.

"Blaire, do ye remember the time ye shot me in the arse? Did ye really think it necessary? All I did was tell ye that you could not come down to the village with me and Arran." He turned to watch her closely, hoping she would correct him. He knew why she'd really shot him. His father had spent what seemed like half a day explaining to him why he was never to speak to a lady in such a hurtful way ever again.

"Nay, Eoin. That isn't why I shot ye, that day. I shot ye because ye told me I was the ugliest lass that ye'd ever seen, and ye'd rather kiss Griffin's arse than be married to me someday. It was the summer we walked in on our fathers discussing the betrothal."

"Aye. That's right. I do apologize, Blaire. I was young and foolish. At that age, I'd rather have kissed Griffin's arse than any lass." He laughed, thinking himself foolish for giving Arran's notion any thought.

They reached the castle grounds and Eoin stashed their equipment away. He thought of one last question as Blaire turned to make her way up to her room in the castle. "I canna remember which ear it is that yer father canna hear from. Which is it?"

"It's his right."

Blaire walked inside the castle, and Eoin felt his heart drop into the deepest depths of his stomach.

He knew it had always been her father's left ear that failed him.

CHAPTER 20

$\mathcal{S}$*cotland—1645*

$\mathcal{W}$as it his right ear or his left? Oh, why couldn't I remember that one simple thing? I second-guessed myself a thousand times as I made my way back to my bedchamber. Why did Eoin ask the question in the first place? Was it really that he just couldn't remember, or did he suspect something?

It had to be the first. What on earth could he suspect? Surely, even if he found my behavior different than Blaire's, he wouldn't immediately jump to the conclusion that I was someone else. From everything Mary had told me, I looked exactly like her.

It didn't matter at this point. If he asked, surely he wouldn't know whether or not what I'd told him was true. He wasn't testing me; although, the way he went on and on about how great Blaire was with a bow and arrow, it did sort of seem that way. Luckily, I'd had a knack for shooting. Who knew? I'd never been coordinated at anything, and all of a sudden I was an expert archer. The entire situation was just too odd for words, and it made me even more anxious to get back to work in the spell room. I'd spent far too long here, and with each passing day I found myself more reluctant to spend more hours searching through spell books. I'd much rather explore the castle, visit with Eoin, or actually cook with Mary, like Eoin thought I was doing.

And while I missed my mother, homesickness wasn't settling in like I thought it should have. I loved it here—the lack of cars and modern technology, the way I didn't hear car horns and sirens each time I stepped outside, the way life was quieter and, as a result, more simple. People had to work so much harder for everything, resulting in an overwhelming sense of pride and a work ethic that radiated from them.

I was also beginning to love everyone at the castle: Mary, Eoin, even Kip and Arran—both of whom seemed dead set against getting to know me. It was okay. I still felt more at home here than I did in my newly-remodeled former bachelor pad of a home back in Texas, where I'd spent so many nights alone. It was comforting to know that there were people just down the hall from me. That somehow made every second feel less lonely.

Yeah, it was definitely time to get back to work in the spell room. As nice as it was to escape reality here for a few weeks, this was not where I was meant to be. If that was the case, I would've been born here, hundreds of years ago. I was an unnatural imposter, and it was vital that I find the spell that would return me home.

Estimating that I still had a couple of hours before everyone gathered for the evening meal, I made my way down into the kitchens to let Mary know where I'd be. Her hands were busy, pulling away at some nameless animal I was certain would be staring up at me from a plate come dinnertime, and as she nodded in acknowledgement that she'd heard me, I made my way into the secret spell room in the back of the basement.

Walking to the side, I scooted past a pile of books I'd already gone through, which were now serving as a secret hiding nook for my beloved normal clothes. Now an expert at laces, I whipped myself out of the heavy gown I was wearing and quickly slid on my jeans, bra, t-shirt, socks, and tennis shoes, smiling as I instantly felt more like me.

I'd methodically sorted through every book in the spell room, and had separated them into stacks according to language, age, and probable relevance. I was now on my last pile of books written in English, and I hoped with everything I had in me that what I needed would be in this one. If nothing turned up, I was going to be forced to enlist someone who could read Gaelic to help me with the rest of the books. But I knew that doing so would significantly increase the risk of Eoin discovering the truth.

I let my head fall loosely toward my chest and rolled it around in both directions, trying to release some tension and get myself into work mode. Crawling onto the old wooden bench that sat in front of the desk, I pulled both of my legs toward me, turning them in so that I sat crisscross on the bench.

The ability to move my legs freely after being trapped under heavy layers of fabric was so refreshing that I found myself sitting in odd positions every time I came down to the spell room to work. Throwing my arms high above me to stretch before reaching for the top book on the large stack, I felt the back of my shirt rise with the movement of my arms, exposing the lower half of my back. It stayed bunched there as I reached for the top book and opened it on the desk, bending forward to begin my examination of its contents.

I knew Mary would have keeled over at the sight of so much exposed skin, but the coolness of the room felt nice on my back, and what did I care, anyway?

I was alone in the room and would be until dinner.

The first book I pulled off the top of the stack was one of Alasdair's old journals, and while the majority of entries held nothing of great relevance, there was an entry at the end of the volume that had me leaning far over the desk in anticipation.

In it, Alasdair referenced his last conversation with Morna. And while most of it left out details of their conversations, he did say that it was vital to ensure that Eoin marry Blaire. He wrote of the spell his sister had cast and how Blaire and, I could only assume myself, would switch places in time, and that I would help save them.

From what exactly, I wasn't sure. And while I could feel a thought tugging at some part of my brain, I couldn't think of any real reason for my presence here. Besides, I didn't intend to stay long enough to find out, and the further I got into the entry, the more excited I became. At the end of the journal entry he had spelled out the title of a book, three words written in Gaelic, prefaced with the words, "Morna said to remember this, if the time comes that it is needed."

It had to be the name of one of the Gaelic books stacked on the other side of the room, and it had to have something to do with the spell; I just knew it. I stared at the three words. They sounded completely foreign as I worked to pronounce them as best I could.

* * *

*E*oin was certain Blaire hadn't seen him peeking out from behind his chamber door as she exited her own and made her way down into the kitchens. He knew he was making a mistake by following her. What did he expect to find her doing? She was on her way to help Mary in the kitchens, the same as she did everyday around this time.

Still, she'd misspoken about her father's ear, and it caused a sense of dread and unease to build in his stomach. Eoin couldn't do or think about anything else, with the last three words she'd said to him churning in his mind.

He knew Arran was wrong. He was married to Blaire, not a different-but-similar-looking lass. But he did now see what Arran had been trying to tell him the other day; something was different about her. She was keeping something from him and everyone else in the castle.

Eoin paused and sat down in the small hallway outside the entrance to the kitchen, content to listen to their conversations as Mary and Blaire worked side-by-side. Perhaps she'd been more open with Mary, and listening to them speak would give him a better sense of what was happening with her.

But the lass didn't go all the way into the kitchen, and as he heard her stop at the doorway to tell Mary she was going below to work, his blood ran cold.

Mary's belated, "Aye, lass. I'll come and warn ye when the food is nearly prepared," did nothing to calm Eoin's growing sense of unease.

He waited until he was sure she was far enough ahead of him not to hear his footsteps. From the direction in which Blaire went, he knew there was only one set of steps that led below the castle.

Hesitantly, he made his way into the one-roomed basement. He hoped to see her working on some task for Mary, but when he saw the light flickering from the doorway at the back of the room, he knew he would find nothing good beyond that door.

There could be no good explanation for why Blaire was in his late aunt's spell room. She shouldn't even have known the room existed. Besides their late father, Arran, Mary, and himself, no one else on the castle grounds had ever seen the inside of that room.

Slowly, he crept toward the entrance, barely pulling at the door so that it opened only slightly, allowing him to see inside. Confusion filled his mind as his gaze poured over the lass sitting, rather twisted, in front of his aunt's old desk. The clothes that the woman had on were completely senseless. Why, the lass had fabric that went up in between the length of her legs! For a moment, he assumed she wasn't Blaire, but a lunatic that had made her way into the castle tunnels.

Then he caught a glimpse of something black and odd spread across a bare space on her back. Swirling and dark, the shapes seemed to spell out something permanently etched into her skin. Surely something like that could only be accomplished with witchcraft.

When he heard the strange lass speak, as if trying to sound out something written within the book she was staring into so intently, he couldn't help but swing the door open with a crash, the shock of all he'd seen reverberating through his veins.

"For all that is holy, Blaire! Ye are a witch!"

I was just finishing the end of the last word written in the book when a crash from behind me caused me to whip around to see Eoin's angry presence in the doorway, his thunderous voice screaming something about me being a witch.

Before I could get out a word in protest, he jerked me up by both arms and roughly dragged me away from the small room. He trembled with anger. I could feel it in the grip with which he held onto my arms. I would be bruised tomorrow. As he dragged me up the stairs toward his bedchamber, screaming in Gaelic every step of the way, I found myself hoping that Mary would hear him. Perhaps, she could at least help me explain the situation, not that I was very optimistic about him giving me the opportunity to do so.

He flung open the door and nearly threw me across his bedroom as he let go of his hold and slammed the door shut behind him.

Eoin came toward me, seeming larger than he actually was, and stopped in front of my hunkered-down figure. I stood shakily, refusing to let him bully me until I'd told him all that I knew.

"Let me explain, Eoin. I'm not a witch. I –"

He immediately interrupted me with more words in Gaelic that I didn't understand before he turned and walked over to the window seat to stare outside.

"What do ye expect me to do with ye now, lass? I should've left ye down in the dungeon to rot, but I expect ye spelled me so that I would relent and release ye, aye? What did ye plan to do, Blaire, place spells on us to do yer bidding and torture me for having married ye? I canna believe Arran was right! What a wicked lass ye are!"

Anger flared within me, and I made no effort to continue the accent I'd tried so hard to use over the past weeks. "Are you crazy? Have I done or said anything to anyone since I've been here that would make you think that I wanted to hurt you? If you'd just stop all of your insane ranting and listen to me, I could explain what I was doing in the spell room."

"How did ye even know about the room, Blaire? Ye had no business being in that part of the castle at all!"

"Mary showed me. It's where she found me when I showed up here."

"Ye are a liar, Blaire! Do ye not remember the day ye arrived? Ye insulted just about everyone in the castle, and ye nearly broke poor Kip's back with the inconsiderate load ye piled onto him!"

"No!" I was no longer afraid, but I was so angry I was on the verge of tears. Each breath seemed painful in my chest. "I don't remember the day Blaire arrived because I'm not Blaire! I don't understand why or how I got here, but I've spent almost every minute since I showed up in this godforsaken place trying to get back home to Texas."

"Not Blaire? Texas? God, Arran was right! How could I have been so blind? Well, I'll no more be fooled by ye, and I'll not have ye causing havoc here anymore."

He reached as if to grab for my arm, but I evaded him, jumping quickly to the left and chunking the nearest object I could reach at his head. It hit him square on the nose. With a ferocious growl, he leapt in my direction once more.

If Mary didn't get up here soon, I was seriously doomed.

---

*D*usk descended over Conall Castle, slowly covering every inch of the grounds, creating the perfect shade from which the two Kinnaird servants could hide. They stopped their horses nearly a mile away from their destination, tying them securely to trees far enough away so that the animals wouldn't be alarmed by any sounds the horses in the Conall stables might make when they carried out their deed. It wouldn't do for them to spook their own. They needed them to get back quickly to Kinnaird Castle.

They had camped along the way, and following Ramsey's instructions, each night they'd collected and saved the blood of the wild game they shot for their dinner in flasks. They retrieved the flasks now from their packs

"I thought ye said there would be over a dozen horses here. There's only nine. The three stables at the end are empty."

"Aye. There should be, but we're only to worry with what's here. We doona have much time to begin with. We must do it quick, do ye understand? They'll not be without someone in the stables for long. We must come while they are all at dinner. The old stable master eats with his wife in the kitchens, while the laird, his lady and brother dine in the grand hall. We shall only have a few short moments to accomplish the task."

The youngest servant, a lad of no more than sixteen, reached to wipe the sweat from his brow. It was a chilly evening, but he felt strangled by the heat rising from his own body and breathed in deeply to try and still the frantic thumping of his heart. It was a cruel crime for which he was about to be responsible. These horses were some of the finest he'd ever seen, healthy and strong. It broke his heart to harm them for no real purpose other than to stoke Ramsey's pride.

As he watched his older brother approach the first steed, he caught his brother's hand. "Be gentle with them. I know we must do this to save Mother, but I willna have them be frightened more than necessary."

As his brother nodded, the younger of the two released his grip, and a knot of emotion hardened in his throat.

With tears streaming down both their faces, the brothers moved quickly, trying to finish their horrid task as mercifully as they could.

When finished, the two boys fled into the night with their souls and minds heavy and their hearts filled with hate for Ramsay Kinnaird.

The trip to get the horses had been shorter than expected, but Eoin had been right; Arran needed to calm down, and getting away from the castle for a day or so with Kip helped tremendously. He had been drinking too much, and he was certain it had impacted his feelings about Blaire. She wasn't someone else, someone trying to harm his brother. She was simply as lost as he was, trying to deal with her new marriage in the best way she knew how.

It was time that he followed her example, and with his mind set on doing just that, he smiled and pointed so that Kip would look out over the horizon where they could see Conall Castle off in the distance, bathed in moonlight.

He was feeling better than he had in ages, and he knew the last time he felt this good was before his father's tragic death. Perhaps Blaire's hold on him was not as strong as he'd thought. He only needed time to heal from the changes of the last few months.

The stables were only a short distance away, and it startled Arran that instead of picking up their pace in their anticipation of getting home, both horses reared up on their hind legs and tried to turn in the other direction. Both men steadied their mounts, and Arran reached down to soothe Sheila as Kip did the same to Griffin.

Arran scanned the distance to the stables, looking for something that would have caused the horses to start. Suddenly, out of the corner of his eye, he saw Angus charging in their direction.

"Ach. Angus! I doona know how else to keep that animal in the stables. If he knows we've taken other horses out, he willna stay put. I expect he's been loose since we left."

"Kip, he looks frightened. I know he's wild, but I've never seen him behave so."

Angus didn't slow his pace as he reached the two men, instead charging in wide circles around them, whinnying and making other noises of distress.

"It's not too far to the stables from here. Let's leave the horses here and take a look first. Aye?" said Kip.

He was already dismounting Griffin and walking him over to the nearest tree to secure him as Arran nodded in agreement, easily swinging himself down from Sheila as he patted the side of her neck. "It's alright, sweetheart. Ye stay here with Griffin and Angus, and I'll come back for ye shortly."

Fear lodged securely in Arran's gut, and with each step closer, it grew. "Something isna right, Kip. I fear someone's been in the stables." He turned to see the old man slowing his pace, his face still and pale.

"Aye, I believe ye are right, son. I smell blood, lots of it. I doona know if I can make myself see. Would ye mind going on yer own? I'll stay right here."

Kip's words did nothing to soothe Arran's fear. He'd never known the old man to back away from anything, but as he saw the distraught expression on his old friend's face, he sensed that whatever he was about to see was terrible. Kip loved nothing in the world more than his horses, except perhaps Mary, and Arran could feel it in his bones that it would be best to spare Kip from whatever awaited him beyond the stable doors. He reached out and placed both hands on the older man's shoulders.

"Aye. O' course. I'm sure tis fine, but I'll go and see by myself. Ye stay here and keep an eye on the others." He nudged his head toward the top of the hill where Sheila, Griffin, and Angus, along with the other four horses they'd acquired, stayed tied to the trunk of a tree.

Turning, Arran made his way to the side entrance of the stable. With each step, the smell of blood became stronger, causing his stomach to churn uncomfortably. It was too quiet inside the stables. Disturbingly so. Arran slowed his pace. Heaven help him if – he cut the terrible thought off short before it could take root in his mind and proceeded quickly again, unwilling to let it paralyze him.

Arran stepped inside the dark center walkway of the stables, grabbing the burning flame from outside the entrance to set light to the first lantern in a long row that hung outside each stall door. Filled with dread, he walked from lantern to lantern, slowly illuminating the horror that filled each stall.

His heart sank, then rose again, pummeling the wall of his chest with a force that almost knocked him to his knees. Every horse lay still inside – still and covered in blood. Arran grabbed onto the post to his right to steady himself. He closed his eyes, but after only a moment, opened them again when he heard a muffled snorting.

The horse in the stall in front of him was stirring, trying to stand. Gasping, Arran ran from stall to stall, quickly checking each of the horses.

They were alive! All of them. And he could find no wounds to account for the blood. Still, something wasn't right with the beasts. They were as sluggish as he himself after a night spent with a bottle of ale in his belly.

Somberly, he made his way back to Kip, his face showing what he could hardly bring his voice to say. "I'm so verra sorry, Kip."

"Ye canna mean it. They're dead?" Kip staggered forward toward the stables.

Reaching out, Arran grabbed the old man's arm, stopping him. "No – no, they're alive."

"What is it then? Ye look as if ye've seen a ghost, son." I think they might've been poisoned, Kip. All of them. And covered in blood, but not their own. They're coming around, though. If we're lucky, we found them in time to save them. Maybe Mary can—"

Kip frowned. "But the blood. What do ye mean it's not their own?"

"I canna find any wounds on them. It's as if they've been doused with some other poor animal's blood."

"How do ye know the blood is from an animal?" Kip asked, his eyes flashing fear as he glanced in the direction of the castle. "Mary . . . " he said quietly, choking on the name.

Arran followed his gaze and went still. "No," he whispered, thinking of Mary, of Eoin . . . of Blaire.

He started running with Kip at his heels, the old stable master trying his best to keep up.

* * *

I had no idea how long Eoin and I had been screaming at one another. Half of his words I had no meaning for, and I was equally sure he could claim the same about the things I was saying to him.

I held nothing back now, screaming in my normal accent, using modern words for which I knew he had no context. I did everything I could just to talk and talk, hoping that he would eventually stop screaming long enough to listen to what I had to say.

It didn't work.

And as we continued to yell at each other, he continued to try and forcibly remove me from the room. We played an odd sort of cat-and-mouse game—me dancing out of the path of his reaching hands, him bobbing out of the way so that whatever object I hurled in his direction didn't bludgeon him in the eye.

He now stood in front of the door, blocking my path to any exit, while I stood on top of his bed, reaching for some sort of metal object that sat beside it. When my hand closed around it, I lifted the object and chunked it across the room. Eoin swiftly moved out of the way just as the door opened and the projectile sailed past Mary's head.

"What in God's name do ye think the two of ye are doing? Bri, get down from that bed this instant, and for God's sake, stop throwing things! Eoin, stop ranting in Gaelic. The lass has no idea what ye are saying. It's time we had a talk, all three of us, but I will have no part in it while the two of ye are acting like ye have gone and lost yer minds." Mary stared us down from the doorway, as an uncomfortable hush settled over the room.

Embarrassed, I slid off the top of the bed and moved to stand beside her. "I'm sorry Mary. He walked in on me while I was working in the spell room. I was trying to sound out the name of one of the books, and he saw me in my normal clothes. I'm pretty sure he saw my tattoo, as well. Then he yanked me up and accused me of being a witch. He won't listen to me."

Eoin moved out from behind the door and, with both fists on his hips, looked at Mary and me. "Tattoo? Mark of the devil, ye mean. Why, I've never seen such markings in my life. And Mary, did ye just call her Bri? Do ye mean to tell me that ye knew that we were being fooled by this witch?"

Mary left my side, moving in front of Eoin and slapping him right across the face. I couldn't stop a grin from spreading across mine, and a giggle escaped my lips at the sight of his reddened complexion.

"Have ye forgotten just who ye are talking too, Eoin? Aye, I did call her Bri, because that's the poor lassie's name. But she's no witch. And the only fool around here is ye, ye thickheaded, stubborn arse! Now sit down and not say a word until the lass has finished telling ye everything she knows. Aye?"

Silently he nodded and sat down on the edge of his rumpled bed. I was definitely going to have to take lessons from Mary. She would've made one heck of a teacher.

A breathless voice screaming, "Mary!" from out in the hallway caused us all to file out of the bedchamber. Arran was struggling down the hall, carrying a panting Kip over his shoulder.

"What's happened?" Mary ran toward Arran, grasping her husband's arm where it hung limply down Arran's back.

"It's alright, Mary. He's fine, just out of breath from trying to match my pace.

Kip nodded and gasped as Arran set him down on his own two feet.

Arran's gaze swept the room, moving from Mary to Eoin and finally settling on me. "Thank God ye are unharmed. All of you."

"Unharmed?" Eoin stepped toward him. "Why wouldn't we be, brother? Has something happened?"

"The horses," Kip managed to rasp from where he stood doubled over next to Arran. "The stables..."

Alarm etched Eoin's brow. "What's happened in the stables?"

"The horses. . . " Arran said, "I think they've been poisoned, brother. All but Griffin, Sheila, and Angus. Whoever did it covered them with blood, as well, but I canna find any wounds. Kip and I, we feared the blood was –" He turned away, unable to finish the sentence.

"Ours," I whispered, horrified as I met Arran's darkened gaze.

"The poison," Eoin said, his voice filled with dread. "Did it do its job?"

Arran shook his head, filling me with relief. "No, they're alive. At least for now. We should check on them." He nodded at Kip. "Have ye caught yer breath enough to go back? They'll be needing yer skills if they're to be saved. Yours, too, Mary."

"I'll go right away," she said starting for the door. "Ye help Kip make his way again, Arran. I fear all this excitement has been too much for him."

"I'll come with you, Mary." Eoin followed her out of the room.

Arran wrapped an arm around Kip and helped him to the door.

"Is there anything I can do to help?" I asked.

"No." Arran glanced back at me, his eyes filled with concern. "Stay put, Blaire. The horses were a warning from someone. Nobody's safe here, least of all ye."

With that, he and Kip stepped out and closed the door, leaving me alone in the room.

Why did Arran think I was most at risk? It took only a moment for me to realize it was because I'm a woman. I shook my head and smiled at the outdated belief that women were the weaker sex. But quickly, my smile fell away as I thought of what had happened to the horses and tried to determine what it might mean.

My skin was clammy, and I reached out a hand to fan myself as the full realization of what was going on came to me. I remembered Mom pointing out a special site for horse burials down away from the ruins where she'd said the Conalls had buried their animals. Her research told of horses that had died of unnatural causes in a feud between the Conall's and another clan. She didn't know how the horses had died, but believed that whatever had happened to harm them had been carried out as a warning of the darker trouble that was still to come to the Conalls.

I realized that was the reason I now found myself in seventeenth-century Scotland surrounded by the very people Mom had spent years trying to learn more about. It hadn't crossed my mind until this very moment that I knew how it would end for all of them.

The fire at the wedding had been the first warning, the horses the second.

I'd been sent back in time to help change their fate, and if Mom's research was correct, everyone I'd come to care about here would be dead within a month.

CHAPTER 23

I'd fallen asleep in a cushioned chair situated close to the fireplace in Eoin's bedchamber, only waking when I heard the door open and close and his voice speak behind me.

"Alright, lass, I'm far too tired to scream at ye. Mayhap, now would be a good time for ye to tell me what's going on."

I sat up and reached backward to squeeze my neck, sore and stiff from sleeping in an odd position for far too long. Eoin and the others must have spent the entire night tending to the horses, as light was already beginning to stream through the window on the other side of the room.

"Is everything alright? Did you . . . ?" I couldn't bring myself to finish the question. If they had been forced to put the horses down, it would have been done as an act of kindness. But I could only imagine the emotional toll that act would take on him and the other men, and I didn't want to stoke a wound.

Eoin sat in the chair opposite mine. "No, all but the oldest horses survived. Mary knew of a potion that my aunt had used to counteract the poison."

"And the others?"

"We buried them."

"How many?"

"Three. They were not long for this world anyway, but 'tis still a cruelty and a crime against both the beasts and our clan."

"I think I know why it happened," I said cautiously, half expecting another outburst like I'd witnessed earlier. But he was far too tired for it now. I could tell by his eyes that it was all he could do to stay sitting upright.

"Do ye, lass? Did ye use one of yer spells to give ye the answer?"

I rolled my eyes as I leaned forward in my seat, staring at him straight on. The door swung open once more as Arran came to sit on the floor next to Eoin's side.

"If ye doona mind, lass, I'd like to hear what ye have to say, as well. Mary tried to explain a little, but I found I could not make sense from what she said."

"It's fine, Arran. I already told you, I'm not a witch. But it was one of your late aunt's spells that brought me here."

"And how exactly do ye expect she could've done that? She's been dead for nearly thirty years."

"I have no idea how she did it. All I know is that she did. Now, please, just listen to me. I promise you, I'm every bit as confused as you are, so let me explain the best I can."

"Aye. Go on." Eoin leaned back in his chair, settling in for what I guess he expected to be a long explanation. Truth was, I knew far less than he assumed I did.

"I'm not Blaire. I've never met or seen her in my life, but from what Mary tells me, we look very similar."

"That ye do, lass. Exactly."

"Right. Well, anyways. My name is Brielle Montgomery. Most everyone I know calls me Bri. I was born in the year nineteen hundred and eighty-five. I'm a kindergarten teacher in Austin, Texas. My mother is an archaeologist, someone who studies and tries to find objects from historical sites. Nearly three weeks ago, she asked me to accompany her to Scotland, to help her with a dig on the ruins of this castle. It was the middle of October 2013. Are you following me?"

"Nay, lass. I canna understand half of what ye say. What is 'kindergarten' and 'Texas'?" Eoin frowned.

"Kindergarten is just a school for very small children. I teach five-year-olds how to read, count, and write. Texas is the name of a state in North America. It doesn't exist yet."

"Aye?" Eoin scratched his forehead, exhaling loudly and leaning up into his seat so that our body positions mimicked one another.

I glanced quickly at Arran, who'd said nothing since entering the room and looked far more confused than Eoin. He saw me staring and nudged his head forward as if wanting me to continue.

"Yes. So anyway, we were digging at the ruins and found access into the old spell room. It held all of its original contents that were unharmed by the fire and undiscovered during previous digs. Inside, I found a portrait of myself, the same one that sits on the table there today. It frightened me terribly, and when I started to sound out the inscription written beneath it, I felt as if I was being torn apart. Then everything went black. Shortly after, I woke up here, with Mary looking at me as if I was an alien from outer space. She gave no real explanation at the time, and quickly rushed me upstairs to prepare for our wedding. Until you threw me in the dungeon, I thought perhaps I was dreaming."

Both men sat unmoving, staring at me as if I'd sprouted three heads. "That's all I know," I continued. "I've been sneaking away to the spell room to try and find a spell that could return me to my home. And return Blaire here."

Eoin was the first to speak. "If Mary dinna seem to believe ye, I'd think ye were the craziest lass I'd ever laid eyes on. Still, she seems certain that she saw ye appear here, and ye do speak verra strange."

"Yeah, well, I can't help it. Sorry."

"Ach, lass. I'm sorry, too. I should not have screamed at ye so. I still doona understand, but perhaps we can all work together now to get ye home."

"Please. And maybe I can help you, as well."

"What did ye mean when ye said ye knew why the horses were poisoned?"

"You remember that I said my mother studies things that happened in the past? She works to find objects that will help people understand events that have occurred back in time. She's spent years working on the ruins of this castle, trying to find answers to who killed you all." The words lodged in my throat, and I could barely get them out as I finished the sentence. It alarmed me how much the thought of that happening caused my insides to hurt and tears to fill my eyes.

"Killed, lass?" Eoin lifted his chin out of the palm of his hand and sat up to look at me more alertly. "The castle in ruins?"

"Yes. Your entire clan was destroyed at the end of December, this year. I think your aunt knew that and that's why she cast the spell. Maybe we can stop it from happening. All we have to do is figure out who's going to do it. They left no clues. It's still a mystery, even in my own time."

"I assure ye that we will do all that we can to prevent it," Eoin said firmly. "But what do the horses have to do with this?"

"I think they were a warning or an omen of what's to come. As terrible as it is, it's nothing compared to what will happen to everyone else, unless we stop them. The fire at the wedding was the first warning, the horses the second. I don't know if there will be a third."

Eoin stood and grasped my forearms, lifting me so that I stood in front of him. He gently wrapped his arms around me in apology. "Thank ye for telling us all ye know, lass. I doona see how I have any choice but to believe ye, and I'm glad ye are not a witch. We shall work together to find whoever poses a threat, aye? And then, once our safety is secured, we'll find a way to send ye back to yer own time. Though, I must say, I will miss . . ." He said no more, letting his words span the distance now growing between us.

I allowed myself to fall into him, letting my head lie firmly against his chest as I wrapped my arms around his waist. "Deal. I'm sorry for not telling you sooner. I'd forgotten about the ruins, forgotten about everything but trying to get home."

He placed one of his large hands on my head, calming me as he might a small child. "Hush, lass. I doona think I would've believed ye if I hadn't walked in on ye in these awful rags. The truth has come out, as it was meant to. Now we have no choice but to make the best of it. We are all too tired to speak more of this now. Let's all find our way to our own beds and sleep a while. We can discuss this more at the evening meal. Today shall be a day of little activity around the castle, I expect. We've all had a day of it. Aye?"

I nodded against his chest and pulled out of his embrace as Arran stood from his place on the floor, coming alive for the first time since I'd stopped talking.

"Does this mean Blaire is in the time and place that ye came from?" The pain and fear on his face was evident, and I finally understood why Arran had seemed so displeased with me over the past few weeks. He loved Blaire, and it had hurt him to see me so pleased in Eoin's company when Arran thought her heart was his.

"I assume so. I expect she's with my mother. If that's the case, you have no reason to worry about her. She will be working just as hard as we are to get us switched back. I'm sure my mother's also thrilled to speak to someone she's devoted her life to learning about."

"Forgive me, lass, if that does nothing to ease me mind." As he turned and walked out of the room, I said a silent prayer that Blaire was safe and in the overbearing arms of my mother.

---

*P*resent Day

"*I*s it really true what ye say about women reading and writing in this time?" asked Blaire. "Can most of them really do it? I can, but only because I begged Father until he agreed to let me learn. Very few women are allowed to do so in my time."

Adelle grinned at what must have been at least the thousandth question Blaire had asked that day. Over the past weeks, they'd spent every day working through the contents of the old spell room, and while they'd learned that a spell had caused the switch, they'd yet to find one that would switch the two girls back. "Yes, all children are taught to read now, and they all go to school from the age of five until they're eighteen. A woman doesn't have to be married to find success in this time. I divorced my husband nearly twenty-five years ago, and haven't been married a day since, and I think I'm doing just fine."

"Aye, I believe that ye are."

"I think we are both about to be doing even better, Blaire! I think that this might be the right spell." Adelle stared down at the faded, aging page, double-checking to make sure she was translating the Gaelic inscriptions correctly.

"Do ye think so? What will we have to do?"

"Yes, this is it. Your aunt even wrote notes in the margins about what she intended to use the spell for. It's amazing, really. She knew that Bri would be born, and that the two of you would look identical. She hoped that by switching the two of you, Bri could help stop the tragedy that befell everyone at Conall castle all those years ago."

"Do ye think that she can?"

"I don't know. I hope she's listened to me speak of the event enough to know that she's approaching the time of the tragedy. But I don't intend to wait and see if she stops it. We are switching the two of you back as soon as we can gather the materials." Adelle didn't miss how Blaire's smile shifted into a rather uncomfortable position at the mention of returning home. The girl's heart was hurting from something recent, and although Adelle didn't know the cause of her pain, she'd seen the same expression on her own daughter's face enough times to recognize it.

"What do we need?" Blaire moved about the small room, trying to look as helpful as possible.

"Most of the items shouldn't be too difficult to find. Herbs and things grown locally, which I'm sure Gwendolyn will have no problem helping us locate. We also need the portrait, which we already have. The only thing that we don't have is Alasdair's ring. Morna says here that she gave it to him, and that he would've passed it down to Eoin. We didn't find any such item in our original dig, so we better hope that it's down here in this room somewhere, or we may have a problem."

"Oh, doona worry yet. We've spent our time looking through the books that could hold the location of the ring."

Adelle leaned to the left as Blaire approached her right-hand side, giving the girl a better view of the spell.

"Adelle, did ye see this? It looks as if the spell may only work for a short time."

"What?" Adelle leaned forward to stare down at the page once more, her veins suddenly flooded with panic. Sure enough, scribbled in tiny Gaelic letters, the paper stated that once the original spell had been set into motion, it could only be reversed until midnight of the night before the anniversary of the massacre.

One month from today.

1645

Just passing through on his way back to Kinnaird Castle, the stranger sat silently in the back of the tavern. He watched as Arran Conall downed one goblet of whiskey after another, until he couldn't begin to contemplate how the lad was still conscious, let alone rambling on as he was.

"I doona think I should give ye another, lad. Ye are far enough gone into the cup as it is, aye?" said the tavern master, trying to discourage the lad from drinking more.

"Nay, not nearly far gone enough," Arran argued. "We shall all be dead within the month, according to my brother's wife, and I dare say I've not had nearly enough to drink to let me forget that."

The stranger stood and slipped quietly outside into the cold night air. It was time he finished his journey with haste.

He had very interesting news to share with his master.

CHAPTER 24

orning brought particular success down in the spell room and we'd only been working for a short amount of time. We'd finally found the spell book with the title that matched the one I'd been trying to sound out when Eoin walked in on me a few days earlier.

The process of searching through the Gaelic books in the spell room moved much more quickly once Eoin knew the truth. Since our heart-to-heart talk a few days prior, our days were spent either in the spell room sifting through books or meeting with Arran to discuss the best way to find out who was to be responsible for the upcoming tragedy.

It was nice to live openly among them and to finally be able to behave normally. It seemed to me that the friendship I shared with Eoin grew stronger with each passing day. I enjoyed every moment I spent with him, and the realization made me even more anxious to return home before I surrendered my heart completely.

I hovered uncomfortably around the spell room while Eoin read each page, searching for whatever spell might be helpful. I was unsure of how to help, most of the books already having been gone through, and found myself staring at him while he worked.

God, he really was beautiful. I'd never in my twenty-eight years in the twenty-first century seen a man that looked so much like a man. He oozed masculinity, but not in a way that seemed to diminish his intelligence. He was smart as a whip, no doubt, and his eyes displayed a sort of hidden kindness; the kind that, while hard to get to, would change your world if you were able to get him to open up and show you his true self.

"

He must have felt me staring at him, and he turned to catch me red-faced as I scrambled to look as if I were doing something productive.

"Come here, lass. This is it."

I walked over to his side, surprised when he turned toward me, opening his arms and prompting me to sit on his knee. Hesitantly, I took a seat, trying to think of spilled finger paint, runny noses, and sticky fingers—anything to keep me from concentrating on the hard chiseled body I now found wrapped around my own.

"What does it say?"

"This is the spell she used. See, her notes are written along here." He grabbed my hand from my lap and, using his hand, guided my fingers along the side of the page. Tingles swam over every inch of my body. *Cheetos in the carpet, boogers on the chair backs, pink eye outbreak.* No thought helped.

"I see. Will it work to switch us back?"

"Aye. I think it will." He didn't let go of my hand as he continued. "We need a few items. Mary can locate most of them. But it speaks of my father's ring, and I doona know where that is. I believe he always meant to leave it to me, but his death was sudden, and I doona think it crossed his mind."

"Well, we can find it, right?"

"Ach, lass. I suppose we shall have to. But it says something else, as well."

I looked up into his eyes, waiting for him to continue.

"The spell will only work until midnight on the twenty-eighth of December, then ye canna return home."

"Well, we have to find it by then anyway. That's right around when they think the massacre happens."

"Aye, we shall. Doona worry. Knowledge is the best defense we could have. It willna come to that."

His left hand laid casually upon my knee while his right wrapped around my back, his palm now resting just above my hip on the curve of my waist. He squeezed me in closer to him, drawing his right hand up to my shoulder so that it brought the side of my face closer to his lips.

"I know I've given ye no more than trouble, lass, but I shall be sorry to see ye go." With that he leaned in as if to kiss the side of my cheek, and I nearly turned us both onto the floor with my quick leap out of his lap.

"Yes. I'll be a little sad, too. I think of you, and Mary, and Arran as friends, and it will be odd to no longer get to see you." I awkwardly patted him on the shoulder and turned abruptly to make my way out of the spell room, cursing my heated cheeks with each step. I knew they'd given me away.

innaird Castle

"Why would the lass have told him such a thing?" asked Ramsay. "She has no way of knowing they will be attacked."

"I doona know, sir. I'm only telling ye what I heard. Arran said that Eoin's new bride believed they'd be dead within the month."

"Perhaps she's got more brains about her than I would've expected, being Donal's daughter. The old sot is the silliest fool in the shire. She must've known that the fire and horses were to serve as warnings."

"Aye. I suppose she must've, though Arran dinna seem to know what the lass meant. He was quite drunk. I could not understand how he was still conscious."

"Aye? Well ye did right by making haste to come tell me. Now go, and keep in mind what will happen to ye and yer family if word of our conversation spreads."

Ramsay watched as the man turned and made his way out of the room. He'd intended to warn them, to make them fear what was coming, but now that he knew the Conalls were suspicious, he found himself less comfortable with the idea of a straightforward attack.

"Gregory, find yer way in here at once!"

Quickly the man burst through the doorway and stood before Ramsay, awaiting his instructions.

"Ye are the most cunning lad I have in my command. Ye know how to surprise an enemy, how to throw them off course of yer plan. I need ye to advise me on a matter."

"Of course, sire."

"We will soon be planning an attack against Conall Castle. It is my intention to destroy all who reside under the castle's protection. It seems Eoin and his brother have heard news of a possible ambush, and I doona want them to suspect us in any way."

Ramsay watched as the young lad took in the news with a look of shock. An attack on Conall Castle would be a surprise to all who served him. The two clans had been allies for decades.

"Give them cause to suspect another clan. Send me to Conall Castle, but dress me in the tartan of a distant clan. I will say I am a runaway criminal, seeking refuge with the clan for the information I bring to them. I will tell them that my laird is planning to attack them."

Ramsay clasped the boy on the shoulders. "Aye, perfect. Ride out come morning."

CHAPTER 25

"Where's Arran? I haven't seen him all day." I sat down in my usual place as we gathered for the evening meal. I'd spent the day with Mary, gathering the herbs needed for the spell, while Eoin had searched through Alasdair's things looking for the ring. Although I'd finished the day with an armload of needed herbs, Eoin's hunt had been less successful.

"I sent him to the village to see if any travelers or townspeople might have heard anything about a possible attack. He was also going to meet with some men to discuss our defenses. It will be important to let the villagers know so that we can be as prepared as possible."

"Good idea, but we will figure out who's planning the attack and stop it before it gets to that point." I gave him a reassuring smile across the table, quickly averting my eyes when his smile turned upward at the corner, his eyes staring flirtatiously.

I simply couldn't allow myself to get any more attached to him than I already was. If someone had told me six months ago I would be doing everything I could to "friend zone" a man this good looking, I would have thought they were out of their mind, but that was exactly what I was dead set on doing until I made it back home. He was making it incredibly difficult.

Just as Mary exited the kitchen to set out supper, Arran burst through the back doors, dragging another man roughly along behind him.

"I found him trying to climb over the castle gate. I started to throw him in the dungeon before I came to get ye, but he swears he has news that we will both want to hear." He released his grip on the man, who stood upright and brushed his arm where Arran had gripped him with his hand.

The man threw a very unpleased look in Arran's direction. "Aye, sir. I come to ye seeking refuge in return for news."

Eoin stood from his place at the table, briefly holding a palm up in my direction as if asking me to stay seated. Naturally, it did nothing but encourage me to stand and join him in front of Arran and the stranger.

"Refuge from what? Are ye a criminal? Ye will not find refuge here, if that be the case."

"Nay, sir. I was held a criminal, but the only crime I was guilty of was loving the laird's daughter. He caught us kissing in her garden and locked me away."

"As right he should."

"Ach, Eoin! Doona be so noble. If kissing were a crime, there's not a lad over the age of fifteen who wouldna be locked away!" Arran chuckled, stopping when he noticed Eoin's serious expression.

"Aye, sir. I wanted to wed her, but he wouldna consent. I was too lowly for the old man." The stranger reached up to grab his heart as if in pain.

"Ach, well yer crime may not have been so bad, but I've yet to hear the news that ye think is worthy of a place here for ye."

"Aye, sir. Laird MacLyrron is staging an attack on ye."

Both Arran and Eoin's expressions conveyed their shock, and I was sure I looked no different.

"I've never even met Laird MacLyrron. His territory is far to the south of here. Why would he attack us?" Eoin stared at the man suspiciously.

"He's a foolish man. He wants to expand his land, and yers is one of the most beautiful parts of the country."

"How can we know if ye tell us the truth?"

The stranger shook his head as he looked down at the floor. "Ye doona know. I canna give ye more than me word. Allow me to stay here, and perhaps with time ye will see that what I've told ye is true."

A long silence stretched out as the stranger, Arran, and myself watched and waited for Eoin to make his decision. I could see with every twitch of his hand or pull of his eyebrow that he was trying hard to determine what was the smart thing to do. He knew that, if correct, the information the man had just given him was vital. If wrong, the man was too dangerous to have in the village. Finally he cleared his throat before speaking.

"Ye will stay on castle grounds and work with Kip on the new horses until ye have earned our trust. Then ye may choose to move to the village if ye wish. If Kip is dissatisfied with yer work, however, ye will be returned to MacLyrron at once. Do ye consent?"

"Aye. I canna begin to express my gratitude for yer kindness."

Eoin shot the man a hard look, his eyes cold. "Doona make me regret my decision, lad. It will not end well for ye." He paused and turned to look at

Arran. "Introduce him to Kip, and get him situated in the hut near the stables."

Arran nodded and grabbed hold of the man's arm once more as they started to leave the dining hall.

"And Arran." Eoin raised his voice so that he would hear him before he made his way out the door. "Meet me in my chambers after ye have seen him put away for the evening."

"Aye. O' course." As Arran left with the still nameless man, Eoin motioned for us to return to our places at the table.

We passed dinner in silence, only glancing up at one another occasionally by accident.

I could see how distracted Eoin was, and it was evident in the way his facial expressions seemed to continually shift throughout the meal that he was still wrestling with his judgment.

While I understood his decision, I wasn't sure if I would've made the same one myself. Granted, the young man had relayed the most promising piece of information we'd received, and it would be much easier to reach out for help in preparing a defense if we knew where the attack would be coming from.

But there was something about the stranger that made me uneasy. Something queer about the delivery of his story that planted seeds of doubt deep in my stomach, seeds that were starting to take root.

***

*E*oin turned his gaze away from the fire as he heard his brother enter into his chamber. "What did Kip say about the lad?"

"Well, he was not too pleased to be tasked as caretaker, but I expect twill be good for him to keep busy," Arran replied. "He's still taking the loss of the older horses quite hard."

"Aye, I doona blame him. Do ye think the lad was telling us the truth?" He watched Arran's face, trying to read his expression as his brother sat down in the seat across from him.

"I doona know, brother, but I'd have made the same decision," said Arran. "What do ye think we should do now?"

"We canna confront MacLyrron. For if they've planned no attack, that's a fine way to start a war, no? I think we must reach out to our most trusted allies, ask them to bring their forces here to help us mount a defense a few days before the expected attack. That way, regardless of who is planning it, twill be more than us alone to defend ourselves."

"I think ye are right. What clans will ye call on?"

"Blaire's father, o'course. And although he's a wretched old fool, Ramsay Kinnaird. Our father considered him a friend and ally, and I know that both of them would be willing to come to our aid." Eoin waited cautiously for his brother's reaction, still unsure of his place as laird.

"Aye, tis the finest chance we have. Do ye want me to make a trip to both Donal and Ramsay?"

Eoin shook his head. "Nay, I need ye to stay here and train the men in the village, strengthen our defenses, and work with Mary to help prepare the castle for so many guests. Bri and I will travel to both territories. Donal will be anxious to see his daughter, and Ramsay may not yet know that I am married."

"But ye doona have Donal's daughter. He will be able to tell the difference!"

"I doona think that he will. Bri was able to fool the whole castle for weeks, surely she can fool Blaire's father for only a few days. The two lasses are identical."

"They're not so identical as ye seem to think, brother, but ye do whatever ye must. I'm happy to stay and work here. I'll keep an eye on the runaway, as well."

"Aye, please do. I'm not so sure if I made the right choice, but I'm glad ye think so. Bri and I will leave in the morning."

Arran stood to leave. "Aye, brother, I do. But ye should tell Bri tonight. Lassies like to know things ahead of time."

Eoin chuckled and stood to stretch as his brother walked out the door. "Ye are right, o' course. I'll go and tell her now."

My skill with horses had not improved since my last little journey with Eoin away from the castle, and so with no other alternative, we rode together on Griffin for our journey to MacChristy Keep and Kinnaird Castle.

The proximity of our bodies was doing nothing to help my "friend zone." In fact, Eoin was holding me closer every hour into our journey.

The nerves caused by my ever-tingling insides, the soreness of my bottom from riding a horse all day long, and the fear of not being able to pull off 'Blaire' in front of Donal MacChristy had me on the verge of a nervous breakdown.

I nearly spooked the horse with my erratic jerk at the sound of Eoin's voice in my ear. "What's the matter with ye, lass?"

"Nothing is the matter. Why would you think something was the matter?" I exhaled rather loudly.

"Because I've been listening to ye breathe like that for some time now. Ye sound like Griffin."

"Right. Sorry."

"Ye doona need to be sorry. Ye need to tell me what's bothering ye so. I'd like to help if I can."

"You can't help. My backside is sore from riding, and I'm about to have a freaking panic attack at the thought of fooling Blaire's father into thinking I'm her."

Eoin's laughter did nothing to help my mood. "Lass, ye say things so verra strangely. But ye doona need to worry about Donal. He canna hear well, and ye look just like Blaire. He willna be able to tell the difference."

"I hope you're right." I exhaled loudly once more just for good measure.

"I am right, lass, so ye doona need to worry about that. And as for yer sore 'backside,' I'd be more than pleased to help ye with that," he said in a teasing tone that scattered goosebumps over my skin. I felt a blush heat my cheeks; until winding up in this time and place with Eoin, I hadn't blushed so much since middle school. No, thank you," I squeaked. "My bottom is just fine, thank you very much." He laughed heartily in my ear. "Whatever ye wish, lass. Let me know if ye change yer mind."

"I will. I mean, I won't. Change my mind, I mean."

For some reason, this made him laugh harder, and I crossed my arms in annoyance as we continued our journey to MacChristy Castle.

---

*I*t was just after dusk when Eoin spotted MacChristy Castle off in the distance. With luck they'd arrive just in time to dine with his father's old friend.

He couldn't wait to dismount Griffin and stretch his tired, aching muscles. He had no doubt the lass did have a sore bottom. His was sore as well, and he was much more accustomed to riding. He'd most likely have to help the poor lass out of bed in the morning, a torturous task to be charged, he was sure. He smiled at the thought as he quickly squeezed his arms around Bri to get her attention.

"Ye see that just on the other side of the hill? We are almost there. Would ye like to stop for a moment so we can relieve ourselves and make ready?"

Her response was immediate. He'd expected no less. "Yes, please. I'm about to pee myself."

He smiled widely into her hair. The lass said the most peculiar and wonderful things. He led Griffin over to the base of a large tree and dismounted before helping Bri off, as well. He scooted nearer to Griffin than was really necessary, so as to increase his closeness to Bri as he lifted her off the horse.

She rewarded him with a knowing look, and he let out a small laugh before walking away to find his own tree behind which he could relieve himself.

He was back at Griffin's side before Bri, and after a few moments of waiting for her to appear from behind a tree, he hollered after her. "Bri! Where are ye, lass? Are ye alright?"

A loud exclamation came from behind the tree.

"Lass, what's happened? Are ye covered? I'm coming yer way!"

"No! Don't! I just . . . I sat on a sticker!"

The sound of his laughter rippled through the trees surrounding them. "Come on out, lass. Do ye need my help?"

He did his best to keep his composure as Bri made her way from behind the tree. Carrying the back of her dress with both hands, she hobbled slowly until she stood in front of him.

"I can't get ahold of it. I think it's in pretty deep. I need you to grab it."

He couldn't keep the corners of his mouth from twitching upward.

"But I swear, Eoin. If you look at anything but that sticker, I'm going to give you a swift kick where it will hurt the most. Do you understand me?"

"Aye, lass. I give ye my word! Now turn around."

As soon as she faced away from him, he let go of the tight rein he'd been trying to keep on the corners of his mouth and gladly let them slide upward, grinning at her white rear end, beaming in the moonlight.

The sticker was easily visible and, with one swift pull, he dislodged it, flinging it onto the ground.

"Alright, lass, ye can let yer dress down now, even though I'll be sorry to see ye do it. Now, let's get back on Griffin and make our way to see yer da!"

I'd never been more humiliated in my entire life. Not only did I get a giant sticker stuck in my backside while doing my business in the middle of a forest, I had to have the most beautiful man I'd ever seen pluck it out.

At least it would be easier to keep him in the friend zone now.

We'd just arrived at the castle, and Eoin was handing Griffin off to the stable master when a man I could only assume was my "da" burst through the large main doors of the castle.

"Blaire! Ach, I'm so pleased to see ye, lass! I doona like not having ye here by my side." Mary was right about his screaming, and as he picked me up around the middle and swung me in a circle, I was sure my eardrums would burst.

Finally, he set me down and stepped toward Eoin, and I nearly choked as I got a good look at his face. No wonder Blaire and I resembled one another so strongly. The man looked exactly like my own father. Same dark hair, same blue eyes, same small, circular patch of gray which stood out among his otherwise ebony-colored hair.

I had to blink quickly, swallowing hard to fight back tears at the sense of nostalgia that swept over me. While my parents had divorced when I was young, I'd stayed incredibly close to my Dad up until his death only three years ago.

It turned out that I'd no real reason to worry about fooling Donal. He gave me little time to speak or respond to him in any way, immediately jumping into a conversation with Eoin and ushering us inside for supper.

We sat down at the grand dining room table, and I was given a glass of ale that I sipped gladly while listening to the two men converse.

---

*A*s Eoin had expected, Donal had immediately consented to bring all of his men to Conall Castle to help with their defense on December twenty-sixth, two days before the expected attack. In fact, the agreement had been made before the first course was laid out, and the rest of the evening passed easily as the two men reminisced about Eoin's father and years past.

Eoin had known Bri had no reason to worry. Donal did not converse easily with women, and he'd had little to say to his daughter, despite his claims of how much he'd missed her.

Still, worry about Bri filled Eoin. He frowned at the servant who was silently refilling her goblet for at least the sixth time. Bri's eyes were visibly glazed, and she looked unsteady as she rested her chin against the hand she'd propped on top of the table. She'd said nothing throughout the meal, and with the amount she'd now drunk, Eoin hoped she would continue to stay silent now.

He'd never seen her drink more than one cup-full during meals, but then again, Mary never allowed any of them more than that. Mary always said that Arran did a fine job of finding drink on his own. She wasn't going to aid him in his task.

A large belch from Bri's end of the table was enough to make him certain it was time for him to make his excuses and take her away to their shared bedchamber. He could only hope no one else had noticed the unladylike sound.

Raising his voice so that Donal would hear, Eoin stood from the table. "I find myself weary from the long day's travel, Donal. If it pleases ye, I believe I will take my wife upstairs so that we may retire for the evening."

His old friend stood and clasped him on the shoulders. "Aye, o' course! It was wrong of me to keep ye so late after the long ride. We will talk more tomorrow. Would ye accompany me on a hunt?"

Eoin smiled and nodded as he walked to Bri's side. "Aye! I shall look forward to it."

He bent to place his hand under his wife's arm and help steady her as he pulled her up out of her seat.

"Goodnight, daughter. I'm glad to have ye home, if only for a short time." Donal stood waiting for Bri's response, and Eoin bent to whisper in Bri's ear.

"Tell him, goodnight. Doona say anything else."

"Goodnight." She smiled sloppily, and Eoin found himself glad that the old man's sight wasn't much better than his hearing as he watched him turn and leave the room.

"God, lass!" Eoin whispered harshly. "What do ye think ye're doing? I've not had that much to drink since I was a young lad." He took one step away from her, but quickly reached to grab her once more as she swayed on her feet.

"What are you talking . . . ?"

She left off the end of her sentence, but Eoin understood her meaning well enough. "Ye are mighty drunk, Bri. Ye have not stopped drinking since we sat down to eat!"

"I am not! I've only been sipping. What was I supposed to do while y'all were visiting?"

"Well, not drink them dry, Bri! If ye're not drunk, why doona ye walk a few steps and show me, aye?" He stepped out of her way while she grasped onto the edge of the table to support herself.

"Fine."

He watched as she took three or four wobbly steps in his direction before swaying widely and falling into his side. "Ye are not drunk, ye say?"

"Ok, fine. But I didn't mean to drink so much. The servant just kept refilling my glass, over and over again, and this hasn't been my most favorite day."

"Aye, I saw that, lass, and I doona suppose that it has." He bent to scoop her up into his arms, cradling her against his chest as they made their way up the stairs to their guest bedchamber.

She was asleep by the time he lay her on the bed, and gently tucking the covers around her, he moved to find himself a spot on the floor.

As much as he wanted to cradle her in his arms all night long, he wouldn't share her bed until she asked.

CHAPTER 27

*P*utting aside my monumental hangover, the trip to visit Donal MacChristy was an indisputable success. Over the two days that we'd spent there, Eoin had kept Donal so busy that I hardly ever saw either of them. I spent my time lounging around the castle, tenderly caring for my wicked bad headache.

We were now on our last day of riding to visit Ramsay Kinnaird, an ally according to Eoin, but a man I knew very little about from either Mary or history. It was a longer journey from MacChristy's to Kinnaird's, and we'd been forced to camp two nights along the way.

Eoin was slowly-but-surely chipping away at the rock wall fortress of my friend zone. The first night the weather had been warm enough for us to sleep on opposite sides of a fire he'd built in a small clearing.

On the second night, the wind blew too roughly through the trees to start a fire, and we were forced to snuggle together to stay warm. It had started out as a necessity, with both of us covered by the same blankets and me curling into the nook of his arm with my head against his chest. But as the night progressed he turned his body so that our fronts were flush against each other, his breath wafting against my face, shaky and warm, as he pressed closer against me.

I'd feigned sleep, refusing to open my eyes and give myself away. Always a gentleman, Eoin only kissed me lightly on the forehead when I didn't appear to awaken or respond to him in any way. He rolled quickly onto his back, shifting me into the crook of his arm once more.

I slept maybe half an hour the entire night.

The next day, I couldn't keep from squirming in the saddle. Eoin seemed concerned. "We are almost there, lass. Do ye need me to stop?"

"If it's alright with you, I'd rather not. Don't want to risk getting another sticker stuck in my bum."

"Aye, it's fine. I'm anxious to finish the ride, as well."

When we arrived at Kinnaird Castle, we weren't greeted by Ramsay at the entrance as we were Donal. Instead, we were escorted into a long study, and expected to wait until Ramsay chose to bless us with his presence. I'd never met the man, but I was already sure I wouldn't like him.

After nearly two hours, he burst through the doors. "Ah, Eoin! What an unexpected surprise. I was verra sorry to hear about yer father's death, but I'm sure ye will make a fine laird yerself."

Eoin stepped almost protectively in front of me, and it did nothing to make me like the man more. "Thank ye, Ramsay. It's been too long. I'd like ye to meet my wife. This is Blaire, Donal MacChristy's daughter."

"Aye, I'd heard that ye'd married, but I never imagined she'd be so beautiful. I bet it is lovely to have her warm yer bed at night." Ramsay chuckled.

Surprising me, Eoin reached out and laced his hand with mine in a gesture of respect. Or perhaps to keep me from doing our host harm. If I'd been in reach of anything heavy and solid, I would've chucked it at the ugly, rude man's head.

"Ach, Eoin, doona fash yerself, I'm only fooling with ye," said Ramsay with a chuckle. "Come, join me for food and drink, and ye can tell me what has brought ye here. Sylva will escort Blaire up to yer bedchamber and will have food brought to her." Ramsay didn't give Eoin a chance to reply before charging through the doors from which he'd come.

I whirled on Eoin, jerking my hand free. "What? You don't seriously expect me to eat dinner in my room like a punished child, right?"

Eoin reached forward and grasped both of my hands and brought them to his lips. "I'm sorry, lass. Ramsay's an arse, but we are guests. We must do as he bids. I need his men if we are to have adequate protection against the attack."

"Fine." I pulled my hands free of his grasp and started moving toward the door. "Show me to my room, please. I'm a woman. I'm sure it's too hard for me to find on my own."

Eoin laughed and rolled his eyes as he moved past me to direct me upstairs.

*A*t first, Ramsay assumed that Eoin had found him out. Perhaps the man he'd sent to fool them had betrayed him, revealing the truth of his murderous plan to Eoin and his brother. But no, as he sat across from Eoin over their evening meal listening to what he requested of him, he knew his secret was safe.

Actually, it couldn't have been better. Eoin inviting him to come and help protect them from an outside attack made his own plan even more easily accomplished. He wouldn't have to gain entry to the castle; he'd already have it. And it would be that much more rewarding to see the look of shock at his betrayal as he plunged his sword through Eoin's heart.

"Aye, ye know that you needn't ask. The Conalls and Kinnairds have been allies for years. Ye have my word that we shall march to help defend ye."

The young, foolish laird had just sealed his own fate.

---

*T*hankfully Eoin and Ramsay's conversation was much shorter than Eoin and Donal's, and I'd just finished my own food when I heard the bedchamber door open and close as Eoin walked in.

"How'd it go? Will he come?" I turned to him from where I sat in a chair close to the fireplace.

Eoin walked up behind me, placed both of his hands on my shoulders, and squeezed gently.

"Aye. He'll come, but I'm not so glad that we have to ask him. He's a wretched man. I'll never understand why my father kept him so close." He continued to massage my shoulders, working his way up and down my back as I released my neck and allowed my head to fall forward, relishing the feeling of his strong hands on my sore and tired muscles. Traveling in this century was hard work.

I unintentionally let out a small moan of delight, and I caught my slip as his hands stilled at the base of my throat.

Obviously taking it as a sign of my enjoyment, Eoin resumed the massage, swirling his hands over my neckline with light touches that sent tremors down my body and caused my breathing to speed up.

There was no chance I could pretend to be asleep now, and I was quickly losing any willpower I had to keep him away.

"Do ye like that, lass? I love the way yer skin feels."

I didn't answer him. Instead I leaned my head back so that my neck was elongated, allowing more space for his fingers to roam.

He stopped abruptly and came around to kneel in front of me, taking both of my hands in his.

"I know that ye must return home once we find the ring, Bri. But would ye mind so much if we behaved as husband and wife just for now? I willna ask ye again, but I want ye badly. Ye have not made it easy for me to maintain my reputation as a man of honor, sleeping so close to ye these past nights."

No one had ever looked at me with such need, such passion, and beneath his gaze, I felt more beautiful than I ever had before in my life. But it was much easier to be brave with him when I thought I was dreaming. Now, as his words sent my heart racing, I had a difficult time choking out any sort of response.

"All right."

I didn't have to say more as his lips found mine instantly, his arms wrapping around my waist. When the kiss ended, Eoin leaned back to look at me again. I felt as if he saw all the way to my soul, and I to his, and when he brushed more kisses across my lips, his eyes still on mine, I lost myself in the depth of his gaze, in the mingling of our hearts and sighs, in our whispered words of longing.

CHAPTER 28

He needed to find the ring. It was Arran's only chance at getting Blaire back, and he wasn't going to let the time window close before they tried the spell.

Arran knew Bri had been searching for the ring since they'd learned it was needed for the spell. And while Eoin claimed to be helping in the search, Arran knew a part of his brother hoped they would never find it.

If the spell did work and Blaire returned to him, he wasn't going to give her up again. She wasn't actually married to Eoin. It was Bri who'd said the vows, and he refused to let her go again.

If he located the ring before Eoin and Bri returned from their trip, perhaps she would have no reason to stay any longer.

He'd searched everywhere—each bedchamber, each study. He'd even turned Morna's spell room upside down in his desperate search for the ring.

The ring was buried with his father. He'd known it all along but had wished ardently that he was wrong, that perhaps his father had removed the ring from his finger before death.

He couldn't do this himself. Arran knew he wasn't that strong. Even going to the gravesite seemed impossible to him, but the ring had to be found.

His stomach rolling uncomfortably, he made his way down to the stables to enlist help from the runaway, now under Kip's command. He hadn't bothered to learn the lad's name. He didn't trust something about the fellow and didn't expect him to stay long enough for it to be worth learning.

When Arran entered the stables, Kip was leaning back against the doorway, looking pleased as he watched his new worker shovel out manure.

"Kip, may I speak with ye a moment?" Arran asked.

"Aye, o'course ye can." The old man pushed himself off of the doorway and made his way to Arran.

"Kip, do ye mind if I borrow the stable lad for the rest of the day? I have an unpleasant task that I'd rather not do myself if I can have someone do it for me."

"Aye, there's not much for the lad to do here anyway. We've fewer horses now, and I managed just fine on my own. Ye are welcome to use him as long as ye wish."

"Thank ye, Kip. Send him to the graveyard."

Arran turned before he could see the questioning look on Kip's face as he solemnly marched toward his father's grave.

They dug for hours, each shovel of dirt opening the poorly sealed wound of grief that crossed right through the center of Arran's heart. When they finally hit the wooden box set low beneath the ground, Arran dropped his shovel and faced the man beside him.

"Ye are to get inside the box and get the ring that's on his right hand. Doona disturb anything else that ye find inside the coffin. Once ye have it, make sure that the box is closed before ye ask me to come help ye fill in the hole. I doona want to see anything inside it."

"What makes ye think I do? I doona want to upset a man's resting place."

Arran grabbed the runaway roughly, shoving him against the side of the deep hole. "I doona care what ye want to be doing. Ye can either do as I've asked ye, or we can send ye back where ye came from."

Arran didn't wait for the man's response as he crawled out of the hole and sat on the grassy patch next to his mother's grave, covering his eyes to push away the memories each thrust of his shovel had dug up.

---

*E*ven Laird Kinnaird wouldn't have asked him to dig up a buried man. It was mighty bad luck.

But as he pushed away the heavy lid on top of the box, Laird Kinnaird's spy saw an opportunity that pushed all of his guilt away. For upon the decaying remnants of Alasdair Conall's right hand were two rings.

The first was a thin band topped with a wide oval. Noting the feminine look to its setting, he determined that this was most assuredly the ring that Arran sought. The second was larger and held the seal of the Conall clan, a signet which Alasdair most likely used to seal and sign letters. It was this ring that caught the man's interest. Such an item would be of great use to Laird Kinnaird, a way to swing the odds of the upcoming battle even further into his master's favor.

Turning his head, he reached and removed the rings as quickly as possible, holding the first in the palm of his hand and silently slipping the second away, out of sight.

Present Day

"I don't know where else to look, but we have to find that damned ring. It's only two more weeks until the anniversary, and I will not let Bri be left there." Adelle sat down. Dirty, exhausted, and on the verge of panic, she placed her head in her hands to cry.

She was surprised to feel Blaire's arm come around her shoulder to offer her comfort. "Doona worry, we will find it."

"Yes, we will. I can't allow myself to consider that we won't. She's my only child, Blaire. She's all I have, all I've ever had. She's the only person I've ever known that could put up with my flakiness and still love me. I was never the mother I should've been to her, and I won't fail her now."

"Oh, ye should not say such things. I doona believe that Bri thinks that ye were a terrible mother. Why, ye have treated me with more kindness and allowed me more freedom than anyone I've ever known."

Adelle lifted her head and patted Blaire on the knee. "Thank you for that. I'm so glad that you've been here to help. And you've handled everything beautifully. You're a wonderful girl. Now, we have to think about where else the ring could be. Everything else on site has already been excavated and is in the Edinburgh museum, and the collection of items does not include the ring."

"We know that the spell book is powerful. Tis what brought me here and sent Bri back in my place. Do ye think tis possible that we could convey a message to yer daughter through it?"

Adelle stood, shaking her head. "I doubt it. I didn't read a spell for anything like that."

"I think ye should give it a go, anyhow. Why not write a note to her in the margins of the spell we are working on? Perhaps, she will see it when she looks at the spell book."

It was too much to hope for, and Adelle didn't want to get her hopes up over such a ridiculous possibility. Blaire was trying to help, and it wouldn't hurt to humor the girl, pointless as the act would be.

"Alright, why not give it a try? I'll just tell her that we are working on the spell, but we haven't been able to find the ring." Adelle opened the spell book and obligingly flipped to the appropriate page.

Blaire didn't believe her own suggestion would work any more than Adelle did, but it bothered her to see her new friend so distressed. She couldn't imagine the pain the woman must be feeling after having her daughter ripped away from her so inexplicably.

She desperately wanted Adelle to get her daughter back. But—just as desperately—she never wanted to return home. She couldn't bear the thought of it—being married to Eoin and living in the same place as Arran. Every glimpse of him would break her heart all over again.

If Arran didn't want to be with her, she'd rather stay here in this strange and foreign time, where at the very least it was acceptable to live independently. She would be free to live her life without putting her heart in the hands of someone else. She could live a guarded, simple life all alone. And, with her heart and soul broken, she couldn't think of anything she wanted more.

Even if they found the ring, she wasn't going to go back. They'd simply have to find a way to bring Bri forward without making a switch.

1645

I was as happy as I'd ever been when we set out on our return journey early the next morning. I'd fallen asleep wrapped in Eoin's arms, only to be awakened a few hours later by his lips kissing the side of my cheek and trailing down my neck.

I smiled and faced him, wrapping my arms around his neck. "I don't have the energy for more than kissing, Eoin. As delicious as the thought of a repeat performance may be."

He kissed the tip of my nose before pulling back to prop himself up on his elbow. "Is there a man in your life, lass? Back in your own time?"

"No." I shook my head. "There's no one. I work too much. I haven't found the time for a relationship."

"So, you've never fancied anyone?"

I understood the meaning behind his politely worded question, and was a bit taken aback. At my age, it seemed odd that he would assume that I'd never had a man in my life before him. At second thought, I realized just how surprising it would be to Eoin if he knew of the freedom modern women enjoy. While most men in this time gained experience with women before they married, no respectable woman would let herself be "ruined" prior to marriage.

" It's different for women in my time," I said, choosing my words carefully. "We have more freedom than women in this time. The same freedom as men, if we want it."

"Freedom?" He lifted a brow in question, and I answered him by nodding. Eoin frowned. "I see, lass."

"Does that bother you? That I've fancied other men before you?"

"Nay, I canna fault ye for the life that ye lived before ye came into mine. But, I'll not say it pleases me. Thinking of another man holding and kissing ye stirs a rather dreadful feeling in my chest."

I smiled, pleased at his jealousy. "You can rest assured I was far less free with my affection than most women my age. Mitsy, for instance."

"What's a Mitsy, lass?"

"Mitsy is a person. A friend. Who, come to think of it, is probably worried sick about me."

He draped an arm over me as he snuggled in closely. "I'm sorry, lass. I suspect there are a good many things that I doona know about ye that would surprise me."

"Yes, I'm sure there are. We are from different worlds, Eoin."

"Aye, lass. But for a time, they are the same world, and that's all I can bear to think of now."

* * *

*T*hought back on those words as I rode in front of him, now only a short distance from arriving back at Conall Castle, as we could see it in the distance. It surprised me how much I could relate to what he'd said. Like Eoin, I found it hard to think of our worlds separating.

Thankfully, he pulled on Griffin's reins, slowing him to a stop before I could allow my thoughts to descend so negatively. He said nothing as he dismounted and turned to lift me off of the horse.

Eoin backed me up against a nearby tree, and his mouth was on mine.

After kissing me ruthlessly, he pulled back, his eyes hungry. "When we get back to the castle, we shall all be busy with preparations. I doona want to end this constant companionship with ye, Bri."

I reached forward to pull him toward me, as glad as he to prolong our time alone together.

God, Eoin wished he could spend his life beside her. He leaned forward, deeply breathing in the smell of her hair as the breeze lightly lifted it toward him. Each time he kissed her, he never wanted to stop. He wanted to claim every inch of her for himself, to make her his forever.

In past experience, he'd found that once he slept with a lass his fascination disappeared. Not with Bri. She'd captured a part of him he'd never lent to anyone, and if he let her go, he knew that she would take that part of him with her when she returned home.

He squeezed her tightly around the middle as they pulled reins at the stables where Kip was waiting for them, ready to care for the travel-worn Griffin.

As they made their way up to the castle, hand-in-hand, Eoin caught sight of Mary waiting at the entrance. Mary glared at him as she saw him and quickly called Bri to join her, for there was something she wanted to discuss with her.

Knowing better than to deny Mary, Eoin squeezed Bri's hand, encouraging her to leave him. As the two women entered the castle, worry started to build inside of him. Whatever Mary was going to tell Bri, Eoin had a feeling it wasn't going to mean anything good for himself.

J was definitely about to get into trouble. For what, I had no idea. But from the look on Mary's face, I could tell she was not overjoyed to see Eoin and me back at the castle so soon.

She didn't let go of my hand, nor did she stop moving until we reached Morna's spell room deep below the castle. Once inside, she released my hand and pointed to the wooden stool in the corner.

"Sit."

I finally understood how my kindergarteners felt when they had to sit out during recess. "Is everything all right, Mary?"

"Nay, lass. What exactly do ye think yer doing?"

I couldn't for the life of me figure out what she was talking about. "I don't think I'm doing anything. What's the matter with you?"

"What's the matter with me, lass? What's the matter with ye? Ye and Eoin were up to no good while ye were away, and doona try to tell me that ye were."

I couldn't repress a smile. "Define 'no good.'"

"Ach! Why, ye have been enjoying the privileges of man and wife, have ye not?"

There was no reason I should've felt guilty for my recent activities with my sort-of husband, but Mary was quickly succeeding in making me feel so. It instantly made me defensive. "I don't believe that's any of your business, Mary."

"Oh, ye doona think that it is, do ye? Well, pardon me, but while ye've been away, the whole castle has been running ragged trying to find the ring for the spell so that ye can return home, and ye go off and act like ye doona want to go."

"I do want to go home." I paused, unsure if I believed my own words. "I think."

"Aye, there ye go, lass. That's the first truth ye've spoken. Ye doona know if ye want to go home. And would ye like me to tell ye why that is, lass?"

"I feel quite sure you're going to anyway." I smiled, but she seemed unamused.

"Aye, that I will, lass. Ye doona know if ye want to go home because ye have let yerself fall in love with Eoin. How could ye be so foolish? Ye know that it canna be so."

I stood, feeling angry and inexplicably on the verge of tears. "It's not like I meant to fall in love with him, Mary. Have you seen him? I don't think I had much say in the matter at all. And why can't it be so? If I look just like Blaire, what's the problem with me staying?"

"Ach, lass, I doona know the lass well, but I expect that Blaire is ready to return home. I'm sure she's right scared out o' her mind being trapped in yer strange time, where she's most likely been forced to dress with cloth that rises up between her legs! Not to mention that yer own mother is desperate to have ye back!"

I was sure that my heart nearly stopped at the mention of my mother. "Wait! Why would you say that?"

Mary reached for the spell book, which still lay open on the table, and thrust it in my direction.

"She wrote to ye. Look around the edges of the spell. I noticed it when I was down here looking for the damned ring. A handwriting I dinna recognize caught my eye. I could not read it, o' course, but I had Arran come and look, and he told me what she said. She's working on the spell, too, Bri. And she needs the ring, as well. She's worried sick that ye might not be safe."

I held it before me, reading my mother's words over and over, a mixture of emotions flooding me. I was thrilled to know that she was safe and that she'd figured out that the spell was the key to switching Blaire and me back. I was also horrified to know how worried she must be for me, and I was certain she'd spent every waking second trying to get me home.

"How do you think she was able to do this, Mary?"

"I doona know, lass. Perhaps, the book's magic allowed the writing to show through."

"Do you think it would work both ways? I need to let her know that I'm safe and that I'm looking for the ring, as well." I held the book tightly to my chest as if by cradling it I was holding on to a piece of my mother.

"I doona see why not. It willna hurt for ye to try. But do ye mean it, lass? Are ye truly looking for the ring?"

I understood her meaning well enough. She seemed to have a better understanding of my feelings than I did, and she knew that part of me didn't want to return home.

"Yes, Mary. I am looking. I know that we have to find the ring. I can't deny the feelings I have for Eoin, but I won't share them with him. It's too selfish for me to stay here. My mom deserves to have me back. Blaire deserves the chance to be able to return to her home. And besides, I doubt Eoin feels the same way I do."

Mary reached forward and rubbed the side of her thumb down the side of my cheek in a motherly fashion. "Ach, lass. I believe he does care for ye as ye do him. That's why it troubled me so to see ye walking toward the castle so happy with one another. I doona want this to hurt both of ye."

"It's too late for that, Mary. It hurts me now just to think of it."

Mary smiled as she turned to leave me alone in the spell room. "I know it does, lass. It hurts me to think of ye leaving, as well. I've come to love ye like I would a daughter. Write to yer mother. It will do her good to know that ye are safe."

"I will. Thank you, Mary."

Once she was gone and I could no longer hear her footsteps on the stairs leading out of the basement, I placed the spell book back on the desk and crawled on top of the stool, pulling my knees in toward me as I buried my head and cried.

I wasn't accustomed to allowing my emotions to affect me so drastically. Living alone for so long, I'd made it a habit of pushing away anyone who dared interrupt my set routines and the comfortable, albeit lonely, life I'd created for myself. If I allowed myself to feel too much, I made myself vulnerable, and that was a feeling that my control-freak personality absolutely rebelled against. Hence, why none of the countless men Mitsy had set me up with ever made it past date three.

So, how was it that Eoin had been able to slip inside the confines of my heart so easily? I didn't know, but I loved him. I knew it without question. But I also knew that it didn't matter. This decision affected the lives of too many others, and I couldn't be so selfish as to only consider my own heart.

If no one else were involved—not my mother, not Blaire, not Arran and his love for Blaire—I would gladly cease searching for the ring and stay here forever. But that wasn't the case, and no number of tears was going to change that.

Drying my eyes on the sleeve of my dress, I unfolded my legs and stood to go and look for a pen and inkwell with which to write a message back to my mother.

I found them quickly and, leaving as much room around the edges of the spell as I could so that we could communicate further if the message worked, I scribbled simply, *"I'm safe, Mom. We haven't found the ring yet, but we are searching. Take care of Blaire. I know she must be ready to return home. I love you. Write back if you get this."*

Inhaling deeply to push back the remnants of unshed tears, I turned and walked out of the room, leaving the message for my mother to see.

It was time to find that freaking ring. Or, apparently, we would all die trying.

"Come in." The knock startled Eoin. He'd expected to be left alone until morning. When Arran walked through the doorway, Eoin was sure his face showed his disappointment. Part of him had hoped Bri would seek him out before bed.

"May I talk to ye a moment, brother?" Arran walked through the room, stopping to sit in one of the two chairs situated in front of the room's fireplace.

Eoin joined him, sitting opposite. "O'course. How did the meetings and training go while we were away?"

"All went well. Everyone in the village has been informed, and they are working together to strengthen defenses. All people outside castle grounds will come to stay at the castle the same night as Kinnaird and MacChristy's men. We will leave the village empty so that they have no one to attack there."

"Good. With both clans coming, I'm not so worried about the upcoming attack. How's the runaway lad been? Is he working well for Kip?" Eoin leaned over the side of the chair and, grabbing a poker, stoked the dulling fire.

"Aye. Kip said he's caused him no trouble, but there's little to keep them both busy. I borrowed him for a task once while ye were away. That's actually why I came to speak with ye."

The fire now burning full flame once again, Eoin returned the poker to its home and sat back in his seat to look at his brother. "Aye?"

"I spent some time looking for the ring that ye need for the spell. I found it. It was buried with father." Arran reached out and placed it in Eoin's hand.

"Arran . . . tell me ye dinna do it?"

Arran stood defensively. "Aye, I could not bring myself to do it, so I had the lad retrieve the ring once we unearthed Father. Ye had to know that's where the ring was. It was the only place we had yet to look."

"Aye, I'll not lie and say I dinna know it was a possibility. But I doona think we need it anymore."

"Doona need it? Christ, Eoin, have ye gone mad? The lass canna stay here."

Eoin cringed as the thought of her leaving caused an uncomfortable pain to hit him right below his ribs. "Aye, she can. She's my wife, Arran, whether I knew it was her that I married or not. If ye hadna gone and pried the ring off of our father's dead finger, then she wouldna had a choice. I canna lose her, Arran. I'm not going to give her the ring."

Arran paced the room, obviously shocked by Eoin's words. "Ye doona have a choice, Eoin! I know that ye care for the lass, but it is not fair to leave Blaire there. I willna let ye do it."

"Ye have no say in it, Arran. And why do ye care about leaving Blaire where she is? She's a wretched lass." Eoin watched Arran prowl the room, struggling to rein in his anger. Arran's passion on the subject confused him greatly.

"Blaire's not so bad, Eoin. What makes ye think that Bri no longer wants to go home? Has she told ye that?"

The question threw him. It hadn't until that moment crossed his mind that she wouldn't want to stay. He knew he'd tried to make it sound as if he knew she was planning on leaving once they found the ring, but deep down he thought she'd choose not to go.

But Arran was right. She'd never said anything to him about staying here. Still, she'd shown him with her affection how much she cared for him.

"No, but I doona think she's too concerned with finding the ring now. She will not mind having to stay."

"Do ye really think so? Go and see where she is right now, Eoin. Ye will find her in the spell room, looking desperately for the ring that ye hold in yer hand. She will never forgive ye if ye keep it from her. She must at least be given the choice."

Eoin stared down at the ring, not looking up as his bedchamber door slammed shut at Arran's abrupt departure.

Surely Arran was wrong. After the long journey back from Kinnaird Castle, the lass would be too tired to search for the ring tonight. And after the way she'd allowed him to hold her through the night, would she even want to?

It didn't really matter. Even if she still did want to return home, he knew he couldn't bring himself to let her go. She'd captured his heart completely and he didn't want to spend his life with any other woman. If she didn't love him already, he could make her love him with time.

He just had to make sure she didn't find out that Arran had found the ring.

With re-hiding the ring set as his task, he left his bedchamber to head for the outer wall of the castle, intent on throwing it into the ocean. He paused briefly at Bri's bedchamber door, hoping to catch a sound of her moving about the room.

When he heard nothing, he quietly lifted the handle to peek inside, expecting to see her sleeping soundly in the large bed. She wasn't there. His heart sank as he took in the vacant room. Changing his direction, he turned to make his way to the spell room in search of her.

As he descended into the castle's basement, he found himself hoping she wouldn't be there, either. He desperately wanted Arran to be wrong.

He heard her moving about the room before he saw her. Frantically lifting books and shuffling through shelves, she jumped when he spoke to her. "Ye should be in bed asleep, lass. It's been a long day."

"Eoin. Gosh, you scared the crap out of me. What are you doing down here?"

"I looked in on ye in yer bedchamber, but ye were not there."

"Oh. Yeah. I'm about to go to bed. Here, wait and I'll follow you up." She blew out the candle and reached out for his hand in the dark.

He took it as he walked toward the staircase on the other side of the basement. "What were ye doing, lass?"

"Just going through the things in the spell room, looking for the ring."

The words cut through him, just as if she'd run a dagger straight through his heart. He couldn't keep the lass here against her will. Arran was right. He knew he had to give her a choice.

He stopped and pulled her close to him just before they entered the staircase. He wrapped his arms around her, kissing the top of her head as she murmured into his chest.

"Is everything alright, Eoin?"

"Aye, lass, all is well. Tomorrow evening, would ye accompany me somewhere? I'd like to surprise ye with something."

He felt her grin against his chest. "Of course. I love surprises."

Tomorrow he would tell her everything; tell her that Arran had found the ring, tell her that he loved her, tell her that he didn't want her to leave. He would place his heart in her hands. And the choice would be hers.

I woke early the next morning, anxious to get to the spell room to see if the message had worked and Mom had replied. I did my best not to get my hopes up, but it didn't work well as I threw on the simplest dress I had and hurried down into the basement.

Carrying the lantern from my room, I shared the flame with the candles scattered around the work table and waited for the room to light up as I nervously glanced down at the parchment.

It had worked, and I smiled and dragged my finger over her markings as I read the words aloud to myself:

"Sweet Mother of God, I'm glad to know that you are safe, baby. I'm sure one of us will find the ring, and we will have the two of you switched back soon. Now that I know you're safe, I can tell you how jealous I am that you're there, getting to meet and live with the very people I've spent my life trying to learn about. I can't wait to hear all of the wonderful stories you must have. I miss you, darling and I love you more than you will ever know."

No doubt that was Mom. She wrote just like she spoke, and it relieved some of my anxiety to know that she would no longer be as worried for my safety. I was reaching to grab the ink and pen and write back when handwriting different from the others on the page caught my eye.

Scribbled in fine lettering beside my first message to Mom, the words were so tiny that I'd almost missed them. I was sure Blaire had scribbled them, and the words caused my breath to catch in my throat.

Right next to my own mention of how much I knew Blaire must be ready to return home, she had written,

"I cannot go back. I want to stay here."

I sat down on the bench in front of the table and read her words once more for good measure. An uncontrollable excitement spread through me as I took in her words a fourth and fifth time. If Blaire didn't want to come back here, was there really any reason why I had to leave?

I already knew deep down that I didn't want to return home. Strangely enough, I fit here in this time, with these people, with Eoin. But I couldn't bring myself to make that decision for the others involved. I couldn't deny Blaire the right to return to her home, I couldn't deny Arran the chance to see the woman he loved again, and I couldn't deny my mother the knowledge that I was okay.

Now that I was able to communicate with Mom, no matter how small the form, she would at least know that I was safe and happy. That's all she wanted for me anyway, and if she knew that I'd found happiness here, she would be able to make her peace with that in time.

It would be hard for Arran to accept Blaire's absence, but if her writing was any indication, it didn't seem to me that she reciprocated his feelings. Perhaps it would be easier for him to move on believing she still loved him but couldn't return home, rather than have her returned to him and find he was unwanted.

I'd left the spell room the night before heartsick, knowing that each time I went to sleep, I would wake up with one less day that I would get to spend here. Today, the possibility of being able to spend all of my days here had me on the edge of pure elation.

But there was still one factor I wasn't taking into account. I was assuming, most likely foolishly, that Eoin wanted me to stay. He was kind, attentive, loving, and seemingly sad when the topic of my leaving came up in conversation. That being said, I knew that knowing he would miss me and him wanting me to stay beside him forever were two very different things.

I wasn't the woman he'd agreed to or thought he had married. And he'd yet to verbally express his feelings for me. Was I willing to make myself so vulnerable to him by telling him how much I loved him, how desperately I didn't want to leave him, with the hope that he would match my own feelings?

The thought terrified me, but I didn't see how I had any choice. I knew myself well enough to know that the regret I would have over not taking the risk would be far more painful than the heartbreak I would feel if he didn't want me in his life.

I loved him too much to leave him. Whether we had years to love or just days left, I would treasure my time with him forever.

I was unsure of where he was taking me tonight, but it would allow me the perfect opportunity to tell him I no longer wanted to go home.

With my mind set, I nervously made my way out of the spell room and went in search of Mary. I was going to be an anxious wreck all day, and I knew she would keep me busy. Plus, maybe she could help me find a sexier dress. I was going to need whatever I could manage to help me keep my cool.

***

*A*rran was already past his boiling point, and his anger over Eoin's selfishness had him ready to spring on the first person unlucky enough to cross paths with him. Unfortunately for himself, it was Kip who he decided to unleash his anger on. He couldn't have made a worse decision.

It was early afternoon when Arran stormed out of the castle, planning to get some fresh air. As he walked toward the stables, he saw Kip's runaway walking casually in the direction of the village. It was the only excuse he needed.

Making as much noise as he could manage, he walked into the side door of the stables, knowing it would draw Kip's attention. Kip held a pitchfork and was working on maneuvering hay around to the different stalls.

"So ye just let the runaway go about his business unchaperoned, do ye, Kip?" Arran yelled angrily.

He was rewarded with a smack right in the middle of his forehead as Kip brought the end of the wooden stick forward, slamming it into his face.

"Now, what did ye say, Arran? I do believe ye thought ye were talking to someone else for a moment."

Rubbing the now red and tender spot in between his brows, Arran blushed with embarrassment at his behavior. "I'm sorry, Kip. I'm not in the best humor. Now, where is the lad off to? Do ye not need him today?"

"He said he had some errands he needed to attend to in the village, and I saw no harm in letting him go. I doona ever need him. I do a fine job running the stable all on my own."

Arran poked his head around the stable door to make sure he could still see the runaway off in the distance. "Do ye trust him, Kip?"

The old man stopped fussing with the hay and leaned against the stall door as he spoke to Arran. "The lad has given me no reason not to, and I think it's best to let people prove ye wrong before ye go about mistrusting everybody."

"Do ye? Well, I'm not as good a man as ye, Kip." Arran turned and followed along the path leading to the village. The runaway was up to nothing good. Arran could feel it, and he intended to find out what the lad had up his sleeve.

"I'm not gonna cut the neckline any further," said Mary with unconcealed exasperation. "Do ye not want them to stay in the dress at all?"

I rolled my eyes as I glanced down at the very modest v-cut I'd spent the better half of the afternoon talking Mary into cutting into the gown. "It's not even that low, Mary, but to answer your question, I'm not all that concerned one way or the other."

"Oh, hush, lass. Ye will make an old lady blush with such talk. I'm glad that ye have decided to stay, but ye doona need these alterations to entice Eoin into wanting ye around."

"I'm not trying to entice him. I'm trying to make myself feel as pretty as I can so I feel confident before I tell him what I have to say. With no make-up or hair straightener, a girl's got to do what a girl's got to do around here."

"Fine, lass, but please tell me ye decided not to wear that strange object ye wear under yer shirt when in the spell room."

I smiled and reached over to grab my bra off the top of the bed. "No, Mary. I'm definitely still going to wear my bra. He knows I'm not from here now, so it won't be a huge surprise for him to see something odd on me. Besides, it lifts the girls up, and they'll look better in the dress. Watch."

I turned my back to Mary, discreetly scooting the dress down off my shoulders so that my breasts sprang free. I then secured them into place within the bra. Reluctantly, Mary had washed all of my modern clothes for me. They'd started to get pretty ripe after weeks of not seeing a washing machine.

Slipping the dress back on, I triumphantly faced her. My breasts perfectly filled in the dress's new v-cut, and the cleavage was just enough to draw attention, without completely giving away the farm. "What do you think?"

Even Mary couldn't hide her amazement at the difference the bra made. "Aye, lass. I regret what I said before. Do ye think we could make me one? I believe I underestimated the size of yer breasts, lass. They're a good deal higher now."

"I told you. And I bet you could fashion something that would work the same way. Just look at what you've done with this dress!" I spun, feeling dainty and beautiful, and my nerves subsided slightly until I heard a knock on the door.

"Ach, lass, there he is." Mary paused and came to place a hand on each of my shoulders. "Doona worry, lass. If he tells ye anything other than what ye want to hear, then I doona know the lad as well as I think I do." She gave me a brief hug and surprised me by giving me a quick swat on my bottom. "And ye look beautiful. Have a good time."

With that I opened the door to Eoin, and as he took my hand, I followed him outside.

---

*E*oin couldn't stop staring. Ach, the lass looked beautiful! But what had she done to the top of her dress? Did she want him to make love to her in the middle of the hallway? Nay, of course he would not allow himself to do any such thing. At least, not until he'd told her all that he needed to, and she'd chosen him as her own.

If Bri rejected him, he would allow her to enact the spell tonight. He didn't think he could bear to have her stay here even a moment longer if he knew she didn't want him in the same way he longed to have her.

It was a long walk to the cave at the base of the shoreline, and he was anxious to get her there quickly. Each second of wondering was more torturous than the last. It was a chilly evening, but the small cave blocked the wind and provided a perfect place from which to watch the waves as the tide rolled in.

As Eoin led her onto the sand, he smiled as she paused to hike up her dress, gathering it in her arms and revealing the pale skin of her legs. He didn't know of another lass who would so unashamedly expose her legs while walking, but he'd expect no less from his strange lass, and he loved every odd thing about her.

He could only hope she loved him in return. As he led her into the candlelit cave, he breathed in a deep ocean-filled breath for courage. It was time for the truth to be known.

*E*oin said nothing as we walked away from the castle, and while I knew we were headed to the shore, he gave no clues as to where he was taking me.

He seemed nervous, and it did nothing to help my nerves. Part of me wondered if he was dragging me away to tell me privately just how ready he was for me to return home. It was easy for my mind to always drift to the worst scenario.

When we reached the sand I jerked loose from his grip, apologizing as I kicked off my shoes and gathered the bottom of my dress. I didn't care how ridiculous I looked waddling through the sand with fabric gathered up in my arms; I wasn't about to dirty this dress after all the work Mary had put into it. She would've killed me, no doubt.

It was getting darker along the beach, and I found myself hoping that we'd reach our intended destination soon. In a horror film, this was exactly the point in which the man would turn around and kill me, tossing my body into the approaching waves.

Eventually we made our way inside a narrow cave hiding along the rocky coast at the back of the beach. It was filled with candles, which illuminated the circular haven. And when I noticed an assortment of cushions and blankets lying on a rock ledge near the back, most of my fears subsided. It was a romantic setting, not the kind of place you would take someone before sending them away, and not the kind of place you would take someone before chucking their lifeless body into the ocean.

Inside the cave the ground was rocky, and without the fear of sand getting caught in the dress, I relaxed my arms and let the skirt fall down to my feet once more. Eoin smiled and took my hand as he led me to the blankets at the back of the cave. Once I'd comfortably crawled on top and situated myself next to him, he turned to me to speak.

"Lass, I need to confess something to ye, but I'm not so sure I can bring myself to tell ye."

Maybe I was wrong about this being romantic. Maybe he was about to tell me he loved someone else, and he was ready for me to go home so that he could get on with his life. A million thoughts ran through my mind as all the fear from earlier came rushing back, and I suddenly felt foolish for thinking I would be brave enough to tell him I loved him.

Instead, I squeezed his hand, encouraging him to proceed. "All right. You have to tell me now. Just get on with it."

He could see that I was shivering, from nerves more than cold, but he couldn't tell the difference. He politely wrapped one of the blankets around my shoulder.

"Lass, I know that ye have been searching for the ring so that ye can go home. While we were away, Arran found it."

"He did?" Shocked, I tried to normalize my expression as he continued.

"Aye." He paused to retrieve it and held it out to me, eventually setting it between us when I didn't reach out for it. "I almost threw it in the ocean."

"You what?" The pitch of my voice was oddly high and screechy, making me sound angry rather than shocked.

"Aye, lass. I'm verra sorry, but I dinna want to give ye the ring. I know that I canna keep it from ye, but I'd like to ask ye something before I let ye have it."

"Of course." My heart restarted as hope began to crawl through the fear rooted in my stomach.

"Doona go, lass." He squeezed my hands tightly between his own, and I was sure my heart was going to burst with happiness. "I've fallen in love with ye, Bri, and I doona wish to be parted from ye. If ye doona love me, I shall give ye the ring, but I could not let ye leave without telling ye."

My voice cracked as I spoke to him, and a tear broke free from my left eye. "No."

He didn't give me a chance to finish. "I'm so verra sorry for keeping the ring from ye, lass. I just wasna ready to let ye go."

I pried my hands loose and reached up to grab hold of his face. "No, listen. Let me finish."

He stopped talking, pursing his lips awkwardly like a fish, and I couldn't help but laugh.

"It's not so funny, lass. Ye're breaking my heart. I only ask that ye do it swiftly."

"Hush. It is funny. Your face looks ridiculous. I meant, 'no,' I'm not mad at you. I had something to tell you tonight, as well."

"Aye?"

"I was going to tell you that I wanted to stop looking for the ring. I can't leave here. This is my home now and I've fallen in love with everyone. Mary, Kip, Arran, Griffin, even you." I winked at him before continuing, "Before, I only thought I had to go back because of my mother and Blaire. She deserved the chance to return to her home, but she doesn't want it."

"How do ye know, lass?"

"It's the spell book. We can write messages to one another that cross over through time. My mother knows I'm safe here, and as long as she knows that, she'll be okay with my decision. And Blaire said she wants to stay in my time. That means I'm free, Eoin. I'm free to stay with you. If you'll have me?"

"Have ye, lass? Did ye not just hear what I said to ye? I'll have ye and ye alone."

We fell into each other then, our lips meeting with a sort of elation that comes from knowing your feelings are matched to the feelings of the one you love.

The ocean waves crashed against the stones outside the cave, mimicking the pounding of my heart as we expressed our love for one another throughout the night.

CHAPTER 34

$\mathcal{A}$rran squatted behind the first building on the edge of the village, peering around the corner as he watched the runaway wait for someone to join him outside the ale house. The lad reached into a small bag he carried around his shoulder and removed an item that he'd wrapped in a cloth.

Arran knew he'd been right to follow him. The lad had been given no chance to acquire anything for trade, unless he'd stolen it from Kip or from some other area of the castle.

Only a few moments passed before a man Arran had never seen before walked out of the ale house and extended a hand in the runaway's direction. He watched as they spoke quietly for a few moments, ending their conversation when the runaway patted the stranger and handed the unknown item over to him.

Arran couldn't make sense of the strange transaction, but he knew he'd just witnessed the runaway betray them.

As he watched the runaway turn to head back toward the castle, Arran pulled his head back around the corner, out of sight from anyone walking by. He waited until the lad moved past him, then quickly ran up behind him, ramming his fist over the back of the runaway's head. Arran caught the man around the middle, shrugging his unconscious body over his shoulder.

He'd take the betrayer to the dungeon, and he'd get the truth out of him by whatever means necessary.

J moved about the spell room, putting away books and materials for what I hoped would be the last time. With my mind made up that I would be staying, and now knowing the location of the ring, I saw no reason to leave the room in such a state of dishevelment.

With each lift of a book, my thoughts drifted to the night before, spent in Eoin's arms. We had talked and kissed and loved one another late into the night, and I'd gotten very little sleep. I'd never been so happy to be so exhausted. As I continued to shuffle books around the room, I realized that the real reason I was so preoccupied with re-organizing the space is that I was doing my very best to put off the inevitable. I had to write to Mom and let her know I wasn't coming home.

I was completely confident in my decision. Regardless of the unusual circumstances that had brought me into this time, it had landed me exactly where I was supposed to be. That being said, it didn't make it any easier for me to go about saying goodbye to my mother for what was most assuredly forever.

The thought brought forth a familiar lump inside my throat. The same lump that had lodged itself into place when I'd attended my father's funeral, the same lump that I'd been forced to choke down after laying eyes on Donal MacChristy.

I knew my mother wasn't dying. She would undoubtedly go on to live a happy life, endlessly dating men either too young or too old for her, and traveling the world on whatever dig caught her fancy. But she'd not only been my mother but my very best friend for my entire life. And while I knew she would understand, I also knew it would hurt her to know that I'd chosen not to return to be her partner in crime.

Once I'd rearranged every book in the room at least twice, I knew it was time to sit down and just get it over with.

I tore a blank piece of parchment from one of Morna's old journals and practiced what I would say to her.

Twenty-five drafts later, I knew that the truth was that it didn't matter what I wrote. It was going to hurt her regardless. It was best that I keep it simple and only touch on the most important things: that I was safe, that I was happy, and that I hoped she would understand.

In the end, I wrote only four sentences, ensuring that I left room in case she wanted to write a reply.

"I don't want you ever to doubt how much I love you, Mom, but I found it. That love you talked to me about at the inn? He's here, and I have to stay with him. I'm safe and happy, and I know that's all you've ever wanted for me."

It was done. And while I knew I'd made the right decision, it had cost me the best mom in the world.

I was unsure of how long I sat there, staring blankly at the wall, feeling oddly cold and hollow. I'd been shattered when my father had been killed in a boating accident. Losing someone so suddenly wraps you in a sort of black shock that takes years to shake off.

Somehow, this seemed harder. It was just as sudden a break, and the knowledge that she was alive and well and would go on living and sharing her fun, witty, and wild self for the world to see, but not for me to get to witness, left me feeling utterly lost.

The hand that touched my shoulder was my anchor, and I gladly turned into Eoin's embrace. He, too, understood the grief of loss, with his father's death occurring shortly before my arrival. He didn't ask what I'd been doing. He looked around at the tidy room and at the words on the page and silently sat down beside me, wrapping me in his arms.

He held me without saying a word, silently stroking my back, bending occasionally to plant a gentle kiss on the top of my head, letting me know that he was there for as long as I needed him.

Eventually, I pulled away and managed a smile to reassure him that I wasn't re-thinking my decision. He smiled back and reached for my hand.

"I know it may not be customary. My parents kept separate bedchambers throughout their marriage, but how would ye feel about moving into my bedchamber? I doona like the thought of ye being so far away. I want to fall asleep each night with ye next to me, wrapped in my arms."

I stood and pulled him toward the doorway. "I would love to. I already asked Mary this morning if she would have someone move my belongings across the hall. In my time, it would be uncustomary for us not to share a room. Besides, I don't want to be alone tonight."

CHAPTER 35

*K*innaird Castle

"*W*hat does the lad want with me?" Ramsay marched from his bedchamber, furious that someone would dare have the nerve to arrive unannounced.

"I doona know, sir. All he said was that he must see ye straight away. He had an item to give ye."

"The fool had better be bringing me Eoin Conall's head on a spike if he's to wake me at this hour." Ramsay burst through the doors of the study where the father of his two stable lads stood uncomfortably at the end of the room. "Well, what do ye possibly have that ye think is warranted to disturb me?"

"I . . . I met with the man ye sent to Conall Castle. He gave me this ring to give to ye. Said it's the signet of the late Alasdair Conall, and he believed it could be of some use to ye since Eoin has asked that the MacChristy clan gather at the castle, as well."

"Give it to me." Ramsay thrust his hand eagerly in the man's direction. He knew he'd done right by sending the lad. He was a quick thinker, and had just proven that he was worth more than Ramsay had previously expected. Ramsay studied the ring, recognizing Alasdair's signet immediately. "Thank ye, lad. Now, get out."

The man's face dropped with his obvious disappointment at a lack of reward, but he retreated quickly, leaving Ramsay alone in the study with one of his messengers.

"Dress in the colors of the Conalls and take this ring to MacChristy Castle

167

at once. Doona give this ring to anyone but Donal, do ye understand? Ye will have no trouble gaining an audience. Donal will welcome any Conall. Once ye have given him the ring, tell him that Eoin no longer requires his men or his presence for the battle. The situation has been taken care of, and there is not going to be an attack."

"Aye. O' course, sir."

With one less clan to worry about, Ramsay was certain his plan to annihilate the Conalls would succeed. In three days' time, he would gather his men and everyone at the castle. Together they would march to the aid of the Conalls, gladly assisting them in their bloody deaths.

---

*C*onall Castle

"*I* assure ye, lad, I'm in no hurry," Arran said to the runaway through the bars of the cell. "I'll gladly spend as many nights visiting you down here in the dungeon as ye wish. But you willna be leaving until ye tell me what it was that ye gave to the stranger in town and where ye got it from."

The runaway glanced around his dark, dank quarters with wary eyes. "I already told ye. The man was my uncle, and I was only returning an item I borrowed from him."

"Ye lie. The man was not old enough to be yer uncle, and ye had no such item when ye arrived here."

"I did so. I keep it in my bag. Ye dinna search me when I arrived. I've had it with me all along."

Arran narrowed his eyes. "What was the item ye borrowed from him?"

"Only . . ." the man swallowed convulsively, his panic at being left in the dungeon apparent. "It was only a coin."

Arran shook his head at the runaway's pathetic attempt to lie. Sighing, he said, "Doona expect to see daylight until ye tell me truth."

The days following my decision to remain here passed by in a blur of hurried activity, with everyone in the castle and village rushing to make preparations for the arrival of the MacChristys and Kinnairds, as well as preparing for the upcoming battle.

It was the night before the expected attack, and while both Eoin and Arran seemed confident all would be well, I found my anxiety building. They'd not seen the devastating ruins of our home, as I had. And while I was confident that having two clans join us for the fight increased our chances, knowing what happened before made me uneasy and made me wonder why there were still ruins on Mom's side of time, if we were going to succeed in battle.

Mom had responded to my message the following morning, playing it upbeat as always, but I could see the tear stains on the parchment where she'd cried. She was happy that I was happy, but she was as heartbroken as I was at our separation from one another. We'd written back and forth over the days leading up to the battle as I did my best to assure her that the fate of the Conalls would no longer stay the same now that we had reinforcements headed our way.

I wondered how it would affect everything on the other side of history if we succeeded. I hoped that I would still be able to use the book to communicate with my mother if the castle never ended up being destroyed. If we were defeated, it didn't really matter.

Dusk had long since crept over the castle, and with each passing hour the tension within the walls heightened. Both the MacChristys and the Kinnairds should have arrived by now, and although Eoin was trying his hardest to remain calm, I could tell that my hovering, nervous energy was doing nothing to help the situation.

I walked over to him and placed a hand on his shoulder as he sat in one of the studies on the main floor staring out the window for any sign of the clans' arrival. "Would you like me to leave you alone for a while?"

He reached up, latched onto my hand, and pulled me down onto his lap. "Aye, lass. It's not that I doona want ye here. But there's no need for ye to stay up so late worrying with me. I'm sure they were only delayed and will arrive sometime during the night. Go on up to bed, lass, and I'll join ye once both clans have been settled around the castle. It will calm me to know that ye are soundly asleep."

I knew I wouldn't close my eyes until Eoin came up to the bedchamber, but he was doing his best to politely tell me to beat it, and I didn't blame him. Leaning in to give him a quick kiss, I turned and made my way upstairs.

<hr>

*I*t was well into the deepest part of the night when Arran alerted him that Ramsay's men were almost to the castle. Eoin stood from the seat in his study and went to the castle's entrance to greet them.

He'd expected Ramsay to burst through the doors with some elaborate tale which would explain their late arrival and have them all laughing and breaking into the ale within minutes. Instead, as Ramsay Kinnaird pushed his way into the castle's main foyer, Eoin knew instantly something had gone terribly wrong.

Ramsay and his men, their clothes wet from the rain and splashed with mud, looked as if they'd been riding hard through the night. Their faces were panicked and frightened.

Eoin didn't bother with greetings as he rushed to grab Laird Kinnaird, who appeared as if he was about to fall over from exhaustion.

"What is it, man? What's happened?"

"Ach, Eoin! I'm afraid we've all underestimated Laird MacLyrron's forces. We only just escaped in time. And I was forced to bring not only my men, but my daughter and all the women and children."

Eoin blanched and suddenly felt unsteady on his feet as he took in the news. "So they doona only plan to attack us. They tried to attack yer territory, as well?"

Ramsay spoke in between gasping breaths. "Aye. I believe he split up his men and sent half to my keep and half to the MacChristy's. For when we passed through Donal's territory . . ." Ramsay paused, as if unable to finish.

A terrifying sense of dread crept over Eoin's heart.

"What is it, man? What did ye find at Donal's?" Eoin ushered Ramsay over to the staircase in the center of the room, and they both collapsed next to one another onto the stone steps.

"The MacChristys will not be coming to our aid. They're all gone, Eoin. The clan MacChristy has been completely wiped out. Women, children, livestock, all. Laird MacLyrron left nothing alive. And now he's headed in our direction."

Bile rose in Eoin's throat. If what Ramsay said was true, their hopes of surviving the attack were greatly diminished. "Do ye think with our combined men we can stand against them?"

Eoin took in Ramsay's pained expression and knew his response before he spoke.

"Nay. I doona believe we can. He has three times the number of men we do. The best we can hope for is to hide our women and children as long as we can, and not let them take us without a fight."

"How far away are they? Do we have time to prepare at all?"

"Aye. A group of my men were scouting their location. Tis how we were warned they were headed our way. They are reconvening to gather after splitting directions. They've camped for the night in between my castle and what was the MacChristy's keep. They canna make it here before tomorrow night."

"A small mercy, but at least yer men shall be able to get a short time of rest before we hide the women and prepare for battle tomorrow. We shall all need our strength. While I know sleep is likely to escape us all tonight, I think we should at least try. Tell yer men they are welcome to set camp anywhere on castle grounds. I will show ye to yer chamber. Yer daughter may stay in my mother's old room. Blaire resides with me."

"Thank ye, Eoin. It calms an old man's heart to know he will die beside such a fine laird and ally. Let us reconvene in the morning."

---

*E*oin opened the door to his bedchamber as quietly as he could, although he knew Bri would still be awake waiting for him. He kept his back to her as he blew out the candles next to the bed. Then he undressed and crawled in beside her.

If he let her see his face, she would know something was wrong, and he couldn't bear for her to know just yet. He wanted one last night, as sleepless as it would be for him, to hold her in his arms and thank the heavens for sending the lass through time to find him.

He finally knew the love that his own father had shared with his mother. When his mother had died, it had taken every fiber of strength his father possessed to keep on living. His love for her never ceased, and Eoin knew it had been her name on his father's mind and heart as he'd drawn his last breath.

He'd never understood how a lass could have such a hold on someone's heart. Eoin grew up wondering why his father never remarried. He thought he would've if it had been he who'd lost his wife. It was unnatural for a man to live alone so long, and how many years did it take for a heart to heal, anyway? Surely not a lifetime.

But all of that was before Bri. And now, as he held her in his arms, feeling the warmth of her skin so vibrant and alive against him, he knew exactly the power a woman could wield over a man's soul.

He loved her beyond reason, beyond hope, beyond time.

Her voice in the darkness rattled him from his thoughts, and he pulled her in closely against him, kissing her hair.

"Did they finally arrive? What kept them so long?"

"Aye, lass. Only some bad weather slowed them. All is well."

It was the only lie he would tell her, but he would allow himself to be selfish, just this night. For Eoin loved the lass too much to watch her die. And after sunrise, although it pained him more than the thought of his own death, he would take the lass down into the spell room one last time. And whether she wanted to or not, she would do the spell and return home.

CHAPTER 37

M acChristy Castle

D onal MacChristy found himself unable to sit still. He felt an unexplainable sense of unease as he paced back and forth down the halls. He suspected this was what life felt like for the many ghosts that roamed the halls of this ancient castle, and when he unexpectedly collided with a figure around the corner he thought momentarily that perhaps he'd run into a real one.

He started at the sight of his most trusted housekeeper, Blaire's old maid and tutor, reeling back from the impact. "What are ye doing awake at this time o' night, lass? Ye should have been away long before now."

The elderly woman nodded and extended a plaid cloth in his direction, nearly screaming to accommodate the laird's bad ear. "Aye, perhaps. I've not been sure whether I should show ye something, but I've decided tis best that I do."

Donal took the strip torn from the bottom of a kilt into his hands and turned it over as the sense of unease crept back into his mind. "Where did ye find this?"

"It was in the bedchamber of the lad that came from Conall Castle."

"Aye?" The colors on the tartan were not the same as the Conall colors.

"Aye, sir. And there is something else as well."

"Get on with it then. Tell me, please."

"When the lad set out this afternoon, he didn't ride in the direction of

Conall Castle. He rode in the opposite direction. I thought it odd at the time, but when I found this in the room, my suspicions grew. Are these not the colors of Ramsay Kinnaird?"

Donal instantly understood, and his heart nearly stopped for fear over his daughter and allies. "By all that is holy, the old fox fooled us! Sound the alarm and gather all the men at once. We must ride for Conall Castle immediately and hope they are not all dead already!"

onall Castle

Once Arran was certain Eoin was retired for the evening and Ramsay and his men had set up camp, he quietly snuck away to the dungeon to continue his interrogation of the runaway. He took a flask filled with water, as well – something he'd withheld from his captive.

Arran had stood quietly in the castle's main entrance, listening to Ramsay's story, and while it was worrisome, Ramsay's sad words and somber face were unconvincing to Arran—even if Eoin was too besotted with his wife to see anything else clearly.

His brother was a good man, better than himself, but at least Arran knew that sometimes a person's eyes told more truth than their mouth. Eoin was too trusting of the man their father had called friend, but Arran could see the almost pleased expression in Ramsay's eyes as he told Eoin his tale of woe.

And Arran was now more certain than ever that the lad he kept in the dungeon knew something about what was going on.

"It seems that yer master has already attacked one of our allies. Why did ye not tell us that he would attack other territories, as well?" Arran took a long drink from the flask, his gaze trained on the lad's hopeful expression.

When Arran lowered the flask, the runaway leaned forward, staring at the leather pouch with longing, but Arran did not offer it to him. "He's not my master," said the lad, his tongue darting out to swipe across his cracked lips.

Arran smiled at the small progress. "Nay? Well, that's a start at the truth. Let me leave ye with something to encourage ye to tell me the rest." Arran lifted the flask to the other man's mouth, tilting it so that only a dribble of water poured out. The runaway lapped at it eagerly, but the flask was withdrawn before he had more than a tease of a sampling of what could quench his desperate thirst.

Arran stepped back, closing the flask and tucking it under his arm. "I'll visit ye in the morning, and if ye tell me all you know, you can have the rest. But if ye are not ready to speak the truth, expect to become even thirstier after I've gone."

Even if he had to parch the deceiver until his tongue turned to leather, the lad would talk tomorrow. He would tell what he knew. The truth would come out.

J did my best to feign sleep, and while I did drift occasionally, Eoin's tense arms wrapped around me told me everything his reassuring words hadn't. Something was definitely wrong, and I suspected he was just waiting until daylight to tell me.

Anxious to hear whatever it was he didn't want to confide in me, I stirred in his arms at first light, trying to make it seem as if I was just waking up.

"Did ye sleep well, lass?" He didn't release me from his hold, and I was forced to look up at him awkwardly to respond, my head pressed against his chest.

"Better than you, I think. Something's wrong. Just tell me."

He stood then, and I was able to see just how dark the circles under his eyes were. Not only had he not gotten any sleep, something was bothering him terribly.

"Aye, lass. I need to take ye somewhere. Put on yer clothes and join me. I'll wait for ye out in the hall."

Once he'd gone I leapt out of the bed, throwing clothes on as quickly as I could manage, desperate to put an end to my wondering. I knew men had arrived late into the night; I'd listened to the commotion from the windowsill and watched as they'd set up camp. With reinforcements here, I couldn't imagine what had Eoin so upset.

He led me down the hall quickly, then yanked me into the stairwell leading to the spell room, an imaginary knife slipped into my side. No way was he about to do what I thought. No way was he about to send me home after everything. He was a fool if he thought I was going anywhere.

I jerked free from his grasp as he reached to light the candles around the dark room. "What do you think you are doing, Eoin? There's nothing for us to do down here. We should be upstairs, preparing for the battle."

He pulled out Morna's ring and set it on top of the open spell book. "There's not going to be a battle, lass. All that's left is a slaughter, and I'll not let ye stay here to die."

Shock coursed through my system, making it hard for me to understand his words. "What are you talking about? Everyone's arrived. Odds are they'll show up here, see your numbers, and there won't be a fight anyway. I know you're worried, but don't be so dramatic."

He shook his head somberly. "Nay, love. Not everyone did arrive. The MacChristys were slaughtered, lass. All. The Kinnairds barely escaped before their own castle was taken. Even with Ramsay's men, we will be outnumbered. All within the walls of this castle will greet death today, and I canna let ye join us. Ye had a life in yer own time. Return to it. Leave, so that I can die knowing that I at least saved ye from my own fate."

I ran to him them, shock and desperation making me cold as I threw my arms around him, seeking his warmth. "No. I won't go, Eoin."

"Ye must, lass. I'm not a controlling man, but I canna give ye a choice. Ye will do the spell."

Tears broke loose, and I sobbed uncontrollably against him, my fear of losing him pushing away any embarrassment over my behavior. "I can't . . . I can't go back to my life before." Sobs racked through my chest, and my head throbbed as if it might explode. "Not after you! I didn't know before. I didn't understand how little I had. I'd never be able to survive there now."

He pried my arms loose from around his waist so that he could look down at me. He shook me roughly. "Now, listen to me. Doona ye tell me that ye won't survive. Ye must. Knowing that I've kept ye safe is the only thing that will allow me to fight and die with my men and not flee from here like a coward. If ye love me, Bri, ye will go. And ye will live a long and happy life in yer own time."

I shook my head as I sobbed, wailing uncontrollably, all rationale gone. "This is my time now. Don't make me do it, Eoin. Please. Don't send me away. If you loved me, you wouldn't ask it."

He shook me, stunning me enough that my sobs subsided briefly.

"Doona ever say that I doona love ye. Do ye not understand what it takes for me to send ye back?"

"No! Because I would never ask it of you." He'd released his grip on my arms, and I crushed myself against him once more, holding on less tightly, slowly surrendering. I knew his mind was made up.

"Aye, I expect ye would, love, but I know tis hard for ye to see now."

"I'm scared, Eoin. I can't stand the thought of leaving you. I'd rather die here."

"Nay, lass. I'd be no help to my men if I had to worry about ye. Ye must go now so that we can prepare the best we can. If by some miracle we are spared, I swear to ye, I shall find a way back to ye. Even if I must don awful shreds of clothing like the ones ye love so much and travel into that strange place to get ye."

I laughed against his chest. "I would love to see that. Eoin?"

"Aye, lass?"

"I need you to hold me. Please. Just for a little while. I need one last moment with you to keep with me, always." I could hear how corny I sounded, but I didn't care. Looking up at him, I continued, "Hold me so tight I'll never forget the feel of you and will always know that you were real."

Eoin's arms came around me and he lifted me so that my feet left the floor and we were eye-to-eye. I couldn't imagine losing this–losing *him*. Not after all I'd been through to find him. I'd crossed time so that we could be together. We were meant to be, and now . . . I couldn't bear to think of it. Eoin was the love of my life. I would never love another the way I loved him. *Could* never. It wasn't possible. "I am glad I shall die tonight, lass," Eoin whispered, scattering kissing across my tear-stained face. "For I doona think I could live a day without ye by my side. With each kiss I take a piece of ye to keep with me, and when I take my last breath, however it may find me, it shall be yer face that I see when my eyes close the last time."

"Eoin," I sobbed, placing my hand in his hair, coaxing his lips to mine once more.

"It's time, love. I canna stay to watch ye do the spell. I'm afraid I would stop ye from doing it. But ye must, just as I must now go to prepare the men. When I leave, change into yer strange clothes and do the spell as quickly as ye can."

He lowered me until my feet were solidly on the floor again, then stepped back. "I shall always love ye beyond time itself, Bri. Even after I'm dead and buried, ye shall feel my love for ye wherever ye may go."

I reached out to him, but it was too late. He went out the door and didn't look back. Dutifully, I set about to follow his last instructions.

CHAPTER 39

should've been gone by now. Hours had passed since Eoin had left me standing alone in the spell room. And while I did break down and cry for the better part of an hour after he'd left, I was now strangely calm and collected.

I'd really had every intention of doing what he asked. I'd changed into my jeans, bra, t-shirt, and tennis shoes. I'd gathered all the materials for the spell and even started burning the herbs. But when I sat down to read the spell out loud, I realized the words just weren't going to come out of my mouth.

There was no way I was going through with the spell. I didn't care that Eoin wanted to die knowing I was safe. That would be no comfort to me as I moved miserably through life without him, scrubbing snot off the backs of school chairs. I'd said vows, albeit while I thought I was in a coma. But I meant them now, and I was not going to oblige him. Deep down he didn't really want me gone, even if he was too noble to let himself admit it.

Blowing out the burning herbs, I quickly changed out of my modern clothes and back into the dress I'd put on this morning. I didn't know what time the battle would begin, but I wanted to be certain I saw Eoin before the men took their positions. If he wanted me to hide with the other women during the fight, fine, but he needed to know I hadn't completed the spell.

---

was running up the stairs in my rush to get out of the basement and find Eoin when voices from around the corner caused me to slow my pace. Stopping only a few steps away from the noise, I listened to try and make out what they were saying.

After a moment, I recognized the first as the always-slurred voice of Ramsay Kinnaird. The second, I could only assume was the daughter whom had oddly been absent from our sight during our stay at Kinnaird Castle.

"Unless ye want me to beat ye half to death, doona ye dare let me find ye talking to someone from Conall Castle again. Do ye understand?"

"I wasna going to tell them anything, Father. I was only visiting."

The mousy voice sounded quiet, frightened, and I immediately felt uncomfortable with the situation. I heard Ramsay's hand as it made hard contact with the girl's face, undoubtedly bruising her, and I stepped out from around the corner so that they both could see me.

Ramsay instantly stepped away from the young girl, and I was shocked at how quickly he was able to change his face from one of malice to one of pure sugar. "Ah, Lady Blaire, my daughter and I only stepped away from the crowd for a moment to have a private conversation. If I'd known ye were down here, we would not have disturbed ye."

"Yes, I can see that." I turned to the girl, whose face was already red and inflamed. Not attempting any semblance of a Scottish accent, I said, "What's your name? We haven't met before."

The girl hesitated, her gaze darting between her father and me. When Ramsay stayed silent, she spoke. "Edana. Pleasure to meet ye."

I smiled at her. "The pleasure's mine. Are you all right? Would you like to accompany me on a walk?"

Ramsay reached out and grabbed Edana by the arm. "Aye, she's fine o' course. Just worried about the battle, is all. And I'm afraid she's been a bit ill. Best if she does not leave the castle."

"Thank you, Ramsay, but I didn't ask you if you'd like to walk. Edana looks old enough to answer for herself."

Ramsay turned his cold eyes on me, all semblance of kindness gone. "Ye overstep, Lady Blaire. Tis not yer place to tell me when my daughter may speak for herself. And if I may say so, I believe ye are overtired yerself. Ye are speaking quite strangely, lass."

Ramsay was accustomed to obedience from women, and he expected me to apologize at once. He didn't know me very well at all. "No, Laird Kinnaird. You overstep by laying foul hands on your daughter. If I see another bruise or red mark on her while you are staying here, I can assure you Eoin will no longer be requiring your assistance, battle or no. It would suit you to remember whose home you are in. Do I make myself clear?"

Ramsay's face flushed red, but he managed to keep his anger under control as he replied curtly, "Aye. Now, if ye will excuse me." He released Edana's arm, and after flashing her a look of indisputable warning, turned and stormed from the stairwell.

I reached forward to touch Edana's shoulder. "Are you really okay? He shouldn't have touched you so."

"Aye, miss. Ye should not have spoken to him as ye did. It will not mean good things for ye."

Her fear for me was evident in her eyes, and I was certain that what I'd witnessed was little to what often occurred between them. "I'm not afraid of your father. He seems a quite cruel, though. Listen, if you need anything while you're here, just come and find me. You don't have to go back with him after the battle if you don't want to."

"Thank ye, miss. It's best that I go now."

With her head down, she followed in the direction of her father, and I wondered briefly if perhaps I'd made things worse for her.

I hoped not, but I couldn't allow myself to think much on it right now.

I had to find Eoin.

CHAPTER 40

*A*rran left his brother's bedchamber with a heavy heart. He'd never seen Eoin so devastated, and it made him realize how wrong he'd been about Bri. Eoin loved her just as much as he himself loved Blaire, and seeing that made Arran feel guilty for how ardently he'd tried to send Bri away.

It was selfish behavior, and now that Bri was gone, he found himself wishing that he could do something to get her back. Even if Eoin was right and they'd all be dead come evening, Arran knew Eoin was weaker without Bri by his side.

He nearly jumped out of his skin, then, when he passed Bri on his way down to the dungeon. She said nothing to him; she only smiled briefly in his direction before hurrying on her way. It was such a normal interaction that it took Arran a moment before he realized that she shouldn't have been there. He whirled around to catch her attention before she got too far away. "Bri! Come here, lass."

He met her halfway in the middle of the room.

"I'm sorry, Arran. I don't have time. I've got to find Eoin."

Arran reached to grab her arm. "What are ye still doing here? Ye should be gone by now."

"I'm not going, Arran. I know Eoin wants to keep me safe. But I can't do it."

Arran smiled and waved her away, dismissing her. "Get on with ye, lass. Ye will find him in his chambers. I'm glad ye dinna listen to him. He needs ye here."

With Bri remaining here during the battle, it was even more important that Arran get the truth out of the runaway. He went to retrieve the leather flask, filled it with water, then started down to the dungeon.

Shivering and mumbling in his sleep, the lad lay curled on the floor in the far left corner of his cell. He was close to breaking, Arran had no doubt. He walked over, opened the flask, and dribbled water onto the unconscious man's face.

"Time to wake up. I've no more patience for ye, lad. It's time for ye to make a choice. Ye can either tell me who yer real master is and the real reason that ye're here, or yer about to face another long day alone in this cell with no food or water. And did I mention we're soon to be under attack? If I die, you might not be found down here for days. It would be a slow, miserable death for ye."

The runaway groaned and raised his head to look Arran in the eyes. "Please." His gaze shifted to the flask in Arran's hand. "Just a sip. I will tell ye what ye want to know after. Just one, I beg ye."

Arran raised his brows. "The talk comes first, the sip after."

"Aye. . . aye." The lad's head fell to his chest and he sighed. "I work for Laird Kinnaird. He's the one that plans to attack ye, not Laird MacLyrron."

"Is what ye say true, lad?"

"Aye, I swear it on me father in heaven." He reached out a trembling hand toward the flask.

"Aye? Well, ye shall meet him there another day, for now ye drink." Arran handed him the flask and the runaway drank deeply.

"Ye will be letting me out of here now, aye?" he asked between gulps.

"Not so fast. I said ye drink, not that I'd be freeing ye so soon." Arran let himself out of the cell, locking it again behind him. "If what you've said proves true and I live to tell the tale, I'll be back for you, lad. Until then, ye may as well get comfortable." Arran climbed the stairs leading out of the dungeon. Bri wasn't the only one who needed to find Eoin. Perhaps now that Arran knew the truth, they would have time to stop Ramsay's treacherous plan.

CHAPTER 41

P resent Day

"What did you say, Blaire? I can't hear you up here!" Adelle continued to plunge her shovel into the soft moist earth, intent on digging up Alasdair Conall so that she could get the ring. It was the last day the spell would work, and daylight was fading fast. She'd resigned herself to the fact that Bri was going to stay, but she would be damned if she allowed Blaire to stay separated from her home forever, as well.

Blaire's voice was suddenly clearer, and Adelle poked her head out of the hole she was digging to see Blaire standing at the top of the entrance to the basement.

"I said, stop digging. I doona know how, but the ring is here. Right on the spell book. Come and see."

It was impossible. She must've set her own ring down in the room, but no, she glanced down at her own hand to see all of her rings securely in place.

"Are you sure, Blaire?" Adelle followed Blaire down into the spell room, nearly swallowing her own tongue when she saw the ring sitting right on top of the switching spell.

"I told ye. Perhaps, it works the same way as the writing. I doona know what made me come down here, but I saw it right away." Blaire smiled at her, and Adelle rushed to envelop her in a large embrace.

"I'm so happy for you, Blaire! This means you can go home. We should start the spell right away." She pulled back when she felt Blaire stiffen in her arms. "What is it, Blaire?"

"Aye, we should start the spell, but I'm not going back."

Adelle's voice came out even higher than usual. "What? Blaire, if you don't go now, you'll be trapped here; the spell won't work after tonight."

"Aye. I know. I canna go back, but ye can. We are gonna do the spell for ye. I doona know if it will work, but we must try."

"Me? It never crossed my mind. The portrait is of you and Bri. It won't work, I'm sure."

"Perhaps if ye hold a piece of me. Here." Blaire reached for a small knife, quickly cutting a lock of her hair and extending it in Adelle's direction.

Adelle took it, cradling the gift as she allowed herself to consider the possibility that she might be reunited with her daughter. Not only that, she would be able to live in the very time and with the very people she'd dedicated her life to studying. It was an archaeologist's dream come true.

"Adelle, if ye want to try, we must try it now. Daylight is almost gone."

"Are you sure you won't go back, Blaire?"

"Aye. There's nothing left for me there. I shall start anew here."

Adelle smiled, hope and fear of disappointment building as they quickly gathered the materials for the spell. When all was in place, Blaire turned to leave.

"I think it best I go. I doona want to risk the spell taking me back. I shall wait in the car. If it doesna work, join me there. Thank ye for yer kindness. I shall never forget ye."

They hugged briefly, and once Blaire had gone and she heard the car door slam in the distance, Adelle placed the ring on her finger and slowly sounded out each word in the book.

---

*1*645

Mary ran through the castle as fast as her short legs would carry her. The moment Kip had informed her of Eoin's decision to send Bri back, she'd fled from her own chambers at the edge of the castle grounds and raced to stop the lass.

How Eoin could be so foolish, she couldn't begin to understand. Did the lad not understand that their love made them both stronger? Passion was wasted on the youth, she was certain.

She nearly slid down the stairwell in her rush to get there before the lass started the spell, and as she ran through the spell room door, she was afraid she arrived only moments too late. The room was humming with an unseen energy, just as it had done the day she'd watched Bri arrive.

Suddenly the room trembled, and Mary found herself staring at the second-oddest looking lass she'd ever seen, next to Bri. The woman looked about with an expression of awe, scaring Mary nearly to death as she cackled gleefully and jumped around the room.

Taking in the lass's strange clothing, Mary could only draw one conclusion.

"Ye must be her mother, aye?"

CHAPTER 42

$\mathcal{E}$oin took his time dressing for battle in the solitude of his bedchamber. All his men were as prepared for the attack as they could be. It mattered not anyway; his men would fight valiantly by his side. He had failed them all, and he knew the ground would run red with the blood of all his clansmen in a few short hours.

He was no longer afraid to die. He'd sent his heart to live hundreds of years away from him. Eoin would gladly meet his death on the battlefield. He glanced out the window, watching his men prepare. A reflection in the glass caught his attention, but he quickly closed his eyes against the vision. It was good he was not long for this world; he'd lost his mind, and was seeing his strange, lovely lass in places where she was not.

A hand on the middle of his back caused his eyes to spring open as he spun to see the most genuine vision he had ever seen standing before him. His feet grew suddenly unsteady and his throat was dry as he worked to choke back tears. "Lass, if ye are not real, leave me be and doona torture me so. My heart canna bear it."

Her slender arms wrapped around him, and his tears ran freely as he scooped her up tight.

"I couldn't do it, Eoin. I know you told me to, and you're going to be angry. But I just don't care. My place is here."

"Nay, love. I'm not angry with ye. Why, I doona believe I've ever been so pleased in all my life." He pressed his lips against hers.

A squeaky noise at the doorway caused him to break his kiss as they both turned to see Ramsay Kinnaird's daughter in the doorway, looking uncomfortable.

*T*hank God Eoin wasn't angry. I knew eventually he would be glad I'd decided to stay, but I was worried that his fear for my safety would be enough to make him react negatively to my unexpected reappearance.

When we broke our kiss, I started at the site of Edana Kinnaird watching us from the doorway. I pulled away from Eoin and went to greet her.

"What's the matter, Edana? Is everything okay? Did your father hurt you?"

Eoin interrupted and walked over to join us. "Hurt her? Why would he do such a thing?"

"I accidentally walked up on them in the stairwell. He hit her hard across the face, Eoin. Look at the mark."

Edana obligingly turned her head to the side to show Eoin, and the angry grumble from Eoin's throat was a sure sign he was angry. "Do ye have something to tell us, lass? I willna stand for it if yer father is hurting ye."

Edana looked down at her hands, fidgeting nervously. "Aye. I know he will kill me if he learns, but I could not live with myself if I let him do what he plans."

"What is it, lass?"

"There's no . . ."

She was interrupted by Arran in the doorway, hollering for Eoin even before he entered the room. "Eoin! I must speak with ye!" He stopped when he caught sight of Edana and me standing together alongside his brother.

Eoin held his palm up in Arran's direction, as if to stop him. "Wait just a moment, Arran. The lass has something to tell us."

Arran shook his head, making his way to stand among us in the circle. "It canna wait, Eoin. Laird MacLyrron is not the one attacking us. It's Ramsay."

I immediately looked in Edana's direction, seeking either a confirmation or denial of Arran's words.

Hesitantly, she spoke up. "Aye, he tells the truth. That's what I came to tell ye. Laird MacLyrron sits comfortably at his home, and the MacChristys are not dead. My father plans to attack ye this evening."

I reached out to gather Edana in my arms, who now cried freely, terrified of her father's wrath.

Eoin touched Edana briefly on the shoulder. "Doona worry, lass. We willna let him hurt ye again. I'll not say I'm not relieved, despite the betrayal. Now that we know he's planning to turn on us, we should have a much better chance in battle."

Arran nodded. "Aye. Would ye like me to go and kill the wily old goat now? I doona think his men will fight us, unless under his command. They all know the wretched soul he really is."

Eoin shot Arran a look of disapproval before glancing in Edana's direction. "Nay, we need to discuss a plan of attack first."

Before anyone else could respond, yet another visitor entered the room hurriedly, and I was nearly knocked to the ground as Mary threw her arms around me.

"Oh me God, lass. I thought for certain I'd missed ye. I'm so pleased ye were smart enough not to listen to the foolish lad." She reached out from my side and whacked Eoin in the side of his arm. "What is the matter with ye? Ye are a foolish boy!" She returned her attention back to me. "I went down to the spell room to stop ye from doing the spell, but ye were gone. I found someone else in yer place."

It was only then that yet another figure in the doorway caught my focus.

"Mom?" I broke free from Mary's grasp as I charged in her direction. I could feel everyone's eyes on us as we clung to each other tightly, both of us weeping into the other's hair.

After what seemed like ages, she pushed me away and smiled. "If you weren't going to come back to me, I decided I was just going to have to come to you."

"Oh, I'm so glad. Is Blaire with you, too?" I didn't miss Arran, as his eyes grew wide at the mention of my look-alike. "I placed the ring on the spell book, hoping it would possibly transfer to her."

Mom shook her head, and Arran quickly masked his expression, doing his best to hide the pain that only I could see. "She didn't want to come. She allowed me to go in her place."

"Oh." I was unsure of what to say and was glad when my mother interrupted, easing the tension in the room.

"Bri, honey. I can certainly see what made you decide to stay. Which one's yours, and is it okay if I touch them both?"

*A*fter taking a few brief moments to introduce my mother to everyone in the room, Eoin hushed us all, taking his place as leader among us so that we could make a plan of attack.

"It's nearly dark, and we must decide on our plan of action."

Arran gave him little chance to continue before interrupting. "I doona see why we need to decide anything. The best thing to do would be to cut Ramsay down, at once."

"Nay. I want to allow him the opportunity to change his mind. Perhaps, he will take it, and no blood will be shed."

It was Edana's turn to speak up, albeit nervously. "He willna do it. Once he's set his mind to a task, doona expect him to back down only because he's been found out."

"Ye may be right, lass, but I will not kill a man for something he's yet to do. Mary, do ye think tis too late to prepare a meal?" Eoin looked in Mary's direction, smiling at the irritated expression on her face.

"Do ye really think that's what we should be speaking of now, lad? I know I'm no warrior, but that seems a shoddy battle plan."

"Aye, Mary. Ye are quite right about that. But if Ramsay willna change his mind, he will call his men to battle when I confront him. If we are sitting down for a meal, at least it will take them a moment to gather for a fight. It will give us an advantage. Ramsay will wonder why I would have us sit to eat when we should be preparing for battle. It will make him nervous, and I'd like him to be so."

Mary crossed her arms and looked exasperatingly in his direction. "Aye. I expect he shall think ye've gone and misplaced yer brain, and I'm not likely to disagree with him. But if ye want food, ye shall have it. I know better than to try and change yer mind, ye stubborn fool."

Eoin smiled. "I'd ask something else of ye, Mary, as well. We canna let Ramsay see Edana again. Give yer kitchen maid instructions as to the meal, and then make yer way up to the top tower to hide with Adelle and Edana."

"Aye, o' course. Where do ye expect Bri to be?" Mary glanced in my direction as if she thought he'd forgotten me.

"Ramsay will expect to see Bri at the table. He knows that at Conall Castle, the laird dines with his wife. He thinks it mad, but he knows tis our custom. 'Twill arouse suspicion if she is not there." Eoin paused and turned his gaze to Arran. "If fighting begins, ye are to take Bri away at once. Doona let anyone harm her. I must handle Ramsay myself."

Arran nodded. "Aye, she will not be harmed, Eoin."

Once everyone knew our plan of action, we all dispersed into our positions. Mary quickly attended to dinner and then escorted my mother and Edana up to the castle's top tower. It was difficult to get to and was certainly the safest place for them to stay.

Arran left to ensure that men would be waiting outside every door of the dining hall, ready for entry into battle if it came to that.

I sat nervously in our bedchamber, waiting for Eoin to come back from his talk with Ramsay. He'd left shortly after making plans to invite Ramsay to dinner. I glanced up as Eoin made his way into the room.

"What did he say?"

"Well, I doona think he believes I suspect him. He only said I was a fool to worry over my stomach at a time such as this, but if I wanted to spend the last moments eating before Laird MacLyrron's men arrived, then he'd not stop me."

"So he's coming?"

"Aye. It's of no concern to him when Laird MacLyrron's men should be arriving, since it is he who shall start the bloodshed."

I walked over and leaned gently into his side. "When is it starting?"

He took my hand and made for door. "Now, lass. I'm eager to end this; I doona like waiting for the unknown. And the sooner ye are truly safe, the better."

CHAPTER 44

Tension laced every inch of the dining hall as Ramsay made his way to seat himself on Eoin's right hand side. I sat on his left, and as we positioned ourselves at the table, I could see in Ramsay's eyes that perhaps he was more suspicious of this impromptu and poorly timed meal than Eoin had thought.

Ramsay's dark, blood-shot eyes, consistently glazed from too much drink, made my skin crawl as he glared at me across the table. I'd angered him earlier, and he was not one to forget someone crossing him.

I met his gaze head on, determined not to flinch from his sight. Finally, he tore his eyes away from my own and turned to speak to Eoin.

"I see not much has changed under Conall Castle's new laird. Ye have yet to learn that meals should be shared in the company of men."

Eoin's face was hard, no longer concerned with placating him for the sake of maintaining him as an ally. "It is ye, Ramsay, that have yet to learn that the company of women makes everything more pleasant."

He reached over to squeeze my hand, and it immediately released some of my tension, if only momentarily.

"Aye? If that be the case, why doona ye have my daughter join us, as well?" Ramsay gestured with his hand at the other empty chairs at the table.

I could see by the way he glanced around the room that Ramsay knew something was off. His hand rested uneasily to his side, giving himself quick access to some sort of weapon concealed from my sight.

"She wasn't feeling well," I explained. "I had Mary take food to her bedchamber."

Ramsay ignored me, offended that a woman dare talk in his presence.

"Yer wife speaks verra strange, Eoin. I dinna notice it before when ye came to visit me."

Eoin was finished putting off the confrontation. I could tell by the way he shifted in his seat, leaning forward so that he could leap into action at a moment's notice. "Ramsay, before I tell ye what I have to say, I'd like to remind ye that our two clans have been allies for generations long before us. We have both come to the other's aid, and I know my father considered ye a friend. It would be a shame for that alliance to come to an end, aye?"

Ramsay had an unsettling ability that made the words coming out of his mouth drip with sincerity while his eyes oozed poison. "Aye, lad, that it would. Good thing we have come together to fight our shared enemy."

"I doona know if that is so, Ramsay. I have reason to believe that it is ye who plan to attack us—that perhaps Laird MacLyrron is not on his way here at all."

Ramsay stood quite suddenly, throwing his fist violently down on the table. I could hear shuffling outside the dining hall doors, and I knew the action had been his signal to his men. Outside these doors, the sound of battle was already ensuing.

"Do ye now? And why would I do that?"

Each door to the dining hall swung open as our men collided with Ramsay's in a horrific dance of death. Metal clashed around us as I stood watching the interaction between Ramsay and Eoin, neither of whom had yet to draw a sword.

"I doona know, Ramsay. Perhaps, ye could explain it to me. Surely there's no reason for bloodshed."

"Ye are wrong, Eoin. There is a need for bloodshed, and there will be plenty of it this night. Ye are a damned fool, just like yer father. He knew that it was expected that ye wed Edana. Instead, he married ye to this strange lass! Our clans would have been made stronger by such an arrangement. Without it, I've no desire to stay allies. Instead, I shall claim the Conall clan and castle as my own."

Eoin didn't have a chance to respond as I screamed at the sight of a sword swinging in his direction. Eoin unsheathed his own just in time. There was no doubt that battle had begun.

I knew my life was in danger, but every swing of a sword and every horrifying sound of a man groaning as he met his death seemed to slow down in my mind as I kept careful watch on Ramsay.

I could see Arran making his way toward me out of the corner of my eye, but he was delayed as he worked to cut down two of Ramsay's men. I'd expected Laird Kinnaird to head straight for Eoin, but instead he snuck away from the crowd.

I knew he could be headed in only one direction.

I ran as quickly as I could, hating floor-length dresses with every step. I was unsure if Ramsay knew that his daughter would be in the tower, but I knew from Eoin that the man was familiar enough with the castle for it not to take him very long to figure it out.

I was worried for Eoin, but at least he had the means and skills to defend himself. Edana, Mary, and Mother were defenseless, and I was not going to allow him to hurt any of them. With each step, I feared I was going to be too late. I was still a good distance from the tower, but when I passed the small hidden door at the end of the corridor, I knew I could take the shortcut Eoin had shown me on that one stormy night.

I stumbled up the stairs in the darkness, ripping off the wooden door that concealed the window entrance, slicing open my fingers as I threw it aside. Though it was dark, I could still make out the castle wall, and it was thick enough that I knew it left me plenty of space to walk along it.

As I scooted along the outside perimeter of the castle, I counted windows until I was almost sure I stood in front of the window that would place me in the tower staircase. I didn't have time to second guess myself. Unable to pry the window open, I reared back and shattered the glass with my heel, cutting wide gashes down my leg as the blood spread over the end of my dress.

It was the right window, and as I made my way up the spiral staircase I could hear Ramsay fumbling with the lock.

"Edana, it will be far worse for ye if ye doona let me in. Now open this door!"

I could hear all three women screaming on the other side of the door as Ramsay budged it open a half an inch with the impact of his shoulder. I screamed at him as loudly as I could to draw his attention away from the doorway.

"Stop! Leave her alone!"

He spun toward me, sticking a finger in my direction. "Doona ye tell me what to do with my daughter. I shall slit yer throat after I'm through with hers!"

I ran, throwing myself in between his oncoming shoulder and the door.

His shoulder hit me square between the breasts. I cried out as all the air in my lungs rushed out of my body. Gasping for air, I struggled to speak. "No . . . take me! Eoin will surrender if you have me! You've won the battle if you take me captive." I hoped to God I was wrong, but I could think of nothing else that might tempt him to leave Edana, Mary, and my mother in peace.

"Aye, lass. Ye are right."

I didn't struggle as he pulled me against him. Holding the edge of a dagger across my neck so tightly that it broke the surface of the skin, he dragged me back down the stairs and into the ongoing battle.

***

*A*rran scanned the room in between swings of his sword. He'd lost Bri in the crowd, and he was certain his brother would never forgive him. Not that it would matter. He couldn't find his brother or Ramsay in the crowd of fighting men.

They were losing too many. He glanced around to see men he'd known his entire life open and bleeding onto the stone floor as their lifeless eyes gazed upward. With each lad he watched fall, his hope of their success waned.

Just as one of Ramsay's men narrowly missed sending a sword straight through his stomach, a surge of men from all surrounding doors shocked Arran into dropping his own sword.

The room suddenly filled with men he knew not to be Ramsay's or their own, and he smiled as he watched Donal MacChristy walk into the center of the room, his booming voice successfully slowing the pace of men clashing their swords against one another.

"Clan Kinnaird, if ye doona wish to die, ye should lay down yer swords at once. For we fight for the Conalls, and ye are far outnumbered now." Donal paused to scan the room, and Arran knew he was looking for Ramsay. "Look around, yer laird is not even fighting with ye. Doona lose yer life for such a cowardly leader."

It only took moments for Ramsay's men to see the wisdom in Donal MacChristy's words. They'd lived under fear of Ramsay for far too long, and there were not many willing to give up their life for his.

Arran smiled as he allowed it to sink in that the battle was over. Laird

Kinnaird must have fled in an act of cowardice, but that mattered not. He was no threat without an army of men at his side.

Arran's relief at their survival was short-lived as he scanned the room twice more, still unable to locate his brother or Bri.

A strange hush settled over the room as men who'd only just been engaged in battle stood awkwardly, unsure now of how to act.

Just as Arran was about to leave the dining hall to go in search of Bri and Eoin, a figure shouted from a shadowy corner of the hall. Ramsay stepped into the light of the room, his arms wrapped around Bri, his knife ready to slice her throat.

*I*t had only taken Eoin a few short moments after the battle had broken out to register Ramsay's and Bri's absence. He'd not hesitated to set out in search of them. Arran could lead the men. Eoin would not lose Bri again.

He'd just made it to the bottom of the stairwell leading to the back tower when he heard someone moving down the stairs. He silently slipped around a corner, unseen, as he watched Ramsay drag his beautiful wife out of the stairwell with a knife at her neck.

It had been all he could do to keep from launching himself at Ramsay that instant, but he knew that once the devil entered the dining hall, Ramsay would expect to see him fighting the battle. When Ramsay realized Eoin was not in the room, that was when he would be at his weakest.

Eoin stayed covered in the darkness as Ramsay stepped into the light in front of the silent crowd. He was only a few short steps from Bri, and his hand twitched on the handle of his sword, desperate to run it through Ramsay's heart.

Ramsay screamed for him as he revealed himself to the onlookers, but Eoin didn't move from his location behind his adversary.

"Eoin! Surrender yer castle and yer men, or watch yer wife bleed to death in my arms."

Eoin watched as Arran cautiously took a step in Ramsay's direction. "He's not here, Ramsay. And surely ye see that ye are outnumbered. This is finished. Doona shed blood when ye have already lost."

Eoin could tell Ramsay was on the brink of panic. He worried that the fool would slide the knife across Bri's throat in a fit of madness. Slowly Eoin crept up so that he stood directly behind the man. Locking eyes with Arran, he shook his head so his brother wouldn't alert their foe to his position.

"Where is he? Someone find him at once," Ramsay shouted at the top of his lungs.

Eoin could see the man's hands shaking on the handle of his blade. The time for him to act was now. He nodded at Arran, giving him a silent signal to make ready to grab Bri when the time was right. He only hoped his brother understood the message.

Making swift use of his sword, Eoin did what he had to do to save his wife. "There's no need to look for me, Ramsay," he said quietly. "I'm already here."

EPILOGUE

February

I scooted myself out from under Eoin's heavy arm as gracefully as I could. He grumbled as the bed shifted, and reached to grab me toward him, but he was too late. I crawled out of the bed but leaned forward to kiss him gently on the forehead.

"I'll be back in a while. There's something I need to work on."

Taking one of the candles from my side of the bed, I slipped on a thin gown and wrapped a blanket around me as I slipped into the night-filled corridors.

It had been several months since the defeat of Ramsay, and while peaceful relations ruled the clans once more, Ramsay's men still remained camped on our castle grounds as they tried to find a solution to whom would now be their new laird.

Despite the flurry of people in and out of the castle each day, things were back to normal, and everyone was safe and happy once more—everyone except Arran. I'd watched him as he dutifully put on a brave face in front of his brother but silently fell apart in private. Each day, he found his way to the bottom of more goblets of ale than he had the day before. I couldn't stand to see him so unhappy a moment more.

It was for this reason that I snuck my way into the spell room in the wee hours of the morning.

I'd stumbled across a promising spell book this afternoon but had fled the room after I heard a noise at the top of the stairs. I didn't want to tell anyone what I'd found until I was certain.

Situating myself on the bench, I held my candle carefully over the yellowed page, reading the words as I smiled wide.

There were other spells that could reopen the portal. Perhaps Arran could find his way to Blaire after all.

MORNA'S SECRET

CHAPTER 1

Just Outside the Ruins of Conall Castle—Scotland—Present Day

Three days I'd sat in the small room at the inn located only a short distance from the castle ruins. Surrounded by what were now considered artifacts of the castle, I took my time, spending days feigning illness so I could decide what I should do next.

Gwendolyn and Jerry, the kind innkeepers, were growing impatient. I knew they wouldn't allow me to stay in the room much longer without explanation, but what was I to tell them? I could hardly believe the truth myself.

With Adelle's help, and by remaining mostly silent when interacting with them, I'd been able to fool the innkeepers into believing I was Adelle's daughter, Bri. But with Adelle no longer here to speak for me, I knew they would notice my lack of an American accent.

A knock at the door meant it was evening, and Gwendolyn was bringing my supper. She'd graciously and unquestioningly brought each meal and left it outside the door since I'd arrived back at the inn claiming to be quite ill. She'd given me the privacy I'd desired, and so it surprised me to hear her speak from the other side of the door.

"I'm sorry to disturb your rest, but Jerry and I are both worried about you, dear. You've spent far too much time inside this room, so you've left me no choice, I'm afraid. You can either clean yourself up and join us for dinner downstairs, or I shall be calling a doctor to come see to you."

Gwendolyn paused, waiting for my response. I wasn't ill, only worried, and I wouldn't have them send for a doctor for a non-existent sickness.

"Twill be...I'll be down shortly." A brief response was best. Perhaps my accent wouldn't be as noticeable with only a few quick words. Not that it mattered. I was going to have to tell them all I knew, although I doubted they would believe me.

At this point, I had nothing left to lose.

I walked down the stairs and into the small kitchen to be met by kind smiles from both Gwendolyn and Jerry. The old man gave me a thorough look-over before speaking bluntly, true to form.

"Ye must be feeling much better, lass. Ye doona look sick at all. Now sit down here and tell us where yer mother is. We know something has happened, and it is time that ye tell us what that is. Gwendolyn is too polite to ask ye, but I've no problem with tellin' ye that yer behavior has been quite strange."

The old man stood to usher me to a chair across from both of them. Once I was seated, he resumed his place next to his wife. I sat silently for a moment, quite unsure of where to begin. I knew my accent would garner questions from them right away. "Aye, I'm no longer feeling ill, but I do need to tell ye both something."

Gwendolyn pinched her eyebrows together. "Well, my goodness, Bri. I know it's tempting once you've been here awhile to try and speak like everyone around you, but I've never been very successful at it myself. You sound as if you've lived here forever."

Jerry laughed in response as he patted Gwendolyn on the shoulder. "Aye, my lassie's voice holds nothing of Scotland, although she's lived here for forty years now. She still speaks as if she arrived in the country only yesterday."

Gwendolyn leaned sweetly into Jerry before glancing back at me. "The accent really is great, but why are you doing it?"

I looked down at my plate of untouched food, not quite ready for either of them to think I'd lost my mind.

Jerry reached across the table to gently squeeze my hand and, as I looked up at him, I could see the concern in his face. "Where's yer mother, lass?"

"She's not my mother. And I'm not Bri. I doona think ye will believe what I must tell ye, but will ye listen to all of it before ye decide that I'm mad?" I lifted my head to look them in the eyes as I waited for their answer.

Jerry and Gwendolyn exchanged an unreadable sideways glance before Jerry spoke first. "Aye, lass. O'course we shall listen to ye. Let us move next to the fire, though. The chairs in there are much more comfortable."

Gwendolyn simply nodded before they both stood and led me into the next room.

Once seated, I fumbled uneasily with my words, unsure of how to begin. One question had sat at the forefront of my mind since the first night I'd left Adelle at the castle ruins. I'd been too afraid to ask, for if the answer was not what I hoped, it meant everyone I'd known and loved had died only days ago, unable to change history. I knew that I must learn the truth before I explained anything further to Jerry and Gwendolyn.

"Might I ask ye a question first?" I dinna wait for their response. "The castle ruins, I suppose they're still ruins, aye?"

Hope fluttered in my chest at their quizzical expressions.

Jerry pointed in the direction of the castle. "Do ye mean Conall Castle, lass? If so, I wouldna go calling the place a ruin. It's still beautifully intact—a fine structure and a popular visit for tourists."

I was unsure of what a "tourist" was, but if what he said was true, it meant that they'd been successful at stopping the attack. Adelle, Bri, Eoin, Mary, and Arran had most likely all gone on to live for many more years. That knowledge was enough to rid me of any other fears I had about moving on alone in this time.

"Do ye really mean it? The castle is not just a pile of rocks? It wasna destroyed long ago?" I needed just one more reassurance in order to fully believe him.

Gwendolyn nodded. "Yes, dear. The Conalls have been one of the most powerful and beloved clans in Scotland for centuries. Descendants still own the castle, but they've partnered with the historical society to open it up for visitors. Are you sure you're not ill?"

I nodded, relieved beyond explanation. It was time to tell them what had happened. Then, regardless of their reaction, it was time for me to move on from this place and start a new life on my own.

"Aye, I feel fine. But I need to tell ye what's happened, and 'tis a long story." I sighed. "I doubt ye will believe me."

Jerry smiled and sat back in his chair, settling in. "Why doona ye just get on with it, lass? Then we will decide what to believe."

"Aye. I'm not sure of where to begin. The first thing I should tell ye is that I'm not Bri. My name is Blaire MacChristy. My father was laird of MacChristy Castle during the seventeenth century. I was betrothed to Alasdair Conall's eldest son, Eoin. But on the day of our wedding in the year sixteen hundred and forty-five, I found myself swept up by a spell cast by Alasdair's late sister, Morna Conall, a witch who died when I was very young. As you can see, Bri and I look verra much the same with our hair dark and our eyes blue, and Morna knew that we would. She cast the spell so that if Bri and I ever laid eyes on the same spelled plaque in a room beneath the castle, we would switch places in time. Nearly two months ago, her spell worked. Bri was sent back, and I was brought forward." I paused to look up at them and was stunned that they both seemed rather unsurprised by my words.

"Lass, why did Morna want ye to switch places?" asked Jerry, as if we were having the most normal of conversations. "And where is Adelle?"

Was it possible that he believed me? It took me a moment to find my voice. "That's why I asked ye if the castle was in ruins. When I arrived here, it was. When Adelle and Bri came here, it was, as well. According to Adelle's research, only a few short months after my wedding, the Conalls were murdered and the castle destroyed. No one ever found out who murdered them, and that was why Bri and Adelle came to Scotland—to search for something that might reveal who had murdered the Conalls. 'Tis the same reason that Morna cast the spell. She hoped that if Bri and I switched places, Bri's knowledge of what was to come would enable her to stop the attack, or at least change the outcome of it. And she did. If not, then the castle would still be in ruins now."

"And Adelle?" Jerry continued to stare at me as if he wasn't shocked by my story.

"Once Adelle realized that we'd been switched, we spent weeks searching for a spell that could switch us back. We found one, but Bri dinna want to return. She married Eoin in my place, and they fell in love after the wedding. I dinna want to go back either. There's not much left for me there." I paused as an uncomfortable knot lodged itself in my chest. Swallowing hard, I continued, "Adelle wanted to be with Bri. So she did the spell instead, and it worked. She's with Bri now. 'Twas three days ago when I arrived here alone telling ye I was sick. I dinna know what to do." I leaned back in my chair and crossed my hands in my lap.

Gwendolyn remained silent, and I could tell nothing by her expression.

The three of us sat in silence for what seemed like an eternity. Eventually, Gwendolyn stood and walked to the other side of the room. Reaching up to the top of the bookshelf lining the wall, she pulled a small box from the shelf.

She returned to her seat next to Jerry and smiled at him quickly before extending the box in my direction. "I'd like to tell you a story myself if you don't mind, dear."

Confused, I only nodded and took the box, placing it in my lap.

Gwendolyn pointed at the box. "Open it, and pull out the photographs."

I lifted the small metal latch that kept the lid closed and looked down inside the box. I remembered the first time I'd seen a photograph on the first day I'd arrived in this time. Adelle had shown me one of Bri to emphasize just how much we resembled one another. Despite all the strange and wonderful things I'd seen, it was still miraculous to me that moments could be captured forever on a small piece of parchment.

Only three photographs lay inside, all facing down, and I lifted them out and closed the lid before turning them over. As I gazed at the images, the air around me chilled suddenly.

The first was of Conall Castle, but not as I remembered it. It was the castle in ruins as it had been when I arrived in this time.

The second was of the spelled plaque, still painted with my portrait. A reminder of the day my life had changed forever.

The first two images were shocking, but it was the third that caused my hands to shake and my breath to come out unsteadily as I glanced up at Gwendolyn. She only smiled softly, waiting for me to speak.

The third photograph was less a picture and more of a painted portrait, depicting people I'd known in my old life. Alasdair, young and vibrant, holding a baby Arran in his arms, while Eoin, no more than five and only knee-high, stood next to his father. Alasdair's other arm was draped around a woman's shoulder, squeezing her tightly with affection. The woman was not Alasdair's late wife, who had died giving birth to Arran, and I knew there was only one other person the woman could be. She was the witch, Morna.

While her face in the portrait was younger, it matched Gwendolyn's exactly.

---

*G*wendolyn eventually gave up on waiting for me to respond. Laughing heartily, she reached out and squeezed my hand. "Come, dear. Surely after all you've been through, nothing can be too much of a surprise to you."

I looked over at Jerry, and he nodded in confirmation.

I gasped. "Do ye mean? How could ye be her?" I asked Gwendolyn. "Morna died when I was a verra small child."

"There are a far manner of things, dear, that seem impossible. Surely this is no more impossible than you sitting here in this century when you were born in another, aye?"

Gwendolyn slowly lost the American accent she'd been using the entire time I'd known her. She was right. After all I'd been through, I had no trouble believing her, but I didn't understand how or why she was here.

"If ye could end up here after yer own death, then why would ye bother with the spell for me and Bri?" I asked. "Could ye not have stopped the massacre yerself?"

Gwendolyn, or Morna, I wan't sure which name was now appropriate, smiled as if she had expected my question.

"Because, lass, there are more important things than life and death. My spell put into motion other things just as important as saving the lives of my family members. Souls needed to meet. Souls that belonged together, despite being born centuries apart. Without my spell, that could never have been."

"Do ye mean Eoin and Bri?" Looking at her more closely, I noticed for the first time her resemblance to Alasdair, Eoin, and Arran. The shape of their eyes, the slant of their smiles, all strong Conall traits that made me trust her story even more.

"Aye. Eoin and Bri. Not to mention, there was my own lad, who dinna exist in my own time. Instead of saving my family myself, I chose to sit back and watch over those who would save them, while at the same time finding the man I was meant to love."

"Ye mean, Jerry isna like ye?" I asked.

Jerry cackled and coughed before he spoke. "No, lassie! I was born right here, in this time. And if I had the gift of magic like my wife, I'd have stopped my knees from cracking long ago."

Morna frowned at her husband. "I've told ye before, I could stop it for ye myself, but ye willna let me." She turned toward me once more. "He accepts the truth, but it all still makes him a wee bit uncomfortable. He willna let me use magic on him."

"So ye mean ye knew I wasna Bri?"

"Aye, lass. But I'll tell ye, I dinna expect ye to stay here and Adelle to go back. My visions dinna show me that. Perhaps they dinna want me to try and stop it from happening. Are ye certain that ye wish to stay here?"

Panic shot through me at the thought of going back. "Aye! I canna go back." I answered too quickly, startling both Morna and Jerry.

Morna's face softened, her eyes showing that she understood. "All right, lass. Well, what is it that ye want to do now? We shall help ye get settled wherever ye'd like to go. Do ye wish to stay in Scotland?"

I'd given it no thought. I'd been too concerned with what I was going to tell them, and whether or not Adelle and Bri had been able to stop the massacre, to think much further than a few moments into my future. "I'm not sure. I doona know what to do."

Jerry leaned over and squeezed my hand, and there was no doubt in my mind that Morna had chosen well. Her husband was the best of men—kind to his core.

Morna waved a hand in the air, as if dismissing my concern. "Doona worry. Why doona we help ye get settled in Edinburgh? We could get ye a job and a place to stay, and ye can see how ye like it for a while. If ye decide later that ye'd like to go elsewhere, then we'll be more than happy to help ye."

"Aye, that will be fine. Thank ye. I suppose ye shall be glad to have another empty room for guests, aye?"

Morna stood and motioned for me to do the same, and then we made our way to the stairs. Clearly, we were all about to retire for the evening.

"Lass, we doona allow other guests. Ye are the only one who knows this house is here. Only yerself and those I wish to see it can see this house along the side of the road. We'd be overrun with tourists, otherwise."

CHAPTER 2

onall Castle – Scotland – 1646

*A*rran Conall made his way down to the stables for his daily ride. The remaining men of what was formerly the Kinnaird Clan still camped out on the castle grounds nearly two months after the demise of the clan's wretched laird.

Laird Kinnaird had given birth to no sons, and with his daughter still unmarried, the clan remained at Conall Castle under Eoin's blessing while they tried to sort out a way to name their next leader.

Arran found himself stifled while standing in an open field. With guests tucked into every free corner of the castle and its grounds, his daily rides and work in the stables were all that kept him from insanity.

He needed to keep busy, anyway. The loss of his beloved Blaire to a century beyond his comprehension occupied his thoughts every moment. He was happy that his brother had found love in his new wife, Bri, but with her face so similar to Blaire's, Arran was reminded of his own heartache every time he laid eyes on his new sister-in-law.

If he'd known his rejection of Blaire would send her so far from him, he would have defied his brother and never let her go. He would live with the regret of hurting her for the rest of his life.

Arran shook his head, doing his best to dislodge all thoughts of his beloved from his conscious mind. He saw enough of Blaire in his dreams. It was torture to see her in the recesses of his mind when he was awake, as well.

Rounding the corner of the entrance to the stables, he found Edana

Kinnaird, the daughter of the late, villainous laird, feeding an apple to his brother's old horse, Griffin. The stables were usually occupied by only the castle's fleet of horses and the old stable master, Kip. But Arran was surprised to find that his spirits lifted at the sight of his new friend.

While many women and children of Kinnaird's clan had stayed inside the castle, Edana was the only one who had her own room upstairs, where members of the Conall family resided. For the past months, Edana had stayed in Arran's late mother's room, just down the hall from his own. He saw her often, and although she always kept their conversations short, he could tell by the way she watched him that she fancied him.

He could never return her feelings. His own heart had been swept away to a different time with another lass. If he'd met Edana only a year ago, he'd have already broken her heart without as much as a second thought. But Blaire had changed him irreparably, and it caused him to look at Edana's feelings toward him in a kinder light. He liked the lass, and he respected her. He wanted to do all he could to show her friendship.

She'd been through much as a child, living with her brute of a father. Arran was certain Kinnaird had abused the young girl physically, and maybe in even more unthinkable ways, as well. She seemed a kindhearted lass, and with all her family gone, Arran knew she must be terrified over the uncertainty of her future.

Smiling wide, he made his way toward her, reaching up to rub Griffin behind his ears as he stopped beside the horse.

"Ah, Griffin. Ye are a lucky lad today. I'm sure ye are glad to be receiving such a treat from a lady rather than from me or Kip, aye?" Arran turned and winked at Edana. "Ye shall spoil him, lass. I fear he shall never take an apple from me again. He'll always want to eat it out of yer delicate hands."

Edana blushed, and Arran didn't miss how she averted her eyes from him before speaking.

"Nay, I doubt it. He doesna seem too particular about who's giving him the apple. He only wants to eat it."

"I doona know about that. I canna think of a time I've seen him look so pleased." Arran continued to stroke Griffin, hoping that if he looked distracted with the horse, it would ease Edana's nerves. "What are ye doing down here? I doona believe I've seen ye in the stables before."

"I'm grateful that ye and yer brother have allowed me to stay here. Lady Bri is exceedingly kind, but I tire of being indoors, and I canna stand to hear the men speak any further about how they shall replace my father." Edana's brow creased in a pained expression.

Arran reached forward to place a hand on her shoulder to comfort her. She jerked away from him as if touched by fire, and Arran quickly went back to stroking Griffin. "I doona blame ye for needing to get away, but doona be worried about yer clan, lass. No matter who takes over as laird, ye shall not lose yer place in the castle. I promise that I'll see that ye are provided for just as ye have always been."

Edana fumbled with her hands nervously, obviously unsure of how to respond. Arran didn't press her. As he turned and began to walk away to see to the other horses, she called out to him. "Thank ye, Arran. I doona deserve yer kindness. I'm not as good as ye think I am."

Arran stopped walking and spun to face Edana. "Doona talk in that manner, lass. Ye deserve every kindness in the world." He paused, deciding that he could attend to the stables later. Perhaps what the lass needed most was to be left alone. "Now, I'll leave ye in peace. Spend as much time with the horses as ye wish. If ye decide ye would like to go for a ride, Kip would be more than happy to assist ye."

Smiling briefly, he turned and left. Perhaps it was time he talked to his brother about their guests. The Kinnaird clan needed to choose a new leader and return to their own castle and territory. He didn't like to see Edana so distressed. The least he could do for her was to see her safely settled.

---

*E*dana Kinnaird watched until she was sure Arran was out of sight. Shivering beneath her clothes, she reached up to brush her shoulder harshly where he'd touched her. She could scrub the spot all day and it would never be enough to rid her of the Conall filth that he'd placed there.

She couldn't stand another moment in captivity here. Each day she spent with the ever-kind and polite Conalls made her hate them that much more.

Her father had been a horrible man. Violent, angry, and disgusting, he'd beaten her mother's spirit until she'd died of sadness. He'd spent much of his life trying to do the same to Edana. But she was far stronger than her mother. Her father had even admitted that much.

Edana had always hated her father, but he was all she'd had in the world, and she would never be able to forgive the family responsible for his death. She had even gone to the Conalls before her father's planned attack, warning them that he planned to murder them. She'd been confused, torn between misplaced loyalty to a father who hated her, and an unbidden wish to see him fail because she hated him, too. And that confusion had caused her not to think straight. It didn't occur to her then that trying to do the right thing would cost her everything.

Despite Arran's well-intentioned promises, she knew now that as soon as a leader rose up among the cowardly men of her father's clan, she would lose her place as lady of the keep. The new laird would marry, and Edana would be cast out, hated for her father's crimes.

Edana was through helplessly waiting to see what would take place. She'd learned enough of manipulation from her father to know that she had Arran just where she wanted him. With each quick glance away from him and each blush of her cheeks, she knew he grew to believe she cared for him. That belief would make him weak, as love does to all people, and then she would be in the perfect position to save her legacy for herself.

With each bat of her lashes in Arran's direction, the desperate seed of revenge took root, twisting its way through every last corner of her mind as she worked out a way to continue her father's work and destroy the Conalls.

She'd failed her father once by giving away his plan. She would not disappoint him again.

CHAPTER 3

"Just stay still for a minute, Mom. Can't you tell I'm trying to talk to you about something?" Bri reached to grab the side of her mother's dress, hoping it would deter Adelle from continuing the raid on her closet—a habit her mother had developed in the twenty-first century. Now, Bri only owned a handful of dresses, yet her mother still enjoyed stealing her clothes.

"Do you think I could talk Mary into making a few more gowns for me?" her mom asked. "She does such lovely work."

Adelle turned and joined Bri at the end of the bed. Quickly hiking up her dress, she kicked off her shoes and jumped up onto the feathered ticking so that she sat cross-legged, facing Bri. Both women, while now considered beloved members of the family, stood out as oddities in this century. Their relaxed social manners and American accents branded them as the foreigners they were.

Bri smiled, amazed at her mother's vanity when they now lived in a place where mirrors were few and far between. The mere fact that they had all their teeth set them apart as rare beauties here. "I'm sure Mary would be happy to sew for you, Mom, but I expect she will have you chipping in on a lot of the work."

Adelle laughed. "Oh yes, I expect that she will. Now, what is it that you were wanting to talk about?"

"Blaire." Bri paused, knowing that the mention of her lookalike would cause a reaction from her mother.

"Oh. Why?" Adelle sighed. "I miss the sweet girl terribly, but there's nothing I can do for her here except hope and pray that she's happy and has adjusted well." Her eyes shifted downward, an odd occurrence for such a forthright woman and a sure sign she truly was heartsick over the idea of Blaire being left in the twenty-first century all alone.

"Well, maybe there is something we can do. I've been spending a lot of time in the spell room—"

"What? Bri, you have no business ever entering that room again. It's already taken you from me once," Adelle exclaimed, interrupting Bri, her voice shrill and panicked. "Besides, I like it here. I don't want to have to follow you if you're sucked back through time again."

Bri rolled her eyes at the expected melodramatics. "It isn't some big wormhole with a magnetic pull that's going to suck me in. It's all based on Morna's spells, Mom. And there are others that can work, that could bring us back and forth as we please. I'm sure there are risks, but I think they might be worth taking."

"What for? I didn't keep Blaire from returning here, Bri. She suggested that I go in her place. She didn't want to come back. She chose to stay."

Bri nodded. "I know all that, but *why* did she not want to come back? Did she ever tell you?" When Adelle shook her head, Bri added, "I think she was heartbroken."

Adelle's face blanched and her eyes widened with surprise. "She never spoke of it, but I think you might be right. She said that there was no longer anything here for her, as if she had lost something dear."

"Have you noticed the way Arran avoids me at almost all cost? When we do run into each other, the look in his eyes breaks my heart." Bri sighed, and at the sight of her mother's confused expression, continued, "I guess I never told you about what happened with Arran, did I?" Bri smiled as she watched the color return to her mother's face with the anticipation of a juicy story.

"No, I've never noticed. And no, you never told me! But, I expect you to right this instant," Adelle said, her eyes lighting up.

Bri adjusted herself on the edge of the bed, reaching for a cushion to prop herself up more comfortably, knowing she was prolonging her mother's impatience. "The night of my wedding to Eoin, Arran came to our bedchamber door thinking it was his own. He was very drunk. Anyway, Eoin was helping put out a small fire at the reception, so I had to help Arran down to his own room. To make a long story short, he kissed me. Granted, he thought I was Blaire, but it was clear that the two of them had been involved. And that he loves her very much."

"Oh, wow. So you're telling me that you've kissed both of them?" Adelle paused and waved her hand in the air in dismissal. "Never mind, that's beside the point. But you know, I do remember that Arran seemed upset the day I arrived and told you that Blaire chose to stay."

"Yes, he was, and I'm worried about him. Each day he drinks a little more than he did the day before. He's broken. I want to go and talk to Blaire, let her know that Arran is still in love with her and see if she would want to come back. Do you think that she would, Mom?" Bri sat patiently while her mother thought about the question. Finally, Adelle looked up and into Bri's eyes.

"I don't know, honey. She was very private. The two of you may look alike, but you are quite different. She was curious about modern things and did her best to keep our conversations on that topic. She didn't ever want to talk about herself."

Bri shifted uncomfortably, her resolve regarding her decision to meddle in Arran's affairs shaky. "There is another reason why I'd like to go back—some unfinished business that I feel I should take care of."

Adelle's eyebrows rose, nearly reaching the top of her hairline. "What's that, dear?"

"Several things, actually. School, Mitsy, and putting an end to the missing persons report I'm certain Mitsy has filed. I need to clear things up with her and stop any police department searches for me that might be underway."

Adelle shook her head. "Nobody's searching. While Blaire and I were at the inn, the police called looking for you. I instructed Gwendolyn and Jerry to tell them you were fine but did not wish to speak to them. I called the station back later pretending to be you so they'd close the missing persons report. I also falsified reports from the dig and scheduled them to be sent out at different intervals for the next three months. Most likely, the grant committee is just now starting to realize that something is off."

"Well, that's good to know. I'm glad my disappearance didn't make national news."

Mom studied me for a few minutes, then asked, "Are you sure you want to do this? Eoin will never let you go."

"Eoin isn't going to keep me from going anywhere. I'm sure he will be against it, but it's something I must do. Arran needs Blaire, and Mitsy needs to know what happened to me. It's only weeks until her wedding. I won't have her ruin her big day by worrying over me."

Adelle stood, and Bri remained on the bed as her mother made her way to the bedchamber door. "I know you will do what you feel is right. Good luck telling this to Eoin. You are far braver than I."

<hr>

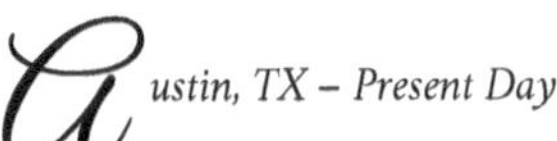
Austin, TX – Present Day

itsy soon-to-be Fredrickson stood across the desk from Principal Hendricks, the twin of Mr. Clean. With her arms crossed firmly across her chest, she tapped her foot.

"Look. I didn't come here to ask your permission, Principal Hendricks. I've already booked the flight. You can either approve the days, or I'll quit. But either way, I'm going to Scotland to look for Bri. I'm only asking to leave a week earlier than I was originally scheduled to be off for my wedding, anyway. The substitute has been here for months now. She doesn't need me in the classroom with her. Now, are you going to sign off on it, or do I need to submit my resignation?"

Principal Hendricks crossed his own arms and looked her up and down as if gauging the seriousness of her words. "You know that the police have already closed the case, Mitsy, and we've already terminated Ms. Montgomery's contract here with the district. The police chief told you himself that they have confirmation in Scotland that Bri is unharmed and still in the country. Ms. Montgomery did this to herself. Why do you feel the need to seek her out?"

Mitsy's head pounded as her blood pressure rose. When she spoke, her voice came out harsher than intended, but she couldn't rein in her frustration. "Some old innkeeper telling the police that the girl they've described is staying with them is not confirmation that she's all right. Neither is them speaking to someone who is supposedly Bri on the phone. The innkeepers said she wouldn't take my calls. Bri wouldn't refuse to talk to me. She knows me, and she knows how worried I'd be. Don't you understand my concern? The couple the police talked to could have murdered her!" Mitsy sat down in the chair opposite Principal Hendricks, her legs shaky and unsteady.

"The police also contacted the archaeological society that Bri's mother worked for. They said that they've received reports on the dig regularly, the last one arriving only a week ago. Bri accompanied her mother on the dig."

Mitsy reached up and tucked a fistful of springy red curls behind her ears, the principal's words doing nothing to calm her down. "I know. I know all of this, but something has gone wrong. Bri is the least impulsive person I've ever known. She lives every day by a strict schedule, and she's my best friend. She would not abandon me without good reason, and she wouldn't miss the wedding. She knows I'd kill her myself."

As Principal Hendricks drummed his fingertips on the top of his desk, Mitsy had to grab onto both of her elbows to keep from slamming her palms down hard on top of his hand. She fidgeted impatiently as she waited for him to respond.

"I'm not going to change your mind, am I?" she asked when she couldn't stand to wait another second.

"You know the days off aren't the issue. I'm just worried about you, is all. As a friend, not as your principal. I don't think you are going to be happy with what you find in Scotland. I truly believe that Bri just decided to abandon her life here. It's best that you move on and forget about her. Try and enjoy the wedding and this new phase of your life."

Mitsy knew he was wrong. Every fiber of her being screamed it. She stood and made her way to the door, pausing there to turn back toward him briefly. "So the days are approved? Great. I'll see you at the wedding."

Slamming the door of his office behind her, she made her way home to pack for her flight.

CHAPTER 4

S cotland – 1646

"Y e canna mean it, Bri!" Eoin's eyes flared, relaying his grave concern. "Morna's spells are unpredictable. Father told me countless stories of how they often went awry, causing havoc around the castle. Ye canna be sure that all will proceed to your liking, love."

Bri hesitated before speaking, knowing that she needed to be careful of how she approached this conversation with Eoin. She was going to do the spell regardless of his liking; she'd already made up her mind. But already in her few short months of marriage, she'd learned that if she wanted to get what she wanted, it was best to make her husband feel as if he had come up with the idea himself.

"The spell has worked correctly several times, has it not? You were even prepared to send me back using it when the Kinnaird clan planned to attack us. Surely you wouldn't have done so if you weren't certain all would go smoothly, right?" Bri placed a hand on his broad shoulder, snuggling in close to weaken his resolve.

She smiled as Eoin buried his face in her hair, kissing the top of her head. "Aye, love. I did believe that the spell would work, but I'm so verra glad that ye dinna do it. By the time she died, Morna was a great caster."

Bri breathed in the heady scent of her husband before shaking her head to bring herself back to task. "So, you see? It would be safe for me to go. You've basically just said so yourself."

A squeal escaped Bri's lips as Eoin trailed kisses along the side of her neck, then nipped her earlobe gently between his teeth.

"Ye are twisting my words, lass," he murmured, his deep voice scattering goosebumps over her skin. "While I do believe the spells willna cause ye harm, that doesna mean I think ye should go. Are ye so sure that Arran feels the way that ye say? I've not heard him speak of Blaire."

Bri stepped back so she could look into Eoin's face. Just the sight of his ebony eyes and hair took her breath away. Smiling, she continued, "Do you not remember the night of our wedding?"

"Ye think I could forget, love?"

Eoin's smile warmed her from the inside out. "Arran may have been drunk, but he wouldn't have kissed me so if he didn't feel there was a reason to," she said. "He and Blaire had kissed before. I believe they were in love."

Bri repressed a laugh as she watched Eoin's eyebrows draw together and his lips twist in muddled confusion. "Nay! Are ye telling me that my own betrothed and my arse of a brother were together before the wedding? I should tear the lousy sot to bits."

"Oh, hush. It's not as if you loved Blaire. From what I've gathered, you couldn't stand her, so what does it matter if Arran could? It's very difficult to control who you fall in love with, Eoin. Besides, if things hadn't happened as they had, it's very possible I wouldn't have ended up here. Surely you wouldn't have wanted that?"

Air quickly escaped Bri's lungs as Eoin crushed her against him, pressing his mouth to hers in a desperate kiss, leaving them both breathless. "Nay, lass, I wouldna want that. I canna stand the thought of ye not being by my side. So, I must ask one thing of ye, if ye are to do this."

Bri stepped away from him, her insides weak and fluttery from his kiss, her curiosity piqued. "What is it?"

"I shall come with ye. If the spell goes wrong, and ye are trapped in another time, I will be with ye."

"You can't be serious, Eoin. For starters, we have no modern male clothes to put you in. I, at least, still have the clothes I was wearing when I arrived here. You would stand out like a sore thumb!"

"A sore thumb, lass?"

Bri couldn't help but laugh aloud at the look of confusion flickering across Eoin's face. "Forget it. But that's another reason why you can't possibly come. You wouldn't be able to communicate. Not to mention how confused you will be by cars, cell phones, ATMs."

Eoin placed his hands on her shoulders. "Aye, lass. It doesna sound so different from the way ye were when ye first arrived here. And ye survived. I shall have ye to help me, and I find myself curious to see the world belonging to my strange, bonny lass."

He smiled sweetly, and Bri found herself softening to the idea. It would be nice not to be all alone. And she agreed with him; if something did go wrong with the spell, she couldn't stand the thought of being separated from him. Besides, watching his reaction to the conveniences of modern times was sure to be a humorous and fascinating experience. Now that he'd presented the idea, she found herself eager to take him up on it.

"Fine. But on one condition," she said.

"Anything."

"While we are there, I am the boss. Life is very different in my world. For your own safety, you need to do whatever I tell you to do. Understood?"

Eoin rolled his eyes, and Bri smiled, anticipating what he was going to say even before he spoke.

"Aye, lass. As if ye are not my master already. It shall be little adjustment from daily life now."

"That's right." Bri winked playfully. "And don't you forget it, mister. Now you'll need to think of something to tell Arran. He will have to know we are going somewhere, but it's best he doesn't know the truth. He would try to stop us from going."

"Aye, he would. I shall talk to him now."

---

*A*rran made his way through the castle's winding hallways, stopping to briefly poke his head in the kitchen to pester the beloved housemaid, cook, and mentor, Mary. He stepped inside the long room and sneakily stuck his hand out to grab at one of the loaves of bread set aside for the evening meal.

He was rewarded with the expected quick smack on his hand.

"How many times do I have to tell ye? Ye are not going to get food from this kitchen until 'tis served to ye, as long as I am here. And doona get yer hopes up, I intend to live many more decades still."

Arran laughed and bent to scoop Mary up in a large embrace, roughly kissing her on the cheek. "Aye, I surely hope that ye do. The castle would fall apart without ye, Mary." He continued to squeeze her, her feet dangling inches off the ground, refusing to set her down until she screeched and reached over his shoulder to swat at something behind him.

He quickly set the plump woman back on the floor and spun to see what had her in such a fuss. Eoin stood with his hand extended toward the bread, guilt spread across his face.

Mary waved Eoin away from the aromatic loaves. "Ye shall drive me mad! The both of ye. It doesna matter how many times I repeat myself, ye doona seem to hear it. Now get." She paused and extended both of her arms out in front of her, palms up, and briskly shooed them from the kitchen. "I doona want to see yer faces until the evening meal. Get on with ye."

"Aye."

"Aye."

Their voices echoed as, in unison, they each kissed Mary on the cheek and quickly made their leave of her place of worship.

Once outside, Arran walked alongside Eoin. "I've been looking for ye, brother. I need to speak with ye about the visiting clan. It's been months, and they've still made no decision regarding a new leader. We canna allow them to stay here forever."

"Aye, ye are right. But that shall have to wait for a few days."

Arran paused, turning to lean against the wall so that his brother would do the same. "Has something happened?"

Eoin shook his head, and Arran instantly felt relieved. He didn't think he could bear any more tragedies so soon after the death of his father and the loss of his beloved.

"Nay, but Bran – from the village – ye remember him, aye?"

Arran nodded. "Aye, o'course. What of him?"

"He has asked that I come to help him with the building of a stable. He canna afford to pay anyone to help. He knew, as his friend, I would. Bri shall go along with me and help his wife with their brood of children."

Arran was certain Bran already had a stable, but he decided not to question his brother's story. With Eoin gone, perhaps he'd have ample time to resolve the situation with their guests on his own.

"Aye, 'tis kind of ye to agree to help him. Do ye need me to go along, as well?" Arran hoped Eoin would say no, but it was formality that he should offer assistance.

"Nay. I need ye to stay here and serve as laird while I'm gone," Eoin responded. "I shan't be far, but I doona want ye to try and find me with castle issues. I trust ye to see to anything that may arise while I am gone."

"O'course. Wish Bran and his family well for me. When will ye be leaving?"

"Tomorrow, I believe. I shall leave ye now. I left my wife in our bedchamber all alone. I am anxious to return to her."

Arran smiled and waved his brother off. "Aye, I'm sure ye are."

Once Eoin left, Arran slowly made his way back to his own bedchamber. While his brother was away, he would focus his time and attention on finding a solution to their guests' dilemma regarding a new leader. And he would focus on solving Edana's problem, as well. If he succeeded, he knew his brother would be pleased.

At the very least, Eoin would be happy to have things around the castle resume a more normal pace. And Arran knew it would be good for him to have something else to focus his mind upon other than Blaire. He might not love Edana, but he could make sure that she was taken care of. Aye, as far as he was concerned, his brother's trip to the village could not have come at a better time.

CHAPTER 5

was certain I'd never heard such language from a lady. I did my best to listen to the angry woman, but with each breath Danny's voice grew louder, and I found my mind drifting away from the conversation. Not that I was given much chance to speak. The old lady—my boss—waved her finger at me in such a manner I was certain it would fall off.

A momentary second of silence caused me to refocus my attention.

"'Ello? Are ye daft in the head, Blaire? Have ye been listening to a word I've said?" Danny threw her hands violently up in the air only to bring them down swiftly so they sat snugly on her hips. She glared at me, unblinking.

"Aye. I did hear ye, but I doona understand. There's no reason why the two of them should have been asleep so late in the day. They werena sick, and 'tis dreadful behavior." I knew my words would be met with more screaming, and I felt the tips of my ears pull back, readying for the inevitable attack.

"Ye are a bloody fool! If only I had the luxury of sleeping in one day in my lousy life, I would take full advantage. It is not yer place to decide how long our paying guests sleep in the morning. I've told ye before, if they are in the room, skip it and go on to the next room for cleaning. Come back to it later, after they wake and leave for the day."

"Aye, I willna do it again." I turned to leave, hoping that if I slipped away fast enough the lecture would be over. But I only took one step before Danny grabbed my arm.

"Ye turn back around. I dinna dismiss ye. Ye are right, ye willna do it again because ye are no longer employed by this hotel."

Danny looked at me, satisfaction evident on her face, but as I continued to adjust to the many unfamiliar words of this time, I dinna understand what she was telling me. "I'm sorry. I doona understand ye. No longer employed?"

"Fired. Doona show up for work here again. I doona want to see ye around here. If this was yer first transgression, then ye would only be getting a warning, but there have been many complaints."

It was cold, but sweat beaded on my forehead as understanding settled in. I no longer had a job. "Complaints?"

"Aye, lass. Complaints. Many. More than one family said they saw ye sweeping the carpet rather than using the vacuum. Another said they saw ye hanging the sheets up in the room to be beaten with the broom handle. Who taught ye to clean? Yer great-great-great grandmother?" Danny laughed slightly, pleased with herself for the odd joke.

"No one taught me to clean. I doona like the sound of the vacuum; it hurts my ears. And I doona know how to use the cleaning barrel for the sheets."

Danny's eyes grew wide at my ignorance.

"Cleaning barrel? Do ye mean the washing machine? Gracious! I'd hate to see what yer house looks like, and I bet yer clothes smell something dreadful. Now, collect yer things and be gone with ye."

She gave me no further chance to speak as she turned and left, leaving me alone in the small storage room beneath the staircase. I knew I'd been in trouble when she pulled me into the broom storage, but I never expected to be left without a job.

Without it, I had little means to pay for the small apartment Jerry and Morna had found for me, and I was unsure of how to search for another job. What could I do? I had few skills, and those I did possess would serve me little in today's time.

I'd held the job for only two weeks. With each passing day, I found myself regretting my decision to stay in this time just a little bit more.

But it didn't matter. I alone had chosen my path. Breathing in deeply, I tried to suck back the tears threatening to fall from my eyes. I lifted my head up and left the closet.

"*W*ait up!"

I heard the shout from behind me but continued to make my way home, assuming the words were meant for someone else.

"Blaire! Slow down. Ye walk so fast I canna catch up with ye."

I stopped walking, causing a man who seemed to be in quite a big hurry to walk right into my back. After he told me what he thought about me in a few short, fairly shocking words, I turned to see one of the other maids, Isla, lifting her dainty, short legs up in an effort to reach me.

"I'm sorry," I said. "I thought ye were calling after someone else."

Once Isla was next to me, we moved off of the main walkway so we could stand without blocking the way of others. Isla rubbed her gloved hands together and cupped them around her mouth, blowing air into them to warm them.

I continued to be amazed at how cold everyone here seemed to always be. 'Twas no colder than Scotland always was. With the thick coats and protective clothing that people now wore, not to mention my favorite modern invention—heaters, I found the temperature to always be quite pleasant.

"No, I was talking to you," Isla told me. "I just got off work, and I heard about what Danny did. I'm sorry about yer job, but ye did do things awful strange. But what I wanted to say is, I might could get ye another job, if ye like."

"Aye, I would like. I doona know what I will do, otherwise."

Isla smiled and put her arm around me as if we were much more closely acquainted. "I thought that might be the case. There is a catch, though. Ye canna do this job looking like ye do. It would only cause trouble for ye."

I stepped away, still uncomfortable with the familiarity people of this time used with one another. "What do ye mean? What is the job?"

"My cousin owns a pub not far from the hotel. I've been bartending there as a second job, but I canna juggle both at the same time. He's looking for a replacement for me. I would train ye myself, and I know he will give ye the job if I ask him. All ye do is mix drinks, but ye look too pretty and sweet with yer long hair and clean face. I know ye have enough spunk to handle the job, but yer appearance needs to reflect yer no-nonsense attitude. I'll help ye change yer look. What do ye say?" Isla smiled and shrugged her shoulders, raising her hands, palms up, as if awaiting my answer.

I knew it would be foolish to tell her no. "Aye, I canna thank ye enough, Isla. What do ye want to do about my appearance?"

I fidgeted uncomfortably while Isla looked me up and down, deciding how to best alter what was apparently so unacceptable about me. "How would ye feel about cutting yer hair? And maybe piercing yer ears? And eyeliner, ye definitely need to learn how to employ the use of eyeliner. It will make ye look more intimidating instantly. Believe me, when tending bar for a bunch of rowdy Scots, ye want a look that says 'doona even think about it'."

"Aye, if ye say so. But I doona wanna look like a man. The hair goes no higher than my shoulders." I reached a hand up to run through my long locks. Mayhap a change would be good.

"Deal."

With that, Isla led me in another direction, away from my new home. We walked for what seemed like miles. My feet felt heavy and tired from working all day at the hotel. At last, Isla turned us onto a dimly lit street where we made our way into what she called a hair "salon."

I was seated quickly. As the woman behind me snipped away at my long, dark hair, I kept my eyes focused on the floor, not wanting to see my reflection in the mirror. Each snip of her scissors caused my heart to beat a little faster.

After cutting what I was sure was every hair off the top of my head, the woman took out a large and frightening object that shot out warm air that she blew onto my wet strands. Once dry, she continued to mess and spray odd potions into my hair as I sat nervously in the seat. By the time she finished, the city was engulfed in darkness, small street lamps the only visible light outside the window.

"Are ye ready?" They were the first words the woman had spoken to me. With my mouth dry, I simply nodded, keeping my eyes squeezed shut as she turned me to face the mirror. "Open yer eyes, dear. If ye doona like it, it's only hair. It'll grow back."

Her argument was sound. Slowly, I opened my eyes, unable to stop the wide smile that spread across my features as I took in my glorious reflection.

While I was certain I was going to find myself without hair, she'd actually kept a good amount. With the ends lightly curled around my shoulders, each strand of hair seemed to find new life, no longer weighted down.

"Oh, 'tis lovely." I smiled and stood, hesitantly reaching a hand out to pat the woman on the shoulder. Twas a gesture that seemed acceptable in this time, and now that my hair seemed to fit, I thought I could at least make an effort to make my behaviors fit, as well.

"Great. Now, on to make-up and piercing." Isla stood, extending money toward the hairdresser before motioning that I follow her out of the shop.

We found our next stop one block further down, on a street even more dimly lit than the last and situated in between two shops claiming to draw pictures on people's skin. We made our way inside.

Once again, I was thrust into a seat, and the proprietor obeyed Isla's orders and held different shapes and sizes of shiny objects up to my ear. Once Isla found one that satisfied her, I was told to sit back and not move, as there would soon be a prick to my earlobe.

I relaxed, certain that a prick would be no worse than being stuck by a pin while being fitted for a dress. The proprietor squeezed his fingers together over a foreign contraption he'd placed over the lobe of my ear, and I felt the rod of the object pierce my skin. I let out a howl I was sure the Conalls could hear all the way back in 1646.

CHAPTER 6

Conall Castle – 1646

"Are ye sure that ye wanna go through with it? I willna be able to sleep a wink while ye are both away. I think ye are being foolish, but ye never wish to listen to me." Mary fluttered nervously around the spell room, rambling as she listed reasons why Eoin and Bri should not try and go forward to retrieve Blaire, only stopping when she was interrupted by Adelle, who stood anxiously in the doorway.

"She's right. I miss Blaire, but I'd rather the two of you didn't risk your own lives to go look for her."

The two women continued to rant back and forth, talking more to each other than to Eoin or Bri, each doing their best to proclaim themselves as alpha among the mother and mother-figure duo.

Bri looked over her shoulder at Eoin, who had his arms wrapped around her to hold her close. "They aren't going to stop until we are gone, you know that, right? It's best that we get going. It will take us a few hours to walk to the inn, and we are going to have some explaining to do about your clothing if we run into anyone at the castle or along the road."

"Aye, lass. I suppose ye are right. What are we to tell them again?"

Eoin squeezed Bri tightly, and she sighed in response to the comfort of his warm arms around her. "Well, let's hope that we don't bump into anyone who works at the castle, like a tour guide. If we do, we will just tell them that you wanted to dress up to get into the spirit of things. They will think you're crazy, but any girl that sees you is just going to be so pleased to have the opportunity to gaze upon you shirtless, I doubt they will care much about your sanity."

Bri smiled as he chuckled deeply into her ear. "I doona think that is so, lass. I'm not so uncommon looking."

"Pfff…yeah, whatever." She paused to twist and give him a swift kiss on the lips. "Let's shut these two yappers up and get out of here. You ready?"

"Aye. Do ye wanna get their attention or should I?"

"I'll do it. I know just how to get a response out of Mom." Bri smiled before she shouted, "Adelle!" in her mother's direction. Instantly, her mother's eyes widened and she whipped toward her, awarding Bri with a stern expression.

"What? I know that you didn't just call me 'Adelle,' right? I'm your mother."

Bri stepped away from Eoin and looked up at him. "Told ya," she whispered before moving to pull her mother into a hug. "We're leaving now, Mom. It's going to be fine. Morna's spells seem to be pretty reliable." Bri pulled away from her mother's vice-like embrace and moved over to hug Mary. "Now, both of you try not to worry while we're gone. It may be a few weeks before we return. Just keep yourselves busy."

It was Mary's turn to react. "Do ye not think that I always keep myself busy? Do ye think I just lie around the castle, trying to dream up things to do?"

Bri rolled her eyes and stepped back so that Eoin could bid both of the women farewell. "No, of course I don't think that, Mary, and you know it," she said. "Now remember, don't let Arran find out where we've gone off to. He'll find out soon enough if Blaire wants to return. But in case she doesn't, I don't want him getting his hopes up."

Both women nodded. When it was clear that Bri and Eoin were about to begin the spell, they quietly retreated from the small room.

Standing in front of the old, faded book, Bri took Eoin's hands. Together they lit the candles and read aloud the words from the book. Momentary shock waves of pain coursed through them. They wrapped their arms around one another and, together, vanished from the room.

———

*M*uffled voices became audible above their heads. Both groggy and confused, they leaned against the walls of the once familiar room until they found themselves reoriented. Having already made the trip through once, Bri knew instantly the headache Eoin would have and went straight for her mother's backpack, still tucked neatly behind the bench in front of the table, out of sight from the eyes of wandering tourists.

Opening the inner zipper pocket, she pulled out the bottle of Advil and dumped out five round pills into her hand, two for herself and three for her beast of a husband. They had no water, but if either of them were to function, they had to medicate the head trauma that always seemed to occur when traveling through time by way of Morna's spells.

"Here." Blaire moved to stand in front of Eoin, her legs still slightly unsteady and discombobulated. "Put these in your mouth and swallow them. They will help with your headache."

Obligingly, Eoin held open his hand and looked down at the pills questioningly. "What are they, lass? They look too small to do much for my head."

Bri slowly raised his hand to motion for him to put them in his mouth. "Trust me. They'll help. At least it looks like we made it. Look at how old everything in the room is."

Bri smiled as she watched Eoin wander about the room, awestruck. She reached a hand in his direction as she moved to the door leading to the staircase out of the basement. "Did you hear the voices above us just a moment ago? I think they must be conducting a tour. No surprise, since we were able to stop the castle from being destroyed. I'm sure it's quite the tourist attraction today. Which means it's going to be difficult for us to get out of the place unseen."

Eoin winked, and Bri smiled at the playfulness in his eyes. "Aye. I expect since I have ye with me, it shall be impossible. Ye are talented at falling down. I'm certain I will have to scoop ye off the floor at least twice before we make our escape."

Bri leaned her ear against the spell room door, listening for any sign of movement on the other side. "What about you?" she whispered. "You're not so light on your feet yourself. Now, let's go. I don't hear anybody on the other side."

Cautiously, Bri pulled the door open, finding the main basement room empty. As she closed the secret door to the spell room behind them, she could tell that it had remained unfound despite the years of tourism at the castle. The only sign of entrance within the basement was an "employees only" sign that was draped across the floor in front of the staircase leading up and out of the room.

Hesitantly, Bri climbed the stairs and gently pulled at the door. The ridged nature of the door's hinges showed her that not even castle employees went down into the basement very often.

But as luck would have it, just as Eoin had securely shut the spell room door, hiding it from view, they both heard the door at the top of the basement stairs open. Listening to the sound of footsteps descend the staircase, they soon found themselves staring back at a very official-looking castle employee whose eyes widened in shock at the sight of them.

*S*cotland – *Present Day*

*M*itsy soon-to-be Fredrickson angrily slammed the car door and stood to smooth her shirt and pants before making her way to the front of the small roadside inn. Her connecting flight out of Chicago had been delayed a whopping six hours, cutting the time that she could spend searching for Bri in Scotland short by almost an entire day.

Not to mention the time it had taken her to rent a car and find a decent map, none of which seemed to show the location of the inn. Hours later, frustrated, tired, and worried sick, Mitsy found herself standing in front of the last place Bri had supposedly been seen.

She hoped Bri was safe, but part of her knew that if she walked into that inn to find her AWOL maid of honor lounging around as if on vacation, she was going to kill her on the spot. Determined to find an answer, she rapped her knuckles against the wooden door with as much authority as she could muster.

The door swung open so quickly she nearly pummeled the head of the old man who now stood before her, smiling. "Come in, lass. Why do ye seem to be in such a hurry? We've plenty of rooms if ye are looking for a place to stay."

Mitsy stepped inside, her angry resolve slipping slightly at the friendliness in the man's eyes. Surely he couldn't be responsible for anything that might've happened to Bri. Stopping just inside the doorway, she said, "I'm not looking for a room. I'm looking for a person. Brielle Montgomery. She supposedly stayed here. She's been missing for some time now, and the police have closed the investigation because they spoke to you and your wife, and you told them that she was fine. She can't be fine. She wouldn't just leave without giving me an explanation." The man's brows creased together, as if he was unsure of how to respond, and Mitsy immediately grew suspicious. "Where is she?"

"Why doona ye follow me into the kitchen, lass, and we can talk about yer friend?"

Mitsy lightly stomped her foot against the ground in an effort to root herself firmly in place. "I don't think so, sir. I think you need to tell me whatever it is you know about Bri right this instant."

"Gwendolyn, can ye come in here, sweetheart? We have a visitor who is looking for Bri." The man paused and, while waiting for his wife to arrive, extended a hand in Mitsy's direction. "My name is Jerry. And ye might be?"

Mitsy didn't accept his hand, only curtly giving her name before his wife rounded the corner from the kitchen and came to stand in front of her. "I'm Mitsy," she said to the older woman. "Now, tell me where Bri is."

Gwendolyn smiled.

"I'm afraid she's not here. She moved to Edinburgh only a few weeks ago. She's working as a maid in a hotel, I believe. If ye like, I can give ye directions to the place."

Shock coursed through Mitsy as she took in the old woman's words. Hotel maid? Moved? Why would Bri suddenly decide to drastically change her life? It didn't make sense. Her voice was shaky when she tried to speak. "Y-Yes. Please. I would appreciate directions."

Holding the small pad in which Gwendolyn had written directions to where Bri was supposedly staying, Mitsy turned and made her way back to the car. She didn't care that she was so tired she could hardly keep her eyes open and so hungry that the sheep in the fields looked appetizing, she was going to find Bri tonight.

"Why did ye tell the lass that Bri was in Edinburgh? Doona ye remember that it is Blaire living there?" Jerry looked at his wife with concern, only to be rewarded with a soft smack on his arm.

"O'course I know 'tis Blaire. Doona ye worry about it, dear. The real Bri is on her way to us as we speak. Once she gets here, we will send her in the same direction as Mitsy."

CHAPTER 7

I glanced out of the corner of my eye, watching Mik as he gathered his coat and made his way to the door. Nearing half past ten, we were supposed to remain open until midnight. I had every intention of closing down the pub as soon as Mik left.

He paused at the door and turned to me. "Are ye sure ye doona mind closing alone, Blaire? I know that it was yer turn to leave early, only some of my friends are throwing a party and--"

I held a hand up to stop him. "Aye, 'tis fine. I doona mind."

Smiling, he opened the front door, sending a blast of frigid air through the room. He paused before walking out, and turned to look at me.

"Ye are welcome to stop by after if ye'd like."

Mik didn't wait for my response. As the door shut, I reached behind me for a wet cloth, and hurriedly began wiping down the counters. If the owner found out I'd closed early, I'd be sure to take the blame. I didn't want Mik to get in trouble, but it was Thursday evening and the pub's only customer was the ancient drunkard who had spent every night here since my first evening tending bar.

Once the counter was wiped clean, I circled the tables, gathering glasses to put in the dishwasher. Every time I started the strange machine, I couldn't help but smile. It was a miraculous invention and much more pleasant than the vacuum and other cleaning instruments of this time. It was much more quiet, and the swishing of the water was a sound I found soothing.

Giving the room another glance to ensure that everything was clean and ready for those working the next day's opening shift, I made my way to the telephone hanging on the side wall. Pulling out the number Isla had given me, I called for a taxi. Telephones were a convenience quite useful on evenings like this when I had no one to help me make sure the old drunkard found his way home. But other than those types of occasions, the ease with which people could contact one another in this modern time made me uneasy.

Having grown so accustomed to remaining in constant contact, people in the twenty-first century became anxious too quickly after not hearing from a loved one or friend. It is much easier to wait for news if you know it will be a long time in coming, than to constantly be aware that every second could bring change.

Pushing my musings aside, I walked over to the old man, who now lay slumped over and snoring. I did my best to rouse him from his slumber as I waited for the taxi that would take him home.

---

*A*fter well past twenty-four hours without sleep, Mitsy's exhaustion started to addle her brain. "What do you mean she doesn't work here? I was just told that she did." Well past twenty-four hours without sleep, Mitsy's exhaustion started to idle her brain. With each word that she spoke, she grew more frustrated and had to blink back tears. It took all of her willpower not to throw a temper tantrum in the middle of the small hotel lobby. She glared at the nervous-looking girl behind the front desk.

"I do apologize, miss. I only started last week, and I've never heard of anyone working here by the name of Bri. It's possible that she does, though. Maybe we've never worked the same shift. Give me just a moment, and I'll ask a few of the maids."

"Yes. Please." Mitsy spotted a lounge chair in the corner, made her way to it, and collapsed onto the worn seat. She placed her fingertips on her eyelids, prying them open and staring blankly at the carpet in an effort to stay awake. A hand on her shoulder caused her to jump, poking herself in the eye. "Ouch!" She stood, straightening and pulling at the hem of her shirt before looking up at the person in front of her.

"Sorry, miss," said the front desk clerk, stepping back to allow another young woman to move up alongside her. "This is Isla," she explained, by way of introduction. "She knows the person ye are looking for, but the girl no longer works here, and her name isna Bri."

Isla nodded. "Hello. Is it perhaps Blaire that ye are looking for, miss? Dark hair, blue eyes, terrible maid. I doona know a Bri who has worked here, but Blaire most certainly fits the description."

Mitsy swallowed the lump in her throat and pushed her hair behind her ears as she repressed the frustration building once again inside of her. "No. I'm not looking for someone named Blaire. I'm looking for a Brielle

Montgomery. Everybody calls her Bri. She's American. She does have dark hair and blue eyes, but I'd be very surprised if she was a terrible maid. That woman is the most anal, organized, nasty-nice person I know. Now I just spoke with an elderly couple who told me that they'd helped secure her job here. It's very important that I find her."

"Hmm." Isla frowned and shook her head. "I doona know a Bri, miss. The only person that I can think of is Blaire. She wasna American, but her accent was a little odd, and she never told any of us where she came from or why she was here. Do ye think that she could have been your friend and pretending to be someone she isn't? Is she running from something?"

Mitsy sat in the chair once again as the woman's words sunk in. She didn't think that Bri would go to the effort of changing her name and using an accent, but then again she never would have thought that she herself would go traipsing all over Scotland looking for her best friend, either. She gathered her things. "I don't know. Can you tell me where this Blaire is now? It won't hurt for me to meet her and see for myself."

"Sure. She's working at my cousin's pub," said Isla. "It's not far from here. I can point ye in the right direction. I doona know if she's working now, but ye can at least go and check."

Minutes later, after being shown the way by Isla, Mitsy uttered a thank you and took off as quickly as her sleep-deprived body would carry her.

* * *

*T*he taxi arrived in just under half an hour, and the old drunk man still sat slumped over a small table at the back of the room. After I agreed to pay the taxi driver double what it would cost to get the man home, he came inside and helped me get the old man into the cab.

Twenty minutes later, I gathered up my empty wallet, put on my coat, and flipped the lights off as I made my way to the front doors to lock up for the night. Due to my bulky gloves, I fumbled to get a grip on the correct key. Finally giving up, I bit the fingertip of one of my gloves, allowing me to slip it off so I could get a better grasp on the slippery keys.

The street around me was dark, and I hurried at my task as best I could, not wanting to linger any longer than necessary. I twisted and pulled on the door handle to ensure it locked, and was just slipping my glove back on when a loud voice to my left caused me to drop the glove and keys.

"Oh my God, Bri! It is you. I am going to freaking kill you! Open that door back up right now, because we are about to have quite the conversation, and I'd rather not freeze to death while doing so."

Not moving to pick up my belongings, I stared back at the strange, red-haired woman. The only word I'd been able to understand that she'd spoken was the name Bri, and I wasn't sure of how to deal with the woman's assumption that I was Adelle's daughter. She seemed to know my look-alike quite well.

"Oh. Surprised to see me, are you?" the woman said, her voice oozing sarcasm. "What? Did you really think you could just skip out on your entire life and not expect anyone to come looking for you? You weren't that much of a loner, Bri. There are people who care about you. I care about you! Now, quit staring at me like I'm the one who's lost my mind. Open that door, or I will open it myself."

In an effort to allow myself a few moments to think about my best course of action, I bent to retrieve my glove and the keys to the pub. Then I obeyed the woman's orders by opening the door. Assuming she would follow, I made my way inside and flipped on the lights. I knew I couldn't pretend to be Bri. If this woman knew her well, it would be impossible to fool her.

Turning to her, I said, "I'm not Bri. My name is Blaire." I paused, guilt at causing her pain and confusion making me shift nervously.

The woman's eyes bulged, and her face reddened. "You have got to be joking. You do realize that coming to find you has cost me several months' salary, don't you? That's something I really can't afford considering I've been busy planning a wedding for the last year and a half. Or did you forget about that, too?"

I wrinkled my nose, knowing whatever I said was going to upset her. "I'm verra sorry, miss, but I truly doona know who ye are."

"Sorry? Well then. I'm sorry for what I'm about to do, as well. But I bet that when I'm finished, you'll remember who I am and who you are just fine."

She lunged toward me, but I managed to move quickly out of her path, beginning an odd dance of lunge and dash around the empty room.

CHAPTER 8

*P*resent Day – *Conall Castle*

*B*ri glanced uncomfortably at her half-dressed husband before turning back to face the shocked custodian. "Hello," she said, smiling as sweetly as she could and reaching for Eoin's hand. "We were just leaving," she told the silent man, pulling Eoin toward the stairs behind them.

She hoped they would be able to exit without further explanation. Her mother had told her once that if you walked with authority and pretended like you were somewhere you were supposed to be, people were less likely to question your behavior. It had worked well for her mother, allowing Adelle to ransack through more museum displays than Bri could count. However, she sensed she would not have the same success as her mother, and knew she was right when the custodian moved to stand in front of her, blocking their exit from the basement.

"Now, I know that ye both must have seen the 'Do Not Enter' sign on the front of this door. What made ye think the sign dinna apply to the two of ye?"

Eoin started to speak, but Bri quickly threw an elbow into his ribs to silence him. The feeling of his bare chest against her skin gave her an idea. Before allowing herself to think it through, she threw her right arm over Eoin's shoulder and snuggled in close to reach over and kiss his cheek. "I'm sorry, sir. You see, we are visiting the area on our honeymoon, and the castle is just so romantic. We are having a hard enough time keeping our hands off each other as it is. When our tour group walked by here, I just decided to take the opportunity to slip away for a few moments with my new husband." Not waiting for the man to respond, Bri turned and pressed herself up against Eoin, kissing him hard on the mouth.

She allowed the kiss to go on for a few moments, intent on making her point to the castle employee. Finally, hearing the man clear his throat, Bri pulled away from an open-mouthed, grinning Eoin.

"Ah, well," said the custodian, "um . . . there are certain places for such things, and this isna one of them. I should have ye escorted out immediately, but seeing as ye are newlyweds, I'll cut the two of ye a break, aye? But I doona want to catch ye somewhere that ye shouldn't be again." He frowned at Eoin. "And why are ye not wearing a shirt, man?"

Again, Bri nudged an elbow of warning into her husband's ribs. She waved a hand flippantly in the air. "Oh. That. It's a costume. He wanted to, ya know, get into the spirit of things."

The man didn't respond, only moved out of their way so they could exit the stairwell. Shutting the door behind them, Bri started to thank the custodian but stopped as the man chuckled once, muttering "Americans" under his breath before shaking his head and turning to leave them alone in the empty hallway.

"Lass, I know I agreed that ye would be in charge during our journey here, but do ye really think that was the best way to handle it? That man thinks that we are both mad, and the way ye dinna allow me to speak, why he must think I'm a mute."

Bri laughed, slightly shocked at her own behavior. "I'm sorry. I didn't know what to do. When I felt your bare chest behind me, it was the only thing that popped in my head. But what does it matter, anyway? It worked, didn't it? Now, let's get out of here before another tour passes by. I don't want to have to explain your clothing again." Dragging her husband along behind her, they made their way out of the castle without seeing another soul.

---

*E*oin frowned at his wife. "Do ye think Blaire will still be here? If she wanted a different life for herself, this hardly seems the place."

Bri knocked on the door of the inn before answering his question. "No, I doubt that she is, but maybe they'll know where to find her. Either way, it might be a bit of a tricky situation. They thought that Blaire was me, so I'm not sure how we are going to explain my sudden appearance, not to mention yours."

The door opened, startling both of them. Before Bri could utter a hello, she was pulled into Jerry's rail-thin arms.

"Bri, it's good to see ye again, lass. And Eoin, ye sure are quite the big lad, are ye not? My wife will be quite pleased to see ye. Now, come inside." Jerry waved them into the living room and shouted toward the kitchen. "They're here, dear."

Bri was certain her mouth hung open as she glanced back at Eoin, whose pinched brows and wide eyes matched her own. Once seated, Jerry excused himself, and Bri leaned over to whisper to Eoin, "Did he just call you by your name? How could he possibly know that?"

Eoin answered absent-mindedly as he glanced around the room. "I doona know. Bri, how is the room lit? I doona think the flames above our heads would be easily lit or put out."

Bri smiled and pointed to the light switch on the wall. "They aren't flames. It's electricity. All you have to do to turn them on is flip that tiny switch over there. Flipping it in the other direction will turn the lights off."

"Ye canna mean it? What a change from our dark, candlelit rooms. Tell me, will we be alive to see lights such as this?"

"No, I'm afraid not. You'll see lots of amazing things while we are here, and I can't wait to watch you discover them, but first..." Bri paused as Jerry entered the room, Gwendolyn trailing him. She stood to give the old woman a hug, then returned to the couch and sat again.

"Bri, you don't need to worry about how you are going to explain your situation to us," said Gwendolyn. "We know that while you were here with your mother at the beginning, it was Blaire for most of the time. In fact, I believe I have some things I must explain to both of you. But first, I'd like to kiss my nephew."

Before Bri or Eoin could react, she moved across the room, grabbed Eoin by both cheeks, and brought him near to her, kissing him on the forehead.

Bri's mind reeled at the spectacle, and only Jerry's voice brought her back to her senses.

"Ach, lassie. That's not even half of it. Ye best settle in and prepare yerself for some interesting news."

*I*t was almost eleven when Bri and Eoin parked the car they'd borrowed from Jerry in front of the pub where Blaire supposedly now worked. The lights were on inside, and while she couldn't see Blaire through the windows, Bri hoped that their search would end here, and their evening of overwhelming surprises would be over.

"Are you ready?" Bri asked Eoin as they made their way to the entrance. "Blaire knows you, so I think it might be best if you speak to her first." She reached for the door handle but paused at the touch of Eoin's hand on her forearm.

"Did ye believe her story, Bri? Do ye think 'tis possible that she really is my Aunt Morna?"

"Yes, I do. After all that we've been through, I find it very difficult to be surprised anymore." She tilted her head to one side, studying his strained expression. "Are you all right? Does it upset you to know that she's been here all this time, while letting you all think she'd died?"

He shook his head. "No. I only wish my father was here to see her. He missed her dearly. He'd be so pleased to know that she is loved and happy. He was the only one around her that dinna fear her witchcraft."

"Well, it seems your father was right. I don't think there is any reason to fear Morna. I, for one, will be forever grateful for all she has done. I wouldn't have you otherwise." Bri leaned in briefly to lightly kiss Eoin on the cheek. "Now, let's get in there and see to Blaire."

"Aye, I doona like cars. Nothing should be able to move so quickly. 'Tisna natural."

Bri laughed as they exited the vehicle and walked to the door of the pub. "You go first. I'm nervous to see my lookalike." She gently nudged Eoin's back, urging him to try the lock.

"Aye, fine. But I doona believe ye should be nervous. I should, however. I doona expect the lass will be too pleased to see me."

The door was unlocked, and they stepped inside to the chaotic scene of overturned chairs and tables. Blaire lay sprawled in the corner, straddled by some red-haired woman whose face they couldn't see. The two women screamed incoherently at one another.

"Eoin!" Bri exclaimed. "Help her! Get that woman off of her. What is she doing?"

Eoin bolted toward Blaire while Bri approached cautiously, standing back to watch as her husband separated the two women.

Blaire stood quickly, glancing down at her disheveled clothing, brushing dust off the bottom of her pants. Bri knew that her lookalike had yet to see her, or to recognize the man holding her assailant. "Thank ye. The woman is mad," Blaire said, out of breath.

The woman in question screamed in protest and threw her head back, sending the red curls that covered her face backward, revealing her face.

Bri gasped aloud in recognition as she rushed toward her old friend. "Mitsy?"

"Bri?" In an effort to escape Eoin's hold on her, Mitsy lunged, and Blaire looked up for the first time since they'd entered the pub.

"Eoin?" Blaire gasped.

I'd witnessed many surprising things since arriving in this century, but none had shocked me more than seeing my ex-fiancé staring back at me, and a woman who looked like my duplicate standing beside him. I knew she must be Bri.

When I made the decision to stay here, I felt certain I would never see anyone from my past life ever again. To find Eoin standing before me now meant that Morna's spells were not as close-ended as Adelle and I had originally thought.

When the woman who had attacked me saw Bri, she shrieked and chaos ensued. Bri shrieked, too, and a tremor of shock reverberated throughout the room. Only Eoin remained calm. He eventually quieted everyone by slamming his fist down so hard against the table that the entire room seemed to shake.

"Quiet, all three of ye!" he boomed. "It has been a long day, and I doona think I can take such noise any longer."

Recognizing the seriousness of his tone, the three of us quieted instantly. But only a moment passed before the redheaded mad woman spoke again.

"Somebody better tell me what's going on here, or I'm going to lose it on every single one of you." Her voice trembled, and she pointed a shaky finger in Bri's direction. "Now, you are Bri, right? If you tell me you're not, I swear I will jump on top of you like I did this one." She nodded her head at me, adding, "How did I not know you have a twin?"

I leaned against the wall behind me, confused as to the circumstances surrounding Eoin and Bri's arrival here, as well, yet quite entertained with the exchange taking place between the two women.

"She's not my twin," said Bri. "I'm not related to Blaire at all, as far as I know." She stepped closer to the other woman, her brows knitting together. "Mitsy, what are you doing here?"

Anger flashed in the redhead's face. A redhead who now had the name of Mitsy. For a moment, I was certain she was going to try and escape Eoin's restraining arms again.

"What am I doing here?" Mitsy hissed. "You have got to be kidding me! What are *you* doing here? God, Bri, I thought you were dead! You've been gone for months with no word or explanation. Your trip to Scotland with your mother was only supposed to last a few weeks. I've been trying to locate you ever since the police stopped their investigation. You're supposed to be in my wedding, Bri! I can't believe you just left everything. Were you really just not going to show up without any excuse whatsoever?"

Mitsy collapsed into a fit of sobs, and Eoin relaxed his hold on her. Bri moved in to comfort her friend, gathering Mitsy into her arms. "I'm so angry at you!" Mitsy choked out through her tears. "If I thought I could get away with it, I'd kill you myself."

Bri ushered her friend away from Eoin and me. "I know," she said in a soothing voice. "Let's move over here out of the way so we can talk in private. I need to explain what's happened, and Eoin and Blaire need a chance to get reacquainted."

As the two women moved toward the bar, I didn't miss the apologetic look Bri shot in Eoin's direction, presumably for leaving him alone with me. Without doubt, my relationship with Eoin had always been slightly contentious, but only because I didn't want to marry him. If I'd known him under any other circumstance, I suspected we would've gotten along just fine. I found myself a little embarrassed to know that Bri had heard of my terrible behavior toward him.

"Eoin." I nodded once, determined to let him initiate any conversation. Always the gentlemen, he moved to pick up my hand and kiss it lightly before stepping away again.

"Blaire, ye look well. Do ye enjoy being here in this time, lass? It's verra different from our own. Are ye happy?"

His question surprised me, and I couldn't help but wonder if perhaps I wasn't doing as good a job at looking happy as I had hoped. Truth was, I was lonely. And while I loved the independence women enjoyed in this time, I missed my home. But I knew it was most likely impossible for me to return. Even if I could, I didn't think I could stand the heartache that would come with being near Arran and knowing I was unwanted.

It took me a moment too long to answer Eoin, and I knew he could read the untruth behind my words. "Aye. O'course I'm happy. Why wouldna I be? Why are ye here, Eoin? I'm verra surprised to see ye."

Eoin chuckled. "Aye, I suppose ye are. I'm surprised to find myself here, as well. Bri wished to come to take care of some things that were left unfinished from her life here. I wouldna let her go alone. If something happened, I doona think I could go back to a life without her."

"I'm glad that ye are happy, Eoin. Is all well with yer family? Have ye heard from my father?" I didn't mention Arran, but something in Eoin's eyes made me wonder if he knew it was Arran I was asking about. Was it possible that Eoin knew about what had occurred between his brother and me? If so, perhaps Arran had not closed his heart so completely to me. The thought gave way for a small trickle of hope to rise within me, one which I quickly pushed down while I waited for Eoin's response.

He waved me to a table in the corner of the room. Pointing toward Bri and Mitsy, he said, "It looks as if they may be a while. Let us sit, and I'll tell ye all that has happened while ye have been away."

I nodded and followed, glancing quickly at the two women visiting at the bar. As I watched them, I remembered the shocked expression on Bri's face when she realized the woman Eoin was holding back was Mitsy. Bri hadn't known her friend would be here. Eoin had lied. They had not come to the pub so that Bri could give Mitsy an explanation, they'd come here looking for me.

***

"Did you tell her why we came here?" Bri led the way to their hotel room as Eoin slowly followed, stopping every so often to stare at something new that fascinated him. Several hours after arriving at the pub, they'd all left together, first dropping Blaire off at her apartment, and next, securing two hotel rooms for the three of them just across the street from Blaire's place of residence. With Mitsy shut away in her room for the evening, Bri and Eoin were finally able to discuss what had occurred over the last few hours.

"I dinna tell her all of why we came here. I told her ye needed to see to some things ye'd left unfinished, but I dinna tell her that we'd come to see if she would return home."

Bri stopped in front of their room and pulled the plastic key card from her pocket. Smiling, she extended it Eoin's direction. "Here. You see that slot above the handle? Stick this card in there and then slowly pull it out. It will unlock the door."

It took him three tries but Bri remained patient, enjoying the look of awe that radiated from her husband's face. Once inside, she decided to tell him the news she'd dreaded sharing with him since they'd left the pub.

"Well, I suppose it's fine that you haven't told her the other reason we came here just yet. You'll have plenty of time to do that."

She heard her husband stop playing with the toilet in the bathroom, and she knew she'd caught his attention. "What do ye mean by that, lass? Now that ye have spoken with yer friend, we should be able to return home in only a few days, aye?"

Bri shook her head and turned a guilty face toward her husband. "No. I'm afraid not. You and Blaire are going to have the next week all to yourselves. I made a promise over a year ago that I would be Mitsy's maid of honor. I'm leaving with her tomorrow to go back to the States for her wedding."

onall Castle - 1646

ormod Kinnaird left the clan gathering more determined than ever to find a way to take over as laird. In his mind, the title was his by right. He was the eldest son of Ramsay Kinnaird's younger brother, but a bastard son, and therefore unrecognized as a true Kinnaird by all but his mother and sister.

The same meeting had been held every night since the death of his uncle, and everyone grew restless as little progress was made in determining the best way to declare a new laird. Many members of the clan wished to return home and wait to declare a new leader, but the majority of people knew this would leave the clan without protection and would make them look weak in the eyes of neighboring clans—a sure way to invite further conflict and violence.

The only decision they'd all agreed upon was that Edana would not be placed out of her home, which left Tormod to assume that the new laird would marry Edana. Only a few men remained unmarried within the clan. Although he didn't know for sure if Edana would be given any choice in who she married, he intended to make sure that he would be her first choice.

Though improper for him to be in the castle's bedchamber hallway at this time of evening with Eoin Conall away and his drunk of a brother left to manage things, Tormod was almost certain he would be able to sneak into Edana's room unnoticed.

He had seen Edana enter the room at the end of the hallway enough times during their stay here to know that it was hers. He stood in front of the door, unsure whether to knock or to try the handle. The sound of footsteps down the hallway caught his attention. Humming accompanied each step, and he knew it was the castle's head maid, Mary; he believed that was her name. If she saw him, it was unlikely that she would say anything. Even if she did, who was likely to take the word of such a lowly servant?

Tormod didn't want to alarm her; it was best that the maid not see his true character right away. He knocked softly, hoping that Edana hadn't already retired for the evening.

She answered quickly, and he found himself unsure of how best to explain his unexpected arrival at her door. "Edana, how are ye this evening? I was passing by yer door and thought I would check on ye."

Her pale blonde hair hung loose about her shoulders. Her beady green eyes peered back at him, questioning without asking aloud why he was there. She was shy, or at least she did a fine job of feigning shyness. He'd been around her enough, studied her enough, to notice how she behaved when she believed no one was watching. The girl had far more fire and bite than she let on.

While many people who possessed the same fiery spirit were fueled by their immense passion for life, he recognized that Edana's fire came from a different source. Her fire raged out of an underlying malice for everything and everyone around her; something that she'd inherited from her father, no doubt. He knew she did her best to hide her true nature, but he wasn't bothered by it. Tormod held the same feelings of malice for all those around him, as well, and he could see it in her eyes even now.

He smiled and glanced quickly down either side of the hallway before speaking again. "May I come in? I doona wish to be seen outside your chamber this late in the evening."

Edana looked down at her feet, and then silently stepped away from the door, allowing Tormod entry into the room.

"What are ye doing here, Tormod? Ye shouldna be in this part of the castle." She spoke with her back toward him as she walked away, leaving him to stand just inside the doorway as she took a seat near the hearth.

Slowly, he moved to sit across from her. But when she didn't protest, he sat down, instead, by her side. "I wanted to see ye. I always want to see ye, but I've only just gathered the courage to do so."

"What? Why, I've never seen ye so much as look at me before." Her voice came out high and squeaky.

Tormod recognized that this was not part of her façade. She was genuinely surprised to hear his explanation. His confidence growing, he scooted closer, reaching over to grasp her hand. "Aye. I've looked at ye many times before, lass, and I see ye now, as well." He rubbed his thumb gently back and forth across the top of her hand until she moved away and stood, pushing her hair from her face in a nervous gesture. Making her way to the door, she opened it and motioned for him to leave.

"Ye canna mean it," Edana snapped. "I doona wish to be toyed with. 'Tis not enough that I just lost my father, and that I'm now forced to live in the home of the very people who took him from me? Do ye wish to tease me, as well? I willna allow it. Now, leave." She pointed toward the door and Tormod stood, realizing he'd just learned all he needed to know about the lass.

Not only did Edana hate most everyone around her, she also held herself in great contempt. Only a woman with a very low sense of self-worth would immediately assume that a suitor at her door this late in the evening was there to belittle her. Edana's feelings toward herself would serve him well. It was easy to make self-loathing women fall in love. In the hopes of receiving the admiration they denied themselves, they would heedlessly throw their heart at the first suitor to ask for it.

Passing her on his way out the door, he paused quickly to steal a kiss. The whispery sigh that escaped her lips was not one of protest, and he smiled as he leaned forward to whisper in her ear. "I will never tease ye, Edana. I intend to make ye mine."

He didn't give her a chance to respond, turning quickly to make his leave. He knew his visit had been successful. He'd left the poor lass wanting more, with her heart beating wildly in her chest. In a week's time, she'd want no other man but him. Of that he was sure.

hree Days Later

*W*hen a knock sounded at his chamber door, Arran rolled drowsily out of bed, cursing Kip for creating so many tasks for him to complete in the stables that day. He knew it was unusual for someone in his position to work in the stables, but he didn't care. Kip had worked him from dawn to dusk, and although Arran complained, he knew it was a good thing. Staying busy was the only thing that kept the drinking at bay and the pain in his heart at a safe distance.

He threw open the door to find out who felt the need to disturb him so late in the evening, and he had to blink several times to make sure his vision was clear when he saw Mary standing in his doorway.

"Mary? What are ye doing? Ye should've been in bed hours ago. Ye work too much as it is."

Mary waved a hand in dismissal at Arran's words as she stepped inside without waiting to be invited. "I doona need ye telling me when I should be in bed, and I doona work too much. I work just the proper amount. 'Tis only that ye work too little that ye think anything more than that is too much."

"Ah. O'course ye are right, Mary." Arran knew better than to argue with her, and so he simply smiled and crossed his arms as he prepared to hear what she had to say. "Now, what do ye need? Ye havena been in my bedchamber this late since I was a wee lad."

"Ye are right, and I see ye havena changed yer bad habits at all. Ye still doona have enough common sense to check and make sure ye are properly clothed before ye invite company into yer room. For goodness sakes, cover yerself. I think ye have blinded me." She shielded her eyes dramatically as Arran glanced down at his entirely naked self.

"Ach, Mary! I'm verra sorry." Scrambling, he reached for something to cover himself, finally deciding to simply sit on the edge of the bed so that he could pull the blanket across his lap.

"Doona apologize, lad. 'Tis not like I havena seen a man naked before. Why, I used to clean that little backside of yers when ye were only a wee laddie."

Arran rolled his eyes, wishing Mary would spit out her news so he could return to a peaceful slumber. "Let's not talk about my backside. What's brought ye here?"

"Ah, right." Mary stopped grinning and faced him head on. "I'm verra worried about Edana."

"Aye? Why?" Arran was awake now. He'd been worried about the lass, too, but he didn't understand why Mary would be. He straightened up in the bed, eager to hear her concerns.

"For the past three evenings, I have seen Ramsay's nephew sneaking into Lady Edana's room late at night. It isna proper for him to visit her after dark."

"Ye are right; it is not. But they are our guests, and I doona think 'tis our place to instruct them on how to behave themselves. Besides, I doubt he is doing anything to the lass she wouldna want him to." He believed his own words, but he couldn't deny how uncomfortable the thought made him. He wasn't jealous of Tormod. He didn't care about Edana in that way. But he had seen the lad interacting with some of his men, and Arran had an uneasy feeling when around him.

"No, I doona think he is hurting her, Arran," Mary explained. "I think he is using her so he can become laird. Ye know that our visitors decided that whomever becomes laird should marry Edana. I believe he is trying to make her want to do just that, which would be fine except for I doona think Tormod is a good man. Not even much better than Edana's father."

"Aye, I agree with ye, Mary. I doona like the lad either." Arran lay back on his bed, gathering the blankets to cover himself, drumming his fingers back and forth across his forehead as he tried to think of how to best proceed.

Only one plausible solution crossed his mind. Although the idea didn't thrill him, it was the only way he could come up with that might keep his new friend from entering a horrible marriage. With no hope of his own true love coming back to him, what did it matter whom he married anyway? He sat up. "I know what I shall do, Mary. We shall have a series of games to test the strength and leadership of all the men who enter. The winner shall marry Edana and become laird of Kinnaird's old territory."

Mary drew her brows together, and Arran knew she did not yet understand his plan. "Aye, fine. But how do ye think ye shall get the Kinnaird Clan to agree to such an arrangement, and what if Tormod wins? That will do nothing to keep her from him."

"They will agree because they are all eager to name a new laird. If they do not, they will no longer have the hospitality of staying on our land. And Tormod willna win."

Mary's scrunched eyebrows rose in question. "And just how do ye know that? He's quite a strong-looking lad."

"Tormod willna win because I plan to enter. I will win and marry Edana myself."

CHAPTER 11

*S*cotland – *Present Day*

I was unsure of how Bri and Eoin convinced me to leave with them. It certainly meant losing another job, and I didn't have any other friends that could help me in obtaining another one once I returned to Edinburgh.

I continued to question my decision as I sat in the back of the small, cramped car next to Bri's friend, Mitsy, who had thankfully settled down. I was sure she thought us all mad. How could anyone not after hearing our story? All the same, she was no longer hysterical, and it was undeniable that she'd been in desperate need of a good night's sleep. She looked much better, even quite striking, with her long, red curls fixed nicely, no longer matted down by tears.

As we pulled up in front of the all-too-familiar inn near the castle, I realized that it was a potent mixture of fear and hope that had caused me to agree to stay here with Eoin for the next week. I'd sworn to myself that I wouldn't return to the inn ever again, and I was terrified to do so now, but I was even more terrified of letting this opportunity slip away. I'd suspected last evening in the pub that there was more to Bri and Eoin's visit to this time than Bri's desire to finish some things she'd left undone. Somehow their visit involved me.

My suspicions were confirmed this morning when they asked me to leave town for a week to keep Eoin company and watch over him while Bri and Mitsy left for Mitsy's wedding. Eoin was more than capable of taking care of himself, especially if he was staying with Jerry and Gwendolyn. Or was it Morna? None of us was sure of how to refer to the magical innkeeper anymore. Something remained that Eoin wanted to discuss with me, and my curiosity over that something was enough for me to leave my position in Edinburgh and run toward uncertainty once again.

It seemed likely that Eoin's news might only break my heart further and make me wish I'd remained in Edinburgh. He'd not said much about my father when I'd asked him. Perhaps he was ill or had discovered that I was gone. I hoped he hadn't. I wouldn't be able to bear the guilt of knowing I'd caused my father such pain.

But what if it was something else? What if now that Eoin was married to Bri, Arran wanted me to return home to be with him? The thought made my stomach flutter excitedly, but just as quickly, it turned to an uncomfortable churn as I realized what I knew must be true. Arran didn't want me to return. He probably didn't care that I was gone. If he did, he would have come here himself. He had far too much pride to allow his brother to make such a request of me.

The car had been parked for some time, and everyone else was unloading their belongings as I remained in the back seat, a familiar depression gliding over me as my latest realization drained away all the hope I'd had of Eoin's news being good.

After this week, I would return to the city, jobless once more, and I would start again.

My own reflection in the window startled me, and I jumped as Bri lightly knocked against the window. "Come on inside, Blaire. They have food laid out for you and Eoin. Mitsy and I have to be on our way to the airport. Our flight is in a couple of hours."

Doing my best to manage a smile, I apologized and joined the others inside. Shortly after, Bri and Mitsy drove away, leaving me to wallow in my nerves over what sad news Eoin had yet to share with me.

* * *

*A*ustin, TX

*A*s the song came to its end, Bri smiled at her dance partner, pulling him in for a hug. "Thank you, Daniel. You're a wonderful dancer."

"It was my pleasure, dear." The man, forty years her senior, kissed her hand before showing her back to her seat. "And you're right. I am a wonderful dancer. If we'd only been able to go on our date, you would know that already."

Bri laughed as she sat down at the now empty table. All of those seated next to her were out on the dance floor. "My loss."

Daniel winked and tipped his head as he glided back onto the dance floor, no doubt looking for the next beautiful girl he could impress with his dancing skills. Bri smiled to herself as she thought back on the night, which seemed like so many months ago, when she'd been set up on a blind date with Daniel. Her mother's sudden arrival had kept the date from ever beginning. But thinking back on the shock she'd experienced when first laying eyes on Daniel and realizing his age, the moments of awkwardness that had followed, Bri was reminded that she had some choice words to share with Mitsy's groom.

It had been Mitsy's new husband, Brian, who'd arranged the blind date, and the lack of sense in the match did nothing to help Bri's judgment of him. Something about Brian that she couldn't identify had always bothered her. But tonight was not the time or place to chide the groom. Due to her plans to return to Scotland and, thereafter, back to the seventeenth century the following day, Bri suspected she was just going to have to let this one slide.

Not that she would be able to find the groom to speak to him if she wanted to. The last time she saw him had been at the beginning of the reception during the cutting of the cake and the first dance. Since then, Mitsy singly navigated the crowds of guests eager to congratulate the happy couple. From the beaming smile on Mitsy's face, it didn't seem that she'd taken note of her husband's absence.

Deciding she could go for a restroom break and perhaps for a little groom search and rescue mission, Bri stood and left the reception hall. Arriving at the women's restroom, she was met by the unfortunate staffer who had been dealt the dreadful task of cleaning up some tipsy wedding guest's puke.

"Sorry," said the young woman. "I don't think you want to come in here right now, but if you go to the end of the hall on the right, there's an office. If you enter, there's a bathroom connected to it on the other side. It's fine if you want to use it since you're part of the wedding party. I should have this mess cleaned up for the other guests shortly."

"Thank you, I think I'll do that."

Making her way down the hall, Bri found that her need to use the restroom lessened as a suspicious noise drifted from behind the office door. Upon reaching it, she pressed her ear up against the wooden surface and heard a deep male voice, followed by a feminine giggle.

To Bri's dismay, between giggles, the woman addressed the man by name: Brian.

*B*ri fled before her presence on the other side of the office door was discovered. Back at the reception, she quickly downed several glasses of champagne as she tried to decide what she should do.

In the end, she watched her best friend, laughing and beaming as she moved through the reception hall, and knew that while she couldn't bring herself to tell Mitsy so soon after the wedding what she'd heard, she also didn't trust herself *not* to say anything.

She approached her dear friend on the dance floor, made an excuse of feeling sick, and then hugged Mitsy's neck hard. Fighting back tears, Bri hopped into a taxi that would take her back to her hotel.

Chances were she'd never see her friend again, but she wanted to leave Mitsy the option of a new life if she decided she wanted it one day, after she learned the truth about her louse of a husband. Mitsy would eventually; Bri was certain. She only wished that she could be here for her when she did.

When she spotted a post office ahead, Bri knocked on the plastic panel behind the taxi driver to get his attention. She motioned toward the post office. "Can we stop here for a minute before continuing on to the airport? I need to run inside and get a stamp so I can put something in the mail before I leave."

"Sure thing. Meter's running." The driver pulled to the curb.

Climbing out of the cab, Bri walked inside with a heavy heart, hoping with every footstep that if Mitsy needed it, she would be able to believe the words she'd written and mailed the letter to her.

CHAPTER 12

Tormod's eyes locked with hers as Edana watched him rise from yet another victory, this time in the sword competition. She shivered beneath her clothes at the tingly rush that cascaded over her. She was in love. She could say so without hesitation. Only a week ago, her future had seemed bleak, wrought with uncertainty and a plan for vengeance that she didn't know how to carry out on her own. Now, with Tormod by her side, happiness no longer seemed so impossible.

He loved her, as well, although he'd yet to tell her so. She knew it by the way he treated her. Edana instantly felt she could trust him, and had quickly told him about her true feelings toward the Conalls and her desire to destroy them. She'd expected him to reprimand her, tell her how wrong she was to think that way, but instead, he'd expressed his own hatred. Together, they'd plotted all they could do to destroy the powerful family once they were married and Tormod was laird.

Now, all that stood in their way was the final round of the so-called games that Arran had dreamed up. She found it sickening that her clansmen had so easily agreed to trust her future to a contest. Only a group of men would be so thoughtless. When Arran put the idea to the clan, she'd openly voiced her misgivings on the proposal. However, with the men eager to return home and with no better solutions themselves, they all boisterously agreed to Arran's plan, throwing aside all thought or concern for her feelings.

The only thing that had calmed her was Tormod's reassurance that he would win the competition for her. And she believed that he would. He was close to doing so already. Only one more person would Tormod have to best, and that was by far the most surprising revelation that came out of Arran's idea.

Not only had Arran stood before her clansmen suggesting how to choose their leader, a move that she saw as highly inappropriate and insulting to their intelligence, but he had also asked the clansmen to grant him permission to enter the contest. The people of their clan had worked and lived together for decades and, in time, they would have been more than capable of solving their problem of leadership on their own.

Arran had moved into a lengthy speech, vowing that if he won, as he obviously thought he would, he would be a fair and strong leader, unlike Edana's father. Each word was another dagger intended to destroy any respect her clansmen might have had for her father. Each word stoked the fire of hatred that burned within her for Arran and all of the Conalls, each of them so self-assured in the righteousness of their actions.

To her utter dismay, her clansmen had wholeheartedly welcomed Arran for entrance, many boasting that they would be rooting for him to win, few even questioning the purpose of the competition. Why not just name Arran laird now?

What a fool Arran was. He thought he could trick her into liking him with his kind words and feigned concern for her wellbeing. It was even more foolish still for him to have such utter confidence in his ability to win her and her territory as his prize. Tormod would never allow it, and if he did, Edana was certain she would kill herself before marrying a Conall.

With archery being the only competition left, Edana stood to go in search of her beloved. She wanted to steal a kiss from the man she would soon call her husband and wish him luck.

Tormod stood in the corner of his tent. Hunched over, he carefully examined each of his arrows, looking for any inconsistency, any warp in the wood that might impact his shot. Archery was his strength, but he knew Arran was masterful with a bow, as well. He could leave no room for error if he wanted to become laird. The title was within his grasp. He would be laird by nightfall. Then in a few short weeks, his marriage to Edana would be bound with consummation. He could finally end the dreadful task of pretending to like the disgusting wretch.

The rustle of fabric to his left caused him to spin, eager to see who was entering. He'd asked to be left alone so he could concentrate in silence before the last challenge. His sister entered, and he was not surprised that it would be she who gave no credence to his wishes.

"Fia, why are ye here?"

She ignored his question and moved over to his arrows, grabbing one as she raised it in question to him. "Do ye think ye can win?"

The question angered him, and he ripped the arrow out of her hand before continuing, "Aye, I can and I will. Do ye not think so?"

"I do think that ye can. Tis only, I doona think that ye should."

Tormod couldn't believe what she was saying to him. Fia was just as eager as he for their family to gain a place of leadership once again. She, too, had been denied her birthright due to the sins of their parents. "Why would ye say such a thing, Fia? Tis within our grasp now. We will finally be allowed in the castle that should have always been our home."

"Aye, and we shall be. But doona do it today, brother. The people of our clan want Arran to win today. If ye defeat him, they will only resent ye. Claim the lairdship in a way that will earn the respect of our people."

Tormod shook his head, confused and angry at his sister's suggestion. "How would I claim the role once Arran is named laird?"

"Ye watch him, stay close to him, and find a truth that ye can distort into a believable lie. Make the people believe that their precious laird has perpetrated whatever crime of which ye decide to make him guilty. Then it will be much easier for ye to take over as laird. Ye will have earned the trust of our people, and ye may be able to get rid of Edana in the process, as well. I know ye doona wish to be married to the lass."

Tormod paced the room, shaken by the thought of giving up everything within his grasp. He tightened his jaw as he turned to send his sister away. "Ye are right. I doona wish to marry Edana, but there are other ways to dispose of the lass once I am laird. I willna give this up, and if ye wish to be moved to the castle once I am laird, ye willna ask it of me again. Now leave at once."

He turned his back and waited for his sister to leave, tightening his fists as her last words caused him to vibrate with rage.

"As ye wish, but ye will regret this Tormod, and ye will see that I was right."

---

*T*ormod had just shot his seventh of the required ten arrows. Now it was Arran's turn, and as he drew his seventh and sent it soaring into the center of the target, Tormod didn't miss the roar of his clansmen. Their scores remained tied. With each perfect shot of Tormod's own, Arran matched it. If the routine continued, the two would have to shoot well beyond ten arrows to declare a winner.

Drawing back, Tormod released another flawless shot, quickly turning to take in the crowd that remained mostly silent. His sister was right. There was no denying that the well wishes of his own clansmen lay with his rival. It would be a difficult lairdship if he took over as leader without the support of his people.

Edana would be furious, but he knew he could comfort her with his lies. He would talk her into working with him, and perhaps it would be even easier to destroy Arran if he had an ally that shared Arran's bed.

With Arran sending another perfect shot that matched his own, Tormod drew his bow and jerked his body at the last minute so that his arrow went flying wildly to the side, missing the target completely.

He would allow Arran to be laird for now, but it would be a short-lived reign. Tormod wasted no time in contemplating a dozen ways to destroy the doomed Conall.

CHAPTER 13

*S*cotland *– Present Day*

*B*ri was due back at the inn today, and I still had no idea what Eoin wished to speak with me about. We'd spent the week listening to stories told by Jerry and Morna, who finally had asked that we call her by her real name.

She was a vivid storyteller, and we all enjoyed listening to the adventures of Eoin's father, Alasdair, and my own father when they were growing up. It was a pleasure to watch Eoin discover the aunt he hardly remembered and had envisioned in his mind as a very different woman than she actually was. Her spells and magic were just a small part of this lively, funny, warm woman, and it was easy to see why Alasdair had adored his sister so much, when so many others had feared her.

It was the first morning Eoin and I had spent alone together. Jerry and Morna had left earlier to visit someone they said lived nearby, but I was quite certain the closest thing they had to a neighbor was the castle itself. I suspected they'd left to allow us time to talk.

We sat across from each other in the living room. Eoin tried to busy himself with the television remote, randomly pushing the buttons, watching with fascination as the pictures changed on the screen. I sat silently for a few moments, knowing that my impatience was about to burst forth if he didn't set the remote down and start talking soon. Still, I knew my own fascination with the oddities of this century and so tried to be understanding.

"Eoin. Will ye please turn it off? It's time for ye to tell me why ye and Bri asked me to come here."

He didn't look at me immediately, instead staring at the remote as he searched for a way to stop the moving pictures. I reached over and pushed the red button, taking it from his hands as the television ceased its movement.

Rising up, he situated himself more comfortably on the couch and crossed his arms as he looked across at me. "Aye, I suppose 'tis time. I should tell ye beforehand that this wasna my idea. And I'm not too pleased with Bri for leaving me here to ask this of ye all alone. She knows more of this than I."

Why would Bri know more about anything than Eoin? She'd been living in my time for only a short period, and while I was still adjusting to the many differences of modern day life, I was sure she was still adjusting to the loss of modern conveniences. "Just get on with it, Eoin. I doona care which one of ye tells me. I'm only anxious to know. Ye have left me waiting for the past week."

"I know, and I'm sorry. I'm only unsure of how to explain this to ye." He cleared his throat, searching for a way to delay explanation even further.

"Eoin, if ye doona wish for me to cause ye physical harm, it would best serve ye to tell me right away." I leaned forward, placing my elbows on my knees and resting my head on my clenched fists, doing my best to look as threatening as possible.

"Bri seems to believe that ye were in love with Arran, and that is why ye left," he said, speaking quickly. "Ye dinna want to marry me, and ye couldna marry him, so ye decided to stay here. She believes that Arran is in love with ye, as well."

I stiffened, every muscle clenching as if to strangle me. My heart pounded painfully at the hope-filled words I'd stopped allowing myself to imagine I would ever hear. "Why?" I asked, breathless, my throat suddenly filled with cobwebs. "What reason would Bri have for believing such a thing?"

"Arran's behavior as of late. He has never been a stranger to the drink, but he has been drinking more than ever lately. And I havena seen him in the company of another woman in a long time. I do admit that he seems rather sad, but until Bri mentioned it, I dinna blame his demeanor on a broken heart."

It was hard for me to imagine Arran drinking more than he already did. The very day Arran had sent me away from him, he'd said he would soon share his bed with another. If he had not, perhaps Eoin was right. It filled me with a hope I could scarcely allow myself to believe without proof of his feelings.

"Has he told ye that he loves me, Eoin? Surely he would have told his own brother. Ye have always been his closest friend, and now that ye are married to Bri, what would have been the harm in him expressing his feelings to ye?"

Rising, I moved restlessly about the room, the rush of mixed feelings making the space suddenly seem too small.

"No, lass, he hasna told me, but I think Bri may be right. There was something that happened shortly after our wedding that should have warned me of his feelings for ye."

I paused in front of the fireplace, keeping my back toward him, reluctant to allow him to see my eyes slowly filling with tears. "Aye? What happened?"

"There was a small fire set after the wedding that I was required to attend to, leaving Bri alone in our bedchamber. When I returned, I found Bri pinned to the wall in the hallway, with Arran kissing her madly."

I spun, my desire to hide my emotions suddenly forgotten. "What?"

"Aye, lass. I hit Arran, and he fell to the ground unconscious, and I threw Bri in the dungeon."

"Ye threw her in the dungeon, thinking she was me? On our wedding night!"

Eoin looked down at the floor. Someone else had clearly already reprimanded him for his actions. "I doona wish to talk about it. That is not the point."

"Aye, fine." I smiled at him briefly, urging him to continue.

"Arran blamed his actions on having too much to drink, but no man, no matter how drunk, would kiss a woman in such a familiar way unless he'd already done so many times before."

He quieted, and it was my turn to feel guilty. Regardless of how happy Eoin was with his new bride now, it was I who had been promised to him by my father, and I'd been unfaithful to him by the feelings I'd held for his brother.

"I'm sorry, Eoin. My behavior was disgraceful, and ye did nothing to deserve my betrayal of ye."

"Ach, think nothing of it, lass. Ye and I were not meant for a marriage together. All I want now is for my brother to be happy and for ye to find happiness, as well. If that is something the two of ye may find together, ye have my every blessing. If ye still love him, Blaire, we'd like ye to return home with us."

"Do ye truly believe he still loves me?" The words were already bubbling to the front of my mouth, but I wanted one more reassurance before agreeing to go home.

"Aye, I do. And Bri is certain of it. She's a wise woman. I've yet to find her wrong in anything."

I drew a deep breath, trying to calm my pounding heart. "Then, aye. I will come."

"Well done, Eoin."

Bri's voice in the doorway startled us both, and we stood to welcome her back.

"I knew you could convince her to come without me. Now, let's head to the castle. We've all been gone too long. Mom and Mary will both be in a tizzy."

---

1 646

The wedding was arranged quickly. Only three days following his victory, Arran stood next to Edana in front of a crowd filled with his new clansmen. Eoin would certainly be surprised upon his arrival back home to find that his brother had moved away and was now a married laird. But Arran was sure Eoin would be happy to have the security of a guaranteed ally in the place of Ramsay.

Their ceremony was coming to a close, and while he repeated the words asked of him, in his imagination, each promise was made to the woman who owned his heart, not to the woman who stood beside him. As he closed his eyes to kiss his new bride, it was Blaire's face that he saw leaning into him.

CHAPTER 14

*T*ormod sat on a boulder perched atop the hillside cliff overlooking the ocean. As waves crashed upon the rocks, he scooted back in an effort to avoid the spray of water. It was a cold evening and the water was freezing; just another reason he was thankful he and his fellow clansmen did not live in such close proximity to the sea.

Edana was supposed to meet him here. She'd promised him right before the wedding ceremony that she would, but as the sun dropped lower and lower over the horizon, he began to question her loyalty to him.

While she'd spoken venomous words about Arran and his family, Tormod had seen Edana exchanging friendly conversation with Arran on more than one occasion. As the sun made its final bow against the horizon and night spread across the sky, Tormod stood. Just as he prepared to leave, he heard Edana's voice behind him.

"I'm sorry. I was delayed. What are we to do, Tormod? It will be difficult for us to meet now that I am married to Arran."

He couldn't have cared less about the tears she shed as she moved up beside him, burying her head in her hands. But if he was to maintain Edana's interest and loyalty, he knew he must show her sympathy.

"Come here, lass." He took her by the shoulders. "I doona wish to see ye cry. Yer marriage changes nothing. We shall be together as often as we can, and soon enough I will be laird."

Edana lifted her head. With great difficulty, Tormod kept his expression from revealing his displeasure at her red, tear-stained face.

"How can that be? The men love Arran. They are glad to have him as laird, and they willna take well to someone trying to take away his position."

"Nay, they willna just now," Tormod assured her. "In time, however, we shall find a way to change their opinion of him."

"How?" Again, Edana collapsed against him into a fit of sobs.

Tormod patted her back and stepped away, incapable of soothing the lass any further and weary of her weeping. "I doona know yet, but ye shall be spending much time with Arran from now on. Watch him, find something in his behavior that we can twist into an untruth, something it will be easy to convince others he is guilty of doing. It may take some time."

Edana looked up. Breathing deeply, as if trying to stop her tears, she said, "Aye, I shall do my best." She sniffed. "Tell me, Tormod, I need to know . . . I fear 'tis the only thing that shall get me through every horrible moment I must spend with Arran. Do ye love me? Would ye wish to be with me even if I would not make ye laird?"

He pulled her in close, wrapping his arms around her as he kissed her on the top of her head. "Aye, o'course I do. I love ye as much as I've ever loved anyone."

The second part of what he'd said was true, not that he'd ever loved anyone, save himself and perhaps his sister. The first, his declaration of love, was the lie, but it had slipped out easily. And perhaps he did love the lass a bit. At least, he loved what she would do for him and the power that would be delivered into his hands with her assistance.

Squeezing her once more in farewell, he eased her away and waved her off to the castle.

"'Tis best that ye go. Yer new husband will be searching for ye, and we doona need to give him reason to be suspicious. I shall seek ye out after we have all arrived back home in a few weeks, after ye are both settled into yer castle."

"I shall miss ye every moment that I am not with ye, Tormod."

After she left him, he sat down on the rocks again, laughing quietly to himself. The lass was a fool to believe that he would care for her. He needed to find a way to destroy Arran soon. He didn't know how much more of the pathetic lass he could take.

---

*E*arly the next morning before the sun had risen, Arran snuck out of his room to retrieve his new bride from his late-mother's bedchamber. All castle workers and wedding guests, Mary being the one exception, assumed the newly married bride and groom had spent their first night of marriage together, and that was just the way he wanted to keep it. It wouldn't do if it was found out that neither of them had wanted to consummate their marriage.

After their wedding, Edana had briefly disappeared. When Arran finally found her, the marks of freshly cried tears stained her face. He'd rushed her off to his bedchamber to comfort her, but she'd pulled away, claiming her tears were caused by her fears of their wedding night.

While he suspected all new brides approached their wedding night with some anxiety, Edana's reaction seemed to be caused by more than just nerves. Arran had already suspected that Edana's father had harmed the lass in some way, but her apprehension for their wedding night only solidified his suspicions of just how monstrous Ramsay Kinnaird had been.

The lass's fears aside, Arran was not eager to consummate the marriage either, his feelings for her being only of a platonic nature. Instead, he'd not questioned her, not pushed the ritual they were both expected to complete, but ushered her quietly down the hall to the safety of her own room.

Arran knew the consummation would have to be completed, but that could come in time, when the bonds of friendship were a little stronger between the two of them. For now, he would simply collect her from her room, and together they would make their way to the stables where they would meet with his new clansmen and begin their journey to the new Conall Castle.

*A*delle cast Mary a puzzled frown. "What do you mean they didn't consummate their marriage? How on earth would you know that, Mary? Goodness, I know you're nosy, but I didn't know you were a peeping Tom. What did you do, cut a peep hole into Arran's bedroom?" She laughed at her own wit.

Mary had to refrain from whopping the woman on the nose. Bri, she loved, but it was going to take more time to adjust to the loud-mouthed, say-anything ways of her mother. "I doona know what a 'peeping Tom' is, but I doona believe I like what ye are suggesting. O'course I dinna spy on them. I know they dinna consummate the marriage because Arran had me prepare his mother's room for Edana to stay in. They dinna spend the night together." Mary continued kneading the dough as her nosy kitchen visitor sat across from her, watching.

"No! Why? It's because Bri was right, isn't it? He does still love Blaire. I knew we should've stopped that marriage, Mary! Perhaps, it's not too late to do something. If they've not consummated it, it's not actually binding, is it?"

"I doona know why they dinna spend the night together, but aye, I do believe Bri was right. But it doesna matter, there is nothing we can do because everyone else believes the marriage is consummated, and we are not going to tell them anything different. Do ye understand me?"

"Why? We must. Bri is going to kill us both when she gets back here with Blaire, and we've let Arran run off and marry somebody else."

Mary threw her hands up in exasperation, sending a cloud of flour soaring into the air. "What do ye think she would have expected us to do to stop him? Arran listens to no one, especially when it is someone trying to stop him from doing something foolish. If Blaire returns, which I doona think she will, she will overcome it in time. I doona like it for either of them, but both have made their own choices. 'Tis not our place to meddle."

"Not our place? That's what mothers do, Mary. And regardless of your position here in the castle, you know as well as I do that you are just as much a mother to those lads as their real mother was. They were young when they lost her, and you've been there for them and loved them since they were babes."

Mary couldn't help but smile. Adelle was right; she loved Eoin and Arran as if they were her own.

Movement in the doorway caused her to glance up from the heap of dough. Kip approached her, carrying a letter. Mary turned to dip her hands into a bucket of water to cleanse them of the flour.

"What is it?" she asked, shaking her hands dry. She reached for the parchment in her husband's hand.

"I doona know. Saw a lad riding up to deliver it, so I stopped him and told him I'd take it here myself. It's addressed to Eoin. Seeing as both lads are gone, I expect that 'tis ye that should open it."

"Aye, o'course." Mary broke the seal and unfolded the parchment. She shook her head as she read the words. "It wouldna do for Old Mary to have one day of rest. One day with both of the lads gone for me to pretend that I live a life of leisure. Nay, such a small wish is too much for me to receive." She paused and pointed at her husband. "Kip, ye will need to gather every one near us to help get the castle in order. We doona only have to clean up the mess our guests left us, but we have a new batch of visitors arriving. Lady McMillan and her three sons will be here the day after next."

he Castle Formerly Known As Kinnaird

The first evening Edana spent at what was now considered Conall Castle but was once Kinnaird Castle, she felt her father's presence everywhere. The remains of his hatred, his abuse, his insanity weighed upon her, taunting her, pleading with her to finish what he'd started.

Her father had given his life to defeat the Conalls, and it had all been for nothing. His worst nightmare had come true. A Conall now led, and his only daughter was now married to one, as well.

Edana moved through the hallways haunted by the memories of her childhood, a childhood filled with fear, filled with manipulation, filled with abuse. Now that her father was gone, she wanted to move on, to live a happier life than the one he had provided for her. But with her father's plan for the Conalls' demise unfinished, she knew his presence would remain over her, tempting her to the madness that he'd surrendered to. The only hope she had of finding peace and ending his control on her life, was to finish what he'd begun.

The Conalls were too confident, too powerful, and too trusting for their own good. Those reasons alone would have been enough to make her hate them, but their defeat of her father had chained her to him. Until she was released from his hold, she would never be able to find the happiness she knew was possible for her with Tormod by her side.

Arran had already retired for the evening in her father's old room. While he'd given her permission to spend the night elsewhere, Edana knew it was best not to put off the inevitable. The marriage had to be consummated or be considered invalid. She knew the servants of this castle well enough to know that they would speak if she did not visit her husband's room.

She couldn't allow questions to arise about the marriage. She needed to do as Tormod had bid her, to spend time with Arran and find a weakness they could exploit to his demise.

Edana paced back and forth, pausing in front of Arran's door with each passing. She was certain that what must follow would be some of the worst moments of her life. Thinking of it brought back flashes of horror from her past that she did her best to push away. This would be different than the times before. She was older. No longer a child. And she was now choosing this of her own free will.

Tormod had yet to touch her beyond a swift kiss during their stolen moments together. Still, she knew the scars of her past would have caused her to be just as frightened as she was now if it were he she must bed tonight, rather than a man she didn't love.

She hoped Arran wouldn't notice the lack of blood. It could mean the end of their marriage if he did. For many men it would, but she suspected Arran would be different. Just another reason he could be easily defeated. He was caring and kind, and that made him weak.

Gathering her courage, she glanced at her reflection in a piece of armory hanging on the wall. Pushing her hair out of her face, she pinched her cheeks to bring up a blush. Before she could change her mind, Edana knocked on her husband's door.

---

*T*he dark castle lacked access to sunlight, unlike Arran's childhood home that was filled with such great light. It wasn't only the structure's positioning in relation to the sunrise and sunset that made this castle dark; the scarred remnants of Ramsay's legacy were etched deep into every piece of furniture and tapestry. Arran wouldn't allow that to be the case for long.

He planned to turn the castle into a place of happiness, a place his children would enjoy for many, many years. A place where his new clansmen could rest assured that they were now represented by a fair and just leader rather than the abomination who'd ruled over them before.

He'd been in his bedchamber for hours, composing a letter to send to his brother, hoping to provide Eoin with more explanation on his surprising choices as of late. He had just finished the letter and was preparing to retire when he heard a soft knock on the door.

Glancing down at himself, a new habit he'd formed thanks to Mary, and finding himself decently clothed, he went to greet his visitor.

Edana stood before him, draped in her nightgown, hair down and pushed back behind her ears. She held a candle which shook lightly in her hands, a sure sign of her nerves, and Arran knew instantly why she'd come to him.

He invited her in, but his insides twisted. He was sure his former self, the Arran before Blaire, would think him mad, but he still found himself rather uneager to bed his new wife.

Despite his misgivings, it would be impossible for him to deny her. He knew what courage it took for her to come to him, and it was an act that must be performed. It was the only way to secure his place as laird, to legitimize their marriage, and he knew that Edana was offering him a kindness by recognizing that fact and offering herself to him without his bidding.

But there was no need to hurry into the act right away. He suspected that she would be much like a frightened animal. If he wished her not to bolt, he would need to take his time and move gently.

He walked to a table near the doorway and poured her some wine, extending it in her direction as he moved to stand away from her, leaning his back against the wall.

"How are ye this evening, Edana? I am surprised to find ye here so late. Is there something the matter with your room?" He needed to be certain he was right about her reasons for coming to see him.

She downed the wine quickly, and Arran couldn't keep his eyes from widening in surprise.

"All is fine with my room. 'Tis the same as it has always been."

She extended the cup back to him, and he quickly refilled it before resuming his place against the wall. "Ye know that ye are welcome in here, Edana, but might I ask - is there a particular reason for yer visit?"

She set her wine down and moved toward him. He tensed all over, unsure of how to proceed. She leaned into him, gently kissing him on the cheek and whispered softly as her lips lingered near his mouth. "I think ye know, Arran. I'm no longer afraid of ye."

She kissed him then, softly, slowly, doing her best to seduce him, but he could feel the soft tremble in her lips. Gently lacing his fingers with hers, he pulled away from her.

"I doona believe ye, lass. I can tell ye are frightened by the way ye are shaking, but that is fine. 'Tis not an uncommon thing for a woman to be quite scared when she is unaccustomed to sharing her bed with a man. But ye do know that this is something we must do, aye? Tis why ye have come." She looked up at him, her eyes hesitant, and his sympathy for her made his heart ache.

"Aye. Ye are now my husband, and 'tis yer right to have me. It would be improper for me to deny ye."

He brought his right hand up to her face, cupping her cheek gently as he tried to reassure her with his eyes. "Nay, lass. 'Tis not my right, but it shall be my pleasure, and I am honored that ye offer me the gift of yerself. Please know that I would never hurt ye, lass, and I will never do anything ye doona want me to. Doona ever be afraid to tell me no. Ye doona belong to me, lass. Ye belong to none but yerself. Doona ever forget that or let anyone make ye believe differently."

Arran pulled her in close so that he could place his mouth to hers. He slowly warmed her lips with soft, feather-light kisses. He wanted it to be her choice, something she wanted of him. It would be difficult enough for him to be the lover to her that she deserved with the image of Blaire burned forever in his heart, but he feared the task would be impossible if he knew Edana offered herself to him out of duty.

As he continued to press gently against her lips, her mouth gradually opened to him, matching his rhythm as he increased the intensity of the kiss.

Accepting her invitation, Arran pulled back and turned to put out the fire and candles.

$\mathcal{A}$delle rushed frantically around the castle, ensuring that each job placed on Mary's task list was completed perfectly. She knew as well as anyone that Conall Castle was Mary's ship to run, but with the quick succession of guests leaving and new visitors arriving today, the mess around the castle was more than even the great Mary could accomplish on her own.

Adelle knew that she gave the old, uptight drill sergeant a hard time. Truth was, the woman simply amazed her. Adelle suspected that despite the older woman's crusty exterior, Mary was pretty fond of her, as well. Seeing the stress that the news of their arriving-any-minute guests had brought to the other woman, Adelle wanted to do all she could to help her new friend.

Satisfied that the castle sparkled enough for even the most discerning eyes, she followed her nose to the kitchen where the salty smell of stew caused her stomach to growl.

She'd expected to find Mary bent over a large pot, stirring and seasoning away until whatever concoction she'd worked up for the evening meal was to her satisfaction, but instead she found the kitchen unmanned. The room was completely empty save for the loaves of bread laid out and the bubbling, steaming, saliva-building stew warming over the fire. It was all too much for Adelle's over-eager stomach to take. With a quick glance around the area to confirm that she truly was alone, Adelle tip-toed into the kitchen.

She was doing Mary a favor by attending to the food herself. Who knew what sort of contaminants or poisons could have been slipped into the pot while Mary was away? The only proper thing to do was to test it herself, to make sure that it was safe for the consumption of their guests.

Reaching up toward one of the room's many shelves, Adelle grabbed a wooden bowl that she swiftly dipped into the steaming stew, filling it to the brim with yummy goodness.

She seated herself with her back to the doorway. She didn't want to get caught red-handed if someone decided to come down into the kitchen. She glanced around for a utensil to eat her stolen prize. Finding nothing, she quickly brushed her fingertips on the hem of her dress and, judging them clean enough for the time being, dipped her fingers inside to pick up a juicy slab of meat.

Mary had outdone herself with this one. Each bite seemed more delicious than the last, and Adelle lost herself as she ravenously chowed down on Mary's creation. She would forever be grateful for the rapid metabolism she'd inherited from her own mother. Without it, Adelle knew without doubt that she would weigh three hundred pounds as opposed to her slight, size two frame.

When she heard voices coming from the floor above her, she stopped her prize-winning chow-down. Straining to listen, she heard Mary's voice welcoming the guests. Knowing her appearance would be quickly expected, Adelle swallowed the last piece of meat whole and raised the bowl to her mouth, tipping it high so that she could drink the last of the stew.

Adelle shoved the bowl back onto the shelf, telling herself she would do her best to remember to come back and clean it. She took the stairs two at a time, hoping she would be able to greet their new guests before Mary showed them to their rooms.

When she made it to the top of the stairs, she paused quickly to catch her breath. Finally, moving with as much grace as she could muster, she stepped into the main entranceway to greet their guests.

"*W*hat did I tell ye about getting into the kitchen when I'm not in there? No one eats before mealtime." Mary ground out the words to Adelle between clenched teeth as soon as they'd seen their guests to their rooms and they began making their way down to the kitchen together.

Adelle's eyes widened as she turned to glance guiltily at Mary. "I have no idea what you are talking about."

"Aye, ye do. Doona lie to me. Look!" Mary moved in front of her, effectively blocking Adelle from taking another step down the small staircase. Taking her by surprise, she reached up and brushed a finger on either side of Adelle's mouth, pulling her hand away to reveal light brown globs of stew.

Adelle sat down on the step behind her and threw her forehead into the palm of her hand.

"Oh, no. Please don't tell me. I didn't spend all that time visiting with Lady McMillan and her sons with that goopy mess all over my face, did I?"

Mary chuckled loudly, obviously pleased with herself as Adelle continued to sink further into a state of mortification.

"Aye, ye did. I canna believe ye dinna notice them staring at yer mouth. I think poor Baodan almost wiped it for ye more than once, but he never worked up the nerve." Mary collapsed into hearty laughter again.

Adelle stood and stormed off, continuing to make her own way down the stairs. "Why didn't you tell me?" she called back to the other woman. "I don't think I've ever been this embarrassed in my entire life."

"Why dinna I tell ye? Because that's what ye deserve for sticking yer mouth in things that ye know ye are not meant to. And as wild as ye are, 'tis certain ye have embarrassed yerself far worse than this before."

"That is completely and totally beside the point." Adelle reached the kitchen first, and before Mary could protest, retrieved her used bowl and filled it up with stew once more. "And don't you say a word about me getting another bowl."

Mary smiled, then broke into laughter. "Aye, go ahead and eat all ye like, Adelle. Why, the look on their faces. Well, I havena enjoyed myself so much in quite a long time. Yer foolishness has brought me great joy. I no longer care what ye eat."

*P*resent Day

"Ye look a fair mess, Eoin. Do ye think we could have Morna take a photo of ye in that outfit that we could take back with us? I think it would provide much entertainment." I smiled as Eoin, moving uncomfortably in the restraint of his denim jeans, rewarded me with a quick but vicious glare.

"Ye are a cruel woman, Blaire," he said.

Bri had been wary of taking him back to the spell room dressed in his usual attire. While Eoin was far too tall to fit into any of Jerry's clothes, Morna had been able to come up with a pair of jeans, tennis shoes, and a dark blue sweater that fit Eoin perfectly. I suspected casting up clothes was a simple task compared to making it possible for people to travel through time.

Morna turned to address all of us as we gathered in the entranceway of her home, preparing to make our exit back to the past. "I shall miss ye all dearly, but remember that ye can find me if ye need to, aye?"

We nodded in unison, and Bri stepped forward to squeeze Morna's neck.

"Thank you. And you'll help Mitsy if she needs it, right? You remember what she looks like, don't you?"

Morna hugged her tightly and gave her a comforting pat on the back. "Aye, o'course we do. And the inn will always be available to yer friend to find if she needs it. The spell room, as well. Now, ye best all be on yer way so that ye can sneak into the room before they lock the castle up for the evening."

Bri had remained unusually quiet since she'd arrived from her trip and, after the exchange I'd just overheard between her and Morna, I suspected it had something to do with Mitsy. I would have to remember to ask her about it once we were home and things were settled.

We each said our goodbyes and, within the hour, found ourselves in the spell room once more. The spell was easily cast, and we clung to one another as the all-too-familiar pain ripped through us and we all disappeared into dust.

CHAPTER 17

646

Our re-entry into the past brought with it the expected headache and a short moment of confusion. It took me a little longer than Eoin and Bri to recover from the travel. They adjusted almost immediately back to their usual selves.

Eoin scowled at his wife. "I doona care how much ye like the way my bum looks in jeans, I willna wear them again. As soon as I can pry them off me, I shall burn them until every last scrap has disappeared."

"Don't you dare!" Bri exclaimed. "You don't have to wear them all the time, but for God's sake, don't burn them! That's the only set of modern male clothing we have. What if somebody else ever needs to go forward again?"

"We are all here now. I doona have any plans of going forward ever again."

Bri returned Eoin's scowl. "Neither do I, but seriously, quit being such a child. You're not going to burn them. Just take them off. I'm folding them up and storing them with our clothing."

With my vision clear again and my headache slowly receding, I slipped into a dark corner of the room to change my clothes in privacy. "She is right, Eoin," I called out to them. "I doona know why ye would want to burn them. I would love to stay in my jeans forever. I doona wish to go back to wearing my old clothes at all."

Bri smiled at me as she extended a dress for me to slip on in place of my modern clothes. "Don't worry. You can still wear them some. Sometimes I sneak down here just to put them on. If we can ever get Eoin and Arran to leave us alone in the castle, we will put them on and just strut around all day and shock the bejeezus out of every person we see. It will be great fun!"

I laughed, twisting to the side so that Bri could help me with the laces. "Aye, I look forward to the day. I hope my hair grows fast. Being back here, it suddenly feels too short."

"Doona worry about that, lass," said Eoin. "Tis not that short, but as to the clothing, ye both would be fools to do such a thing. If the wrong people were to see ye dressed in such a way, they'd have ye burnt for witchcraft, and they wouldna all together be lying. Now, let's go and make our return known." Eoin turned and left, leaving Bri and me alone in the small spell room.

Bri turned to follow her husband, but I reached out to stop her, placing a hand on her arm. "Bri, do ye think Arran will be pleased that I am here? I'm quite nervous to see him." She reached up and squeezed my hand.

"I really think he will be. Don't be nervous. We will look for Mary and my mother first. I don't expect Arran will be in the castle, anyhow. He spends most of his time either in the stables with Kip or drinking in the village."

Taking a deep breath, I followed her out of the spell room. Nerves were senseless. I knew they would do nothing to change the outcome of whatever reunion was about to occur.

The room grew warm as Eoin, Bri, Adelle, Mary, and I sat surrounding the work table in Mary's kitchen. That's where we'd found Adelle and Mary, and the excitement of their welcome had quickly become a muddled chaos as everyone seemed to speak at once.

Eventually we'd sat together, each person eager to hear a different set of news. I feigned attention for most of the time as I anxiously awaited the answer to the one question I was too afraid to ask.

When Mary finally said it aloud, my entire body went numb.

"He isna here, Eoin. All of Kinnaird's clansmen have left, and his former territory shall now be known as a Conall territory, as well." She cast me a wary glance. "Arran is laird there now. He has married Edana."

I felt as if a thousand pins pricked my skin at Mary's response, and my heart sank to the pit of my stomach.

"What?" Bri's voice was shrill and panicked as she glanced my way.

Mary cast her eyes downward. "Aye. I'm afraid 'tis true. They left here only a few nights ago."

I could tell she was not pleased by the news she had to share with us. I was helpless in discerning my own feelings, the excited hope and bright future I'd been imagining suddenly dying like the candle flame I found myself staring into. At least Arran wasn't here to tell me the news himself. The words from his mouth would have felt like rejection all over again. Perhaps now I could simply leave, return home to my father whom I was sure would be more than happy to marry me off to another man of his choosing.

"Why didn't you stop him?" Bri snapped at her mother.

"There was nothing we could do, Bri. You made us swear not to tell him where'd you actually gone. We couldn't give him a good reason not to marry her without telling him what the two of you were up to."

"I don't care. That was the one reason good enough to break your promise." Bri looked to be on the brink of tears.

Wanting to stop her from blaming her mother any further, I let the one question at the forefront of my own mind slip out. "Does he love her?"

Silence rewarded my question. Adelle and Mary exchanged knowing glances, both obviously unsure if they should give me an answer.

"No." Bri answered for them. And Mary and Adelle nodded in agreement.

For some reason, both women apparently thought that it would be even more devastating for me to learn that Arran had married Edana if he was not in love with her. And perhaps it was.

For if Arran had married for love, I would have been left with no choice but to move on with my life. To grow old, certain in the knowledge that there had never been any hope that I might spend my life at his side.

But knowing that he didn't love her would make healing and moving on more difficult. I would live every day wondering, hoping and wishing that he was thinking of me, wanting me by his side instead of Edana. I would live every day imagining what my life could have been like if his marriage had only been delayed by a few days.

Mary cleared her throat. "Yer Aunt Kenna arrived yesterday, Eoin. Baodan, Eoghanan, and Niall, as well. I am unsure of the reason for their visit, but I think 'tis time for ye to go and greet them, let them know that ye are back."

Eoin stood and nodded. "Aye, o'course. I suspect they've come to pay their condolences about Father. They were in the midst of their own grief when he died. I should have reached out to them myself."

Bri reached for his hand. "I'll let you visit with them a moment. I'll come up shortly. I want a chance to visit with Blaire alone." Bri dropped his hand and turned to her mother and Mary, sending them an unmistakable message with her eyes. Understanding, they stood and followed Eoin out of the kitchen.

I rose and moved to the seat across from Bri, silently looking down at the table as I waited for her to speak.

"I'm so sorry. I'm so very, very sorry, Blaire," she said after a time. "When we left, there was not the least bit of talk of Arran and Edana marrying. I scarcely saw the two of them together, and he never flirted with her. I never would've come to get you if I'd known."

I wasn't angry with her. Of course she wouldn't have known, and Eoin certainly wouldn't have asked me to return if he'd had any idea. "Ye doona need to apologize to me, Bri. I know that ye dinna know."

"If you want to go back, I'll go one more time so you don't have to do it alone. I'll help you get set up wherever you like. I can stay with you, teach you some things, get you a good job. I'll even have all of my bank accounts transferred to you. Whatever you'd like."

"I doona wanna go back, Bri." I looked up at her as she stood, sensing she had more to say and that I wasna going to like whatever it was.

"I was hoping you would say that. We're going to go pay Arran a visit. You and me. We're leaving in the morning."

I shook my head as forcefully as I could. "I will do no such thing, Bri. Are ye mad? What good would that bring?"

"I don't know, exactly. But I do know that you have to see him. You'll wonder forever about him, if you don't. You'll wonder if he still cares, or even if you cared for him as much as you'd thought. If anything, perhaps seeing him one last time will bring you closure."

I'd only known Bri a few weeks, but I could recognize enough of her mother in her to know that arguing would not change her mind. "Is this not my decision to make?"

She smiled and shook her head. "No. Not at all. And don't tell Eoin. He'll only try to stop us from leaving. Meet me at the stables at dawn."

She exited the kitchen before I could respond, and I was left to ponder through a sleepless night just what new humiliation and heartbreak would await me at Arran's new home.

CHAPTER 18

*E*arly the next morning, with dawn still some time away from peeking through the night's blackness, I heard a knock on the bedchamber door.

Still wide awake, I answered quickly to see Bri with a small bag draped over her shoulders. She couldn't have looked any more excited.

"Come on, let's go! I told Mary of our plan last night so that she could have Kip ready some horses. Don't worry. She promised she wouldn't tell Eoin. I think she's trying to make amends for letting Arran get married."

I shook my head in disagreement. "She has nothing to make amends for. Arran isna a man that is easily kept from doing what he wishes."

Bri's smile briefly disappeared as she stepped into the room to help me gather a few things for the journey. "You're right. I shouldn't have been so harsh with Mary and my mother. I owe them both an apology. And I'll give them one just as soon as we get back, but right now, we need to go before Eoin rolls over and realizes I've gone."

"Doona ye think he will be furious when he finds out? Do ye not think he will come after us?"

Bri's smile returned, and I found that I was changing my opinion of her. I'd first thought her to be a rather serious-mannered, laced-tight kind of person, but upon spending further time with her, I was learning that she was more mischievous than she let others know. "Well, normally I believe he would come after us immediately. But there are guests here now, and I don't think he will leave them. He'll be spit-fire angry, but he'll get over it."

"Aye, well he's not my husband. If ye are certain we should go, I willna worry myself over it." I picked up the bag Bri had filled. Moving as silently as

283

we could through the corridors of the castle, we made our way out the back door.

A torch burned outside the stable entrance. As we approached, Bri called out, "Kip, are the horses ready?"

"Aye!" came Mary's response from inside, surprising us both. "I already sent Kip back to bed, but they are all ready for us to leave."

Bri and I exchanged a questioning look. "Mary, what are you doing?" Bri asked as we hurried inside. I stood back, trying not to laugh at the sight of the short, round woman balancing astride a horse, beaming the brightest smile I'd ever seen.

"What does it look like I'm doing? I'm coming with ye. I've been telling Eoin and Arran for years that I needed a break. After the past few weeks, I feel I've earned it. Besides, I need to see with my own eyes how Arran is faring in his new home." She nudged the horse with her pudgy heels, and it took off at a slow trot out of the stable.

Neither Bri or I argued. After mounting our horses, we followed Mary. And away from Conall Castle the three of us went.

It turned out that Bri was perhaps a tad less adventurous than she wanted to be. By midday, she'd worried herself into such a state of guilt that she rode in complete silence, offering only her pained expression to keep us company.

I, on the other hand, enjoyed every minute of being astride a horse again. The feeling of being out of the city without the car horns and other modern-day noises that had kept me consistently nervous had me feeling more like myself than I had in ages. As long as I tried to keep our journey's final destination out of my mind, I found myself even feeling happy.

Mary remained cheerful but consistently complained about the torture her backside was experiencing from riding atop a horse for such a long time. My own backside was feeling the effects, as well. The months I'd spent away had softened my previously horse-accustomed bum.

As the day progressed, Mary's good humor found a way to crack Bri's worry-creased brow, and the mood lightened. By the time we drew our horses up at the side of a small break in the trees to camp for the evening, all of our middles ached from laughter.

We dismounted, our bodies stiff and achy, and slowly hobbled along to make camp. Each of us moved as if decades older than our given ages. I started a fire while Mary lay out the bread and cheese she'd packed for the journey. Bri went in the direction of a nearby stream to gather some water. Shortly thereafter, we each lay under the stars, our stomachs full and our bodies sore.

I was on the edge of sleep, and I expected Bri was, as well, due to the loud snort that burst forth from her, when Mary's loud, overly-excited voice caused us both to sit straight up.

"What is it, Mary? Did something frighten ye?" I scooted closer to the fire so that I could see the expression on her face more clearly. She looked more excited than anyone should have been after riding for hours and sleeping on the ground.

"Aye, me bum was so sore I almost forgot what I took from Arran's old room. Wake yerselves up, lassies. I have just the thing to soothe our aching bodies."

Bri, who was sitting up but hunched over in a half-asleep position, looked up at Mary from under heavy eyelids. "Sleep? Yes, I believe sleep will do the trick just fine."

"Nay, 'tisna sleep, though I expect we shall all sleep quite soundly after we partake of what I've brought for us. Now wake yerself up." Mary stood and made her way over to her bag, which was propped against a nearby tree. Reaching inside, she withdrew a large bottle of something undoubtedly stronger than wine.

"Mary!" Bri's shocked voice echoed through the open space around us, sending the maid into a fit of giggles.

"I told ye I was in need of a break from my work and a break is what I shall have. I doona think there is anything wrong with Old Mary allowing herself just one night to be foolish. Now, ye lasses will join me whether ye like to or not." She extended two wooden cups to us and we took them without protest.

Once they were filled, we all sipped silently, our exhaustion making us far less enjoyable company than Mary seemed to desire. Eventually, I could take no more of Mary's disappointed glares and turned to address Bri.

"Do ye know of any games? I couldna make sense of most of them, but when I was serving drinks in Edinburgh, people would at times play games while they were drinking."

"Well, I'll confess to my lack of drinking knowledge. Teaching gave me little time for a social life, but I suppose I know of one or two games we could play, if Mary still wishes to continue her wild night."

Mary nodded, smiling widely as she poured more liquor into her cup. "Aye, o'course I do. Have ye yet to see me change my mind about something once it has been set?"

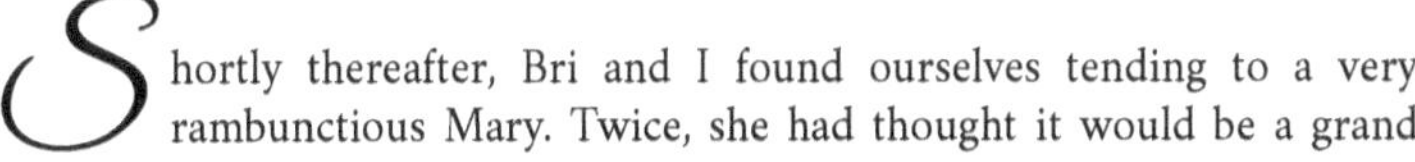

Shortly thereafter, Bri and I found ourselves tending to a very rambunctious Mary. Twice, she had thought it would be a grand idea for us to take off our clothes and run naked through the break in the trees where we'd set up camp.

Each time, we'd quickly diverted her attention elsewhere.

The game *Never Have I Ever*, as described by Bri, had started off innocently enough. We'd given Mary the opportunity to ask questions first. In her effort to get both of us drunk, she'd asked questions that she knew would require us to take a drink, such as, "Never have I ever travelled through time." But soon the questions were turned over to Bri and me. It seemed no matter how wild our inquiry, Mary had participated in the activity. Soon, I'd learned things about Mary that not only shocked me but made me slightly nervous to be in her company. It was certain neither of us would ever look at the woman in quite the same way again.

Thank goodness, what seemed to be a never-ending bottle of whiskey finally ran dry. Shortly after, an exhausted and bleary-eyed Mary succumbed to sleep.

CHAPTER 19

*B*efore sunrise, I rose to gather water. The trip didn't take long, and while I'd expected to find both Mary and Bri still asleep when I returned, Mary was fully awake and busily ordering Bri to get up and help her pack up camp. Mary showed no signs of suffering after her bountiful whiskey consumption, instead seeming rather more rested than either Bri or me.

"How do ye feel, Mary? I was sure that ye'd sleep for quite a while longer." I bent to roll up my belongings, following Mary so that we could strap them to our horses.

"I doona know why ye would ask such a question. I feel fine, o'course."

She wouldn't look at me, keeping her head down as we gathered another load to bring back to the horses. Bri joined us, and having heard the beginning of our conversation, joined in. "How could you possibly feel fine, Mary? You drank more in the course of an evening than Arran drinks in a day. Do you even remember anything about last night?"

Mary stopped walking and whirled on both of us, quickly setting down her load. "Nay, I doona, and it doesna matter. Both of ye are never to mention what happened last night ever again. Do ye understand? I've never behaved in such a way, and I find myself feeling a wee bit ashamed this morning."

I shook my head. "Doona feel that way. There's no need."

Bri nodded. "Yes, please don't feel that way, Mary. You've been under a lot of stress with Eoin and me being gone, Arran leaving, and then the visitors. Not to mention, my mother."

Mary smiled, seeming to forgive herself a little. "Aye. We shall blame it on yer mother. Now, let's finish gathering camp and be on our way. I doona wish to spend another night on the ground. I believe that neither of ye will speak of this, not that anyone would believe ye even if ye did."

She was right. No one would. Laughing, we packed up, then Bri and I hoisted Mary's short legs up onto her horse. After we mounted our own beasts, we moved on in the direction of the new Conall Castle. I tried to keep my mind on anything other than the knowledge that I would be seeing Arran again – and meeting his new wife – come nightfall.

The Castle Formerly Known as Kinnaird

"Did we know that visitors were arriving?" Arran followed the messenger to the entranceway of the castle, all the while wondering if his new guests were just one more thing he'd forgotten. The many duties required by the laird were far more than he'd realized, and each day he found himself more impressed with the way his brother had handled the responsibilities back home so soon after their father's death.

"Nay, sir. Ye would have been informed if we had received news of their arrival beforehand. 'Tis three women, sir."

Arran stopped before opening the castle's main doors and faced the messenger. "Three women? Do ye know who they are?"

"They say they are from yer old home, sir. An old lady and two women who look like the same person, but they doona talk the same. One of them talks verra strangely."

Arran clasped the man on the shoulder more in an effort to steady himself than to gain attention. It couldn't be true. Blaire was gone, that painful ache in his chest a reminder of her absence every day. "Ye must be mistaken. 'Tis only two women, aye?"

"I'm not mistaken. There are three. The first two insisted I let them in right away, but I told them I wouldna do so until I spoke to ye. The third woman was verra quiet. I noticed her for that reason. See for yerself."

The man pulled the large doors open, giving Arran no time to prepare himself for what he both hoped and dreaded he would find. He found Blaire's eyes right away—the pain, passion, and yearning there, a sure reflection of what she saw in his own.

He wanted to run to her, to gather her in his arms and tell her he was sorry for sending her away, sorry that he hadn't denied his brother and married her when he'd had the chance. He almost did just that, but was stopped by a slight touch on his back.

He jerked away involuntarily, and he looked to his side to find Edana standing there.

"I dinna know that Donal had two daughters. They look remarkably similar. Are ye not going to show them inside? They're family, aye?"

"Aye, o'course I am. Would ye go inside and have our table readied for three more? I shall escort them in at once." Edana nodded and turned from him, and he silently chided himself for briefly forgetting the existence of his new wife.

Bri dismounted her horse quickly and came over to him, throwing her arms around his neck and smacking him lightly on the back of his head.

"It's good to see you, but you are a damn fool, Arran." Whispering in his ear, she added, "How could you go and do such a stupid, stupid thing?" When he pulled back to explain, Bri quieted him by pulling him in close again. "Don't you dare try to explain it to me right now. We can talk about it after we eat. Go and squeeze Mary. She's been missing you like crazy. And don't say a word to Blaire right now. You can't upset her before she is forced to sit with Edana. You can speak with her later."

She finally loosened her grip, and Arran stepped away. Quietly, he murmured, "I doona understand. How is Blaire here? Why?" Questions coursed through his mind, questions he knew would have to go unanswered for the moment. "What will we tell Edana? She doesna know about the spell room. No one does."

Bri smiled at him reassuringly, but it did nothing to soothe his uneasy mind. "Don't worry, I'll think of something to tell her over dinner. We need to come up with a story, anyway. We will have to tell it a lot. No one has seen the both of us together yet. Now, go to Mary and help her down from her horse, then see her inside. Blaire and I will find our way shortly."

Arran nodded and walked toward Mary. After helping her slide off of her horse, he yanked her into a large embrace. He kissed her soundly on the cheek before rearing back at the smell that rose around them. "Ye smell like an ale house, Mary. Did ye bathe in a basin of whiskey?"

The old woman flailed in his arms, and her face reddened as she smacked him hard on the arm. He seemed to be having that effect on the Conall women this evening. Both Mary and Bri had hit him since their arrival.

"What do ye mean by that? Do ye not know me well enough to believe that I would do such a thing? Why, ye are most likely smelling yerself!"

Arran laughed and stepped away from her. "Aye, I'm sure ye are right, Mary. Now let me show ye inside to yer room where ye shall rest as long as ye are here. Ye work hard enough at home. I want ye to do naught but breathe for a while."

She laughed, and Arran pulled her in close again. Then, doing his best to avoid Blaire's gaze, he looked down while showing Mary inside.

A knock on the bedchamber door caused my breath to lodge in my throat, but upon hearing Bri's voice on the other side, I released a sigh of relief. I swung the door open to be greeted with the hefty smell of meat and wine as Bri carried my dinner inside.

"Here you go. It was difficult for me to explain why I needed to bring you food when supposedly you were too ill to go to dinner. I'm sure Arran knew I was lying."

I sat quickly, shoveling the delicious meal into my mouth as it eased my grumbling stomach. "I shouldna have come here. It was wrong of me to do so. Did ye not see the way Edana looked at him when she came outside?"

Bri crossed her arms as she stared down at me. "No. I didn't. I was too busy looking at how Arran couldn't take his eyes off you."

"He dinna even speak to me." I quickly finished off the food and stood, moving to the door. "I canna stay here, Bri. I'm going back tonight."

I made to open the door but was stopped by Bri's tight grip on my arm. "Ok, if you want to go, that's fine. We will leave tomorrow, but you can't go anywhere tonight. You don't know the way back by yourself anyhow. I'm sorry. It was wrong of me to make you come here."

I could see the sense in her words. It would be foolish for me to travel at night all alone, but I knew that I couldn't spend another moment inside the castle. "Doona be sorry. Ye have no reason to be so. Ye are right. I willna leave, but I need to get outside of the castle. I dinna know seeing him would upset me so. I'll be brushing the horses in the stables."

I shut the door before Bri had a chance to speak.

CHAPTER 20

rran knocked lightly on the door, hoping that Bri would open it quickly before Edana saw him sneaking into the room of their female guests. She'd been away in her own bedchamber for some time, but he knew her to be a nighttime wanderer. She was finding her way into his bed much more frequently.

Blaire's absence at dinner had surprised him. He knew she wasn't ill, not that he could blame her for not wanting to see him. She must think he truly didn't care for her, to be able to marry so soon after what they had shared together. If only Blaire knew how she occupied his every thought, pained his every breath when he wasn't near her.

"Come in. Did you not hear me calling you through the door, telling you that you could enter?"

He'd lost himself in his own thoughts of regret and self-pity, forgetting that he was standing outside the door until he heard Bri's voice in front of him. He looked up, pulling himself out of his trance as he stepped inside. "Nay, I dinna. I was thinking."

"I'm sure you were. What did you think about what I told Edana about Blaire and me? Do you think she bought it? Will everybody else?"

Arran frowned as he tried to remember what story Bri had told. It was the last thing on his mind. All he could think about was Blaire. "Forgive me, I doona know what ye told her. I am not feeling like myself."

Bri reached out to lay a hand on his back, and he smiled, knowing she understood.

"I know. I'm sorry. We can talk about it later. She's not here, Arran. She said she was going to the stables."

291

He nodded, briefly shutting his eyes as he pictured her there, slender fingers running gently down whatever horse was lucky enough to share her company. "O'course she is. The lass loves horses as much as I do. She willna want to see me, though. Why is she here, Bri? How did she get back to this time?"

"Eoin and I went for her. That's where we were, not at Bran's."

Arran had suspected as much. Not that they'd traveled into the future, but he knew they weren't at Bran's. They would have learned about his wedding much sooner if they'd only gone as far as the village. "Why did ye do so?"

"Because I could see that you were miserable, and I believed that Blaire was still in love with you, as well."

"And is she?" Arran turned away from her, his heart nearly stopping at the anticipation he felt at his question. It was wrong of him to ask, to care. He'd promised himself to another, but Blaire had claimed ownership of his heart long before he ever knew of Edana Kinnaird.

"Of course she is. She would never have dreamed of coming back here if she wasn't. We didn't know you were going to run off and get married. You don't love Edana, do you?"

"I'll not speak poorly of Edana, but I'll not lie to ye, either, and tell ye that I love her. It matters not. I am married to the lass, and there is nothing that can be done to change it." The truth of his own words hit him square in the chest, and he found himself leaning a hand against the wall to keep from doubling over. "Ye know the truth of my words. Why did ye bring her here if ye knew I couldna be with her?"

"Because things didn't end properly between the two of you. Now she needs closure, to know that it is finished and that you have both said your peace. You need it, too, Arran. Then you can both move on with your lives."

He inhaled deeply, trying to catch the breath that seemed lodged in between his ribs. "I shall go to Blaire. I must speak with her and see her once more before I lose her again. I've spent every moment since she left believing that I would never see her again. Now that she is back, I canna deny myself what I've been yearning for every moment. I know we canna be together, but I must see that she is well and apologize for the hurt I've caused her."

"Yes, go. But end it, Arran. Don't allow either of you to walk away, hoping for something that can no longer be. It would only make it harder for both of you."

He nodded, turning away from Bri as he silently opened the bedchamber door to make his leave.

---

*T*he ground behind me crunched, the coldness in the air hardening all of nature. The noise was a sure sign someone was approaching.

Part of me hoped it would be Arran, but another part of me hoped that the footsteps behind me were a figment of my mind. I was furious, hurt, and humiliated by my presence here. It was wrong of me to have come to his home, to be in the place he shared with his new wife. But I wanted to see him, to hold him, to know that it wasn't only me that was pained by our last moments spent together before I traveled forward in time.

"Bri told me I would find ye here. I dinna think I would ever see ye again, Blaire."

My hand froze as it moved down the side of the chestnut-colored mare. "Aye, I suppose ye dinna."

"I'm pleased to see ye. It has been verra hard for me since ye went away."

He was lying, I was certain. Speaking words meant to make me weak in front of him and cause me to confess my true feelings. I'd done so once before, only to be sent away heartbroken. I wouldn't allow myself to be so foolish again. "Oh, has it? I dinna believe ye were that fond of me."

He grabbed me by the arm, pulling me away from the mare as he spun me so that I faced him. I was close to him, our chests nearly touching. Arran stared down at me angrily. "Doona do that, Blaire. I came here to apologize to ye, but I willna allow ye to behave as if ye believe that I dinna care for ye. Look into my eyes and tell me if ye believe that I doona still."

I held my breath. His grip on me was tight, and all I could see were his eyes, pained and hungry. My own chest started to rise and fall rapidly, and I yanked away from him. "Ye doona need to apologize for not wanting me. Ye canna help who ye love. I hope that ye and Edana will be verra happy together." I walked toward the stable doors as quickly as I could, desperate to get back to the safety of the castle. We were too alone here, and if he touched me again, I was afraid I wouldna be able to make myself push him away.

But Arran was too quick. This time he dinna only grab my arm but gripped me tightly by both wrists, pulling me back into the confined shelter of the stable. Once inside, he leaned against the door of an empty stall and pulled me against him, my wrists and front flush against his chest. I kept my hands clenched into fists, unwilling to allow my palms to rest against him, certain I would unravel at such an intimate touch.

He was tense, as if suppressing something deep within him. He didn't speak, didn't move. He only held me close to him as we stared silently at one another. Slowly, our breathing quickened, my chest matching the rise and fall of his. Arran's eyes dropped to my lips, only to dart upward again.

I felt danger rising, feelings unsaid threatening to express themselves through touch, and I squirmed within his grasp, hoping that I could move away and break the tension surrounding us.

He didn't allow it and only pulled me closer, leaning forward to plead breathlessly in my ear, "Doona move, lass." He pulled his head back so that his eyes pierced my own. "I know…I know I canna have ye, but ye were right.

I canna help who I love and, married or not, I love ye, Blaire. I should never have sent ye away. To be separated from ye these past months has been hell. Ye have to know that I dinna mean a word I said before you went away. If I were a better man, I would never have done what I did to ye. If I were a better man, I wouldna allow myself to hold ye in my arms now."

His lips, trembling and warm, pressed against my forehead. I melted, allowing the man for whom I'd yearned for so long to hold me, as I'd dreamed of him doing for what seemed like ages.

I should've pulled away and run back to the safety of the castle. Around such company, he would never have been so bold, but here, with no one to serve as witness to our actions but our consciences, he held me tightly against him, his eyes hungry whenever they met mine, his body trembling as he struggled with his conflicting emotions.

My heart was beating such that I could scarcely think. Arran was a good man, an honorable man, a married man. I felt his struggle in the tension in his arms, hard muscles holding him back from surrender, back from the act that would undoubtedly sever his sacred marriage vows. Despite his past philandering ways, it was not in him to decide to do such a thing now that he had wed. It was not in me to ask him to betray his wife

He held back, his body as tight as a bow string. In that instant, I saw the future that lay ahead of me, one of solitude. Arran and I couldn't be together in the way we both desired, as husband and wife. But our love needed to be validated, to be expressed in such a way that we could both hold on to the memory that our hearts belonged to one another even as we made our way through life apart. I couldn't deny myself one kiss, one to take with me and cherish for the rest of my days and long, empty nights.

"Arran," I whispered his name softly, opening my fists so that the palms of my hands rested against his chest. It was enough—too much. He pulled away, his eyes red and heavy, glassy and moist with unshed tears. Although we stood apart now, he kept a tight grip on my wrists, silently pleading with me to send him away. But I could not.

"Aye, lass?" His voice was dry and cracked as the words struggled to find their way out of him.

"I know the truth of what yer marriage means for us, but I doona have the strength to walk away from ye this night without one kiss. Please, Arran."

He crushed his mouth to mine, his arms moving around me as he released my wrists and pulled me hard against him. I moved my hands up to the sides of his face, running my fingers through his hair as I heard him swallow a hard lump in the back of his throat.

I rubbed my thumb gently across his cheek, pausing as I touched a droplet of wetness that quickly found its way onto my tongue, its salty bite bringing tears to my own eyes. I'd known Arran all of my life, and had never seen him cry until now.

I pulled my lips away from his, and then kissed each one of his eyes. He pulled away, rubbing his hands quickly over his face as he smiled, embarrassed that I knew he'd been crying. "I'm sorry, lass. What a fool I must look to ye."

I cupped either side of his face and kissed him gently. "Ye are not a fool. Ye are the man I love."

He smiled, the look in his eyes warming me all the way to my toes. "Aye, and you are the woman I love." His lips roamed over my face as he kissed my brows, my cheekbones, my chin. "I have been a frozen shell since ye left, Blaire. Tis only in this moment as I feel the warmth of yer skin that my heart begins to thaw."

I shut my eyes reveling in the feeling of his fingertips brushing against the skin on my face, my neck, my collarbone. I wanted so much more – we both did – but knew this would have to be enough.

"God, Blaire. Ye canna know how beautiful ye are."

Our lips met again with a heated passion, no longer restrained by our previous hesitation. With the knowledge that we could not be together in even this small way ever again, desperation filled us.

Our lips danced in a heartbreaking frenzy.

For a time, there was only this night, this moment, the two of us. All thoughts of tomorrow or yesterday faded, became as distant as the future that had separated us from each other for far too long.

CHAPTER 21

*A*rran, the fool, thought he and his lover had gone unseen, of that Tormod was certain. But he had kept a tight watch on the castle, waiting for anything he could use against the man who had stolen his birthright, and

his waiting had paid off. He'd long heard of Arran Conall's philandering ways, and such a man was unlikely to change his habits after marriage. Tormod couldn't have dreamed up a better partner for Arran's betrayal of Edana. For it wasn't just any woman with whom Arran was dallying; he had snuck into the stables with his brother's wife.

The two had handed him a grand opportunity, one if played properly would likely destroy both Conall brothers. Edana already hated them. Once he shared what he'd seen last night, Tormod knew she'd be willing to do whatever he asked of her to help him ruin them.

He waited inside the home he shared with his sister, watching for any sign of his pale-haired and plain-faced pawn to make her way through the village. She met him there each morning while Arran went on his daily ride. Their moments together were short, but each moment he was forced to spend in her company, talking and kissing, made him hate her all the more.

What a pathetic creature, so willingly giving him her trust at the first sign of his forced affection. She was ignorant, stupid, and Tormod found nothing less attractive in a woman.

"I see Edana coming this way," said his sister. "I shall be away now."

"Wait." Tormod called out for her to stop before she made her way out the door. "Do ye think 'tis wise to ask her to do what ye suggested? If she isna pregnant, Arran will surely know before too long."

Tormod flinched at the look Fia cast in his direction. "Aye, Arran will feel guilt over his betrayal of Edana, but 'tis not her place to forbid him his dalliances. If she tells him she's carrying his child, his remorse will multiply on its own, making him weak, just as we need him to be." She glanced away from Tormod, adding, "Edana is coming. Go kiss yer fool."

Once his sister left, Tormod moved to the doorway, looking each direction down the street to ensure that none would see the laird's wife enter his home. It was unlikely, he knew. People kept away from him and Fia. His sister's company was a pleasure most did not seek, for she was a woman of strength, not a woman of pity like the wretch that now made her way inside.

"Tormod."

He stiffened as Edana threw her arms around him. Pulling away from her, he motioned for her to sit next to him. "I have something to tell ye, Edana. Something we can finally use against Arran."

"Aye, are ye going to tell me that Arran has been with someone else? I know he dinna stay in his room."

Tormod's brows lifted in surprise. Perhaps the lass was visiting her husband's bed more often than he'd realized. It was all the better. It would make their tale all the more believable. "Aye, he has, but not just with anyone. He spent the night with his brother's wife."

Edana shook her head, and Tormod lifted his brows even further. He'd been certain it was Eoin's wife he'd seen with Arran.

"Nay, 'twas not Bri, 'twas was the other one. Blaire. The one he couldna keep his eyes off of when they arrived. It seems that Donal MacChristy is more interesting than most people believed. He had two daughters, twins, and he sent one of them to grow up with his brother."

"Ye canna mean it? How could no one know of this?" His brows were about to lift off his head, and Tormod did his best to straighten his face into some semblance of normalcy. This was the most interested he'd ever been in Edana's words.

"They said that Donal was afraid he couldna care for both girls after their mother died. He sent Bri away, and she spent most of her life traveling in the care of her uncle, which goes a far way toward explaining the odd way in which she speaks. Blaire stayed here, and it was she that was supposed to marry Eoin. But before the wedding, Bri returned home, and it was she that Eoin fell in love with, not Blaire. But it seems that Arran has stepped in where his brother failed."

"I've never seen two lasses so similar in appearance." Tormod leaned back and shook his head in surprise.

"Aye, 'tis quite remarkable. But it was most certainly she that ye saw with Arran, not Bri. I saw Bri after I noticed that Arran was not in his room."

"Aye, I suppose it must have been. Regardless, I know what we must do to weaken Arran." He leaned forward and grabbed Edana's hands, knowing the effect his touch had on her. She yearned for him, and any intimacy he offered her, however slight, would only make her more amenable to his plan.

"What is it?" She stood from her chair and moved to his lap, looping her arms loosely around his neck. Tormod had to keep himself from grimacing as their bodies touched.

"Ye have been sharing his bed, aye?"

"Aye, but each time 'tis only ye that I see in my mind. Arran is only the vessel I use to reach ye when we are apart." She kissed him then, but Tormod cut the contact short, standing swiftly. "What is it?" Edana frowned. "Have I displeased ye?"

"No, no. You couldn't, lass." He touched her hair. "All's well and good. My mind is just preoccupied with my plan to overthrow yer husband. He should believe ye when ye tell him that ye are with child. I shall find a nurse to confirm yer story."

"Why? I am not with child, and it wouldna take too long before Arran would notice the lie." The pitch of her voice was high and painful to Tormod's ears. He turned away from her to grimace at the wall.

"By the time Arran would notice, ye may very well actually be with child, whether it be mine or his," he said. "And any remorse that Arran feels for having slept with another will only cause him more pain if he believes ye are carrying his child. His love for his unborn child and his guilt over betraying ye will make him weak." He could sense that she was about to protest. Rather than listen to the sound of her voice once again, he crushed himself to her and set about his daily task of making the fool love him.

onall Castle

"**S**low down, Adelle," said Eoin. "I canna understand ye when ye speak so quickly."

Adelle threw her hands up in exasperation. Her son-in-law was decidedly too calm over their present situation. It was clear that he hadn't heard her, or she was certain he would be much more panicked.

"Donal MacChristy is here. I've never seen a man who so closely resembles my ex-husband. I nearly jumped out of my skin when I saw him. He came to visit with Blaire. He said he wants to see her! I didn't know what to tell him so I just had Kip take him down to the stables so that they could get his horse situated." Adelle watched as her words sunk in, and Eoin's formerly calm face began to match her own.

"O'course he would show up whilst Bri is away. She canna even pretend to be Blaire if she isna here. How will I explain to him that his daughter went to visit my brother without me? He will hardly think it proper. And it isna! That's why she left without me. She knew I wouldna have let her go."

Adelle cleared her throat to interrupt him. "That isn't our only problem. When they do get back, how are we going to explain to him that there are two Blaires?"

CHAPTER 22

The Castle Formerly Known as Kinnaird

Morning came much too quickly, and with it the sadness that had been momentarily lifted slowly seeped back into my heart. As light started to peek through the small cracks in the stable doors, I felt Arran shift beside me, and I turned my head so that I could kiss his brow.

The tilt of my head sent a tear that sat dormant in the corner of my eye running down my face, and I quickly reached up to brush it away.

I'd not slept a wink through the night. Arran was too honorable a man to betray his marriage vows, and even if he hadn't been, I would not have let him. He would not have been able to live with himself had we made love. And so we simply held and kissed each other, which I knew was a betrayal of Edana, as well, if I were honest with myself. Sometime during the night, Arran had drifted away into the slumber of a man who'd not slept soundly in quite a long time. He'd held me tightly, squeezing his arms around me if I shifted only a little, as if he was afraid I would get up and leave him during the night.

Perhaps I should have, but my heart was torn into two very distinct pieces, and the confusion of feelings left me frozen and as trapped in the stables as I was trapped by Arran's heavy arms. I had never felt such love, such joy, never known just how deeply two souls could connect simply through touch. I had also never been so heartbroken. The sadness I felt at knowing what we shared could never be more—could not even continue as it was—caused me to ache all the way down to my bones.

"I doona wish to move from this place, lass. Do ye think we could hide away here and live with the horses?"

I smiled and kissed him lightly before forcing myself to stand and adjust my dress. "Nay, as much as I wish it, we canna. If I doona return before Mary awakes, ye know she shall have everyone in the castle looking for us."

"That she will, lass."

He stood, brushing hay and dust from his clothing, as I had done. "How will I get back into the castle unseen?" I asked him.

"I doona expect that anyone will question ye. If they do, just tell them ye went out for a morning walk. I shall leave from here to go out on my daily ride. I shall see ye, Mary and Bri before ye return home." He gathered me up in his arms, pulling me in so close that I could scarcely breathe. "I love ye, lass, and I doona believe that I can say goodbye to ye. When I am able to arrange it, I shall come to ye. From now on, my marriage to Edana will be only for her protection, but my heart shall always be yours. In time, Edana will learn to accept it. And perhaps she'll come to see that her happiness would be greater if she had her freedom. I would still watch over her, just—"

I stopped his words midsentence by tensing and pulling away from him, unsure of what he was suggesting. I couldn't have him make promises to me that I knew could never be. Arran was a good man, and though he spoke of a future freedom, he was not free now and never would be as long as they both lived – he and his wife. Soon, he would feel remorse for our actions. True, we had not consummated our love, but he had betrayed his wife, nonetheless, simply by holding me, kissing me, declaring his love. Once he admitted that to himself, he would not come to me again. "Tis best for ye to not leave me with hope when it isna there."

He grabbed me quickly, silencing me with his mouth, causing my head to spin and my knees to buckle. "I willna let ye go, Blaire. I canna do so again. Tell me that if I come for ye that ye will see me. I must live with the hope of holding ye in my arms once more."

The tears fell freely now. Any resistance I had shattered. If he came to me, I would welcome him. Though his honor and mine would not allow us to come together completely as lovers, I was not strong enough to deny myself the pleasure of his kisses, or the comfort I found in his arms. All that I was had been his for quite some time already. "Aye, I will. Now, leave. Bri and Mary will be awake soon. I should make my way back inside."

"I love ye, Blaire. When ye left this time, ye took my heart with ye, and it has belonged to no one else."

He kissed me once more, then moved to open the stable doors so he could mount his horse and depart on his ride. He smiled back at me as he left.

Once he was gone, I scanned the horizon. Seeing that all was clear, I made my way back to the castle.

*B*ri was awake when I arrived at our shared room. 'Twas apparent she'd been so for quite a while.

"Oh, Blaire. I'm glad you're back. I couldn't sleep a wink after Arran came by here looking for you. Are you okay?"

She stood from where she was seated on the edge of the bed and pulled me into a quick embrace.

"Aye, I shall be, in time. We should make our leave today."

She was kind enough not to question me further before going to wake Mary.

Once Bri had left, I cleaned myself using the small basin of water that sat at the back of the room. After changing, I did my best to pin my hair so that it didn't look like I spent the night in the stables.

I struggled with an unruly strand that was difficult to reach at the nape of my neck. It stuck out in a way that defied gravity, but unable to see it, I found myself useless when it came to securing it into place.

Bri entered the room. Seeing my difficulty, she came to offer her assistance. As she grabbed the long strand of hair, combing through it with her fingers, I asked her about Mary.

"Was she still sleeping when ye went to wake her?" While Bri worked on the back of my hair, I kept my hands busy trying to soothe the frizzing strands around my forehead.

"She was awake, but lounging in a steamy tub while three ladies waited on her hand and foot. Arran wasn't joking when he said she wasn't to lift a finger while she's here."

I laughed, picturing Mary ordering the poor lasses about. I was certain she would not be too pleased with having to leave Arran so soon. "What did she say to ye when ye told her we were leaving?"

Bri chuckled, and I caught her eyes in the small mirror before us. "Nothing that I wish to repeat. She said that we were welcome to leave if we wish, but she was making this her permanent home because Arran was the only one to show her any appreciation in ages. But don't worry, she'll come. In fact, I expect she will be ready for departure before us. Whether she will admit it or not, it's driving her crazy not to be ruling over her roost." Bri lowered her hands from my head and moved back. "There. Does that feel better?"

I reached behind and smiled as the piece was no longer floating toward the ceiling. "Aye," I said, nodding in approval. "Thank ye."

A knock at the door and Mary's boisterous voice from behind it signaled that Bri was right. Soon we would take our leave from the castle, from Arran, and from the place my heart would always remain.

*E*dana stood back after saying her own polite and expected farewells, watching closely as Arran made his own. He'd given her no explanation, made no excuse for his absence from his bedchamber the night before. Perhaps he thought she'd not come for him and believed his absence had gone unnoticed.

Even before Tormod's damning news, Edana had taken notice of her husband's empty bedchamber, and she'd suspected that he'd spent his night with another. She could not say she was surprised. The wandering ways of Arran Conall had been legendary as she was growing up, and she didn't know a single lass who didn't dream of having him woo her. But this knowledge did nothing to slow the torment of anger that spread its fiery touch over her each time she pictured them together. It didn't matter that she was in love with another. Arran was a fool. It was only right that she should find a true man elsewhere, but she should have been enough for Arran.

At first, she'd been resistant to Tormod's suggestion that she lie to Arran about a pregnancy. But as she watched him lean into Blaire and pull her close, unable to stop his lips from lingering near her cheek and the undeniable yearning that shone in his eyes, she realized the awful truth. Arran had not only spent the night with Blaire, he'd given her his heart. Whatever loyalty Arran had once felt for Edana, it had diminished overnight. In order to keep him close, malleable to her plans, she had to regain his loyalty.

She would do as Tormod bid, and by sundown she would win back Arran's heart by pretending to be pregnant with his child.

CHAPTER 23

The first day of our journey back to Conall Castle was a pensive one. I remained wrapped in my own thoughts of loss and guilt. Although I had broken no vows to Edana, I couldn't deny the guilt I felt over her. She was an innocent victim of Arran's and my love for one another, albeit an unpleasant one. I'd only spent a few moments with her, but I was certain a friendship would never have been possible between us under any circumstance.

She was entirely miserable-looking, and something about her made me uneasy, as if she knew what had occurred between Arran and me. The glare Edana shot at me as we departed made me question whether or not my love and I had been alone the night before, as we'd believed.

The second day of our journey, the day we were due to arrive back at the castle, proved to be more eventful.

Mary complained regularly about us ending her rare treat of luxury so soon, but it was easy to detect the jest in her words. With each hoof step that brought us closer to Conall Castle, Mary's smile grew. I could tell she was itching to resume her duties as the true leader of the castle.

After at least a dozen complaints, she suddenly changed the subject and addressed me so bluntly that I nearly fell off my horse in surprise. "Ye slept with him, dinna ye?"

"Mary!" Bri's shocked and elevated voice echoed throughout the countryside.

"What?" Mary dismissed Bri's rebuke with a wave of her hand. "Ye have been thinking the same thing, have ye not? I saw the way Arran looked at her, and she at him, when we left. 'Twas not a look that people share unless they are intimately acquainted." Mary gave Bri an expression that dared her to disagree.

"I may have been thinking it, but I have the tact not to say it or ask," said Bri, cutting her eyes in my direction. "Goodness, Mary, I swear you get nosier with each passing day."

"I'm not nearly nosy enough!"

"Aye, we did sleep together, but not in the way that you think," I said. "I doona wish to discuss it further." I lifted my chin, knowing I'd merely piqued Mary's interest even more with my curious statement.

Mary narrowed her eyes at me. "What other way is there, lass? I wasn't born yesterday." She shook her head and smiled. "Doona ye worry, lass. I'll not be judging ye for it. Arran's marriage is not one built on love, and it never should have happened."

Sympathy was evident in her eyes, and it only increased my longing for Arran. It pained me to say it, but I couldn't bear for them to think that Arran had broken his holy promise to his wife. "I slept all night in his arms, Mary. But Arran did not dishonor his marriage vows any more than that," I said quietly.

Both women were unable to hide their surprise. Mary opened her mouth to say something but was interrupted by the appearance of

a rider off in the distance. We were nearing the castle, and Bri groaned and slowed the pace of her horse.

"Crap, it's Eoin. I bet he's so angry, he's ready to lock me away."

She laughed, but it was an uncomfortable sound. I could tell she was nervous for his reaction.

"Doona worry. He may be angry, but I've known the lad all his life," said Mary. "He knows by now that ye canna control women. He will just be glad that ye've returned. Besides, it looks as if he is riding for us. He must have news he hoped would reach us before we arrive back home."

Mary's revelation caused us all to pick up our pace in our eagerness to hear what Eoin had to say.

He met us quickly, reining to a halt beside us. "Ach! There ye are ye three naughty lassies. Why, I should throw the three of ye in the dungeon where ye canna cause any more trouble." He smiled, showing his jest. "But first, I want to kiss my wife. Come here, ye awful scoundrel." Eoin maneuvered his horse so that it was next to Bri's and deftly lifted her off her own horse so that she straddled him on his. He smacked her behind softly and proceeded to kiss her as Mary and I watched awkwardly.

Eventually Mary interrupted. "All right, that's enough! Stop it, the both of ye. I was feeling quite hungry and ready for a meal once we arrive back at the castle, but I think ye've spoiled my appetite."

"Hush, Mary. There's some remaining for ye, as well." Eoin dismounted, pulling Bri down from the horse with him. Once they were both on the ground, he moved to Mary's side, reaching for her and pulling her off the horse and into a tight embrace. He kissed her soundly on the cheek. She squealed and protested in his arms, but her red cheeks and wide smile showed her joy at reuniting with one of her boys.

"Tis good to see ye, as well, Blaire," Eoin said with a nod in my direction. "I'm glad ye have all arrived back safely, although ye should never have gone alone." Eoin set Mary on the ground and stepped away to regard us. "Ye left Adelle and me with quite a mess to trouble ourselves over. Not only our guests, but yer father arrived last night, as well."

"My father?" My voice croaked as I said the words. I hurried to dismount, afraid I might faint and fall to the ground, otherwise. As far as I knew, my father believed that it was I married to Eoin. He had no idea that I had spent the last months in a different century. He would have to be told the truth. Whether or not he would be able to believe it, I knew not.

"Aye, his arrival was unexpected. He said he was eager to see his daughter. I've done what I could to distract him, but he is verra disgruntled and losing patience. 'Tis best that we get all of ye back as quickly as possible so that the two of ye," he pointed to Bri and myself, "can give him whatever explanation ye choose."

"So ye told him nothing?" Part of me hoped Eoin would have explained everything to him, but it seemed that he'd left that unpleasant task undone. Not that I could blame him.

"Nay. I told him that ye'd accompanied Mary into the village to gather some supplies for the castle, and he was not too pleased to hear it. He thought it unwise of me to allow ye to go alone. I canna imagine what he would think of me if he learned I'd allowed ye to travel as far off as ye did."

Eoin ran his hand over his face, clearly exhausted after dealing with my father. I'd yet to see him, and fatigue was already overcoming me at the prospect.

He was a good man, and I loved him, but my independent spirit had made me a difficult child to manage. He'd been pleased when he'd finally been able to marry me off into the hands of another to oversee my behavior. He would not be pleased to know that his efforts had been unsuccessful. I was afraid he would feel it meant that he had ownership over me once more. If so, he would be disappointed. I would not be going back home with him, even if I had to work with Mary in the Conall's kitchens. I remounted my horse and gestured to Eoin, Bri, and Mary to do the same.

"Let's be on with it, then. I doona wish to keep him waiting."

"*I* canna believe it, truly. If ye dinna both stand before me now, I would never be able to believe such a story. I always knew Morna was a witch, but I never believed she would be capable of such a grand spell. Why, ye've given an old man the shock of his life."

My father laughed deeply as he gave me a warm hug. His reaction to our story after bringing him to the spell room was astonishing. Rather than doubt us or become angry, he'd accepted our explanation with pure curiosity.

"Ye are not angry with me?" I asked, returning his hug. "And ye will go along with what we told Edana, claiming us both as yer daughters?" It was a relief to be free of my nervousness over his being here. Now I could simply enjoy the feeling of safety that came with being wrapped in my father's arms.

"Nay, I'm not angry. I doona see how either of ye had a choice in what happened. And aye, I shall be pleased to call Bri as my own. I've thought she was for some time now." He smiled at Bri. "Ye did a remarkable job of fooling me. Ye are a magnificent trickster."

Bri laughed and shook her head in disagreement. "With all due respect, I believe your bad ear went a long way to making my performance believable to you."

"Ach, I'm sure ye are right, lass." Father reached up and touched his left ear.

Bri stood and excused herself to give us some privacy. We'd brought Father down here, hoping that the presence of Morna's spell books would help him to believe.

"I'll leave the two of you to visit alone for awhile," Bri said. "You know, I think it's fitting that I should be known as your daughter. You bear a striking resemblance to my real father."

She winked at both of us. Once she was gone, my father stood and grabbed my hand so that he could lead me out of the spell room.

"Let's go for a walk down by the sea, shall we? I'm anxious to hear of my bonny lass's adventures while she was away."

I nodded, and together we left hand-in-hand. In that moment, I felt closer to my father than I'd ever felt before.

CHAPTER 24

The Castle Formerly Known as Kinnaird

"Ye have been drinking less of late, have ye not?"

Edana's voice startled him. Arran turned away from the window he'd been staring out of, imagining where Blaire was, what she was doing, wondering if she was thinking of him, as well. One week had passed since she had returned to Conall Castle. Although she was days away, his world seemed brighter just knowing he could get to her, that she was no longer out of his reach in another century.

Every night since their departure, Edana had come to him, softly knocking on his door in the middle of the night. He'd ignored it, never giving explanation, hoping that within time she would give up and cease seeking his affection.

Tonight was the only night she'd entered his room uninvited. He faced her, doing his best to feign a smile. Over the past days, he'd come to learn more about his new wife, and what he'd discovered made it easier for him to push aside any guilt he felt over his feelings for Blaire.

Edana screamed at the servants and ordered them around as if they were criminals rather than loyal, hardworking members of their household. It was a habit she'd learned from her father, no doubt, but a needless act of malevolence, nonetheless.

Her moods shifted suddenly. It was impossible for him to tell when he was seeing glimpses of her true self. He hoped the real Edana was the one he saw in her rare moments of kindness, but something warned him that her other moments of ill-tempered outbursts ran deep to her core.

With each day, he grew more certain that she was not a shy, helpless victim, not a beaten woman who needed his aid, as he'd once believed. If only he'd not been so foolish, rushing into a commitment when he knew not to whom he was committing. He could be welcoming the woman he loved into his bed rather than denying his wife entry into it.

"Aye, ale is not so appealing to me as it once was. Why are ye awake so late in the evening, Edana?"

"I needed to speak to my husband. Have ye not heard me knocking on yer door these past nights? Have ye already guessed what it is I'm here to tell ye, and ye no longer find me so pleasing?"

He didn't know what she was talking about. He'd noticed little about her as of late. In fact, he hardly saw her when he looked right at her, so occupied his mind was with thoughts of Blaire. "Aye, lass, I heard ye knocking, but I have been tired. I have not been in the mood for company at night. But nay, I have not guessed anything about what ye have to say to me. What do ye mean by that?"

"I'm with child, Arran."

Shock coursed painfully through him, and he found that he was gripping the edge of the table so tightly that his knuckles shone white beneath his skin. "Nay, lass. We have not been married long enough for ye to be carrying a child. Even if ye were, it would be too soon for ye to know it." He hoped that he was right, but he knew little of such things, and he knew that his words were born more from wishful thinking than true knowledge.

"Aye, 'tis true that we have not been married long, but 'tis still verra possible for it to be so. I have not bled, and I have never missed doing so before. My nurse has confirmed it, as well."

Arran pulled the stool out from the small desk and plopped himself down on it, his head suddenly heavy and throbbing.

Edana motioned to someone standing in the doorway. Shortly after, a woman who looked to be about Mary's age approached him. She was short and slight. There were dark circles beneath her eyes. He thought she looked too unhealthy to be a nurse to anyone but still rose to greet her. Before he could speak, Edana interrupted.

"Go on, tell him. Tell him what ye just told me. That I am carrying his bairn."

Edana's tone caused him to look attentively toward the nurse who stood before him. There seemed to be an underlying threat with Edana's words, and the look of fear on the poor woman's face was enough for him to be sure he was right.

"May I speak to yer nurse alone for a moment, Edana?" He expected her response and fumbled quickly for an answer that would placate her.

"Do ye not believe me? What reason would I have to lie?"

"Nay, lass, I believe ye. If ye say that ye are with child, I believe that ye are. Tis only I have a private matter of a personal nature I would like to have seen." He smiled politely at the nurse.

Edana rolled her eyes as she slowly made her way toward the door. "Fine. Suit yerself, but ye know that she is not a real doctor. She deals only with birthing and such matters. If something troubles ye, ye should see the man in the village."

"Tis only a small matter. I suppose any woman with knowledge of herbs could help me with this. Go on. I shall come to ye shortly, and we shall talk."

With Edana gone, Arran motioned for the nurse to sit on the stool in front of his desk. "What is yer name, miss?"

The woman's voice was quiet and shaky. It pained Arran to know that she must have been mistreated by the people of this castle for some time to be so frightened in his presence when he had given her no reason to distrust him.

"My name is Gara, and I'm afraid that she is right, sir. I doona know much of healing and only a little of herbs. Perhaps ye should seek help elsewhere. I wouldna want to mislead ye."

Arran crouched down in front of Gara, smiling to ease the woman's nerves. "Doona worry, lass. All is well with me. I only wanted to speak to ye without Edana being present. Now I wish that ye tell me the truth. Do ye know Edana to be with child?"

"Aye, sir."

"Ye doona have to worry, lass. If she's threatened ye, all ye need to do is tell me so. I'll believe ye, and I will ensure yer protection. Has she done so?"

Surprise flickered in the woman's eyes, and Arran allowed himself to hope that perhaps Edana's words had been a lie.

"Nay, sir. She is carrying yer child, as ye shall see soon enough. Now, may I be excused from ye, sir?"

Arran stood so that the woman could move from her seat and extended his arm out beside him. "Aye, lass. Ye are not being held against yer will. Thank ye for speaking to me and for yer honesty."

"'Tis my pleasure to be of service to ye, sir."

Gara stood and nodded before turning away from him, but Arran called out to her once more before she could leave the room.

"I know that things have not always been good for the people of this castle, and while I claim no responsibility for yer suffering, I am sorry for it. I vow that I will do all I can to change things from now on. Doona ever be afraid in my presence."

"Thank ye, sir."

She slipped out quickly, leaving Arran alone to think about the unborn child that was seemingly on its way to him.

*C*ara hurried down the hallway, breathing in deeply and swiftly wiping at her face to hide the tears.

Arran Conall was a fine man. He would be a good laird to her and to her people. It did not sit well with her to lie to him, but she needed the payment for her family. The death of her husband had placed a burden on her that she'd been unable to adequately meet for some time. This lie would guarantee her family a roof over their heads for a long while. She was willing to put aside her morals for the sake of her children.

Still, it was not right, and she'd live with the guilt over such an injustice for all of her years to come. With each passing day, she would search for a way to make amends.

CHAPTER 25

"*D*id she do it, Tormod?" asked Fia.

He walked through the doorway of his home, not surprised to find his sister there waiting. She did her best to make him feel as if each new plan was his own, but he was no fool. He knew his puppet master well, and he needed her. Without Fia to guide him, he had no chance of destroying Arran Conall so that he could take over as laird and put a Kinnaird back in power over their territory.

She was talented at deceit and quick to think of each new step in their plan. He hoped today her ideas would be at their best. He had to find a way to rid himself of Edana for good.

"Aye, she told him last night, but his reaction was not what we had hoped. He was not so pleased to hear about his coming child."

Fia waved her hand dismissively in front of him. "'Tis no matter to us. Such news is difficult for any man when the woman carrying his child is not the one he loves. The newness will wear away. Soon he will fall in love with the child, real or not. Why do ye look so upset, brother? The wretch did as ye bid, did she not?"

"'Tis not enough to destroy Arran. I canna be with Edana. We must rid ourselves of her and find another way to ruin Arran." Tormod paced around the room, frustrated and tired of his act with Edana. Each time he saw her, she clung closer to him. His patience was growing thin.

"Nay, ye are too filled with haste. As long as Arran believes that Edana is carrying his child, she is of use to us. If we were to end her life now, Arran would not have the attachment to the thought of a child as he will in a few months. When it comes time for her pregnancy to show, we shall release ye from her so that Arran doesna find out that she wasna truly carrying his child."

Tormod could see the sense in her words, but it did nothing to ease his impatience. Still, he would have to spend the months until Edana's death imagining it, savoring each image of her slowly taking her last breath. "How will we kill her when the time comes?"

His sister turned to him slowly, a smile spreading across her thin face that sent chills down his spine.

"I know a woman, a witch really. She has given me a poison that will kill Edana. When it comes time that Arran could see that she is not carrying his child, ye will give it to her and tell her that it is an herb that will make it appear as if she lost the child by starting a bleed. She willna know when she takes it that it shall kill her. When it is discovered that she is dead, it will look as if she died from an early labor with the child."

It would be perfect, far better than any plan Tormod could have devised on his own. Not only would the lass die in a way that would appear natural, but she would realize before she died that she'd been betrayed, that Tormod did not love her.

He could tolerate Edana a few months more. Then her perfectly tragic death would be the reward for his patience.

CHAPTER 26

After his conversation with Gara, Arran sat inside his bedchamber absorbed in his own thoughts of regret and self-pity. He knew it was wrong for him not to go to Edana, not to express to her how pleased he was that she was carrying his child, but he couldn't bring himself to lie to the lass anymore.

Their marriage was pretense, the reasons Arran had married her invalid. For Edana was not the woman she'd made herself out to be while staying at Conall Castle. Not only that, but each time he'd taken her to his bed, he'd been dreaming of another, a lass so special to him that the only children he'd ever imagined himself having were hers.

He was a man torn, sworn by law and his marriage oath that he would stay by Edana's side, but promised by soul and heart to a lass who was waiting for him at his brother's home.

He'd yet to seek out Blaire, afraid that each moment spent together would only make the moments apart more difficult. And now, with the news of his unborn child, he was afraid it would be impossible for him to go to Blaire without being crushed by the weight of his guilt.

If it were only Edana, his love for Blaire might have been enough to push away his feelings of guilt. But now, with a child on the way, he knew he could not be unfaithful in any way.

Arran would not allow himself to be the sort of man to teach his children that such behavior was acceptable. It was bad enough the way he'd treated women before, using them for his enjoyment and then discarding them before his bed grew cold.

Blaire had changed him. He could now see the value of owning a woman's heart, the strength, responsibility, and the pure happy misery that came with possessing such a gift. He wanted to teach his sons to view women the same way, but he would be unable to do so if he continued to dishonor their mother through his relationship with Blaire.

It didn't matter that he did not love his wife. His conscience didn't care. It would be the hardest thing he would ever have to do, to give up his heart so quickly after having it returned to him. But his child would need a parent who lived a life of honor, more so than most if the child's mother was to be Edana Kinnaird.

He would tell Blaire face-to-face. It was the least he could do. His heart demanded that he see her one last time, to hold her and give her whatever explanation and apology he could offer. He knew nothing would be enough to heal the hurt he would cause her with his farewell. It had been she, after all, who'd tried to speak reason, saying that they should not meet again after their last night together.

He'd been a heedless fool. Unable to see the cards that fate would deal him when he'd promised Blaire he would come to her as often as he could. Now he would have to break her heart all over again.

His spirit broken, he sat down at his desk to pen a letter to her. He would tell her nothing of why he needed to see her, only ask that she meet him at the small cottage not far from Conall Castle in one week's time. She would come, her smile illuminating the four walls in which he would meet her. That smile he would soon snuff out, the smile he was afraid, once gone, would send him plummeting into the darkness he'd once known so well.

***

Conall Castle

Several weeks had passed with no news from Arran. I found myself growing more certain that news would never come. I'd suspected as much when we'd said our goodbyes, but I hadn't realized how miserable waiting for him would be.

Despite Arran's promise that we would see each other again, I knew what kind of men the Conall lads were. I knew the kind of man their father had been. It would not set well with Arran to break his wedding vows, regardless of the quality of his marriage, and even if our relationship was only one of the heart and soul and never consummated.

For most, marriage had little to do with the love of the two people joined, anyway. Not in this time. One of the things I'd found most fascinating about the twenty-first century was one's ability to easily dissolve a marriage. If only Arran had married Edana there.

But he hadn't, and such a wish could never be. So as I continued to tear the handful of herbs Mary had given me, tossing them into the stew as she stirred, I talked to ease my mind of thoughts of loneliness.

"What do ye think of Adelle and my father? Do ye think that if they spent more time together, they could get on well?" I already knew the answer, but I also knew the reaction such a question would garner from Mary, so I let it slip out innocently, trying not to grin as I waited for her overzealous response.

Instead of Mary, Adelle's voice answered from the doorway. "Oh, gosh no, sweetheart. Your dad is a nice enough fellow, but truth be told, he looks so much like my ex-husband, it's hard for me to spend more than a few minutes in the same room with him."

I smiled and winked at Adelle as I nudged my head toward Mary. "Aye, I know. I only wanted to hear Mary ramble on about how ye do not deserve my father. If I dinna know better, I would say that Mary has taken a fancy to him herself."

Mary whacked her wooden spoon hard against the table. "And what of it if I find him to be a fine looking man? There's no harm in looking at him when he passes by. I dare either one of ye to spend forty-five years married to Kip and see if ye doona find other lads pleasing to the eye. Kip appreciates a pretty face, as well, and I'll not be one to deny him the pleasure of looking."

Adelle walked around the table and tugged on the sleeve of my dress, as if requesting that I accompany her. "Right you are, Mary. It's healthy to recognize beauty when you see it. I'd be lying if I said I wasn't green with envy over my daughter's new husband. Within the next few centuries, there'll be few men like him around."

I laughed and brushed my hands against each other to rid them of the remaining herbs. "I'll be back shortly, Mary, to help plate the meal for supper."

Mary nodded and turned her attention back to the stew. "Aye, that will be fine, lass. Ye know that ye doona have to be down here cooking away with me, anyway. I appreciate yer help, though."

Once we were outside the basement kitchen, I noticed the folded piece of parchment Adelle concealed in her hands. Flashing it before me, she waved it in the direction of the stairs. Grabbing a lantern outside the kitchen door, we walked halfway down the flight of stairs before stopping to sit down on the steps next to one another.

"This came for you this morning. I saw the messenger riding in and went to greet him before nosier eyes saw it."

I couldn't repress an eye roll as I reached in the direction of the parchment. "As if ye are not the nosiest person in all of the keep, Adelle?"

"Well, I'll not disagree with you, but would you have rather Eoin retrieved it? It's from Arran."

My heart thumped painfully at the mention of his name, and I found that my hands were shaking as I snatched his letter from her hand. "I suppose ye will be waiting until I share what's inside of it with ye?"

Adelle nodded and grinned widely. "What kind of a question is that? Of course I will be waiting."

It took me little time to read the contents of his letter. It contained only a few lines of his jagged script. "He wants me to meet him at a cottage he says is near the castle grounds. I doona believe I've been there before." I paused, unsure how to express how I truly felt over his request. "I doona know if I should go."

Adelle sat quietly, as if thinking over the best advice to give me. "Do you want to see him, Blaire?"

The words slipped out easily, without hesitation. "Aye, o'course I do. I miss him every moment that I am not with him. But he is married, and I doona wish to tempt him to break his vows."

Adelle reached over and squeezed my hand gently. "You are making him do nothing. Would you like to hear my opinion? I'll only give it if you wish me to."

I nodded, enjoying the feeling of her hand around mine. I'd been small when my mother passed away, and Adelle was the closest thing I'd ever had to a mum. "Aye, I wish it greatly."

"I don't know how wise it would be for you to listen to an old, modern heathen like myself, so take what I have to say with a grain of salt. Relationships are far less black and white than some people wish to make them appear. There are some instances when life causes us to make decisions we wish we didn't have to make, but those things should not be used as an excuse to deny ourselves happiness. Arran's marriage to Edana was one of those decisions." She hesitated, as if unsure of how to express what was in her heart. "Do you understand what I'm saying?"

"Perhaps. Ye believe I should meet him, aye?"

She nodded slowly, squeezing my hand more tightly before standing. "If you want to, then yes. Don't deny yourself moments of joy with the one you love. It is Arran's decision to make, and it seems he has made it already by asking you to meet him. Guilt is a useless emotion. Do as your heart wishes. You will regret it when you're older if you do not."

She started back up the stairs, leaving me alone in the stairwell as I called up to her. "Thank ye, Adelle. I'm not sure if ye helped me at all, but I appreciate yer words nonetheless."

Adelle stopped at the top step and laughed loudly. "I'm not very good at advice. Ask Bri. She'll vouch to the truth in that. She was always more of a mother to me than I was to her. My point is that I regret the things that I didn't do more than the things that I did. And believe me, I was a wild child in my younger years. There weren't many things that I didn't do."

With that, she turned and left. I, though, continued to sit in the stairwell, allowing the candle inside the small lantern to burn away as I gripped tightly to Arran's written words.

Adelle was right. Even if it was the last night I could ever spend with him, I would regret not seeing Arran more than I would regret the guilt of our time spent in each other's arms. Besides, I'd promised him already that, if he sent for me, I would come.

CHAPTER 27

*C*onall Cottage

I arrived at the cottage just before sunset, knowing Arran would not arrive until after dark. The day after Arran's note had arrived, I'd ridden in search of the small cottage, finding it only a short distance away, in the direction of my father's castle. I couldn't believe I'd never seen it before during my many trips to Conall Castle as a small child, but Arran had chosen well. It was beautiful and secluded among the lush, steep hillsides.

I secured my horse and unloaded the basket of Mary's baked goods that I'd stolen from the kitchen just before leaving the castle. Making my way inside the one-roomed cottage, I started a fire and dusted out the rarely used room as best I could. I spread the food out on the small wooden table and was trying to catch a glimpse of my reflection from a sword that hung upon the wall when I heard the sound of a horse approaching outside.

However my face and hair appeared would have to do. Taking a deep breath for courage, I stepped outside to greet Arran.

He was as beautiful as I'd ever seen him. The last rays of sunlight cast down upon him as he rode in, illuminating his blonde hair and striking, deep blue eyes. He smiled, but it was not the unrestrained smile of excitement that I'd expected. Tension etched his face. And as he dismounted, I sensed that something was very wrong. His desire to meet me was not for the reason I'd believed.

Suddenly embarrassed by the spread I'd laid out for us inside, I moved to block his entry into the cottage, no longer wishing for him to see what I'd

321

brought for us. He didn't say hello as he moved toward me, but silently pulled me into his arms as I stood in the doorway of the cottage.

He held me closely, not kissing me nor speaking as my head pressed snuggly against his chest. His hold frightened me. He clung to me as if he feared he would not ever see me again. "Arran." His name came out of me rather breathlessly. He held me that tightly. "Are ye well? Are ye ill or injured? Ye are frightening me."

I turned my head to look up at him as he finally loosened his hold and lowered his eyes to meet mine.

"Nay, lass, I am not ill or injured, and I dinna mean to frighten ye, but I am not so well, either."

"Come inside. 'Tis getting cold." I was no longer worried about him seeing the food spread out for him. He was far too troubled to notice.

I held onto his hand as I led him inside. We both sat on the edge of the bed that was against the back wall of the room. I turned to him, taking both of his hands into mine, each moment of silence a warning that my heart was about to break once more. "What is it, Arran? Ye canna stay silent any longer. What has happened?"

***

*H*e couldn't begin to know how to tell her what he must. The words lodged in his throat, content to stay there forever if his conscience would allow it. Once he said the words aloud, he would be forced to watch Blaire's heart break all over again, the same as it had the day she'd disappeared into another century.

He'd sworn that if he ever got her back, he would never let her go. That if it meant he would burn in hell, he would do so to be with her. But all of that was before his child came to be, an innocent in all of his mistakes. Arran could no longer allow himself to be selfish.

"May I kiss ye, lass? And then I will tell ye what I must, though I wish dearly that I dinna have to do so."

***

I nodded, but as his lips touched mine, the room grew colder. Instead of the warmth that his touch always evoked in me, an icy winter spread through my limbs, snapping every branch of hope I'd held for this evening spent with him. This was a kiss of goodbye, and my body rebelled against it. I pulled away from him, shaking my head as tears threatened. "Nay, Arran. I willna allow ye to do what ye are about to do. I canna lose ye again."

He stood abruptly, running his hands over his face and through his hair as he often did when he was nervous. He'd done so ever since he was a child. "I'm so verra sorry, lass. Ye canna know how much it pains me."

I stood as well, anger suddenly replacing any sadness. I'd known that he would be unable to live with the guilt, but why had he not agreed with me when I'd warned him our last time together? It was cruel of him to allow me to hope, only to destroy it once more. How many times could one man break and heal a heart?

I moved in front of him, shoving him as roughly as I could in the chest, determined to express my frustration and pain in any way other than tears. "Doona ye dare apologize to me. Why did ye ask me to come here only to tell me that ye can no longer do this? Ye had to know that I would believe ye were asking me to come and be with ye as ye promised me that ye would."

He grabbed me roughly by both arms.

"Perhaps I shouldna have asked ye to come here, but I couldna keep myself from seeing ye one last time."

I jerked out of his grasp. "Ye are selfish and cruel, Arran. What changed since I last saw ye? Ye should have told me then that we couldna be together, even if only to hold one another as we did that night. I knew ye were too good of a man to allow yerself to do even that any longer while married to another."

"Edana is with child."

'Twas not what I'd thought he would say, and the shock of his words must have shown on my face for he quickly continued.

"I expect my expression was quite similar to yers when she told me, lass. I have not touched Edana since I knew ye were back, but she says it happened shortly after our wedding."

I could think of little to say and slowly moved to sit down on the bed once more. "So that is why then? Ye can no longer meet with me for the sake of the child?"

"Aye, lass. I shall be a good man for my child, even if it shall break my own heart to do so, leaving me a shell of a man. If she wasna carrying my bairn, I swear to ye I would spend every moment possible with ye for the rest of my life."

He sat down next to me on the bed, crawling into the middle of it as he pulled me into his arms. Silently, I lay with my head against his chest, savoring the last moments I would hold him in my arms. I couldn't fault him for this. If he didn't act with honor now, he would not be the man who owned my heart.

"Can ye forgive me, lass?" He whispered the words into my hair as he gently kissed the top of my head.

"There is naught for me to forgive. Ye couldna have known I would return to ye, but I willna lie to ye and tell ye that my heart is not shattered, and I'm mighty jealous of yer wee wench of a wife."

He shifted in surprise, tilting my head up so that I was looking into his eyes. "Ye have nothing to be jealous of, love. 'Tis only ye that shall ever hold my heart."

I shook my head in disagreement. "Nay, ye are wrong. I'm not jealous of Edana, only that she carries yer child. If only we'd both not been so foolish, that was a joy meant for me. And I willna be the only one to hold yer heart. The child she carries will and already does, or ye would not be here ending this thing that is between us."

He couldn't argue. He knew the truth in what I said. Instead, he simply held me close to him, rubbing my back as his lips lay on top of my hair.

Eventually, I fell asleep. When I awoke the next morning to the first rays of light shining into the space around the doorway, Arran was gone.

J was not surprised to find that he'd gone sometime in the night, but it made the finality of his farewell all the more painful. As far as I knew, there was no rush for me to get back to the castle, so I spent the morning inside the cottage with my arms wrapped around my knees, curled up in the bed, weeping.

I wept for Arran and his foolish choices that had gotten us to this point. I wept for myself and my ignorance. I wept so that once I gathered the strength to leave this place of refuge, so separated from anyone else, that I would not cry for Arran Conall ever again.

Midday, I rose and tidied things before splashing my face with the cold water from the washstand, scrubbing away any remnants of tears. The iciness of the water brought forth an idea. I quickly stepped outside to see if the weather would allow it. Summer was upon Scotland, and the weather, usually damp and cold, was now pleasant and tolerable. I twisted in my dress, missing the freedom that clothing in the twenty-first century had given me. Unfortunately, 'twas still many years before women would wear trousers.

I walked in a circle around the cottage to ensure my solitude as I set my mind to going out to the sea. A place I knew of along the beach on the way back to Conall Castle was just as secluded as the cottage. It had been years since I'd swum in the ocean; not that I had done it verra many times, anyway. The seawater was much too cold. But today it seemed a good idea, the appropriate medicine for my tender heart.

The water would hurt at first, its icy touch like a thousand pinpricks in my porcelain skin, but the pain would quickly fade and a numbness would replace it, a numbness that I hoped would work its way into my heart.

Ensuring that everything inside the cottage was just as it had been before my arrival, I mounted my horse and set out for the sea.

* * *

As I'd expected, no one else enjoyed the shore. Although the waves were larger than I'd hoped, I was not going to let that keep me from a swim. I stripped bare, leaving my dress and underclothes on a mossy rock as I descended into the shallowest part of the water.

Two grassy hillsides on either side separated an inlet of ocean from the vast openness of the rest of the sea. A secluded strip of water, perfect for my chilling dip.

The first touch of water was so shocking I was afraid I'd pull my foot away to find that my toes had fallen off, frozen by the water's tight grip on a winter long over. The air outside might have begun to warm, but the ocean had yet to catch up to the changing of the seasons.

Intent on not changing my mind, I decided it was best to plunge right in, and I dove headfirst into the sea.

I'd expected the ocean depth to deepen quickly, but instead, my head cracked hard on a rock on the sea floor. As I pushed myself up to break the surface of the water, I reached up to touch my head and gasped as my hand came away covered in blood.

I could taste the saltiness of it dripping into my mouth. I struggled to catch my breath due to the frigid water. The sky began to swirl above me, and I feared I was bleeding heavily. Before I could drag myself out onto the shore, darkness closed in around me.

* * *

The jostling of the horse that carried me caused me to open my eyes, but the effort that it took to do so sent such a pain traveling down my head and through my back that I shut them quickly once more.

I was naked; I could tell by the feeling of the horse's hair upon my calves. But I was discreetly covered by a tartan that I recognized as that of the Conalls' guests. "Where are my clothes?"

The man cradling me in his arms as he steered the horse answered softly, taking care that no loud noise would hurt my head further.

"I expect they are wherever ye left them, lass. I dinna take the time to look for them. Ye were bleeding something awful. I thought it best to get to ye before ye drowned or bled to death."

"Thank ye." The words sounded distant, as if it was not me that said them. Although I wondered who my rescuer might be, I was too weak for any more conversation. I could see Conall Castle up ahead, yet still I closed my eyes and drifted away once more.

he Castle Formerly Known as Kinnaird

ormod had not actually been in the castle since he was a small child, but he remembered the hallways well, and he had no trouble finding Edana's bedchamber.

Everyone in the castle was asleep and, if the rumors in the village were true, Arran Conall had been away for days visiting his brother at Conall Castle. For this reason, he'd decided to make this unexpected visit to Edana.

He knew Edana would be furious that Arran had gone and would assume that their plan to claim she was carrying Arran's child had not gone as hoped. It seemed she was right, but Tormod could not allow her to believe so. She had to continue to feign the pregnancy so that she could ignorantly take the poison at just the right time.

He knocked softly on her door, not wanting to draw attention from elsewhere within the castle. There were many men on duty, and he'd been lucky to make it so far undetected. It took a moment for Edana to answer. He couldn't keep his eyes from widening at the sight of her.

Her eyes were red, glassy. She was deep in her cups. Drunk. The longer he spent time with her, the more he knew that the lass had more in common with her father than she realized.

She stepped out of the way, nearly tripping, and Tormod quickly darted inside to help steady her. "What are ye doing, lass? Tis not appropriate for the lady of the castle to drink so much."

Edana sat down on the edge of her bed and patted the cover to suggest he should join her. "No one will know how I'm behaving. I am all alone here. My husband doesna care that I carry his child. He still finds time to visit his lover."

Tormod sat next to her, taking the goblet of ale from her hands. "Edana, ye are not really with his child."

"It doesna matter. The plan dinna work as ye hoped it would."

He forced himself to reach up and stroke her hair. "Just give it a while, lass. As time moves on, he will grow accustomed to the idea of a child, and he will love what he believes is growing inside of ye."

"And what will we do when he realizes that there is no child? Ye said we would think of something, but I canna continue to do this if I doona know that there is a safe way out of it. He canna know that we lied to him."

Tormod nodded and pulled his hand away. "Aye, lass, I know. 'Tis why I've come to ye. I have acquired an herbal drink that will make ye bleed when the time comes that Arran grows suspicious. It will appear as if ye lost the child. Then he will never know that ye dinna tell him the truth. He will only be lost in the grief of his unborn child. He will then be at his weakest."

"So it will do no harm to me?"

He stood and helped move her up higher onto the bed so that he could settle her for the night. Her eyelids were starting to droop. He was thankful that he would not have to take her into his arms this evening. "Nay, lass. It will do no more harm to ye than ye've done to yerself this night. Now, rest. I believe Arran is due to return home tomorrow."

Once her eyes closed, he slipped out silently, grinning at how easily she'd accepted his lie.

onall Castle

"So you will stay then?" Bri and Adelle sat on either side of me, grinning, while a smiling Mary stood at the end of the bed. I gingerly nodded so as not to hurt my aching head.

It had been one week since I'd knocked myself unconscious during my ocean swim. While the wound on the top of my head was healing and hurting less, my chest worried me. It rattled with every breath I drew, and I felt more ill each day. I'd yet to mention my concerns to anyone; I had already caused them enough trouble.

"Aye. If ye will have me, I shall. I love my father, but I doona wish to return home with him. Have any of ye spoken to him about this? He will not be happy that I wish to stay here."

I watched as the three of them shared glances back and forth. Finally, Mary spoke up. "Aye, lass. He said that he would leave the decision to ye, but before ye make up yer mind, he has something else he wishes to speak to ye about. I believe he will be in shortly. 'Tis why we've come to ye now. We wished to ask ye to stay before he has a chance to talk to ye."

"And what is it that he wishes to ask me?" The rattling in my chest built. I swallowed hard to repress the cough that threatened to burst forth. I was being fussed over enough by these three ladies and didn't see reason to cause them more worry.

Standing, Adelle rolled her eyes dramatically, reddening with frustration.

"He made us promise we wouldn't say anything to you, but I told him I think he's a fool for even bringing it up."

"Mom." Bri's voice served as a warning of the sound of footsteps approaching my room.

Baodan, Lady McMillan's eldest son and my watery savior, stepped inside the doorway, leaning his tall body into the wood frame. "Ach, excuse me. I dinna know that Blaire already had visitors. I shall take my leave and return at a later time."

"Oh, nonsense," said Bri. "We were all just leaving." She stood and smiled at me quickly before waving toward Adelle and Mary, indicating that they should follow her.

Adelle called back to me over her shoulder as they walked out of the room. "We'll be back this evening. I want to hear what you told your father."

I scooted back in the bed so that I could sit up straight. As Baodan approached me, he pulled his left hand out from behind his back, revealing my rumpled dress inside his grasp. "I will not disturb ye long, lass. I only wished to return this to ye. How are ye feeling?"

I took the dress, smiling at him in appreciation. "Thank ye. I feel much better. My head only aches a little now." As if to refute my claim, the cough that I'd held back earlier would no longer be repressed, and I lost myself in a fit of painful hacking that caused my head to pound severely.

Baodan quickly moved beside me, placing one hand on my shoulder and another on my back to steady me. "There ye are, lass. Yer head may feel a wee bit better, but ye are not well, are ye? Have ye told anyone of this cough?"

I shook my head guiltily. "Nay, I havena. Tis nothing, I'm sure."

"Tis not nothing, lass. Ye breathed in too much of the cold sea water, and ill ye are. I'll send for someone to see to ye."

He moved away from me, and I instinctively reached out to grab his hand to stop him. "Nay, please doona do so. If it gets worse, I shall tell them, but I doona want a fuss over nothing."

"As ye wish, lass, but please promise me that ye will stay abed and rest until 'tis gone. I wished to speak with ye further, but I'll leave ye be for a while. Ye look as if ye could use some sleep."

"Fine, I promise. But what did ye wish to speak with me about?" I was curious, but he was right. I was exhausted, and the coughing had caused my head to ache dreadfully.

"Tis not urgent that I speak to ye about it now. We'll have time to do so later." He smiled at the confused expression on my face and ducked his head as he retreated from the room.

Twas the first time I'd actually spoken to Baodan alone aside from the moment on the horse, but I wasna nearly conscious enough then for that to constitute conversation. I couldn't imagine what he seemed so keen to discuss with me.

I quickly drifted into a restless and short-lived sleep, stirring as I felt my father's lips lightly touch my forehead.

"Ye scared me badly, Blaire. When Baodan rode up with ye, yer head bleeding so fiercely, I thought for a moment I would lose ye. Ye are all I had after yer mother died. I canna bear the thought of losing ye, as well."

I reached up to dash away a rogue tear running down his face, and he quickly grunted in embarrassment. "Ach, I am not a crying man, but a father's love for his children is enough to bring a man to his knees. How are ye feeling, love?"

"Better." I dinna say more, not trusting my cough to stay silent otherwise.

"I'm sure that Bri, Mary, and Adelle have already been to see ye. Did they tell ye what I've come to speak with ye about?"

"Nay, but Adelle seemed none too pleased about it."

Father smirked rather uncharacteristically. "Aye, I suppose she dinna. She's a strange lass, but I canna say that I doona like her. She's fiery like ye, Blaire. I am glad that she was there to take care of ye in yer time away."

I smiled. "Aye, me too. Now what is it, Father?" A small cough escaped, but I was able to hold off any more so that it seemed as if I had only cleared my throat.

Intuitively, he stood and moved to the water basin to pour me some water. Returning to my side, he said, "Baodan has asked me for permission to marry ye."

I spit up all of the water in my mouth. "What?" I struggled to get the word out in between a fit of coughing.

Worry creased Father's brow as he scooted in closer, cradling me as Baodan had done earlier. Eventually, the coughing subsided and father shook his head in dismay. "That must be seen to, lass."

I dinna argue as I had done earlier. He was right. Each fit of coughing grew louder and lasted longer than the time before. "What did ye just tell me, Da?"

"Baodan came to me a few days ago and asked permission to marry ye."

"Why would he do such a thing? Are ye sure that ye dinna arrange this? Ye did it once before. What did ye tell him?"

He took both of my hands in his own, stroking them tenderly. "Nay, lass, I did no such thing. I was wrong before to send ye here to wed Eoin, but please believe me, I only did it because I thought it best for ye."

"I know." And I did know. I was the most precious thing in the world to him. He was simply at a loss as to what to do with me.

"I told him the choice was yers, lass. I will not make such a decision for ye again."

That was at least some relief. "Thank ye. Ye doona think that I should do it, do ye, Father?"

He looked down and shrugged. "I doona know, lass, but I believe him to be a good man." Meeting my gaze again, he asked, "What will ye do if ye doona marry? Ye are welcome to return home, but I doona believe that ye wish to do so. What is here for ye? Ye were not meant to work in the Conall's house. Ye deserve a family and keep of yer own."

His question was fair, but one I'd given little thought to. "I'm unsure, Father. But I doona know Baodan. I doubt I could ever love him."

"Ye canna know that for sure, lass. I dinna love yer mother at all when we married, but she was my very soul by the time she left this world. I will not advise ye what to do. Ye are a sharp lass. I shall let ye decide. All I ask is that ye think on it. Speak with him. Get to know him before the McMillans leave in three days time."

I nodded, unsure of what to say. Father could tell that I needed rest. He bent to kiss me once more. "I love ye, lass. Sleep now and think of it come morning."

After tucking the blankets around me, he poured more water into my cup then blew out the candles, leaving me in darkness. Before sleep finally took me, I lay awake for hours, all that he'd said turning over in my mind.

CHAPTER 30

The Roadside Inn – Present Day

"What's the matter, love? What have ye seen?"

Morna jumped at the sound of her husband's voice. Slowly she opened her eyes, pulling herself out of the dream. "Ach, Jerry. It doesna seem to matter how often I help them, they always find a pathway to trouble."

He sat with her, wrapping his frail, bony arms around her as she'd known he would, acting as the supporter he'd always been for her. "Who, lass? What has happened?"

"Blaire is verra sick. I doona think she will heal on her own. She needs modern medicine to keep her from dying. I believe Bri will look for a way to heal her. If I can only leave something in the spell room for her, she will find it without having to travel forward. It takes a toll on the body, and I doona think Bri should go through again."

"Why dinna ye say so, love? Give me what ye need to leave for her, and I shall go at once. I know ye doona like to return to the castle. I'll go and be back in time for supper."

Morna stood and kissed her husband firmly on the mouth. "I knew there was a reason I married ye."

Leaving him smiling in the living room, she went in search of the antibiotics and all of the other medications needed to rid Blaire of the sickness that threatened her life.

1 646

*B*y the next morning, I was coughing up blood and my skin was so warm to the touch that sweat covered my body. I drifted in and out of sleep, delirious, nonsensical dreams dancing before my eyes.

When the visions stayed present while awake, my worry increased. My vision remained constantly blurred, and I could hardly register when someone was in the room with me or when water was being poured down my throat. I knew that someone stayed in my company, washing me, trying to coax me to eat, changing my sweaty bedclothes and bloodied cough rags, but didn't know who. I could hardly speak, I was so overcome with fever. And I couldn't move without the aid of another.

Fluid built deep within my lungs. I knew death was coming for me.

Each morning, Bri would come to dose me with medicine. Advil that she'd brought back with her the last time she'd passed through the portal. It helped in breaking the fever only for a little while. With each passing day, the medicine seemed to burn off more quickly, and I found myself in delirium once more.

On the fourth morning, I prepared myself to say my goodbyes. The fever had receded slightly, and only one person demanded the forefront of my mind. After Bri came to administer the pills, I asked her to stay so that I could take advantage of what I assumed would be a brief respite from my delirium.

Knowing I would not last long, I gave quick instructions. "Bri, I need ye to get me some parchment and a pen. I need to write to Arran and tell him what is happening. I need him to come and say goodbye."

I could sense that Bri wanted to argue, but she looked me over and held her tongue. She, too, could tell that there was not much life left in me. I scribbled the note with haste, grimacing when a slight splatter of blood landed on the parchment as I coughed. I handed it over to her, and she sealed it without reading, respecting my privacy, as I'd known she would.

"Ye will send someone with it right away, aye?"

She nodded and placed a moist rag on my forehead. "Of course I will. Now rest. I'll take it to a messenger now."

"Thank ye." I shut my eyes as she left, feeling more peaceful than I had in days. I only had to hold on until Arran could come and bid me farewell.

*B*ri ran through the castle and out the back doors in search of Kip, calling out to him before she even reached the stables. "Kip, can you call one of the lads that helps you with the horses straight away? I need one of them to ride to Arran."

She slowed her pace as she rounded the corner into the stable to find Kip already ordering a young lad to mount up for the ride.

"He shall take good care of it. Won't ye, lad?"

The boy nodded, and Bri gratefully handed the parchment up to him, only pausing to kiss Kip lightly on the cheek before taking off at a full run back to the castle. It was time for her to enter the spell room again. She'd be damned before she let Blaire die.

Flying through the castle, Bri nearly slipped on the steps leading down into the basement. She recovered quickly, not pausing to catch her breath until she stared, open-mouthed, into the contents of Morna's spell room.

Sitting on top of the spell book was everything they needed—syringes filled with antibiotics, more Advil, medicine to break up the fluid in Blaire's chest. All of it sat atop the faded, yellow parchment as if it had always been there.

She almost turned to stop the messenger, but decided it best to let him go. Modern medicines would help greatly, but as sick as Blaire was, she didn't know if it would be enough to save her. In case they didn't, she couldn't deny Blaire's last wish to see Arran.

Smiling, Bri moved into the spell room to gather up the treasures. Morna's days of magic had not ended with their last trip into the past. She was watching over the Conalls and her beloved home still, centuries away from them all.

---

*T*he messenger rode fast, only stopping for a few hours of rest and to relieve himself when necessary. He'd seen the panic in the lady's eyes as she'd brought the parchment to him. He knew not what information Arran Conall needed so desperately, but the lad's family had been loyal to the Conalls for decades. He would not be the first of his people to disappoint them.

He made the journey in half the time it would have taken most. Knowing his horse was in desperate need of rest, he stopped at the edge of the village and knocked on a stranger's door to see if he could pay for a stall for his horse while he attended to his duty.

The knock on the door surprised Tormod. Surely Edana would not be visiting at this time of day, and everyone else in the village knew better than to come to his home. He swung the door open to find a travel-weary young lad with dirt on his face and clothing.

"What do ye want?" Tormod stared down at the lad, hoping that his size alone would be enough to strike fear in the boy.

"Excuse me, sir. I'm traveling from Conall Keep and am on my way to deliver a message to yer laird. I was only hoping ye would allow my horse to rest here for a bit whilst I complete my task."

"Conall Keep, ye say? Let me see this note that ye carry." The boy backed away from him, and Tormod floundered for an explanation for his request. "I only want to make sure that ye come from where ye say, and then I shall return the letter to ye and allow yer horse to rest here."

Hesitation crossed the boy's face, but eventually he extended the parchment toward Tormod. Tormod snatched it out of the lad's hand before ripping it open to read its contents. He then tossed the letter into the fire.

The boy lunged at him, but Tormod caught him swiftly by the throat, pushing him into the wall. "I suggest ye get on yer horse and ride back to Conall Castle. Tell whoever sent ye that ye delivered their message just as intended. Ye would not want them thinking that ye failed them, would ye?"

The boy shook uncontrollably under Tormod's heavy hands, and his face looked conflicted as he took in his words. "Aye, sir. Ye are right. If ye will only allow me to leave, I shall do as ye ask."

"O'course ye will, lad. Now get out of here and doona ever knock on my door again. Understand?"

The lad nodded and quickly mounted his horse, fleeing in the direction of Conall Castle. Tormod smiled ghoulishly as he shut the door. Not only was Arran about to lose his wife and child but his lover, as well. And he would believe she died without him bidding her farewell.

Everything was beginning to lean in his favor.

CHAPTER 31

Two months had passed since the day Bri, Adelle, and Mary had come charging into my room and rather excitedly poked me in the bum with some sort of sharp instrument. That day and the days following, I'd been too overcome with fever to question or worry about what it was they were doing to me. Eventually, though, the fever broke for the last time. Slowly but surely, I started regaining my health.

Still, there was no doubt just how close to death I'd come. People seemed nervous around me, avoiding much in the way of conversation, as if they were afraid I would break if touched or spoken to. I'd still not left my bedchamber. The closest to the outdoors I'd come were the few short moments each morning that someone helped me to the window, where I sat and enjoyed the summer breeze.

Only the past few weeks were fresh in my memory, but I knew my days had settled into the same routine for months. Mary brought meals throughout the day, staying with me to ensure that I finished every bite. Afterward, she told me stories while combing my hair or rubbing my feet.

Each morning, my father visited, but he only stayed a short while before heading out to help Eoin with whatever task needed doing. He would not return home until I was well, but he refused to be a guest in the Conall home without contributing in some way to their well-being.

The afternoons were spent with Bri and Adelle. This was my favorite time of day, for the two women were the only ones who had enough faith in Morna's medicines not to tiptoe around me, fearing that any stress might cause my death. They talked freely, and I usually ended up laughing so much that the coughing fits returned. Whenever that happened, Mary appeared to shoo them from the room.

I could tell by the angle of light through the window that it was almost time for Bri and Adelle to arrive. As if summoned by magic, they appeared just as theys crossed my mind.

"Hello, hello!" Adelle clapped her hands together, smiling broadly. "You look much better today, hon. Soon it will be time for you to get outside and stretch your legs. It's certainly nice enough for you to do so, and you've spent so much time in bed. It's important for you to start rebuilding your muscle strength. I'm sure you're as weak as a new babe. I think tomorrow one of us will get you outside." She moved across the room to open the window wide, allowing the sunlight and fresh air to seep inside.

"I'll not argue with ye. My legs have shriveled away to nothing. Come and sit with me."

Both ladies hiked up their dresses and sat with their legs crisscrossed on the end of the bed.

"Mom's right. You're looking much better." Bri laughed as she patted me lightly on the knee. "What did you think that first night I came and stuck that needle in your rear end?"

"I dinna know what ye were doing, but I was far too ill to care. Truthfully, I doona remember much of these past months. Only the past few weeks are clear to me."

Adelle fidgeted, and I could tell she had something she really wanted to say but didn't know if she should.

"What is it, Adelle? Please doona be like Mary and speak to me like I might die from real conversation."

Adelle laughed and stopped bouncing the bed with her jittery movements. "Fine. What have you decided about Baodan? You do remember your father telling you that Baodan asked him for your hand in marriage, right?"

"Aye, I do remember, but Father has not mentioned it again, and Baodan does not speak of it when he visits. He has come to sit with me each evening the past few nights, but says little." I nibbled my lower lip and frowned. "I'm not so keen to bring up his proposal."

Bri's brows drew together as she studied me. "Is that all you remember of your time with Baodan? Only the last few days?"

"Aye, is there more that I should remember? If there is, I am lost to it. The fever made everything a dream."

Bri stood and went to shut the door to my bedchamber so that no passerby would hear our conversation. "Yes, but I'm not surprised that you don't remember it. Baodan has been at your side every day. When you were at your worst, it was he that replaced your bloodied rags with clean ones and lifted you so that we could clean you and change your bedding. He wiped your cheeks with a wet cloth and brushed the hair out of your face, only leaving you when we instructed him that he must. It's only been since you've been more yourself that he's stopped visiting as often."

It was surprising to me that he'd done so, and I didn't understand his reasons. "Does he feel that much guilt over what happened, do ye think? Twas not his fault. I jumped into the water all on my own. If he'd not been there, I would've died that day."

Adelle shook her head. "No, I don't think he feels guilty. I think he's quite taken with you, dear. I think perhaps I was wrong to react the way I did to your father's news that Baodan wants to marry you." Adelle winced with remorse.

I felt the heat of a blush creep up my neck. "What are ye saying, Adelle? Ye believe I should marry him? He's not even asked me. Perhaps he's changed his mind."

"I'm not saying you should agree to marriage. Not yet. Just get to know him. See if anything is there between the two of you. And I don't think he's changed his mind. I heard him asking Mary earlier if he could take you for a short ride tomorrow, just the two of you. Go with him and think about whatever he says to you. I think he's a good man. It's rare to see someone be so attentive when he hardly knows you."

"Mom's right," Bri agreed. "He's been incredibly caring toward you. But Blaire, just know that you are welcome to stay here forever if you wish. Truly. Do not say yes to him because you feel you have no other choice." She stood and motioned to her mother to do the same. "We should go. I expect he will be along shortly."

I called out to stop Bri from departing, hoping to speak to her alone about the one thing that had hung at the edge of my mind even during the worst of my fever. "Wait, Bri. Can I speak to ye a moment alone?"

"Of course." Bri stepped back inside, and Adelle waved at me before disappearing through the doorway. Sitting on the chair next to my bed, Bri crossed her legs. "What's up?"

I hesitated, not wanting to show how much I cared what her answer would be. "Arran... did he...did he come at all while I was ill?"

I knew she would not lie to me. As I'd hoped, she answered without hesitation. "No, he didn't. And he sent no letter back in response to yours."

"Is it possible that he dinna receive it? Mayhap the messenger lost it along the way."

Bri blinked sad eyes at me. "No, I'm so sorry, but I spoke to the messenger we sent myself after he returned. He told me that he delivered it to Arran's hands directly. The man has no reason to lie."

"Aye, I suppose 'tis true. Thank ye. That's all I needed to know. If ye doona mind, I'd like to be alone now."

Bri stood and nodded once. "Absolutely. I'll see you in the morning. Get some rest."

She'd only just made it to the doorway when Baodan appeared, and they passed each other as she made her way out of my room. He smiled at me but remained in the doorway. I was thankful; it seemed he would not be staying long.

"I'm sorry I dinna come to see ye earlier today," Baodan said. "I've been working on something for ye that kept me away. Do ye think ye would feel up to accompanying me somewhere tomorrow? We willna go far from the castle, and I've received Mary's blessing to get ye out of doors for awhile."

Images of Arran reading my note, learning that I was dying, and choosing not to come to my side, pierced my heart. He was truly gone from my life. I pushed away the pain and smiled as brightly as I could at Baodan. "Aye, I would like that verra much."

"I am pleased to hear it, lass. I will see you soon, then."

With a nod, he ducked under the doorway and left. I rolled over so I could stare into the setting sun. Perhaps the light would burn all images of Arran from my mind.

CHAPTER 32

$\mathcal{M}$ary lay the dress she'd picked out for me over the back of the chair next to my bed then pulled back the curtain so that the morning light streamed in. "Nay, lass. I doona think 'tis a good idea for ye to strain yerself by bathing right before ye go outside. The outing will be hard enough on its own."

"Do ye want me to call for Adelle and Bri, or will ye oblige and help me yerself? I'm sure they would be more than happy to do it."

"Nay, lass," Mary said, sounding flustered. "Please doona go hollering, ye will only make Adelle do the same. If ye insist, I shall have a bath drawn for ye, and if ye wish to wear another dress I shall retrieve it."

I smiled triumphantly as I pushed myself upright and swung my shaky legs over the side of the bed. "I insist. I doona wish to be proposed to while looking a mess. And I can smell myself. It has been far too long since I've had more than a cloth bath."

"Aye, fine. I do agree that ye smell a wee bit like old cheese. Do ye have any other demands of me?"

Mary feigned annoyance, but I could tell she was happy to help and glad that I was feeling well enough to bathe. "Aye, can ye have Bri and Adelle come? I'd like Bri to pin up my hair, and Adelle willna like it if she is left out of the preparations."

"Aye, I suppose ye are right about that, as well. Give me a moment. I shall fetch them."

"No need," came Adelle's voice from the doorway. "We're here. We saw Baodan this morning, and he told us you agreed to accompany him. We thought we would come and help you get ready."

Adelle crossed the room and gave me a light hug. Then she helped me to my feet as a smiling Bri extended a treasure in my direction.

"Look what I've brought for you! I went down into the spell room and retrieved it from your pile of modern clothes. It will make you feel more human, and you'll like what it does to the way your dress looks."

"Aye, I know. It can work miracles." I reached for the bra, pressing it tightly to my chest. "But do ye not think that he will notice it?"

Adelle laughed heartily, garnering a lower-yer-voice-before-I-thump-ye look from Mary. "If it was me accompanying Baodan today, then yes, he might. But I don't think you're the sort of girl to let a man pass a base on the first date."

"Base?" Mary and I said in unison, sending both Bri and Adelle into a fit of laughter.

"Never mind, dear," exclaimed Adelle between snorts. "Let's start getting you cleaned up."

Adelle led me toward the tub while Mary instructed the men who brought in steaming pails of water. Before long, I was being tugged and pushed and prodded in different directions as all three women worked diligently to prepare me for the outing.

* * *

he Castle Formerly Known as Kinnaird

*I*f Arran was counting correctly, Edana should have been swelling more beneath her clothing than she seemed to be. It was true that he was no expert in such matters, but it had been at least four and a half moons since he'd shared her bed, and he could not see the slightest change in her physical appearance.

He'd also taken notice of how well she seemed to be feeling. She'd not been troubled by the bouts of ill stomach he knew many women suffered during their beginning stages of being with child. It had been bothering him for days, the wondering, and he knew he could not keep his questions at bay any longer.

He reached across the table where they sat while eating their evening meal. Placing his hand gently on her shoulder, he said, "Edana, I wish to ask ye something, but I doona want ye to be angry at the question."

She sat back in her chair, malice clear in her eyes. Each day he could sense her disdain for him a little more sharply.

"Why would ye think I should get angry? Are ye suggesting that I'm angry often?"

There was no reason to be gentle with her. Arran knew that regardless of what he said, Edana would find a reason to be upset by his words. "Aye. Exactly. Ye stay angry all the time. Ye scream at people who have done naught but help ye, and I believe ye are a liar."

Her face blanched, and something deep within told him his suspicions were right.

"What do ye mean?" she said, her voice so low and breathless he almost didn't hear the question. "What could I have lied to ye about?"

"I doona believe ye are with child, Edana. Ye havena swollen at all, and it has been too long for ye not to have done so."

She pushed away from the table and stood, and Arran could see that her hands shook with rage. "I canna believe that ye would insult me so," she said, her voice rising. "'Tis only that ye canna see how I've grown with my clothes on. Kinnaird women never swell much with their children."

Arran stood, as well, his confidence in his suspicion growing with every word she uttered. "Aye? Is that so, lass? Fine. Why doona ye take yer dress off right here and show me how yer belly grows?"

She stepped away from him, as if afraid he would rip her dress right off of her body. He couldn't deny he was tempted, but he was not the sort of man to disgrace a woman in such a way. Besides, he didn't need to. Her reaction was more than enough to make him certain she was not carrying his child.

"I'll do no such thing, ye wretched man. Do ye think ye cannot touch me for months and then have me take my clothes off? I willna allow ye to do so. When yer child arrives, ye will see what an ignorant fool ye have been."

She turned her back on him and fled the room.

Arran did not go after her. He sat down to finish his meal. She was right about one thing. He was a fool. A fool to have ever believed his wretched wife, and a fool to have denied the one woman who had ever truly loved him. Deep down in his soul, he had sensed from the beginning that Edana had lied to him, from the very night she'd come to him with news of their child.

Whatever misery life with Edana would bring to him, tonight he felt as if he deserved every bit of it.

***

A knock sounded at Tormod's door. If it was the Conall messenger again, he decided he would kill him. Surely the lad wouldn't be so foolish as to knock upon his door twice. And not so late. Night had long since settled over the village.

Tormod opened the door and was nearly knocked to the floor as Edana threw her arms around him, weeping. "Arran knows. He knows I am not carrying his child."

He unwrapped her arms from his neck and pushed her away from him. "Slow down, lass. What do ye mean? Did ye tell him?"

His face flushed with anger at the thought. If she'd been so stupid, he would kill her this night. If she'd ruined their plan with her words, he would not put up with her one moment more.

"Nay, I dinna tell him anything, but he told me that he doesna believe that I am carrying his child. He has noticed that my belly hasna grown, and he thinks I have lied to him."

He turned away from her to grab the glass bottle he'd patiently held onto for months. "Then doona worry, lass. All is fine. If he suspects that ye are lying, it only means that now is the time for ye to take the herbs. Once he believes ye have lost the child, he will blame himself for upsetting ye so. Here." He gave her the bottle. "Take it tonight, lass, once ye are abed. Take every last drop. I shall see ye in a few days after all is done."

Again, she wrapped her arms around him, kissing him quickly on the cheek. "Aye, I shall drink it as soon as I return to the castle. I love ye, Tormod."

He opened the door to show her outside. "Aye, lass, I know ye do."

Once she'd departed, he shut the door and waited. When he was sure she'd be far enough ahead of him that he could follow her unnoticed, he left the house. This promised to be a wonderful night. Edana's death was finally upon him.

CHAPTER 33

$\mathcal{E}$dana took her time returning to the castle after obtaining the herbal solution from Tormod. She wandered the streets of her small village, the only home she'd ever known, battling an inexplicable sense of unease. The village and the people in it came alive for her in a way they never had before, as if she were saying goodbye.

As a young girl, she'd taken after her mother. She'd had a sweet spirit and never understood why her father became angry when she played with the children in the village. She couldn't see the difference between herself and the people that lived under her father's protection outside of the castle walls.

She'd had many friends. Her mother ensured it, taking her out daily to interact with the people of the village, doing her best to make sure Edana understood how blessed she was to live a life in which things came to her easily.

If only her mother had lived, Edana suspected that she would have become a better woman—a woman like her mother. Her father had always been a terrible man, but her mother's death released him from his cage. When that happened, darkness descended over her life.

Her father had never allowed her to leave the castle. Surrounded by the evil that seeped from him, Edana had sensed that her soul was beginning to warp. Her thinking changed, too. The people who had been her childhood friends began to seem unworthy of her attention. She was a Kinnaird, and there were few worthy of her time.

Tonight she felt a shift in that mindset she'd held for so long. As she passed the candlelit windows, she wished she could join the people behind them. To live a simple life, free from the ghosts of her father, was a dream Edana had long since stopped allowing herself to hope for.

But perhaps Tormod was right, and once Arran was gone, she would be free. Together she and Tormod could create the simple life she longed for. He had to be right. Her trust in him was the only thing that kept her moving closer to the castle, even as a small voice in the back of her mind told her to smash the bottle onto the ground and flee from her life here.

Arran spoke the truth when he said that she was easily angered, but it pained her to have it stated so plainly. She wished she could change, but she knew she could not. Her father's grip held tight inside her still, and words of anger and hate slipped off her tongue when words of kindness would not.

She was tired of not being the person she wanted to be. As she entered the castle and climbed the steps to her bedchamber, she vowed to herself that once Arran was gone, she would put all of the past behind her and start anew.

Her bedchamber was empty, as she knew it would be, but she felt uncomfortable at the unease she felt at finding it so. If Arran had decided to wait for her there, she would have been unable to take the herbal solution.

She set the bottle down next to her bed, undressed, and then donned her nightgown. Crawling into bed, she propped the feather pillows so she could sit up. When Arran found her there, it would appear that she'd been in pain and forced to endure an early labor on her own.

Edana knew she would have to drink the contents of the bottle quickly so that she would have time to stash it away, out of sight, before the bleeding began. Once she'd bled enough to raise alarm, she would scream for someone to come to her aid. She only hoped the cramping wouldn't be too painful.

Shaking, she reached for the glass bottle, then wiggled the top off. The scent was potent, and it made her stomach churn. It smelled nothing like any herbs she'd been around, but she was uneducated in such matters. There was no reason for her to believe that the mixture was anything other than what Tormod had told her.

Pinching her nose, she touched the bottle to her lips and quickly tilted it upward. She had to swallow hard and fast to keep from immediately retching out onto the bed. Once she'd drained the bottle's contents, she bent over to place the vial under the bed. She resumed her position—legs spread wide apart—and waited for the bleeding to begin.

At first nothing happened. Other than the foul taste in her mouth, she thought perhaps the process would be a painless one. But just as quickly as she'd begun to hope, a pain settled deep in her belly. She opened her mouth to scream, only to find that no sound would emerge.

The pain spread fast. Fire seared through every inch of her body. Holes burned through every vital organ. Finally, the sounds came—inhuman moans

—so quiet she wondered if her vocal chords had melted when the potion touched them.

She glanced down between her thighs to see blood draining out of her, and knew. Poison. Not the herbal mixture Tormod had promised her.

Just as quickly as the pain had begun, it stopped. Her heart beat slowly in her ears. Her limbs hung lifeless and cold. Blood continued to drain from her body as she realized the mistakes she had made. So many mistakes.

Her father's spirit had never coaxed her to seek revenge on the Conalls. Instead, his spirit had rooted for her demise. The same black presence he'd been in her life had cheerfully led her to her death.

What a fool she'd been to believe Tormod. To believe that a man could love her and want to care for her. To want him to—a man no better than her father.

The one soul who could've given her all she needed, and who would've kindly done so even though he didn't love her, was the man she was about to hurt the most.

Arran would not know that she'd done this to herself. That she'd lied. Once he found her, Edana knew Arran would blame himself and live with the guilt always, a fate he did not deserve. She'd been too foolish to admit that before.

She took her last breath, praying that Arran would one day learn the truth.

Her prayer didn't include herself. She got no less than she'd earned. Casting aside her hopes for a new life, Edana shut her eyes as death took her.

CHAPTER 34

C *onall Castle*

W e'd all expected that Baodan would call for me sometime in the morning, but as the day passed with no sign of him, we quickly learned that we were not as sure of his plans as we thought.

I was ready before midday, all cleaned up, hair pinned back, looking as presentable as I had in months with nowhere yet to go. The morning's preparations exhausted me, so shortly after I was ready, and Bri, Adelle, and Mary were satisfied with my appearance, I lay down and fell quickly asleep.

It felt as if I'd only drifted for a few short moments, but when I awoke to the feeling of a hand lightly grabbing my own, I opened my eyes to see the light from the setting sun fading out my window.

"I'm sorry, lass. I should have been more specific as to when I planned to come for ye. I feel terrible that ye've spent the whole day waiting on me. Ye must be exhausted already."

I was, but I sat up with as much energy as I could manage. I swung my feet over the bed and stood, only slightly shaky. "Nay, doona be sorry. I needed to get up and behave as a human for a while."

I was certain the back of my hair was a mess after sleeping on it most of the day, but I didn't want to fix it in front of him. What did it matter, anyway? I had no real feelings for Baodan; there was no reason to try and impress him.

"Are ye ready, lass? If ye doona feel like ye are ready to leave the castle for a bit, we doona have to go. I wouldna like for ye to make yerself sick again by doing more than ye are ready to do."

I reached up to grab his arm, the thought of spending one more moment in my bedchamber torturous. "Aye, I couldna be more ready to get outdoors for a while. I shall gladly go wherever ye wish to take me."

"That is my hope, lass."

His words made me nervous, and I instantly regretted my previous enthusiasm. I didn't want to make him believe I felt something I did not. If he intended to ask me what everyone around me seemed to think he was going to, I had no answer for him.

I didn't know the man well enough to love him and, even if I grew to know him well, I was certain my heart was not capable of surrendering to another. Regardless of Bri's insistence that I was welcome to stay at the castle as long as I wished, I knew it would not be right to live a lifetime with her family, relying on their charity and friendship.

And Father was right. Even if I could not have the love that I longed for, I did still someday want children—a notion which, before Arran, I had found repulsive. I used to think the idea of children a dreadful thing, but Arran's love had opened a part of me I had not known existed, and even though he was gone from my life, those parts of my soul remained open.

Baodan held tightly onto my hand as we moved slowly down the castle stairs, stopping often to allow me to rest, each step a struggle after being off of my feet for so long.

There was no question that Baodan was a good man. I knew Arran well enough to know that he would not have been as patient with me, and I did not get the feeling that Baodan struggled with drink as Arran sometimes did. Baodan would be a good father. Perhaps if I did not want to be alone forever, Baodan would be a fine choice of a man with whom to spend my life.

I set my mind to consider the possibility. I would listen to all he had to say and hope that the right decision would come to me.

---

*B*aodan lifted me onto his horse with ease. Whether I wanted to or not, I was forced to lean back against him. My muscles were so weak and tired. I trembled terribly from the effort it took just to make it out of the castle.

My weak muscles were enough to make me shake, but within moments of leaving, I became certain I knew where we were headed. Not that Baodan could have known I'd been there before. It wasn't possible that he knew the memories this place would bring up for me, the pain that I had suffered here. No one at the castle, save Adelle, would have known that I'd been here before, and I was certain she didn't know that the cottage was where Baodan planned to take me.

He'd been here today, readying it for this evening. Candles burned inside the windows. The entire place was alight with the soft glow of tiny flames.

Baodan reined in the horse next to the cottage, dismounted, and then carefully helped me down. He continued to hold on to both of my elbows, helping to steady me as he led me inside.

"If I know the three lassies that spend every spare moment by yer side, I expect ye already have some idea as to why I've brought ye here. But I doona wish to speak of that right away. First, I'd like simply to share a meal with ye and visit so that we may get to know one another a bit more. Would that be acceptable to ye, lass?"

"Aye, it would." I sat down in the chair he pulled away from the table for me. I did my best to push away all memories I had of the last time I'd been here.

As soon we started eating, Baodan said, "I know that I do not know ye well, lass, and ye do not know me, either. But 'tis my ardent wish that we both grow to know each other better."

"Aye? Well, anything ye wish to know, I shall tell ye. Many think I am much too free with what I say." The food was delicious, and I relished in the enjoyment of eating at a table rather than in bed.

"I do not mind straightforwardness in a lass. My beloved wife was much the same way."

I certainly had not suspected that he'd been married before. While I knew him to be at least five years older than me, he did not look it. To imagine him with a wife in the past proved difficult.

"I did not know that ye were once married. How did she go, Baodan?" My wording was off, but I was unsure of how to ask what I wanted to know in a way that wasn't rude or painful. I was sure he would understand my meaning well enough, though, and I was right.

"How did I lose her, lass?" Briefly, he closed his eyes. "Six years ago, 'tis been. We'd only been married a year when the sickness came for her. I was away on a short trip, gone for only a fortnight to help a man with acquiring a piece of land. I knew not that she'd been ill until I returned home to find her dead. I live with the guilt of not being there with her those last days."

That went a long ways toward explaining his attentiveness while I was so ill, and I felt uncomfortable at the thought that my stupidity had caused him to relive such pain. "I'm verra sorry. I doona know what else to say to ye, save that."

He shook his head and took a deep breath, pushing the dark memories away, it seemed. "There is naught to say but that, but I appreciate yer kindness. I thought that ye should know before I ask ye what I intend. Yer father has spoken to ye of it, aye?"

I nodded, swallowing my mouthful of food and scooting my plate away so that I would not be tempted to eat more. "He has, but if ye intend to ask it, I'd prefer to hear it from ye, as well."

He smiled and stood, dragging his chair so it was in front of mine. Then, resuming his seat, Baodan gathered both of my hands in his. "Aye, lass, that would only be right of me, would it not? I shall ask ye what I asked yer father, but I wish to be honest with ye first, if ye would allow me to be so."

"O'course. I would wish nothing less than whatever truth ye have to give."

"I am not in love with ye, lass, and I doona know if I ever will be. My heart was buried with my wife long ago, but that doesna mean that I doona want a family, and I doona wish to spend the rest of my days alone."

He paused, but held my gaze, as if unsure he should continue. "Go on," I coaxed. "Say whatever ye wish, and I will take no offense to it." Truthfully, I was pleased that he dinna offer a confession of love. It would have been unkind of me to accept it when I had none that I could return to him.

"Verra well, lass. I've heard some talk that ye yerself have lost a love. Nay on purpose, but yer three bonny friends doona speak as quietly as they sometimes think they do. I've come to believe that perhaps yer heart is in much the same place as mine, that it belongs to another and always shall. There was one name that ye whispered during yer fevers over and over again, and I doona wish to cause ye pain by speaking it here."

My intake of breath was sharp, and he could see that he'd surprised me. "I did not know that I'd done so. Bri, Adelle, and Mary never said."

"I know that ye did not, lass, and I doubt that they were privy to seeing ye do so, as well. They were often with ye only when ye were awake. I was afraid to speak much with ye, so I kept ye company often while ye slept."

"Ah."

He laughed softly before continuing. "Perhaps, I should have kept that to myself, aye? That may be unsettling to ye, but I assure ye, lass, I was only watching over ye to make sure ye were safe and as comfortable as ye could be."

I squeezed his hand. "Aye, I know. It comforts me that I was so well watched after. Thank ye. I have not told ye thank ye enough for saving my life."

"I deserve no thanks, lass. Any man but the worst would have done the same. But this is really what I've brought ye here to ask of ye." He fidgeted nervously, and I rubbed my thumb back and forth across his hand to calm him. He smiled as he looked down at our entwined fingers. "I believe we are both of similar hearts and minds, lass. While I know I canna give ye what ye once had, I can give ye companionship. And I swear to ye that I will offer ye protection and a happy home. As for any children that we may have together, I will love them and serve them for all of my days. Will ye marry me, Blaire?"

Arran was gone. Whether he was happy in his marriage or not, he was now expecting his own child. When he'd said goodbye to me the last time I was in this cottage, he'd certainly meant it. Even word that I might die was not enough to bring him back to my side.

Baodan was a more honorable man than the one who owned my heart, and I would not be lucky enough to come by a better offer ever again. "Aye, lad. I'll marry ye."

He smiled as he leaned hesitantly forward, gently sealing my promise with a kiss.

The Castle Formerly Known As Kinnaird

*A*rran woke in the middle of the night, his heart beating quickly, panicked and filled with a sense of dread. He rose, drenched in sweat, and paced around the room to try and calm his breathing.

He couldn't understand what caused him to feel this way. He was a sound sleeper, and he'd not been having nightmares. Just the opposite, actually. Blaire had come to him in his dreams, as she did most nights. He delighted in the time he spent there holding her in his arms, kissing her over and over again. No matter how unreal or fleeting those moments were each night, he clung to them, wishing each day away so that nighttime would come and he could be with the woman he loved once more.

But tonight his dreams were interrupted. He could not shake the feeling that something was terribly wrong. He dressed quickly, then opened the door to his bedchamber so he could listen for any sign of trouble that might be brewing below the stairs.

The castle was silent and dark, save for a few candles still burning. Reaching for the candle closest to him, he hesitantly made his way out into the hall. He knew not why he was headed her direction, but every step forward brought him closer to Edana's bedchamber.

The lass should have been asleep long before now, and he knew he should not disturb her without reason, but something deep inside him lurched with fear as he stood before her room. He pressed his ear against the outside of the door, hoping to hear her snoring or moving about.

When he heard nothing, he breathed deeply and quietly pushed open the door. He looked first not at the bed, but at the candles, still lit, scattered throughout the room. It was unlike her to leave them burning after she'd gone to bed. Perhaps she still had not returned to the castle. He knew he'd angered her greatly in the dining hall.

Slightly relieved, he stepped all the way inside and had to swallow hard to choke down the bile that rose in the back of his throat.

Her head lay oddly back against the pillow, the upper half of her body propped up, as if she were sitting. Her eyes were wide open and lifeless, her legs spread awkwardly open. It was then Arran noticed the blood slowly dripping off the end of the bed.

A deep, animalistic groan escaped his throat at the gruesome sight, and he fell to his knees in the doorway. He knew not how long he sat there, but eventually the castle began to stir. He was pulled to his feet by two servants, but he quickly jerked away from them and fled the room, not stopping until he burst outside the castle doors.

With his first deep breath of the cool air, he vomited, then sobs overtook him. He knew it was his fault. The lass hadn't lied to him about the baby, and his screams and horrible accusations had caused her to lose the child, and ultimately her own life.

How soon after he'd gone to bed had Edana fallen ill and begun to bleed all alone in her bedchamber? How long had she suffered before dying? The questions that tormented him made him ill. No one, not even Edana, deserved to die such a death, all alone with no one to come and provide aid to her or answer her cries for help.

She must've screamed. How could one not when going through pain such as that which was so clearly etched forever on her face? If only he'd drunk less during their last meal together, perhaps he wouldn't have been sleeping so deeply not to hear her cries.

Arran knew he was not a good man. Not like his brother, not like his father. He'd battled demons of guilt and remorse for past decisions for much of his adult life, but nothing compared to this transgression for which he would now have to hold himself accountable.

He'd killed her. Whether it was by his own hand or not, he knew he would feel responsible for the lass's death and for the death of his unborn child for the rest of his life. Rising, he straightened himself, roughly brushing away his tears. The least he could do for her now was to see her properly laid to rest. Then he would beg God for forgiveness for all that he'd done.

Making his way back inside the castle, he began giving orders, stopping the castle's messenger as he passed him on the stairwell. "Ride for Conall Castle at once, lad. Speak only to my brother, Eoin, and let him know of what has passed here this night. He will wish to be here as we lay Edana to rest."

ormod watched from his hiding place just on the edge of the castle gates. He'd left shortly after Edana, silently following behind her so that he could keep tight watch on the castle. He wanted to know the instant his plan succeeded.

It had taken longer than he'd expected. Eventually, he'd drifted off the sleep as he crouched low to the ground, out of sight from anyone who might pass by him. Late into the night, a cold breeze stirred him. Tormod looked up to see the castle slowly fill with light. He suspected then that someone had found Edana's dead body.

He hoped that was the case. He still wasn't sure if the lass had found the nerve to go through with the plan. She'd been quite shaken earlier when she knew that Arran suspected her lie.

It wasn't until he saw Arran's shadow burst through the castle doors, saw him retch all over the ground, that Tormod knew for certain Edana was dead.

He was finally free of the young, foolish, ignorant lass, and his soul smiled at the knowledge of it.

Tormod remained in his hiding spot, watching the activity in the castle throughout the night, enjoying every moment of knowing how Arran would blame himself for his wife's death for the rest of his life. The plan had played out exactly as his sister had predicted. Arran would be at his most weak and vulnerable in the weeks ahead.

There would be many in the village that would find Edana's sudden death surprising. All Tormod had to do now was plant the seed of suspicion as to the cause of it. If he could make the townspeople turn on their new leader , it would go a long way toward ensuring his own place as laird once he did away with Arran Conall once and for all.

He was so close to all that he wanted he could almost taste it. Ridding himself of the wretched Edana had been the hardest part. His sister would know just the right way to proceed to finish his task. Within a fortnight, he planned to be residing within the very castle he was lurking outside of now.

onall Castle

"So you said aye to him, love?" asked Father. "And ye are at peace with yer decision?"

He appeared at my doorway late in the night, shortly after we returned from the cottage. I'd just made my way to bed. It was clear that he'd waited up so he could learn of my decision.

"Aye, Da, I did. 'Tis the answer ye hoped I would give him, is it not?"

He surprised me by shaking his head. "Nay, lass. I did not wish for ye to say aye if 'twas not what ye wanted, but I cannot deny that I am pleased that ye will be taken care of. Baodan is a good man. He will treat ye well."

So tired I could scarcely keep my eyes open, I yawned widely, speaking to him in between deep breaths. "Aye, I believe he will."

"Well, I'm happy for ye, lass. Baodan is anxious for ye to marry so he can take ye away to yer new home up in the McMillan territory. If it pleases ye, I told him I'd like ye to be married at home."

"Aye, I would like that verra much."

"Good, lass. We shall all set out the day after tomorrow – the McMillans, the Conalls, and us. Sleep well, daughter."

He turned and left, and I chuckled lightly to myself. He was more pleased than he cared to let on that I was to be married. He'd been quick to make the arrangements, not wanting me to run out on another wedding.

he Castle Formerly Known as Kinnaird

Gara waited until all of the other servants were to bed in the wee hours of the morning, after Edana's bedchamber had been cleaned and her body removed for burial preparation, to seek out Arran. She knew the new laird would not sleep tonight.

For the sake of her family, she'd done as Tormod and Edana had bid her. But she had not known the malice behind their plan. She'd gone to assist in the cleaning of Edana's room once she heard news of the lady's death, and as she'd bent to scrub the pool of blood off the floor, Gara had spotted the small bottle turned over on its side.

She'd picked it up, tucking it away as she tried to understand why the poor lass would've done something so vile to herself. Then she noticed from where on Edana's body the blood had come, and realized that her death had not been self-inflicted.

It was Tormod who'd killed her. The monster had played Edana for a fool, and she'd fallen for it, drinking the solution as he bid her. She must have thought it would feign the loss of the child so that Arran would not find out she'd lied to him.

Gara's realization caused her to fear Tormod even more, and she slipped the bottle away so no one else would see it. But her guilt over the lie she'd told for him was more than she could bear. She couldn't allow Arran to be fooled by his wife's deceit – and her own – and forever blame himself. Perhaps she could tell him the truth about the child without revealing the real cause of Edana's death.

At first Arran thought he imagined the knock at his door. The previous commotion throughout the castle had long since settled, and he'd assumed he was the only one still awake. When the soft rapping began again, he moved from his stupor of self-loathing and guilt to see who was at the door.

When he opened it to find Gara, he was certain she'd come to tell him what he already knew – that Edana's death was no one's fault but his own.

"Verra sorry to disturb ye, sir, so late and especially on this night. May I speak to ye a moment?"

He stepped away to grant her entry. "Aye, o'course ye can. What is it, lass?"

Her gaze lowered. "Before, sir. I lied to ye."

He was too tired to think of what the lass could have lied to him about. "What do ye mean, Gara?"

"The night Edana brought me to ye months ago, she was not carrying yer child. Not that night, not this one, either."

"What?" Her words hit him square in the chest. They were too much for his sleepy, guilty, grief-stricken mind to absorb.

"I'm telling ye that Edana lied to ye, sir. She was not expecting a child."

"If that's true, lass, then how did she die?"

"I doona know, sir. Women sometimes do bleed unexpectedly. She just lost too much blood too quickly."

Arran paced around the room, unsure of how to take what the lass was telling him. He was hesitant to believe her, even though he himself had questioned Edana for so long. "How can ye be certain that she was not with child?"

"I examined her myself. There was no child inside her. Never was."

Relief washed over him. He was not pleased by Edana's death, but if what Gara told him was true, at least he could rest in the knowledge that it was not he that had caused it, and there had not been a child lost, as well.

"Thank ye, lass. So when ye told me she had not threatened ye, I suppose ye also lied about that, aye?"

"Aye. I could not risk her harming my children, sir, and we were in desperate need of the payment she gave me. I apologize for any hurt I have caused ye."

"Doona worry. It was not yer fault. I'll not speak ill of the dead, but it was wrong of Edana to have ye do so." He placed a hand on her wrist. "Before ye go…"

She stared at him hesitantly. "Aye?"

"Is there more ye are not telling me, lass?" Arran needed desperately to know everything. "Anything else ye can share about why this happened?"

Her eyes grew wider as she shook her head in denial. "Nothing at all," she whispered.

He nodded. "Then ye may leave me now."

After Gara departed, Arran sat alone in his bedchamber, wrestling with a flurry of emotions. To go so quickly from overwhelming guilt and loss to possible relief and optimism about his future brought on a different sense of guilt.

He had known that Edana was a horrible person. But now, after Gara's admission, he realized he had not imagined just how low his wife had been willing to stoop in order to have her way. Still, it felt wrong for him to feel relief because she was dead.

The lass had lied to him for some time. He couldn't deny that he'd lost respect for her long ago. Still, he would lay his wife to rest. Anyone deserved that much.

He was now free from a union that should never have been. As soon as he saw Edana laid peacefully to rest, he would ride to Conall Castle to retrieve his heart.

To retrieve Blaire.

Conall Castle

Arran spent the few days leading up to Edana's burial in solitude, silently making peace with her death and his own regrettable decisions that had linked him to her. But now that he knew the truth of Edana's lies, he realized there was only so much responsibility he could take in what happened to her.

He would not allow himself to be haunted by her any longer. Once she was buried, he rode immediately for his home. He'd been surprised when Eoin had not come to be with him after receiving the news of Edana's death. He'd carried out the burial quickly, so perhaps his brother simply hadn't had time. Arran would explain it all to Eoin upon arriving home.

Some of his new clansmen would undoubtedly question how he could move on so quickly to a new wife, but Arran believed that anyone who'd spent time in Edana's company, or that of her father's, would understand.

He couldn't wait to see Blaire, to run to her and beg her to come back to him now that they could truly be together as husband and wife. They could have the family they'd long dreamed of having together.

Arran nudged his horse with the back of his heels when he saw the stables ahead of him. He was so close. Only a few more moments and he would be able to hold her again.

He rode into the stables at full speed, pulling up hard on the reins so he could fling himself off the side of his horse. He didn't notice Kip standing in the corner until he heard the old stable master's voice.

"Arran, 'tis good to see ye, lad, but what brings ye here? The castle is empty save myself and a few other servants."

Arran walked toward Kip and clasped his dear friend on both shoulders. "Have they gone down to shoot arrows then?"

Confusion filled him as he watched Kip shake his head. Where else could everyone have gone? Not far, surely. "Where can I find them?"

"Slow down, lad. I'll ask ye again. Why have ye come here? I only just received word about yer wife three days past. I'm truly sorry, lad."

Kip's words brought back the sharp pain of Edana's death. No matter how he'd felt about her, he could not help but regret the loss of someone so young. If only she'd had the time, he thought perhaps she could've become a better person than she was when she died. "Ach, thank ye, Kip. But ye know as well as I that I should not have married her in the first place. 'Twas an awful mistake, and one that I doona wish to repeat by allowing myself to spend one more moment apart from the lass I'm meant to marry. Where is she, Kip? Where's Blaire?"

Arran's nerves built as he watched Kip turn his face downward and awkwardly pick at the ground with his foot. Kip hesitated to tell him something, and it frightened Arran greatly. "What is it, Kip? Doona tell me that something has happened to her. Is she well? Ye must tell me at once."

"Nay, lad, naught has happened to the lass, but she is not here. She's at MacChristy Castle with the rest of yer family. She's set to marry yer cousin Baodan in two days."

"What? How could this happen?" Arran set to mount his horse, not wanting to stay a moment where Blaire was not.

"What do ye mean, lad? He asked her, I suppose."

"So, she doesna know of what's happened to Edana?" He turned the horse in the stables so that he could ride in the direction of MacChristy Castle.

"I do not know, lad. She may by now, but I was the only one here when the messenger arrived with the news. I sent him straight for MacChristy Castle to find Eoin. He is probably just arriving."

Arran spurred the horse forward, calling back to Kip over his shoulder. "Thank ye, Kip. I shall see ye soon. I doona intend on staying away from Conall Castle so long ever again."

---

*M*acChristy Castle

*T*he messenger arrived late in the evening on the day before I was to marry Baodan. I was away in my old bedchamber with Bri. She was playing with my hair, teasing it into different arrangements for the wedding, when Adelle burst through the door, red-faced and breathless.

"Mom, what is it?"

Bri dropped the strands of my hair and rushed to her mother's side. Certain something was terribly wrong, I nervously twisted in my seat so that I could face her.

"Edana is dead. The man Kip sent with the message said that her child tried to come early. Both she and the baby have died."

The room suddenly felt much too small. As tears threatened, I stood to make my way outside, but Bri reached out and grabbed my hand to stop me. I didn't know what to think of Edana's death. I'd been so jealous of her for having Arran when I could not, for carrying his child. But I would not have wished such a fate upon anyone.

"Blaire, are you all right?" Bri asked quietly.

I nodded and pulled out of her grasp. "Aye, only sad. Arran does not deserve such pain. Does Eoin know?"

Adelle nodded. Addressing Bri, she said, "Yes, he plans to ride out in the morning. He shall miss the wedding, but he wishes to be at his brother's side."

"As he should. I'm going to go outside to sit in the garden for awhile. I think it best I spend some time alone."

I did not wait for either of them to respond, holding back tears that burst forth the moment I stepped out the back side of the castle and into the garden. I sat down on a splintered wooden bench, poorly crafted by my father when he was a young lad. Placing my head in my hands, I wept.

I didn't know for whom I cried, but the tears fell freely. After some time, I felt a strong hand touch my back. I'd been certain I was alone, and I'd heard no one approach. Brushing away tears with my sleeve, I opened my eyes and looked up into the face of Arran.

*A*t first I thought I'd imagined him, that after too many nights of him haunting my dreams, he had now come to torture me while awake, as well. I leapt out of his grasp, staring, open-mouthed, as he gazed at me.

"Blaire, why are ye crying, lass?"

He moved forward to touch me, but I jerked away from him. "Doona touch me. Ye should not be here, Arran. Is it not true what I just heard about Edana and yer child?"

"Nay, only part of what ye heard was true. I'm here to tell ye the rest and to make sure that ye do not marry Baodan. Now tell me, why are ye crying?"

"Ye ask that as if I have naught to cry over." I could not choose just one reason for my tears, for there were many. I was heartbroken for Arran's loss, heartbroken for myself, and angry that he would choose now to reappear in my life.

"Ye doona have reason to wed my cousin anymore, lass. Now that Edana is gone, I am no longer married. Do not marry Baodan. Marry me, as ye are meant to."

Feelings of heartbreak disappeared. Disgust filled me at Arran's callousness over the death of his wife. I'd known that living with her would not be easy for him, but he was a man quite changed from the Arran I had once known and loved. "How can ye speak to me so when she has not been dead a week? I know that ye did not love her, but ye disrespect us both by speaking of her so now. Did ye think I would rejoice over her death and claim ye as my own?"

His brows pulled together, and I could see he was struggling with his words. "Forgive me, lass. I do not mean to sound so cold-hearted, but believe me there are things that ye do not know. Things that I wish to tell ye now. Ye know me well. I have no way about me with the right saying of words."

He sat down where he'd found me and motioned for me to do the same. Hesitantly, I did so, keeping some distance between us, for I knew all too well the power his touch wielded over me. "Then tell it, but I will not marry ye, Arran. I have promised myself to Baodan, and I shall marry him tomorrow."

He shook his head, unbothered by my words. "Nay, ye will do no such thing, lass. If I have to bind ye and carry ye off from here myself, I will do so. Ye will not be marrying anyone save me."

I did not know what to say to that. Part of me wanted to kiss him and tell him how much I'd missed him, while the other part of me wanted to hit him over the head with something large and heavy. I decided, instead, to stay silent and listen to what he had to tell me.

It did not take him long to oblige. "Again, lass, forgive me for sounding cold about Edana's death, but she was a wretched woman, and I canna claim that I am not glad to be free of her. She lied to me, lass. She was never carrying my child."

"Then how did she die?" Twas small relief to know Arran had not lost a child, but I knew that if he'd believed a child was coming, he would be pained to learn that one was not.

"I do not know for sure, lass, but I know that it was no fault of my own. I should not have married her, and I'll regret any pain I caused her always, but I will not be so foolish twice."

I reached out and patted his hand, only allowing my touch to linger for a moment. If this had been all, I would have followed him into marriage this very night, but that was not the case. Part of me was unwilling to forgive him. "I'm so sorry, Arran."

"Sorry for what, lass?"

"I'm sorry that my leaving caused ye to marry her. I'm sorry that she died. And I am sorry, but I cannot marry ye now."

As before, he seemed unconcerned with my denial of him. "Ach, lass, I know that ye do not wish to hurt Baodan, but he is a strong lad. He will find the lass that is meant for him. But ye, Blaire . . . ye are meant for me alone."

I stood and moved away from him, tears threatening once more. "Aye, once that was true, Arran. But Baodan is a better man than ye, and he was there for me when I needed him, when ye refused to come, although I lay dying."

"Dying? I know naught what ye speak of, lass."

He was lying, I was sure of it. But the pained expression on his face did not seem feigned. "How can ye say that ye do not know, Arran? I sent ye a letter when I believed I had only days to live. Bri spoke to the messenger that delivered it straight into yer hands."

He moved too quickly for me to evade him. Grabbing both of my hands into his own, he pleaded, "Believe me, lass, this messenger did not tell Bri the truth. Had I known that ye might die, no matter the cause, there is naught in this world that would keep me from ye. Tell me that ye believe me, Blaire. Ye possess every bit of my heart and soul. Had ye died, I would have, as well. I will not wait to have ye as my wife a moment more."

He kissed me then, and I returned it before moving my lips to his ear so that I could whisper to him. "Aye, I believe ye. It hurt me more than I care to tell ye when I thought that ye knew and did not wish to come."

"Ach, lass. . . "

He sighed heavily into my ear, his breath shaky. I could feel how much he longed for me. Pulling away slightly, he kissed me gently on the lips as he stared into my eyes. In his gaze, I saw everything I'd ever wanted to hear from him. His eyes said more than words ever could.

"It pains me to know that ye could think it of me, but I know that I havena treated ye as I should," he said quietly. "If ye will have me, lass, I shall spend the rest of my life making it up to ye."

"Aye, Arran, I'll marry ye." I kissed him briefly, moaning as his hand on my lower back pulled me to him.

Suddenly, a voice to my left caused us both to grow still. "Will ye, lass? I doona believe that my wedding day will turn out as I'd hoped."

I turned to see Baodan standing close by. While his face gave none of his emotions away, his eyes, deep brown and beautiful, were sad. My heart filled with guilt as it broke for him.

CHAPTER 39

*A*rran left us, understanding that I needed a moment alone with Baodan to explain the best I could what had taken place since we'd last seen each other. I could not tell if he was angry; Baodan was a man whose face was impenetrable. I sensed, though, that even if he was angry, it would take much to get him to express it.

"Baodan, I believe I need to tell you what's happened . . . " My words sounded foolish and obvious, but I knew not what to say. My face felt flushed with heat from my embarrassment and shame.

He surprised me by reaching for my hand, then he led me through the small garden, the two of us walking side-by-side.

"Nay, lass. I doona think ye have as much to explain as ye think ye do."

"What do ye mean?" I allowed him to lead me as we slowly made our way out of the garden, meandering through the castle grounds in the moonlight.

"He is the one, is he not, lass? The one who laid claim over yer heart even when he was no longer with ye? I knew it was my cousin, lass. As I said, ye spoke his name many times when ye were delirious with fever."

"Aye, and I'm so verra sorry, Baodan. I would not have agreed to marry ye if I believed there was any way for Arran and me to be together. But now that there is, I cannot marry ye. It would not be fair to ye for me to do so."

"Aye, I know that ye cannot, lass. I wouldna wish for ye to."

I stopped walking so that he would stop, as well. Facing him, I clasped hold of his other hand. "Truly? Ye are not angry with me?"

He smiled, squeezing my hands gently. "Nay, lass. I am sad that I shall not share in the pleasure of yer company. I think that we could have been bonny friends, aye? But I cannot be angry with ye for doing as yer heart bids. Ye are lucky, lass. Ye have been given the chance to be with the one ye thought ye'd lost. If I was given the same opportunity, not even the fiery pits of hell could stop me. I am happy for ye, Blaire."

I had not expected such a reaction, but after listening to him, I was not surprised. Baodan was the best of men. If I had more brains than heart, I would have married him rather than Arran. I stretched, having to stand on the farthest tips of my toes to reach him and kiss him on the lips. Then I pulled him into a hug. He squeezed me tightly, and my feet came off the ground. Together we stayed there for only a moment.

Once he set me back on the ground, I stepped away from him to walk back to the castle, but I turned to bid him one last farewell. "Goodbye, Baodan. Ye are a good man. There is someone else out there who ye will find, and she will heal yer heart. I have no doubt of it, and there is no man more deserving of finding true love again than ye."

He shook his head shyly. "Nay, lass, I doona know about that. If such a time comes, I shall welcome it, but I will not expect it as I journey forward."

I turned away and went in search of Bri, Mary, and Adelle, silently throwing a prayer up to the heavens that love would find Baodan again. I knew the women in my life would not be pleased with me if I kept all that had happened from them for very long.

*P*ure commotion filled the castle by the time I made my way back. Eoin, Mary, Bri, and Adelle were thrilled to see Arran. They were also all ready to resurrect Edana and bury her again after learning of the lies she'd told him. Baodan's family members were so angry with Arran and me over my cancelled wedding to Baodan that I feared a brawl might erupt. Thank goodness Baodan showed up shortly after I arrived and calmed them down, taking them away so they could make their preparations to return home.

As the chaos ensued around me, only one person's reaction concerned me. I searched for my father, and found him leaning casually against a doorway, observing the screaming spectacle with ornery amusement.

He smiled as he spotted me, then quickly made his way over, pulling me into a side corridor before I could be swept away by the flurry of activity in the main hall. "So, I hear that ye've changed yer mind on another wedding, have ye, lass? Please tell me that this one to Arran shall be yer last, and that ye will truly marry him."

I laughed into his chest as I hugged him. "Aye, Father. If I do not, I shall let ye send me away to a convent."

"Doona tempt me, love. Now, let us leave this place. The two of ye can be married at the top of the river near here. It runs into a deep valley and is the prettiest place in all of Scotland. Yer mother and I were married there. If we leave now, we can make it by morning."

We set out in the middle of the night—my father and I on our own horses and Arran and Adelle atop another. She was not an excellent rider, but she was no novice, either. When Arran told her she could ride with him if she wished, she'd wasted no time in accepting his offer. I had a feeling her decision had more to do with her desire to be close to my handsome husband-to-be than her not wanting to ride alone, but it did not bother me a bit. How could I blame her? Her infatuation with handsome men made me smile. And I was secure in the fact that I, and I alone, would be the lucky woman to share Arran's bed from this night onward.

<hr>

*B*y the time we arrived at the river, the sun was just beginning to rise, casting beautiful shades of pink and yellow across the shimmering water that gently trickled down the valley, slicing beautiful curves in the green landscape.

The ceremony was short and simple, rather unlike the pathways we took to reach the spot my father had chosen. Adelle cried loudly throughout our exchange of vows, garnering multiple looks of horror from my father. But at the ceremony's completion as we sealed the vows with a kiss, I didn't miss the small trickle of tears that fell from Father's eyes, as well.

Arran pulled me in close, running his fingers deep into my hair as he placed a trail of tiny kisses up to my ear. "I dinna think I would ever be able to call ye wife, but in my heart I always thought of ye as such."

I shifted my head and brought my lips toward his once more. Quickly saying our farewells, we left Father and Adelle to make their way back to MacChristy Castle alone. Mounting Arran's horse together, we set off down the valley, not knowing what direction we sought and not caring, as long as we were headed there together. . . and alone.

CHAPTER 40

ormod waited until the group had split in two and each had departed – Arran and Blaire off toward the north, and Laird MacChristy and an unfamiliar lass riding back toward MacChristy Castle. Only then did he crawl from his hiding space and walk far off to the west where he'd left his horse tied to a tree.

Immediately after Edana's death, Tormod had gone into the village to spend time in the ale house, hoping that he would be able to spread suspicion of how Edana had met her death among the townspeople. His efforts had been fruitless.

Everyone he spoke to had lived under the miserable leadership of Ramsay Kinnaird and were not as sympathetic as he'd hoped toward Edana and her untimely fate. Most were also suspicious of him. Wretched man or not, Ramsay's blood pumped through him. Knowing this, the townspeople were unlikely to trust him unless given real reason.

The people saw Arran and all of the Conalls as saviors who had finally delivered them from the all-powerful hold of his uncle. It had only taken him upsetting a small handful of villagers before he'd been run out of the ale house. They would not allow him to speak ill of their new laird or suggest that he'd done something so heinous.

Arran hadn't, of course, but the truth of Edana's death could never be known if Tormod was to ever take over as laird. He had left the ale house angry and defeated. The next few days were spent sulking, until he saw Arran ride from their territory in the direction of Conall Castle.

It didn't take him long to guess where or to whom Arran was riding. Tormod knew he was traveling to see his lover, anxious to fall into her arms now that he was rid of his wife. Not that he could blame him. There was no denying that the lass was a great beauty.

Tormod knew not how Arran's new marriage to Blaire could contribute to his downfall, but he was sure that once he told his sister, she could figure out a way to turn it to their favor. He rode quickly, anxious to arrive home so a plan could be made and a trap set before Arran and his new bride returned to their stolen castle.

***

"Ye are certain they are married? He dinna just take her to his bed?"

Tormod ground his teeth in frustration. She was smarter than he, but he was no fool. Fia often spoke to him as if he were a small child, not the man who would soon serve as her laird. "Aye, I would not have ridden so fast to ye if I was not absolutely certain. I saw it with my own two eyes."

"Aye, good. Ye shall use his new bride to turn the people against him."

"How? The people doona wish to hear talk against him, especially if it should come from either of us."

"Aye, 'twas foolish of ye to try and sway anyone yerself to begin with. All we need is to pay someone else to do our bidding as we did before. The people are too loyal to Arran and the Conalls, but they have not had as much interaction with the MacChristys. It will be easier for them to believe ill of Blaire if the news comes from someone that lives among them and they accept as part of the village. We are outsiders, ye and I. Go and gather the midwife who confirmed Edana's lie to Arran. If she is not willing to help us, take her children."

***

Tormod reared back to kick in the door of Gara's home with as much force as he could muster. The small wooden shack was dark, and he hoped to scare Gara and her family out of their beds. When the lass saw him with his lit torch, ready to set her home ablaze, she would come with him willingly, and he would not be forced to take her beastly children.

He moved throughout the small space, holding his torch in front of him, slowly realizing the shack was empty. Not only were Gara and her children not there, it was evident by the lack of personal belongings that they never planned to return.

Perhaps the lass had more brains than he'd realized. She'd not taken his threats idly. Still, he knew that his sister would not be pleased to know that they no longer had Gara under their control. But tonight was not the night for her to upset him. Tormod was itching for violence. One day his sister would push him too far.

"What do ye mean, she is not there? God, how could ye be so daft, Tormod? To let her go after what she knows? I told ye we should have disposed of her after she served her purpose the first time."

Tormod threw his fist hard against the doorway, his frustration at his sister reaching a point where he was afraid he could no longer control his anger. "Are ye not the one who suggested that we go to the lass and enlist her service now? I am tired of ye speaking to me as ye do! Ye doona know to whom ye speak. Soon, I will be laird of this territory. If ye doona wish to stay in the ruins in which we live now, you willna speak to me so ever again."

He blanched when she slapped him hard across the face, and his fists began to tremble as the world around him disappeared. All he could see was her screaming. He knew not what she said, only making out an occasional word that escaped her vile mouth as rage filled him. There had been too many years of her belittling him, of her ordering him about and behaving as if he was useless without her.

Fia might have been quicker to think of ideas, but Tormod always followed them through. Suddenly he knew how to bring down Arran. All he had to do was find another castle servant he could coerce to do his bidding. He had no further need for his sister.

"Doona ye threaten me," Fia hissed. "Ye're a fool. Ye were born a fool, and a fool ye shall stay. Any triumph that ye have ever seen has been owed to me. Ye are as useless as our horrid father and as daft as our mother."

As quickly as Tormod's rage had risen, an eerie sense of calm replaced it. Suddenly, it was all clear to him. Fia was no more than an obstacle, one that he could no longer allow to stand in his way.

"Goodbye, sister." He reached forward, ramming her head hard against the doorway. She was knocked unconscious at once, and when Tormod felt for a pulse, there was none.

He stepped over her lifeless body and made his way to the castle. It would be easy to find someone willing to do his bidding, and if they would not, they would meet the same fate as Edana and his sister.

*A*rran and I rode casually, not making haste to anywhere as we followed the river deeper into the valley. We were both as happy as we'd ever been, but equally as exhausted. Arran, especially, had gone days without sleep, and I could hear his soft snoring against my ear as I rode in front of him on the horse.

I laughed quietly, just loud enough to wake him and send him jerking upright in the saddle.

"I think 'tis time for us to take a rest, aye? If ye start to topple off the horse, I will not be able to keep ye from falling." I leaned back and turned my head to kiss him as he pulled up on the reins to slow the horse's pace.

Dismounting, he tied the horse to a tree. Hand-in-hand, we made our way to the river. After searching for a few moments, we found the softest patch of earth and lay next to each other to rest our eyes for awhile.

I curled into the nook of his arm, imagining that while we intended to sleep, Arran would first suggest that we partake of another enjoyable activity. But no sooner had I settled myself comfortably next to him than he was snoring loudly.

I reached up, lightly kissing his brow before I rested my head against him to try and sleep awhile myself, but I dinna drift long before I grew restless and stood to stretch. I would let him sleep as long as he needed. It was a beautiful summer day, and I'd taken a fancy to sticking my feet into the running stream so I could feel the water swish between my toes. My last experience with water briefly crossed my mind, but I dinna fear the river with Arran by my side.

The water was cold, but it felt nice in contrast to the warm sun that beat down on my face. I leaned back, extending my neck to spread the warmth over me. I knew not how long I lay there, but I heard Arran approaching before I felt his hands on my shoulders.

"Ach, lass, ye look beautiful with yer bare feet splashing in the water and yer bare neck red from the sun. If I wasna a gentleman, I would take ye right here."

"Gentleman? Ha! Where might my husband be? I know not of this gentleman that ye speak of." I kept my back to him, smiling as he sat behind me. His arms wrapped around my waist and he laced his fingers together, leaning in to lightly blow warm air into my ear and down my back.

I laughed at the sensation, squirming as he held me tight, tickling me with his warm breath.

We went still after a time, and I turned my head to kiss him, but nipped his earlobe, instead.

I smiled as I heard his breath catch. He had not expected me to tease him so.

"Oh, do ye not know what that does to me, lass? Doona tempt me," he crooned in my ear."I do not wish to treat ye like an animal and have ye in the middle of nature for any passerby to see. But if ye continue, I may lose all sense of restraint."

I wiggled closer against him, turned my head again, and stuck my tongue in his ear, intending to torture him so that he would change his mind. "I do not care if anyone sees. But look around, I think we are all alone save for the birds and fishes."

He disappointed me by bending his knees so that he could jump to his feet. "Nay, lass. Ye are my wife. I want to honor ye in a bed with a roof above us. I willna take ye until we have found shelter for the night."

I raised my toes out of the water, shaking them dry. Then I stood quickly making my way back to the horse. "Let's ride then, and I do not wish to make as slow go of it as we did this morning. I am not a patient lass, husband, and I'm anxious for this honoring that ye speak of. Where shall we stay this evening?"

He smiled, following suit as we made our way to the horse, him mounting first and then assisting me so that I sat in front of him, mimicking our positions by the river. "There is a small village nay far from here, and there is an inn where we will stay for the night. 'Tis a common place of rest for travelers so they doona often have rooms, but my father knew the owners well. They shall have a room for us, I am certain."

"Sounds lovely."

"Aye, lass. Lovely is too tame a word for what I have in mind."

"'Tis some promise ye make, lad," I teased. "I hope ye are up to the task." I smiled, squealing as he released the reins with one of his hands and gently pinched my bottom.

"Do ye doubt it, lass? Well, I shall prove ye wrong soon enough."

———

*A*rran was not a liar. After giving the old couple who owned the inn a generous number of coins, we were provided a comfortable room at the farthest corner of the establishment. He'd certainly intended to assure that we would not be disturbed for the evening.

We had waited much too long for this moment, and for most of that time, we thought it would never arrive. I always imagined that I would be nervous my first time, but I was not. As we lay side-by-side across the bed, facing one another, our eyes locked, and Arran stroking my hair, my longing for him left no room for nerves. He was my love, my husband, my life. We had overcome many obstacles, and I had crossed time and come back again so we could be one. For me, it could not happen too soon.

He sent me a mischievous smile and I returned it with one of my own. "Before we arrived," I said in a teasing tone, twirling a strand of his golden hair around my finger, "I seem to recall ye mentioned honoring me, aye?"

"Aye, and I seem to recall ye doubted me being up to the task," he said in a tone that mimicked mine. "I'll have ye know, I have been with many women, lass, and I know what each one of them desires."

I stiffened, not liking the direction he'd taken the conversation. I'd always known that, though he was mine, I would not be his first. Still, I did not wish to be reminded. "If ye wish to honor me, mayhap it would be best for ye not to tell me just how many women ye have treated thus. It does nothing to make me feel special, aye?"

He placed one finger across my lips to silence me. "Hush, lass. Ye dinna let me finish. I know what they want, but I have never given it to any of them."

"Ye are too sure of yerself, Arran. How can ye know what all women want?"

"What they want, lass, is to be worshiped, for a man to surrender himself to them, giving them his soul so that he will nay love another for the rest of his days." He kissed me thoroughly before adding, "It has been asked of me many times in the way a lass would touch me, opening her heart, begging me to give her that most precious part of myself. But I always tucked it away, never understanding why I couldna let that part of myself go. Now I know."

"Aye?" My heart fluttered so wildly in my chest, the word came out of me breathlessly.

"Aye, lass. 'Twas for ye. My heart waited for ye before I knew ye were to come into my life. I shall worship ye now, love, and as I do so, know that I share with ye my soul, for there is no other in my life but ye. For the truth is, lass, that ye've possessed my soul since the first time I saw ye. By the end of this night, I shall lay claim over yers, as well."

"Oh, Arran, do ye not know by now that ye already do?"

"Ye are my first love, Blaire. My first and my last," he said then, his voice a deep caress in my ear.

"And ye are mine," I whispered, as tears of joy filled my eyes. "I will never let anything keep us apart again."

"Nor will I."

The night faded away around us, and for me there was only Arran. His eyes, his warmth, his whisper of my name. All mine, this night and forever more.

CHAPTER 42

"*N*ow what did I tell ye, man?" Tormod stepped away, releasing the old man who'd served as gardener at the castle for three generations of Kinnairds, allowing him the chance to speak as he'd bid him.

"If I doona do what ye ask, ye shall kill my wife. Ye have her locked away and gagged where I canna get to her."

Tormod groaned at the trembling man. "Nay, ye fool. I shall certainly do all that ye have said, but I intended for ye to tell me what ye are to say to the villagers after ye gather them together this evening. Are ye certain they will come if ye send for them?

He glared at the old man, watching as he reached up to rub the side of his cheek, now red from the impact of his palm. "Aye, sir. I know all in the village and all know me. They shall listen to whatever I have to say to them."

"Good and what is it exactly, man, that ye have to say?"

"That…that Blaire MacChristy is a witch. That I've seen her steal herbs from my garden so she could cast her spells. That I believe she has bewitched Arran for some time, and it was she that killed Edana, not the loss of a child."

"And what will ye tell them of Arran if they should find him innocent in Blaire's wrongdoing?"

"That the spell she cast on him is too strong and has addled his brain such that his bond to her will only be severed by death. That if we are to keep our village and children safe, we must rid ourselves of both Arran and his new bride, the MacChristy witch."

"Aye, man. Now doona ye forget what shall happen to ye if ye should waver in yer story. I will be in the crowd listening to yer every word. If ye should waver, 'tis yer wife that shall suffer."

Tears rolled down the old man's face, and they brightened Tormod's heart. Finally, he was the man he'd always hoped to be. People feared him. If his ancestors had taught him anything, it was that with fear came power.

He sent the man away to gather his clansmen.

$\mathcal{W}$e spent two more nights at the inn, then started for home, where we hoped for nothing more than to have at least a fortnight of peaceful nothingness.

It took us mere moments as we neared the castle to know that we would not get our wish. It was night, but a large crowd gathered. We heard angry voices while still a good distance from the stables.

"What do ye think has happened, Arran?" Fear gripped me in the belly, and I fought back the urge to beg Arran to turn the horse around so we could flee from here. Something in the back of my mind warned me that the crowd awaited us.

"I doona know, lass, but surely there is need to worry."

His words were meant to comfort me, but tension hardened his body. Even the horse was hesitant to continue marching forward the closer we got to the village.

"I think ye are wrong, Arran. They've spotted us, and some of them are now headed in our direction. Perhaps we should leave."

"Nay, lass. I am laird of this keep now. Whatever has occurred, 'tis my duty to see to it and see that my people are cared for. I'm sure that all they need is leadership to assist in whatever has occurred."

"Aye, I'm sure ye are right." I knew that he was not, but I did not wish to cause him to fear the approaching crowd any more than I knew he already did.

Slowly, we drew closer. As soon as I heard the words the people chanted, my blood ran cold.

"Witch. Witch. Witch." They screamed it over and over, fingers pointing at me while their pity-filled eyes turned toward Arran.

"What is the meaning of this? Who among ye will step forward to tell me what has happened whilst I was away?"

An elderly man standing apart from the crowd hollered out, gesturing wildly at me. "That be her, the witch. We should bind them at once."

I couldn't make sense of what the man said, but I didn't miss the way he cast his eyes downward after he finished speaking, not looking up again as the crowd poured in around us. Two men stepped forward with chains, roughly dragging us off of the horse, chaining us before either of us had time to scream or protest.

Our mouths were gagged and our eyes covered as they led us away to somewhere deep below the castle. Not until we were thrown into cells did they remove our coverings, but it was too dark in the cell for me to see anything. I called out for Arran, feeling frantically around the darkness. "Arran! Arran, where are ye? What has happened?"

A voice that I had not heard before teased me in the darkness. Malice dripped from the deep, unsettling tone, and I screamed as large hands gripped me hard by both arms.

"Arran is not here, lass, and I doona think that ye shall ever see him again."

CHAPTER 43

"There is no need for ye to do this, sister. Yer children need ye, and ye shall all be safe here if ye will only agree to stay."

Gara pulled her sister into a large embrace but shook her head, resigned to the decision she knew she must make. "Nay, I canna continue to live with the wrong that I've done. I lied once to provide for my children, and it resulted in the death of a lass who'd seen naught but heartache her whole life. I lied once more to protect them, but I canna be the mother they deserve if I am not willing to do what is right."

"But ye doona know for certain what Tormod plans. Why do ye think ye shall be able to stop it?"

Gara didn't respond right away, squatting so that she could kiss each of her three children, holding them tight as she prayed it wouldn't be the last time she got to hold them in her arms.

"Go inside my dear ones, and be good for yer auntie whilst I am away. I love ye more than ye shall ever know."

She controlled her sobs until the children were inside her sister's home. Struggling to catch her breath, she gasped, "I doona know what I shall do, but I know that I must try. I heard Tormod in the ale house doing his best to make the men believe that Arran killed Edana. He did no such thing, but Tormod willna rest until he has succeeded in turning my people against them. 'Tis time that I share the truth with my clansmen."

"But ye must know that he shall kill ye if ye do so," her sister warned.

Gara nodded, pulling her cloak over her so that she could be on her way. "Aye, but I am not living now with the guilt tearing me into pieces. If I should die, at least my soul will be at peace knowing I have made amends for the sin I committed."

"God go with ye, sister."

Gara turned, fleeing into the night so she would not be tempted to turn back and live as a coward. She could only hope that one day her children would know of her bravery and grow up to be the men and women she'd given her life to allow them to be.

---

*A*rran would not allow himself to lose Blaire again. If he had to break his own legs and ribs to get out of his cell, he would find a way to save her. Any man that got in his way would find himself dead, clansman or not.

He rammed his shoulder hard against the metal. If only he could get one of the bars loose, he could somehow squeeze his way out. It was so dark he could scarcely see, but a noise at the end of the hallway alerted him that he was no longer alone. He stilled instantly, patting himself down for anything he could use as a weapon.

"Sir, are ye there? Tis Gara."

He could think of no reason for her to be down here. His first thought was that she must have been one of the ones to conspire against him. He knew that she'd already lied to him at least once before. Had she lied again when she said she knew nothing else?

But on second thought, he remembered that she'd come to him, risking her own safety to tell him the truth of Edana's lie about the child.

He called out to her, doing his best to be loud enough so she could hear him, but restraining somewhat so he would not draw attention from elsewhere in the dungeon. "Aye, lass. Do ye know why I was placed here?"

He listened as she made her way toward him. When she stepped into the small beam of moonlight streaming into his cell, he saw fear on her face and knew that she was not there to harm him.

"Aye. Tormod has convinced everyone that the lass ye are with is a witch, and she killed Edana. He says she has ye under a mighty spell."

Anger boiled inside of Arran. He'd wanted to kill Tormod the moment he'd first laid eyes on him, able to see the lad's evil spirit through the hatred that shone in his eyes.

"Why would he do it? What does he have to gain from it?" Arran believed he knew the answer, but it was hard for him to imagine anyone wanting to be laird enough to go to such lengths. Ruling a keep was hard work, and if he could go back, he would gladly give up his position as laird, but not to a man like Tormod.

"He wishes to be laird. He believes it is his right because he is the bastard son of Ramsay's brother."

"Do ye know where they've taken Blaire? What does he intend to do to her?" His heart beat quickly at the thought of Blaire being harmed. If Tormod hurt her in any way, Arran would return whatever pain he inflicted on her, tenfold.

"Nay, sir. I doona know where she is, but the clansmen intend to kill her. That is clear from the mob that awaits ye outside."

Arran beat his fist hard against the stone wall, growling at the pain. "I am not so worried about the mob. All I can think of now is Blaire. I must get to her before Tormod causes her harm."

The woman blinked troubled eyes at him. "I dinna tell ye the whole truth last time I spoke to ye. I was too afraid that Tormod would hurt my children, but now I have seen them safely away to be with my sister, and I have come to right the wrongs I have played a part in."

"What is it, lass? What dinna ye tell me last time we spoke?"

"Edana dinna die naturally. Poison killed her. A poison Tormod instructed her to take. I doona believe that she knew it would kill her. I believe she thought it would only mimic an early birth and the loss of a child."

Arran shook his head in the darkness, disgust rising in the form of bile in the back of his throat. "How could anyone be so evil? Do ye know of a way to get out of here, lass? 'Tis urgent that I do so before Tormod can cause harm to anyone else."

"Aye, sir. I have worked in the castle most of my life, and I know where a set of keys is kept hidden. I've fetched them for you."

Arran breathed a deep sigh of relief as he watched Gara pull the keys out from under her dress and begin to work on his lock. Once he was free, he pulled her into a quick embrace, then departed in the direction of the other cell block.

CHAPTER 44

I dinna know the man who held on tightly to me in the darkness. He pushed me back hard into the cell wall and growled a sound so inhuman that the evil in it caused me to shiver uncontrollably. I was certain that my life was about to end.

A sound in the distance caused him to pull away from me, and I had to swallow to keep from emptying my stomach onto the cell floor.

"I did as ye bid me. Now, tell me where I can find my wife."

The voice sounded old and frightened, and I knew that whatever he asked of the creature next to me, he would not receive what he hoped for.

The stranger spoke, calling the man to approach him. "Come here, gardener, and I shall tell ye where ye can find yer wife."

My eyes slowly opened themselves to the darkness, and I could see the outline of the old man as he approached the cell. I also saw a glint of metal as my captor pulled a knife from his boot. I charged him, jumping on his back and bringing my fist down on the top of his head with as much strength as I could muster.

The beast was too strong. While it caused him to shift his arm so that his blow to the man wasna fatal, the dirk still slipped easily into the old man's side. I screamed loudly, hoping for anyone to hear me and come to my aid, for I knew that the dirk would be headed for me next.

My captor was on me in an instant, grabbing my throat with one hand and pinning both of my wrists above my head with the other. I could hear footsteps headed in our direction, but it didn't seem the choker could make out the sound. His face contorted with rage as he did his best to squeeze the life out of me.

He was succeeding. As my vision faded, I was unsure if it was truly Arran that I saw reach to grab the dagger out of the man's side, then charge through the open cell to send the weapon deep into my assailant's neck.

The monster's hold on me instantly released, and I sank to my knees, desperate to catch a breath as the blood from the man's neck continued to spray over me. I retched at the taste of it dripping into my mouth, and I stepped away, not wishing to be near him as he took his last breath.

His eyes remained open, the same evil expression forever plastered on his face. Even in death, the beast beneath the man shone through.

It took me a moment to catch my breath. By the time my head cleared, I could see Arran and a woman I didn't know bent over the elderly man who gasped painfully at the knife wound in his side.

"Doona worry, lad. We shall get ye the care that ye need. Only hold on a moment more, and we shall find someone to tend to ye."

I watched as the man reached out to grab Arran's arm, preventing him from going for help. "Nay, lad. If ye leave here before the clan knows the truth, they shall murder ye on the spot. I am not long for this world, and I doona wish to be, either. I understand now that Tormod killed my wife before I even agreed to do as he asked. There is no place in this world for me if she is not here at my side."

Arran shook his head, intent on helping the man. "Nay, lad. Ye shall live many years still."

The woman on his other side shook her head, interrupting him. "I'm verra sorry, but ye are wrong, sir. The old man is right. He has only a few moments left, and there is naught that we can do to help him."

I dinna know the elder, but tears sprang up in my eyes. If he hadna arrived when he had, it would be me lying on the cell floor dead. This man had saved my life.

"Aye, I told ye, lad. I know that I am dying, and I doona wish for it to be any other way. At least help me to fix the wrong I've done to ye. Ye and yer lady must stay hidden until the people have heard what I have to say. Gara, will ye help me to my feet and let me lean against ye so that, together, we can address them? Once we have both spoken, ye will be free to leave here, and I will die knowing that I dinna let the monster win."

I could see that Arran knew he would not change the old man's mind. He rose from his knees, pulling the man up with him so that he could situate him on Gara's shoulders. He helped them to the doorway. Then, sending them out on their own, he returned to my side.

"God, lass, I thought I had lost ye."

"And I ye." I threw myself into his arms, sobbing as he reached to wipe the blood from my face.

A sudden hush outside the dungeon told us that our saviors now had the attention of the crowd. Hand-in-hand, we moved to the doorway and hid in the shadows as we watched them inform the crowd of all Tormod's evildoings.

The clansmen did not seem surprised. Once the truth was known, the crowd gathered in close around the gardener, no longer in anger but to comfort their friend as he took his last breaths.

Arran and I remained hidden in the shadows as the clansmen left the village to grieve their friend and hero. Gara came to us as they carried the old man's body away to prepare for burial. Relief etched her face. I could tell then that she'd risked her own life for us, as well, not knowing if she would come out of it alive.

"Thank ye, Gara. We owe ye a debt that we can never repay." Arran clasped the woman's shoulder, unsure of how to express his gratitude.

"Ye owe me nothing. I am more fortunate than I thought possible. My conscience is now clear of the wrong I did ye, and I will return to my children when I dinna believe I would ever be able to do so. If ye follow this pathway through the dungeon, it will lead ye back into the castle where ye can clean yerselves up and rest, away from everyone. Now, excuse me, I have bairns that I need to gather in my arms."

Once she was gone, we silently made our way through the dungeons, not stopping until we were inside the castle. We knew that we would not sleep, despite our fatigue. We were both eager to await the sun, for it was the only way this day would truly feel over.

"Are ye sure that ye are fine with this, Arran?" I asked. "For if this is something that ye want, I will stand by yer side. I know there are many dark memories in this place, but I believe that we could make new ones here." I walked up behind him as he finished penning his letter that detailed to his clansmen why he was to step down as laird.

"Aye, lass, I doona doubt that we could, but I doona wish to. This is not our home, and these people are not our people."

"They did accept you at first, did they not?"

He twisted in his seat, wrapping his arms around me as he buried his head in my breasts. "Aye, lass, they did, but they turned on me rather quickly, as well. I dinna wish to be laird to begin with. I rushed into it foolhardily because I believed that I was helping another. If only I could have seen all the trouble that decision would cause us."

I kissed the top of his head. "There is no sense in thinking that way. No one can know just where their decisions will take them. All we can do now is make the best of our future."

"Is this decision pleasing to ye as well, lass? I wish to please ye and, if ye wish to stay, I shall."

I shook my head, unable to repress the shiver that traveled through me at the thought. He squeezed me tightly in understanding. "Nay, I doona wish to stay. I wish to return to Conall Castle to live in the happy chaos with yer brother, Mary, Bri, and Adelle. And then, when it is time that my father can no longer serve as laird, ye can replace him. But for now, let us live more simply, with none of the responsibilities and troubles that come with a lairdship."

Arran stood, sealing his letter and slipping it away to give to Gara. She would be sure to share it with the clan, who in time would find a laird from within their own group of men.

The people would not be surprised to learn of our decision to leave. Few would approach us still, their guilt from their accusations toward us making them hesitant to speak.

"Ach, lass, ye are a mind reader, I'm sure, for there is nothing that I wish to do more than all that ye have just said. Come, let us leave this place."

---

*A*rran was not deserving of the blessings given to him, of nothing he'd ever been more certain. Many men better than he were more deserving of Blaire and her love, but he would gladly spend the rest of his life trying to make himself worthy of her.

She'd healed him from a broken spirit, forgiven him of his wrongs again and again, and shown him the value that comes with finding someone with whom to share all of life's struggles.

He leaned forward to smell her hair as she rode before him, stunned by how just her scent alone could elicit emotions in him he'd never known existed before. He couldn't wait to give her a babe—a son or a daughter with eyes just like their mother's. As soon as they returned to Conall Castle, he planned to immediately begin work on that task.

Or mayhap, even better, he would begin tonight as they stopped at the McMillans' to rest on their journey home.

---

*W*e took the long route back to Conall Castle and, much to my dismay, Arran insisted that we stop at the McMillans' on our way home. Baodan was Arran's favorite cousin, and he'd not had the chance to make peace with him the night Baodan found us together in the garden.

'Twas not Baodan I worried about seeing, but I knew that his mother wouldna welcome me with open arms. By a happy coincidence, she was away when we arrived. It allowed us to spend a pleasant evening with Baodan and his brothers, all of whom I was certain would become my dear friends.

The next morning we set off early, determined to make it back to Conall Castle within two more nights. I'd settled comfortably in my seat in front of Arran, nearly falling asleep as I leaned back against his shoulder, when an odd flash of red caught my attention out of the corner of my eye.

I sat up so quickly, my heels unintentionally went hard into the side of the horse, and Arran had to pull hard at the reins to get the beast back under control. "What is it, lass? Ye nearly scared the poor animal to death."

"Did ye not see that woman, Arran? In the pond?"

Arran pulled back so that the horse came to a stop, and he twisted to look back on the pond that sat just at the edge of McMillan Castle. "Nay, lass, I doona see anyone. Ye saw a woman, ye say? Perhaps, someone is only taking a dip. The morning's nice enough for it, would ye not agree?"

I shook my head; the notion was mad. "Nevermind. I must have dozed for a moment and dreamed something strange."

Arran slowly nudged the horse forward. "Nay, lass. Ye were not asleep; I can always tell by yer breathing when ye are. Tell me. Who do ye think ye saw?"

"The woman looked just like a lass I met in the twenty-first century. A dear friend of Bri's."

"Aye? Well, I will tell ye that does sound mighty strange, but tis not so impossible, either."

He was kind enough not to call me mad, but I wasna eager to discuss it with him further. "Aye, 'tis strange. Doona mind me, I am only overtired." I nudged him playfully in the ribs.

He laughed into my ear, and I smiled, the imaginary figure quickly disappearing from my mind as he kissed the back of my head and tightened his grip around me. We rode toward Conall Castle—to our home—where we would finally be able to build a future together.

EPILOGUE

The Roadside Inn – Present Day

"Jerry, 'tis time for us to make ready once more." Morna stood, stretching after her dream as she smiled wide. It would be fun to tweak her spells, and necessary if the new lass were to cross paths with the one she was meant to.

"O'course, love. What have ye seen?"

"We need to make our home visible once more, but it shall be different from the times before. The redhead is coming our way." She smiled, knowing Jerry would be pleased. He loved company, and he'd taken a liking to the fiery lass who'd come so valiantly in search of her friend.

"Ah, 'tis verra good news, but why should this be different? Do ye not think the lass will stumble across the spell on her own? Bri and Blaire managed quite nicely."

Morna shook her head. It was unlike any dream she'd had before, but she was certain as to its meaning. "Nay, 'tis not that. The lass will find the spell, but she canna use the same one that's been used before. For while my spell room shall be her portal, it doesna need to be her destination."

"How do ye know?"

"Because one of our lassies has already caught sight of the lass elsewhere, even before she's actually arrived. It seems that a force more powerful than myself sees fit to warn the Conalls of the girl's arrival."

THE CONALLS' MAGICAL YULETIDE

CHAPTER 1

onall Castle, Scotland - December 1646

here's nothing quite like the soft thump on your palm as you press it against a swollen, pregnant belly, allowing the small infant tucked safely away in its mother's womb to kick at the inside of your hand. The surreal experience filled me with joy as I pressed my hands flush against my daughter's stomach, smiling widely as tears brimmed in my eyes. I'd felt the child's movement more than once, but it didn't matter. I had the same reaction every time. My baby's baby had completely captured my heart, even if it would still be weeks before I would know she could be safely delivered without the conveniences of technology and medicine from our own time.

"All right, Mom. You simply cannot keep your hands glued to my stomach every moment of every day."

I smiled as Bri stepped away, grabbing the end of the blanket and tossing the other end in my direction, signaling for me to help fold it. "Oh, but I wish that I could. I think the babe moves even more than you did, dear, and you were quite active."

"Really? Well, I sincerely apologize. I'm beginning to feel miserable."

As if to emphasize her point, she collapsed onto her freshly-made bed and threw her hands up over her head as far as her dress would allow. I kicked off my own shoes, hiking up my dress as I sat crisscrossed on the end of the bed. Pulling Bri's legs across my lap, I removed her shoes so I could massage her swollen, most-assuredly sore, feet.

She sighed, wiggling her toes as I squeezed them, and I suddenly saw her as the little girl she'd once been. She was more than ready and capable of taking care of a child, but I found it hard to believe she'd grown so quickly, and that I was old enough to be a grandmother.

I continued to knead the arches of her feet and heels until she drifted off to sleep. When she began to snore lightly, I carefully lifted her legs so that I could scoot out from under them, and crawled off the bed as gently as I could. I walked to the fireplace, poking the logs until the flame took a firm root over them once more. I curled into a small wooden chair that sat before the blaze, gazing first into the flames before glancing about the room.

Every inch of the castle oozed magic. I sensed it in the air. As I sat with the fire warming my bare toes, I could almost feel Morna's eyes watching over us across the centuries.

No surprise, really. I imagined it only made sense that magic be palpable throughout the castle. Magic had, after all, brought both Bri and me to live in this place and century when we'd been born hundreds of years in the future.

Before my trip into the past, I'd been an archaeologist who specialized in Celtic finds and history. The Conall Clan was my specialty, the last twenty plus years of my life spent trying to solve the mystery behind who'd murdered them in December of 1645.

My continuing efforts to solve this mystery brought my daughter and me to the ruins of Conall Castle only one year ago, in the year 2013. I'd pestered her until she'd agreed to accompany me, not knowing that a spell cast by a beloved Conall ancestor, Morna, would rip Bri from our time and bring her into the past to live with the Conalls right before the devastating massacre was supposed to take place.

Thankfully, Bri was meant to be here. Not only did she help them change the course of history by stopping the massacre, but she also fell in love with the man of her dreams, Conall Castle's new laird, Eoin. I'd been unwilling to be separated from my daughter, no matter how happy I was for her. So when Bri decided to stay in this time with her husband, I used Morna's spell to travel back to the seventeenth century, as well.

The greatest dream of an archaeologist's life is to live with the very people he or she has devoted so much of a lifetime to learn about. And I now lived that dream-like existence. However, it was slowly becoming a reality I accepted. On top of it all, I would soon become a grandma.

I was as happy as I'd ever been, with only one lingering thought keeping me from overwhelming joy. I'd always been a social person. I liked to date. I liked to flirt. While it had become more difficult to find a date with someone my age even in the twenty-first century, I was certain that in the seventeenth century men considered me hopelessly over-the-hill, with one foot deep into the grave.

I would most likely spend the rest of my days alone, something I'd realized shortly after arriving in this time, but a fact of life that took me a bit longer to accept than I had hoped.

No matter. I had much to be thankful for. Christmas time, my favorite time of the year, had arrived. I was anxious to discuss preparations for the holiday with Bri. So when I saw her stir, I stood from my place by the fire and went to her side.

"What?" I knew the pitch of my voice rose too high, almost to a squeak, but if that old bat thought she could stifle our Christmas, she had another think coming.

"Mom, is it really that big of a deal? We didn't even notice it last year."

The hormones were messing with Bri's head. She loved Christmas as much I did. I couldn't imagine how she seemed to be so fine with skipping Christmas. "Yes, it's that big of a deal! Of course you didn't notice it last year. You were all too busy trying to stop the attack on the castle. What's Mary's problem with Christmas?"

I didn't miss the look of frustration in Bri's eyes as she answered my question. "Mary likes Christmas very much. She loves cooking. You know that. It's only that after Eoin's mother passed away, Christmas became less of an event as the years went on. Not to mention, it's been outlawed in Scotland for the last four decades."

My expression mimicked my daughter's frustration. "Darling, you know as well as I do that Christmas continued to be celebrated, just a little more quietly. Besides, who is there to enforce it when your husband is laird?"

"Well...no one really. Look, I love Christmas, but I've no desire to put Mary into more of a tizzy than she stays in constantly. If you can get her to agree to it, then I will be the first to jump on the Christmas bandwagon with you."

"Oh, I'll get her to agree. As much as she likes to fight it, I'm Mary's closest friend, and she's all bark, anyhow. Go and get Eoin. While I know that Mary will eventually get on board, we may need him to intervene in the argument she's sure to put up."

Bri nodded and laughed as I turned and left her bedchamber. This was no laughing matter. Whether the child was present or not, my first grandbaby would have a Christmas to rival any other. I would make certain of it.

CHAPTER 2

hree Days Ride North of Conall Castle

now built outside Hew's window, and his creaky joints told him a bad storm brewed. Still, he left his home at this time every year. He'd not missed his trip to her gravesite once in the twenty-plus years since his beloved had passed away. He did not intend to let the snow deter his plans.

Hew walked around his small home, tidying up before his journey south. He lived alone, far away from the nearest village. He'd not seen another soul in months, and that was just as he would have it. He knew his shyness held him back. It had been a wonder that he had ever married at all.

---

ew had not expected it, the day his sister's best friend, Mae, had approached him while he chopped wood for the fire at the back of his family home, grabbing his face and kissing him squarely on the mouth. He'd been a young lad then, and that kiss had changed his life. Hew had grown up with Mae constantly underfoot, as she and his sister were inseparable. While he had silently admired her for many years before that kiss, he was far too shy to ever express the way his heart beat for her.

That night so many years ago, he'd felt her watching him, but did not turn to greet her. His heart pounded uncomfortably just having her near. He continued to swing his ax down into the blocks, swiftly chopping the wood into two pieces. Her hand on the lower part of his back caused him to jump, and he nicked the edge of the block of wood before he threw his ax to the ground and whirled to face her.

"Mae, ye startled me, lass. Ye should be inside. 'Tis far too cold for ye to be out of doors." He could remember every word spoken between them, the scene held captive forever in his mind.

She'd touched his arm then, smiling as she shook her head, dismissing his worry. "Hew, if 'tis not too cold for ye to be out here, then I doona think I shall freeze to death, either. Did ye know that I shall turn ten and eight tomorrow?"

He'd stepped away from her, too nervous to simply stand there with her hand lying on his arm. "Nay, lass. I dinna know. I shall make ye something. Carve ye a piece of jewelry, perhaps?" He didn't know what to say to her – never did.

"I would like that verra much, but that isna why I mentioned it to ye."

He'd gathered the freshly chopped logs of wood into his hands, desperate to keep busy in her presence. "Nay? Why did ye then?"

He stilled when she moved to stand in front of him, blocking his path. "Will ye set all that down for only a moment, Hew? I'm trying to talk to ye."

He reddened and obeyed. "Aye, lass. Why doona we sit for a moment?"

They'd moved to the pile of wood, stacked just high enough to serve as the perfect chair. He trembled as she grabbed his hands, but he swallowed his nerves and forced himself not to flinch away from her touch. "What is it, lass?"

"As I just told ye, I shall be ten and eight tomorrow, and I doona wish to become an old maid."

Hew couldn't still the twitch of his hand as he realized where she headed with her words. "Nay, lass, I doona believe ye will. There are many lads who would eagerly wed ye."

"Aye, I doona believe that I shall become an old maid, either. Still, most my age are already married. While yer sister is several years older than me, she was married at ten and seven. And ye are right, many lads would be willing to wed me, but I am not so eager to marry them."

"Why is that, lass? Is there no one that catches yer fancy?" It was too much for Hew to wish that Mae would answer as he wanted, but to his everlasting shock, she did.

"Aye, there is one, and I willna allow him a moment longer to behave as if he doesna care for me as much as I care for him."

His heart began to beat so quickly he feared she could feel its quick pulse in his fingertips. Though a cold night, sweat beaded freely on his brow. "Is that so, lass? And who is this lad ye speak of?"

"If ye doona know, ye are as daft as yer sister seems to think ye are."

She paused and reached in quickly to kiss him. He was so stunned, she pulled away before he could react and kiss her back properly. "Nay, lass. Ye canna mean it. 'Tis some other lad that ye mean and ye are simply using me for practice, aye?"

She laughed before kissing him again. This time he pulled her close as she melted against him. Breathlessly, she pulled away from him so she could whisper into his ear. "Nay, Hew, there is none other but ye. There never has been. Ye are going to marry me."

He smiled against her cheek, her confidence somehow diminishing his shyness. "If ye insist, lass."

"Aye, I do."

"And what shall ye do with me once we are married?" His hands found their way to her hair, and he cradled her against his chest, pulling her into a tight embrace.

"We shall move north, find a piece of land for only the two of us, and together we shall build a home where we will spend all of our days together."

They married within a fortnight and proceeded just as Mae had wished. After moving north, they built a home for the two of them, one isolated from the rest of humanity. Five years flew by in a haze of love in which they spent every moment at each other's side.

Eventually, they planned a trip to visit their families in Conall territory. They left in winter, and Mae fell ill on their journey. She fought hard, but the sickness was too much. She died only two days after they arrived at their destination. Hew chose to bury her there, at the place in which she'd grown up. Afterward, with a broken heart, he returned to their home alone.

Hew saddled his horse, pushing away the memories of his past as he headed out into the storm. It had been many years since Mae passed. While he would feel her absence always, his heart had now healed as much as it ever could from such a wrenching loss.

Each year, he continued to make the trip to her grave on the anniversary of her death. He did so to pay his respects, to speak to her, to remind himself that there was once a time in his life when he had not been so completely alone.

CHAPTER 3

$\mathcal{C}$*onall Castle*

$\mathcal{I}$ tried to make as much noise as I could as I made my way downstairs into the castle's kitchen. I was certain Mary would be there, busily working away on the evening meal. I was right, and she instantly knew it was me creating the commotion.

"Adelle, ye doona always have to make such a ruckus when ye move about. Come in here and help me plate the food."

I knew I was normally no louder than anyone else in the castle, but Mary constantly looked for something to nag me about, so I obliged her by being purposely obnoxious in her presence.

In many ways, Mary was the castle's most important resident. She'd worked there for nearly forty years. Everyone, especially Eoin and his brother Arran, accepted the cook and head maid as the castle's true boss. She ran the castle like the captain of a ship. Nothing happened within the walls without her notice or approval.

I stuck my head into the kitchen, smiling as I reached up onto the shelf just out of her reach to grab the plates. I thought it best to test her mood before immediately jumping into what I wanted to discuss with her. "How are you today, Mary?"

Mary motioned for me to lay out the plates, saying, "Ach, I'm fine. 'Tis a bonny day. I enjoy the snowfall, but I feel a bit of guilt for loving it so. 'Tis sure to mean more work for Kip in the stables to keep the horses warm."

"Oh, don't feel guilty about enjoying anything, Mary. You know that Eoin

411

and Arran will both do whatever they need to do so that Kip's load in the stables is not more than he can handle. I have a wonderful idea that I think we should all consider doing together before the snow outside gathers too much."

"What might that be?"

"I think we should all go out and find a tree to cut down for Christmas." I looked down at the plates, busying my hands as I awaited her reaction. Perhaps if I pretended I didn't know her thoughts on the matter, she would be more willing to discuss it.

Mary turned away to grab the bread, and then began breaking it into pieces. "Nay, I'm afraid 'tis not possible. Lovely thought, though."

In the year that I'd known her, Mary had never referred to anything I'd ever said as "lovely." I was unsure of how to respond. "Umm…why 'tis not possible?"

She didn't appreciate my attempt to mimic her accent. Casting a frown at me, she said, "Well, Christmas is no longer openly celebrated in Scotland, and after Elspeth passed away, Alasdair dinna find the joy in the season he once did. The two lads dinna grow up with it being a grand celebration."

"Do you not enjoy Christmas yourself, Mary?" Eoin and Arran's history with Christmas seemed irrelevant. Alasdair had been dead for over a year, and I couldn't imagine either of his sons having a problem with the festivities. Their mother had died when they were very young. While Christmas might have brought up painful memories for their father, it would not have the same effect on either of them.

Mary shook her head and returned to help me with the plating of our meal. "Nay, lass. I enjoyed Christmas verra much when I was a young girl. My brother always made me the most beautiful presents. He was quite the craftsman."

"Mary." Her words surprised me. "I didn't know you had a brother. Is he… is he still living?"

"Aye lass, verra much so, but I doona see him often. He lives far away from here and is a bit shy. Always had a difficult time interacting with others. Only certain people had the ability to draw him out."

She looked down, as if saddened by some memory. I interrupted her thoughts to try and lift the mood. "Are you certain he's related to you? How could one sibling end up so shy while the other does nothing but talk?"

Mary rewarded me with a quick whack on the arm as she chuckled and resumed her work in the kitchen. "Aye, I'm certain. I suppose he was shy because I never gave him much of a chance to speak. As he grew, he simply grew accustomed to his own silence."

I couldn't help but wonder about Mary's brother, about her family, and what she would have been like as a child. I felt close to my dear friend now, but I honestly knew very little about her. She was always so busy caring for everyone else that I feared we often forgot about the woman within her. I shook my head, remembering my reason for speaking with her. "You have very cleverly changed the subject, Mary. If you enjoy Christmas, then why are you against us celebrating it? I'm sure you have some wonderful traditions you could share with us, and Bri and I could share ours with all of you, as well."

Mary tried to hide the smile that pulled at the corners of her mouth, but I could sense her resolve dropping.

"I'll not say that it wouldna be a pleasant time. I just doona wish to upset the laddies if 'tis something that should bring up memories of their parents."

A deep voice in the doorway caused us both to turn our heads. I smiled as Eoin and Bri poked their heads into the kitchen. Eoin's strong hands rested gently on Bri's shoulders as she leaned the back of her head lovingly into his chest. "It will do no such thing, Mary. Ma made Yuletide a spectacle and, while Da did try, it wasna the same after she passed. I think 'tis far past time for us to restore the celebrations to their former glory."

Mary let her smile pull free now, and I could see that the idea excited her.

"If that is what ye want, my dear lad, then I shall be as pleased as anyone. I only dinna want to upset ye or Arran."

Eoin moved across the room, each step accentuating his strength. His hair was even darker than Bri's, his eyes the color of obsidian glass. My grandchild was going to be beautiful.

He wrapped his arm around Mary, drawing her near before bending to kiss her on the cheek. "Aye, I know. Ye are always watching out for us, and I love ye for it, Mary."

He released her and stepped away to regard us. "Do ye think the two of ye can work together to make the preparations?"

I smiled, bobbing my head up and down enthusiastically. "Of course we can." I could sense that Mary was about to intercede with some jab as to how difficult it would be for her to put up with me, so I quickly added, "Do we have permission to do whatever we wish?" I already had a grand idea, but I didn't want to mention it to anyone before I'd convinced Mary.

Eoin grinned and glanced cautiously at Bri. "I feel that I may come to regret this but, aye, I shall not tell either of ye lassies what to do. It would be wrong of me to do so, and it would be a fruitless effort anyway."

"Absolutely right." I scooted over and draped an arm around Mary's shoulder. She glared up at me in response. "Don't you two worry. Mary and I are going to make certain this is the most magnificent Christmas Conall Castle has ever seen."

CHAPTER 4

"*A*delle, ye have lost yer mind if ye believe for one moment that I would do such a foolish thing as follow ye into that God-forsaken time that ye came from!"

Listening to Mary rant, I crossed my arms and sat down on the steps leading down into the castle's basement and spell room. It was impossible for her first reaction to anything that came out of my mouth to be a positive one.

"What is so important that ye would feel the need to do such a thing? I know ye are daft, but gracious, 'tis a horrible idea. What if we were unable to return home? I doona think I could stand to spend one day there."

"Calm down, Mary," I said, deciding it was time to intercede before her head exploded. "Morna's spells are reliable. Now that we know she lives in the inn near the castle, we will go straight there to stay with her. You don't even have to go into Edinburgh with me if you don't wish to. Wouldn't you like to see Morna again?"

Mary's face changed from red to white much too quickly. I was afraid I was about to have to pick her up off the ground. She extended a shaky hand in my direction, letting it hang in front of my face at eye level. "Do ye see what ye do to me? Ye have me so upset, I shall not stop shaking for days. Nay, I doona wish to see Morna again. The lass was a dear friend, but I spent the last twenty-five years believing her dead. 'Tis where the dead should stay. Good and buried."

Breathless, she plopped down next to me. I reached out to pat her on the back but quickly retracted my hand in response to the daggers her gray eyes shot toward me. "She was never dead, Mary. She just moved on to a different time. I'm sure she would love to see you."

"Nay, I doona expect she wishes to see me that much. If she did, could she not just come here herself to visit?"

I shook my head, regretting the direction I'd led our conversation. I didn't know enough about Morna or her abilities to speak of her so freely. "Nevermind. Don't go for Morna. Go for me. Surely you wouldn't want me to travel there alone?"

I was none too worried about going alone. I'd lived my entire life, for the most part, alone. It would be no problem for me to make the journey to my own time without anyone along. But the temptation of watching rigid, uptight Mary in the twenty-first century was a joy I very much wanted to gift to myself. It would be the best Christmas present I could ask for.

"I doona give two twiddles whether ye go alone. I hope that ye go and get stuck there. Can ye not tell by now that I'm not that fond of ye?"

I smirked at her jab. I spent most of every day at her side. If she truly didn't enjoy my company, I knew her well enough to know that she wouldn't put up with my presence. "Hush, Mary. If you're really so afraid to go along, that's all you had to say. I wouldn't have pressed you further. It's not good for someone your age to upset yourself and get so stressed out." I winked at her. "You're much too old to let fear overwhelm you." Mary was only a few years older than me, but I liked to pretend she was much, much older.

Mary stood abruptly and stomped her foot like a small child. "'Tis not that I'm frightened, only that ye are foolish to do so."

"I'll make you a deal, Mary. If you go, I'll help you with whatever chore you wish for the next month."

Mary hated, more than anything, beating the bed linens. I could already see her wrestling with the temptation of my offer in the way her eyes darted back and forth, calculating the pros versus the cons of saying yes. Eventually her eyes stopped moving, and she said, "Aye, fine, but I willna wear breeches that go up between my legs. I shall be allowed to stay in my dress the whole time, or I will not agree to go with ye."

I smiled. "Deal. You will look ridiculous, but it doesn't matter to me one bit as long as you come. Let's go tell Bri and then be on our way."

Present Day

*B*ri had warned me that, with the castle no longer in ruins as it had been when I lived in the twenty-first century, the site had become a popular tourist attraction. Still, I had underestimated the number of people that might be milling around when Mary and I arrived.

We made it out of the roped-off basement undetected, but the stares Mary's clothing garnered as we made our way were enough to rival an eight-legged horse at a zoo. Luckily, Mary was so bug-eyed at everything she saw that she remained completely oblivious to the pointing fingers and stares.

Once outside, we began the long walk to the inn. "Excuse my language, Adelle, but holy bugger," said Mary. "My head hurts something awful. I knew that it would from witnessing both Bri and yerself come through, but I dinna expect it to be quite so bad."

I winced. "Yes, I'm sorry. Morna will have something we can take to get rid of the pain. I'm certain of it." I tilted my head, studying her expression as we walked. "What do you think so far?" I asked.

"Well, I was surprised to find the castle looking much the same. But 'tis lighted much more, and oddly."

"Yes, electricity is amazing. All homes and buildings have it."

"Is that so?" Mary took in the scenery around us. "As we walk along this path, it doesna look so different."

She was right; besides the gravel road leading to the castle, this part of Scotland was still very much untouched by the conveniences of modern times. "Yes, unless you decide to accompany me into Edinburgh, your shocks will be less than they could be. Morna's home will have many things to surprise you, but nothing like the city."

"Aye, well I canna say that I doona enjoy the adventure of it. Perhaps I *will* join ye when ye leave for the city."

We walked in silence for the remainder of the way until we arrived at Jerry and Morna's. I was none too surprised to find both of them waiting for us at the front door.

"Ach, Mary!" Morna exclaimed. "I canna believe it! I nearly spit up my food when my vision showed me yesterday morning that ye two lassies were on yer way to see us."

Morna charged Mary, who blanched at the shock of laying eyes on the dear friend she'd thought lost forever. The two pulled each other into a tight embrace.

Jerry made his way over to me, then wrapped his rail-thin arms around my neck. "Adelle, it is lovely to see ye again, lass."

"You as well, Jerry. So, Morna saw us coming?"

Morna's voice answered me as she and Mary walked toward us, arm-in-arm. "Aye, I did. And I've not been so pleased by a vision in some time. I'm also thrilled to know that our dear Bri is with child, is she not?"

"Yes, and she's close to popping. Only a few more weeks, and my grandchild will make its appearance. I simply cannot wait." I smiled, leaning in to give Morna my hug of greeting.

Morna waved us inside her home. "I'm sure 'tis true, lass. I have something I wish for ye to take back with ye. It's an herbal potion I've mixed. 'Twill help her greatly with the pains of labor."

"Oh, thank you so much. I've been worrying myself sick thinking about the ordeal that's ahead of her. I thought I was going to die when I gave birth to Bri, and I let them drug me up with every medicine they had."

Morna laughed as we made our way into the sitting room. Mary's eyes bulged at the sight of every odd trinket. When Morna pointed at a box in the corner, tears immediately filled my eyes.

"I also retrieved something else for ye, lass," Morna said.

I had to keep from running toward the large box of ornaments, each a special memory of the Christmases Bri and I had spent together while she was growing up. Every year our collection grew, and each new ornament was a new, precious memory. "Morna!" I hadn't a clue how to express my gratitude.

"'Tis what ye really wanted, is it not?"

I nodded in disbelief. "Yes, but it never crossed my mind that I would actually be able to get them. I just planned to go into Edinburgh and buy a brand new set. All of this was in the States, at Bri's old place. How did you... how did you do this?"

She laughed heartily. "Did I not just make it possible for the two of ye to come here from hundreds of years in the past? Compared to that, 'twas a simple task to move these to us. Look in the other box. I also included a few other things I could sense were precious to ye."

My hands trembled with excitement as I moved to open the lid of the next box. I opened it to find an old CD player that could be operated with large DD batteries, packs and packs of replacement batteries, and our entire collection of Christmas music. Bri's baby blanket, knitted by my own mother, gently padded the Christmas items. Tears fell freely at the sight of it. "Oh my God, Morna. Are you a mind reader, as well?"

Jerry interjected playfully, "Aye, she is lass, and 'tis terribly annoying. I canna silently begrudge her anything without her finding out about it and charming me into forgiving her."

Morna laughed and leaned gently into her husband. "I am not that good at it, but ye are quite open with yer thoughts. 'Twas easy to see the things ye desired most from your trip here."

She was spot on. There was nothing more that I wished to retrieve. Everything I thought I would be unable to find was here. As far as I was concerned, we could make our way back to the castle immediately. But as I glanced over to see Mary in the kitchen, gleefully playing with the running water coming from the faucet, I thought better of suggesting we leave right away. "I cannot thank you enough, Morna. There's no need for me to make a trip into the city now, but would it be all right with you if we stay here tonight and leave in the morning?"

"Of course, lass. I wouldna have it any other way. I'm anxious to catch up with Mary, and I canna wait to hear her cries of excitement when we allow her to take a hot shower."

CHAPTER 5

he wind blew icy snow roughly into his face, and Hew could barely see the path in front of him. His fingers and nose burned from the pain of the harsh wind and bitter cold. With each step forward, his horse slowed his pace.

He didn't wish to stop for the night. He was so very close to the end of his journey, but he knew that his four-legged companion would not be able to go much further. He groaned at the thought of where he knew he must stop—Conall Castle—his sister's place of residence. The castle was so close that he could make out the silhouette of it in the distance, its grandness evident even through the storm.

It had been far too long since Hew had paid a visit to Mary. Nearly ten years by his count, possibly longer. He missed his sister, but he knew she would treat his arrival as a celebration, and the thought of such attention caused him to cringe inwardly.

Still, there was hardly another choice. Bracing himself for the torture he knew was about to ensue, he leaned down close to Greggory's ear, whispering words of encouragement as he nudged the old horse to the right. "Just a wee bit further, lad. There shall be a fine stable and blankets to keep ye warm just ahead. I'm sorry to have taken ye out in such a storm. I shall see ye well fed tonight, old fellow."

*F*lames flickered in the stables, so Hew knew before he approached that someone was still at work within them. They were most likely preparing the horses for the evening, making sure they were properly tended to in the cold weather.

He rode straight into the stables without seeking permission. He knew enough of the Conalls' generosity to know that they would not protest anyone seeking shelter for their horse on such a night.

Hew dismounted, quickly brushing the snow off of Greggory's coat, jumping at the sound of the voice in the far-end stall. "What sort of a fool would travel in this weather? 'Tis not so good for yer horse, sir. What be yer name?"

Hew's cheeks suddenly warmed. For a moment, he feared he would be unable to utter a word. He'd not spoken to another person in many moons. He swallowed, steeling himself for the task. "The fool's name is Hew. I apologize for the intrusion, but I must ask yer permission to allow me and my horse to rest here for the night. The poor lad willna be able to go much further."

A strong man as tall as him, with long, shaggy blond hair stepped out of the stall and smiled as he walked toward him. He knew it must be the youngest Conall brother, Arran, but the lad had been much younger when last Hew had seen him.

"Aye, of course ye can. It would be a wretched man to turn away anyone in a storm such as this."

Hew continued to rub the sleeves of his covering over his horse's coat, doing his best to dry the animal. "Thank ye, sir. I shall help ye in the cleaning of the stables come morning in payment for yer kindness. Ye are Arran, are ye not?"

Arran reached for a blanket draped over the doors of one of the stalls and moved to help Hew in his efforts. "Nay, that willna be necessary for ye to clean the stables. But, aye, I am Arran. Should I know ye, sir?"

Hew shook his head as they worked alongside each other, warming and drying the beast. "Nay, I doona expect that ye would remember me, but I believe ye know my sister, Mary. Is she still in service to yer family?"

The strapping lad next to him patted the horse gently on the backside before casting a rather surprised expression in his direction. "Nay, ye canna mean it? Ye're Mary's brother? Well, 'tis a pleasure to meet ye. And aye, we know Mary well, but I wouldna say she is in our service. This castle is more hers than my brother's."

Hew laughed. It seemed his sister had changed little over the years. "Aye, lad, that sounds verra much like she would have it. I dread the fuss she shall make over my arrival, but I feel I must make my presence here known to her. Where can I find her?"

Arran fidgeted uncomfortably. For a moment Hew worried that perhaps his sister was unwell, but the lad recovered quickly. "Well, it seems that she herself has gone on a bit of a journey, but doona worry about the weather, we know that she is quite safe and out of the storm. I shall let her explain to ye where it is she has gone once she returns."

Hew didn't understand what the lad meant, but he wasn't disappointed to learn that he would be able to rest before reuniting with his sister. "Ah, well, I'm certain she will be pleased to tell me all about it. She used to talk a great deal. I doona imagine that has changed."

Arran laughed and motioned for Hew to lead his horse into one of the empty stalls. "Nay, sir, she hasna changed. She's talked a lot for all the time that I've known her. Now, let us get yer horse settled, and ye shall follow me inside so that ye can have a room of yer own."

Hew stiffened and stopped moving forward. He would not be comfortable staying inside the castle. It was not where he belonged. He'd rather stay in the stables, with only the horses for company. "Nay, lad, I shall stay here with the horses. It would not be proper for me to accompany ye inside."

"Nay proper?"exclaimed Arran. "I willna be letting ye stay out here in this weather. If Mary learned I'd done so, she'd kill me herself, I'm certain."

Hew didn't wish to be impolite to his host, but staying in the stable was something he knew he must insist upon. He wouldn't sleep a wink in the presence of so many people. "I doona wish to offend ye, lad, but I simply canna stay in the castle. If ye willna allow me to remain out here, I'm afraid that Greggory and I will have to be on our way and take our chances with the snow."

Guilt filled Hew at the look of shock on Arran's face. If only the thought of company didn't paralyze him so.

"Nay, please doona leave in this storm. Mary would rather me allow ye to sleep in the stables, I'm certain. But perhaps, I can provide ye with something a little more comfortable than stable floors."

"Truly, lad, 'tis no trouble for me to stay here. I've slept in worse many times before."

Arran shook his head as he draped Hew's horse with coverings. "Just listen to me before ye say nay to it. We have a cottage not far from here. 'Tis empty. No one stays there, and ye are welcome to do so if ye wish. Ye can build ye a fire, and there is a proper bed. Please, sir, at least stay there."

Hew couldn't deny how pleasurable a warm fire and a soft bed sounded to him. As long as it was truly separate from the castle as the lad said, he thought he could find rest for the night there. "Aye, lad. I shall gladly stay in yer cottage. I'm sorry to be a bother to ye. I appreciate yer kindness."

Arran clasped him tightly on the shoulder. "Nay, sir, 'tis no trouble. I apologize for saying so, but ye're rather a strange fellow, are ye not?"

Hew laughed at the truthfulness in Arran's words as the young Conall showed him the way to the tiny cottage. "Aye, lad, that I am, verra strange indeed."

CHAPTER 6

Getting back to the seventeenth century was mildly tricky, but Mary and I managed. Because we brought with us two boxes of belongings and the precious vial I hoped would provide Bri with much relief once she went into labor, we were forced to sit on the floor of the spell room while we balanced the boxes in our laps. We chanted the words aloud together and reached over our boxes to link hands right before the spell began to work.

When we arrived back, we nursed our aching heads for a few short moments and then made our way up to the kitchen, where we heard Bri and her lookalike sister-in-law, Blaire, working together.

"We're back! What are you two girlies up to?" I set the box I carried down just past the doorway and went to give both of the girls a quick hug. I lingered an extra second with Bri, pressing my hands against her stomach to see if my grandbaby would give me a quick kick. For the moment, it seemed the infant slept soundly.

"We're trying to cook," said Blaire, in answer to my question. "But it isn't going so well. Eoin and Arran will be thrilled that yer home, Mary. They're convinced that if they have to go another day with us as cooks, they shall starve to death."

Bri winked at Mary and then bobbed her head in the direction of the box. "What did you get?"

I grabbed her hand and anxiously dragged her over so I could reveal all of the precious goodies we'd brought. "Morna knew what I wanted. She gathered up our ornament box. Isn't it wonderful?"

Bri moved to her knees instantly, her belly getting in the way, but I knew nothing would keep her from rummaging through the boxes. Each item was as special to her as it was to me. "Oh, Mom. You're joking! This is amazing, truly."

"Yes, it is, dear. She gathered a few other items for us, as well, but I'm going to wait until later to show those to you. It can just be a surprise for everyone." I placed my hand on her shoulder as I squatted down next to her. Then we lifted each tiny memory out of the box.

Blaire walked across the room to stand next to us. "The storm has slowed a bit. 'Tis still impossible to go too far from the main building, but not much is falling right now. Mayhap we should all go out together and find a tree to cut down for the decorations."

Bri leapt to her feet with more energy than I'd seen her exert in the last two months. "Yes, that's a perfect idea. I'll get Eoin. Blaire, you find Arran. Mom and Mary, go get Kip and meet us out back. Stat!"

She scurried off quickly, Blaire following suit. Mary and I laughed together, walking out of the kitchen so we could prepare for our outing.

---

*B*oth girls had apparently already decided that we would go tree hunting today if we returned from Morna's in time. The gathering of everyone went entirely too smoothly, as if they all waited on pins and needles for us to get home. The excitement of Christmas was starting to move through our merry little group.

The snow was beautiful, covering every inch of the castle grounds. I found myself wishing more than once that I'd enlisted Morna to cast us all a pair of sturdy snow boots to bring back. But we were all having such a wonderful time, none of us thought much about our ice-cold toes.

It took us some time before we found a tree that everyone agreed upon. We'd decided against many with the perfect shape that had proven far too large. And then some of perfect size had not been the right shape. Eventually, the perfect tree stood before us. While Eoin, Arran, and Mary's husband, Kip, worked at chopping it down, all of us girls huddled together, watching.

The landscape remained silent, save for the crack against the wood as the men took their turns driving the ax into its base. For a moment, I thought I'd imagined a soft whining sound coming from somewhere behind me, but as I listened I felt certain that I had not.

An animal, of that much I was sure, and a young one at that, made the noise. I couldn't tell what kind of creature it might be. My heart squeezed uncomfortably at the thought of anything so tiny and helpless being trapped out here in the snow.

Afraid that too many people approaching would cause it fear, I slowly crept away from the group and went off in search of the soft whine.

*H*ew stepped out in front of the small cottage, frowning as he looked out over the snow-drenched landscape. He'd hoped very much that he would be able to leave today, but it would be impossible. Even though snow no longer fell, he feared his horse might break a leg if he forced him to trudge through snow so deep.

He threw his arms up above him, stretching and groaning at his frustration. In response to the noises he made, something whined not far from him. Compassion compelled him to go in search of the creature.

Turning, he draped himself in thick coverings, the chill from his ride yesterday still set deep within his bones. Grunting, he took off in the direction of the noise. He stepped only a few feet away from the cottage when he caught sight of the dark, whimpering ball of fur at the base of the tree.

Hew bent, gently picking up the puppy, cradling it as it shivered uncontrollably in his large hands. He wrapped the pup up in his own furs, rubbing his hands back and forth over the small creature to warm it. It was a miracle the pup still lived, for it must have spent the previous night out in the storm.

Waiting for the puppy to stop trembling, Hew held it closely to his chest. When he felt its warm tongue start to lap at the inside of his fingers, he knew the pup was only cold, not injured. He uncovered the tiny animal, smiling as he took in its handsome features.

Hew raised him to check the gender and, finding him a boy, set him back into the cradle of his hand. The dog was fluffy with thick hair that made him look much bigger than he seemed. Its coat was dark on back, with a beautiful mixture of gray, brown and black spots covering his chest and feet. Warm brown eyes oozed kindness, and above them, small patches of light brown hair stood out, giving the illusion of brows.

"Why, ye are a handsome pup, are ye not?" He pulled the creature in close to him once more, reaching down to pick the clumps of icy snow from between the pup's paws. He stilled when another small whine caught his attention. "Ach, it seems that ye have another wee friend close by. Let's go find him together."

*I*t had not taken me long to find the source of the noise. If not for the weak bark that the creature let out as I approached him, I would have probably stepped right on top of him, as the white of his fur matched the snow.

The puppy lay hidden close to the Conall's small cottage, with only his black nose and mouth sticking up out of the drift. I gasped when I saw him, quickly reaching down to snatch him out of his icy home, brushing the snow off of him with my bare hands. "Oh, you poor thing!"

The creature responded with another small bark. Once he was free of the snow, I lifted him, examining his coloring. His hair was straight but full— beautiful, but he was the kind of dog I was sure would shed easily. White fur covered most of his body, but his backside was black. With the exception of his white mouth and snout, each side of his face and both ears were black, too.

I'd expected the creature to squirm in my grasp but, once he became warm, he collapsed, relaxing completely, his small legs dangling on each side of my arm. I grinned as I pulled him in close. I hoped very much that Eoin would not object to having a dog in the castle because the pup would come with me, regardless.

A voice behind me caused me to jump, jerking my arm so that the puppy came awake, yipping in displeasure.

"Ah, I thought I heard another one making noise. Seems our two little friends must be brothers, aye?"

I turned around to face the most handsome man I had ever seen.

CHAPTER 7

"*O*h my, you scared me. Hello there." I lifted my knees high as I moved closer to him. I didn't miss the strange expression that crossed his face when he heard me speak; everyone in this time had a similar reaction to my accent and twenty-first century way of expressing myself.

"'Ello to ye too, lass. I apologize for frightening ye. 'Twas not my intention. I heard this wee lad and found him not far from the one ye hold in yer hands. I still heard whining so I knew there must be another close by." He pointed to the black squirmy ball he held. His pup was far less content than the one cradled like broccoli in my arms.

Once close to the man, I extended my hand to touch the wiggly pup he held. The dog's fur felt soft like baby hair. As I rubbed him, the man reached his hand across to pet the pup I held.

"They are both fine looking pups, are they not?"

I nodded, and we simultaneously pulled our hands back to our sides. "Yes, beautiful dogs. Look at the markings above their eyes. They look quite different, but they must be out of the same litter."

"Aye, lass, I believe ye are right. They are the same size and age. Forgive me, miss. My manners are not what they should be. My name is Hew. To whom do I find myself speaking?"

I reached out to shake his hand. My stomach fluttered as he grabbed my fingertips and briefly touched them to his lips. I was far too old to have such a reaction to a man, but God he was a beautiful being. "Um…" I faltered and blushed, totally out of character from my normally over-confident, over-flirty self. "Um…Adelle. My name is Adelle."

I guessed he was only a few years older than me, if not the same age.

Thick, dark, wavy curls, only lightly sprinkled with salt, covered his head. He kept it cropped short, unlike many men of this time who wore theirs longer. I preferred his. I didn't see the appeal in being with a man who had more hair on his head than I do.

Tall and broad shouldered, every inch of Hew was covered in clothing, but I had a feeling he would not be soft beneath the layers, like so many men from my time were by the time they reached my age. He worked hard; that was evident from the tone of his skin and the light crease of wrinkles across his brow. A light shadow of a beard only added to the manliness he exuded.

His awkward stance hinted at shyness. Now that we'd introduced ourselves to one another, he seemed uncertain of how to continue the conversation.

I had to shake my head to recover, yanking my stare away from the deep green abysses of his eyes. "Um…are you from around here? Do you live in the village?"

The puppy Hew held had stopped squirming and had fallen asleep in his arms. Bending his head to look at it, he said, "Nay, lass. I doona live anywhere near here. I'm on my way elsewhere but had to stop here due to the storm. I am staying in this cottage here." He pointed behind him. "The Conalls were kind enough to grant me refuge from the snow. My sister lives with them and works in the castle."

Only one woman worked for the Conalls, and other than myself, only one woman that wasn't a Conall actually lived in the castle. Mary was both. But there was no possible way the god that stood before me could be the brother Mary had been talking about. "You wouldn't be speaking of Mary, would you? Your sister is someone else, yes?"

Hew's eyes sparkled a brilliant green, creating another flurry of flutters in my stomach. "Aye, lass, 'tis Mary that I speak of. Do ye know her?"

Stunned, I stared at Mary's brother. I had based my mental image of him on her appearance, envisioning a short, round, aging bald man who talked loudly. This man was none of those things. His voice was deep, but he spoke quietly and said nothing more than required by the conversation. "Yes, I know Mary quite well. She's just around the corner here, along with everyone else from the castle. We've been cutting down a tree for Christmas. Does she know that you're here? Mary and I were away yesterday, we only just returned this morning."

He shook his head. "I doona know if she is aware of my presence yet, but I guess 'tis time that she is. Will ye lead the way to her for me, lass?"

"Of course." I turned and waved so he would follow me. I felt self-conscious with my back exposed to him. With every step, I damned myself for pinning my hair up into a hideous bun before we trekked out into the snow.

The group saw me first, and Mary immediately tore into me for stepping away from their company. "Adelle, what is the matter with ye? Why did ye run off without telling us where ye'd gone? Ye could have frozen to death…"

She paused when she caught sight of her brother, then moved her short, stumpy legs faster than I'd ever have thought possible. Charging through the snow, she threw herself into his arms.

Hew let out a puff of air as she squeezed him, and then pushed her away as gently as he could. "Be careful, Mary. Ye shall squish the wee pup I hold in my arms."

Mary glanced briefly down at the sleeping dog but seemed unaffected by the adorable bundle. Bri and Blaire, on the other hand, immediately went to snatch the pups from each of our arms.

"What are ye doing here, Hew?" Mary exclaimed. "I havena seen ye in years. God, ye look good, brother!" Once Hew was free of the puppy, she threw her arms around him again.

"I was on my way to Mae's grave, but the storm caused me to seek shelter here," he explained. "I only arrived last evening."

The sadness I'd seen earlier in Mary briefly crossed her face again, and I wondered greatly about the identity of Mae. The pain showed only for a moment before Mary whirled away from her brother to face the crowd that had gathered, all of us watching curiously.

"I see," she said, her eyes narrowing. "And which one of ye knew he was here and dinna tell me the second I arrived this morning?"

Bri, Blaire, Eoin, and Kip all looked back and forth at each other, clearly in the dark, while Arran glanced sheepishly at the ground. "'Twas I, Mary," he said, after a moment of silence. "I apologize. I'm a fool. I got so caught up in the lasses' excitement over finding a tree that I forgot to tell ye."

I thought for a moment she would march through the snow and smack him, but her happiness at seeing her brother seemed to override her annoyance at not learning of his presence until now.

Mary tsked. "Shame on ye, Arran, but 'tis no matter now. Why doona the rest of ye go on back to the castle with the tree? I shall join ye shortly after I spend some time speaking with my brother, aye?"

"Aye, Mary," said Eoin, as he motioned for us all to head back. "Spend as much time as ye wish. I suppose we willna starve from only one more night of Bri and Blaire's cooking. Yer brother is welcome to dine with us, but if ye wish to spend some time alone together, I can bring ye food later this evening."

I was surprised when Hew responded to Eoin instantly. "I would be much obliged to ye if ye would allow us to dine in the cottage. I shall repay yer kindness in some way."

I couldn't blame him for not wanting to dine with everyone. We were a bit much to take. Still, his quick rejection seemed a little odd. He walked over to Blaire, who was holding his new puppy. After she handed it to him, he and Mary turned to make their way back to the cottage.

As we made our way the short distance back to the castle, both Bri and Blaire squeezed in tight on either side of me while I balanced my puppy in between my open palms. The girls leaned in close so that they could hear the other's whispers.

"Mom, holy cow, would you ever have thought Mary's brother would look like that?" Bri nudged my side playfully.

I smiled, laughing as I shook my head. I leaned into her, nudging her back. "No, not in a million years would I have expected that."

"Ye did find him a handsome lad, aye Adelle?" Blaire's voice was as quiet and excited as Bri's.

"Oh yes, very much so. He's quite striking. Why do you ask?" He must be married, of course. All the good ones were.

"He's a bit of a hermit from what Eoin and Arran told us," said Bri. "His wife died decades ago, and he lives all alone far away from anyone else. Seems a bit crazy to me, but Eoin seems to think he's just shy. Regardless, does it matter if he's crazy when he looks that good?"

The three of us laughed loudly, garnering questioning glances from the three men walking in front of us. Bri liked to think she was my polar opposite, but she was more like her Mama than she wanted to admit. "Well, it does matter a bit, yes, but I don't think he's crazy." We were approaching the castle. "Let's not gossip anymore now, the boys will give me a hard time." I lifted the puppy. "I'm going to find some food for this little one to eat."

Once inside, the girls dispersed. I carried the sleeping pup down into the kitchen while I thought over what I'd just learned about our new visitor. He was unmarried.

And I was not displeased to hear it.

All was abuzz within the confines of Conall Castle the next day. It was decorating day. That, along with her brother's visit, lifted Mary's spirits as high as I'd ever seen them. As a result, everyone else in the castle couldn't help but be merry, as well.

I'd not expected us to put the tree in the castle's main entrance. I worried that the modern ornaments we planned to put on the tree might raise suspicions of other castle workers. I could not have been more surprised when I made my way down in the morning to find that Eoin, Arran, and Kip had placed the tree there.

"Wouldn't it be best if we set up the tree in the basement? I won't be able to hang the ornaments on it otherwise."

"Aye, ye will. Feel free to hang anything that ye wish from the tree. I willna have us hiding our celebrations. All who work within the castle know of Morna's legacy and her spells." Eoin walked up to me and bent to briefly kiss me on the cheek. "Good morning, Adelle."

I smiled, so very pleased that my daughter found such a wonderful man. "Oh great, that's wonderful. It will look beautiful in the corner there, next to the grand fireplace."

"Aye, it will. Look." Eoin pointed to the staircase behind me. "Here come the other lassies. Let us eat and then we will begin the festivity of decorating."

*O*ver breakfast, I couldn't help but notice Hew's absence from the table once again. I was fairly sure he hadn't left already. The snow still had not melted enough for travel, and there was little way for him to get food in the cottage without someone bringing it to him. I didn't understand why he seemed so set against joining us in the castle. Leaning closer to Mary, I asked, "Why won't your brother join us here to eat? He knows that he's welcome, doesn't he?"

Mary pulled one corner of her mouth to the side before casting sad eyes in my direction. "Aye, he knows it, but he insists on being alone."

"Why is that?" I looked down at my food so that my interest wouldn't seem too eager.

"He's painfully shy. He's spent so much time alone, I'm afraid he doesna know how to be around other people anymore."

That was a hard concept for me to grasp. I loved spending every second in the company of others. It was unhealthy for someone to live in such a way. It might be one thing for a person to spend time alone by their own choice, but another to feel that they were prevented from joining others due to shyness. "Well, the only way to become less shy is through practice. Will you see him this morning?"

Mary nodded. "Aye, I shall bring him something to eat as soon as we finish here and before we begin decorating."

"Ask him to join us and help in the decorations. It's going to be a lot of fun. Insist on it, Mary. You can be very persuasive."

Mary chuckled but shook her head. "That may be true with many people, Adelle, but nay with my brother. I can insist until the stars have risen, and it will not persuade him to do something he doesna wish to do."

I frowned. I didn't like the thought of Hew all alone in the cottage while the rest of us spent a joyous day decorating. "Well, will you at least ask him?"

Mary stood, covering a plate to take to her brother. "Aye, lass. I'll ask him."

---

*P*erhaps he'd been too short with his sister, Hew thought. It wasn't unreasonable for her to wish that he spend some time with her by joining in the Christmas festivities. He would make time to see her later when she was alone but his shyness would have done nothing but dampen the spirits of everyone else.

Hew no longer knew how to feel comfortable in front of one person, let alone an entire family of people who evidently were quite close to one another. He'd managed well enough when he'd bumped into Adelle the day he'd found the pup now sleeping at his feet, but that was an unusual occurrence. They'd had the discovery of the pups in common, which had given him something to talk to her about. Hew decided he would be certain to make an effort to spend a little more time with his sister before he left.

He reached down to rub on the sleeping pup, thinking back on the strangest thing his sister had told him. She'd said more than once that Adelle had insisted that he come to the castle and help them with the decorations. Why would the lass desire such a thing?

She must feel sorry for him. Any other possibility seemed too unrealistic for him to consider. There'd only been one woman to fancy him in his whole life. It wouldn't make sense for another lass to decide to do so now.

Would it?

I waited until all of the men started trimming the tree, working it into the perfect shape, before sneaking away to grab the surprise I had in store for all of them.

Mary's trip to see her brother had been quick. When she arrived back at the castle without Hew, I knew he had rejected her invitation to join us. I couldn't help the small pang of sadness that lodged itself in my chest, but I did my best to dismiss it. I hardly knew the man, after all. What did I care if he chose to be such a fuddy duddy?

Blaire had already helped Bri carry the large box of ornaments upstairs, so while the men shaved away at the tree and the girls marveled at each ornament as they pulled them out of the box, I went down to the basement once more.

Opening the box, I pulled out the large boom box, flipping it over so that I could install a fresh set of batteries. Placing the CD player under one arm and a stack of CDs under the other, I made my way upstairs.

Once I got into the great room, I walked with my back toward everyone so as to shield the contents in my arms. Then I set the player discreetly next to the fire, hidden away behind a large chair. I thought it best to select a classical Christmas mix first. I was afraid anything too modern would frighten the bejeezus out of Arran and Kip, both of whom had never made a trip through time.

I started the music with the volume turned low. It played just loud enough to cause everyone in the room to glance around, as if they were imagining the sounds in their heads. Slowly, I increased the intensity until Kip threw both his hands to his ears and looked up to the ceiling in horror.

"What in the name o' God is that? I've told all of ye, I doona like the magic that seems to go on in this place. Make it stop."

Mary laughed and walked over to grab her husband's wrists. Prying his hands away from his head, she said, "Doona be such a fool, Kip. 'Tis not magic, only a music maker we brought back from our journey. Do ye not think it sounds lovely?"

When Kip didn't answer, Arran said, "I've never heard such beautiful noise in my life. Leave it be, 'tis magical."

Eventually, Kip surrendered and joined in with the humming and singing as we spent the day turning Conall Castle into a Christmas wonderland. The tree didn't take all that long, and after it was complete, Mary led us girls downstairs to make garland and wreaths to hang up around the castle.

It was hard work, twisting the leaves and branches into arrangements that pleased the eye. Mary, Blaire, and Bri took to it quite well, though. All of my projects, however, were undisputed disasters.

I'd not been a crafty woman in the twenty-first century, where craft stores on almost every other corner sold glues and tools to help with projects. Without such conveniences, I found even trying to attempt the endeavor to be pure misery.

After three failed wreaths and a string of garland only the *Grinch* would appreciate, I was taken off craft duty and given the measly task of taking the mistletoe that Bri had created and hanging it above the dining hall entryway.

Mary thought the tradition of mistletoe to be a brilliant idea. "Ye mean that if I can somehow trick Kip into standing beneath the doorway with me, he will be forced to kiss me? Why, I shall stand there all day and wait for him to pass through! I doona believe the old bugger will even remember what part of yer body that ye use to kiss, 'tis been so long since he's done so."

I laughed, but as I did so, Mary's brother crossed my mind. If his life was anything like what Bri and Blaire had described, I imagined that it had been quite some time since Hew had been kissed, as well. For some reason, I wished to be the person to change that for him. "Mary, would you mind if I took Hew some food to eat after the evening meal?"

She clucked her tongue at me knowingly. "Ach, I knew there was a reason ye wished me to ask Hew to help with the decorations. Ye have taken a liking to him then, have ye?'

I reddened—something that seemed to be happening much more frequently than normal. I didn't like it one bit. "Well, what if I have?"

Mary laughed and looked down, concentrating on the bunch of stems in her hand. "Nothing, dear. It has been far too long since Hew has shared his company with another. Please, I would love for ye to take him his food. I doona like getting out in the snow anyway."

"Will he be angry, do you think? I don't want to upset him. I just thought perhaps I could bring some of the decorations that we didn't use, and I could leave them for him to set up at the cottage. It would give him something to do. With the snow still piled up, I don't think he will be leaving us anytime soon."

"Right ye are, lass, and he willna be angry at all. He's a kind man, although I'll admit that he is slow to warm. But once ye reach the man behind his shyness, the man he really is, why..." She paused, smiling down at her wreath. "Hew is a man worth getting to know."

The cottage stood silent in front of Arran and me. I feared Hew had already gone to sleep for the evening. But when the puppy I cradled underneath my arm let out a high-pitched yelp, the door to the cottage flew open.

"Ach, evening, Adelle. Evening, Arran. I thought there was a third pup who had found his way out of the snow, but I see 'tis only yer little fellow, Adelle."

"Ah, yes." I paused and waved Arran away. Earlier, we'd cut down a small tree, and Arran had dragged it to the cottage, as well as helping me carry the food and decorations, which we'd set beside the door. "Thank you, Arran. I'll make it up to you somehow."

"Good night," Arran told us. "There is no need to make anything up to me, Adelle. Ye are quite welcome." He turned and started off, calling back to me over his shoulder, "Be careful on yer way back to the castle." Then he disappeared into the darkness, leaving Hew and me alone.

I silently thanked Arran for following my instructions to leave as soon as he dropped off all of the items. I wanted a chance to be alone with the quiet, strange man, and I didn't want to take the chance that Hew might ask Arran to stick around.

Not that I should've been concerned. With the look of surprise on Hew's face, I wondered if I would even be invited inside. I lifted up the basket of food I held in my left hand as I set my pup down on the ground. He immediately ran inside the cottage to join his brother. "Um...Mary was busy so I told her I would bring you something to eat. I hope you don't mind. Also ..." I pointed to the items behind me, " ... I brought some decorations. We had some left over from today, and I thought it would give you something to do, ya know, if you wanted to decorate the cottage for Christmas."

He scrunched his brows together. I couldn't tell if he was confused or disgusted. I'd not given much thought to the fact that he was a man and probably didn't give two flips about beautifying anything. I'd simply been trying to spread the cheer.

"I...you don't have to take the decorations. I can come back with Arran in the morning and get them," I stammered. "But at least take the food. I'll just head back to the castle now." I squatted awkwardly, whistling to my pup to come, but to no avail. The two brothers wrestled playfully on the floor with no intention of ending their little games anytime soon.

Hew surprised me by reaching out to put his hand on my shoulder. "Nay, lass, I shall enjoy the decorations. Please, come inside."

He stepped aside to usher me in, and I immediately complied, running my hands up and down my arms to warm myself.

"Come sit by the fire while I set the table," Hew instructed. "Surely ye are in no hurry to return to the castle. Why doona ye stay and eat with me? I'm sorry if I gave ye the feeling I wished for ye to leave. 'Twas simply that I was surprised by yer presence."

"Oh." I wanted to smack myself square in the forehead at my inability to speak like a grown woman in front of him. My behavior was absolutely ridiculous. No man, not even Bri's father, had the ability to render me speechless so completely.

"Did ye already eat, lass? If so, I shall wait until after ye have gone. Perhaps ye can at least warm yerself by the fire for a little while, aye?"

For someone so shy, he tried to be talkative. And I rewarded his efforts by appearing far less friendly than I actually was. I needed to get a grip! I loved to talk and, by golly, I intended to do so. I set my mind to acting human again before I opened my mouth. "No. I haven't eaten."

He stood and moved to the small table, laying out the spread I'd brought for him. "Come and join me, lass."

---

*W*e ate quietly. I searched my mind for ideas of what I could speak to him about, but came up short. I knew that Hew sensed my hesitation, as sometimes I would utter a syllable, only to stop before forming a complete word. He took pity on me by speaking himself.

"I apologize for the way I behaved when I opened the door. I am verra much accustomed to being all alone. Although I am a visitor here, visitors of my own are verra unexpected. Might I tell ye something?"

I nodded. "Of course."

"It occurred to me that perhaps ye keep stopping yerself from talking to me because ye are worried that I might notice the odd way in which ye speak."

That had nothing to do with it, but I didn't want to object when he had obviously put so much thought into my silence. Instead, I remained quiet and waited for him to continue.

"I confess that I did take note of it when I first met ye. But then Mary told me yer story about where and when ye came from and I understood. So doona worry, lass, I willna judge the way ye speak. I'm not so good at speaking with others myself."

Surprised by his words, I smiled. Mary hadn't lied. Her brother was a kind man. "How is it that you seem to have so easily believed what Mary told you? It is hard for even those of us who have experienced Morna's magic to accept it."

"Ach, ye have found yer voice. I am glad for it." Hew smiled slightly.

If I'd been standing, I expect my knees would have grown weak at the beauty of that smile.

"I knew Morna when I was a child, and I grew up hearing stories of her powers," Hew explained. "I know my sister well enough to know that she wouldna lie to me about such a matter. Besides, life is such that many things happen that we canna explain. It must have been quite a change for ye to come here, aye?"

Our food was now gone, and I knew I would be expected to take my leave soon. "Yes, it was, but one I welcomed. With my daughter being here, there's nowhere else I'd rather be. I love it here very much." I stood, pushing my chair in before walking to the door. "Why don't I help you carry the rest of these things in? Then I'll leave you be for the evening."

The same unreadable look that had crossed his face earlier resurfaced, and I was afraid I'd somehow upset him. He cast his palm out in the direction of the empty room. "Are ye not going to stay and help me? It seems ye have brought enough trinkets to decorate an entire village, and I havena celebrated the holiday since I was a small child. I'm afraid I shallna know what to do with all of it on my own."

I beamed and stepped out into the darkness so he wouldn't see my reddened face. "Yes, I would love to."

For someone that didn't like the company of others, he seemed to be in no hurry to rid himself of mine.

---

*H*ew thought the lass must still carry Morna's magic with her for her to have such an effect on him. He'd been surprised by her slim presence at the door. And pleased when she'd quickly sent Arran away, her blonde hair blowing wildly in the breeze. She wanted to be alone with him. While Hew wasn't sure why, the thought made something deep within him warm for the first time in ages.

At first, Adelle had seemed even more nervous than he. That fact somehow helped to calm his nerves in the beauty's presence. In fact, he felt very much himself with her and talked as freely as he did with anyone.

The lass's shyness had not lasted long. After he'd asked her to stay and help him with the decorations, she'd talked with him at length, telling him grand stories of all that had happened at Conall Castle within the last months. For the first time, Hew found himself wishing he had not stayed away from his homeland for so long.

When all that Adelle had brought him was set up just as the lass would have it, he walked her back to the castle, his heart more sad than he would allow himself to admit that their evening together had come to an end.

"Thank you for allowing me to interrupt your evening," she said. "I hope I wasn't too much of a bother."

The lass was mad if she was unable to see how much he had enjoyed her company. Perhaps his feelings dinna show clearly on his face. He had kept them locked away deep inside himself for a verra long time, after all.

He stared directly into her green eyes now, eyes so vibrant and alive that he couldn't help but realize how little he'd allowed himself to truly live for far too many years. She was the most beautiful woman he had ever seen, her pale face pink from standing out in the cold. He wanted to do nothing more than warm it with the touch of his lips.

"Nay, lass, ye were not a bother at all. I had a wonderful time," Hew said quietly.

Mustering all the courage he had left in him for the evening, he quickly leaned in to kiss her on her cheek. Turning before he could see her reaction, he marched back into the darkness, his heart beating faster than it had in decades.

CHAPTER 11

Carrying my pup, I left my bedchamber early the next morning to join everyone in the dining hall for breakfast. Still high on the endorphins Hew's lips had stirred in me the night before, I reminded myself that it had only been a kiss on the cheek, but the reminder did nothing to push the giddy flurries away. What would I have done if he'd given me a proper kiss?

I found myself imagining such a kiss, then pushed the vision from my mind. I was going to be a grandmother for goodness' sake. I had no business acting like a silly schoolgirl with a crush.

But honestly, who was I kidding? Even though I was a grandmother-to-be in my fifties, I'd always been young on the inside, immature some would say, and I didn't have hope that a grandchild would change that about me any time soon. I'd given up acting my age—whatever that meant—long ago.

I walked into the dining hall and felt my eyes widen in surprise. Hew sat at the table along with everyone else. Doing my best to hide my shock, I sat at my usual place, setting my puppy on the floor at my feet. Then I turned to listen to Eoin, who was addressing the table.

"Are ye finished with yer meal, lads? If so, let us be on our way. I'm not so inclined to leave Bri's side, but she was verra insistent that we make this trip."

Bri nodded and waved him off, patting her stomach with her other hand. "Yes, I was. Be gone, all of you, and have a wonderful time. The baby seems content where it is. I'm certain it will be days until the birth."

"Where are you going?" I asked. I'd obviously missed the front of this conversation. Regardless, I was not willing to be left out of the loop.

"Since Christmas Eve is only days away, the men are leaving us for a few days to go on a hunt," Bri responded from across the table. "Hew has agreed to stay with us until after the holiday. He's going to help them on the hunt. Mary says he is a fine shot with an arrow."

I glanced at Hew, then quickly away. "Wonderful. Are you boys certain you trust us to have free run of the castle while you're away?"

Eoin laughed as the other men rose from their places at the table. "Oh, Adelle. Ye all have free run as it is, do ye not?"

I had nothing to say to that. He was right. We most certainly all did exactly as we wished. Headstrong women filled Conall Castle.

As the men prepared to leave, Hew walked around the table to stand at my side. He carried his puppy, which had been hidden underneath the table at his feet, just like mine.

"Will ye watch over him for me while I am away, lass?" My pup had ventured out from beneath the table and Hew set his beside it. They instantly began gnawing at each other's faces playfully. "They seem quite attached to one another."

I grinned, nodding emphatically, pleased and surprised that he'd decided to join the men on their hunt. "Of course. I'll take excellent care of him."

"Aye, I'm sure ye will, lass."

He turned and left without bidding farewell to anyone else in the room, even Mary, and I could almost see the steam coming from her ears.

---

*M*ary waited all of five seconds after the men left the dining hall to tear into me. "Did ye lead my brother to believe that ye care for him more than ye do, Adelle? Are ye not bothered that he will be hurt by yer pretense? Hew is not like other men who are amused by a woman's teasing."

My mouth fell open in response to her attack. "What? Are you mad? Of course I didn't pretend any such thing! I didn't do anything save talk his ear off. He was very kind to put up with me. I enjoyed his company very much."

Mary's expression changed from one of anger to sheer surprise. "So ye swear to me then, ye are not simply amusing yerself by teasing him into thinking the likes of ye would enjoy being with such a shy man? What did the two of ye talk about? My brother hardly speaks two words in a week's time."

Whatever anger that had faded from Mary had moved into me. "Mary, if I weren't afraid you would knock me flat on the floor, I'd be half tempted to throttle you right now. It is absolutely none of your business what your brother and I talked about. And you insult me by thinking I'd toy with his feelings."

"Since he willna talk, did ye fill the time by trying to kiss him, then?"

Bri and Blaire glanced nervously at one another, and I could tell they wondered if they should stand in between us to keep us from attempting to strangle one another. Both of us needed to calm down.

"No, I did no such thing, Mary."

"Oh." Mary stood and walked around the room, as if trying to accept my words as truth.

"Oh, is right. You should feel mighty ashamed of yourself for assuming such a thing." I leaned back in my chair, crossing my arms to show my frustration.

Bri blinked at me. "Mom, in Mary's defense, Hew is her brother. He has been alone for a long time and he's a gentle and sensitive man. She's only looking out for his best interests, and it's not as if what she accused you of doing would be completely out of character for you, besides."

I shot my daughter a look that must have been frightening for she sank down into her chair and didn't say another word as we all waited for Mary to speak again.

Eventually, she exhaled exaggeratedly and moved to resume her seat at the table. "Well, if the two of ye dinna even kiss, my brother must fancy the oddest of women, because he's mighty taken with ye."

"Why do you say that?" My face warmed, and I reached up to fan myself. At least at this age, I could use hormones as an excuse.

"I all but begged him to join us as ye bid me to yesterday, and he would not come. He spends one evening in yer company, and he shows up at the castle this morning without being asked. He's always welcome o'course, but 'tis shocking behavior from him, Adelle. He even suggested the hunt. He went to Eoin early this morning and told him that he thought he'd found some great places for hunting on his way here."

"Is that so?" I looked down at myself. If only there was air conditioning in this century.

Bri smiled and pointed at my face. "Mom, you're blushing. You like him, don't you?"

My daughter was skating on thin ice this morning. "Yes, I do, but I am not blushing. I'm far too old to blush. It's just very warm in here, is all. I think I'm having a hot flash."

"Nay, Adelle," said Blaire, ganging up on me along with Bri. "'Tis not warm in here at all. I doona believe ye are having a flash of warmth. I think Bri is right, ye're blushing."

"Why don't the two of you just bugger off?" I stood, determined to go find some cold water to splash on my face. At the doorway, I paused and looked back at the threesome. "Oh, Mary," I said, my old spunk returning. "I didn't lie when I said that I didn't kiss your brother." Smiling, I added, "*Hew kissed me.*"

CHAPTER 12

The men stayed close to the castle, finding shelter for themselves and their horses in the village. The hunt had done them all good. Hew was accustomed to spending his days working hard on his land. He didn't like being cooped up in the confines of the small cottage each day.

He'd wanted to learn more about Adelle from his hosts while away, but had hoped to keep his growing feelings for her a secret. He'd been completely unsuccessful. It seemed all of the men had assumed that his sudden eagerness to join in the castle activities had something to do with her.

As they made their way to the rooms they'd rented at the inn for the evening, Arran nudged him in the ribs as if they'd known each other forever. "Did ye enjoy Adelle's visit last night? Ye must have, for I had no luck convincing ye to step inside the castle walls, while she had no problem doing so at all."

Hew couldn't lie to him. Just the thought of Adelle made something deep within his chest hum with an excitement he'd thought himself no longer capable of feeling. "Aye, lad. I verra much enjoyed the time we spent together."

"And ye find her a bonny-looking lass, do ye not?"

The lad was forward, but Hew expected it was how he was with everyone. Arran didn't seem the kind of man to mince words, no matter with whom he conversed. "Aye, she's as beautiful a lass as I have ever seen. Do ye know her well, Arran?"

"Aye. I've spent much of the last year with her. She's wonderful, although a bit more forthright with her words than most lasses. I wouldna have her any other way, though. Mary, Blaire, and Bri are much the same, so perhaps that is why I doona mind her so much. I find fiery lasses to be the best company."

"Nay, I doona mind it, either. My wife was verra much like that. She always said whatever came to her mind. 'Twas a treasure to be with such a woman. I never had to guess what she was thinking." Hew smiled, slightly surprised at himself. It was the first time he'd spoken of his wife that sadness hadn't crept into his heart.

"Well, ye never have to wonder what Adelle is thinking, 'tis certain," said Arran with a chuckle. "Ye shall be joining us for the meal on Christmas Eve, aye? It would disappoint her if ye dinna, and I can tell by the sparkle in yer eye when ye speak of her that ye doona wish to do that."

The last thing Hew wanted to do was upset Adelle in any way. Slowly but surely, he found himself wanting to do nothing less than please her. "Aye, lad, I'll be there. Ye are right, I doona wish to disappoint her at all."

*

The men returned to the castle midday on Christmas Eve. The prizes of the hunt were such that I was immediately forced to join Mary in the kitchen so that we could get started preparing the meat. Bri and Blaire somehow evaded the kitchen. I suspected they were both spending private moments with their husbands, whom they'd not seen for an entire three days.

It seemed a bit ridiculous to me that such a short period of separation seemed to cause them both such distress. Even so, I was a little envious of the relationships they had found. I'd never had that sort of bond with Bri's father. We both celebrated at the absence of the other. Even after our divorce, I'd never dated anyone long enough to allow my feelings to become very strong.

By the time all of the food was prepared, everyone but Mary and I waited anxiously in the dining hall, ready to devour the feast that was about to be placed before them. I'd just stepped into the room when I tripped on the bottom of my dress, causing me to lunge forward.

I was certain I would land on the floor, spilling the precious bread basket I held, but Hew's quick reflexes suddenly set me right. He'd jumped up to pull a piece of garland out of his curious puppy's mouth and had passed by me just in time to prevent my fall.

"Are ye all right, lass? Mary would kill ye if ye dropped the food."

"Yes, she most certainly would. Thank you." I looked up at him, instantly lost in the greenness of his eyes. He didn't let go of my forearms, and it took Arran's voice from the table to break the lock of our gazes.

"Look up," Arran said, pointing above our heads. "Ye have both found yerself beneath the mistletoe. Ye must kiss her, Hew. 'Tis bad luck if ye doona."

Our eyes met again. I was certain Hew wouldn't kiss me. It had seemed a major accomplishment for him to have kissed my cheek in private. Mistletoe or not, a public display of affection would be too much to ask of him.

He didn't glance away. Instead, leaning in so close that his lips were only a hair's width from mine, he whispered, "It seems that I must. I willna have bad luck following ye, lass."

His lips pressed warmly against mine, soft and shy. I melted into him, winding my fingers up into his hair as the butterflies in my stomach took flight, coursing through every inch of my body.

"Well, now ye have gone and ruined it," Mary said, her voice causing Hew to break the kiss and pull away from me. She pointed up at the mistletoe. "Now that Kip has seen what that is for, I shall never be able to trap him beneath it."

Hew laughed, but leaned in close to my ear after Mary passed by us, whispering so quietly that no one but I could hear him. "I intend to finish that kiss later, lass," he said, sending chills of delight up my spine.

I smiled, not caring about the eyes focused on us. "I surely hope so," I whispered back to him.

*C*hristmas morning was all that I'd hoped it would be. Presents, a beautiful tree, a warm fire, and lots of love and laughter filled the castle. Together, we lit the candle to place in the window, lighting the way for strangers—a New Year's tradition Mary shared with us. I'd heard of the custom through my archaeological studies, but it was a treat to be an active participant in the ritual.

When Bri opened the baby blanket, she cried big fish tears that soon had all of the women, even Mary, blubbering like babies. My grandbaby was due to arrive any day now, so I'd also wrapped up the vial Morna had sent along with me. Bri's reaction was just what I had expected.

"Oh, thank God! For weeks, I've been so terrified about the pain I would experience without medication." She placed both palms lovingly on her belly and laughed. "I'd about made up my mind that I was not going to let this child come out. If the medicine came from Morna, it's certain to help, don't you think?"

I suspected she might be getting her hopes up a little too high. While I was sure Morna's potion would help to take the edge off somewhat, I knew from my own experience that even with modern medicine, childbirth was seldom, if ever, a pain-free experience. I didn't imagine that's what she wanted to hear, though, so I simply smiled and nodded. "Yes, I'm sure it will help."

Hew had joined us but remained standoffish. I assumed he didn't want to make any of us feel guilty for not having gifts for him. I did, however, have something for him. It just wasn't quite ready yet, and I didn't want him to know about it until later. I would need to enlist Mary's help to finish it, as I'd done a fantastic job of thoroughly screwing it up.

I walked over to him, gently reaching out to touch his arm. "Merry Christmas."

He smiled and gently squeezed my hand. "Merry Christmas to ye, as well, lass. It has been many years since I have been able to witness such a wonderful celebration, but now I believe I shall take my leave and return to the cottage for awhile."

"Oh, please don't. We all enjoy having you here. Do you feel uncomfortable?"

"Nay, lass. I am surprised to say that I am verra comfortable with all of ye. 'Tis only that I have something I'd like to give ye but 'tis not quite finished. Would ye stop by the cottage in a little while?"

I smiled, but panic rushed through me. "Yes, of course I will." I wasn't going to accept a gift from him unless I had something to give him in return. That meant I didn't have much time to convince Mary to help me fix the disaster I had tried to sew together yesterday morning.

Hew smiled, squeezing my hand once more before he slipped away. As soon as I saw him gone, I crossed the room to yank Mary up from her chair.

"You have to come help me, quick. I tried to make Hew something, but I've messed it all up. Now he's going to give me a gift, so I need you to repair my disaster so I'll have a present to give him in return."

"Ach, I see how he is. He will give you a gift—a complete stranger until just a short time ago—but has nothing for his sister. Did I just hear ye say ye tried to sew something, Adelle?"

"Yes," I said, adding, "I know. It was a horrible idea."

Mary looked at me begrudgingly but stood. I knew she would be happy to help. "Aye, lass." She laughed heartily. "Ye are a fool, but I'm so happy this Christmas morning, I doona mind telling ye that I love ye dearly. Now, let's go fix the mess ye've made. My brother deserves a proper gift."

radling the puppy close to my chest, I knocked on the door to the cottage with numb fingers, my red nose sniffling as I waited. It had started snowing again and the wind blew bitterly cold. Hew opened the door quickly, smiling wide.

"Come inside, lass. Ye and the pup both. 'Tis freezing outside."

A large fire burned from the hearth, making the room warm, almost toasty, inside. Hew wore less clothing than usual—long pants, a thin linen shirt that exposed the upper part of his chest. I swallowed hard at the sight of the dark hair peeking out just beneath his Adam's apple.

Once I stepped inside and lowered the pup to the floor, Hew pulled me into a warm embrace. I breathed in the masculine scent of him, my face pressed so closely to his chest I could feel the beat of his heart. "I'm sorry it took me so long to get here," I said softly. "I had to coax Mary to help me finish your gift. I made quite a mess of it on my own."

Moving away from me, he crossed the room to grab a small box that sat on the windowsill next to the tree. "Ye doona need to give me a gift, lass."

"Well, same goes for you, then. But, it seems that we both did anyway, so let's exchange them."

I didn't wait for him to give me mine before extending the two folded pieces of cloth I held in my hands. He took them, and after unfolding them, stared down at the odd pieces quizzically. "Thank ye, lass, but what exactly is it that I'm holding?"

I bent down and snatched up my puppy, which had been snuggling next to his brother near the fire. Reaching out, I took one of the cloth pieces from

Hew and gently slipped it over the puppy's head, pushing each leg through the tiny holes.

He laughed loudly. "Did ye truly make a shirt for the pups? Is this a common thing where ye come from?"

I smiled. I knew he would find it silly, but there was no denying how precious both of them would look in their small, wool onesies. "Yes, I surely did. Not all that common, but a few crazy people like me do sometimes dress their dogs. You can't deny how cute they look."

He grinned, picking up the other pup and slipping my other small creation over the animal. "Nay, lass, I canna deny it. They shall be the bonniest, most ridiculous-looking pups anywhere. It seems that our gifts will complement each other."

"Oh, really? How?"

He placed the box inside my hands. "Open it and see, lass. I hope ye like them. It has been some time since I carved anything."

The box itself was exquisite, crafted by fine hands. I could only imagine how magnificent the contents inside would be. I lifted the top gently and took off the small piece of cloth covering the items. When I saw what lay beneath it, I had to choke back tears.

Two wooden ornaments lay nestled within, each perfectly carved into the shape of a dog—a puppy, to be exact. The ornaments dangled from two matching crimson ribbons. I glanced down at the pups snuggling on the floor at our feet, marveling at how closely the ornaments resembled the two creatures that had first brought Hew and I together.

I'd not had a gift so touching in many years. It wasn't the ornaments themselves, although they were certainly impressive. The attention and thought that had gone into such a gift touched me deeply. Hew had obviously listened to me the night we'd decorated the cottage together, and taken special note of my love for such objects.

"Do ye not like them, lass?" he asked, his voice startling me. "I'm not as good at crafting wood as I once was. I'm a bit out of practice."

"No." I reached out to grab him firmly by the hand. "They're amazing, Hew, truly. I love them. It's only that . . . I'm a little disappointed." I grinned flirtatiously at the concern in his expression.

"Disappointed, lass?"

"Yes, disappointed. I was hoping your gift to me would include finishing that kiss we started."

He laughed, ripping the box from my hands, tossing it onto the bed across the room, and pulling me tightly against him. "Aye, I'll finish it, lass, and then I'll begin another. And another."

This kiss held none of the shyness of the first one. Hew's lips moved confidently against my own as, with one hand pressed to my lower back, he brought me closer to him. The fingers of his other hand wound into my hair.

"Ach, lass," he said into my ear when he finally pulled away, the touch of his breath sending a cascade of shivers across my skin. "Doona tease me so again about being disappointed. If ye want me to kiss ye, all ye have to do is ask..."

I laughed at the tickling sensation his words spread down my neck and back. "I'm sorry. I didn't mean to tease you, Hew. Next time, I'll know."

"And when will this next time be, lass?"

"How about now?"

He cocked a brow. "What did I tell ye?"

I smiled and narrowed my eyes. "Kiss me," I said coyly.

He kissed me lightly at first. I kissed him back just as gently. We learned the feel of each other's arms, the texture of lips, the taste of one another. I felt lightheaded as his breath merged with mine, and I had the oddest feeling that despite the delicious newness of our relationship, he was familiar, someone I'd known deep down in my heart for a very long time. Someone I'd been waiting for, that I was supposed to meet.

If I didn't pull away and change the subject quickly, I was afraid I would allow this experience to go to a place I was not ready for yet. Not that it wouldn't be nice, but something in my mind screamed that this man needed to be different than the men I'd known in the past. He *was* different. Special. And I wanted our relationship to be different and special, as well.

Slowly, I stopped the kiss and pulled back. "I just thought of something."

His green eyes were hazy, nearly blurred with the pleasure that I was certain mirrored my own gaze. "Aye? What is that, lass?" he asked. "Do ye think perhaps ye could tell me later? With you in my arms, I can't think at all."

I laughed and tried to step away, but he held me close to him. "No, it's very important. We have yet to name our puppies. We found them together. I think we should name them together."

Hew remained quiet for a moment, then said, "Aye, lass, ye are quite right. We should do it together. And I know just what I wish to name the dark one."

I tilted my head to one side, studying him. "Really? What?"

"He's quite a masculine pup, do ye agree? His fur makes him look like an exotic beast. I think we should name him Tearlach. It means that he is a manly creature."

I smiled. I didn't think the puppy looked manly, only adorable, but he was right. As the pup grew, the fluffy hair around his head would make him look like a lion. "It's the perfect name for him," I said.

"Ye should be the one to name the lighter one. 'Tis ye that found him."

I thought for a moment, but every name I came up with sounded too American. My pup needed a name as noble and Scottish as his brother's. "Do you see how his tail always sticks up? It looks like he is waving a flag. Is there a word for that?"

"Aye, lass, I see. What about Bratach? It holds much the same meaning."

"Bratach. I like it!" I stood on my tiptoes and kissed Hew's cheek. "I think it's perfect, and with that I will take my leave. You are too much of a temptation for me to stay a moment longer."

He laughed, a deep, grumbled sound that shook his whole chest and made my knees go weak.

"Temptation, lass? Nay, 'tis ye that are the temptation. I have been alone for a long time. Ye have awakened feelings within me I fear I am too old to handle."

"You are not old," I said indignantly. "You're the same as me, I'd imagine, and I am in no way old, which means neither are you." I moved to stand by the door.

"If you say so, lass. Will ye accompany me somewhere tomorrow afternoon?"

"Yes, I think I could manage that. Where?"

"'Tis a surprise, lass. I shall meet ye at the back of the castle come midday."

He opened the door to the cottage, taking my hand so he could walk me back to the castle, leaving me to wonder just what tomorrow held in store for me.

CHAPTER 15

*H*ew rose early the next morning to work on carving the large piece of wood left over from the ornaments he'd made for Adelle. He hoped to shape it into a sort of sled that he and Adelle could take on their outing this afternoon.

Just thinking about spending more time with her made his heart beat more quickly. He'd lived alone for too long. He realized now that he had convinced himself that a solitary life was the only way to honor the memory of his late wife. And so he'd remained wrapped in his memories of their brief time together. Memories that should have been a blessing instead of the trap he'd made them into. Adelle had changed all of that. Since meeting her, he felt released from his self-imposed prison, and more alive than he could ever recall feeling. He was slowly learning that choosing a solitary life had not honored his late wife; in fact, nothing could have been further from the truth.

Mae had not been a jealous woman. She knew she held his heart and lived her life with more light and love than any other lass he'd ever met. She would've wished more for him. She wouldn't have been pleased that he'd spent so many years all alone.

It saddened him that, for so long, he'd not realized the mistake he was making.

All he could do now was to try and move forward, living the rest of his life as Mae would've wished it. She would be very pleased to know that he'd found happiness once again. He could almost hear her whispering in his ear, pleading with him not to let Adelle slip out of his grasp.

He didn't intend to do any such thing, but he also knew it would be best that they spend their afternoon together out of doors. He was a man who'd gone too long without the company of a woman. He would only make his situation more difficult if he allowed himself to be alone with her for an extended period of time within four walls. Adelle was too special a woman to dishonor her, and he was not the sort of man to do so, anyway.

For this reason he worked, chipping away at the wood with as much force as he could muster, crafting it into the perfect seat for two. He must exert whatever physical activity he could to help keep his mind off of his need for her.

*E*ither Hew hadn't told Mary what he planned for us to do this afternoon, or she was simply determined not to reveal what she knew.

She and Bri insisted on grooming me for my outing with Hew, and they'd decided to dress me in the finest frock I owned. "Are you sure this is appropriate? I feel very overdressed," I said.

"It's always better to be overdressed than underdressed," my daughter quipped. "I believe you are the one that taught me that. Besides, we have no way of knowing, do we, since Mary refuses to reveal her brother's plans?"

As Bri continued to pick away at my hair, doing her best to pin it into place, Mary threw her hands up in exasperation. "I already told ye, I doona know what his plans are," she screamed. "I havena spoken to him about it. Ye are a couple of thick-headed lassies, the two of ye!"

She turned and left us, stomping her feet on the way out the door. Once she was gone, laughter burst out of us. "I should not have pestered her so. There. What do you think?" asked Bri.

She stepped away so that I could turn and look in the mirror. "Thank you," I said, eyeing my reflection. "My hair looks nice, but I feel ridiculous in this dress. I'd rather be in jeans and a nice blouse."

Bri laughed and bent down to squeeze me while placing her face up against my own. "I'm sure you would, but those days are over, I'm afraid. At least it's not expected that we shave our legs in this time."

"Thank God for small mercies." She was right. It would have been considered quite strange for us to do so in this time and that was fine with me. I always thought it a pain in the rear anyway.

"Are you nervous, Mom? You like Hew quite a lot, don't you?"

I stood, wishing I could shorten the dress a good eighteen inches just so I would be able to move more freely. "I do like him a lot, and I admit to being a little nervous. But every time I'm around him, whatever nerves I may have had before dissipate quickly." I averted my gaze, suddenly embarrassed. "I'm probably being foolish. Once the snow melts, he'll no longer want to stay here."

"I wouldn't be so sure, Mom. I think if he had reason to stay, he would. You may just end up being that reason."

I hoped she was right. The thought of him leaving filled me with sadness, but I would not worry about that now. Today, I was simply going to enjoy his company.

CHAPTER 16

Sneaky Mary had known exactly what activity Hew had planned for us. When he arrived at the back entrance of the castle carrying a sled, I caught sight of Mary hiding around a corner, cackling like a banshee.

"It is not the least bit funny, Mary! Now he will be forced to wait on me while I change. There's no way I'm going to get this dress sopping wet."

Mary stepped out from her place in the shadows, laughing as she waved her brother inside. "Oh, doona be such a grumpy bairn, Adelle. Hew, get yerself inside whilst the lassie changes."

Hew stomped his snow-covered feet off outside before following Mary's instruction, casting me an apologetic glance before reprimanding his sister. "'Twas not kind of ye, Mary." He turned to me. "But I willna say I'm not pleased to see ye in such a fine dress, lass. Ye look lovely."

Mary piped up once again, not giving me a chance to thank him for his kind words.

"Ach, if ye find her pleasing in that, I'm sure ye shall fall over when ye see what she will come down in next. I'm certain she will use yer idea of playing in the snow as the perfect excuse to don her horrific garb from her own time. I doona see what the lads seem to see in it, but every time Adelle, Bri, or Blaire decide to squeeze themselves into their modern clothes, all the lads, my own Kip included, can hardly keep their tongues inside their mouths. 'Tis truly pathetic."

Hew's brows pulled together quizzically, but he said nothing. I ignored her, as well, and turned to make my way back upstairs.

I was almost out of sight when Mary called out to me, "I'm right, aye? Ye are going in search of yer 'jeans?'"

I smiled at the anticipation of ripping this burdensome dress off and sliding into the comfy denim. I yelled over my shoulder back at her. "Yes, Mary. You are very right, indeed."

Mary had also been right about Hew's reaction to seeing a woman in such clothing. It was certainly a sight men in this time were unaccustomed to seeing. His mouth nearly fell open when I came back downstairs. Though entirely covered from head to toe, and bundled up for our snowy activities, I suddenly felt self-conscious under his gaze.

"Ach, lass, I doona know if ye should trust yerself with me when ye look as ye do. Do women commonly dress in such a manner where ye come from?"

I laughed and marched out into the snow ahead of him. "Yes, all the time. This is quite a conservative outfit, I assure you. Would you rather I put my dress back on?"

He caught up to me quickly, throwing his arms around me from behind and kissing me roughly on the cheek. "Nay, lass," he said, his facial hair tickling my ear. "I wouldna let ye go and change even if ye wished it. Come. I found a bonny hill near the cottage that shall be perfect for sledding."

I was both excited and surprised by his choice of activity. Hew was much more fun than he'd originally let on. Taking his hand in my own, we made our way to the snowy hill.

The lass meant to torture him. No other explanation made sense for her to have dressed the way she had. There was no hiding her shape in the trousers, and what a fine shape it was. Curvy in all the right places, as a woman should be.

Hew breathed in deeply through his nose, hoping the chill in the air would cool the fire that burned inside him. Thankful when they reached the hill, he promptly placed the sled down onto the snow and instructed Adelle to sit in the front so that he could join her on the back end.

Pushing off hard, they flew down the snowy landscape, both of them howling with delight as the cold wind rushed across their faces. When the sled finally reached the bottom of the hill, it stopped rather abruptly, uprooting both of them from their seats, sending them tumbling out into the snow.

They landed in a twisted pile. Adelle was on top of him, laughing so hard that the trembling of her chest shook his own.

"Are ye all right, lass?" Their fun would be spoiled quickly if his idea of going sledding had caused her harm.

She smiled brightly, bending to quickly kiss him on the tip of his nose. He found himself wondering how a lass could manage to keep her teeth so brilliantly white. They were stunning, just like every other part of her.

"Yes, I'm fine. Let's go again!"

She leapt off of him and was halfway up the hill before he could manage to roll over and climb his way out of the snow.

CHAPTER 17

"*W*akey, wakey…"

Bri's voice lured me out of a deep sleep. I awoke to find Bri and Blaire sitting on either side of me, grinning in anticipation.

I rolled onto my stomach, shielding my face from the both of them, groaning as I spoke. "What do you want? Just leave me alone. I'll wake up sometime tomorrow."

Bri stuck her hand into my hair, mussing it about so that I would turn over onto my back. "You missed breakfast. So did Hew. Mary's not pleased with either one of you, and she said that you will just have to wait until evening to eat because she wasn't going to warm anything for you once you woke up."

I obliged her and rolled over, sitting myself up so that I was eye level with both of them. Endlessly hungry, I could out eat almost any man. No way would I wait until evening to eat. "That's not happening. I am more than capable of feeding myself. Mary is not going to dictate when and what I eat."

Bri looked over at Blaire who laughed knowingly. "What did I tell you, Blaire? I knew she would say something like that."

"Hicumm…excuse me," I said, clearing my throat to gain control of their attention again. "I'm right here, you know. Now, what are the two of you doing in here?"

I knew well enough why they'd come, but Blaire obliged me by answering my question. "Why do ye think we have come? We wish to hear all about yer afternoon yesterday."

Thinking back on the day, I couldn't help but grin. It had been a wonderful afternoon and ages since I'd laughed so hard. My stomach would be sore for a week from the effort of it. I ached from head to toe, bruised from the many spills I'd taken into the snow, but every tight muscle was worth it. "Well, we honestly didn't do much of anything except sled down the giant hill near the cottage about a thousand times."

Bri smiled as she held on to her swollen belly. "Did you have a good time?"

"Aye, o'course she did. She canna keep from grinning." Blaire winked at me, but her expression quickly shifted to concern. "But ye seem to have had a wee bit too much fun, Adelle. Ye are mighty red."

I reached up and touched my face, flinching at the pain. My cheeks felt quite swollen. There was little in the way of sunscreen in this time, and I'd not thought to cover my face, even after I learned we were to spend the day sledding. "I'll have to see if Mary has any herbal salve I can put on this to calm it down a bit. How bad do I look?"

"Completely terrible," said my daughter.

My eyes widened in surprise. With each passing day Bri grew more uncomfortable in her pregnancy, and she was becoming increasingly blunt with her words. "Ouch. Thanks, Bri, but I suppose it's my own fault. I really didn't think about sunscreen, at all."

Blaire glanced at Bri with shocked eyes and did her best to comfort me. "It isna all that bad, Adelle. It shall heal itself eventually."

"Eventually?" That was not okay with me. It needed to be completely healed by tonight. Once our afternoon of sledding had concluded, Hew had very seriously and nervously asked that I dine with him in the cottage this evening. He said he had something very important he wished to tell me.

"Aye." Blaire sent me a cautious glance.

I knew it wasn't her fault, but she could tell I was agitated by her response that it would take some time for my sunburn to heal.

"I know that 'tis not pleasant for ye, but it shall take at least a week for ye to look like yerself, I'm afraid."

"Awesome." I didn't know what else to say. Nothing could be done for my stupidity. I would look scary when I arrived at the cottage this evening. Perhaps we could dine outside in darkness. Even if we turned into icicles, it would be preferable to frightening the poor man to death with the abomination which was now my face.

"*A*re ye certain, brother?" Mary asked. "Ye havena been acquainted with Adelle verra long. 'Tis no small decision to decide to leave the home that ye have known for so long."

Hew moved about the cottage nervously. He knew it was a rash decision, but nothing had felt so right to him in a good many years. He loved the lass greatly, and he would tell her so tonight. "Aye, Mary, I am certain. There is naught left for me at home, and there hasna been since the day Mae left me. 'Twas foolish of me to stay there so many years after her death. It pains me to think on all the joy I have missed because I was too frightened to take a chance on being happy again. I wasted much time."

His sister reached out and placed a comforting hand on his arm. "Nay, brother. Ye dinna waste time. Things happen as they are meant to. If ye truly feel the way ye seem to about Adelle, then I doona believe ye were meant to leave yer home until now. If ye had, it wouldna have been her that ye found."

Mary's words comforted him. She had a kind way of looking at all the mistakes he had made. Regardless, he was thankful he had met Adelle now. "Aye, Mary. I canna imagine not knowing the lass. If I agree to work here at the castle, do ye think that Eoin and Arran shall agree to let me make this cottage my home?"

Mary's laughter made him smile. He should've expected such an answer from his fiery sister. "There is no need for ye to ask either of them," she said. "Ye are welcome to stay here because I say so and that's all the permission ye need. Both of the laddies know it and have since they were bairns. 'Tis I that am truly laird over Conall Castle."

"I believe ye are right, Mary. They all seem to bow at yer feet, regardless of the hard time ye seem to love giving them. Now, allow me to walk ye back to the castle, Lady Laird. I have much to think on. It will take me some time to decide the perfect manner in which to say what I must."

CHAPTER 18

"What in the world is the matter with ye, Adelle?" asked Hew. "Take that covering off the top of yer head."

I knew I looked ridiculous, like I was wearing a cheap Halloween costume with the gauzy fabric over my head, but there was no way I was taking it off. I was a vain woman and not afraid to admit it. Whatever he had to say to me, he could say it to me as I was or not at all. "Sorry. I will do no such thing." I kept my head down, my gaze on the pup in my arms.

Stepping into the cottage, I walked past Hew, setting the growing Bratach on the floor, where he joined Tearlach in their usual game of "who's the toughest brother?"

Hew shut the door to the cottage and walked around to face me, frustration clear in his expression. "Ye look ridiculous, lass. I wish to tell ye something important, and I doona wish to address ye while yer covered like a wee ghost."

I glanced up at him, only barely able to see him through the small holes in the fabric, but I could make out enough of his face to know it was perfectly perfect. Speaking a bit more loudly than might've been necessary to compensate for the fact that the fabric covered my mouth, I said, "How is your face not red as a beet? You were out in the same snow and under the same sun that I was in yesterday, and there is no sign of it anywhere on you!"

He laughed, understanding. "Ach, I see. Did the sun blister yer skin a bit, lass? I should have insisted that ye cover it, but I dinna think of it. I spend much of my days outdoors. I suppose my skin has grown accustomed to such sunlight."

"Well, how wonderful for you. Let's eat." It wasn't only the way my face looked that put me in a sour mood, but the pain from it felt something awful. I'd never been burned so badly in my entire life.

"It shall be mighty hard for ye to eat properly with that cloth covering ye. Just take it off, Adelle. Do ye really think that I'm so concerned with the way yer face looks?"

I nodded emphatically. "Of course you are. All men are."

He rolled his eyes, sat down at the table, and started eating immediately, not waiting for me to join him. "Suit yerself," he responded in between mouthfuls. "But if ye truly believe that, Adelle, ye havena been around the right kind of men. I like yer face verra well, but 'tis not my favorite part of ye."

"Oh, fine. So you're one of those," I said grouchily, unsure why I felt the need to provoke him so.

He gave me a little smirk. "'Tis yer mouth that I was referring to. I enjoy it verra much."

Underneath the veil, my brows met in the center. "My mouth? My lips are quite thin. You have strange tastes."

He stood, and I thought perhaps I had pushed him too far.

"Aye? And ye are a silly lass, Adelle. I dinna mean yer lips. I mean the surprising words that ye always seem to form with them. I have never known a lass so forward."

I looked down, embarrassed. "Yes. I know. That's always been a problem. It's a bit of a turn off, isn't it?"

He frowned once more and came to crouch down next to me, taking my hands into his. "I doona know what ye mean by 'turn off' but, nay, I love the way ye speak verra much. Now, I willna tell ye what I must with that damned cloth covering yer head."

He yanked it away before I could grasp it, then reeled back in disgust, almost falling onto his bottom. "Ach, lass, ye look dreadful. Never ye mind, I doona wish to say what I once wished."

My eyes widened with shock and pain. He quickly scrambled up on his feet to gather me into his arms, laughing softly. "Oh, lass, forgive me. Doona look so upset. I couldna resist it after ye berated me just a moment ago. Ye look mighty fine, lass. Ye always do."

I didn't pull away from him but narrowed my eyes. "No, I do not honestly think I look fine. My face is so red I look like I was born on the sun, and it's quite swollen, as well."

"Doona tell me what I think, lass. I wouldna lie to ye. I doona care if the redness never fades, although it shall. I would still think that ye looked mighty fine. Now, hush. Let me tell ye what I wished to when I asked ye to come here."

I didn't believe a word he said about my face at the moment, but I didn't wish to argue with him anymore. I was eager to hear what he had to say. "All right, fine," I relented. "What is it?"

He stepped away and sat on the edge of the bed, holding my hands so that I would sit next to him. "I've decided that once the snow melts, I am not going to return home."

Hope fluttered in my chest. I'd spent every second trying not to think of the day when he would leave here and praying that the snow would stay forever. "Really? Why?"

"Do ye really not know the answer to that question, lass?"

He looked into my eyes. I could see all that he wished to say deep within them, but I desperately wanted him to speak the words. "Maybe, but I won't know for sure until you tell me."

He took a deep, shaky breath. He was nervous, but I was not about to intervene and let him get away without saying what he felt. I'd let too many men do that before. If he meant it, he could find the strength to say the words. "I…I know that I havena known ye long, Adelle, but it doesna take so long for the heart to know what it wants. I'm in love with ye, lass. Verra much so."

I smiled, staring deep into his eyes. Tears threatened to fall, but I held them back. I must have remained quiet for one moment too long for when he spoke again, his voice was shaky.

"I doona expect that ye should feel the same so quickly. Perhaps 'twas rash for me to tell ye so soon, but I have spent too many years alone. I willna deny myself love a moment longer if I can have it."

"No." I reached up and lay my hand against his cheek. "Hew, no. It wasn't too quickly at all. I love you, too."

"Do ye truly, lass?"

"Yes, I do. I think I loved you the first moment I saw you in the snow, holding that sweet little puppy firm against your chest." I leaned forward and kissed him but had to pull away at the pain that shot through my lips at the pressure.

"Ach, lass. I'm verra sorry that ye are hurting so. Doona kiss me now. I hope there shall be plenty of time for that later."

"There's nothing for you to be sorry about, and yes, I do too."

His face grew serious again, filling my heart with worry for a moment.

"I willna return to where I came from, but before I make this my home, I must finish the journey I started. I must bid Mae farewell one last time, lass. I hope that ye doona mind."

I shook my head, surprised that he thought I might. "Of course I don't, and of course you must. When will you leave?"

He looked out at the snow, hesitating. "At sunrise," he said, finally. "I know that the snow isna melted yet, but no more has fallen in days. I am anxious to finish my journey so I can begin a new chapter in my life."

Something twisted uncomfortably in my stomach, but I could not determine its source and did my best to ignore it. "You will be careful, yes?"

He smiled, rubbing his hand gently up and down my back. "Aye, lass. I will. I have someone most precious to return to now."

I wished to stay with him until morning, but I left shortly after learning he would be taking off at sunrise. I wanted him to be rested before traveling out in the snow. He'd sent both pups with me, entrusting Tearlach to my care for the duration of his journey.

I slept fitfully. While I tossed wildly throughout the night, both pups slept soundly in the bed with me, snuggled tightly to my side. They didn't move all night, only stirring at sunrise. Just as the sun broke over the horizon, they stood on all fours in the bed. Looking toward the window in the direction of the cottage, they whined mournfully.

The knot in my stomach returned.

CHAPTER 19

$\mathcal{A}$s planned, Hew left at sunrise. It was not a far journey to Mae's resting place. In fair weather he could have made the trip there and back in a day, but with the snow still so deep, he knew it would take him at least two.

Just two days away from Adelle seemed too many. He wondered if she'd been disappointed that he hadn't asked her to marry him. He hoped she was not, for he intended to do so as soon as he made it back from bidding Mae one final farewell.

He wished to marry Adelle with all his heart, but some small piece of him would not allow himself to ask it of her when Mae still lingered in the back of his mind. He knew his wife would be pleased for him, finding someone to share the rest of his life with, someone he loved. He'd come to that realization soon after he arrived at Conall Castle and met Adelle, but he wished to spend a few moments alone with Mae so that he could truly put the past behind him.

The day trickled by slowly as he lost himself in a sea of past memories. Memories of loneliness and the choices he'd made that had caused him to be so. A new future lay ahead of him. He couldn't wait to embrace it with all that he had.

He stopped often to allow his aging horse to rest and to clean the icy chunks from the horse's hooves and coat. He asked much of his beloved beast to accompany him on this trip. His horse was old. Hew knew the animal would not make it another year. It seemed appropriate that Greggory's last journey be to Mae's grave.

Slowly, dark descended over Hew and the great beast. He knew he should stop for the night, but no good place offered shelter from the snow. There was a small village just outside of the Conalls' territory, so against his better judgment, he nudged the horse on, praying with each soft kick of his heels that his companion could make it into the village.

It happened quickly. The horse stepped upon a rock buried out of sight, deep within the snow. He heard the creature's leg snap and did his best to throw his own leg over the side so that he could dismount before the Greggory fell, but Hew was not quick enough.

The horse fell in the direction Hew dismounted, and Hew's left shoulder dislocated on impact with the frozen ground. He was pinned beneath the injured animal, the weight on top of him squeezing the breath from his lungs.

Pain coursed through him. The stars in the sky melted together, turning into darkness as he lost consciousness.

*P*resent Day

"*M*orna…Morna, wake up, lass!" Jerry shook his wife's shoulder with as much force as his thin arms could afford. He watched, terrified, as she tossed in her sleep. The noises she made indicated she was injured. He could see her eyes darting back and forth beneath her closed eyelids, and he held his breath in fear.

"I must gather my spells," she finally said, opening her eyes to look at him. "They are in need of us, Jerry."

He sighed in relief, his whole body trembling from the remnants of his worry. Jerry had often seen his wife stir in discomfort during fitful dreams, but never so much as he'd just witnessed. For a brief moment, he'd worried that it hadn't been magic that caused her to do so, but perhaps old age.

He had every intention of passing from this life before his beloved. He knew he would not be able to live a day without her. "Ye scared me to death, Morna. I was afraid…well, I doona wish to speak of what I thought."

He smiled against her hand as she laid her palm against his cheek, knowing what he meant well enough. "'Tis not a worry ye should have. I shall not leave this world until I am good and ready to, and that willna be for a long time. Come."

She stood and gestured for him to follow her. He did so without question. His wife carried a great burden, one he was eternally grateful he didn't possess. "What is it, lass?"

"A lad I knew as a child has taken a fancy to Adelle, and he finds himself in need of help. I must warn them, send Adelle the dreams that were just shown to me so they may have a chance of reaching him in time."

She didn't stop to explain more to him, and Jerry didn't ask any further questions. This was an urgent matter, but he didn't worry over such things as his wife did. He'd yet to see one of her spells go awry.

477

CHAPTER 20

I'd slept so little the night before Hew departed that I would have been on edge the next day even if the pups had not chosen the exact moment of his departure to whine as if wounded. I spent the hours after his departure sick with worry, and it exhausted me. My only relief was that my face no longer ached, and the swelling had diminished greatly throughout the day.

As I traveled upstairs to my bedchamber, a pup under each arm, I was sure I would spend another sleepless night worried over Hew. Much to my surprise, a sense of drowsiness so strong that I could barely make it to my bedchamber door without losing consciousness overcame me.

It seemed a great effort to change into my nightgown. As soon as my head hit the pillow, I fell asleep.

I woke in the middle of the night with sweat beaded on my brow. The covers were off of the bed, mangled on the floor as if I had fought a great battle in my sleep. Screaming had pulled me out of the horrific dream I was having, and for a moment I thought I had heard my own yells.

I felt the need to scream now. Visions of Hew crushed beneath the weight of his horse, unable to scoot from beneath the animal, burned in my mind. I stilled in the bed, sitting up so that I could listen.

For a moment all remained quiet, but it took only a second before another scream ripped through the castle corridors.

I leapt out of the bed. Bri. She must have gone into labor sometime in the night. I could only hope that it was just starting, and I had not missed being there for her.

I burst into her and Eoin's bedchamber, relieved to see that Mary was already making preparations, ordering others about while Blaire administered Morna's mixture to Bri.

I ran to my daughter's side, giving her my hand. She squeezed it tightly as a contraction gripped her. "How are you? Is everything well?"

She grunted in between words, her expression set in determination. "Yes, as well as it can be, I believe. Will you go tell Eoin he better get in here this second? I don't care that it's unusual for men to stay at the bedside during delivery during this century. If he misses the birth of his child, I shall never forgive him."

"Of course." I had to pry her fingers loose from my hand. Turning to Mary, I asked, "Is she close, or do we have some time before the baby arrives?"

Mary must have been able to tell something else distressed me for she answered quickly, waving me on to whatever other task sat on my mind. "Nay, she isna as close as she wishes. We have some time still."

I nodded and ran out of the bedchamber, nearly colliding with Eoin, Arran, and Kip, who all huddled together in the hallway. I knew I must do as Bri bid first. Although I was certain my dream had meant something, I couldn't know for sure that what I had seen had been real.

I grabbed Eoin's arm and pulled him away from the circle, smacking him lightly as I scolded him. "What on earth do you think you are doing? You better get in there with Bri right this instant or I am going to drag you there myself."

He looked back at me nervously. "I am afraid to, Adelle. I doona think I can bear to see her in such pain, and I couldna live with the guilt if something happened to her and the babe."

I softened, feeling sorry for him. It was easy for women to forget what a terrifying ordeal childbirth was for the father. "Nothing is going to happen to them. Morna's drink will help with the pain soon and all will go well. Trust me, if you miss this Bri will not understand. Go. Now."

He nodded and hurried down the hall, leaving me to turn my attention to Arran and Kip. "I need to ask something of both of you. I know that you may think me mad, but please I beg you, listen to me before you dismiss me."

Kip stood silently, giving me an expression that I knew meant he dreaded whatever I was about to tell him. He knew it would only mean more work for himself.

Arran nodded and reached out to lay a reassuring hand on my shoulder. "Aye, of course, Adelle. What is it?"

"I had a dream, a terrible one. I've never had one quite so vivid. It was dark, and Hew was lying on his back in the snow. His horse had fallen on top of him, crushing him, and one of his arms hung oddly to his side." Saying what I'd seen out loud made it seem more real to me. As I finished, my voice cracked. I couldn't keep a tear from falling down my face.

Arran glanced quickly at Kip and then back at me. "Do ye think that he is in danger, lass, or did ye only have a dream that has upset ye?"

I shook my head. "I don't know, but I'm afraid that he might be in trouble. I know it seems crazy."

Arran squeezed my shoulder. "Nay, it isna crazy. We have all seen too much of what Morna can do to disregard what might be a warning from her. Kip and I will ride at once."

"Thank you. I'm sorry to send you, but I can't leave Bri right now."

Arran was already moving down the corridor, Kip following silently behind him as he called back to me, "Of course you canna. Doona worry. We shall find him in time."

I believed that they would. They had to. I couldn't bear to think otherwise.

CHAPTER 21

Once Morna's medicine worked its way through Bri's system, her screams lessened substantially and things began moving rather fast.

She dilated more quickly than Mary had expected. Much to her dismay, she was forced to enlist the help of each of us in some way. Blaire did whatever Mary asked of her, while Eoin and I sat on either side of Bri, coaching and calming her with each set of pains.

When it came time for Bri to push, I watched in awe and astonishment at her strength. It was a miraculous thing. The love that filled the room in the moment the tiny bundle arrived into this world was enough for me to momentarily push away my worries over Hew.

While here, there was nothing I could do, and my heart nearly burst through my chest when I held my granddaughter in my arms for the first time.

I'd heard it said before that grandchildren filled you with a kind of love that was not even matched by your children. I'd always thought it a crazy notion, but as I latched on to her tiny fingers, I finally understood.

To hold a little human, one that came from a very piece of me, allowed me for an instant to believe that I would truly live on forever. In Bri, in her daughter, and in whatever children this child would one day have. It was all that one could ask for in life, more than I ever thought I would receive.

"Mom, you're crying more than I am, more than Eoin."

I glanced over to see Eoin practically blubbering in the corner and laughed as I carried the child to Bri's loving arms. "I don't care. I have never seen anything more perfect in my entire life."

Bri smiled, bending to kiss her daughter's head. "I know. Me, either. Where's Arran? I'm sure he's ready to meet his niece."

I didn't wish to burden any of them with bad news, but I knew I must tell them. "It's nothing to worry over I'm sure, but I had a dream about Hew. I became worried that perhaps something had happened to him on his journey. Arran and Kip rode after him to make sure that he is all right."

Bri looked up at me closely, clearly seeing past the calm façade I was doing my best to maintain. "Go."

I shook my head, dismissing her. "No, I'm not going to leave you so soon. You just had a baby, for goodness' sake."

She raised her left hand and shooed me from the room. "Mom, go. Everything is fine here. I know you need to be there. Just promise me you'll be careful."

I couldn't deny she was right. I bent quickly to kiss both her and the babe on the forehead before turning to leave the room. "I will."

I ran to the stables, mounting the first horse I saw, and took off at full speed away from Conall Castle.

I'd left the castle before sunrise, and it neared dusk when I finally found them. The vision before me was just as I'd seen it in the dream. I had been right about Hew. I was certain it was Morna who'd sent the warning to me.

"Is he..." I could hardly force the words out of my mouth. "Is he alive?"

"Aye, lass. I am verra alive and intend to stay that way."

When Hew's voice answered, the relief that washed through me was enough to nearly bring me to my knees.

My legs were shaky as I approached him, the adrenaline that had allowed me to ride to him so quickly suddenly receding. I knelt next to him, grabbing both sides of his face as I examined him for injuries. "Why haven't you moved the horse off of him?" I asked Arran and Kip, who stood behind me. "He's going to lose his legs if the horse stays on him much longer."

"We only just arrived a few minutes before you, lass. Ye must have been riding verra quickly to have caught us."

Hew reached his right hand up to touch my face, his other arm dislocated. "Nay, lass. If I hadna thrown my shoulder out of place, I would have been able to scoot out from under Greggory. I willna lose my legs."

"I'm glad to hear it." I stepped out of the way so that Arran and Kip could get on either side of him. Together they lifted him, avoiding his injured shoulder so that they could pull him out from under the horse, whose breathing was shallow. My heart winced in sadness at the creature's pain. His suffering would have to be ended.

Once Hew's legs were free, Arran had me move to his right side so that I could hold him down and steady while Kip secured his feet. When he was still, Arran asked him to bite down hard on a rag, then he jerked the shoulder into place. It was a horrible sound, but after the initial pain, the relief became instantly visible on Hew's face.

With help, the two men pulled him to his feet, and after a few moments of allowing his blood to circulate, he moved about to get his footing under him.

Eventually, he turned to address all of us. "I am verra grateful for yer help. I hate to ask it of ye, but would ye all mind riding ahead a ways, only for a few moments?"

"Why?" The word slipped out quickly, but as I looked at the way he stared down at his horse, sadness in his eyes, I knew.

"It must be I that end this for him, and I wish to do it alone."

Silently, we turned and left him.

He did not prolong the task. Once Hew joined us, we made plans to stay in the village where he had been headed when his horse had fallen. The village was located close to Mae's grave. Hew was determined to complete the journey he had intended.

Although I couldn't stand the thought of leaving him alone once again, I understood his need to do this one last thing.

---

*A*rran, Kip, and I had been at the small inn a few hours when Hew arrived. He said little as he entered, only asking which was his room and leaving us in the dining hall to retire for the evening.

We followed him shortly, separating as we each made our way to our rented rooms. We were all exhausted, and I couldn't blame Hew for not wishing to speak with us when he'd arrived. I was just happy to know that he was safe.

He'd suffered much over the last few days. He was sure to be sore, tired, and heartsick at the loss of his beloved horse, not to mention the melancholy I knew he must feel after having visited Mae's grave.

For this reason, I expected it to be Arran or Kip at the door when I heard a soft knock right as I blew out all but the last candle for the evening. Instead, when I opened the door, Hew stood before me.

CHAPTER 23

"You should be in bed. You're injured and it's been a long day."

He didn't answer me, only moved into the room shutting the door behind him. He reached out to me with his good arm, pulling me close to him as he kissed me desperately.

After a moment, he drew back breathlessly. "Doona tell me what I should do, lass. I had to see ye."

He released me, and I stepped away, hoping that putting some distance between us would dim the fire he'd lit within me. "Is everything all right?"

"Aye, lass. Will ye marry me?"

The words caught me off guard. He spoke them so quickly, I wondered for a moment if perhaps he hadn't meant to say them. "What? What did you just say?"

It took him only two strides until he stood before me, clasping tightly onto both of my hands. "Ye did hear me, lass, but I shall ask ye again. Will ye marry me, Adelle?"

A pleading in his eyes nearly broke my heart. After everything, he still worried that I might say no. "Yes, of course."

"Really, ye will, lass?"

"Aye," I said, mimicking his brogue in jest, reaching up to kiss him gently before standing on my tiptoes to whisper into his ear. "I want nothing more than to be your wife."

He kissed me wildly, without restraint. And then we were laughing. Laughing and kissing and holding each other. Now that I'd found him, my soul mate, I never wanted to let go.

Hew didn't leave my room that night, and we didn't take the time to re-light the candles I'd extinguished before he arrived. It didn't matter; the room was ablaze with our love for one another.

CHAPTER 24

e were married in the great room of Conall Castle on New Year's Day, surrounded by all of the people we loved most in the world. The vows were simple, but I'd never meant anything more than the few words we spoke to one another.

Hew's eyes never left mine as I made my promises to him. "I doona know where life will take me, but I choose ye to be at my side. From this day forward, my soul belongs to naught but ye. I now bind myself to ye in the present and for all the times to come. Together we are now one."

I didn't know where the vows came from, and I'd undoubtedly messed up the accent badly, but Hew didn't care, and neither did I.

As he leaned in to kiss me, baby Ellie Adelle Conall, named in honor of Eoin's mother, Elspeth, and myself, squealed as if she'd been pinched. Our pups howled loudly in response.

A happy chaos surrounded us, and it was just as we wished it to be.

I had been right. It had proven to be the best Christmas season that Conall Castle had ever seen.

MORNA'S MAGIC

CHAPTER 1

Austin, TX—Present Day

Two thoughts flashed through my mind as my trembling fingers gripped at the letter and the set of keys my husband held out to me. The first was that if Brian said one more word, I planned to take off my shoe and ram the pointy end of the heel deep into his skull. The second was that I was so ashamed of my own stupidity that I was just as inclined to ram the heel of the other shoe into my own head.

How could I have let so many months pass with him making the most ridiculous excuses to stay away from home? How could I not have caught on? What a silly, desperate fool I must be to have made it so easy for him to break his vows. It must've thrilled him to discover he'd married such an unassuming, trusting wife.

Now that I knew what he'd been up to, over a year's worth of clues seemed glaringly obvious. While we'd never truly been happy, I never thought him capable of such a betrayal. He was an ass, but a cheat? A liar? I'd not seen this in him.

I'd had plenty of time to come to terms with his affair. Weeks of lawyer negotiations and packing my belongings had quickly made me glad to be rid of him. But what had me shaking with anger and unshed tears was the revelation I held in my hand.

"Are you really so surprised, Mitsy?" Brian said defensively. "Bri left too quickly to sell the place, and it's not like she had that many friends. She left it in your care so why shouldn't I have used her house? What did it hurt?"

I squeezed the key so tightly that its ridges buried deep into my hand, indenting the skin. I was sure he could see the steam coming out of my ears, but I refused to scream at him as he expected me to. Brian would call it another one of my "ginger" moments and use it as justification for the affair. I would not give him the satisfaction.

"No." I said the word calmly and slowly released my breath so that it didn't come out as a loud sigh of frustration. "I'm not surprised she left me the house, I'd just never given it much thought. What I'm surprised about is how you thought it was okay to keep this letter from me. This is not addressed to you."

He chuckled, and I ground my heel into the floor to keep myself from ripping it off and attacking him.

"You're right. It isn't, but we were married when it came in the mail, and what's yours is mine, yes? Besides, Leah and I needed somewhere to go. It's not like we could come back here when you were always sitting in the house waiting on me."

My face could not have grown any hotter, but still I did not raise my voice. "You can justify anything, can't you? Bri would strangle you herself if she knew you'd been using her house to cheat on me."

Turning from him, I walked across the room to swing the last of my belongings, all thrown messily into a large duffle bag, over my shoulder so that I could make my way out the door. I'd not even read the letter yet. As soon as I saw Bri Conall's handwriting and the key tucked inside the envelope, I knew that my friend had left her house in my care. The date at the top showed just how long Brian had kept this from me.

There was so much more that I could say to him, so much more I wanted to say, but I knew none of it would do any good. He would never see anything wrong with the kind of man he was, and I was tired of him. I was tired of everything, really. I only wanted to get out of this house without saying another word. I didn't ever want to see him again.

"I wasn't the only one who cheated," Brian said behind me. "Maybe you didn't do it physically, but in your mind you did. Every time I held you, I could see *him* behind your eyes. It's too bad for you, really. He didn't want you, either. That's why you ran to me, isn't it?"

I didn't respond. If only Brian would let me be and not say anything else, I might be able to make it out of the room and to my car without bursting into tears. But I knew he wouldn't be so kind.

"Bri is nuts," he continued. "She rambles on in the letter about you coming to visit her at the castle and how much you would love the seventeenth century. Bri's completely out of her mind. No wonder you two were such good friends."

I kept my back to him as I reached for the door handle, and I swallowed the lump in my throat when he chuckled again. "Goodbye, Brian." I didn't look back as I walked out the door, climbed into my car and started the engine, then pulled out of the driveway.

In the rearview mirror I saw Brian's mistress, Leah, pulling into the spot I'd just deserted, replacing me so quickly at our home it was as if I'd never been there. I couldn't bring myself to feel any hatred toward her—only pity. God help her, the poor girl had no idea what she'd gotten herself into.

---

*A*s much as I didn't want to spend the night at Bri's old house, especially after learning what Brian had used it for, I was relieved to cancel my hotel reservations. Classroom teachers don't make much money, and as a teacher's aide, I made even less. I couldn't move into my new apartment for another week, and with no family to offer me shelter until then, I had no choice but to reserve a room at the shabbiest of hotels.

If it meant saving a little money, I could push away the memories that would flood over me at Bri's—Brian's love nest. Memories of nights spent with Brian there when it had been his and we'd been dating, before he sold the house to my friend. Memories of helping Bri paint and refurbish the old bachelor pad until it was beautiful and perfect, just as she wished it. It's not as if I planned on sleeping much anyway.

The flowers on the front porch that she once tended so carefully had long since died, and an uncomfortable pang knocked on my heart at the thought of how much I missed Bri. I still didn't fully understand what had happened to her. She was the classroom teacher, and I worked directly under her. She was also the closest friend I'd ever had. When she disappeared after accompanying her archaeologist mother on a dig in Scotland, it's no stretch to say that I lost it a little.

When I finally found her after flying to Scotland, it was clear that she'd fallen madly in love. I saw how much her new husband, Eoin, adored her, and I couldn't blame her a bit for leaving everything behind. I would've done the same.

I'd experienced love like that once, but it hadn't been with Brian. What he'd said to me was true. The loss of Jep—the man I'd loved—led me to settle for Brian.

I understood Bri when it came to the love thing. What I didn't understand was why she'd lied to me about it. She had lied so confidently, weaving a story so detailed that I truly did want to believe it, but I couldn't. People do not—and she did not—travel through time.

Anxious to read her letter, I turned the key and stepped inside the entryway. To my surprise, the place was immaculate. Well, at least the front part of the house was. Most likely only one area of the house had been regularly used, and I would stay clear of that room.

I dropped my bag in the doorway, carrying only the letter into the living room with me as I slowly made my way around the space, turning on lamps and lighting a few candles.

Once the room was properly lit and the smell of pumpkin-scented candles wafted sweetly through the air, I went into the kitchen and put a kettle of water on the stovetop to heat, preparing to steep a large cup of tea. I was in desperate need of something to soothe my frazzled nerves and angry heart.

It had been weeks since I'd slept properly. Now that the divorce was final and Brian was out of my life, all of the stress, sadness, anxiety, and insomnia of the past weeks seemed to hit me at once.

After the kettle whistled and I poured the steaming water over a large cup filled with several tea bags, I all but collapsed onto the oversized sofa that sat in the middle of the living room. I found a coaster and set my tea cup on it, then propped the pillows up behind me so I could sit comfortably while reading Bri's letter.

I was incredibly curious to do so. I'd not heard a word from her since the wedding. She'd not even taken the time to say goodbye, slipping away during the middle of the reception. I was still angry about that, but I supposed Bri had her reasons. And she did leave me a house, which certainly counted for something. Not that she could've known just how much I would need it. Or perhaps she had, and that was the very reason she had left it for me. Bri had never really liked Brian.

I didn't need to open the envelope. Brian had already done that, and the rumpled edges showed just how many times he'd read through it himself, clearly trying to make sense of Bri's words.

The letter was short and the handwriting definitely Bri's, although it looked hurried. Something told me her idea to write the letter had been a last minute thought before she returned to Scotland. The first part was what I'd expected—an apology for leaving so suddenly and an explanation that the house was now mine to use as I saw fit. She spoke of how much she loved me, how much my friendship meant to her. Then she launched into what Brian had mentioned, speaking of her love of life in the seventeenth century and suggesting I might love it, too.

After that, she changed subjects quickly, only writing a few sentences at the bottom of the page. She'd not even bothered to sign her name.

"The house is yours while you need it, Mitsy, but when it comes time for you to get away and you're ready to start a new life, come and find me. You're welcome here. You will need the help of the innkeepers you met in Scotland. I'm not going to bother trying to tell you what happened again. I know you didn't believe me last time, and I don't expect you will believe me now...not until you experience it. Call them when you're ready."

Staring down at the odd message with fascination, I flung my feet over the edge of the couch, suddenly needing a large gulp of tea. Bri's statement was written as if she knew that I would want to leave here one day, that I would want to leave Brian. There was no *if* in her hastily scribbled message. Not only that, it suddenly seemed to me that perhaps she didn't intentionally lie about time traveling back to the seventeenth century. Bri actually believed she'd done just that.

Which changed things and made me worry for her all the more. Even after I found Bri and she told me the elaborate tale, even after I met Blaire, the woman who so closely resembled her that I was certain they had to be related in some manner, I still could not believe my friend's story. There was a reason she felt the need to lie. Frankly, I was so glad to know that Bri was alive and not murdered, buried in a ditch in the middle of Scotland, that I had decided to let it go. Begrudgingly, I'd accepted the fact that I might never know the truth of what happened to her after she disappeared. But if Bri truly believed that she'd traveled back in time, then something terrible must've happened to her.

Her brain was addled, disturbed, and I owed it to her to find out just what and who had done this to her. Not that I didn't need to get away from this place for personal reasons – I certainly did. But a trip to Scotland to find Bri and try to talk her out of her delusions would be the perfect excuse to leave. Better to help someone else out of a problem than to wade in the self-pity I felt at my own.

Making my way back to the front doorway, I found my duffle bag and withdrew my wallet and cell phone. I recalled writing down the phone number for the strange innkeepers I met the last time I searched for Bri. The old couple had been nearly impossible to reach, and I was not altogether sure that I'd be able to make contact with them again. I got the impression that their phone number and address were not readily available.

Finding the slip of paper in my wallet, I clicked the call button on my phone and punched in the number as quickly as I could, not waiting a moment so that I could change my mind. The phone rang once and was answered by the unmistakable voice of the innkeeper herself.

"Why, Mitsy, how are ye, dear? Jerry and I have been expecting a call from ye any minute. I suggest that ye start packing up yer things, though ye willna need much once ye get here."

My mouth hung open. How did she know it was me who'd called? I doubted that she had caller ID at the little inn. How did she know that I planned on coming there? I'd yet to say a word to her, and I didn't know what to say now. "Um…hi. Why would you expect a call from me?"

The old woman at the other end of the phone laughed softly. "Well, dear, I know a large number of things that I doubt ye would expect me to. Best ye get yerself here and then I will tell ye more. I'm sure ye willna believe a bit of it, though, until ye see it for yerself."

She was certainly right about that. "Ok...uh, is Bri there? May I speak to her for a moment?"

I knew she would tell me Bri wasn't there, but obviously she was. How else would the woman have known that Bri suggested I come there?

"Ye know that she isna here, love. She's a far time away from here to be sure, but ye will see her soon enough. She told me to tell ye when ye called that she doesna wish for ye to pay for yer plane ticket on yer own. She knows your budget is limited. I've already called the airline and purchased a ticket for ye. Yer flight is at 3:00 p.m. tomorrow. All ye need to do is check in at the counter. Yer rental car has been arranged, as well. I suppose since ye found yer way to our inn once before, ye are capable of doing so again. We will see ye soon. Safe travels, Mitsy."

She hung up the phone, and I stared at the wall in confusion. Thank God it was summer. As long as I didn't stay gone for more than a month, I wouldn't have to make arrangements at work.

It seemed that by this time tomorrow, I would find myself on a flight headed to Scotland.

CHAPTER 2

*M*cMillan Castle, Scotland—July 1647

Baodan McMillan glanced in Niall's direction, the two brothers' eyes locking over their mother's words. She was leaving McMillan Castle, the home she'd known for over three decades.

Baodan could make no sense of her sudden announcement. His mother had fallen ill nearly a month ago. With each passing day, she grew weaker. It did not sit well with him that his mother had decided to find a home elsewhere. The people in their territory would not understand it, and he wished to be near her so he could help care for her during her sickness.

Leaning across the dining hall table, he wrapped his fingers around both her hands, squeezing them gently. "Are ye saying that ye wish to go on a journey, Mother? Ye must know that ye are too weak, but surely it would do ye some good to escape the castle walls for a while, aye? If ye wish, I shall take ye for a ride so that ye may spend the afternoon away from the castle tomorrow."

Baodan glanced up to see Niall nod at him across the table, showing his approval at the suggestion. Out of the corner of his eye he saw Eoghanan, his youngest brother look down at the table angrily. Eoghanan's red hair and pale face were so different from his own dark brown wavy curls or Niall's ink-colored tendrils. His youngest brother's coloring labeled him as the outcast he was, and Baodan knew he would speak out in disagreement.

"No, Baodan. It willna do for her to only leave here for a short while. She needs to reside elsewhere. She wishes it."

Baodan's teeth ground together as he gripped the edge of the table with his free hand. "I doona think that is for ye to decide, Eoghanan." He started to continue but stopped as his mother pulled on his hand.

"I willna allow ye to speak to him so, I doona care how old ye are. He is right. I shall be leaving to reside elsewhere for the foreseeable future. I leave in the morning."

Baodan stood, unable to sit calmly. How could his mother allow Eoghanan to influence her so? Of all her sons, she heeded the words of the one who had betrayed him, causing him to lose the person dearest to him. He paced the room, circling the table where his mother and two brothers sat. He knew he would be unable to change her mind, but he'd be damned if he allowed her to make the journey without him. "Where is it ye plan on going, Mother? Ye do know how unusual this is, aye? Who will care for ye?"

"I miss my sister. Too much time has passed since I have seen her. She resides in a private cottage on the grounds of Cameron Castle and has done so ever since her husband passed away. She has invited me to live with her, and I shall. She says they have a talented healer in their territory. I suspect the woman will have me feeling better in due time. Ye doona need me to run the keep, and I will be but a three day journey away from here. While I am ill, and until I have grandchildren that need spoiling, I doona see a reason to stay here tending over ye three boys like ye are all too young to tend for yerselves. And I doona wish for any of ye to tend over me."

Baodan hadn't realized he held his breath until he exhaled, softening his resolve as he moved to sit by his mother once again. His worry for her expressed itself through frustration, and he knew she didn't deserve such treatment from him. "I appreciate yer confidence in us, Mother, but we all still depend on ye much more than we realize. I know I willna change yer mind, though I canna say that I think it a good idea for you to leave. At the verra least, I will travel with ye and see ye safely settled."

His mother spoke quickly, too quickly, and it only served to increase his suspicions. "No. Eoghanan has already agreed to travel with me. There is no need for both of ye to leave here."

He ignored her, facing Eoghanan. "I canna imagine yer reasons for convincing her to do this, but I'll be damned if I let ye take her there. I doona trust ye, especially not with the women I love."

He expected his brother to react angrily, to show some form of self-defense. He'd not directly addressed Eoghanan in months. Instead, the look of pain in his brother's eyes made him feel guilty for his hasty words. Baodan knew he placed more blame on Eoghanan than was fair but, try as he might, he couldn't stop the resentment he felt toward him.

"I'm sorry that ye doona trust me, brother, for there is no one in the world that I trust more than ye. If ye wish to accompany Mother, then I shall remain here with Niall, but doona ever again suggest that I would harm her. No matter what ye blame me for, surely ye know I wouldna do that."

Baodan cast his eyes downward, ashamed and guilty. "Aye, o' course ye wouldna. Still, I will be the one to see her safely to the Camerons'."

Eoghanan stood and turned, speaking with his back toward the table as he exited the room. "As ye wish. I'm retiring for the evening. I'll come down in the morning to bid ye both farewell before ye leave."

Once Eoghanan left, Baodan faced Niall, whose dark hair hung loosely in his face, covering eyes just as dark. He knew Niall expected what he was about to ask of him. "Can I count on ye to stay here and run things while I am away? To keep an eye on Eoghanan?"

"Aye, ye know I will."

Their mother stirred, drawing Baodan's attention. "There is no need for ye to watch over Eoghanan. Ye have punished him for too long." Her words shocked him nearly as much as her sudden decision to leave their home.

Baodan wouldn't allow himself to speak angrily to her, but he couldn't sit quietly while she defended his brother. "Why doona ye go up to yer bedchamber, Mother? I will send someone to help ye gather yer belongings. I need to be out of doors."

Not giving her a chance to respond, Baodan moved quickly from the room. It was a beautiful night, and he wished to sit out by the pond, to stare into it. Perhaps some of his bitterness would drift away on the water's rippling surface.

***

*B*aodan kicked off his boots as he reached the water's edge, grinning as one of the leather footings splashed into the water. Perhaps part of him had kicked it into the water on purpose. It was a pleasant summer evening, hot for Scotland. Although it was never good to have a wet shoe, it gave him the perfect excuse to go for a swim.

He glanced around to ensure that he wouldn't be revealing himself to any castle maids or female servants. Finding the pond and surrounding area empty, he swiftly stripped down and dove into the chilly water.

The water proved a balm to his skin and soul, instantly relieving his flustered spirit and angry mind. He reached the shoe quickly, throwing it onto the shore to begin the slow process of drying, before diving beneath the water's surface once more.

He swam as if racing, moving his arms in and out of the water, bobbing his head up and down as fast as he could manage. With each gasp of breath he pushed himself harder, each stroke of his arms helping to push away his worries and resentment of things past and present. He was in his element, his favorite place in the world; only when his fingers and toes were wrinkled and freezing from being too long in the water did he feel most at peace in the world.

He found that peace now, as all worries washed away with each stroke. *Dreamlike* described the joy he felt as he pushed himself forward in the water, eyes closed to what lay before him.

The dream ended abruptly as he kicked himself forward, and the corner of a rock tore its way into his flesh. He knew the pond well, but he'd gotten carried away, forgetting all about the patch of rocks that lay beneath the surface at the center.

He knew his foot bled, the sting of the water's touch told him that much. Breathing between gritted teeth, he stroked his way back to the shore, crawling out onto the grass to check his injury. It wasn't a bad cut and would heal quickly, although it would be sore for at least a few days.

Baodan leaned back onto his elbows and stared out across the black pond, only lit by the full moon hanging high above him. He was a good swimmer. Good thing, too. If he hadn't been, it was likely that Blaire Conall would have drowned the day he found her unconscious in the freezing ocean only a little over a year ago.

Thoughts of that day drifted away as he laughed softly to himself, thinking of his throbbing foot. His life seemed to be much like his unexpected cut. The times when things seemed most peaceful, everything usually fell apart.

That was the case with his late wife, although only his family knew what had truly happened to her. Everyone else believed Osla had fallen ill, taken quickly by an aggressive illness. In Baodan's mind, it wasn't all that far from the truth.

They'd only just married, and he'd thought himself so in love with her that she occupied his every thought, but he couldn't help but see the changes in her shortly after they wed. Osla grew dark and unhappy, miserable. She stopped speaking to him and would hardly leave her bed. She waged battles within herself, and he knew of no way to help her.

During one of her darkest spells, he was forced to leave for a fortnight to help a man acquire a piece of land. He left her in Eoghanan's care, and his brother swore to watch after her.

The night he returned to the castle, Baodan found her hanging out of one of the castle windows. Eoghanan claimed to have fallen so ill only hours before she killed herself that he couldn't move from his bed.

Baodan lived always with the guilt of not being able to save her. If he had been home, he would not have let a sickness keep him from protecting her from the wickedness that had invaded her mind.

Years later, the same sort of abrupt turnaround in his life had occurred when his father died. Everything had just begun to take on some sense of normalcy following the turmoil of Osla's suicide, when his father's sudden death sent Baodan spiraling downward again. He had always been optimistic in nature, but after that, Baodan released all hope of having the life he had once dreamed possible.

He did his best to remain kind, not to harden his heart against all of humanity, and in that he succeeded. He still found joy in his family, in running their home and land, and in serving their people. He still offered a helping hand when needed, but that was all the joy he allowed himself to feel. He took pleasure in the happiness, security, and friendship he could bring to others, but closed his heart to any of those same things offered to him in return. His hope had been broken too many times for him to allow it to creep back into his soul ever again.

He thought he'd found a person of similar mind and spirit in Blaire Conall. She was Blaire MacChristy when he rescued her from the freezing water, and the hurt in her eyes was enough to break his heart. She was broken, defeated, and a reflection of what he'd been years ago. He wanted nothing more than to help her, to heal her heart with friendship rather than love.

For that reason, he proposed to her. Love was a horrible misery, one that he intended to never fall prey to again. He suspected that Blaire felt much the same way, and for two people who didn't want love, perhaps friendship was best.

She accepted his proposal, and he found himself happy that he would spend the rest of his days with someone he could share mutual companionship and respect with, free of heartbreak or hope.

In what seemed to be a pattern in his life, that smaller dream ended, as well. Hope had still flickered within Blaire, and she was far luckier than him. Her heartbreak was healed when her love, Arran Conall, came back to her, suddenly free from the confines of his own marriage.

Baodan let her go willingly. He couldn't begrudge her happiness if she could find it. If he were less broken, less hard and more lucky, he would gladly leap in the direction of love as Blaire had.

Friendship was really all he'd offered her; friendship could remain although she was married to another, and so it had. He considered her to be his closest friend, a confidant when he had few. They wrote to each other often and, because she was married to his cousin, both families used the other's home as a stopping point when traveling. It became a happy friendship and one of the things in his life for which he was most grateful.

Thinking of Blaire, he stood. He kept his left foot off of the ground and tried to shake away the water from his body and the self-pity from his mind. Then he donned his clothing so he could go inside.

He had much to be thankful for. He could almost hear Blaire's voice telling him to quit his sulking and get on with his life. It would be what he made it, and he would fill it with kindness, friendship, and a safe lack of love.

*E*oghanan glanced up from his writing desk to see his eldest brother staring into the pond outside his window. Baodan's tall frame and broad shoulders intimidated everyone at first glance, but his brother had the kindest of hearts, and the bitterness Eoghanan knew Baodan held toward him didn't suit his kind demeanor. If only Baodan knew the truth, perhaps years of pain would finally come to an end. For years, Eoghanan had gladly carried his sister-in-law's secret, but he could do so no longer.

He suspected it even on the night of her death, but not until their mother fell ill did he realize the whole truth of what had occurred that tragic night. No illness prevented him from protecting her; a poison did. And now his mother exhibited the very same symptoms.

Baodan was too blinded by his need to lay blame for Osla's downward spiral and tragic death to see the truth, but soon Eoghanan would have the proof he needed. Osla had not taken her own life that dark night so many years ago. Someone within the castle killed her, the same person who poisoned him to prevent him from saving her, and the same person who slowly poisoned their mother now.

All he needed to do was ensure his mother's safety.

To gather proof of the unthinkable.

Niall's secrets wouldn't keep much longer.

CHAPTER 3

ustin, TX—Present Day

As anticipated, sleep eluded me. I spent the night tossing and turning and glancing at the clock every five minutes, hoping the sun would soon rise so that I could get up and start my day.

I was ready for it to be three o'clock so I could escape this house, this state. Every inch of the city contained a memory I'd rather forget. When it was finally six a.m., I jumped out of bed, put on my workout clothes, and left for a good long run.

I ran without direction, hoping it would clear my head and exhaust me enough that I would, at the very least, be able to sleep on the plane. I enjoyed running and ran as fast as my feet would carry me, logging at least six miles before I rounded the block leading back to the house.

I stripped just inside the doorway, anxious to get into a steaming hot shower. Hoping that Brian and Leah had confined their affair to the master bedroom, I showered in the guest room. It was a good thing Bri didn't seem to have any intention of coming back here. I was sure she would want to burn every last sheet, washcloth, blanket, and towel. I wanted to do the same myself, but knew that with my luck I would probably end up burning the entire house to the ground.

Sufficiently pink and warm from the hot water, I dressed in comfortable sweats for the plane and went about the business of packing the few items I thought necessary to bring. I didn't have much here. Most of my belongings were in storage, and I didn't want to go and collect them just for a trip.

Packed and ready to go by ten and not wanting to stay in the house a moment longer, I decided to go ahead and make my way to the airport. I didn't want to pay for parking, especially considering I wasn't sure how long I would be gone, so I called a taxi. It would be about a half hour wait before a driver could arrive, so I picked up my mess, locked up the house, and went to sit out on the front porch to wait for the cab.

It wasn't surprising, but still seemed quite odd to me, that Bri would leave me an entire house. I always thought that was something people did only after they died, and thank God she hadn't. I couldn't make myself stay in the house. Once I found Bri, I intended to try and talk her into taking it back. If she wouldn't, I would simply sell it and use the money to restock my savings, which had been painfully depleted by the divorce.

The taxi driver arrived right on time, and I found myself at the airport, checked in and through security by noon. With three hours to kill, I decided to grab some lunch and maybe a drink, or two, or three, in the chain restaurant and bar located just down from my gate.

Eating alone is a strange thing. As I sat there munching on my plate of potato skins and sipping on a gargantuan margarita, I realized quite pathetically that I didn't ever remember doing this before. How does someone reach the age of twenty-eight without ever having eaten in a restaurant all alone?

I knew the answer, but it made me utterly ashamed of my lack of independence. Of all the things in the world, I was most terrified of being alone; just another of the reasons I'd allowed myself to so easily fall under Brian's spell even though I didn't love him. Jep Franks was the only man I'd ever truly loved, and if I was honest, still loved. I married another simply because I couldn't stand the thought of being alone, and didn't expect love like mine for Jep to find its way to me ever again.

Sitting there alone, staring at couples and groups of people coming in and out of the restaurant, I thought of Bri and how we were such opposites. It was a wonder that we ever became such good friends. She would revel in the aloneness, the happy solitude of sitting by herself watching others' lives move around her. Traveling alone made me feel lonely and sad, and I wondered if others judged me for it. Did they know I was simply a runaway with no one to come along for the ride?

I had always given Bri such a hard time for spending so much time alone, but the truth was, I envied her. Although she always had her lively yet flighty mother, she'd grown up just as alone as I. Instead of it making her dependent upon social interaction, she'd become strong and independent.

I'm not saying that I admired everything about Bri. Good grief, it was frustrating trying to get her to go out on a date. Men fawned over her, and she just simply never saw it. She was constantly oblivious to the glances and gawking eyes. Bri never joined me in gawking back. I admit, I did my share.

If I hadn't always been tied to a man, I would've taken advantage of being single. While I did wish to follow Bri's lead on the independence front, I had no intention of ending my gawking days.

The male species, the exception being Brian of course, was made to be admired, and now that I had been released from the prison of being married to the dark, cloudy, negative force Brian had become, I intended to do a lot of admiring.

*O*ith a fresh perspective and a much more upbeat attitude, part of which could be attributed to finishing off that second margarita, I paid my bill and went to freshen up a bit in the bathroom before finding a seat at my gate to await boarding.

Although I wore sweats, I had made an effort to look as pretty as possible, hoping it would lift my spirits. That, and the aforesaid margaritas, seemed to do the trick; I was pleased with what I saw in the mirror. Apparently though, the woman standing next to me wasn't.

I saw her out of the corner of my eye. She wore skintight cheetah print pants, high heels, and a deep v-cut shirt that I couldn't have pulled off in my wildest dreams. She busied herself by applying at least half a case of blush onto her already blushed cheeks. The oddest part of her ensemble were the cowboy boots that went halfway up her calf, and the bright blue cowboy hat that balanced perilously on top of her rolling carry-on. I wasn't sure the hat would fit over the top of her hair, which was styled into a poof at least three inches high.

I turned away to grab some paper towels before exiting the bathroom. I knew I should've felt guilty, or at the very least ashamed, for staring at the woman. Then again, it seemed she'd expect to get stared at, dressing that way.

I'd just finished drying my hands when her voice behind me caused me to jump almost out of my skin. "Oh, my, my, my. That'll never do." The words were aimed at me and drenched in a thick, extremely fake Texas accent. I had lived in Texas all of my life and had never heard such a pronounced Texas twang, except in the movies. "Wait just a minute, sugar. I'd like to offer you some assistance."

I spun slowly, my brows knitted together in confusion. "Assistance? I wasn't aware that I needed any." The words came out a little sharp, and I really felt that second drink had caused my usual filter—however slim it was—to leave the building.

The woman reared back with wide eyes. "Oh, what a feisty thing you are, but yes, you do need assistance. You are far too gorgeous for me to let you go back out there like that. You have the darkest circles under your eyes. You look as if you haven't slept in days."

I remained facing the same direction but cast a sideward glance into the mirror. Although I hadn't noticed it before, deep, dark circles shaded the skin beneath my eyes. No wonder. I suffered from sleep deprivation. "I'm afraid you're right, but there's not much I can do about it. My makeup is in my checked bag."

She smiled wide and reached down to grab a bag sitting next to the rolling carry-on. "Not to worry, sugar, I've got just the thing."

Before I could protest, the stranger unwrapped a fresh sponge and slathered violet-colored cream under my eyes. I glanced down to see a boarding pass hanging out of the bag. Her name on the pass read, *Eleanor Billings*. I looked up at her again, narrowing my eyes. "Hmm...Eleanor Billings. You don't look like an Eleanor. Or sound like one."

Her hand froze on my face, and she instantly lost the Texas twang as she said, "Darn. Not convincing, huh?"

I winced and bit my lip.

She sighed. "I'm an actor on my way to L.A. to audition for a movie. I have to go straight from the plane to the audition so I had to go ahead and get in character." She stepped away so that I could turn to examine her work.

I looked much better, certainly more awake and sober than I felt. "Thank you. And I'm sorry to disappoint you by not being fooled. The good news is, I think I recognize you from a movie, or maybe a television show. Your name sounds vaguely familiar."

"Do you watch any of the daytime soaps?"

"I work during the day, but I record *Sunrise, Sunset*."

"That's it!" She grinned. "I had a brief part in it last year. Mimi Melinski."

"Oh my gosh! You were Mimi?" I widened my eyes and tried to get past the fake wig and all the makeup. "It *is* you! I loved Mimi."

"Thanks," she said, with a sheepish grin.

"Let me guess," I said, tilting my head and studying her. "The part you're auditioning for...southern hairdresser, as in *Steel Magnolias*?"

She laughed hard. "One would think, but no, actually. Well, not exactly. Think *Mrs. Doubtfire*, except more cops and less children, and..." she hesitated and reached up to scratch her head. "Actually, it's nothing like that."

I grinned and laughed. "All right, well that sounds just great." Glancing at myself in the mirror again, I added, "I do look much better, thanks to you. I appreciate your help. Let me return the favor." Before she could respond, I turned to grab another paper towel, wetting it beneath the running faucet. Wringing it out, I reached up to dab it over her cheeks, rinsing away some of the excess blush. "Don't take offense, but it seems that you're much better at doing someone else's makeup than your own."

"None taken. The exaggerated southern hairdresser look is new to me. All you needed was a little light under your eyes, which was simple. This…" she circled her face with her fingers. "This is a little harder for me to deal with."

Satisfied, I pulled away and chucked the paper towel into the trash can. I glanced at my watch and quickly reached down to grab my bag. "I've got to go. Almost time to board. Thanks again for your help, and good luck at your audition."

"My pleasure. Try and get some sleep on the plane. You seem to be in need of it." She surprised me by reaching behind me before I could leave, and quickly grabbing the clip that held my hair into a messy bun at the base of my neck. Her eyes widened as my long, red curls cascaded over my shoulders and down my back.

"That's better. Why on earth would you pin all that up?"

I reached back, fluffing the hair into place and tucking it behind my ears. "It's easier that way. I'm traveling. Who's going to see it?"

She shook her head in disbelief. "Everybody in the airport is going to notice you, sweetie, whether your hair is pulled up or not. Besides, that is some killer hair. I wish I could find a wig just like it." With that, she turned and left me in the bathroom.

After taking a second to laugh at the odd occurrence, I snatched up my bag and made haste to my gate. When I got there, passengers were already lining up to board. Luckily, I was in the first group. Taking my place in the back of the line, I waited my turn for my ticket to be scanned. Smiling at the attendant as she tore my pass, I stepped out onto the walkway leading to the plane.

Amazing the difference a few hours could make. This morning things seemed bleak, but now I felt more excited than I'd been in ages. This trip could be great, and for the first time in the five years since I'd met Brian, I was finally free.

*M*cMillan Castle—Scotland—1647

*B*aodan knew he should still be sleeping. A long journey lay ahead of him once he left with his mother for Cameron Castle, but he wanted to speak with Eoghanan alone before his mother woke.

Eoghanan would be awake. Baodan wasn't sure if his mysterious brother ever slept. He would be in his room, writing away by candlelight in his journals. What he wrote, Baodan was sure he would never know. Not that he cared. It took all his strength just to remain civil around him.

As expected, Baodan found his youngest brother hunched over his writing desk, scribbling away, his shoulders stiff. He didn't look up as Baodan entered. Instead of announcing his presence, Baodan walked across the room, only stopping when he stood next to the desk. He glanced down at the secretive pages, but Eoghanan yanked them away, breaking his rigid stance by standing abruptly.

"These are not for ye to look at. If I wished ye to see them, I would have addressed them to ye, aye?" Eoghanan's eyes—green, gold, and cat-like— challenged Baodan as he widened his stance. His unruly red hair looked like dancing flames atop his head.

Baodan stepped away, not wishing an argument to escalate. He only wanted to find out the truth behind their mother's desire to leave, not to rehash ill feelings. "I'm sorry, I dinna come here to spy on ye. I only wished to speak to ye before leaving."

Eoghanan looked suspicious. Baodan knew he'd given him more than enough reason to be in the years since his wife's death.

"Why? Ye doona ever wish to speak to me."

Baodan reached up to run both hands through his hair and over his face. Eoghanan had once been his closest friend in the world. It seemed odd to him that he should feel so uncomfortable speaking to him now. "'Tis about Mother. I need to know why ye have convinced her to leave. Whether Aunt Nairne wishes to see her or not, Mother wouldna have come to the decision to leave on her own. I canna figure out why ye see the need for her to leave here. Do ye not wish to help care for her? Not even while she is ill?"

"Aye, o' course I wish to care for her. Can ye not see 'tis for that reason that I insist she leave? I doona care what ye think of me. I love her just as much as ye do."

Why did he feel the need to be so vague? Baodan had no reason to assume that the change would be in their mother's best interest. "No, I canna see that her illness would be a reason for ye to make her leave here. I doona doubt that ye care for her, but ye are not telling the truth of what ye mean by all of this."

"No, and I willna tell ye all there is to it, either. 'Tis not my place to do so. Not yet."

Baodan moved across the room so that Eoghanan would not see his frustration, but the tone of his voice gave it away. "Is that so? I doona believe it was yer place to allow my wife to die, but ye did so anyway. Why worry about what is and isna yer place now?"

In a rare show of anger, his brother charged him, slamming him up against the wall.

"Ye are an ignorant fool. Do ye think that speaking to me in such a way will make me inclined to tell ye why Mother must leave? I willna tell ye anything of it, for ye wouldna hear me even if I did. Ye have closed yerself off to me, and ye have punished me long enough. She has been gone for over seven years, Baodan. Do ye truly believe that I wouldna have helped her if I'd been able?"

Baodan could hardly speak as shock coursed through him. Eoghanan released him and backed off, shaking, pain evident in his voice and his eyes watery with anguish. Baodan stepped away from the wall, eager to leave.

Eoghanan brought out the worst in him. He hated the person he became around his youngest brother—the very reason he spent so much time avoiding him.

"I'll bid ye goodbye now, brother. I only wished to learn why she must leave, but I can see that I willna gain the information from ye. I canna believe ye have coerced Mother into doing this. She's so ill she can hardly lift a spoon to her mouth. We will be lucky if she survives the trip."

Baodan moved toward the door, only stopping at the sound of his brother's voice – soft, small, and so different from how he sounded a moment ago. A voice filled with warning rather than anger.

"She willna only survive the trip, she shall thrive from it. Just wait and see how her health improves once she is away from this castle. Then perhaps ye will see that I wasna wrong to persuade her to leave."

Baodan left quickly, more frustrated than he'd been before entering his brother's room. Why had his life become a series of riddles in which everyone around him seemed to know the answers, save him? Something hid from him. If he could get through the next few days without any more surprises, he intended to devote his every effort to finding out what that was.

* * *

*B*aodan wished to make one more stop before he left to prepare the horses. If his mother still rested when all was ready, he would wait until she elected to leave. She would need all the strength she could muster for the trip of several days. He would not be the one to disturb her.

He rounded the corner and knocked on Niall's bedchamber door. Niall wouldn't be awake like Eoghanan, and Baodan found himself hesitant to enter his brother's room unannounced. He wouldn't be surprised to find a lass with him, and Baodan didn't want to embarrass the girl, if so.

Niall was a charmer, but Baodan knew that his brother was also a liar when it came to women. He made love and promises, only to leave each lass he wooed heartbroken and quickly forgotten.

When no response came to his knock, Baodan rapped his fist against the doorway louder, stepping away as he heard his brother's grumbling voice.

"What do ye want? Can ye not see that the sun is still not up? I doona rise until it does."

Baodan stared at the door, annoyed. Everyone in the castle knew the sun to be high in the sky before Niall chose to rise from his bed. When the door finally swung open, Niall stood before him nude, his hair sticking up messily as his black eyes stared up at Baodan. He expected Niall's grumpy reaction and stared down at his brother, who stood a few inches shorter than him.

"Would ye like to have yer nose knocked up into yer skull, brother? I have company and was having the sweetest dreams," Niall complained.

Baodan shook his head, not the least bit surprised. "Ye shouldna treat women so. They are not created for ye to enjoy and toss aside."

Niall laughed, and Baodan reached around his brother to close the bedchamber door so that the lass sleeping in the bed would not hear their conversation.

"Ye are a fool if ye truly believe that, Baodan. 'Tis the only reason they exist as far as I'm concerned."

Baodan chuckled once, throwing his hands up in surrender. "Then I suppose I am a fool, for I doona agree with ye. 'Tis a twisted way to look at any lass, but I know there are many men who think as ye do, so I willna fault ye for it. I only wish ye wouldna tease them so with yer sweet words and false promises."

"I doona wish to be with the lasses who wouldna care if I made my true feelings known. They doona tend to themselves like lassies truly looking for love. Now..." Niall crossed his arms, clearly not pleased with being lectured. "Did ye come here to make me feel guilty, or did ye have something different that ye wished to say to me?"

"Aye, I wished to see if ye know why Eoghanan would want Mother to leave here. I canna see any sense to it. I thought perhaps ye might be able to help me see a reason for this." The look on Niall's face made him regret his decision to speak to him. Niall's relationship with their mother had always been strained.

"No, I doona know, and I doona care. I shall not be sad to see her go."

Baodan's jaw tightened at Niall's words. "Ye should be ashamed of yerself for saying such a thing."

"Why? She doesna like me, and she makes it clear."

The look of disgust on Niall's face made Baodan clench his fists in anger. He turned away, knowing his temper was about to flare. He didn't look back as he walked away, only speaking loudly enough so that Niall could hear him. "Perhaps 'tis the way ye treat women and the way ye lie to everyone around ye that makes her not so fond of ye. I canna say I like ye much myself, at the moment. Watch over the keep while I am away."

Fuming, Baodan exited the castle's main entrance as fast as he could. He shuddered at the thought of Niall's thoughtless words. It made him wonder just how good of a man he himself could possibly be when both of his brothers were the worst sort of men.

CHAPTER 5

O n The Plane To Scotland—Present Day

With my head slumped against the window of the plane and drool dribbling out the side my mouth, attractive was the last word anyone would use to describe me. I fell asleep just as soon as I settled into my seat, and when the unpleasant tickle woke me, I wasn't sure if we were in the air yet.

Eyes still closed, I raised my head off the window and ran the back of my hand over my chin and mouth. With no turbulence or movement, as far as I could tell, I assumed that we'd yet to take off. Planning on resuming my slumber within seconds, I reluctantly opened my eyes and slid the plastic cover on the window up just slightly so I could peek outside.

Sure enough, I saw tarmac rather than sky, and it was clear there had been some sort of delay. I groaned and started to close the window when a familiar voice to my left caused my hand to freeze on the shade.

"Hey there, sleepy. I almost woke you, but you looked like you really needed some shuteye. I couldn't believe it when I got to my seat and saw you sitting there. What's it been, Mits, five years? Surely we will take off soon. We've been sitting here for over an hour."

I didn't turn, didn't even respond, just pinched my eyes shut. Could Jep really be sitting next to me? It was too crazy a coincidence. I quickly tried to think back to the restaurant. I was sure I'd only had two margaritas. But the incident in the bathroom had been weird enough, and now this. This was just too much. The chances of Jep and I ending up on the same plane, in seats next to each other, were so small, I sincerely couldn't believe it was really his voice I'd heard.

"Mits? Are you okay?"

If only I didn't need to pee so badly, perhaps I could simply lay my head down and feign sleep for the duration of the flight. Unfortunately, I did have to go to the bathroom. Besides, it might have been five years since I'd seen him, but I still knew Jep well enough to know that he wouldn't let me deplane without speaking to him. And why would he? He'd been my best friend, and I his, for over twelve years.

We'd been childhood friends, and then young lovers. And he'd smashed my heart into a gazillion pieces.

Knowing I couldn't ignore him forever, I swallowed the lump that formed in the middle of my chest and faced him.

"Hello, Jep." I smiled as I looked him over, hoping he would be unable to see every thought that ran through my mind. He'd changed. His previously dirty blonde hair was darker, and his brown eyes were tired, less hopeful than they'd once been. Small bags pouched beneath his eyes, the kind that men get as they grow older. He was too young to have them already. Jep had aged too quickly in the few short years since I'd seen him last.

I glanced down at his left hand to find he was still married. If his marriage even remotely resembled what mine had been, it went a long way toward explaining why he looked so much older.

If he was a stranger and I was meeting him for the first time, I don't think I would have found him overly attractive, but he wasn't a stranger, and despite the changes in him, I found him just as handsome as always.

I swallowed once more and said a silent prayer that my voice wouldn't come out shaky and weird. "I've never been so surprised to see anyone. Why are you going to Scotland?"

He smiled back and reached across the armrest to pull me toward him. "Business. Now, come here. It's been too long since I've held you in my arms."

He hugged me, but I immediately felt uncomfortable. What an odd thing for him to say. It was a sentiment I'd spent a lot of time thinking to myself over the years, but one I never would've expected him to return. While I found myself thinking of him often, I knew there was no reason for me to ever cross his mind.

Apparently, Jep noticed that I'd become rigid within his embrace. He parted ways with me quickly, pulling one half of his mouth up into a quirky grin while glancing down at the floor. "I'm sorry. That was out of line. It's just..."

A ding above us interrupted his apology. The captain came over the speakers to tell us that the problem with the plane had been fixed, and we would be cleared for takeoff shortly. Once the plane started moving, I would be unable to go to the bathroom until after we were in the air for a while. I couldn't wait that long.

Unbuckling, I stood to make my way to the lavatory. "Sorry, I'll be right back. I've got to go to the ladies' room before the plane takes off."

He nodded, and I made my exit, taking a deep breath for the first time since I'd heard his voice. I couldn't imagine what he wanted to say, but I was sure I didn't want to hear it. Any rehashing of memories would only make me ache, and I'd just set my mind to being much more positive only an hour ago.

His words of goodbye the last time I saw him, while kinder, hurt me more than anything Brian could ever say. I'd cared about Jep that much more than I ever had my husband.

I wet a paper towel in the sink and freshened my face before exiting the restroom. Then, filled with dread, I made my way back to my seat. Jep's nearness made everything inside me hum. When we'd been together, he'd had the same effect on me, but the feeling was more about excitement, anticipation, and love back then; now the humming was different, caused by palpable tension and unsaid words. It wasn't angry tension, but the sort that is usually between two people who have a shared painful history. Or at least one that did not end well.

As soon as I sat down, the plane moved, and for the duration of the takeoff, both Jep and I remained silent. After we were in the air and the atmosphere in the cabin changed back to one in which people visited quietly while others slept or read, I could see Jep's hands start to twitch. I knew he was nervous about something.

I closed my eyes, hoping to ward him off from saying anything, but it didn't work.

Finally gathering his nerve, Jep reached out to squeeze my hand gently. I opened my eyes and he pulled his hand away.

"I know you're not asleep," he said. "Can I ask you something?"

I didn't respond immediately, instead weighing the chances of him actually refraining if I said 'no.' Since I was fairly sure the chances weren't good, I said, "Um...sure." I intentionally sounded reluctant to chat, hoping he'd get the message and change his mind. No such luck.

"Where did you go?" he asked.

"What?"

He shifted in his seat to face me. "After the wedding? Where did you go?"

It seemed rude of me to stare straight ahead while he studied me so intensely, so I looked him square in the eyes. "I didn't go anywhere. Brian and I stayed in Austin. I got a job as a teacher's aide at a local elementary school. Why do you ask?"

He looked down again. I'd never seen him so hesitant about anything. He was usually overconfident, leaning toward cocky. "That's not what I meant, but I'm surprised to know that you didn't leave Austin, and we've never bumped into each other. I don't see a ring on your finger. Are you and Brian...? Are you still...?"

I was tired and cranky. If he insisted on talking, I wished he would just say whatever was on his mind. "No, we're not. Look, I don't want to be rude, but I'm exhausted. After we land, I'll have a several hours car drive ahead of me. Just spit out whatever it is you're talking about. For instance, you said that's not what you meant. Explain that."

His eyes swept downward, which did nothing to gain my sympathy. "I mean, I didn't hear from you again after my wedding."

I was older in both age and life experience than I'd been when Jep and I were together. I wouldn't allow him to guilt-trip me over something that was his fault ever again. "What?" I almost shrieked the word, garnering attention from passengers seated nearby. Leaning in slightly closer to him, I lowered my voice and said, "Did you honestly expect that I'd stay in touch? You married her! I know we'd been broken up a while, but we still talked every day and you got engaged and married, all without telling me you were even seeing someone else! You knew me well enough not to expect I would call or text a married man."

He looked up and locked eyes with me. "I did know, but I couldn't stand the thought of not talking to you. That's why I didn't tell you until after the fact."

"It was a selfish thing to do. And don't tell me that you couldn't stand the thought of not talking to me. The things you said to me after your wedding were meant to guarantee that you would never hear from me ever again." I stopped speaking before my voice could crack. Thinking back on the night I learned about his marriage was enough to take all the breath out of me.

Jep reached his hand up and caressed the side of my face. I almost pulled away, but the touch was comforting, and I chose to lean into it.

"I was lying. I was sure you would know. It was self-preservation, preservation for my marriage. I had to push you away, but I always thought you would know. Surely you do. I always loved you. I did back then, and I do now. I'm not sure that you ever truly stop loving someone once you've fallen in love with them."

He dropped his hand, and I twisted in my seat toward the front again. I breathed deeply, thinking on what he'd said. Hearing those words was like being released from a set of chains I didn't consciously even know had bound me.

In that moment, I realized it wasn't so much the loss of Jep that had wounded me all those years ago, but the loss of love. For me to have known how much I loved him and to hear him say that he'd never loved me, despite all the years we'd spent together, was more painful than him moving on to someone else. If I'd at least known that my love had been reciprocated, it would have been easier to move on.

Sleepy, I closed my eyes before speaking to him again. "What you're saying doesn't change anything, you know. You were an important part of my life, but it wasn't ever supposed to be you and me, in the end."

His voice was quiet, but I could hear the same relief in his voice that I felt in my soul. "I know, but I needed to tell you."

I smiled, eyes still closed, as I spoke through a large yawn. "I know, and that's all I ever needed to hear."

Why then, with this settled and Brian out of my life, did I feel the future would demand more than my past ever had?

CHAPTER 6

he Roadside Inn, Scotland—Present Day

"hy do ye look so pleased with yerself, love?" Jerry asked. "Yer cheeks are sure to be sore if ye go on grinning like that."

Morna Conall stepped inside the doorway of their charming home to plant a sound kiss upon her husband. He stood waiting for her in the entryway. Grayed hair framed his wrinkled face, but his thin mouth smiled against hers as she kissed him. His wrinkled, plaid blue shirt hung loosely on his slim frame, and the smell of pipe tobacco lingered near him. No matter that his knees creaked and his ears required that she speak up, he would remain ageless in her eyes, always.

"I doona know what ye mean, Jerry. I'm just pleased that Mitsy arrives today. 'Tis good to feel useful, and I'm anxious to see how the spell works now that I've tweaked it." She was aware that her husband would know she wasn't being completely honest, but she found Jerry charming when he was all riled up.

"Aye, but that isna why ye are grinning so. If I know ye as well as I think I do, and believe me I do, then I would say that ye've already been making yerself useful and using yer spells a bit, aye? Now, what is it that ye have done?"

Stepping out of her shoes, Morna moved into the living room and sat on the couch, patting the seat next to her so Jerry would join her. She reached to brush her red hair out of her face. It turned a bit whiter with each passing year, streaking the flame-colored strands. With Jerry seated, she reached for his hands. "All I did was rearrange a flight ticket so that a certain lad would be on board with her."

"Why would ye do that? What is the purpose of her coming here if the man she's supposed to meet resides in the States?"

Jerry's voice came out high and confused, and Morna laughed as she squeezed his hand. "The lad she's meant for isna in the States. I only wished to learn what occurred in her past that led her to us. So I did some casting to find it. Ye see, there's always much more to the end of a marriage than the actual end of it."

If only all relationships were lucky enough to be matched by her, Morna was certain there'd be many less hurting hearts in the world. She was a master at it, and she believed that to provide aid in the creation of love was the best use of her magic.

"Aye, that there is, dear. Did ye put Mitsy's husband on the plane?"

Morna shook her head. "Ex-husband now, and o' course I dinna! In Mitsy's case, her deepest wound was not from her marriage but from someone that came before it. She needed that wound to be healed before she goes back in time. I believe allowing her and her love from the past a chance to speak to one another did just that."

"Now, why is that, love? Why did she need to be rid of her hurt? Hurt is something that we all must learn from, and time heals our hurts well enough on its own."

Morna smiled. She found her husband to be wiser for his lack of magic. "Perhaps ye are right about time but, in this case, I thought time needed a little help."

"And just why is that? Ye are goading me by finishing every sentence without giving a full explanation, and I doona like it."

Morna laughed as her husband's voice rose. He was always quick to grow frustrated. She kissed him swiftly on the cheek and leaned into him. "Aye, I know that I am, but I canna help it. Ye make it too much fun."

He glared at her, only causing her to laugh more.

"Fine, fine. I'm finished. I just believe that now that Mitsy is free of the feelings that were holding her back, she will be more able to help someone who will need her assistance to free himself, as well."

A sudden knock on the door caused them both to jerk their heads toward the entranceway.

Jerry stood, moving slowly toward the foyer. "How did ye not see that she was about to be here?"

Morna moved to join her husband. "The casting distracted me. I was eager to see the results of my efforts with the plane tickets. Not to mention..."

"The fact that ye will have to lie to the lass," Jerry's voice finished her sentence, and Morna looked down regretfully.

"Aye, we shall both have to. 'Tis the only way to get the lass where she truly needs to be, and that place isna with Bri at Conall Castle."

*J*ep and I both left the plane as quite different people than those who boarded it. With the mutual feeling that the past was truly behind both of us, we parted amicably and happily. It didn't take long to gather my luggage, as I'd checked only one bag. Since this was my second time to rent a car to go in search of the odd innkeepers, the process went smoothly.

Several hours later, I found myself parked outside of the inn, anxious to go inside so I could speak to Bri. If she wasn't there, I knew she must be somewhere close by.

Rather than the furious and frantic knock of my previous visit, I knocked softly and stepped away from the door. The last time I arrived at the inn, I'd been in a bit of a panic and had not been on my best behavior.

It took a moment, but as soon as the door swung open, I was pulled into a surprisingly firm embrace.

"Ach, lass. I'm pleased that ye made it safely. Come inside, Mitsy. It's good to see ye, dear."

Once the elderly man released me, I managed to smile, despite the overly-familiar greeting. "Thank you. It's good to see you…Jerry, is it?"

He beamed and patted me firmly on the shoulder, taking my purse to set it beside the door. "Aye, it was kind of ye to remember my name."

I stepped inside just a little bit further so I could glance around for any sign of Bri or her husband, Eoin. "Yes, I remember your name, but I'm afraid I'm not sure of your wife's name. When I met her, she was Gwendolyn, but I heard Bri refer to her as Morna?"

As if summoned, Jerry's wife stepped into the entranceway and embraced me in much the same way Jerry had. "Call me Morna, dear. And ye did remember my names, both of them. 'Tis only that ye dinna remember which one to use."

Friendly folks, I thought to myself, but truthfully, I didn't mind the affection. I was merely surprised by it, especially considering how terribly I'd treated them both during my first visit here. "I'm afraid I owe both of you an apology. The first time I came here, well, I was very rude. I was only—"

"No need to apologize," Morna interrupted, waving me inside the kitchen. "You were worried about Bri. It only goes to show what a good friend ye are. Come, sit and eat a bit. I've made chicken pot pie. Not a Scottish dish, to be sure, but when my American friends come to visit, I like to try American recipes."

Jerry wrinkled up his nose, and I laughed at the disgust on his face.

"Aye, well at least ye dinna make the lasagna this time."

Morna ignored him. As soon as I was seated, I dug into the delicious dish. "It's wonderful. Thank you. Might I ask you a question?"

Morna sat down across from me and Jerry followed, sitting next to her. "O'course ye can. I suppose ye are anxious to know how things are to happen now?"

I frowned but stared down at my food so as not to show my utter confusion. "I just wanted to ask you if Bri was here."

The pitch of Morna's voice caused me to look up. She seemed as shocked as I was confused. "Well, o'course she isna here, dear. She told ye where she was, dinna she?"

Was everyone around here smoking the same thing? Surely, she didn't believe that Bri was living in the seventeenth century? "Well, she did tell me something, but come on. It was obviously some sort of weird joke. I don't know why she wouldn't tell me the truth."

Morna stood and excused herself. When she returned seconds later, she carried a plain, brown dress and a smooth, black rock. The dress looked like something you would put on at a carnival to take an old-timey photo. "She wasna lying to ye, Mitsy, and if ye wish to see Bri, ye must go back, as well."

I didn't say anything. I just sat there, looking at the old couple as if they were crazy. I half expected a camera crew to pop out of the woodwork at any moment to tell me I was on some sort of hidden-camera reality television show.

Jerry reached across the table and squeezed my hand, obviously trying to comfort me, but he only served to make me jump out of my seat.

"Okay, seriously, what is going on? You two are freaking me out. Bri's had her fun, but I am really not in the mood for her nonsense after the long flight and drive to get here. So, if you would, please tell her to get her skinny self out here."

The odd couple glanced uncomfortably at one another and then back at me. I canna make Bri come out here," Morna said. "I'm sorry, lass. I doona blame ye for thinking us mad. All of it seems so commonplace to me that I forget 'tis truly traumatic for those unaccustomed to the idea. I have magic, dear. I'm a witch, if ye like. Bri truly is living in Conall Castle, but in the year 1647. Ye willna believe it until ye are there, I'm sure. While it will be a rough adjustment, I can see that there willna be another way. Here's the long and short of it, Mitsy. If ye really wish to see Bri again, ye will step into the bathroom, change into the dress, and do as we bid ye."

"Trust us," Jerry whispered softly.

---

*M*orna's eyes flashed when she ordered me into the bathroom and, while I believed her to be harmless, if there were really such things as witches, I almost believed she was one in that instant.

I did as she asked, the whole while trying to figure out any plausible cause for what she was talking about. Perhaps it was a role-playing thing. That nerdy thing that video-game people do, gathering in fields and pretending to be things and people they're not while engaging in fantasy-type battles. Surely Bri wouldn't be involved in such a thing.

My next thought, and the only one that truly made any sense to me, was that it was some sort of creepy cult, something that Bri had gotten sucked into after she met Eoin. Could he and this old couple have somehow managed to brainwash her so that she actually believed all this time-travel business? If it was a cult, I imagined the only way I would ever see Bri again was to play along and act as if I believed them so they would bring me into their secret gathering place. I wasn't sure I could do it, but I could try. If it meant bringing Bri back into reality, I would do it wholeheartedly.

Once I stripped myself of the sweats I wore, I climbed into the dress, squirming against the hard package of something I could feel on the inside of the dress. I couldn't do up the laces myself, so hesitantly I stepped back into the kitchen.

"Look." I pointed a finger at both Morna and Jerry and put on my angriest "ginger" face. "This is obviously some sort of crazy cult thing, and while I'll play along so that I get to see Bri, I don't want you to think for a moment that you're going to be able to brainwash me. You got it?"

Morna rolled her eyes dramatically, and Jerry started laughing so hard he doubled over. Neither reaction did anything to calm me down.

"Believe what ye wish, lass, but in due time ye will see that ye are the one who is mad for dreaming up such a ridiculous notion." Morna paused to raise her palm toward me. "But aye, lass, I swear not to try and brainwash ye."

I spun my back toward her. "Well, good. Just so it's clear. I'm only here for my friend and then we are both getting out of here as quickly as possible." Realizing that I sounded crazy, too, I lowered my voice and spoke much more sweetly. "Would you please help me with these laces? I couldn't do them on my own."

"Sure, dear."

Each time Morna pulled on the laces, the lump on the inside of the dress pushed into my side. "What's inside the dress? Is it some sort of tracking device? If so, I can assure you the dress is coming off as soon as I leave here."

With the next tug, I was certain she pulled on the lace a little tighter than was absolutely necessary. "Ye no doubt have a bit of Irish ancestry in ye, doona ye dear? For ye are as mad as a wee banshee. I sewed some ibuprofen and a few other medicines into the dress. Believe me, ye will need them once ye travel backward."

"Looney tunes, every one of you," I said, muttering the words under my breath. Morna must've heard because she tugged so tight on the laces, it knocked the air right out of me.

"What was that ye said, dear?" she asked innocently.

"Nothing." I sounded weak and breathless, and knew I should've kept my thoughts to myself.

Morna stepped away and motioned for Jerry and me to follow her. "Come along. It will take us several hours to get where we need to go. We best get on the road."

I thought Bri was living at Conall Castle?" I asked the question sarcastically. No one lived at Conall Castle. It had been a tourist attraction for many years and was no longer inhabited by anyone.

"Ye are going to Conall Castle, but ye must travel there by way of the pond at McMillan Castle. It has magical qualities."

"Of course it does." I stared out the window, enjoying the green beauty, despite being held hostage by two crazy bags. The landscape was so different from Texas, and in the best possible way.

We turned down a secluded gravel road, and I knew the instant we had reached our destination. The beauty of the place took my breath away. A grand pond sat off to the right of the magnificent castle. It was smaller than Conall Castle but equally as exquisite. For a brief moment, I imagined being one of the ladies who'd been lucky enough to live there during its prime.

As quickly as the odd thought came, I rejected it. Lucky? They didn't have toilet paper, electricity, running water, or tampons. Or birth control! 'Lucky' was entirely the wrong word, but staring at the beauty of the place made it easy for me to romanticize the past in a way that was, undoubtedly, unrealistic.

Morna parked next to the pond, quickly exited the car, and motioned for me to follow. Seeing no choice but to do so, I did as she bid. When we reached the pond, I bent to dip my fingers into it. The water was cold, but what was I expecting? This was Scotland, after all.

I turned to throw a frustrated look in Morna's direction. "Just how, exactly, is coming to this pond going to take me to Bri and the band of lunatics holding her hostage?"

"Ye must skip the rock, dear. If it skips three times, it shall take ye where ye need to go. Or, ye can hold it close to ye and float on yer back while we push ye into the water, but I suppose skipping it would be more fun for ye. If ye decide that ye need to come back, use the rock the same way."

I laughed and reared my arm back to chuck the rock, but waited as I asked Morna another question. "And just how do you expect me to do that? After I skip the rock, won't it disappear by floating to the bottom?"

She shook her head and laughed, clearly thinking my question stupid. "No, it will find its way right back to ye. Just like the pond is magical, so is the rock."

"Oh, right. How stupid of me." Again, I faced the water. "Are you joining me, or am I jumping on the crazy train alone?"

Jerry patted me on the back and turned to head back to the car. "Good luck, dear, and good luck to whoever finds ye there first."

"Start the car, Jerry. I'll be there in a moment." Morna bent down to pick up a handful of smooth rocks. "No, we willna be joining ye. This is for ye to do alone. Now, why doona ye practice with these rocks first?"

I dismissed her hand. I'd taken many picnics and jogs around Lake Travis, and I knew how to skip a rock with the best of them. "I don't need to practice." Rearing back, I flicked my wrist and watched the rock bounce. Once. Twice. I turned my head to Morna. "See, three times..."

In that instant, everything went black.

CHAPTER 7

M cMillan Castle—1647

*H*e wouldn't wake her, but Baodan hoped his mother would rise soon. He was anxious to leave here. His brothers had put him in a bad mood, indeed. If only all people were more like animals, perhaps he wouldn't have such a bad taste in his mouth for many of those nearest him. He ran his hands down the side of the marbled horse, leaning his head against the gentle beast.

"Ach, Artair, ye are a fine lad. What would ye say if we moved Niall and Eoghanan out here, and I moved ye and Heather into the castle? Ye could both have yer own bedchamber, and I wouldna mind if ye dined with me at the grand table."

The horse neighed happily and Baodan laughed as he tugged on both horses' reins, walking them out of the stables. "Aye, I expect ye would both like that, but alas, I was only teasing. I do care for them ye know, even Eoghanan. Despite how hard they make it, they're my brothers. Besides, I doona think Rhona would stand for ye living inside. She cleans up after the rest of us too much as 'tis."

A strange movement out of the corner of his eye caught his attention, and he whirled to face it. He was a good distance from the pond, but he could see something floundering in it. A bird, perhaps? He continued to move forward with the horses, straining his eyes to try and make out what tossed about in the water so frantically.

He heard it then—the faint scream so soft he thought perhaps he had imagined it. There were no females around who would have gone for a swim. He turned to Artair. "Did ye hear that, boy?"

The scream reached him once more, and the ears of both horses perked up as they took off at full speed in front of him. Baodan ran in the same direction. Although the horses stopped at the pond's edge, Baodan dove into the chilly water as he reached it.

There was indeed a woman flailing about, right at the center. Baodan glanced up in between powerful strokes to see a lass with bountiful red hair bobbing up and down, yelling angrily.

He slowed as he reached her. The lass wasn't drowning. She treaded water quite well, while shrieking like a banshee.

She had the strangest accent, much like his cousin's wife, Bri. Although he didn't understand half of what she shouted, he sensed it wasn't appropriate language to be coming out of a woman's mouth.

<hr>

The impact of the water as I hit it was unlike anything I'd experienced before. I imagined it to be something like diving off the high dive without any form. I would be sore for days.

I couldn't explain it—what happened from the moment I threw the rock to the moment I hit the water. One minute, I was on the shore. The next minute, everything around me went black. The next, water rushed up into my nose as I slowly sank.

Reacting quickly, I pushed my way up to the surface as soon as I registered that I was under water. I could swim well, although I preferred tiptoeing into the water to being catapulted into it.

My head was bleeding. I reached up to touch it as I treaded to get my bearings, and my hand came away covered in blood. The wound didn't hurt, but I suppose I was in some sort of shock from the sudden jolt. I wasn't altogether sure whether I hit my head when I entered the water, or I'd been wacked by someone behind me and then tossed in.

I spun in a circle, realizing that I was a good distance from any shore. No way had I been thrown into the water. But if not, how else did I end up here? I started to scream. At Morna, at Bri, at anyone who would listen.

"I'm going to kill you, Morna! Crazy old biddy. Where are you hiding, anyway? Don't think I won't find you, and when I do you're going to wish you'd never met me. You said Bri was supposed to be here! Did you put the *Kool-Aid* in that chicken pot pie?"

"What is 'cooo-laid,' lass?"

My back was toward the man who'd spoken, but I spun quickly when I heard his voice. Cheese and crackers, he was freaking beautiful.

"Are ye hurt??"

I momentarily forgot to kick my feet and dipped beneath the surface shortly before popping back up to spit up more water. He was at my side in an instant, his firm hand yanking me upward.

"I'm fine. Thank you."

He reached up and dabbed at the wound on my head. "No, ye are not fine. Ye are bleeding, lass. Do ye need me to help ye to shore?"

I pulled away from him and started to swim. Gorgeous or not, bleeding or not, I didn't know this man, and I had a sneaking suspicion he was part of the *Kool-Aid Club*, whoever he was. "No. I can make it just fine."

"As ye wish, but ye will let me see to it once we get to shore. Ye have no choice in the matter."

No choice? My head would stop bleeding, but my sanity grew more fragile with every second I spent in Scotland. Once I found Bri, we would bounce.

The man was a practiced swimmer and reached the shore minutes before me, but he obviously realized I didn't want his help. He remained waiting on the shore for me to arrive.

He was dripping wet, bare-chested, chiseled beyond belief. And wearing, I kid you not, a kilt. Looking at him, my stomach immediately felt swimmy, even though by this point I was pulling myself out of the water.

I'd seen his face while dog-paddling in the middle of the pond, and while it was stunning, to see the package all together was enough to warm my freezing, wet skin through. His dark eyes slanted out at the ends just slightly, making him look serious and smoldering. His hair was dark brown and blended with different shades of copper, making his wavy hair look shiny and alive. He had lots of it, and although cut short, the glorious mass hung loosely around his ears. Wet, wavy curls hung down into his face and eyes.

I shook my head. No matter how ridiculously handsome he was, he was obviously part of the lunatic gang. I twisted and reached behind me to wring out my own hair. The long ringlets absorbed water like a towel and, as I squeezed, it poured from my locks like a running faucet.

"That's some head of hair ye've got there, lass. 'Tis stunning."

"Umm...thanks. Now, seriously. . . I did what the crazy bat asked. I got dressed in this ridiculous outfit, traveled out here, threw that stupid rock, and somehow ended up in the water. Surely that's enough for you to allow Bri to talk to me. If she really wants to stay here, fine, but I need to see her and speak to her."

He regarded me skeptically as he grabbed my arm and dragged me over to a small rock bench just a few feet in front of us. " Ye must have hit yer head harder than ye thought, for not only are ye bleeding, ye are speaking utter nonsense."

I briefly forgot about my head, but as I felt the blood trickle down my face, I reached up to touch the gash above my forehead and winced at the sting. "Ouch. That hurts like crazy now."

"Now? Did it not hurt ye before, lass?"

He reached forward with his hand, gently wiping away the stickiness from my face. He had no cloth, save his kilt, but he seemed more worried about cleansing the blood from my face than the ick factor of getting it on his hands. "No, it didn't hurt before and it only hurts a little now. It's already about stopped bleeding, I think. It's not a deep cut."

He crouched down so that he was eye level with me and continued to gently wipe my face. By the time he reached the slash, it had stopped bleeding entirely.

"Ye're right, lass, and I'm glad for it. Sit here a moment. I'm just going to wash this off."

He jogged over to the water's edge and rinsed his hands. Before returning to me, he met two horses that were headed in his direction. Gathering their reins, he walked them to my side and patted both gently. "They were worried for ye too, lass. They ran to your aid as soon as they heard yer screams. Now, what was it ye were saying in the water? Did I hear ye mention Bri? Do ye know her, lass?"

The relief at hearing Bri's name was instant. I couldn't have been more pleased. If he knew her, she had to be close. "Yes, I do, and I need to speak to her right away. Where is she?"

"Not here, lass. She resides at Conall Castle and is married to my cousin, Eoin."

So much for relief. "You've got to be kidding me. That's what Morna said too, but she said I would find her by throwing the stupid rock into the pond here. Not that I believed her, but I at least thought Bri was around here somewhere."

He crouched down again, worry evident on his face. "Morna Conall? She's been dead many years."

I stood, angry as ever. He did the same, and although he towered over me, I rammed my fingers deep into his chest. "Look buster, I'm sick of this crap. Morna is alive and well, unfortunately. Not that she's going to stay that way for long. She's the one who brought me here, and she told me that I would find Bri. If Bri's not here, I'll tell you what's going to happen. You are going to go get your car and drive me to wherever you've got Bri, right this instant."

He didn't budge. Amusement danced in his eyes as he stared down at me. "I doona know what a 'car' is."

I smirked at him and walked over to the horses. "Fine! Then get me on one of these bloody animals and we'll ride there."

"Did ye say 'bloody' lass? Are ye from England? Ye doona sound English."

"No, I'm not from England! I'm from the States. I don't know why I said bloody. I've never said it before in my life. I'm tired, my entire body hurts, and I'm ready to get out of this episode of *The Twilight Zone*." My voice cracked, and I swallowed hard to keep from crying. I hated that every time I got this angry, I felt the need to cry. It immediately made me seem less forceful.

He walked up to me and hesitantly tried to wrap his arms around me in comfort, but I jerked away.

Exhaling loudly, he said in a sympathetic voice, "I'm verra sorry I've upset ye, lass. It wasna my intention. What's yer name?"

I sucked up my sniffles and tried to steady my voice. "Mitsy, and yours?"

"Baodan. Now, I believe that ye know Bri. By the way ye are going on about her, I have no doubt. I will take ye to see her, but I'm afraid I canna do it right away."

A new voice answered him, and I turned to see another man approach. He was striking in the most unusual of ways. His hair matched my own in color, and he was tall but didn't move as smoothly as Baodan—each step forward reserved and slightly hunched. His lips were large, and his voice was exceedingly deep.

"No, brother, ye doona need to take her anywhere. Ye can leave her in my charge, and I will see her to Conall Castle myself."

CHAPTER 8

"What?" My voice broke, and my face flushed so quickly I thought my head might burst from the pressure of it. Enough was enough. "I'm not staying in anybody's 'charge.' I haven't joined your crazy role-playing cult circus, so don't try to dump that load of bologna on me!"

I continued yelling, but neither man listened to me as they stared each other down. Finally, Baodan reached out and grabbed me firmly on the shoulder, pushing me soundly down into a sitting position on the bench. "Sit and hush. Doona say another word. Eoghanan needs to explain himself, and I canna hear him with yer screeching. Just calm down, lass."

I tried to stand but his hand still pressed down on my shoulder. He was strong as a bull, and I would go nowhere unless he allowed me to. "Calm down? Are you crazy? You're both acting as if I'm some sort of object!"

"Did I not just tell ye to hush? Would ye like me to gag ye, or will ye cease speaking on yer own?"

I crossed my arms and stayed silent. He was obviously serious, and I had no desire to be muffled.

He faced the other man, an expression on his face as angry as I imagined my own to be.

"Just what do ye think ye are doing, Eoghanan? I wouldna leave ye to watch over a toad. I trusted ye once and it ended with my wife dead. I doona trust ye with women who belong to me."

"What?" I didn't care if he gagged me, he was out of his mind. "You are a sick, deluded jerk. I've known you all of ten minutes. I do not belong to you."

Both men ignored me, and I drew my gaze to the pained expression on Eoghanan's face as he fidgeted uncomfortably.

"I am tired of this between us, brother. How can ye carry such hatred for me within ye for so long? 'Tis time for ye to put this behind us. Ye canna delay Mother's journey, and ye canna take this lass along with ye. If ye wish to be the one to take her to Conall Castle, then ye should be the one to do so. In the meantime, someone must look after her."

Baodan released his grip on my shoulder and stepped in front of me protectively. "And ye think that should be ye?"

I scooted over on the bench, watching the two men intently, now intrigued. Fantastic actors, both of them. These guys took role-playing to a whole different level.

Eoghanan stepped forward, his voice low and just as angry as Baodan's. "Surely, ye doona mean to leave Niall to watch over her? He'll have seduced her before sundown."

Baodan shook his head, casting a glance my way. I assumed he meant to reassure me that he wouldn't let that happen. "I doona like it, but ye are right. I canna leave her with Niall."

"Then give me a chance, brother. 'Tis not the same as it was with Osla, and ye know it."

I very much wondered who Osla was, but neither man gave me a chance to ask.

Baodan all but growled at his brother. If the two men truly were siblings, which I seriously doubted, they didn't resemble each other in the slightest. "If anything happens to the lass, ye will not enjoy what happens to ye."

"Excuse me?" I hardly recognized my own voice, it sounded so screechy with rage. I stood and stepped out of his reach before he could grab my shoulder again, and went to stand apart from them so that we made an odd sort of triangle. "Let me explain something. Nothing is going to happen to me because I am not staying here. I'm going to see Bri, and I don't need anything from you." I squirmed, suddenly needing to use the restroom. Why did I always need to pee at the most inconvenient moments? "Except to have you direct me to a toilet."

"A 'toilet'?" Both men said the word in unison.

I threw my hands up in exasperation. "Stop! Seriously, just cut it out. Press pause for just a moment. Once I'm where I need to be, you are free to resume this delusional little game of yours."

Eoghanan spoke only to Baodan. "Is the lass daft? What is she talking about?"

Baodan shook his head. "I doona think she's daft. She hit her head, though. Perhaps she just needs some rest."

"Aye, I believe she does. She looks a bit wild, does she not?"

Eoghanan glanced in my direction but tore his gaze away after he saw the glare I cast at him.

"Hello? Did either one of you hear what I just said? Of course I'm not daft, you bunch of morons! Quit ignoring me."

Again, neither heard nor listened to me. As I stared, their conversation quickly escalated into a full-out argument, and I stood back, looking around at the castle grounds. I don't know why I didn't realize it after I got out of the water, or even after I asked Baodan to go for his car, but now I noticed the utter lack of modern transportation. And a sudden chill rushed down my spine.

When Morna pulled up in front of the pond, other vehicles were parked at the castle—not around the pond where she parked, but up closer to the castle itself. It was a tourist attraction, just like Conall Castle and many of the other castles in the surrounding area. But now there wasn't a tourist in sight, nor any sign of one.

Although it was still daylight, I wasn't sure how much time passed in between tossing the rock and waking in the water, but it only felt like seconds. It couldn't possibly have been more than a few hours. Could the castle have closed for visitors in that time? If so, was it likely that every employee and security guard had left, as well?

Each second I spent here just became weirder. I glanced over at the horses. They seemed gentle enough, and I'd been on horses a few times. Maybe if I stayed quiet, I could get away atop one of them. Unlikely, but I couldn't just stand here staring at Crazy One and Crazy Two.

Slowly, I backed away. Watching them argue, I crossed over to the horse farthest from them. I imagined I could see the chestnut colored mare's sympathy for me in her eyes. She might cooperate, if only the men would keep arguing long enough for me to get away. I jumped to wrap my arms around her so I could pull myself up.

"I'm going to see her to a room," said Baodan to his brother. "Ye may make sure she's cared for, but doona let her outside of the room. I fear she'll try to leave if ye do so."

Before I could pull myself up onto the horse, Baodan turned and spotted me. He was by my side before I could blink, grabbing me away from the beast, flipping me over his shoulder so that my head bounced up and down against his back as he carried me off toward the castle.

I stopped screaming once he stepped inside the main building. It wasn't doing me any good, anyway. He had a firm grip on me, and no matter how much I banged on him or hollered at the top of my lungs, he didn't release me. Besides, the interior of the castle was so beautiful and quiet, it seemed wrong somehow to disturb the atmosphere by screaming.

My silence seemed to bother him, and he reached up with his left hand that he'd had wrapped around my legs and gave me a quick smack on the rear. "Did ye lose consciousness, lass? I dinna know ye could be so quiet."

The smack elicited a yelp, and he laughed at the sound.

"Where are you taking me?" The words sounded broken, each step he took up the stairs knocking the air out of me.

"Did ye not just hear what I told Eoghanan? I'm taking ye to a bedchamber, where I will ravish ye before leaving on my journey."

"What?" Screaming again, I lifted my leg and swung it down into his lower stomach just as hard as I could. "You will do no such thing. Put me down. Now!"

He grunted at the impact, but then laughed loudly, pinning my legs against him so I'd have no chance of kicking him again. "Shhh, lass, I jest. I promise I shan't touch ye. We are only going to have a little talk, ye and I."

"I don't want to talk. All I want is to find Bri, shake the crazy out of her, and then get on a plane back to the States."

He stopped in front of a large door and released the grip on my legs with one of his hands so he could open it. Once inside, he closed the door and set me down on my feet. My head pounded from my injury, and I felt dizzy from being upside down. He reached out to steady me as I got my bearings. "I doona know what a 'plane' is, lass. Just like I dinna know what a 'car' was when ye mentioned it earlier."

I pulled away from him once my blood seemed to be running in the right direction. "Right, I forgot. We're in the past. Do they have cameras watching you guys all the time and if you break character they put you in a dungeon or something?"

Baodan squinted, his brows drawing together. Crossing to sit in a large chair across the room, he said, "Ye are verra strange, lass. Half of what ye say seems like another language entirely. Why doona ye take a seat?"

I didn't know if it was from hanging upside down, my confusion and rage, or the temperature in the room, but I grew very warm. With a head wound, I thought I'd better be careful. "I'm really hot. Can you maybe turn up the air in here a bit?"

Again, the same confused expression. I wanted to knock it off of his pretty face.

"I could open a window if ye like?"

I pinched my dress in between my boobs and lifted it up and down quickly to fan myself. Baodan regarded me as if I was doing a strip tease in front of him. "Yes, please do. But can you also adjust the thermostat? Hasn't this place been modernized? If you have visitors every day, surely it has air conditioning."

As he opened the window, I moved around the room looking for air vents. With the exception of the window, I noticed no source of circulation anywhere in the room. Only sun rays streaming in through the windows illuminated the room, not electricity. Sunlight and candles were the only source of light.

"What is a thermostat?" Baodan studied me more closely, adding, "Where did ye say ye came from?"

The only explanation I could think of was that they'd not modernized anything to preserve the historical value of the place. Regardless, it seemed odd that there wouldn't be the slightest hint of anything modern in the room.

"I'm from the United States, and I live in Texas. I'm from the same place as Bri." I moved to sit in the chair across from him. My head was starting to ache again from the cut.

Baodan leaned forward so that his elbows rested on his knees, and he clasped his hands out in front of him, regarding me sternly. "Well, ye see lass, now ye have given me cause to worry over ye, for ye are either one of two things. Ye are either daft, as Eoghanan suggests, or ye are a liar."

"Excuse me?" I leaned my elbow against the arm of the chair and allowed the side of my face to rest inside my palm.

"Aye, lass, now which is it? Bri doesna come from this place that ye speak of. She is the daughter of Laird MacChristy, a twin to be exact, although few people knew he had two daughters until recently. While I'll admit that ye speak much like her, she spent her childhood living in many different places, traveling with one of her father's relatives. I doona know her well, but I have met her, and I know this to be true."

I sat up and leaned forward so that we stared squarely at one another. "You don't know squat, because all of that's not even remotely true. I can't imagine why she would have made that up. Maybe you have to tell a cool story to get into this club, but it's seriously time to give me a break. Haven't I been through enough today? I got dressed up in this ridiculous garment, rode all the way out here only to be knocked unconscious, and was somehow dropped into the middle of the pond. I cut open my head, and now I'm held against my will. Please. I am begging you, just cut the crap and tell me what's really going on here." I tried to look as desperate as possible, not that I found it hard to do. I started to feel panicked about the inconsistencies of everything around me. None of it made any sense.

He reached forward and grabbed both of my hands, his touch gentle. I didn't have enough fight left to pull away. It reassured me to know that, despite how crazy he seemed, he genuinely felt sympathetic to my plight.

"Lass, I doona know what ye wish for me to tell ye. Why doona ye ask me a direct question, and I will do me best to answer it. But doona use the strange words ye've been using, or I willna be able to help ye a bit."

"Fine." I moved around in the chair, unable to get comfortable. With my dress still very wet, it grew heavy. "For starters, is there anyone around here from whom I could borrow some clothes? Jeans would be nice, but if you all insist that I wear another costume dress like this, I guess it will suffice."

He looked nearly as tired as I felt. "Ye did it again. 'Jeans?' I doona know what those are. I will send for someone to bring ye a new dress just as soon as I leave ye."

"Leave? You said you would take me to Bri."

"That I did, but ye are forgetting that I told ye I canna do it right away. I have promised my mother that I would see her to my aunt's, and that I shall. It should take me no more than three or four days. Upon my return, I will take ye to Bri at once."

I hiked the dress to just above my knees to allow me to cross my legs. Shaking my head, I said, "Are you suggesting that I stay here for four days while you're gone? You're crazy. That is so not going to happen. You said she's at Conall Castle, right?"

He took in my crossed legs with obvious disapproval. "While I doona believe ye are from where ye say ye are, I do believe that ye doona come from here. I havena seen a lass sit like that in my entire life."

"Good grief. They're just legs. Are you really that big of a prude?"

He laughed loudly, a deep, belly laugh so contagious I couldn't help but smile in return.

"I dinna say that I doona enjoy the sight of them, but ye would be asking for trouble in the wrong company. 'Tis lucky that I found ye in the pond and not Niall." His eyes strayed to my knees again, then quickly back to my face. "And, aye, Bri is at Conall Castle."

"Great! Then I don't need anyone to accompany me. It will take me all day, but I'm pretty sure I can find my way there on my own."

"I'm afraid 'tis not possible, lass."

A knock on the door interrupted us, and quite possibly the oldest woman I'd ever seen stuck her head inside the door.

"Yer mother is awake and ready to leave as soon as possible." The woman glanced over in my direction and took in the puddle forming at my feet. "I'll bring the lass a new dress at once. Will she be staying here?"

I stood and moved toward her. "No, I'm leaving as soon as I get a change of clothes."

She paid me no mind, looking through me as if I'd said nothing. "Baodan?"

"Aye, she will stay in this room until I return. I have left her in Eoghanan's care, mistake it may be, but please have men stay close to the door at all times, and make sure that she is well cared for."

The woman nodded and left, closing the door behind her. I made to follow her, but Baodan quickly moved to block me, looming in the doorway. "I'm sorry, lass, but ye willna be leaving without me. 'Tis too far to Conall Castle for ye to travel alone, and I doona trust my brothers to see ye all the way there."

"Why?" He spoke of his brothers as if they were criminals. I didn't have much experience with siblings or normal families, but his mistrust of them seemed odd.

"Eoghanan is negligent, and Niall would seek to woo and seduce ye simply for the sport of it. Not that ye will have a choice in it, but promise me that ye willna leave this room until I return."

"You're joking? I will do no such thing." I tried to step around him, but he grabbed both of my arms.

"Aye, lass, ye will."

"Look, I appreciate your concern, but you don't need to worry about your brothers. I don't need someone to look out for me, so even if Eoghanan is 'negligent' he won't be a problem, and I am not all that wooable so neither will Niall. While none of you seem to be, I am living in the twenty-first century. And just FYI, it's completely illegal to keep me here against my will."

Genuine worry spread across his face, and he released his grip on my arms. He seemed very sad for me, and it made something deep within me hurt. I didn't want his pity, especially without reason for it.

"Ach, so Eoghanan was right then. Ye are daft. If that be the case, then I am sure ye are truly verra scared. I am sorry for that, lass, but 'tis all the more reason for me to keep ye here. Ye are right when ye say that ye are not mine in the way that ye meant, but ye are mine to care for until I deliver ye safely into someone else's hands."

He ran his palm down my arm as if I was ill. It only served to infuriate me more. "You seriously think I'm crazy, don't you. Well, I've got news for you, buddy. I am not the crazy one. You might want to quit eating the food here. Maybe that's what they're using to screw with your head. Because you, my friend, are the one who has lost it."

He smiled at me pathetically and reached for the door. "Ye shall be well taken care of while I am away. When I return, we will travel to Bri's. Perhaps she will know where and to whom ye belong."

With that, he left the room, locking it securely behind him. I couldn't begin to process all that had just happened. Part of me wanted to laugh hysterically at his assumption, but at this point, I started to feel as crazy as he accused me of being. Maybe the blow to my head had left me confused.

Only a few minutes later, the old woman who had entered earlier opened the door and held out a fresh dress to me. She said nothing and didn't enter the room. I crossed to her and grabbed the garment from her hands, and she closed the door and locked it.

I stripped quickly, eager to get dry and ready to rip open the pouch with the medicine. Morna had been right about one thing; I needed something to ease my aching head. The fact that she'd known I would require it disturbed and puzzled me to no end.

Turning the dress inside out, I pulled at the loose stitching around the pouch. It came open easily. Inside was a small plastic case filled with much-needed ibuprofen. Something else lay in the pouch, and I had to reach inside to grab it. As soon as my fingers touched the smooth, cold surface, bile built up at the back of my throat.

I pulled the object out and threw it onto the bed, truly frightened for the first time since the beginning of all this craziness. In the center of the bed now sat the shiny, black rock—the very same rock I'd sent skipping all the way to the bottom of the pond.

he Grounds of Cameron Castle

*B*aodan and his mother reached the castle grounds three days after leaving home. He couldn't help but notice that his mother seemed far less tired than he. While he took care with her, traveling much more slowly than he wished, she should not have been so full of life this far into their journey, considering her illness.

He couldn't make sense of it, but Eoghanan was right. All it took was half a day's ride and a shabby meal of pheasant to bring his mother back to her old self. She was still weak, but for the first time in months, light filled her eyes, and she started talking as if she'd been starved for conversation for far too long.

They decided to bypass Cameron Castle itself, riding instead straight for his Aunt Nairne's cottage so that he could settle his mother and leave at once for home. His mother could greet his cousins later in the evening. The journey took longer than he'd planned, however, making him all the more anxious to check on Mitsy.

What a strange lass—completely mad, but Baodan couldn't help liking her. Perhaps all of her confusion could be a product of her injured head, and he would return to find her at rights with herself.

He surely hoped so, for it seemed wrong of him to think of someone who was out of her mind in the way he thought about Mitsy. Baodan had spent every moment since leaving his home thinking of that mess of red curls and her whip-like mouth. He dreamed of tugging hard on those locks while claiming every inch of her lips with his own.

"I wish I hadna been sleeping so that I could have witnessed the arrival of the fiery lass who has so captured yer attention." His mother laughed as she turned on her horse to look at him where he rode behind her.

Baodan believed the woman could read minds. "I am worried for her, is all."

"I doona believe ye, although ye worry too much over everyone. The one ye should be worrying about is yerself."

Baodan nudged his horse forward so that he rode next to his mother rather than behind her. "Why do ye say that?"

"Because ye are in danger of growing hard-hearted, my son. Ye have seen more loss and anguish than most, but life is not worth living if ye close yerself off from it."

He didn't answer her. Even if he wished to change, he didn't know how.

"That's all I'll say to ye about it. Now, tell me more about this girl. Ye said she spoke of being from the twenty-first century?"

Baodan shook his head and smiled, thinking back on it. The lass had a grand imagination, mad or not. "Aye, but she hit her head on a rock moments before. Perhaps it did more damage than she believed or than I realized."

His mother looked over at him and grinned nervously. "I swear to ye that my head is fine. I dinna bump it, and I doona wish for ye to start to think that I am mad, as well. But why are ye so inclined not to believe her?"

Surely she played some sort of trick on him. "Heh? I'm sorry, but what do ye mean by that? O'course I wasna inclined to believe her."

"Dinna ye say that she said many words for things that ye have never heard of?"

"Aye." He pulled back on the reins, slowing his horse. They were drawing close to his aunt's cottage, and he wanted to hear what his mother had to say before they arrived.

"And dinna ye say that she mentioned a woman named Morna? Yer uncle Alasdair's sister's name was Morna, and she was a powerful witch."

As a child, Baodan had heard stories of Morna the witch, but for most of his life he'd dismissed them as simple tales. He'd never heard his mother speak as if she believed the rumors to be true. "She wasna a real witch, surely?"

"Aye son, a real witch. I dinna believe the stories either, not until our last visit to Conall Castle. Mary, ye remember her, doona ye? She told me the truth of it all. Bri is no more Laird MacChristy's daughter than old Heather here." She reached down to pat her horse. "She fell prey to a spell put in place by Morna many years ago, and as a result, she fell through time. 'Tis a verra long story and, to be honest, I doona remember all of it, but I spent enough time around yer cousin's strange wife to believe Mary's story. Eoin's new wife is kind and has made a place for herself amongst the family, but 'tis verra clear that neither her nor the lass's mother grew up in the same world as ye and I."

Impossible. No matter how odd the lass seemed, Baodan had never witnessed such magic himself. "Surely, ye canna mean it? How can something so impossible be so?"

"How can the love of two people create another? I doona see how that is any less impossible than this. I have seen magic in my life, son. It does exist, and there is a piece of it held captive in yer home." She gazed ahead. "We are nearly there. I think it is best if ye unload my horse and leave for home at once, for ye owe the lass a grand apology."

---

*M**cMillan Castle*

*T*he smug, beautiful jerk had lied. It was currently night four of being locked inside this room, and he'd still not returned. Not only that, but his idea of me being "well taken care of" differed from my own. Breakfast consisted of some sort of roasted bird, and as far as I was concerned, unless it poured out of a green box and tasted like sugary apples topped with milk, it didn't constitute breakfast.

Lunch and dinner consisted of less food together than what I usually ate in one meal. I liked to eat and made sure that I could do so without gaining a lot of weight by running my fair share of miles every day.

The exception being the last four days I'd spent locked up inside this hole. Perhaps hole was a bit extreme. I'd slept in few rooms as pretty, and the bed was quite comfortable, despite being springless and slightly lumpy. All that aside, any room where I had to go to the bathroom inside a wooden bucket and use scraps of cloth as toilet paper, I could label as a hole.

I had spent the first day in denial, clinging to my hope that all of this was just some sort of nerdy role-playing game taken to the extreme. But by day two, I could no longer deny the unexplainable presence of the rock inside my dress and abandoned that notion. Only two other possibilities remained.

One: the impact of the water and the bump on my head had caused brain damage, and I truly was crazy. Two: Bri, Morna, and Jerry all told the truth.

For some weird reason, the first possibility seemed less plausible to me than the second. After the first day, my headache was gone, and I seemed to be having no sort of other cognitive difficulties—no slurred speech, no dizziness or confusion. Nothing. Only a small scab remained to remind me of the injury.

The second possibility, while admittedly insane, was now what I accepted as reality.

Bri was smart, and not the sort of person to easily fall under the influence of others. I'd used the assumption that Bri was crazy or brainwashed to rationalize the truth of something I simply couldn't wrap my head around.

Truthfully, I was no stranger to magic, the paranormal, or whatever you wanted to call it. In the end, my absolute certainty that the rock had somehow returned to me, along with two incidents that had occurred in my past, finally pushed me to accept the fact that I truly had landed in the seventeenth century.

The first past incident happened when I was eighteen. On the day of my high school graduation, I walked up the steps to the front door of the only real home I'd ever known to collect my foster mother, Lilly, for the ceremony. With my hand on the knob, I twisted it, but for some reason the door simply wouldn't open. I tried again and again to budge it, without luck. Suddenly, I heard a voice, clear as day, beside me say, *"Don't go into the house alone. Call Jep and wait for him to get here."* I glanced over my shoulder but found no one. Again I heard the same words. *"Don't go into the house alone. Call Jep and wait for him to get here."*

I started to cry. Since the door wouldn't budge, I did as the voice insisted. Once Jep arrived, the door opened with ease. Inside, we found the remnants of a break-in, with things smashed and broken everywhere, anything worth value stolen.

We called the police immediately, and Lilly arrived at the house with them. Thankfully, she'd been out getting her hair done during the robbery. From a surveillance camera of a neighbor's house, the men had been armed, and the time stamp showed they were still inside when I arrived at the front door. The thieves fled out the back.

The other incident occurred in college. During Winter Break, Lilly took me to Wales. Her parents moved from Wales to the States when she was a little girl, and she always wanted to make a trip back there to revisit her childhood. It was the most terrifying experience of my entire life.

We spent the day driving through Snowdonia National Park and decided to stop for the night at a small family-run inn in a nearly deserted town. With the hotel virtually empty, we were the only ones in a room on our side of the old house.

The evening passed normally, and both of us slept like the exhausted and weary travelers we were. In the morning, things changed. We packed our bags, rolled them to the door, and opened it to see a female figure staring at us not ten feet down the hallway. An apparition, for we could also see *through* her.

The ghost stared at us as we stood frozen in the doorway, seemingly deciding if she approved of our presence. Neither of us breathed. After a few very long seconds, the woman turned and walked down the hallway, evaporating in the distance. If Lilly hadn't seen it also, I would have been certain I'd imagined the ghost.

Both instances couldn't be explained, yet I knew with absolute certainty that both happened. Confident in the reality of those instances, I didn't see how I could continue to deny the possibility that something truly unexplainable had happened to me now, as well.

If I believed without doubt in guardian angels and ghosts, why couldn't I believe in time travel?

I woke on the fifth morning with a fully renewed attitude about my current situation. Sure, it terrified me to realize that I'd somehow ended up in a time nearly four hundred years before I was born, but I also had hope that when I was ready to return, I would be able to. After all, I had the rock, didn't I?

According to Morna, the entire purpose of the rock was to insure my ability to return. So far, she'd told the truth about almost everything. Skipping the rock indeed sent me back in time, and the rock magically returned to me after I tossed it, just as she'd promised it would. Bri, however, Morna had lied about. While Baodan confirmed that she lived in this time now, the innkeeper had led me to believe that I would find her here at McMillan Castle. And Bri wasn't here. I doubted she even knew I had arrived in the seventeenth century, as well.

I twirled the rock between my fingers. It scared the bejeezus out of me to find it inside the pouch, but now I prized the possession as my lifeline back home. As long as I had that with me, I saw no reason not to enjoy my time spent with Bri in a place and time most people would only ever dream of visiting. I might as well enjoy this place, as well, until Baodan took me to Conall Castle.

I slipped out of the gown I'd been given to sleep in and reluctantly crawled back into the now-dry dress that Morna dressed me in. I found it uncomfortable, which made me self-conscious. I was a jeans and a t-shirt, sweats and hoodie, kind of girl. Dresses were no less than a tolerable form of torture.

I spent half of an entire day trying to manage the laces myself. While I figured out how to keep the dress up, it was sloppy work. As long as I wouldn't reveal myself to the man sitting outside my door, I felt satisfied.

Walking across the room, I knocked at the door and tried to rouse Eoghanan. I knew he sat just outside the door. He'd spent every moment since Baodan left leaning against the doorway. Until now, I'd only managed to coax a few words out of him. I intended to change that today.

"E-o, look. In case you haven't noticed, your name isn't the easiest to pronounce so I'm just going to call you E-o. Is that cool?" As expected, he didn't answer, and I slumped down in the doorway and sat with my shoulder leaning against the hinge. "Come on. I know you're out there. I see you every time a meal's brought, or a bath, or they come to empty my chamber pot. You haven't left, not even at night. I can hear your snoring through the door. Open up. I won't try to leave, I swear. I just want to talk."

He groaned, annoyed, but still said nothing.

"You have no idea what a talker I can be, and I have nothing to do in here. So you can either open up this door and talk to me for a little bit, or you can sit there with the door closed and listen to me talk at you all day long."

"Ye doona need the door open to speak to me, lass. If ye insist on doing so, talk as ye are now."

I shook my head, stopping when I realized that, of course, he couldn't see me do it. "Nope. I'm afraid that's not going to work for me. I like to speak to people face-to-face, not through big wooden doors."

He laughed, but I could tell I made him uncomfortable. I really didn't care.

"I doona think Baodan would want me talking to ye, lass."

"I don't really care what Baodan wants. I'm being held in here like a prisoner when I've done nothing wrong. The least you could do is open the door and talk to me."

I heard him stand, and I smiled. I could out-pester anybody. Although I knew I shouldn't pride myself on it, I usually got what I wanted.

He shouted and I jumped, but then realized he wasn't shouting at me. He told the guards at either end of the hallway to stand down. "If she tries to run, stop her lads. I only mean to talk to her." After a moment of no movement, I heard him slip the key inside and open the door.

Seeing me sitting on the floor, he did the same, mirroring my position so that we faced each other, each of us leaning against the inside of the doorframe.

"Thank you." I smiled and leaned across him to peek down the hallway, but he quickly grabbed my arms and pushed me back inside.

"Did ye not just tell me that ye wouldna try to get away? I'll not hesitate to shut the door again and let ye to talk with only yerself."

"I wasn't trying to go. I just wanted to see what the place looks like. All I saw was the upside-down view coming in. It's beautiful."

He nodded and looked up and around him, as if he hadn't taken the time to appreciate its beauty in some time. "Aye, lass, it is. Now what do ye wish to speak about?"

Where to begin? Anxious to ask many things, I decided to start with what pressed at the forefront of my mind. "Why have you been sitting outside my door? Caring for me and being a creepy stalker are two very different things."

"I'm sitting out here for yer protection."

"Why?"

"Because ye doona want the men of this castle to enter yer room."

"What does that mean? Are you saying that I need to be protected from you?"

He shook his head and looked down at his hands awkwardly. "No, lass. I swear to ye, I willna hurt ye."

"Then who? The other brother? Niall, is that his name?"

"Ye are not afraid to say whatever ye think. 'Tis unusual in a lass."

"Sorry." I wasn't sorry at all. I had no filter, and I didn't imagine that would change anytime soon.

"Doona be sorry. I doona suppose anyone ever has to fear that ye are pretending to be something ye are not, and that's more than most people can say."

"Yes, it's a problem at times, though." I hesitated, then asked, "What's Baodan's problem with you, anyway?"

He waited, as if deciding to share that information, then relented. "He believes that I am responsible for a great hurt, and foolishly he doesna trust me."

E-o wouldn't hurt me. I'd spent all of five minutes with him, and I would stake my life on that fact. A pain in his green eyes made my chest hurt, but a deeply rooted kindness lived within him—a kindness I expected he'd been unable to express for some time. "He's wrong about you."

He looked up from his hands at me, obviously surprised. "Why would ye say that, lass? Ye doona know me at all."

I shrugged my shoulders and grinned at him. "I have a knack for that sort of thing. I'm good at reading people." I thought of Brian and grimaced. "Well, most people, anyway."

He laughed, and I saw his smile for the first time. Large and crooked, his lower lip stuck out in the most adorable way. What could he possibly have done to make Baodan despise him so much?

"Ah, well we all have pasts, doona we? By the look on yer face, I can see ye are thinking about someone in yers."

"Yes, but it's nothing worth thinking about. Can I ask you a question?"

"Aye, for ye will anyway."

"You're not really his brother, are you?"

He turned quite pale but recovered quickly. It couldn't have been that big of a secret. I'd not met Niall yet, but Baodan had dark hair and eyes. E-o looked more like he could've been my brother, with the same red hair and skin tone as myself.

"I am in every way that matters, lass, but ye are right. I am not his brother by blood."

He didn't seem to want to elaborate, so I didn't press him. "Can I ask you just one more? Last one, I swear."

"Aye."

"Is Baodan wrong about Niall, as well?"

Anger flashed across his face, and I knew his answer before he spoke. "No, if anything, Baodan doesna realize how dangerous Niall can be."

"And that's why you sit outside here?"

He nodded somberly. "Aye, but lass," he paused and reached out to grab my hand. "I'm afraid I willna be here tonight. There is something I must attend to before Baodan's return. I shall lock yer bedchamber door, and Rhona will have the only other key. I am sure that I have been over-cautious. Doona worry. The guards will be outside yer doorway, as well."

Suddenly chilled, I nodded and pulled my hands away from him to run them up and down my sleeves as I watched him stand to leave. "What is it that you have to do?"

He crossed to the door. "I'm afraid I canna tell ye that. And lass…please doona call me E-o, I'll teach ye how to properly say my name next time I see ye." He stepped out and shut the door, and I could hear his footsteps fading away.

I laughed, any worry that I'd felt due to his concern for my safety gone as quickly as it came.

---

*E*oghanan reached the alchemist's cottage by sunset. As he slipped off of his horse, he led the beast to the back, securing it safely out of sight so that none would notice it.

He could see the old man working inside. He was alone, just as Eoghanan had hoped. The man appeared small and frail. It wouldn't be difficult to overpower him, but Eoghanan hoped he wouldn't put up a fight. He wished to hurt the alchemist as little as possible.

Peeking around the corner of the house to make sure that no one watched, he stepped inside without knocking. Approaching him from behind, he raised his fist and brought it down hard upon the back of the man's head.

One blow was all it took. Catching him as he went limp, Eoghanan gathered his target and strapped him to the back of his horse then rode in the direction of McMillan Castle's dungeons.

CHAPTER 12

y stomach growled loudly, reminding me that it was past time for another measly meal of some sort of meat I was unlikely to enjoy. Usually food arrived right at dusk, but the sun had set hours ago, and my stomach rumbled in response to the late hour.

Just as I contemplated whether I should holler at one of the guards to ask about the delay, I heard the key jiggle inside the lock. I moved to a small table against the farthest wall of the room and sat with my back to the door to await my food.

The door latched into place, and I froze in my seat. Rhona never stayed long enough to bother closing the door. I knew before I turned that it was not her in the room with me. I'd nearly forgotten Eoghanan's warning and the concern on his face at having to leave me, but as rocks settled in my stomach, I knew who I would find as I twisted in my chair.

"You must be Niall."

He nodded as he moved to set the food down in front of me and then went to lean against the wall beside the small table so that he looked right at me.

I expected him to be tall and menacing. Instead, he stood much shorter than both Baodan and Eoghanan, and his face was unusually pretty for a male. He was good- looking, no doubt, and he knew it, too. He displayed it in the way he held himself. I suspected he denied himself little.

"Aye, lass, right ye are. 'Tis a pleasure to finally meet she who has all in the castle busy with gossip."

Unlike the ease I'd felt with both other brothers, I held my breath in

Niall's presence. I wondered if I would have felt the same way if Eoghanan had withheld his warning. Regardless, something inside told me to tread carefully. "Where's Rhona? She usually brings me my meals."

He waved his hand dismissively and stepped closer. "Eat, lass. Rhona dinna feel well, so she went abed and left yer meal in the hand of her kitchen maid. I told her I'd be happy to take it to ye as I was anxious to introduce myself. When I arrived, I found that both the guards were not feeling so well, either. Seems something has spread throughout the castle."

"Ah." I ate slowly, hardly looking up from my plate in the hopes that he would take his leave. Inside, I knew better. If he had any intention of leaving, he wouldn't have closed the door behind him.

He waited until I finished. With every bite, I could see his eyes raking over me. All my hunger vanished, and eating became a struggle. I no longer wished to finish the meal.

"Thank you for the food." I stood from the table and moved to the door to open it for him. "I'm quite tired. If you don't mind, I think I'll retire now."

I had only just cracked the door open before his long strides met me and he pushed the door closed with his hand. "Just a moment. I willna trouble ye long." He reached to grab a small satchel hanging off of his kilt and dropped it onto the table where I'd just eaten. The bag jingled with coins, and I swallowed a hard lump in my throat.

"What's that for?"

"'Tis yer payment, o'course. There is talk around the castle that yer trade is in the company of men. I doona usually have use for such women, but I heard ye were verra pretty. And ye are."

He stepped closer and took me by the arm. His touch was gentle, but a threat lay within it, a dare to pull away.

I stayed still but turned my head as he leaned in to caress a handful of my hair. "Why would anyone say that?" I asked. "It isn't true. I'm a friend of the Conalls and am only staying here until Baodan returns, when he plans to escort me to Conall Castle."

He stepped toward the bed and held onto me so that I moved with him. "I doona believe ye, lass. 'Tis true that castle servants often form untruths to entertain themselves, but I see no other reason for ye to be here."

"I just told you the other reason. I'm on my way to the Conalls."

"Enough!"

Deep and angry, his voice spread goose bumps over my entire body.

"If that were true, ye wouldna be traveling alone. Now, ye have received yer payment, and I will receive my purchase."

He moved the hand entangled in my hair to the base of my neck and twisted my head until I had no choice but to face him. I closed my eyes, trying to think of what I should do.

His mouth moved to my ear, and he whispered into it. Warm breath touched my skin, but it sent ice crystals running down my spine.

"This can be enjoyable for us both, lass, if ye let it. I am not a selfish lover, and while I know some men doona mind being met with a struggle, 'tis not something I prefer. But struggle or not, I shall have ye. Make up yer mind which it shall be, now."

Niall waited for me to answer, breathing down my neck while pushing his body closer to mine. His words offered me a solution. He enjoyed being a charmer. He took his pleasure by giving pleasure. He enjoyed the act of leaving women with hope when there was none.

I was strong, but he would be able to overpower me if I struggled. If I could pretend to want him until I made him vulnerable, perhaps I could injure him enough to escape.

Terrified, my hands trembled. But I knew if I cried I would lose my nerve. I needed to give an Oscar-worthy performance. Clenching my hands into fists to still them, I moved them up to his wrists, then opened my fingers and wrapped them around his lower arm. I gently tugged so he would release my neck.

He did, but looked at me curiously, apparently anxious for me to give him an answer. I stepped away from him and smiled as seductively as I could. "Have you ever done this before? Paid for someone, I mean?"

"No."

His answer pleased me. Surely the women he was accustomed to wooing, being from this time, were less knowledgeable about men than me, coming from the twenty-first century. I noticed the anticipation dancing in his eyes and knew that if I could just pull this off, I would be able to get away.

I tilted my head to one side, holding his gaze, and said, "Take off your kilt." I was disgusted with myself, but I would not allow him to have the upper hand in this situation. He stared at me, clearly shocked, and the lust in his eyes disappeared. I worried I'd taken it too far.

"What about yer dress, lass? This hardly seems fair."

Taking him off guard, I crushed my mouth against his, kissing him so fervently, I could barely breathe.

He seemed stunned motionless for a few seconds, then began kissing me back. It took all of my concentration not to gag. He thought himself better at this than he truly was.

When I felt him start to reach his hand underneath my dress, I grabbed his wrist and ended the kiss abruptly. "Not so fast," I said coyly. "Your turn first."

He grinned and moved to kiss my ear, laughing at the delight of something unexpected. Stepping away from me only slightly, he looked down to undo his kilt, and I took that moment when both his hands and his eyes were distracted to bring my knee up hard between his knees.

I expected him to scream, and maybe even fall onto the bed or the floor and writhe in pain. Whatever the case, I hoped he'd be out of commission long enough for me to escape. But my plan worked even better than I'd imagined. Scream he did, but only for a moment. Then he dropped onto the bed, clutching himself. Niall turned white as snow, his eyes rolled up into his head, and he passed out cold.

CHAPTER 13

W hat on earth was the lass doing, and why didn't it surprise Baodan that she'd chosen not to wait for him and managed to escape? Baodan just rounded the edge of the pond when he saw her running fast into the woods, her red curls bouncing messily out behind her. He'd never seen a woman move so quickly in his entire life.

He called out to her as he approached but, instead of slowing, she increased her speed as she turned to look at him.

Worry gripped him. Something had happened to upset her greatly.

"Come on, Artair. We need to reach her." The horse sped up as he bid.

A s soon as Niall passed out, I grabbed my shoes and Morna's rock and took off from the castle at full speed. I knew he would send someone after me, but it wouldn't be Niall himself. I expected he would be moving slowly for a while.

It felt good to run, and as the cool evening air hit my lungs, I delighted in the pleasant sting with each breath I took.

I neared the edge of the castle grounds when I saw a horse approaching, but it was too dark for me to discern the rider's identity. I assumed one of the guards had found me. I pushed myself to run faster, although I knew I wouldn't be able to outrun the horse.

Eventually, the horse followed close behind me, and I could clearly hear the rider's voice. Baodan.

"Mitsy, just who do ye think ye are running from? There's no one coming after ye."

I slowed to a jog and then to a walk so that I moved right beside him and the horse. "You are. And there is no way that I am going back inside that castle. If you try to make me, I'll do the same thing I just did to your scumbag of a brother. Then, I'll steal your horse so I don't have to walk all the way to Conall Castle."

"What?" Panic filled his voice.

I heard him jump down, then he rushed to stand in front of me, forcing me to stop. He grabbed both of my arms. "Let go," I demanded.

He did so immediately, but didn't allow me to move around him.

"Lass, ye must tell me what ye mean. Did he hurt ye? I swear I'll kill him if he did."

I wasn't going to stop until I was far away from McMillan Castle. I didn't want to talk about it anyway, not tonight. If he wanted to know, he would have to keep traveling right along with me. I'd tell him after I cooled down a little. "Are you going to take me to Conall Castle? And I mean, like, right now? I'm not stopping until I'm far away from here."

"Aye, lass. If ye wish it, we shall ride through the night and rest in the morning, but for God's sake, tell me what happened to upset ye so."

He walked backward and was about to trip over a stump, so I stopped for a moment and reached out to steady him. He mistook my reach as a desire to draw him near, and he deftly laced his fingers with mine, stepping forward to pull me into an embrace. "What happened, lass?"

I knew if things had turned out differently with Niall, I would have flinched at Baodan's touch, but mercifully they hadn't, and I welcomed Baodan's embrace. He carried no agenda behind it. He worried for me and held me because it wasn't in his nature to do otherwise.

I sighed, laying my head against his chest. With the adrenaline rush of earlier subsiding, I suddenly grew tired. "If it's okay, I don't want to talk about it right now. If you'll take me to Conall Castle, I'll tell you in the morning."

"If ye insist, though I wish ye would tell me now. I willna press ye. Come." He took my hand and led me to the horse. Lifting me up onto it first, he then swung himself over so that he sat behind me.

He didn't hesitate to slip both of his arms around my waist. It felt oddly intimate, but he didn't pull away at my quiet intake of breath, nor did he act as if he were doing anything unusual, two strangers riding so close to one another.

He wiggled the reins to nudge the horse forward. Once we moved, he extended his hand to pat my knee quickly. "Ye are tense, lass. I willna let ye fall off." He squeezed his arms around me to emphasize his point. "Lean against me and go to sleep."

I did allow myself to relax and happily leaned against him. But while I was exhausted, I knew I wouldn't be able to sleep. Not right away. "I'm not sleepy."

"Aye, ye are. I'm sorry that I dinna return as quickly as I thought I would. My mother was ill, and it slowed us down a bit."

I didn't say anything. He couldn't help his mother's ill health, but I couldn't bring myself to say it was all right. If he'd returned when he said, Eoghanan wouldn't have had to leave, and Niall would never have approached me.

He reached up to touch my hairline, to examine my injury. "'Tis not so bad as it looked that first day. Does it hurt ye, lass?"

I shook my head lightly. "Not at all. Just a little scab now."

"Good. I'm pleased to hear it."

We rode in silence for a while. I spent the hours looking up at the stars, picking out constellations in awe. A million changes would occur in the time that spanned from the year I found myself in now to the time I was born in. Everything would change—everything except the stars.

"What are ye looking at, lass?"

He leaned forward and whispered the words in my ear. Unlike his brother's breath that chilled me to my bones, the sound of his deep whisper warmed me all the way to my core.

"The stars. They look exactly the same three hundred and sixty-seven years from now. Well, I'm sure an astrologist would tell you they've changed a little, but I sure can't tell a difference."

His breath caught as I spoke, and I cringed as I awaited more accusations of my insanity. I'd forgotten that he thought me "daft."

"Tell me more about your time. What are some of the things ye mentioned before? A plane and a car? What is a toilet?"

I twisted my head to look at him with pinched brows. "What? When you left, you thought I was crazy. What happened?"

He laughed, and I didn't miss how his eyes lingered on my lips before he glanced upward again. I turned my head back around to face the direction of our travel.

"Aye, lass, I truly did, but my mother told me the truth. I informed her how ye screamed the name of Morna when I found ye in the pond, and she knows of the woman's power. Morna's been dead a long time, but she was a powerful witch. Mother told me of all that the witch did to bring yer friend Bri here to this time, as well. I'm sorry for thinking ye mad. I dinna know any of that until Mother told me."

"Ah, I see. Well, I'm glad that you don't think I'm crazy."

"So tell me, lass. Tell me what all of those things are that ye spoke of."

Truly sleepy now, I found it hard to keep my eyelids open. I started to speak, but the words came out in between yawns. "Tomorrow. I'll tell you in the morning."

I allowed my head to roll to the side as I started to drift into sleep, but it took longer to doze off than Baodan realized. I know he wouldn't have said what he did if he knew I could hear.

As I leaned into him, he bent downward to plant a kiss on the side of my head. "Aye, I shall happily wait until the morrow to hear it. For every strange thing that ye utter from that beautiful mouth of yers is a pleasure to hear."

*A*ch, trouble found him. The lass slept soundly against him, and she made the most unusual sounds in her sleep. The sweetest, softest coos of comfort that made him want to turn her around and kiss that beautiful mouth of hers.

He shook his head to clear it of thoughts of her. Seeing that the sun rose in the distance, he slowed Artair's pace so that he could find a suitable place for them to stop and rest. Temptation was a downfall of being a man, he supposed. No matter that he was no longer capable of love, it didn't stop him from being attracted to a beautiful woman, and beautiful she was.

He'd never seen hair like hers, so red, curly and endless. A man could get lost in it, and he wished that he could do just that. He leaned down to smell it, and his stomach grew taut from the sensation that washed over him. What sort of oils and creations must she have access to in her own time to make hair smell so wonderful?

And her eyes, he couldn't see them now, but they were eyes of such rarity that he need only see them once to remember them forever. They were the oddest combination of green and brown, each color so different and vibrant that, from afar, it looked as if her left eye was completely green and her right eye brown. In truth, at closer view, each eye had colors of both, and they were captivating and magical—eyes of a mystical creature, surely, and not an ordinary human.

Not that she was ordinary, she was anything but. Mitsy was loud and bold. And whether she intended to be or not, he found her quite amusing. He wanted to know more about her, more about her time and what had led her here. He hoped she wouldn't feel the need to sleep too long so he could spend the day talking with her.

"Are ye ready to wake, lass? Artair here needs to rest, and I'll not deny that I do, as well."

She threw her arms up to stretch, sending one of her hands right into his jaw. Instantly swirling around to face him, her quick apology was mixed with a not-so-subtle hint of amusement dancing in her eyes. "Oh, I'm sorry." She laughed and reached up to rub his jaw. "Does it hurt?"

He enjoyed the feeling of her hands on him. While it hadn't really hurt him at all, he was no fool. "Aye, it does, lass. Ye have a strong hand."

She glanced up at him knowingly, and his face warmed at the embarrassment of being found out.

"Well, here." She stretched upward and planted a brief kiss on his jawline. "All better?"

Every muscle in his body went rigid. "What was that for?"

She shrugged as she continued to look over her shoulder at him. "It's just something that you do. Kiss a boo-boo to make it better. I don't know. Sorry, guess that trend hasn't caught on yet."

"Ah, well I know that ye doona know it, but ye stretch while ye sleep. Ye hit me then, as well. Many times."

She grinned at him and laughed, turning quickly around to face forward again.

What had gotten into him? He was jesting her, and it would only lead to trouble for them both.

* * *

I couldn't believe Baodan had actually ridden through the entire night. That's what I'd told him to do, but he'd been dead on his feet after traveling. I expected him to ride until I fell asleep, and then stop to make camp.

Instead, when he woke me at dawn, we were surrounded by landscape I would not have recognized from later centuries. I was immediately grateful he'd seen me fleeing his home. While I would probably have been able to find my way to Conall Castle during my own time, there were currently no roads or landmarks to assist me. Each tree looked much like the last.

He'd flirted with me, whether it had been his intention to do so or not. I'd given him reason to, though, when I kissed him on the jaw, but it just seemed like too good of an opportunity to pass up. Baodan was an incredibly handsome man. As the horse came to a stop at Baodan's chosen place of rest, I slipped off, not taking into account how numb my bottom would be. I was so sore and numb that I couldn't feel it at all. As soon as my feet hit the ground, my knees buckled.

Before I could stand, Baodan lifted me up by both elbows, and my chest grazed his as he did so. I would've found the contact quite flustering if not for the sensation of thousands of pins pricking my bum as my circulation returned.

"Holy moly! My butt hurts!"

Baodan looked down at me and laughed. "Ye have a penchant for swearing, doona ye? And ye are not accustomed to riding, or yer backside wouldna hurt ye so."

He let go now that I had my footing and twisted to stretch, which emphasized every chiseled muscle in his stomach.

"Although, I'm a wee bit sore myself. 'Twas a long ride."

I attempted to move around a bit, stretching and turning as much as the dress would allow, so that he wouldn't see me staring at him with awe. "I'm sorry. I shouldn't have made you ride all night. You have to rest now. I'll keep myself busy somehow."

He looked as if he could fall over at any moment. I wasn't surprised that after riding all night, his need for sleep now outweighed his curiosity of finding out what had happened to me the night before. "I'm sure ye will, lass. Ye doona seem like the sort of person to sit idly. Just stay close and doona get yerself into trouble, aye?"

I smirked at him and turned to walk a few trees down while he settled against the trunk next to where he'd tied his horse. "Yes, sir. Sweet dreams."

He didn't answer, and I looked back to see that his eyes were already shut. I predicted that I had at least a few hours to kill before we would move again, which was fine with me. I was eager to make it to Conall Castle, but my legs were none too eager to get back on a horse.

My stomach growled, and I looked around miserably at the vast emptiness. I'd never in my life appreciated the heart-clogging goodness of any fast food restaurant the way I did in that moment. I'd not had time to think about food when I'd fled, and I expected that since Baodan hadn't intended to leave on another journey seconds after arriving home that he had little in the way of food with him.

He would be forced to hunt or gather something because I didn't know how to do it. I couldn't stand the thought of being totally useless, though. So as I marched around the wilderness, an idea of how I could help came to mind.

As a small child, I had lived in an endless bounce of foster homes until I found Lilly. To be honest, I didn't remember much about most of them. It was a dark, lonely existence, and each time I entered a new home, I knew it would only be for a short period.

I did, however, remember one family very well. They'd been kind enough, but their real children never took to me. In the end, it just didn't work out. They were big into camping and we went often. I hated most of it, but I loved watching the dad build a fire. He created it the old-fashioned way, with kindling and wood, saying he learned how to do it in Boy Scouts.

I'd been far too little at the time to attempt it, but it occurred to me that perhaps I could give it a try now. Unless all Baodan gathered was berries for us to eat, we would need to build a fire at some point. I could go ahead and get it started for him, because there was no way that I would eat raw meat. I hoped that by the time I gathered some kindling and found wood to burn, he would be rested enough to wake up and get me some food.

It took me a long time to find enough small branches and kindling to make anything work, but eventually I thought I had adequate materials to give it a go. I sat down to the task at hand and got to work, very quickly realizing that building a fire wasn't as easy as my foster father had made it look.

I was clearly missing some part of the equation, because no matter how fast I ran my fingers up and down the pointed stick, not even a smidge of smoke rose out of the small pile. I got a little carried away with it though, and I continued to twirl my hands up and down the stick until my palms were red, only stopping at the sound of a stranger's voice behind me.

"Do ye need some help there, lass? Ye are not going to build a fire that way."

I turned to see a rather wild-looking man make his way toward me. He had no horse, and it appeared as if he had traveled for some time. More than that, really, he looked as if his home was amongst the trees. His hair was a tangled mess, and I could smell him as he approached, but he seemed harmless enough.

Maybe the stranger could help me get the fire started and then take his leave before Baodan woke. I could let him think I'd built the fire. "Yes, please. I'm afraid I really don't know what I'm doing."

"Aye, I can see that. Hand me that wee stick that yer holding."

He crouched down beside me, and I extended it in his direction as he pulled out a dirk and went to work on the stick, slowly shaping it into a much more pronounced point. Once he finished, he completely rearranged my pile and then moved to stand behind me. "It should be easier now, lass. Place yer hands back the way ye had them."

I did, and he crouched down and hesitated. I turned around to smile at him. "It's ok. You can show me."

He grinned a nearly toothless smile and scooted closer so that he could wrap his arms around my back and place his hands over my own. Together we spun the stick. Just as smoke started to build at its base, Baodan's voice boomed through the trees.

"I would appreciate it, sir, if ye would take yer hands off my wife."

CHAPTER 15

The Dungeons of McMillan Castle

Eoghanan had hoped to capture the alchemist and secure him inside the dungeons quickly enough so that he could be back outside Mitsy's door by morning, but it had proved to be impossible. While he had secured the man easily enough, he had to sneak him into the dungeon, and despite the man's small stature, Eoghanan struggled to move his unconscious prisoner down that many stairs.

By the time the alchemist was inside a cell and regaining consciousness, most of the morning had passed. Every moment Eoghanan spent away from Mitsy's door, his worry for her grew. He needed to protect her, but he also needed to protect his family from the danger that lived amongst them. He looked up at the small window near the top of the cell. Seeing that the sun was past its midpoint, he decided now was his best time to move.

Niall should be out for his daily ride, which meant there would be a few precious moments to search for the poison to present to his prisoner. Surely if he showed the man his own vial, the alchemist would not be able to deny that he made the potion.

Once he acquired the poison, Eoghanan would check in on Mitsy. He would make certain that she'd been fed and spend a few moments speaking with her in the hopes of lifting her spirits. It would not be an unpleasant task. He found the lass's company rather pleasing.

Surely Baodan would return today and would soon see the lass safely to

Conall Castle. With both of them gone, Eoghanan would be free to resume his questioning of the man sitting in front of him without distraction.

Eoghanan shoved a glass of water in the alchemist's direction. "There is something that I must see to. I shall be back to visit with ye shortly. I doona wish ye harm, but I will have the truth from ye. If ye doona wish to give it freely, ye will leave me no choice but to hurt ye. Think on that whilst I am away."

The man called out to him as he started to leave, causing Eoghanan to pause and face him.

"What is it that ye think I have done, sir? For I swear to ye there is nothing."

"Ye have provided a man with a poison of much harm."

"Do ye have this poison of which ye speak? For I am not a maker of such potions."

"I doona now, but I will." Eoghanan turned and left, praying with each footstep that his brother's room would be empty, and that Mitsy was safe and sound in her own.

---

*E*oghanan held his breath as he opened Niall's door, exhaling only after finding it vacant.

Once inside, he hurried as fast as he could, lifting every object in sight. He pulled open the window draping. Light streamed in, bouncing off of something beneath the bed. Crouching low, he saw the vial standing neatly underneath where his louse of a brother slept.

Niall would notice the poison's disappearance, but what did it matter? In a few days, Eoghanan would reveal all of his brother's wrongdoings.

Slipping the vial safely away on his person, he crept out of Niall's room, rounding the corner quickly in his hurry to check on Mitsy. His heart froze at the sight of the bedchamber door hanging open, and the only person standing inside the room was Rhona.

"*W*hat has happened here? Did I not tell ye to keep her inside?" Eoghanan grabbed the old woman by both arms, shaking her gently as panic coursed through him.

She said nothing, and he stopped as he noticed her trembling. He realized that fear wasn't what caused her to shake. Rhona feared no one. Releasing his grip, he directed her to a chair. "What is it, Rhona? Are ye all right?"

Fanning herself, she looked up at him in confusion. "Would ye believe me if I told ye I dinna know for certain? It seems that most of the castle fell suddenly verra ill during the night. I couldna see in front of me, and I grew too weak to get up off my knees. The guards outside the room said the same happened to them."

Niall. His brother had caused this. Eoghanan had experienced the same symptoms on the night of Osla's death, and his mother had felt much the same for the past months. "What happened to the lass, Rhona? Where's Mitsy?"

She shook her head. "I must have fallen asleep in the midst of my illness for when I awoke, Niall sat beside me. He told me that Baodan returned home and took the lass immediately for Conall Castle."

Rhona was no fool. Unlike most, he knew she didn't fall for Niall's charms. She'd always been suspicious of him. "Do ye believe him, Rhona? Did Baodan come here?"

She shook her head and looked down at the floor regretfully. "No. I doona think that Baodan would have left so quickly with her. At the verra least, he would have spoken to me before he went. 'Twas clear that Niall had not been struck by the same illness as the rest of us, and I have not seen him or the lass since. When he spoke with me, I still couldna move, and he left me quickly."

"Did he take her, do ye think?" Surely, Niall would have no reason to, but if he had, Eoghanan doubted the lass still lived.

"I doona think he took her. He seemed verra angry, and he walked with a bad limp. If he tried to capture the lass, I believe he failed to do so."

"Good." Eoghanan turned to leave, his mind racing with all that he knew he must do. "Do ye know where he went?"

"No. I expect to the village. 'Tis where he likes to find all his lassies, and he seemed in a bad way. I expect he's gone in search of someone to soothe him. I hope that he willna, but I feel sure he shall."

"I have to go, Rhona. Will ye be all right here?"

She nodded and waved him on, so Eoghanan ran back down to the dungeons. If Niall no longer stayed at the castle where he could keep an eye on him, it was more urgent than ever to gather proof of his brother's evildoings. Eoghanan's prisoner would give him answers tonight.

"*P*lease, man. I doona wish to hurt ye, but if ye doona tell me what ye know of this, ye will leave me no choice." Eoghanan extended the man a drink of water. He'd not laid a hand on him as of yet, and he hoped he wouldn't have to. "Have I hurt ye? I doona mean ye harm, but I believe ye have been forced to provide a man something that has harmed others, aye?"

"Ye did hurt me. Ye hurt my head." Slowly the alchemist drank the water, staring back at Eoghanan with dismay.

"Would ye have come with me willingly?"

"No."

"Help me, sir. Of what are ye so afraid?"

For the first time, a spark lit the man's eyes. "How can ye ask that? I have done nothing, but ye have locked me up like a criminal. If ye doona mean me harm, then why have ye brought me here?"

Why did he believe the man? No other in the village held as much knowledge of herbs. Of course, Eoghanan knew his brother to be smart enough to think of looking outside of his own village for the poison. It wouldn't do Niall any good for people to learn the truth about him.

Eoghanan crouched down in front of his prisoner, regret in his heart for the injustice he now believed he'd done. "All right, lad. What are ye called?"

"My name is Durell."

"I'll tell ye the truth of what has happened, Durell, and ye must swear to do the same with me. For if I find later that ye have betrayed me, and it was ye with whom my brother worked, I assure ye that I shall be the last one to see ye alive."

"Aye, I swear it. I have no reason to lie to ye."

"Fine. I believe that my brother acquired a toxic elixir and uses it to slowly poison our mother. 'Tis not the first time he used such a substance on another. My mother is gone from the castle now, so I have hope that she will heal, but she is still in danger until I can prove his guilt."

The man's look of genuine horror convinced Eoghanan that he was not the supplier of the poison. "Surely, the laird couldna do such a thing. Why?"

Eoghanan shook his head, astonished at the man's conclusion. "No, 'twas not Baodan. 'Twas Niall. Now, I believe ye when ye say ye dinna aid him in this. Are there others who could have done so? Here is the poison of which I spoke." He handed the vial to the man and watched as he stared at it.

Eoghanan held his breath while he waited.

Finally, Durell said, "Aye, I know who made this poison. There is a woman who lives not far from the village. She is not much of a healer. Only those who wish to bring foul things upon another seek her mixtures."

Eoghanan clasped the man on the shoulder, hopeful for the first time in many days. "Is there an antidote for this?" He knew this vial would not be the only one in Niall's possession. For him to have poisoned their mother for so long, he must have much more locked away.

"Aye, I can make ye one, but I shall need to be at my home with my herbs and mixtures."

Just as well, Eoghanan needed to get to the village to find his brother, anyway. If he found Niall and he did have Mitsy, or if Eoghanan learned Niall had harmed her, Eoghanan would not wait to gather proof. He would gladly kill his brother on the spot. "Verra well, we shall leave at once." He smiled at the look of relief on the old man's face. "I told ye I wouldna hurt ye. My apologies for yer head."

CHAPTER 16

he Road To Conall Castle

he man released his grip on me immediately and jumped away like someone struck by lightning. "I'm verra sorry, sir," he told Baodan. "I was only trying to help her with the fire. I shall take my leave at once."

I stood and held up a hand to stop the man. "No, wait. Thank you. I needed your help. Stay and have a meal with us before you leave. If you will start the fire, my *husband* and I will go in search of some food." Baodan's eyes met mine at my sarcastic reference to the lie he'd told the bum.

"Only if yer husband finds this acceptable," said our visitor, looking down at his feet, clearly intimidated by Baodan.

I walked over to Baodan and grabbed him firmly by the hand so that I could drag him off to where he had left his horse.

"He insists upon it," I said. "We will be back in a little while with something to eat."

I squeezed Baodan's hand as tightly as I could, but I knew it didn't cause him the pain that I wished it would. Once we were out of earshot, I turned on him. "Are you crazy? What in the world is the matter with you?"

A look of genuine shock flashed in his eyes. "Me? Ye're the one who allowed that vagabond to lay hands on ye, lass. He could have dirked ye right in the side, and ye would have been helpless to stop him."

"He was just helping me. I tried to start a fire to help you out, and I didn't have the slightest idea what I was doing. But all of that is beside the point. Why did you tell him I was your wife?"

"It isna suitable for ye to be traveling alone with a man who isna yer husband."

"But I am traveling with someone who isn't my husband. Do you really think that man cares about what is suitable or not?"

"I doona care what he thinks, lass, but until we get to Conall Castle, ye shall be seen as my wife to anyone we may cross paths with. Now," he reached out and grabbed me by the wrist, dragging me behind him as he traveled farther away from the man and our fire. "Ye have promised this man food to eat, and food we shall give him."

<hr>

*P*lenty of daylight remained by the time we finished eating. We could have traveled a good distance further but our wild man, who later introduced himself as Alec, seemed starved for conversation and chatted our ears off until sundown.

It turned out that Baodan was far less of a tyrant than he tried to make himself appear, for it didn't take long before he softened to Alec. By the end of the evening, he offered the man work at MacMillan Castle.

After hours of listening to the two men talk, I zoned out until Baodan's touch on my hand drew me out of my daze. "I'm sorry. What did you say?"

"Alec just said that we made a handsome couple, and I told him 'twas only because of my wife's beauty."

He winked at me playfully, and I smirked at him in return.

Smiling at the two of us, Alec stood. "Aye, it has done my heart good to witness two people so truly in love. Gives me hope that I may one day find a lassie of my own." He tore his gaze away from me to address Baodan. "Why doona ye just kiss her already? I can see in yer eyes that ye wished to do so all afternoon, but ye have been denied the pleasure of doing so by my presence. Go on and do it now. 'Tis been too long since I've seen a proper kiss."

I stilled where I sat, but Baodan stood instantly and drew me to my feet. Facing me, his gaze holding mine, he said quietly, "Aye, lad. If ye wish to see a kiss, I am in no mood to deny ye."

It was rough and consuming, the way his lips met mine. There was heat in his kiss, a passion that had been suppressed for far too long, and I was more than happy to help sate it. He had one hand woven into my hair, gripping the back of my neck so tightly I could only move my lips in response to him when he allowed it. With his other hand against the smallest part of my lower back, he pressed me closer, so close I felt his heart beating rapidly in his chest.

He had yet to break for air, and I worried one or both of us would pass out from the effort. He kissed like a man too long without love. While possibly less practiced than his younger brother, he made up for it in natural talent.

I found myself wishing that Alec wasn't with us so the kiss could go on and on. But when I could take no more without blacking out, I reached up with my right hand and pressed it lightly on Baodan's face. He stilled, and I realized in that instant that he'd lost himself. It broke my heart to be the one to pull him back to reality. I got the feeling that he didn't often allow such weakness in himself.

An apology lay behind his eyes, and I reached up to kiss him lightly in the hopes that he would know it was okay. How could it not be? I couldn't imagine a woman alive who would have been bothered by that kiss.

Alec started clapping, and I blushed as Baodan released his grip on my neck. Stepping away from one another, we turned to stand side-by-side. But Baodan kept his arm around me, holding me tightly.

"Ha!" exclaimed Alec. "I couldna have ever dreamed up a kiss as wonderful as that. Well done. Now . . ." He stood. "'Tis time for me to take leave of ye both and find camp for the night. Thank ye for yer kindness."

He turned to leave, but Baodan spoke to stop him. "'Tis already dark, and I doona wish to ride at night again. Why doona ye set camp here with us tonight, and we may take our leave of one another in the morning?"

Alec nodded and went about the business of rolling out his small blanket for sleeping. I knew he had to be relieved not to travel elsewhere after dark, but I suspected that Baodan asked him to stay for another reason.

If someone else camped with us, Baodan would insist that we share the space where we lay our heads to sleep. For in the company of others, we had to maintain the façade of being husband and wife.

We had only one blanket and Baodan spread it out across the ground. We stretched out beside one another. Though a warm evening, the wind held enough of a chill to cause me to shiver despite the nearness of him. I lay with my back against his chest. Neither of us spoke until we heard Alec snoring on the other side of the dwindling fire.

"Come here, lass. Turn into me."

I hesitated, but as a breeze whipped through the trees, I trembled and rolled over to face him. He removed a pin from his kilt and held a large portion of it over me like a cape. The kilt had enough fabric to keep him covered.

I did as he instructed and scooted closer, until I was up against him with the kilt snug around me. To clear my head, I glanced up at the dark sky and exhaled every ounce of tension I hadn't realized I'd been carrying.

Somehow, I knew instinctively that Baodan wasn't a threat to me. In fact, I felt more protected with him than I had in ages. I pulled my eyes down from the sky to look at him. "Why did you do that?"

He reached up with his hand to brush a lock of hair from my face. "Do what, lass?"

"Suggest that he camp here with us."

"Ye doona think that I did it so that the poor lad wouldna have to find a place to set camp after dark?"

"No."

"I think 'twas only that I wanted to be near ye. Do ye mind lass? He's asleep now. If ye wish to sleep on yer own, ye can."

I opened my hands that were balled against his chest to lay them flat against him. "No, I don't mind."

He leaned forward and kissed me on the forehead. "Good. Now," he scooted away just a tad so that he could look at me more clearly, "'tis past time that ye tell me what happened back at the castle to upset ye so and caused ye to leave before I returned for ye."

I grimaced at the thought of it. There'd been enough activity today to distract me from thinking of the incident. "Fine, but you have to promise that you'll take me to Conall Castle. No matter what I tell you, you can't decide to turn around and head back home."

He continued to stroke my hair. "Was it so bad as that, lass? Please tell me that he dinna hurt ye. He only said something to upset ye, aye?"

I shook my head, but spoke quickly to clarify. "No, he didn't hurt me. I'm fine. I did, however, hurt him quite badly."

His eyes widened in surprise, but he said nothing so that I would continue. "Promise first. Promise that you'll take me to Conall Castle."

He nodded, but worry filled his face. "Aye, fine lass, I promise."

I didn't want to rehash the whole incident so I spoke quickly, just giving him the highlights. I knew he would need nothing more to get spitfire angry.

Baodan's hand stopped on my hair. Even in the moonlight, I could see his face grow pale. "What did ye do, lass? Did ye kill him?"

I sat up, taken aback by his assumption. "What? No! Of course I didn't kill him."

He seemed to breathe a sigh of relief, but pulled me close to him again "Well, if ye had, there was just cause for ye to do so. If ye dinna kill him, what did ye do?"

"I kneed him where it counts."

He pulled away and sat up on his elbow so that he could look down on me. "Where it counts, lass?"

I tried to gesture with my hands, but ended up just looking ridiculous. "You know. Let's just say there's a slight chance you may never be an uncle—not from that brother, anyway."

A brief moment of silence followed, but apparently Baodan could no longer contain himself, and he erupted into the most ridiculous and inappropriate fit of laughter I had ever heard.

I moved from beneath his kilt and sat with my legs crossed in front of him, frowning. "How is that even the littlest bit funny? If it hadn't worked, who knows how far he might've taken the situation?"

Baodan reached out to try and grab me in between hoots of laughter, but I jerked away, suddenly angry. Eventually, he pulled himself together and sat up in front of me, looking guilty.

"I'm sorry, lass, truly."

"Why were you laughing? It's not funny. It was downright terrifying, and I probably did some serious damage to him."

"'Tis not funny, at all, what he tried to do to ye. Believe me, Eoghanan shall not be welcome inside McMillan Castle after I return, brother or not. I only laugh from imagining the way ye surprised him, lass. He wasna expecting the punishment ye gave him, I can assure ye."

I tensed at his mention of Eoghanan's name. "Wait! Did you just say E-o, I mean Eoghanan?"

"Aye, lass. I willna have him in the castle after what he did to ye."

"But it wasn't Eoghanan. It was Niall."

He flinched. "What did ye just say?"

"You heard what I said. Eoghanan showed me nothing but kindness. Niall did it, the disgusting creep." Baodan looked as if I'd slapped him. "What's wrong?"

He quieted for a moment, then shook his head somberly. "I'm ashamed of myself, lass, for assuming it was Eoghanan. He is many things, but he is not a man who would try to force himself on a lass."

"And Niall is?"

"I have never known him to use force, but he doesna treat women the way they deserve. While I am not too pleased with Eoghanan, either, I feel my assumption to be a betrayal of the man I know he is." He lay down once more, holding out the longest part of his kilt for me again. "Come back here. I am in awe of ye."

"You're in awe?" It hardly seemed an appropriate emotion for the current situation. "Why?"

"Aye, I am. I have never heard of a woman denying Niall a kiss, or anything else. And ye dinna only deny him, ye gave him no less than he deserved. I am proud of ye."

"Well...thanks." I could scarcely stay mad at him for laughing when he'd clearly meant all that he said to be a compliment.

I'd yet to join him back under his kilt, and he waved the edge around like a cape. It looked ridiculous. "Am I forgiven? If so, come and join me here again."

"For laughing? Aye." He shook his head at my attempt to mimic his accent, causing me to smile as I moved to snuggle in close to him again. My cheek pressed against his bare chest, and his chin rested on the top of my head. "What did Eoghanan do to you? What were you two talking about the day I arrived here?"

He didn't move away from me, but his chest gave as he let out a large breath. "'Tis not a happy story."

I reached up to trail my fingertips down his arm in the hopes that it would soothe him. I didn't wish to anger him. I only wanted to know more about the history between he and his youngest brother. "I don't always need stories to be happy. I have quite a few unhappy ones of my own."

"I was married once, lass."

So this was the "her" they spoke of. "But no more?"

"No more. And 'tis a long story, lass, and I find myself suddenly sleepy. Perhaps I may tell ye another time."

His heart beat even more quickly than mine, and despite the sadness in his voice at the memory of his prior wife, I didn't believe he was sleepy. "You're not about to fall asleep, and you have all night to tell it, but you don't have to if you're not comfortable."

He kissed the top of my head but held me close, as much for his own comfort as mine, I assumed.

"It was not for verra long, my marriage. Something forced me to leave her for a few days to assist a man from the village, and I left her in Eoghanan's care while I was away. When I returned, I found her dead."

"How?" The wind seemed suddenly colder.

"A—a sickness."

He tried to hide it, but I saw how he hesitated. I didn't know him well, and he was under no obligation to tell me, but I knew there was more to the story than he said. For while it went a ways to explaining Baodan's feelings toward his brother, it still didn't make much sense to me. If she really passed of a sickness, how was that Eoghanan's fault? Chances were, Baodan would have been no more help to her than his brother.

"I'm sorry." I felt the knot he swallowed and regretted asking the question.

I pulled away so that I could look at his eyes. They were cold and hard, different from how I'd ever seen them look before. I knew then that we spoke of a part of his past that he spent every moment of his life trying to bury deep within himself.

"I'm sorry." I repeated, but the words sounded silly and useless. What good were they to him now? Still, I didn't know what else to say.

"Doona be. 'Twas many years ago. I only regret I wasna there to save her, for the guilt of that has turned me into someone verra hard."

"Hard?" I found him anything but. I thought him kind, funny, and gentle.

"Aye. I doona feel like I once did. I doona allow myself to. I enjoy friendship. It causes me hurt when others are in pain, but I doona care about others the way a man should."

"What does that mean? How should a man care about others? You were kind to me even though you thought me a lunatic when you found me. You offered Alec a place to stay and something to give him purpose. You didn't have to do that. I think you care more than most. You're a good man, Baodan."

"Thank ye, but that is not what I meant. I am not capable of love anymore, of caring for someone enough to allow them to care for me in return. I am hardened irreparably. I now feel that only fools allow such hurt as love into their lives; that's what it is, in the end. All love is a hurt."

Not that I could prove him wrong from personal experience, but even I knew what he said to be total crapola. I didn't think he even really believed it himself, but I didn't want to argue with him. Not when I had initiated the conversation. He wouldn't have told me any of the story of his wife's death, or what he felt about it, unless I had asked him to do so.

So I said nothing and snuggled into his warmth as I let sleep take me away.

S ometime in the night, Baodan roused me by shaking me lightly on the shoulder and whispering in my ear. "I'm sorry to wake ye, but I canna sleep."

I stretched and yawned. "What's wrong? Has something happened?"

He grinned and scooted down on the blanket so that our heads were even. Reaching out with his left hand, he cupped the side of my face and pulled me close. I was wide awake now. His nose touched mine as he stared deep into my eyes. "Can I ask ye a question, lass?"

I laughed and nodded, the tip of my nose tickling the tip of his. "Yes, of course. What is it?"

"If I kiss ye again, will I be in danger of receiving the same punishment ye gave Niall? I doona wish to meet the same fate as my brother." He asked it slowly, his eyes teasing me as he brought his lips closer to mine, only to pull them away just before they touched.

Slow torture, the tension between us. Every limb in my body went weak and fluttery with the anticipation of imagining his lips claiming mine. Our chests rose and fell quickly in a synced rhythm that pained me, as if I ran at full speed.

I didn't answer him. There was no need. Instead I pressed my trembling lips against his. He grinned against my mouth, and I nudged his nose with mine. I returned each of his kisses full force, as content as he seemed to be to relish in the pleasure of exploring one another in only this way for as long as we both wanted, even if it meant going without sleep. Baodan focused all of his attention on kissing me in such a way that each breath I took was not my own but a breath given to me by him as he claimed my mouth. That, in and of itself, proved to me just how capable he was of caring.

After his confession, he would think that to sleep with me would make him no better than his brothers. To show respect for me in such a way negated everything that he believed about himself.

For any man incapable of love, as he'd claimed himself to be, would not have been so considerate, so selfless.

We left at sunrise, bidding Alec goodbye before beginning our final leg toward Conall Castle. We'd fallen asleep wrapped in one another's arms. While I felt a glow from within following my little makeout session with Baodan, he seemed a little worse for wear.

He remained quiet all morning. I expected he wrestled with what he knew to be true. He cared for me, whether he claimed to be able to do so or not. And whether or not I wanted to admit it, I cared for him, too.

I was lost in my thoughts about him when he nudged me, making me jump. He pointed at a stone façade in the distance. "We are almost there, lass. Ye will finally be able to see yer Bri."

I threw my hands up in the air. "Yay! She's going to freak out! Do you think she knows I'm coming?"

He laughed. "I doona know. Most likely, no, but if the witch could send ye through time, I suppose she could warn Bri of yer arrival, aye?"

"Yes, I'm sure Morna could. I hope that she didn't, though. I would like to surprise my friend." When Baodan slowed Artair and turned him off of our trail, I asked, "What are you doing?"

"Do ye mind if we stop just a moment, lass?" asked Baodan. "I need to move my legs a bit."

Baodan dreaded their arrival at the castle. Once there, he would scarcely see Mitsy. He would speak with Bri's supposed twin, Blaire, for a bit and spend the night, but then he would have no reason to stay any longer. He couldn't bear the thought of leaving the lass who had mysteriously appeared in his pond.

He tried to tell himself that he was only worried for her safety, but he knew that to be a lie. She would be safer with his cousins than in his home, for his brothers didn't live with the Conalls.

Last night had him out of sorts with all that he knew about himself. For too many years to count, he'd not experienced joy like that he'd felt while holding her through the night. But it had also been the worst sort of torture, for he knew they could never be together.

He'd known women since the death of his wife, but always lasses like himself—widows who only wanted companionship, a reprieve from their loneliness, not another love. He'd made them no promises, and they had not wanted any.

Something was odd about his reaction to Mitsy. Last night, he'd been unable to bring himself to ask her for the same—a night to quench his need and hers, to make him forget for a few blessed hours that he was alone in the world. He had told her the truth, just as he had told all the other women, but to take it any further would have been to put her aside with all the rest. He wouldn't do it.

He always lied to everyone about the true nature of his wife's death, but repeating that lie to Mitsy had caused his stomach to churn. She was different. She deserved better. Someone who could give her every piece of his soul, not someone who lied to protect himself from speaking of a painful memory.

As much as he wished he could be that person, he didn't have enough left in him to give. He knew once they arrived at Conall Castle, whether she decided to stay in this time or return to her own, he would lose her. If only he could kiss her just once more.

Once Artair stopped, Baodan dismounted quickly, turning to help Mitsy down before taking off into the trees. He heard her call out to him, but he didn't turn around until she caught up to him and reached out to grab his hand.

"Hey, what's wrong with you? Where are you going so fast?"

He spun and pushed her hard against the trunk of the nearest tree, crushing himself against her. To be near her frightened him more than anything in the world. After this kiss, he wouldn't allow himself to be so scared ever again.

Her lips were soft, warm, and sweet—everything that he was not. Abruptly she pulled away, and he forced himself to close off the dream of her.

Stepping back, he looked down. There were words written in her eyes, something she wished to say but hesitated to do so.

He squeezed her hand to encourage her. "What is it, lass? I like the way ye say all the things that enter yer mind. Doona stop now."

"That isn't the kiss of someone who doesn't care. Believe me, I've had them. Men who don't care don't kiss a woman like that."

She let go and started walking back to Artair. It would be too cruel to allow her to hope. "Mitsy, lass, ye are wrong. 'Twas not the kiss of a caring man. 'Twas the kiss of a man who's been too long without a woman."

His throat burned at the lie, a lie even he didn't believe. Not anymore.

She faced him, her expression giving nothing away. "Then don't ever kiss me again, because if you mean it, I deserve a far better man than you."

The truth of her words hurt him to his very soul.

<h1 style="text-align:center">CHAPTER 19</h1>

hat a moron. I truly didn't think that even Baodan believed what he said. Even so, any man should know better than to say something like that out loud to a woman, even if he thought it. It was like saying that he'd used me, but his actions had shown otherwise.

His words didn't hurt my feelings. They pissed me off. I just couldn't understand his mindset. It was terrible that he'd been hurt, but if he thought no one else had ever been wounded by love, he was delusional.

Maybe I was just a serial optimist. All of the modern conveniences that I'd had the pleasure of using throughout my lifetime aside, I knew I'd had a harder life than Baodan. He was a Scottish laird who grew up in a castle, for goodness sake. He had a mother and father who loved him. He'd never been poor.

I was an orphan who spent my childhood without family and with only one close friend. I'd not been born into a family filled with love, and I'd be paying off student loan debt for the rest of my life. I'd been burnt by love more than a few times, but never once had I thought about shutting myself off from all feelings or emotions.

Baodan's cowardice disappointed me, but I refused to let him put a damper on my day. I hadn't seen Bri in over a year. I couldn't wait to squeeze her neck and catch up.

We remained silent for the rest of the ride. It was an awkward sort of silence after the incident in the woods, but thankfully we were close to Conall Castle. As we approached the stables, there seemed to be few people about. I worried for a moment that perhaps they wouldn't be home.

Baodan approached the stables and called out, "Kip? Are ye in there?"

From inside the stalls came a voice I recognized—that of Bri's look-a-like, Blaire, whom I'd met when she traveled forward in time.

"Is that ye, Baodan? What are ye doing…" She popped her head up out of the last stall and looked at me, pausing.

I could only hope Bri's face would look half as surprised. I waved as I spoke to her. "Don't worry. I won't attack you this time."

Baodan dismounted from the horse, and looked up at me in utter bewilderment. "Do ye know her, lass? That isna Bri, ye know."

Blaire stepped out of the stall and made her way quickly over to Baodan, wrapping her arms around him as if he were her long lost brother. "Aye, she knows I'm not Bri. We've met before."

"How?"

Baodan turned from Blaire, and reached up to help me off the horse, but I wouldn't take his hand. Instead flipping over so that my belly touched the horse's back, I slid off onto the ground.

Once I grounded myself, Blaire pulled away from Baodan and moved to give me a hesitant hug before stepping away. She remained skittish around me, not that I could blame her. The first time we'd met, I'd mistaken her for Bri. I thought Bri pretended to be someone else, and it made me so angry I attacked her in one of my most regrettable ginger moments.

Blaire touched Baodan's arm. "Ach, I forgot that ye dinna know. Before we were engaged, I'd been living forward in time. In the same time that Bri and Mitsy come from."

That was news to me. It was my turn to look bewildered. "What? You two were engaged?"

Baodan shook his head and started to move Artair into an empty stall. "Long story and one that doesna need to be told. Blaire, will ye take Mitsy to Bri?"

She hooked her arm through mine, and together we started out of the stables. "Aye, o'course. I was only tending to the new colt here. I'll send Eoin and Arran out for ye, and they'll see ye inside once ye've seen to yer horse."

As we left Baodan, Blaire pointed up to a high window near the top of the castle. "I expect we will find her nursing the baby. I hope the wee thing isna sleeping. If she is, it willna be for long with the way Bri will scream at the sight of ye."

"Baby?"

She didn't answer, only nodded and grinned as she led me inside the castle.

---

*W*e had only just turned down the hallway that held the room where Blaire seemed to think Bri would be when I heard an American accent whisper quite loudly behind me.

"Oh my God! Mitsy!"

I turned to see Bri's mother, Adelle, walking toward me excitedly, a sleeping bundle wrapped in her arms. I smiled as I met her, shocked for the third time in a matter of minutes. "Adelle! What are you doing here? Is there anybody that Morna hasn't gotten her witchy claws on?"

"Oh, I guess you didn't come here on your own then, did you, dear? Don't be too hard on Morna though, she knows what she's doing. She wouldn't have sent you here unless you needed to be here."

I reached over to embrace Adelle, making sure not to squish the sleeping babe. I lifted the blanket to get a better look at the beautiful dark-headed girl. I thought I might cry at the happiness I felt for Bri as I looked down at the small child. Bri always wanted nothing more than a family of her own. "She's beautiful. What a happy grandma you must be."

"Happy, indeed. I'm even married myself now."

"Married?" I'd never seen Adelle look so content. The seventeenth century seemed to agree with the Montgomery women. I winked at her. "Knowing you, you snagged a seventeenth century Scottish hunk half your age, right?"

She chuckled once and then stopped so she wouldn't wake the baby. "A hunk, yes. And Scottish. The other, not so much." She shrugged, letting me know his age didn't matter. "I'm not worthy of him, but I don't plan on letting him go any time soon." Pointing in the direction of the room Blaire and I were headed for, she added, "Bri's in there." I told her I'd get little Ellie to sleep so she could take a nap herself. Go in and wake her up. She'll be so excited to see you, she'll think she's dreaming." She leaned forward and kissed me on the cheek before starting off down the hallway. "Love you, sweetie. We'll talk more later."

With Adelle gone, Blaire waved me over to the doorway and opened it just a crack before whispering, "There ye go. I'm off to find the lads."

I crept into the room and walked over to the edge of the bed, grinning as I looked down at her. She slept as she always did, with her hands above her head and her mouth hanging wide open. It would've been kinder for me to allow her to sleep, but it also would have been totally out of character.

I gave her a light shake. "Wake up, sleepy head. Turns out you're not as crazy as I thought. I really worried about you for a while."

Her eyelids flickered open slowly, and I laughed as I watched her eyes adjust. When they finally did, she all but tumbled out of the bed in her rush to stand so that she could look at me properly.

"Mitsy! Oh, my gosh. I hoped you would come, but I wasn't sure if you ever would. Did you get the letter?"

She wrapped her arms around me in a hug so tight I could scarcely breathe. I patted her back in an effort to get her to release me, but she would only do so when she was good and ready. "I did find your letter. Let's sit down."

Eventually she let me go and crawled back onto the bed, motioning for me to join her.

We sat facing each other. For a while, she just stared at me, smiling as if she had thought she'd never see me again. And I suppose, she could've been right.

"Why did you leave the letter?" There'd been more to it than her just wanting to give me the option. She knew something, something that made her believe that things wouldn't work out between Brian and me.

Her smile faded, and I thought her eyes hinted of guilt.

"Why don't you tell me why you decided to come here first?"

"He cheated, and did for most of our relationship, I think. Not that it was all his fault. I knew he was a jerk. He never really tried to hide that fact, but I married him anyway."

She nodded, knowingly. "Total jerk."

"Did you know, Bri? That he was cheating?"

"Not until the wedding. I caught him…"

She hesitated, and I didn't blame her for doing so. Who wanted to be the one to tell someone that the night of their wedding, their husband had been caught with another girl?

"It's fine, Bri. I don't care anymore. Really."

"I went in search of a restroom during the reception. With the women's being cleaned, the janitor directed me to one in a private office down the hallway. I heard him with a woman inside. I should've told you, but I couldn't bring myself to do it that night. That's why I left the letter. I figured when you found out about him yourself, you would know why I sent it. How long have things been bad?"

I shrugged. The real question was, when were they ever *not* bad? "They always were. I think inside I knew he cheated, but I didn't find out about it until a few months ago."

"When did you get the letter?"

"Oh, that. Brace yourself. I know you're going to blow a gasket. Brian gave that to me the day before I came here to Scotland. He'd opened it the week after the wedding. He stayed in your place with her."

Her eyes tripled in size. "That sorry… Oh, if I was there I would have unleashed a whole barrel of crazy on him. I'm so sorry. I didn't ever think…I wouldn't have…"

I grabbed her hand. "Of course you didn't think about that. Why would you? It's fine. I'm just glad he gave me the letter. I didn't believe a word inside it, of course. I only came to Scotland because I believed you were in some sort of brainwashy cult."

She laughed and shifted her position on the bed. "What? I told you in Edinburgh. Although, I knew you didn't believe me."

"How could I? This is the craziest thing I've ever experienced." My own feet were asleep so I rolled off the side of the bed and moved about the room to stomp the tickle out of them.

"It is crazy, but amazing. I believe I was always meant to be here. What do you think about all of it?"

Many things ran through my mind: the blisters on my toes from uncomfortable shoes that rubbed, the lack of toilet paper, the miserable meals, no hot running water. "I think most of it is completely terrible. Parts of it, though . . ." Baodan crossed my mind. "Some things aren't so bad."

"Some things, huh?" She looked up at me knowingly. "You obviously didn't just end up here. Where did you land, and who brought you here to the castle?"

---

*I*t wasn't his intention to listen in on the lassies' conversation. He'd been on his way to a room to rest and clean up after far too many days out of doors. The sound of his name being uttered from Mitsy's lips stopped him cold.

"What do you know about him? Baodan?"

He pressed his back flat against the wall, only leaning his ear toward the doorway so that he could hear Bri's response.

"I don't know a lot, only that I like him very much. He's very close friends with Blaire, and she adores him. He has to be a pretty good guy to remain friends with someone who dumps him days before she's supposed to marry him."

He probably imagined it, but Mitsy's voice when she answered almost sounded jealous. "About that. How did that happen? Baodan told me yesterday that he isn't capable of loving anymore, whatever that means. Why would he have asked her to marry him? Did they date? Do people do that here?"

Bri's voice was calm, a perfect counter to her fiery friend. With great insight, she seemed to understand his relationship with Blaire better than most.

"I don't think he ever loved Blaire. I think he enjoyed her friendship and wanted to help her when she was heartbroken and alone."

"Hmm…that sounds like something the silly fool would do."

He didn't know what she meant by that, but she was still clearly upset by what he'd said to her earlier.

"Oh, you've got it bad, don't you?"

Baodan couldn't repress a grin at Bri's question. While he didn't understand the exact meaning of it, he understood the connotation well enough. She asked if Mitsy fancied him.

"Why would you say that?" Mitsy asked.

"Oh, come on, Mitsy. Your face is all red just from talking about him. And Mits...everyone is capable of love. If he took the time to tell you that he wasn't, he obviously likes you very much."

"Well, that's what I thought! But when I gave him the perfect opportunity to 'fess up, he was a total wuss."

Wuss? Baodan didn't know what that was, but was he really so transparent?

Quietly, he stepped away from the door, but stopped at Bri's next question—the question he had wanted to know the answer to since soon after he'd met Mitsy.

"What are you going to do? Will you stay here?"

Mitsy stood close to him, leaning against the wall he supposed, for her voice when she spoke sounded right next to him. He could offer nothing, but he wished with every fiber that she would stay.

"I expect I'll leave. I love you, Bri, but I couldn't stay here with you and your family. It wouldn't be right, and there's not much for a woman on her own to do around here."

He shouldn't have expected her to stay, but his heart felt like lead in his chest at the thought of her being centuries ahead of him. If she wanted to leave, it would be wrong of him to stop her.

He moved away from the door and made haste down the hallway. The castle walls suddenly restrained him. He needed to get outside to clear his head, to remind himself that he'd only known the lass a few short days.

***

*B*ri waited until his footsteps disappeared before she looked at me knowingly. "How long did you know he was standing on the other side of that door?"

I laughed, pleased with myself. "I heard him walking down the hallway before he ever stopped. You did too, right? Why did he think no one would notice the sudden lack of movement?"

Bri stood and moved to put her arm around me, grinning. "Yes, I noticed. So you really don't have any intention of leaving, right? Please say you don't."

I reached up to pat her arm. "No, I'm not going to leave right away. I don't know if I'll stay forever, but if it's all right, I'd like to stay for a while. I have this magic rock that Morna gave me so I can go back to our own time whenever I want, but the truth is I have little to go back to. You and your mother are the closest thing I have to family. Until I figure out what it is I really want, I'd like to stay."

Bri squeezed me and stepped away so that she could point at the door. "Good! Now, go and find him and see how upset he is. If he has any sense, he'll talk you out of leaving. I expect you'll find him sitting on the outer wall. He hung out there a lot when he was here caring for Blaire. I'll show you the way."

I hoped I hadn't made a mistake by lying, but I wanted to see if he would be bothered at the thought of me leaving. I suspected by his sudden disappearance from the doorway that he was, but I supposed I would find out for sure soon enough. "Was it wrong for me to do that?"

Bri looked over her shoulder at me as we walked down the hallway. "Not at all, girl. It was very well played."

CHAPTER 20

I found Baodan where Bri had expected him to be, and it pleased me to see that he did appear to be very upset. He said nothing, only glanced backward at me as I crawled out on the edge to sit beside him.

"Thank you." I leaned into him, just barely nudging my shoulder with his to get his attention.

He didn't turn to look at me, instead facing straight ahead as he spoke. "For what, lass?"

"For bringing me all the way here. You didn't have to."

He crossed his arms, and seemed uncomfortable. "Aye, I did, lass. I couldna allow ye to travel alone."

He wasn't going to give me the answer I wanted, not without a little prying, anyway. "And I suppose that's the only reason you brought me? You just couldn't stand the thought of me not being safe?"

"Aye. I did no less than any decent man would."

I crossed my arms, mimicking his stance, and turned to stare at the side of his head. My temper flared, and if he didn't watch it, he would find himself on the receiving end of some serious ginger rage. It was unfair of him to be so cool toward me. "So, when will you return home?"

"At sunrise. I have responsibilities at home. I have been away for too long."

I couldn't believe that he planned on leaving so soon. I thought he would at least stay a few days. "Well." I could hardly utter the lie. "I guess this is goodbye then. I'm planning on returning home tonight."

"Aye? Well, safe journey to ye, lass."

I was about to cry. I didn't want him to see. I spun around so that I could crawl off the ledge and return to the castle. He stared straight ahead, behaving as if my leaving was of no consequence to him.

Perhaps it had only been me who felt something between us, and our few days together were nothing out of the ordinary for him.

A sob bubbled up in my throat. I knew he had to have heard it, yet as I crawled back inside the main building, Baodan did nothing to try to stop or comfort me. It seemed I was the wrong one. He told the truth before. He was incapable of feeling anything.

hy did he feel like crying? Baodan never cried. Not once since the death of his wife had he done so. He stared into the black sky in front of him, trying not to blink so that tears would dry in his eyes rather than fall.

Only the sound of Blaire's angry voice behind him pulled him from his trance.

"Baodan McMillan, if ye doona get yerself off that wall and go after that lass, I shall kick ye off the edge and watch ye fall to the bottom."

"What are ye talking about, Blaire?" He spun and dropped himself back onto the walkway where she stood.

"Doona do that. Ye know what I'm talking about. Ye are a fool. Ye care about her, doona ye?"

He couldn't lie to Blaire, not about this. She would never believe him even if he tried. "Aye, I do, but I doona know how to love someone anymore. I told ye that when I asked ye to marry me. I doona want it, and she deserves to spend her life with someone who can love her. That isna me."

"Are ye saying that I dinna deserve more than that?"

Ach, he didn't know how to speak to women. He only knew how to upset them. "No, o'course ye did. 'Tis only that I believed ye dinna want love, either. Mitsy does, and she should have it."

Blaire shocked him by moving toward him and slapping him hard across the face. "Ye do want love, ye silly fool! Slapping ye may not have been kind, but I doona think kindness is what ye need right now."

His head spun from the impact of her slap. He had a hard head, but she had a strong hand. "Aye, say it. It canna be worse than ye knocking me upside my head."

"Ye say that ye doona know how to love so that ye doona ever have to hurt. 'Tis true that ye may be out of practice, but ye can learn, and she'd give ye the chance to do so."

He reached up to run his hands over his face. "I'm frightened that I willna be enough for her."

Blaire softened and reached out a hand to him. "Do ye remember what I told ye the day I ended our engagement?"

He shook his head. "Perhaps. Remind me."

"I told ye that one day ye'd find the person ye were meant to be with. Although ye told me ye dinna think it would happen, 'twas what ye said last that was important. Ye said that if such a love came, ye would welcome it."

Surely not. He couldn't imagine himself saying such a thing, but then again, Blaire always had a way of making him tell the truth. "And ye think Mitsy is that love?"

"Aye, I do. I know that ye havena known her long, but she was meant to come to ye. I saw it."

He gave her a suspicious frown. "What do ye mean by that? Have ye joined the lady Morna and taken up witchcraft?"

She elbowed him playfully in the side. "No, o'course I dinna, but I do believe that Morna showed me something. Do ye remember when Arran and I came to stay at McMillan Castle after leaving the castle formerly known as Kinnaird?"

He nodded. "Aye, I do. What of it?"

"As we left and rode by yer pond, I saw a redhead swimming in the water. I knew the lass looked just like Mitsy, but I thought at the time that I'd imagined it. I dinna make sense of the vision until ye both arrived here this afternoon. She was meant for ye, Baodan. Now, go and get her before she does something foolish."

---

*H*e found her on the beach, staring into the ocean with enough sadness in her eyes to break his heart. Her hair blew so wildly around her face that he knew she couldn't see him. He paused to watch her before approaching.

She glanced down at a small object she held in the palm of her hand. He couldn't make out what it was, but as she lifted her head and reared her arm back, he knew what she meant to do. His heart stopped.

He ran as fast as he could, diving into the water after the small rock she sent sailing into the air.

For the life of me, I couldn't figure out what on earth Baodan was doing. He floundered around in the water like a crazy man, and the shock of watching him do so made me stop crying.

I looked down at the pile of pebbles I held in my hand and realized. He thought I'd thrown Morna's rock. My heart started beating rapidly, and it frightened me just how quickly my mood shifted from heartache to hope in the flick of an eye. I hadn't been wrong after all.

I shouted after him, but the waves were coming in so strongly that he couldn't hear me. Reluctantly, I slipped off my leather footings and started to step into the water. I would get his attention no other way. There was no point in hiking up my dress, I would get soaked through anyway. Instead, I just walked straight in, grabbing onto his arm as I reached him.

"Baodan." He didn't seem to feel me, his arms swinging wildly, his eyes wet. "Baodan, stop. What are you doing?" I knew, but wanted him to say.

When he finally registered that I stood next to him, he latched onto me, crushing me against him as he wrapped his arms around me. "Ach, Mitsy, how are ye here, lass?"

"What do you mean? Why wouldn't I be here?"

"The rock. I saw ye throw it, and ye just told me that ye were leaving." He carefully kissed the top of my head and stroked my hair, now frizzy and damp from the spray of the ocean.

"No, you didn't. I didn't throw Morna's rock. I just chucked a bunch of pebbles into the ocean."

"What?" He leaned back and grabbed both sides of my face, turning my head upward so that I looked straight at him.

"You heard me. I didn't throw it, but what do you care, anyhow? You didn't seem to mind that I planned to leave."

He kissed me then—a soft and short touch, but my heart danced in response to it.

"Ach, lass, I did care. 'Twas for that reason that I found myself too frightened to tell ye. I have been a fool."

I shivered uncontrollably. The water was freezing, and the windy night made it even colder. "Can we get out of the water? Then you can tell me what a complete and total moron you've been."

I don't think the chill of the water bothered him at all. He looked surprised when I said it and then noticed my trembling arms. Before I could protest, he bent down and lifted me, carrying me like a babe out of the roaring ocean.

Once on shore, he carried me up to a nook in the high towering rocks that blocked the wind quite well. We didn't have anything dry, but he rubbed his hands up and down my arms to warm me and pulled me close to him.

I wouldn't be warm until I got into some dry clothes, but I wanted to finish our conversation before going back inside the castle. "Ok, you can continue now. You were telling me what a fool you are."

He chuckled, and I delighted at the rise and fall of his chest as he did so. He was so sturdy, so beautiful.

"Aye, I was. I canna tell ye how sorry I am, lass. I know that I doona know ye well, but I doona believe I've ever cared for someone the way I do ye. 'Tis a different feeling, an unusual one, and I doona know what to do with it."

He was right. It was different, the feeling that spanned between us whenever we were near one another. "What do you mean you don't know what to do? You don't do anything, just let it come naturally."

"Aye, I wish it came so easily for me. I still doona know if I am capable of allowing someone into my life, but I would like to try. Please, doona leave."

I was so thrilled at his openness, I beamed all over. I knew what a step it was for him. "I'm not going to leave. Not yet, anyway. I never planned on it. I heard you outside Bri's door and I said it to get a reaction. When you gave me none, I became so angry I could have spit fire."

He surprised me by pinching me hard on the rear. "'Twas a dirty trick. It broke my heart to hear ye say that ye wished to leave with not a thought of me."

"Will we stay here a while?" I knew he wouldn't feel like he could.

"I canna do so. There are things at home that need my attention. Will ye come with me and stay at the castle? I know 'tis verra much of me to ask ye to return to the castle while Niall is there, but ye will be safe as long as I'm with ye. He willna be allowed in the castle any longer after I arrive." He shifted nervously. "'Tis not verra customary, but I doona care, and ye doona seem to me as the sort of lass who would mind it."

I would have loved to stay with Bri longer, but she would understand. I couldn't pass up the chance of seeing where this led. "Yes, I'll come, and you're right. I don't give two squats about what's customary."

CHAPTER 22

*A*pproaching *Cameron Castle*

The goodbyes were hard but not nearly as difficult as they would have been if I'd been going back to my own time to return to Texas. At least now, I knew I would see Bri and Adelle again. Even if I did eventually decide to leave here, I would make sure to see them both before I left.

Baodan decided that we should stop at Cameron Castle to check in on his mother on our way back to McMillan Castle. I tried to gently persuade him otherwise, but he'd not relented. I didn't blame him, of course. Naturally, he worried after she'd been so ill very recently.

Still, it didn't make the thought of meeting her any more appealing. He could sense my nervousness and leaned forward to nibble at the base of my neck, but ended up with a mouthful of hair.

"Ye have lovely hair, lass, but how do ye have so much of it? I doona even think Artair has as much as ye do. Did yer parents have locks such as that?"

How little we truly knew about one another. He didn't know anything about who I'd been before I came here, not that I'd been orphaned, or that I'd been married. Yet, I couldn't shake the feeling that it just wasn't very important. Those were all things he could learn in time, and while they played a part in making me who I was, he didn't need to know them to see the person I was now.

He could see what lay inside me without knowing anything, and as long as he accepted that, I supposed it didn't matter how long we'd known one another. After all, I'd known Brian for years, and I would bet money that he wouldn't be able to tell anyone my favorite color, movie, or even birthday. Time meant little if the person you spent it with was a total numbnut.

"No." I leaned into him, relaxing my head against his chest. "Well, I actually don't know. I never knew either of my parents."

"Ach, lass, I'm verra sorry. What happened to them?"

"I don't know. They may still be alive, actually, but part of me likes to hope not. I know that sounds horrible, but if they died, it means they didn't want to give me up."

He reached up to brush my hair so that it draped over one shoulder as he rested his chin on the other, his face pressed gently against mine. "Give ye up?"

"Yeah, it happens sometimes, if the parents feel they can't care for the child. I was bounced around from home to home until I was fourteen."

He dragged his hands up and down my thighs, rubbing them in comfort. "And what happened to ye then?"

"I was placed in the home of an old woman named Lilly, the only home that ever stuck. She was the closest thing I ever had to a mom, and I loved her very much. She passed away a few years ago, right after I graduated college."

"Ye know, we took in Eoghanan much the same way ye speak of. All suspect it, but few know the truth of it. 'Tis not always blood that makes someone kin, aye?"

"Yes." It pleased me to hear him say such a thing about Eoghanan. Perhaps his guilt of assumption as to who assaulted me would soften him toward E-o and help him realize that no fault lay with him.

He squeezed me tight and let out a soft sigh of sympathy, but I could tell he wanted to ask something.

"What?" I turned my head to kiss his cheek, and he grinned against my lips.

"What is college?"

I looked up to see several riders coming toward us. I tapped his knee to get his attention. "I'll tell you later, looks like we have visitors."

He smiled again as he spurred the horse on. "Indeed we do, lass. It seems that we are to cross paths with my mother."

* * *

She traveled in a small group—two men, one of them Baodan's cousin, the laird of Cameron Castle, Griogair Cameron. The other a trusted friend called Henson.

As soon as we reached them and hellos were said all around, everyone dismounted. His mother surprised me by bypassing Baodan and coming straight over to me to greet me properly.

"I'm Kenna. Ye must be Mitsy. I was right about ye, aye? Ye fell prey to one of Morna's spells?"

"Um…yes. And yes I did." Baodan glanced over at me before whisking the two men a little farther away. I supposed he didn't want to have to explain what his mother meant.

"And ye did find yer friend, aye? Did ye not wish to remain with the Conalls?"

I warmed suddenly. What would I say to her? *Yes, I did find her, but now I'm going to live with your son for a while. Just so we can, ya know, see where it goes.* I did not want to be the one to explain anything to her. That was Baodan's job. "I did see them, yes, but Bri is very busy with her baby, and I didn't want to intrude."

"Ah, so ye thought ye would play upon my son's sympathies and rely on his charity, aye?"

I didn't want to get off on the wrong foot with his mother, but her assumption seemed uncalled for, and I wasn't one to stifle what I thought just to make a good impression. "Excuse me? That's not what this is, at all. Perhaps you should talk to your son about it."

She smiled and laughed softly before moving to lace her arm through mine. "I like ye, lass, and so does Baodan. Just look at the way he keeps glancing over here at ye. I haven't seen him look that way in a verra long time. I only spoke in jest. I'm pleased to know that ye are not a lass to be ruled over."

I laughed shakily and smiled down at her, now much more at ease. "Where are you going? We were headed to Cameron Castle to see you."

"I am headed in the direction ye came from, toward Conall Castle. I have yet to see my niece and am anxious to love on the sweet babe."

I grinned, thinking of the fat-cheeked, blue-eyed baby girl. "Well, she's sure a cutie."

"Aye, I'm sure she is. Let's go meet up with the lads so that each of us can be on our way. Griogair will be headed back to Cameron Castle now. He only means to escort me to the edge of his territory. Henson shall accompany me the rest of the way. I'd like us to make it much further before nightfall."

"**W**as she as frightening as ye imagined, lass?" Baodan whispered as we watched his mom and Henson ride in the direction of Conall Castle.

"No. She's great. Much like you. Although, it's hard to believe she fell as sick as you said. She seemed totally fine."

We remounted Artair and set out on our way. "Aye, if I had not watched her wither away in her own bed for so many moons, I wouldna be able to believe it myself. I'm verra glad to see her doing so well, but something told to me before haunts me now."

Worry and confusion echoed in his voice. I twisted around to look at him. "What do you mean?"

"'Twas Eoghanan who convinced her to leave when she was ill. I dinna understand why he would wish it. When I spoke to him about it, he told me to wait and see how much better she would feel once she was away from the castle. He was verra right."

"How could he have known that?"

He shrugged. "I doona know, but 'tis certain I intend to find out as soon as we arrive."

I allowed the evening to pass by silently. Each time I glanced back at him, I could tell that his thoughts were very far away.

CHAPTER 23

As we approached McMillan Castle, I saw nothing of either brother. I couldn't have been more relieved. The closer we got to Baodan's home, the more I sensed that Baodan readied himself to pounce on Niall for what he had done to me. I didn't want to be anywhere around when he found his brother.

The entire situation with his mother also did nothing to help his mood. I had my own suspicions as to why Eoghanan believed his mother would be safer elsewhere, but while Baodan stewed, it was not the time for me to express them.

Eoghanan had been right to try and protect me from Niall, and after the little time I'd spent with the creep, I would put nothing past him. I couldn't imagine what would make any man, even one such as Niall, want to poison his own mother, but if someone inside the castle meant Kenna harm, my bet was on him.

The stables were empty, and I couldn't bear the stress in Baodan's face as he put Artair away in the stall. I walked around the horse and embraced him, kissing him thoroughly. Baodan's mood needed a lift.

When we were both breathless, he grinned down at me, his previous worries gone, if only for a second. "What was that for, lass?"

"Does it matter?"

"No. Are ye ready to go inside? I'll see ye settled so ye may rest while I find my brother."

I sighed, disappointed. I hoped to distract him for a little longer, but clearly he would find no peace until he had dealt with Niall. "Yes, I'm ready."

He grabbed my hand and walked quickly. It pleased me to know that he thought enough not to bring me to the same room he'd placed me in before. He seemed to read my thoughts and looked sideways at me as we continued down a long hallway in the opposite wing from where I'd stayed before. "I will not ask ye to stay in your prior room. I shall place ye in my own room, and I shall find rest elsewhere."

He opened the door but didn't step inside, merely motioned for me to enter. "Go ahead, lass. I shall have a warm bath brought up for ye and a clean dress. I shall join ye later, for I doona want ye to be in my home with my brother about. I willna be able to breathe freely with ye here until I see Niall gone from my home forever."

He started to leave, but I stopped him. I knew he'd be angry with Eoghanan as well, and E-o didn't deserve to be punished for Niall's bad behavior. "Hey, it's not Eoghanan's fault so don't try to make it his. He spent every moment outside my door until that last night. He truly didn't want to leave me, but something urgent required his attention. He was worried about me. Promise me you won't punish him for this."

"Aye, I shall try not to do so, lass." He kissed me softly and left.

True to Baodan's word, a group of women arrived carrying steaming buckets of water so I could have a relaxing bath. I did not find it relaxing. Though nice to get clean, I felt as if I harbored woodland creatures in my hair. I worried endlessly while I sat in the large tub.

Not about Niall. If he still lingered around and tried to come near me, he'd find himself walking funny again. I did, however, worry about Baodan. He held on to too much anger and resentment, and I expected that he had done so for a good many years. I couldn't imagine how it would feel to have such bitterness living inside of me for so long. I had plenty of things to be angry about, but I always wound up utterly exhausted after getting all riled up for all of five minutes. It would be an exhausting life, staying angry all of the time.

Perhaps ridding himself of Niall would help some, but I doubted it. While I still didn't understand the reasons, Niall wasn't the brother that Baodan despised the most. What happened between me and Niall might have evened the playing field a little, but Baodan punished Eoghanan, not Niall, with every thought.

There had to be more to the story about what happened with Baodan's late wife than Eoghanan simply being unable to save her from an illness. At least, I hoped so. If Baodan really did put so much blame on his brother for something so uncontrollable, perhaps he wasn't really the man I considered him to be.

The bath water grew colder with each passing second. Ready to get out, I glanced around the room for something I could use to dry myself off. Seeing nothing, I frowned, stood, and did my best to shake off the water from the top half of my body. After wringing out my hair, I dressed in the clean gown and moved next to the fire to allow my hair to dry.

Five minutes later impatience got the best of me, and I decided enough time had passed. How long did it take to tell someone to leave, anyway? Baodan would be angry if he caught me outside of the room, but he would have to realize that he was not my keeper. I would not be ordered around without good reason, and I could see no reason for me to stay inside his room.

Besides, I wanted to explore the castle, right-side up and not in the hurried fashion afforded me while I was escaping from Niall.

I moved quietly, pausing with nearly every footstep to listen for any sign of Baodan approaching. I hoped I could hear him coming and would be able to run back to his bedchamber before he arrived there.

Only ten steps away from the bedchamber, a hand at my elbow caused me to stop.

"Ach, what are ye doing back here, lass?"

Rhona spun me around to face her. An odd combination of relief and confusion etched her face.

"What do you mean? Baodan brought me."

"Oh, the Laird is back? I am not so pleased to hear it. I canna stand to imagine what he thinks of me now."

I regarded her skeptically. "Did you not know? Who ordered a bath to be readied for me?"

She shook her head. "Baodan must have sent some of the girls up here himself, for I have been in the gardens, and to the gardens I shall return."

"Why? I'm sure Baodan would wish to see you."

"No, I doona believe that he would. I failed him, and allowed something wretched to almost happen to ye. I canna apologize enough for it, lass."

She looked devastated, and I reached out a hand to comfort her. "You didn't allow anything. The fault is not yours, and I don't think Baodan sees it that way, either. Besides, nothing really happened to me."

"Oh, I'm glad that he dinna hurt ye, but it doesna release me of my failure."

Why did so many of these people feel a need to punish themselves for everything? I probably leaned too far in the other direction. I knew how likely I was to mess up pretty much anything, so I learned from a young age to forgive myself everything. "Yes, it does so release you."

"I willna argue with ye, lass, but ye simply doona understand. Baodan is not a forgiving man to those who fail him. I have cared for this family since he was a babe, but I doona doubt that he will wish me gone for not watching over ye while he was away. I am off to the village to gather a few things and pay a visit to my brother. I will be back in a few days. By then, perhaps I will have the courage to face him."

"Um...okay. Well, have a safe trip." I stared at her, wide-eyed, as she walked away. She seemed almost frightened of Baodan, and that made me uneasy.

My first impressions of Baodan, after realizing he wasn't the role-playing weirdo that, at first, I'd assumed him to be, was that he was kind, generous, and a little broken. Broken was okay, but secretive and mean wasn't.

His seemingly unreasonable ill feelings toward his brother, and Rhona's fear of him now, had me second-guessing my decision to come here. To press him about the truth might push him away further, but it had to be done.

I needed to know what he hid from me.

CHAPTER 24

cMillan Territory Village

Eoghanan knew how hard Durell worked for him, but creating the antidote moved slowly. With each day, he grew more concerned that Niall would harm another before he could find him.

Three days passed with no sign of Niall in the village. Eoghanan looked for him the first night, but after failing, he decided his time would be better spent aiding in the creation of the antidote. He spent nearly every moment at Durell's side, assisting him in whatever way he could. Today Durell tasked him with gathering more herbs.

On his way to do just that, Eoghanan saw three young lassies huddled together, whispering. They caught his eye immediately, and it only took him a moment to realize why. Two of the girls, the youngest ones, were Niall's conquests, young girls who'd been tricked by Niall into believing he cared for them, then discarded after they no longer amused him.

The third lass, and by far the oldest, was Greta, a married woman Eoghanan had seen accompanying his brother more than once. It was common knowledge among villagers that Greta was free with her affections, despite her wedded state. Eoghanan saw the women out of the corner of his eye. They watched him and whispered, smiling and laughing between their hushed words. They had no reason to be talking about him. He socialized with no one, and had no liaisons with women, from the village or otherwise. Perhaps they spoke of his brother, and only watched Eoghanan to ensure that he couldn't hear what they said.

He approached them. "Morning, lassies. Do any of ye happen to know where I could find Niall?"

The younger girls said nothing, only stared at him with wide eyes. Intimidated by no one, Greta allowed her gaze to roam him, up and down. "Why would any of us know? As ye can see, he is not with us now."

Eoghanan moved closer so that they stood around each other in a tight circle. He couldn't be easily intimidated, either. "Aye, I can see that just fine. Is yer husband away again?" Greta's face showed nothing, and Eoghanan knew that he assumed correctly. "Aye, I dinna think that he would be home. He stays away often, does he not? If I followed ye to yer home, would I find Niall there? Let us go and see, shall we?"

He started away from them, but stopped as Greta ran to block his path. "No, ye willna find him at my house. While I'll not deny that I did see him two days ago, he couldna join any woman in the way I think ye imply."

"What do ye mean by that, Greta?" He remembered Rhona's mention of his limp. He must have been injured badly. The thought brought Eoghanan great joy.

"'Twas just what I told these lassies about. Niall told me quite willingly about his trouble, though I canna imagine why he would have wanted anyone to know."

"Well, what was it?" Eoghanan needed to know so he could get the herbs back to Durell. If Niall had truly been gone for two days, little time remained to make the antidote. Niall could easily reach many destinations within a few days time.

"I'm telling ye, am I not?" Greta stared at him briefly, looking exasperated. "He said that ye had a lass that makes her living pleasing men staying at the castle." She lifted her brows. "I would think our Laird wouldna need to pay for the company of a lass, but 'tis no matter. Niall tried to purchase her. The lass refused but eventually gave into him when he persisted. But only for a moment. Once she had him distracted, the lass kneed him in the family jewels." She paused and glanced down at herself. "He said it hurt him so badly he couldna stop her before she fled the castle."

Eoghanan let out a large breath of relief. At least Mitsy got away from him. The lass was fiery and smart. No doubt she would have found her way to the Conalls by now. "So he came to ye for what reason?"

"I doona know. He couldna do what he usually wants to when he pays me a visit. He simply rested for a day and then went on his way."

"Did he say where he was going?" Eoghanan feared he already knew the answer.

"He said that he was traveling to Cameron Castle. That he wished to see yer mother."

Eoghanan said nothing as he turned and left them, running as fast as he could back to Durell's. He had known all along that taking their mother away from McMillan Castle was only a temporary solution. Which is why he had hoped to have proof of all Niall had done before Baodan returned. He had suspected that Niall would go after their mother then.

Letting himself into the alchemist's home without knocking, Eoghanan threw the herbs at the old man. "How much longer, Durell? I need the antidote immediately."

Durell shook his head, and Eoghanan's heart sank. "I am close, sir, but it willna be ready for at least another day."

Dread overcame Eoghanan as he slumped against the wall. It would be too late for his mother by then. He couldn't reach her or send her a warning in time. She would most likely be dead before the antidote was ever prepared.

*M*cMillan Castle

*B*aodan was relieved to discover that his brothers were not anywhere on the castle grounds. Niall must have fled after realizing the magnitude of his mistake. Baodan hoped that he would have the sense to never return.

Eoghanan, he suspected, had simply gone to the village; he wouldn't run from his mistakes. Neither would he run from false accusations. Mitsy was right. Niall's attempted rape of her was not Eoghanan's fault. And neither was Osla's death. Why had it taken him so many years to accept the truth?

Anger filled Baodan, anger at Niall, and anger at himself for what he'd become. Too many years of regret and frustration had built up inside him, and he could take it no longer.

Years of expecting more from himself than he expected from those around him, years of believing that guarding his heart would protect him, had saved him from nothing. In the end, he had only robbed himself of happiness, robbed himself of truly living his life.

He would choose to live now. Damn anyone who tried to stop him from doing so. Baodan hoped that confronting Niall would release some of his frustration. Until he could find his brother to do so, he would place himself at the mercy of the lass now in his bedchamber.

He was a man in need, more now than ever before in his life. He had resisted her up until now out of a foolish sense of honor. He would not do so again, not if she would have him. If Mitsy was willing, he would explore every inch of her, lay claim to all that she had to offer. Make her his.

His freedom to live again was tied to this lass who had appeared in his life from out of a future time; Baodan sensed it. He would go to her and voice his desire.

I intended to speak with Baodan as soon as he returned from sending Niall away, to demand that he tell me what had really happened between him and Eoghanan. All of my well-laid intentions flew out the door the moment he walked into the bedchamber.

He looked hungry, needy. There'd been a similar look in his eyes as we lay next to each other the night we made camp with Alec, but it had been a restrained hunger, muffled. There was no restraint in him now, and the intensity of his gaze startled me.

"Are you ok? What did you say to him?"

Baodan tensed. He didn't move from inside the doorway, and more so than usual, he seemed to tower over everything inside the room.

Closing the door behind him, he rolled his neck from side to side, and I found myself unconsciously backing up until my shoulders hit the wall behind me.

"Hello?" The word sounded small, and by the looks of him, I knew he hadn't heard me. I couldn't tell if he was angry or possessed by some other emotion, but I swallowed hard as he moved toward me, every nerve in my body aware of his approach.

He didn't stop until we stood face-to-face. Baodan flattened his palms against the wall on either side of my head, trapping me between his arms. "Niall is not here," he said, finally. "Neither is Eoghanan."

"Oh, okay." I ducked beneath his arms and scooted down the wall, but before I could put any distance between us he moved, blocking my path, leaving me trapped once more.

"Where do ye think ye are going, lass?" He leaned forward and pressed his forehead to mine, his voice deep and slow. The words reverberated down my spine, my entire body trembling at the sensation.

"Um...nowhere. I'm just moving across the room. So . . .did you decide where you're going to sleep?" Not that I wanted him to sleep elsewhere. I wasn't afraid of him, but the intensity of his gaze and the cat and mouse game we were playing intimidated me. I could tell where this was leading, and although I wasn't inexperienced, I'd never been with a man so . . . virile and demanding. I knew he wouldn't hurt me or do anything I didn't wish to do, but I didn't know what to expect and that threw me a little. I was used to being in control of my responses, but I had a feeling that with Baodan, there would be no controlling my reactions to him.

He laughed as he leaned forward and gave a light bite to my earlobe, talking in between the kisses that he trailed down the side of my neck. "I changed my mind. I doona intend to sleep elsewhere, lass. Not if ye doona mind me staying here with ye." He gave me no chance to respond before he moved his kisses lower, brushing his lips along the sweep of my collarbone. "Ye doona mind, do ye?" he asked, his voice a low rumble as he moved up the other side of my neck and proceeded to nibble on my earlobe.

"No, I wouldn't say I mind. What's gotten into you?" I asked the question breathlessly, but I had to know the answer. Something had changed in him. He had such confidence and seemed so unburdened by whatever had held him back before. It pleased me greatly, whatever had caused the change. Bossy Baodan was so sexy it wouldn't have surprised me if my entire gown had melted off my body. My skin burned.

He moved to my lips and kissed me ravenously, then pulled away, keeping one hand at the lowest part of my back, pressing me against him. "Ye, lass.'Twas not only the witch that sent ye here who possesses magic, for ye do, as well. I have spent much of the past years acting as a fool. None have been able to make me see that until ye." He paused, then asked, "Do ye want this?"

I didn't need to think about it. I nodded. "Yes. Absolutely."

Baodan left my side to cross the room and bolt the door.

CHAPTER 26

*B*aodan turned to her once more. Mitsy was the most beautiful woman he had ever known. Her vibrant red hair against the paleness of her skin, the smooth lines of her face, her lovely shape.

She looked across at him with anticipation and a sense of trust so complete that it broke his heart. He could not do what he wanted to most in the world. He could not lay claim to her as he wished, as he had promised himself and told her he would only moments ago. She was not just any woman, nor merely one to whom he was fiercely attracted. He needed her too much. His desire for her was stronger than any he'd ever known in the past. When they came together, he wanted the reason to be more than to sate his lust or to forget his shame for the resentment he had allowed himself to hold onto for so long.

If she were any other woman, it wouldn't matter as much. But Mitsy had the power to pull him from darkness; she'd proved as much. She deserved more than to be used to sooth his frustrations.

She deserved his love and honesty. His love, she had, although he could not bring himself to tell her just yet. She had warmed his cold heart the first moment he saw her, and had captured it completely when she fell asleep against his chest the night he saw her running into the woods.

He suspected she felt much the same way about him as he did her, but it wouldn't be fair of him to allow her to love him, or for him to claim her as his own, when he'd been dishonest with her. She deserved to know the truth about his wife's tragic demise. For if it caused her to feel differently, she would have every right to turn away from him.

Before he could say anything, she crossed the room to him and wrapped her arms around his neck. He kissed her gently, and she tensed in his arms. She was no fool, and he knew she sensed the change in him although he hadn't uttered a word.

"Nope," she said. "You're not doing this again. I'm not letting you beat yourself up over something like sex. You're allowed to have it. People have it all the time, and we are having it tonight. So get that terrible look off your face. This is totally about to go down."

He wrapped his arms around her and laughed into her hair. She said the strangest things, and he loved all of them. Lifting her hair, he gently kissed her neck. "I'm sorry, lass, but I canna do so tonight." He leaned back to look at her.

Her face changed from teasing determination to wariness. "Why?" She lowered her arms to her sides.

She thought that he didn't want her.

Baodan pulled her into his arms and kissed her again until she melted against him. Then he stepped back, took her hand, and led her to the bed. They sat down beside one another. "I canna do this, lass. Not tonight. Ye deserve more than what I can give ye this moment. 'Tis been far too long since I have been with a woman. If I lay with ye now, 'twould be more about satisfying that need than what it should be about. I care about ye too much to do that."

She smirked and snuggled closer to his side. "You are far too honorable, Baodan. I'm not sure any men of your kind exist in my time."

He smiled, then grew serious again. "There is also something that I must tell ye. For once ye know it, ye may feel differently than ye do now. I willna lay claim of ye until ye know what it is."

"Fine. What is it?"

She spoke short, and he couldn't deny that it pleased him to know how disappointed she seemed to be not to have him make love to her.

"'Tis about my wife who died. Osla dinna pass the way I said."

Her face softened as she laced her fingers with his. Baodan felt that perhaps she had suspected his lie.

"We were happy for a while," he continued. "I was, at least. I loved her verra much, but something wasna right inside her heart and mind after we married. She dinna smile or talk often. She would rarely leave her bed and spoke often of her hatred for living."

He paused to gauge Mitsy's reaction, but she revealed nothing of her thoughts. Her gaze remained sure and steady.

Setting aside his nervousness, Baodan continued, "I went away for a short time and left Eoghanan to watch over her. Osla was in the darkest place I'd ever seen her. While away, I worried every moment. I hurried to return to her, and when I arrived I found her dead. She'd hung herself out of one of the windows. I blamed Eoghanan for too long, but he isna the one who deserves the blame for what happened to her."

Baodan swallowed the lump that had formed in his throat at the mention of Osla's fate, and closed his eyes to distance himself from the moment. Mitsy's hand moved to his face, and he opened his eyes to see her staring at him in astonishment.

"Do you think the person to blame is you?"

He nodded, the shame rising within him once again. "Aye, I wasna able to save her. I couldna be enough for her, and the knowledge of that drove her to end her life."

Mitsy surprised him by leaning forward to kiss him. She held her lips against his, unmoving, and he sighed as some of the tension within him fled.

"I don't know what it is with you that makes you punish yourself so completely," she said softly. "You're right to say that Eoghanan is not to blame, but neither are you."

"How can ye say that, lass? 'Twas my job to protect her, and I failed. I dinna make her happy, and she couldna bear it."

Mitsy shook her head. "It was not your job to make her happy. That is something every person must do for themselves. You are not to blame for the sickness in her mind. It is horrible when someone has such sadness inside them, but you are not the cause of her pain."

Baodan said nothing. Perhaps she spoke the truth. He had done nothing but treat Osla with respect and love. Why was it that when Mitsy said it, it made perfect sense, but he'd been unable to reach the same conclusion on his own?

"Is that why you hesitated to love me?" she asked "You were afraid that when I knew the truth I would blame you, as well, and wouldn't want you? That I'd worry that you wouldn't be enough for me?"

He could scarcely look at her. He feared nothing more than what she'd suggested. Never had he cared for anyone in the way he cared for Mitsy – not even Osla. He couldn't bear the thought of her leaving him when their lives together had only just begun. "Aye," he murmured. "That is my fear."

She shook her head, her eyes widening. "You are a silly fool. I'd not given it much thought until now, but seeing as you're so harsh on yourself, I wonder if you're as harsh on others. There's something I haven't told you yet, either. Perhaps when you hear it, you won't find me so appealing."

"No," he said. She could say nothing to make him love her less. "I'm afraid ye are stuck with my affections, whether ye wish them or not. Ye are faultless in my eyes, no matter what it is that ye have to tell me."

"Still, I will say it. Then we will have everything from our pasts out in the open, and we will be free to start over and love one another. That's all I want, Baodan. For us to be free of the past."

He nodded. "Aye. Get on with whatever ye must say."

"I was married once, too."

His eyes widened, and she stared at him. He'd not considered the possibility, but it made sense. Baodan knew her to be younger than him but older than most lasses of his time when they married. Of course she would have a past from her own time. Her life did not begin the moment she arrived here. "Ach, I'm sorry, lass. How did he die?"

"He didn't. Unfortunately, he's alive and well, and carrying on with some girl while living in my old house."

Though not a phrase he knew, he could easily surmise what she meant by "carrying on." However, the part about her husband still being alive made him nervous. "If he dinna die, does that mean that ye are still married to him?"

"No. I'll admit that I'm no history buff, but I'm pretty certain that even if divorce is allowed in your time, it's not very common, right?" When he stared at her blankly, Mitsy explained, "My husband and I divorced, which means that we are no longer married. He was unfaithful to me throughout our marriage."

The idea of any man treating Mitsy so poorly angered Baodan. "I'm verra sorry, lass. If he wasna four hundred years ahead of me, I would verra much like to harm him for the pain he caused ye. But I dinna lie to ye before. It does nothing but make me admire ye all the more. Ye have been through much, and ye have not let it harden ye as I have done."

"You aren't as hardened by your past as you think," she said to him. "I saw through your tough guy act the moment we met."

He loved the lass. Just being next to her made him feel as if he could be the person he yearned to be—the man he had thought he had buried along with his wife. Closing his eyes, he kissed her, losing himself in the comfort of her arms as she wrapped them around him. Feeling, for the first time in his life, as if he was truly in the place he belonged.

CHAPTER 27

"Doona ye move, lass. Stay in bed. I shall find us something to eat."

Still very sleepy, I tried to sit up as he started to leave. My hair must have looked a mess for he grinned, as I did. I patted a hand to my hair, where his eyes strayed, and felt it sticking out wildly in every direction. "Yeah, I know," I said with a laugh. "I'm a messy sleeper, and I look ridiculous when I wake up. Always."

"Ye look beautiful, lass. I'll be back."

Once he left, I stretched myself out over the bed and smiled at the ceiling. We'd fallen asleep in each other's arms and slept through the night. I'd been wrong to question the sort of man Baodan was, and it relieved me that he had chosen to tell me the truth without me having to guilt it out of him.

I looked over to the window. Judging by the height of the sun, I guessed the time to be somewhere around midday. I expected it was highly unusual for Baodan to stay in bed so long.

Before we'd fallen asleep the night before, we had simply held one another and kissed. Baodan whispered in between kisses how he cherished me, how his life had started over the moment he saw me flailing about in his pond.

I'd been content just to be in his arms. Our confessions had changed something between us. A tangible sense of closeness, not quite as strong before, now bound us even more.

It seemed ridiculous to me that I could fall so quickly in love, but it was undeniable that I'd done just that. Baodan was a different sort of man than I would've ever considered to be my type in my prior world. Something about that fact made him seem even more right for me now.

I'd never been around a man who spent as much time thinking and analyzing situations as he did. He worried constantly about screwing up. It caused him constant grief, but it also made him considerate, thoughtful, and concerned. He was a true gentleman in every sense of the word—to the point of annoyance.

I could not have dreamed up a man more opposite from myself. He was quiet while I was loud, careful while I was rash, solemn while I was goofy. We seemed to view life in very different ways. That wasn't surprising, I suppose, since we came from very different worlds.

I felt balanced in his presence, protected and content in a way I'd never felt before with any other man. Although I knew it should've seemed foolish, there was such truth in the way I felt, I knew it couldn't be. I was in love with him.

Just as the thought crossed my mind, Baodan entered the room carrying bread, cheese, and a pitcher of a liquid that I surmised to be ale. It had a strong, pungent scent. Not my usual breakfast, to be sure, but if brought to me in bed, I wouldn't complain.

"'Tis all I could find. It seems that Rhona disappeared along with both of my brothers, and I have told everyone else to enjoy a day in the village. We have the castle to ourselves."

"Oooh, how nice. I do know where Rhona is, though."

He raised both eyebrows as he motioned for me to crawl out of the bed to come eat. Why didn't it surprise me that he would be concerned with crumbs? "Ye do, lass? How do ye know that?"

"Don't get mad, but when you left me here yesterday, I sort of snuck out after my bath. I bumped into Rhona about three steps outside of the door. She said she planned to visit a family member for a few days. She seemed very worried you were going to be angry with her for what happened between Niall and me."

"Hmm...it seems that I have many apologies to make once she and Eoghanan return. She has witnessed my poor treatment of Eoghanan all of these years and undoubtedly expects to receive the same from me."

He looked down, ashamed, and I reached out to squeeze his hand. "Hey. The past is not worth worrying over. If that's all everybody did, nobody would ever accomplish anything. You'll apologize to them later. Don't let it ruin the day."

He smiled and pulled me toward him for a kiss. "Ye are right, lass, as ye seem to be always. I have something planned for ye this evening."

"Will it involve more time alone in this room?" I smiled against his cheek, and my pulse quickened at the thought of it.

"Patience, lass. Ye shall see."

*E*vening could not come fast enough, and I spent the day trying to push the sun out of the sky with my mind. I didn't succeed, of course, but eventually night did arrive.

I watched the anticipation build within Baodan throughout the day, as well. He also seemed nervous, and I suspected I knew why.

I saw the love in his eyes when he looked at me. I heard it in his voice when he spoke, and I felt it in the soft stroke of his fingers as he held me close and played with my hair.

I suspected that he wanted to tell me tonight how he felt about me, but I hoped to beat him to the punch. I wasn't entirely sure if he believed that I didn't blame him for what had happened to his wife, and I wanted him to know that whatever had happened in his past did nothing to change what I thought of him.

As soon as he led me outside the castle, I guessed where he was taking me. To the pond, his favorite place. "What are we doing? Skinny dipping?"

He looked back at me, his eyebrows pinched together as they always did when I said something he thought strange. They stayed pinched a good deal of the time.

"What is skinny dipping, lass?"

"Swimming, but without any clothes on."

"Is there any other way to swim? I doona much like to get in the water with my clothes on."

I laughed as we reached the water's edge. "Well, in my time, most people wear special suits when they go swimming. Just to keep their private parts, ya know, private."

"That's what the water is for, lass. And the moon. It will keep our parts from being seen." Not even remotely shy, he ripped off his kilt and dove into the water before I could blink, his body a blur in the moonlight. It had happened so quickly, I didn't even catch a glimpse of his naked body, anyway.

"How's the water?" I asked.

"Invigorating, lass. Join me."

As I slipped out of my gown, Baodan kept his back to me, ever the honorable gentleman. His old-fashioned morals made me smile. I'd never been modest when it came to my body, but to my surprise, I found myself enjoying these seventeenth century rules of courtship. Or maybe they were just Baodan's rules, who knew? Whatever the case, it was a refreshing change —this level of respect in a relationship.

Taking a deep breath, holding it, I jumped into the pond. "Invigorating" was an understatement; the water was freezing. My entire body tightened in response to the cold, and I breached the surface gasping and yelping.

Baodan laughed and swam over to me. Facing me, he took both of my hands in his. His dark wet hair gleamed beneath the moonlight, his damp skin glistened. I gazed into his sparkling black eyes. "This water is fricking freezing!"

"What did ye expect, lass? 'Tis summer, but ye do know where ye are, aye? 'Tis warm where ye are from?"

"It can get pretty cold in the winter, but most of the time, it's much warmer than this. The summers, oh gracious, they're hot."

I let go of his hands, and we swam circles around each other until I slowly adjusted to the water's temperature.

He started swimming toward the edge of the pond diagonally across from us, and I followed. "Are ye any warmer?" he asked when we reached the shallower part of the water where I could actually stand.

"Yes. It's much better now."

He faced me again, and we both crouched so that only our heads bobbed above the pond's inky black surface. I bumped into a smooth ledge behind me. Placing my hands on top of it, I pushed myself up so that I sat on its edge. It set just deep enough beneath the water to cover my breasts, and its width allowed me to easily lean back into a wall of rock.

Once seated, Baodan moved to sit beside me. "I love the water, lass."

"I know you do. Do you know what I love?"

His eyes met mine and held. Their intensity took my breath away. "What's that, lass?"

"You." I blurted out the truth of my feelings for him rather unromantically, but I'd never been good at expressing my emotions in poetic words. Sounding eloquent wasn't my goal. I just wanted Baodan to know without a doubt that I returned his love.

"Ach, Mitsy." He rarely said my name, and to hear him do so now and in such a loving way sounded like music. Without another word, he reached his hand to the back of my head, spread his fingers through my wet locks, and kissed me.

When our lips parted, he said in just above a whisper, "Will ye look at me, lass? I wish to tell ye something, as well." His voice was shaky, breathless.

Happier than I'd ever been, I turned to hear what he had to say, but the sound of rapidly approaching hooves interrupted us.

Baodan leapt out of the water to retrieve his kilt before the rider arrived. "Stay in the water so that ye are covered, lass," he said, concern apparent in his tone.

Even in the darkness, I noticed something about the way in which the rider approached that hinted at terrible news. As the man drew nearer and slowed his pace, Baodan called out to him, "What is it, lad? What news do ye bring here so urgently?"

"'Tis yer cousin, Laird Cameron. He's dead. And yer aunt, Lady Cameron, is missing."

CHAPTER 28

The details behind Griogair's death made little sense. Nor did the sudden disappearance of his mother. According to the messenger, Laird Cameron had been found collapsed over a plate of food in his mother's empty cottage, with Nairne nowhere in sight.

Baodan stood silently for only a moment, then pushed aside his shock to make preparations. "I need ye to ride into the village for me," he said to the rider. "Gather up Rhona and all from the castle who I sent away from here today. Tell them to return at once, for I must leave verra soon."

Everything but my head remained submerged beneath the water, and without Baodan next to me, the water grew very cold once again.

The rider nodded at Baodan. "Aye, sir." He started to turn his horse but paused. "I forgot to tell ye, sir. Yer brother Niall has stepped in to watch over things until Lady Cameron is found and new arrangements can be made. He must have been only miles from the castle when Laird Cameron passed, for he arrived only moments after they found yer cousin's body. 'Twas fortunate timing."

A shiver travelled through me. I doubted good fortune had anything to do with Niall's timely arrival at Cameron Castle so soon after his cousin's death and his aunt's disappearance. While Baodan knew what a cad Niall could be, I doubted he suspected him capable of murder. I, on the other hand, could imagine it all too well. The timing of his arrival was far too convenient to be a coincidence, in my opinion. Besides, I'd seen in Niall's eyes all he was capable of on the night he'd set out to rape me if I didn't comply with his wishes.

Baodan frowned and stepped closer to the messenger. "What brought my brother there, lad? Do ye know?"

"I believe he intended to pay a visit to yer mother, sir. But she had already moved on to Conall Castle by the time he arrived."

Thank God. I didn't like the idea of Kenna being there amongst the chaos that must surely consume Cameron Castle now. And she would be well protected with the Conalls.

"Ah, I see. Thank ye, lad. Now, ride as fast as ye can to the village, for I need all of the castle servants to return quickly, aye?"

"Aye, sir." With that, the man left.

Baodan quickly grabbed my gown, then moved to the water's edge to hand it to me. He turned away as I emerged from the pond and dressed. Once I completed my task, he pulled me close and wrapped his arms around me. I sensed the move was more to comfort himself than to warm me.

"I'm so sorry." I whispered against his chest, and he kissed the top of my head gently.

"As am I, lass. I canna make sense of it. I can think of none who would wish my cousin dead."

I shivered against Baodan, unsure if I should say aloud what, to me, seemed so obvious. With Laird Cameron dead, Nairne gone, and Niall suddenly in charge at Cameron Castle, I couldn't imagine why Baodan didn't have the same thought running through his mind as did I. This was Niall's doing, all of it. And whatever else he planned to do, could not be good.

"Let's get ye inside, lass," Baodan said. "I canna leave ye here alone, but I willna take ye to Griogair's burial, not with Niall there."

"What about your aunt? Do you think...?" I couldn't finish.

Baodan reached for my hand as we proceeded to the castle. "I think that she is alive and well. She was either not there when Griogair died, or she made her escape. I willna allow myself to believe otherwise until we know for certain. She deserves our help, and I will give it to her. I am only glad that my own mother left before all of this occurred. 'Tis a relief to know that she is in safe hands."

"Yes, I'm glad, too." He walked quickly, and I struggled to keep up with his pace. "What about Eoghanan?" I asked, out of breath.

"I doona know where he is, but it doesna matter. I canna wait for him to arrive here, as I doona know when that will be."

Minutes later, inside Baodan's bedchamber, he quickly started a fire. I wrapped up in a blanket he brought me and tried to get warm. Despite all that had happened since our moments alone at the pond, Baodan still took the time to show me care. It didn't matter that he hadn't had the chance to return my declaration of love with one of his own – I knew how he felt. I was certain he'd been about to tell me when the messenger arrived. And there would be other days for sharing.

"Will they…will they bury your cousin if his mother isn't there?" I asked.

"Aye, lass, they willna wait to do so. As soon as Rhona arrives, I must leave you. I need to be there for Griogair's sisters, and I doona wish to let Niall near Griogair's widow and child."

I nodded. "I don't blame you."

"Aye, he doesna need to get settled in his new position, for he willna be laird of Cameron Castle. Whether it be my own territory or not, I willna allow it."

"Ye willna allow what?" As if summoned, Rhona appeared in the doorway and Baodan rushed over to greet her.

"I willna allow Niall to be laird of Cameron Castle. Laird Cameron is dead, and I must ride there at once." He leaned forward and grabbed the woman's hand so that he could kiss it. "I'm happy to see ye, Rhona. I owe ye an apology, lass. I know 'twas not yer fault, what Niall attempted to do to Mitsy. I never believed it to be. But 'tis my own fault that I behaved in such a way that ye would expect me to be angry with ye."

Rhona's face softened dramatically, and she reached up to lay the back of her hand against his cheek. "I am sorry, as well. I know who ye are inside, Baodan, and in my own distress I dinna trust it. Be gone with ye. I'll take good care of the lass while ye are away."

"Aye, I know that ye will." He moved over to stand next to me, grabbing both sides of my face as he kissed me gently. "Ye are the loveliest lass I have ever known. I shall think of the way ye feel in my arms every instant that I am away. I will return to ye soon. Make no mistake."

He left quickly, and I stood at the window to watch him ride away, not moving until he disappeared from my view.

***

The next morning, Rhona was friendlier toward me than she'd ever been. She busied herself around me in the castle kitchens, eager to prepare whatever I wanted.

"I'm fine, really," I insisted. "I'm no longer hungry, Rhona. But, thanks." I'd already eaten enough food to last me a week. If she tried to force anything else down my throat, I knew I might throw up. Standing to avoid another round of offerings, I moved to the doorway. Pausing, I looked back at her. "Can I ask you a question, Rhona?"

"O'course ye can, lass. What is it that ye need? I'm pleased that Baodan dinna wish for ye to be locked in the bedchamber this time."

"Oh geez, I am too. Listen, I can't stand to do nothing all day. It's not in my nature, and I'm worried, anyhow. Lying around will kill me. Is there anything I can do to help you? Anything I can do to keep busy?"

She smiled wide and moved to my side. Pointing up the staircase, she said,

"I'm pleased that ye are not satisfied to spend yer days abed. Far too many lassies find it pleasing, and 'tis how death finds ye. I doona plan to slow down long enough for it to ever catch me."

"Good plan." Laughing, I waited for her to give me some direction. She grinned. "Lady Kenna is much the same way as yerself, lass. Before she fell ill, she busied herself by working in the room at the verra top of the castle. See." She pointed upstairs again. "All the way to the top. I doona think she would mind if ye piddled in there. Looked through the books. Perhaps ye can find out how she meant to place them and aid her in the quest to clean the room up a bit."

"Perfect." It sounded like tedious work, which was just what I needed—something requiring just enough concentration so that I would not have time to worry. "I'll go there now," I said.

She waved me on, and I smiled over my shoulder at her as I walked out of the kitchen, directly into a very distressed Eoghanan.

"*E*-o! Where have you been?" Dark circles lined his red eyes and his face seemed abnormally pale. He looked as if he hadn't slept in days.

"Ach, lass."

Visibly shaken, he gripped me tightly, pulling me against him in such a way that it seemed like I had known him for years.

"I am pleased to see that ye are well. I knew that ye would be, but I was still verra worried about ye. Where is Baodan? I must speak with him at once. We must leave for Cameron Castle immediately. I have reason to believe that our mother is in grave danger."

"Wait. What?" I pulled back so I could look at him straight on. I assumed that his cousin's death upset him, but he spoke of something else. "Why are you worried about your mother? She's not at Cameron Castle." Shock spread instantly across his face, and I reached out to lay a reassuring hand on his arm. "You don't know what's happened, do you?"

"Oh, God." He blinked and staggered back a step. "I feared I would be too late. But I hoped that…" A sob escaped him, cutting off his words.

I put my arm around him, easing him to sit on the step at the bottom of the staircase. "Hey, calm down. I think you're mistaken." I sat beside him. "Too late for what?"

"She's dead, is she not?"

I sat next to him and grabbed his hand, shaking it against his knee so that he would look up at me. "Your mother? No, she's not dead. I told you, she's gone to Conall Castle. She went to see the new baby. It's your cousin, Griogair, who is dead."

"I'm sorry, lass, I doona understand."

He was such a mess. He needed a bath, a meal, and some sleep. Still, I knew that he would do nothing else but worry about his mother until he knew what had happened. "They found Laird Cameron collapsed over the dining table in his mother's cottage. Nairne is missing. In the meantime, Niall arrived and stepped in until arrangements for a new laird can be made."

Eoghanan's eyes darted back and forth as his tired brain tried to understand all that I'd said. "God, lass. It may be that all of this wasna his plan, but he willna let it deter him for long. Ye said that my mother is not at Cameron Castle? I am pleased to hear it."

"Yes, she's at the Conalls'. Whose plan?" He looked away suddenly, and I knew he'd not meant to say all that he had.

"I should have said nothing to ye, lass. 'Tis not yer concern. 'Tis Baodan with whom I need to speak."

"Baodan's not here, and unless you plan on riding after him, which you are in no shape to do, I think you should just tell me whatever it is that has you so out of sorts." I leaned back so Rhona could see me inside the kitchen, and I waved to get her attention. "Will you get E-o something to eat? I swear he's about to fall over."

For a brief moment, Eoghanan's frown faded, and he grinned at me weakly. "Thank ye, lass. I could use a good meal, but I thought I told ye not to call me E-o. 'Tis not my name, and it sounds foolish."

"Well, then tell me how to say it."

"Another time. When I feel the need to smile, I shall teach ye. There is too much sorrow in my heart now to do so. And I willna tell ye, lass. I'll leave it to Baodan to do so, should he feel the need."

Smirking, I stood to leave Eoghanan in Rhona's care. I loved Baodan, and I liked Eoghanan, but I couldn't stand their mutual belief that it was up to a man to decide what a woman could do or be allowed to know. Besides, I already thought I knew what he was keeping from me.

"There's no need for Baodan to tell me. I already know that Niall had something to do with your mother's illness and with what happened to Griogair, though I'm not sure Baodan realizes it yet. The only thing I don't know is why he did it. If you do know and you'd like to tell me, I'd love to hear it. If not, it's no matter. I'm pretty resourceful. I doubt it will take me very long to figure it out. Now, eat some food and take a bath."

Leaving him gawking after me, I moved past E-o on the stairwell and went in the direction Rhona had pointed out to me.

The darkness of the room forced me to retreat back into the hallway to find a torch to light the many candles scattered about. Once illuminated, I found it far less dusty than expected. Kenna had already done most of the dirty work.

I moved slowly about the room, glancing at the neat piles of books, trying to get my bearings as to how she had categorized the volumes. Many of the books were not written in English, which presented a problem for me. I slowly realized that I was useless to her efforts.

With the promise of staying busy shattered, I settled at the desk that sat at the center of the room. One book lay open in front of me. Encased in leather, the pages were considerably larger than a standard sheet of paper. It was a beautiful book, mysterious. I flipped through the pages, stopping when I realized I recognized the words written within.

Surprisingly, and quite unlike the other volumes scattered throughout the room, this book was written in English rather than in Gaelic. And it was not a book at all, but a journal. I wondered whose.

Baodan didn't strike me as the type to pour his feelings onto the page, and neither did Niall. Eoghanan seemed a possibility, but the script looked too feminine to be his handwriting; the flourished, cursive handwriting made for difficult reading.

My next guess was Kenna, but I wasn't sure if women were able to read and write during this time. Perhaps ladies of means, such as Baodan's mother, were more educated than women from the village.

I started at the beginning, taking note of the first date recorded, written over eight years prior. Scanning the pages, I flipped to the last entry, which was located only a little more than halfway through the journal. The last time someone had put pen to page was seven years ago. I read the entry with interest, stunned and saddened by the dark, disturbed words.

Only one person could have written something so morbid.

Baodan's late wife, Osla.

CHAPTER 30

*C*ameron Castle

"Ye are not going back inside until I have spoken to ye." Baodan grabbed Niall by the arm, dragging him effortlessly to the side of the castle, away from the burial site. He wished to squeeze his brother's arm until the bone snapped, to beat the wretch to a bloody pulp.

Niall struggled to free himself, unsuccessfully. "I'm afraid I doona have time, brother. There is much to be done. With Aunt Nairne still missing, there is none to assist here but me. I now understand what it must be like for ye all the time. I doona envy yer position."

Baodan held him tightly, bringing his face in close to Niall's so that no one else could hear his words. "Doona behave as if ye have done no wrong. If ye hadna, ye would have greeted me as soon as I arrived, not pretend as if ye dinna know me."

Baodan didn't miss the shift in Niall's gaze, the dark energy that cascaded over them as his brother's demeanor changed. A malice festered in Niall's eyes that Baodan had never noticed there before.

"The only wrong I have done is try to bed the lass who has blinded ye. But she is an ungrateful wench who should be taught not to bite the hand that feeds her."

Baodan's fist hit Niall in the side with enough force to crack a rib. He held his brother upright to keep him from doubling over in pain. It wouldn't do for anyone to notice the tension between them. What he had planned for Niall must remain a secret until he learned what his brother had been up to these past weeks, if not longer. "Ye are not to speak Mitsy's name ever again, do ye hear? She is a permanent member of yer former home. Doona dare show yer face there again, for ye willna be welcome."

Shock spread across Niall's face. Inhaling deeply, he stood as upright as his sore ribs allowed. "McMillan Castle is no more yer home than mine, but 'tis no matter. I have been welcomed here with open arms. It shall be many a year until Griogair's son is old enough to take over his duties as laird."

"'Twould be a mistake for ye to get comfortable in yer position here. I will no more allow ye to care for this territory than I would allow ye to care for my own. Do ye think I doona see what ye have done here?" Baodan released his grip on his brother and forced a smile at one of the castle maids as she walked by. Watching until the lass disappeared around a corner, Baodan grabbed onto his brother again.

"Just what is it that ye think I have done?" asked Niall in a goading tone.

A jest lay within his brother's gaze, a dare for Baodan to speak what he professed to know. It infuriated Baodan that Niall was well aware of his bluff. He didn't understand all that had happened to put his brother in charge here, but as Baodan faced Niall's cold and calculated stare, he knew who to blame. "I doona know how, and I sure canna see why, but I believe Griogair's death came about by yer hand."

"My hand?" Niall's angry voice dripped with sarcasm as he glared disdainfully at Baodan. "I can swear to ye that I did not touch Griogair. I rather liked our dear cousin."

"I believe that ye dinna lay a hand on him, but 'twas yer poison killed him, and it wasna the first time ye have used such a potion."

"Oh? And who else do ye think I have killed? Have ye not spent yer entire life side- by-side with me? Doona ye think ye would have noticed if I was capable of murder?"

Baodan shook his head. "No. I remained too blind, too wrapped up in my own selfish pity to see what was right in front of me. I doona know who else ye have killed, but I have come to believe Eoghanan was right to get Mother out of yer reach."

"Ach, Baodan. What reason would I have for hurting her? 'Tis no secret that I despise our mother, but what would I have to gain from her death?"

"I doona know, but everything ye do is for yer own gain, so I know there must be a reason."

Baodan stilled at the wicked smile that spread across his brother's face. Niall finished his jest, enjoying the freedom of not having to hide his hatred.

"Ah, so Eoghanan has said nothing then? O'course he hasna. I can tell by the look on yer face that ye know nothing, and I believe that ye never shall. The fool is too honorable, too caring to hurt ye in such a way."

Baodan closed his eyes and breathed deeply, picturing the lass that awaited him at home. He could not kill his brother, not until he rallied enough forces to push Niall away from Cameron Castle. Away from all that he held dear. "I willna ask ye what ye mean, for it would bring ye pleasure, and ye are deserving of none. Enjoy yer time as laird, for it shan't last long, brother." Baodan dropped his hand from Niall's arm, turning so he could mount his horse.

"Will it not? I doona see how ye shall end it. I will tell ye this and 'tis the truth whether ye wish to hear it or not. Griogair was not the person I wished to harm."

Baodan turned to look at Niall over his shoulder. "Do ye think me a fool, Niall? I know he wasna the one ye aimed for. Ye told many that ye were headed to see Mother, dinna ye? And 'twas Mother's food that ye believed ye'd poisoned."

Niall laughed, and the cruel sound of it chilled Baodan to the bone.

"Aye, but it seems that all has turned out for the best. With Griogair gone, I now have a home when ye have denied me one."

"And what of Nairne, did ye kill her, as well?"

"No, 'tis all that troubles me, for I doona know where she is. I expect she is dead somewhere on the castle grounds, felled by the grief of watching her only son die before her eyes. But believe me, if she is not dead, I shall be the first to find her, and the last to see her alive."

Baodan longed to leave here, to return home to find the truth that he sought, and to wrap his arms around the woman he loved. Yet he had to find a way to protect his aunt. Niall had filled his heart with enough hate and disgust to last a lifetime, and Baodan needed to wash it away before it consumed him. "Do ye think that Nairne's words are all that can end ye? I doona need proof of what I know for men to join me against ye. My word is worth much more than yer own." Baodan turned, but he heard Niall's quiet laughter as he walked away.

"And just what makes ye think that?"

Baodan kept his back to his brother, moving away from the monster behind him as he spoke. "While I have denied myself much, I havena spent my life treating others like they are mine to pawn as I wish. I have many a friend, while ye have none. There is more power in that than ye know."

For the first time in as long as Baodan could remember, his brother said nothing. Baodan rode away from Cameron Castle knowing he must rally his forces with speed, or he wouldn't be able to protect Nairne.

All he could hope for was that Niall had taken his bait and would come after him. Surely Niall would be more concerned with stopping him than finding their helpless aunt.

CHAPTER 31

$\mathcal{M}$cMillan Castle

$\mathcal{E}$very instant spent within Osla's journals brought me closer to her secret. Unable to continue the work Kenna had started, I offered to help Rhona in the kitchens but made sure to sneak away for a few hours each afternoon so I could dive into Osla's sad world.

Eoghanan did not seek me out again after our recent encounter, but I knew he stayed around the castle. Each day on my way to the tower room, I would see him pacing outside, waiting with baited breath for Baodan's return.

The seventh morning after Baodan's departure, I woke early and headed straight for the tower room. We expected Baodan back today, and I wanted to finish the few entries left in Osla's journal. With every step up to the tower room, I prayed that the answers I sought would reveal themselves in the riddles gone unsolved for far too long.

The entries she had written detailed her gentle descent into darkness, and the evolution from happiness to despair broke my heart. At least for a while, Osla's life had been a happy one.

"After much begging, Eoghanan agreed to teach me to write. Baodan would have taught me, but he would not have understood my desire to learn as Eoghanan has. He, too, holds things within and finds release through the written word. We have worked for many months together, and I have left these pages empty until I was skilled enough to grace

635

them. Finally, Eoghanan says I am ready. Now, when I am too quiet to speak, I will pour out my soul to these empty pages."

I wondered if Baodan knew that Eoghanan taught Osla to write. Their lessons must have begun even before they married, for she detailed the wedding.

"Today shall be wondrous. Even if clouds fill the sky, there will be sun in my heart."

I flipped past those entries. The girl seemed likable enough, but I didn't really want to read about how madly in love with Baodan she'd been. Dead or not, the thought caused jealousy to flare within me.

Osla's entries continued happily for the first five days of my search, but on the sixth day, her words took a turn for the worse, revealing a secret betrayal.

"He is the devil, yet I am drawn to him. I know that what he offers I should not take, yet I am tempted."

Two entries later—guilt and despair.

"I have betrayed the man I love most in all of the world, all for a moment in the arms of evil. I was a fool. 'Twas empty compared to the love I receive from Baodan. I should not have listened to his sweet words. I have seen too many lasses enter and leave his chambers. Why did I believe I was different to him than they? I deserve the hell that awaits me."

Osla never mentioned the man's name, but I knew of only one person within the castle fitting her description. Niall.

I sat down on day seven, picking up on the aftermath of their affair. Baodan knew nothing of this, but I suspected Eoghanan did, and kept it from his brother. A few entries down the page, my suspicions were confirmed.

"I wish this to end, but Niall threatens me, and so I must obey. Today our secret was discovered. Eoghanan saw us together. I could not be filled with more shame. There is, perhaps, some good that has come from his discovery. He will not allow Niall to touch me again. Eoghanan told him that if he ever came to me again, he would kill him. It was not an idle threat, and I believe Niall knows that."

I understood why Eoghanan had not told Baodan. Eoghanan had cared very much for Osla. He knew her regret and didn't wish to dishonor her. He also understood Baodan well enough to know that the knowledge would've destroyed him. So he kept the secret, not foreseeing the trouble that would arise from it.

"I am grateful that Eoghanan has kept my secret, but I can bear it no longer. Tonight, I will tell Niall my wish to confess. Perhaps, he will see reason and we can tell Baodan of our betrayal together."

I'd spent very little time with Niall, and even I knew that would never work. Only one entry remained, and it differed from all of the rest. So hopeless were the words, even the handwriting changed. While I was unsure of the exact date of Osla's death, I knew her life ended shortly after these words. This Osla bore no resemblance to the one who had started the journal.

"Secrets lead to death, and I will welcome mine. Then Baodan will be free of me."

If the entry had ended there, suicide would have been a believable end to her life, but the words that followed proved the key to the true secret behind all that had happened to Osla.

"I should end my life, but I am too much of a coward, too selfish to release Baodan of me. Despite my agony, the will to live is strong. Although I try to diminish its flame, there is a spark of hope within me. Hope that, with time, my mind will heal itself. But time no longer exists for me. He comes to end what we started; I feel his approach every moment, and fear has taken up permanent residence within my heart. My moments left in this world are few. Perhaps that is just as it should be."

I sat blinking at the empty pages following her words, the pieces to the puzzle coming together in my mind. Osla hadn't killed herself as Baodan believed. She'd been murdered by the same man who had tempted her into betraying her husband, making the rest of her brief life a living hell.

A few pieces still lay unconnected: Eoghanan's illness on the night of Osla's death, Kenna's sickness that caused her to leave McMillan Castle, and Griogair's sudden death now. They all related to Osla.

I looked at the flickering light that danced on the walls around me. Kenna had worked within this very room before falling ill. No doubt, she had read the words I gazed upon now. As each final piece fell smoothly into place, a voice behind me jerked me out of my thoughts.

I turned to see Eoghanan standing in the doorway.

"Ye canna tell him, lass. Not ever."

CHAPTER 32

"Why?" I wanted nothing more than to tell Baodan. He deserved to know the truth after believing himself at fault for so many years. More than that, he needed to know so that he could move on with his life—with our life together.

Eoghanan crossed the room to the desk where I sat. Reaching out, he closed Osla's journal. "There is no need for him to know. 'Twould only cause him pain."

"He's already in pain." I stood, confused and frustrated. "Keeping the truth from someone doesn't protect them. It only keeps them living a lie longer than they need to. Baodan blames himself for what happened to Osla. He thinks he failed to make her happy."

Eoghanan regarded me skeptically. "How could he think such? Osla loved him more than anyone."

"He thinks that because Baodan thinks *everything* that goes wrong is somehow his fault."

Shaking his head, Eoghanan said, "To tell him would only lay the blame with Osla, and 'tis not her fault, either."

"That's ridiculous."

I pressed my fingers hard against my forehead, willing myself not to lose my cool in a show of anger. I couldn't take another moment of this "women are weak" mindset that all of these men seemed to share.

"I'm sure you've never heard the expression, but it takes two to tango," I snapped. "Niall is at fault more than anyone, but I don't get the impression that Niall forced Osla to have an affair with him. She had her own mind and was responsible for her own choices. I know that you liked her, but she played a part in this. I'm not saying that she doesn't deserve forgiveness, but better Baodan lay the blame on her and Niall than on himself a moment longer."

For a few moments, Eoghanan paced the room in silence, staring down at the floor.

When I could take no more, I said, "Oh gracious, just say something, would you?"

"Ye are the oddest lass I have ever known."

"Yeah, I get that a lot around here." I crossed my arms and glared back at him. We stood in an odd sort of showdown across the tower room, him at one end gripping the journal, me in front of the doorway blocking his exit.

"I mean it, lass. I've never heard a woman speak the way ye do."

"Am I wrong? What I said . . . doesn't it make sense to you?"

Eoghanan returned the journal to the table, and I took it as a sign of his resignation. "Ye are not wrong. 'Tis only that I havena spoken of all that happened in so long. It pains me to do so now."

"I'm sorry. I shouldn't have been so harsh." Of course it hurt him—the death of his friend, the grief of Baodan, the betrayal of Niall. Too much for any one person to hold inside for so long. "Why haven't you told anyone?"

"Join me outside," he said. "This room holds too much sorrow.

We left, but didn't go far. After closing the door, we sat together on the steps leading up to the tower. I waited in silence for him to gather his thoughts.

"For the longest time," Eoghanan finally said, "I dinna see it, what Niall had done. I suppose I dinna really want to. Osla couldna move past what she'd done, couldna bear the guilt of it. It wasna so difficult to believe that she would harm herself."

He stared in front of him and although he spoke to me, Eoghanan's mind roamed far away, lost in dark memories of the past.

"After her death, I could think of no good reason to tell Baodan about the affair. He dinna need any more pain, and Niall had already done all of the damage he could. I was wrong to think so, but I thought 'twould be best to leave their secret in the past."

"How long did you believe she ended her own life? When did you learn what Niall had done?"

"'Twas only after our mother fell ill. She would never tell me, but I knew by the way she started to treat Niall that she'd uncovered his secret. Shortly after, she fell ill. It dinna take long for me to see the similarities in her sickness and the one that felled me the night Osla died. 'Twas much slower moving, but she couldna eat, and could barely leave her bed. That's when I knew what he'd done."

"He killed Osla." I didn't ask it as a question. I knew what he would say.

"Aye. Niall would do anything to keep Baodan from learning what he had done. He knew that I dinna wish to tell him, but Mother would see it differently. Like ye, she would see the need for Baodan to know the truth. He killed Osla for the same reason. In the end, she wished to tell Baodan the truth, but he refused to give her the chance."

"So, why didn't you feel more inclined to tell Baodan what really happened once Kenna fell ill? Surely your mother's well-being was more of a concern than hurting Baodan with the truth, wasn't it?"

He closed his eyes, and I could sense the regret he tried to push away.

"I should have, lass. 'Tis the verra first thing I should have done, but I dinna trust Baodan. Ye have changed him more than ye know, Mitsy. Before ye found him, Baodan blamed me as much as himself. I thought that if I approached him without proof, he would cast me aside for good. 'Tis why I sent our mother away, so that she would be safe until I found the proof I needed to approach Baodan."

Listening to his words, the final piece clicked into place. "But Niall went after her anyway, didn't he? He didn't mean to kill Griogair. He tried for your mother."

He nodded, and glanced somberly in my direction. "Aye, and 'tis my fault that Griogair is dead. Before I sent Mother away, I finally got the truth from her. She found the journal just as ye have. She promised not to tell Baodan right away, to give me time to gather proof. Had I told Baodan sooner, Griogair would not have met such a fate. I doona believe Niall truly wishes to be Laird, but the mishap provided him a convenient place to hide."

I reached out to him, wishing he would understand through the squeeze of my hand just how wrong he was.

"There is no one to blame for Griogair's death but Niall. It's impossible to always see what the right choice is. You did your best with the knowledge you had. Of course, you would expect that Baodan wouldn't believe you without proof. He has treated you poorly for far too long. He knows that now."

"Does he? I doubt it verra much, lass."

Eoghanan carried just about as much self-loathing as Baodan. It broke my heart to see it in both of them. "He does. I know it because he told me."

"If he did, lass, then ye canna know how much he must love ye, for he never speaks to anyone about himself."

"Well, I'm pretty good at extracting information." I nudged him playfully, and a slight smile showed at the corner of his mouth, disappearing as quickly as it came.

"Aye, ye are that, and I see that ye are right. As soon as Baodan returns, we shall tell him. All has been kept secret for far too long. With Griogair's death, Niall must be stopped."

"Ye doona need to wait another moment for me to arrive. I think it best if ye both start speaking at once."

Either his footsteps were quiet or we were too engrossed in conversation, but neither of us had noticed Baodan's approach until he stood before us. Tired, anxious, and scowling, he moved past us on the stairwell and into the tower room.

CHAPTER 33

$\mathcal{S}$tanding with crossed arms, Baodan waited for us to join him inside the tower room. I understood his testiness; he was exhausted and dirty from his journey, and I imagined that Niall's presence at the burial of their cousin had added to Baodan's impatient mood.

"Hey." I made my way over to him, managing a half-smile that I hoped might ease his distress. Standing on my tiptoes, I kissed him gently.

He thawed instantly and exhaled loudly, squeezing me tightly against him. "I'm sorry, lass. I am so pleased to see ye, but my soul is sick. I am tired of all these untruths. If either of ye know something that I doona, please for the love o' God, tell me now."

No matter the stress that hung in the air, I found it heaven to clutch onto him, to know he stood near me and not within Niall's reach. "Sit down. I'll let Eoghanan tell you. The story isn't mine."

$\mathcal{A}$s Eoghanan stepped forward, I leaned against the wall, allowing the brothers their moment of revelation, never tearing my gaze from Baodan's stony face. I knew the ache that started deep in your stomach and spread after learning of a spouse's betrayal. The difference between my experience and Baodan's, though, was that he had loved Osla. I never truly loved Brian, not in the way that a wife should love her husband. I suspected Baodan's wound would be deeper than mine, and I hated that for him.

As Eoghanan revealed all that had taken place, I saw in Baodan's eyes the moment he realized that Niall had the potential for evil. His brother was a

643

sociopath, and Baodan finally understood that fact. Maybe he'd always known it but had simply been in denial. For the realization seemed more to sadden than shock him. I feared that learning of Osla's betrayal would be what stopped him cold. And I was right.

"No." Anger emanated from him as Baodan stood and took a step in Eoghanan's direction. "I know that I wasna fair to ye after she died, and I canna apologize to ye enough. I know that 'twas not yer fault, but I willna allow ye to speak such lies against her."

Eoghanan glanced at me sideways, and my heart squeezed uncomfortably at the pain I knew Eoghanan felt at his brother's lingering distrust. I stepped out of the shadows and pointed at the table and the journal atop it. "Baodan, don't. He has no reason to lie to you. It's all right there, in the book."

He turned and looked down at the closed volume. Raising his hands in frustration, he said, "What's this? And what does it have to do with Osla?"

"It's hers," I said softly. I didn't want him to read it, but I knew he would not believe Eoghanan, otherwise.

"No. She dinna know how to write, nor read."

"Aye, she did, Baodan. I taught her myself."

Baodan's clenched fists were the only sign that he heard Eoghanan's words. Hesitantly, he flipped open the worn cover. Every bit of me wished I could prevent the pain he was soon to confront.

---

*M*uch time passed, and I couldn't breathe with the anticipation of his reaction.

Anguish filled his voice when, finally, he spoke. "'Twas Niall. He killed her, dinna he?"

Baodan turned in his seat to look at us, his eyes red and brimming with unshed tears. I wanted to run to him and throw my arms around him, but I couldn't bring myself to do so. This pain stemmed from a time before me, and in this instant, he didn't want me near him.

Eoghanan stepped toward his brother, pausing when Baodan held up a hand. "Aye, Baodan. It was Niall. But 'twas only after Mother fell ill that I learned the truth myself."

"Ah, 'tis why ye sent her away," he said, in just above a whisper.

"Aye."

Baodan stood, his eyes moving back and forth between Eoghanan and me. The pain etched on his face hurt me to my core. "Thank ye for telling me." He lowered his gaze, as if he couldn't bear to look at either one of us any longer. "If ye will excuse me, I should like to be alone."

"I'm afraid ye doona have time for that, sir," came a voice from the doorway. A maid stood there, out of breath from climbing the stairs. "The entire Conall clan, along with yer mother, has just arrived at yer door." When Baodan nodded, she turned and scurried back down the stairwell.

Baodan stepped toward the doorway. "'Tis good they have come. We shall need them. Rally the keep and make ready for trouble. I've no doubt it's coming for us."

"Ye stay as long as ye need, Baodan. I'll go and see all is done," Eoghanan assured him as he waved his brother back.

I stood still until Eoghanan left. Then I couldn't wait any longer. Whether he wanted me to or not, I needed to touch Baodan. "I know you want to be alone, and I'll leave soon, I promise. But I…I need you to know that I'm here."

One lone tear spilled from his eye, and I reached my thumb up to brush it away. He grabbed my hand and held my palm against his face, not trying to hide the pain. It meant more to me than he realized.

"I'm verra glad for it, lass, for I feel quite out of sorts with the world."

"That's okay, you don't always have to be strong."

He placed his palm against my face and pulled me close, stroking my hair with his fingers. "Aye, today I do, lass, but there is none that gives me strength the way that ye do."

CHAPTER 34

I tried to figure out why Kenna would've brought all of the Conalls with her when she came home. Maybe she'd decided it was time to bring Niall down, despite the fact that he was her son. With distance between them, she no longer felt threatened by him and would no longer keep her silence. Baodan seemed glad that she had brought so many with her; the support of many clans would be needed to end Niall.

Walking hand-in-hand, Baodan and I made our way down to the castle entrance. I grew more nervous with each step. For if the clans gathered, it meant an impending battle.

"I wish I'd used a knife on him instead of my knee," I muttered.

"What did ye say?"

"Oh." I hadn't realized I'd even spoken the thought aloud. "Um…I said, I wished I'd used a knife on him that night. Then he'd already be dead, and we would not have to deal with all of this."

"Ach, lass." Baodan continued walking but looked down at me with a shocked expression. "I am verra glad ye did no such thing. If ye had succeeded, ye wouldna be able to deal with the killing of a man. Ye are too soft-hearted."

"Pssh." I lifted my brows. Niall was a killer. It would've been an honor to give him what he deserved.

"Oh, my God. She's alive." Baodan pulled away from me and hurried across the main entryway, where an older woman stood. He scooped her up into his arms.

I stood back, allowing Baodan and the woman I assumed to be his aunt a moment together.

I heard Adelle approaching—her quick, hurried step and brisk voice—before I saw her. I turned to see all of my favorite girls approaching, accompanied by a shockingly attractive older gentleman who had to be Adelle's husband.

"Oh. My. Gosh." I mouthed the words.

Grinning like a schoolgirl, Adelle hugged me. "This..." we turned in unison, "is my husband, Hew."

I offered him my hand and he took it gladly, his giant palm engulfing mine. "It's very nice to meet you, Hew. You must be quite something to have wrangled in Adelle."

His laugh was a deep, friendly sound, and his smile reached his eyes. The best smiles, from the kindest people, always did.

"Ach, I am verra pleased to meet ye. I have heard much about ye."

"Oh, no." I laughed, unable to draw my attention away from his beautiful brown eyes and shortly cropped hair.

"All good things," he added, retracting his hand and nodding before turning to speak to another in the room. I wondered if he sensed our desire to talk about him.

"Adelle, you hooked a good one," I whispered, and Bri and Blaire laughed, scooting in closer to join the conversation.

"I think somebody's got a little crush on your husband, Mom," said Bri, winking at me. She held her baby close, and I reached out to run the side of my hand across little Ellie's sleeping face. Bri looked beautiful with a baby in her arms.

"Oh, give me a break," I said. "It's just that I'm happy for your mother, is all. I'm happy for all of you."

"Ditto." Bri lifted the baby and nudged her head in the direction of the staircase. "Will you show me where I can put her down? Then we can all resume our visiting while Baodan and the men sit down to make plans."

"Yes, of course." Together we all walked up the staircase. "What did Kenna tell all of you?"

"Most everything, I think."

Bri didn't seem overly worried, which was very odd, but it did help to calm my anxious nerves. Motherhood suited her. I found myself wondering how it would be to have a child with the man I loved.

"Kenna said she told you two she was coming to Conall Castle to see the baby, but she was really coming to ask for our assistance," explained Bri. "I suppose she didn't want to tell Baodan at the time. She wanted him at home to watch over McMillan Castle. If he's anything like the Conall men, he would have turned around to follow his mother had she told him."

"Yes." I nodded. "He would have."

"We were readying to leave when Nairne showed up, exhausted and sick from traveling by foot for days. She is grief stricken, but mainly she's angry.

She watched her son die before her eyes, and she knew instantly Niall was to blame. Kenna told her all she knew before she headed in our direction."

"God, I can't imagine—witnessing the death of her son, unable to stop it, then dragging herself all the way here." I shook my head. "It's terrible."

"Yes." The baby stirred in Bri's arms, and she bent to kiss Ellie gently on the forehead before continuing, "All of it is, and Niall must be stopped. It's scary, you know, how you can spend time around someone and just never see who they really are. Granted, I've not spent much time with Niall, but I always thought him rather harmless."

I shivered at the thought of anyone thinking him harmless. Then again, I'd had a very different introduction to him than most. "No, that's not the word I would use to describe him. Here." I opened the door to Baodan's bedchamber. "You can put the baby in here."

Bri placed her daughter in the center of the bed, and I found myself looking longingly at the sight. Someday soon, I hoped, this would be my bed —mine and Baodan's. It surprised me to realize that I liked the look of a baby sleeping there.

CHAPTER 35

"***M***itsy, lass, wake up."

Baodan's lips brushed my brow and I stirred, grinning into the blanket. I sat in a chair that, earlier, I had moved next to the bed. Only the top half of my body lay on the blankets, my hand extended out toward Ellie, her precious little fingers wrapped around one of mine.

"There is a visitor in my bed." Baodan bent, wrapping his arms around me as his cheek pressed against my own, and I turned to kiss the side of his face.

"Yes. Bri needed to rest after the trip here. I told her to leave Ellie with me. Seems I needed to rest, as well."

"Aye, ye look lovely next to a bairn."

"Hmm…" I recalled my thoughts, seeing Ellie in the bed earlier. I knew I was putting the cart before the horse, as the saying went. Baodan had not even mentioned love, much less marriage, and already I was imagining his baby in our bed. "What's been decided?" I asked, trying to redirect my thoughts. Delicately pulling my finger from Ellie's grasp, I twisted in my seat and stood, wrapping my arms around his waist.

"We will leave in the morning," said Baodan. "My own men, along with the Conalls and many of their men. It should end easily, but I canna say for sure with Niall. I doona believe many at Cameron Castle will follow him should he try to stand against us, but he is cunning. He willna go without one of his games."

"What will you do with him?" I asked, the thought of him leaving again making my heart sink. I wanted nothing more than to stay with my arms wrapped around him forever.

651

"He will be killed, lass. There is no other end for him—no more chance for redemption."

"I'm sorry. It shouldn't be that way. You shouldn't be placed in that position, not with your own brother."

"No, but we all go through things we shouldna have to. Ye taught me that, lass. Ye have taught me many things."

I moved my hands to the side of his face and stretched to plant a kiss on his beautiful lips. "I don't know about that. You give me too much credit."

"No." He grabbed my face so that our positions mimicked one another. Suddenly, his eyes grew very serious. "I doona give ye enough. There is something I must tell ye, lass, something I wished to say to ye many a night ago but 'twas interrupted. The words have been on my heart since that night, and I willna be able to breathe well until I have them said."

Goosebumps covered my skin and fireflies danced in my stomach. "What?" I grinned, hoping my suspicion correct.

"I love ye. Without doubt nor hesitation, none in my life has ever captured my heart as ye have."

"You don't have to say that," I said quietly. "I know that Osla occupied a special place in your heart."

He shook his head, pressing his lips against me before speaking again. "Aye, lass. She did. But the place ye occupy is even more special. Osla was my wife and I did love her, but not like this. 'Twas only that, before ye came to me, I dinna know that love could be any stronger than the love I had before. But, Mitsy, it can. I am hopeless against ye. 'Tis not only my heart ye have captured, but my verra soul. Ye reside here," he tapped his chest, "and I intend to keep ye there forever."

Mr. Darcy himself, in the flesh, could not have beaten that speech. My eyes started watering, and my lip trembled. I must have looked ridiculous, because Baodan's expression fell.

"Have I upset ye, lass?"

"Oh, no! It's just . . . what do you expect a girl to do with words like that? I love you, too. You know that."

He smiled. "Then marry me, lass. Tonight."

An overwhelming feeling of joy filled my heart. "Yes. I want nothing more."

I expected him to kiss me. Instead, he smiled and stepped abruptly away. Directing his words toward the doorway, he called out, "Ye can come in now, lassies. She said aye."

"What?" My eyes widened. "Everybody already knows?" Grinning ear-to-ear, he nodded. "Well, that was a gamble, wasn't it?"

He laughed and shook his head. "From yer reaction, I doona think it was. I canna wait a moment longer, lass. If ye had said no, I doona know what I would have done, for all is ready except ye. I wish to be married right away."

Adelle, Bri and Blaire rushed into the room and hurried over to hug and congratulate me. As exquisitely happy as I was in that moment, a part of me wondered if his hurry also had something to do with his plans for Niall.

Did Baodan fear that he might not return from his reckoning with his brother and wanted to give me the protection of his name and clan?

The thought put me very ill at ease.

653

$\mathcal{E}$veryone gathered beside the pond. The sun set in the distance, dipping into the horizon, casting beautiful rays of light that bounced off the rippling water.

Kenna patted me, then we locked arms. "Are ye ready, dear?"

I shook my head at the sight of the tears in her eyes. "No, you can't cry! I'm already about to lose it. If you cry, I'll cry, then I expect Baodan will cry. It just won't do."

"Verra right, dear."

Kenna laughed and pulled away to sniffle and gather herself. When she returned to my side, her eyes were red but dry.

"I'm very fond of your son. I didn't think... I didn't expect to be doing this again."

Adelle started blubbering on the other side of me, and I forced myself to turn away from Kenna. "Oh, no. Not you too. Go clean yourself up."

I whirled back to Kenna. She laughed quietly. "We are a fair mess, are we not? I am verra glad that ye are fond of him. I am fond of him, as well. And of ye, dear. I doona believe there were ever two people more deserving of the other's affections."

"Thank you. I'm ready. Let's do this."

In a flash, Adelle returned to my side, fresh as a daisy.

As we started our walk toward the gathered group, I smiled, all nervousness gone.

*M*y eyes locked with Baodan's as I drew near to him. From that moment on, nothing else in the world mattered but him.

He reached for my hands, and the ceremony proceeded in a blur. I knew not what I said or how long it lasted, but I knew, for sure, my state of distraction didn't matter at all. Only something so right could be so absorbing.

His kiss at the end came suddenly, and I melted against him as everyone around us erupted into cheers.

For all my chiding of Kenna and Adelle, my own tears flowed freely as we walked down the center of the crowd as husband and wife.

Baodan bent forward and whispered in my ear, "Thank ye, lass."

"For what?"

"Ye have given me back what no man can live without. Love. And hope. Ye have given me back hope, Mitsy, and I couldna love ye more for it. I'd die before I ever lived without ye from this day forward."

"*I* think you must be part fish," I said, teasing Baodan at his suggestion that we have a bath brought up to the bedchamber.

"Part fish?" He wrapped his arms around my waist and nibbled playfully at my ear.

"Yes. It hasn't escaped my attention that you have a thing for water. Which is great, but I think I'd rather just have you take me to bed at the moment."

He worked at the laces of my dress, brushing my hair aside as he kissed the back of my neck.

"That's exquisite." I allowed my head to fall back against him as my dress fell away.

He dropped his hands, drawing circles down my bare back with his thumbs. Then, scooping me up into his arms, he carried me to the bed. "Fine, I doona care where I love ye in this moment. Whether it be in the water, or the bed, or before a crowd of onlookers."

"Eeek. Let's just keep it in the bedroom." I laughed as he threw me onto the bed and dove on top of me.

We kissed and rolled across the bed, laughing and teasing each other. But soon we grew silent, our kisses drawn out, our need for each other too raw and eager to delay any longer. We had waited for this moment, waited to be man and wife, until we were promised only to each other for the rest of our lives. In my time, many would consider it a corny, old-fashioned tradition, unnecessary, silly to wait until marriage. There was a time that I probably would've thought the same thing. But so much had changed—in my life, in me. The fact that we'd waited made this moment so much more special somehow.

Baodan claimed all of me this night, our wedding night, and I claimed him. We took advantage of every instant of our first night of wedlock, making love to one another until dawn. Each moment was a shared gift, a mutual promise. The first night of many nights to come, together as man and wife.

The next morning, Baodan left our bed early, and the carefree haze that had covered the night before evaporated in an instant. Today, the men marched toward Cameron Castle.

Now cold and anxious without him near me, I dressed and went in search of Bri. I found her in the kitchen, kneading dough with Rhona, Blaire, and the Conall's beloved kitchen maid and boss of everyone, Mary.

"Hey there. Aren't you all glowing? Somebody didn't get much sleep," she teased. Bri winked at me, and I blushed before stepping into the kitchen.

"'Tis just as it should be. No bride should sleep on her wedding night. Oh, how I wish I could go back to it, though I'm quite sure I doona remember how it all works." Mary laughed and stepped away from the perfect loaf of bread she had just finished kneading. She dipped her hands into a cool bucket of water to rinse them.

"Bri, can I talk to you for a moment?"

She smiled and stepped away to rinse, as Mary had done. She grabbed my arm as she stood next to me, concern evident on her face. "Is everything all right?"

"Yes." I just . . . there are some things I'd like to ask you.

Bri's brows drew together. "Of course. Let's go."

As soon as I walked back into my bedchamber with Bri trailing me, I spun to face her. "I know it's way too soon after my marriage to be worrying about this, but when you married Eoin, did you consider how it would be—raising a child in this time? I mean, without all the modern conveniences. And the advances in medicine . . . vaccines. And having a daughter . . . do you worry about the prejudices Ellie will face?"

Bri smiled. "It did cross my mind. It still does, from time to time. I just have to believe that everything will work out for the best. I'm with the man I love, and we were meant to be. Ellie was meant to be." She shrugged. "Besides, I can always go back to our time if I need anything, thanks to Morna."

"You mean medicines?"

"Yes. Or anything else. I guess you could say that Morna is my security blanket."

I thought about that for a moment, then said, "But Morna isn't getting any younger. She won't live forever, you know. What then?"

Bri flinched, blinked at me. "I hadn't really thought about that, but you're right. Maybe that's something we should address with her at some point." She placed her hand on my arm. "Don't worry so much. You should just be enjoying being married to the love of your life right now, right?"

I smiled. "Of course. I am. It's just . . . last night when Ellie was sleeping on our bed, I thought how much I want a family. It's something I never really thought that much about before. But I love Baodan and I want his babies. And that got me thinking about our situation—yours and mine. How we're in a position to know just how much a child is at risk in this time in comparison to our own."

"But there are advantages for children living in this time, too. There's a lot of stress on kids in the twenty-first century, Mitsy. You and I know that as well as anyone, having worked with children in our time." She hugged me. "Enjoy being in love, Mitsy. There'll be plenty of time to deal with your worries later."

I squeezed her tight. "I will. Thank you for making it possible for me to come here, Bri. If not for you, I never would've met Baodan."

"I'm glad it worked out. You two were meant for each other."

***

*A*ll the men sat at the ready, awaiting Baodan's command that they begin their journey to Cameron Castle. Eoghanan didn't know how Niall would try to evade him, but he was certain his brother would do his best to outsmart them all.

If Niall chose poison as his weapon, at least Eoghanan would now have the antidote ready. He only needed to retrieve it from his bedchamber. He went to the place where he had left it and swiftly retrieved the precious liquid.

He hurried back down the hallway, but when the vial slipped from his hands as he passed by Baodan's bedchamber, Eoghanan paused to pick it up. Bri's voice echoed inside the large room and drifted out into the hallway. She and Mitsy were talking about having babies in this time. Mitsy seemed concerned.

Suspicion arose within him; his new sister-in-law might very likely be with child. Just another reason why, now more than ever, Niall must die.

CHAPTER 38

"$\mathcal{I}$ doona wish for ye to be frightened, lass. All will be fine. I, along with all my men, shall return safely in a few brief days." Baodan squeezed my hands tightly as he bent to kiss me goodbye.

"I know. I'm not scared." He knew I lied. Thankfully, though, he didn't contradict me. If I allowed myself to voice my worry, I'd fall apart.

"There will be guards all around the castle, but I doona want any of ye lassies to step outside. Stay together when ye can. I expect no trouble here, but I need ye all to stay safe."

I nodded, hoping he would leave soon. The quicker he left, the sooner he could return. "We will. Now go." I reached up to kiss him again. "There's no point in delaying it. I love you."

"And I ye, lass."

He turned and mounted his horse. I looked for Eoghanan to bid him farewell but he was nowhere in sight. "Where's E-o?"

"Right here, lass."

He approached me from behind, and I turned to throw my arms around him. "Stay safe, please."

He patted me gently on the back, and I stilled as he whispered in my ear. "Aye, I will. Ye do the same, lass. I know about the bairn."

I pulled away and stared at him with wide eyes. "What?"

He kept his voice low. I was thankful that Baodan was too far away to hear him. "I dinna mean to, but I heard Bri as she spoke to ye."

"E-o . . . you misunderstood. I was just getting some advice from Bri, for when that time comes."

He didn't look convinced. "Aye, lass. Whatever ye say."

"No, really. Please don't put that bug in Baodan's ear. If he thought I was with child, it would upset him greatly, considering we just married yesterday."

"Why would I put a bug in my brother's ear, lass?" He shook his head and scowled. "Ye do have strange ideas."

I laughed. "It's a figure of speech. I'd explain, but . . . never mind. There's not time now. Maybe when you return."

He smiled. "I will look forward to it, Mitsy. I only wished to ask ye to take care with yerself, whether or not there's a bairn on the way."

"Thank you. I will." I glanced toward Baodan. "Bring him back safely to me, okay?"

He turned to leave but looked back at me. "Aye, I swear to ye I will. There is nothing I would not do to protect either of ye."

CHAPTER 39

*H*eavy hearts filled the grand sitting room at McMillan Castle as soon as the men left. Each of us sat in silent prayer for the men we loved to return unharmed. The numbers were in our favor. As far as we knew, no one at Cameron Castle would deny our men entry. Still, any time there was the threat of violence, there was the risk of death, as well.

Desperate to lighten the mood, I moved across the room to snatch tiny Ellie out of Bri's arms. "Come here to your Aunt Mitz. I want to squeeze those little cheeks of yours until you squeal with laughter." Squeal she did, but not from delight.

"All right, here you go. Just take a chill pill. I wasn't really going to squeeze your cheeks." Embarrassed and feeling foolish, I gave the screeching baby back to her mother while the rest of the room chuckled quietly. At least I had succeeded in breaking the eerie silence. "I'm going to be rotten at motherhood," I muttered.

"What?" The voice belonged to Adelle. "Are you going to have a baby?" she whispered, her expression filled with delight.

"No, I'm just obsessed with the thought of it, all of a sudden."

"Of course you are," she said quietly, hooking her arm through mine. "You're a young newlywed living in a time without birth control. If you're not pregnant already, chances are you will be soon."

"What?" Kenna's voice, much like Adelle's, echoed throughout the room. She rushed over to me. "Ye are with child?"

Before I could respond, she squashed me in a hug so tight I almost couldn't breathe. "No. I mean, if I am, we won't know for awhile since I'd only be a few hours along," I babbled.

I'm not sure that either woman believed me. Like me, they had babies on the brain.

"If ye are worried about what I will think if ye are, don't be, lass," said Baodan's mother.

"No, really. Please . . . I'm not sure how this rumor got started, but I don't want it getting back to Baodan." I sighed. "I was only asking Bri some questions about raising babies during this time. That's all. I mean it. Okay? When I *am* pregnant, you two will be the first to know, after Baodan. And maybe Bri. I promise."

The two women exchanged a smug smile.

"Aye, whatever ye say, dear." Kenna ran her hand up and down my arm in a motherly fashion. "I havena been this happy in a verra long time."

"Don't be." I wanted to smack myself for speaking so loosely to Bri about a topic that was not even relevant yet. "As I said, some day, but not now. Seriously."

"Oh, girly." Adelle threw one long arm around my shoulder, pressing her cheek flat against mine. "If you suspect you are, I expect it's true. Your body has a way of telling you."

"Exactly." Bri winked at me, and I could see she was enjoying this misunderstanding immensely. I scowled at her as she bounced Ellie up and down on her knee to soothe her.

Adelle directed me to sit next to her near the fire. "I know I'm not really your mother, but I consider you my daughter, as I do Blaire." She blinked back tears, taking me aback with her emotional state. "I know you don't want it out yet so you're playing dumb, but just know that I'm thrilled that I may have another grandbaby coming."

Before I could protest again, Blaire joined us, and Adelle said, "Don't you fret, Blaire. It will happen for you, too, when it's meant to."

Blaire smiled politely, but I could see doubt in her eyes. "I hope ye are right, Adelle. I'm verra afraid that all the years I spent saying I dinna want children have come back to punish me now that I do."

Adelle waved a hand in dismissal. "Oh sweetie, that's just not the way things work. Do you know how many people say they don't want children and end up with a horde? Sometimes it just takes time."

Mary, the Conalls' beloved cook and castle maid, spoke up. "Aye, and even if it doesna happen, children will find ye that are not yer own but ye love them just as much as if they were. Kip and I werena able to have children, but Eoin and Arran are no less mine than if I pushed them out of myself."

I smiled at Mary then turned to Blaire. "Have you tried to get in touch with Morna about getting pregnant? I bet she'd be happy to help if she could." Surely the thought had crossed her mind, but I wanted to bring it up in case it hadn't.

Blaire smiled genuinely and nodded, her eyes wide. "Aye, I'm sure she would help, and that is precisely why I doona wish to ask for it. I know the meddling lass too well. She would not only give me one, but three at once if it pleased her. That wouldna please me at all."

All of us who knew Morna laughed and nodded in agreement, only stopping as Rhona entered carrying a tray of food. "'Tis not verra much, lassies, but I doona expect that any of ye have much of an appetite, anyway. I dinna see the need to go to much of a fuss without the men here. Too much of the food would go to waste."

"Thank you. Where are all the other girls?" Despite the lifted morale that talk of babies had generated, a shiver of warning swept down the back of my neck, and I suddenly felt very uneasy.

"They are all sleeping together in my own cottage on the castle grounds. They should be locked up safely for the evening. I wouldna allow them to go far from me while the lads are away."

"Good." I nodded at her. "And you will stay here with us."

"If 'tis what ye wish, I shall." She placed the tray of food in the center of the room. It didn't take long before Adelle dug in, and shortly after the rest of us followed her lead.

I had thought I was hungry, but my appetite died as a sense of unease grew within me. I sat back, casting my attention to the darkest corners of the room where Nairne sat. It was the first time I had noticed her this evening.

She was alone and silent, and it occurred to me that she must be grief-stricken over the loss of her son. Still, her quiet isolation was unsettling. She sat slightly away from the rest of the group, surrounded by shadows, the fire barely casting any light on her.

I stood. Something deep within me warned that I should stay away, but I couldn't allow her to feel excluded. The other women continued to chat; I didn't think they even noticed I'd left the group.

"Nairne," I said quietly, as I drew near enough for her to hear me. I felt the blood drain from my face as I looked into her eyes. They were open, but cold, unseeing. Nairne was dead.

CHAPTER 40

At The Edge of McMillan Territory

Baodan's heart beat painfully in his chest. There was no choice but to go forward, to find his brother and end him before he could harm another person. Yet, something wasn't right; he felt it in the air around him. Each step that took him and his men further away from McMillan Castle made Baodan more certain.

"Halt!" He screamed the word, yanking hard on his horse's reins.

"Baodan, what are ye doing?" yelled Eoghanan. "We doona need to be away any longer than we must. Let us ride and end all of this."

Mitsy's heart thumped loudly in his ears. Nothing else around him, not his brother's voice, nor the sound of the horses protesting their sudden stop could overwhelm the sound of it. He yearned for her presence whenever away from her, but only in his dreams did he sense her presence so completely. Until now. She was frightened and in danger. He could sense it.

"Something is not right. I should have left ye with them. It wasna right of us to leave them alone."

Eoghanan put a hand up to hush the men behind him. "We dinna leave them alone. There are many guards in place outside the castle."

"Aye, but Niall knows the castle too well. He could get inside if he wished." If only the beating in his ears would cease. Each thump drove him further into panic.

"Do ye think it possible?" asked Eoghanan. "Do ye have reason to believe that he is no longer at Cameron Castle?"

"I doona know, but there is trouble at home. I canna tell ye how I know, but I do. As surely as I know my own name, I know it."

"What do ye want me to do? Just tell me. I'll do it."

A scream in the distance ahead of them prevented Baodan from answering his brother's question. A rider approached quickly, a woman—Griogair's widow.

"Baodan!" She screamed his name through the trees. The panic in her voice only heightened his fear.

Baodan sent a pleading look toward his brother. "Go! Ride back home. For God's sake keep her safe. I canna lose her, Eoghanan. I'll follow ye shortly."

Eoghanan turned and nudged his horse, galloping away. By the time Baodan could no longer see him, Wynda was by his side.

"Did ye ride here alone?" he asked the woman, who was clearly distressed. "Ye shouldna have done so."

"Aye, I verra well should have. Doona move any further toward Cameron Castle. Niall isna there. None would join him to stand against ye, and he fled four days ago."

"Four days?" Baodan's ears rang with shock. He gripped tight on the reins to hold himself upright. It took only three days to reach Cameron Castle.

"Aye, and he headed this way. I left as soon as I could, but he is a faster rider than I."

Baodan turned to his cousins, both standing behind him, ready for his orders. "Eoin, Arran, we must return to McMillan Castle at once. I shall ride ahead. See to Wynda's safety."

His entire world lay inside the walls of his castle. To think that Niall stood within reach of Mitsy filled him with enough rage to blind him. He wished to kill his monster of a brother. And kill him he would.

*M*cMillan Castle

"*N*airne. Nairne." I tried to say her name, but it came out as a breathless scratch—the very embodiment of nightmares when the dreamer tries to scream and cannot. "Nairne!" Finally her name found its way past my trembling lips. When not a muscle within her twitched, I knew that it was true. She was dead, and no amount of calling her name would wake her.

Everyone behind me still chatted busily, nibbling away at the small meal. Slowly I moved to grip Nairne's arm. Warm to the touch. She'd not been dead long. At first glance, I thought perhaps her heart had failed or a stroke had killed her, but across her brown dress spread a patch of red, seeping its way through the thick fabric as it crawled across her torso.

Shaking, I took a step backward, scrambling to get away from her as I noticed the point of a blade protruding through her stomach.

A deep laugh started from the shadows behind the chair. I staggered backward again and fell as everyone in the room grew silent and Niall emerged from behind Nairne's lifeless body.

CHAPTER 41

o one screamed as Niall stepped from behind the chair, all of us too frozen with fear to move. Normally smooth and cocky in appearance, he looked utterly mad with his curly dark hair sticking up in every direction, and his sick smile spread wide.

Every tooth in his head showed as he cackled uncontrollably. Slowly, I reined in my terror. Fear would hinder me. I'd stopped him once before. I would do it again.

The room was filled with intelligent, spitfire women, and we outnumbered him easily. He was stupid to approach us while we were grouped together.

"Ach, ye are a fool, Niall. Ye have no place here, and if ye so much as touch one red hair on Mitsy's head, I shall charge ye and sit on yer head until it bursts."

I glanced back at Mary in utter shock. Brunette or not, that old broad was a redhead at heart. She gave me a run for my money in the sass department.

"Hush, Mary." Bri reached to latch on to the old woman's hand, warning in her voice.

Niall laughed even more loudly before thrusting his sword out into the air in Mary's direction. "Ye best shut yer mouth, or I shall run this through it. I mean none of ye any harm. My business is with this one."

He jerked his head toward me, and I pushed myself up off the floor.

"No harm?" Kenna sobbed. "Son, ye killed her. Yer own aunt, and ye laugh at the sight of it. Have ye not caused enough pain? 'Tis over, ye have to know that." Her entire body shook at the shock of her murderous child.

671

Niall trained his gaze on the woman who brought him into this world. "Ach, Mother. Ye are verra right, there has been much pain caused by me, but doona worry, I'm nearly done. I know that I am not long for this world. My brothers will end me, but before they do, I shall tear one more lass from Baodan's grasp. If ye doona wish to join her in death, then ye willna speak to me again."

She said nothing for the moment, and I took the opportunity to step into his line of sight. "Niall, she's not going to say anything else. It's just you and me, okay? I guess you're pretty angry about what I did to you, aren't you?"

Nothing in me accepted that he would hurt me. I simply wouldn't allow it. A sword was propped against the fireplace across the room. If I could distract Niall, I hoped to signal to Adelle, who sat closest to the weapon. One of us needed access to it, and she seemed the logical choice.

"Aye, lass, I am verra angry indeed, and 'tis reason enough for me to kill ye, but 'tis not why I will take great pleasure from doing so."

"No? Then why?" Too riled up, Niall didn't notice the footsteps that approached the doorway, and I swallowed a sigh of relief at Eoghanan's shadow in the doorway.

His finger moved across his lips, signaling for me not to reveal his presence.

"Why?" Niall snorted a humorless laugh. "Because Baodan has taken a fancy to ye, and it wouldna please me to allow him any happiness."

I shook my head. "Has Baodan wronged you in some way? I thought it was you who hurt him."

He threw his head back, scoffing at the question.

I put one hand behind my back and thrust my fingers in the direction of the sword. I had no way of knowing whether my gesture would be noticed. With Eoghanan in the doorway, I hoped it wouldn't be necessary, but couldn't take that chance.

"Has Baodan wronged me?" Niall roared. "He has, though I doona believe he would ever see it that way. I didn't kill Osla, her love for Baodan did."

I tilted my head, studying him. "Hmm…how do you figure?"

"If she dinna love him, then she would have kept our little secret, but she insisted that we tell him. At the time, I couldna allow it. So, ye see, she gave me no choice. The fault in that lies with Baodan."

Disgusted with his twisted reasoning, I said, "Are you listening to yourself? What you're saying doesn't make sense." What was E-o waiting for? I didn't think I could delay Niall much longer.

"Enough!" Niall moved forward quickly, stopping when the point of his sword pressed into the center of my chest. "Eoghanan, I know ye are here," he said over his shoulder. "I am not the fool that ye all seem to think. Come out, or I shall run her through."

Eoghanan stepped quickly from the shadows, his face white with worry, his jaw clenched tight. "Niall, if ye hurt her, I swear I shall kill ye."

"Ye will do so anyway, but I will not kill her right away. I will wait until Baodan arrives. I would verra much like for him to watch her die."

His eyes glinted with madness. "And now so must you."

With the end of his sword pressed against me, I did as he bid, stepping into him. He dropped his sword as he wrapped one arm around my waist and withdrew a dirk tucked away inside his kilt. He pressed it into the flesh of my neck, pushing hard enough to draw blood.

I was rash and stupid to have assumed that he would be unable to hurt me. He did a fine job of it now. I couldn't die here, not like this, not in the first place to ever feel like home to me. Not when I'd finally found Baodan, the love of my life. We had years ahead of us together, children to bring into the world. This could not be my end.

Sobs threatened to overtake me, but I knew if they did, Niall would only push the blade deeper into my skin. So I bit my lip to keep from crying out. I would not give him the pleasure of thinking he'd broken me.

Sound suddenly filled the hallway outside of the room, and Baodan charged in, followed by Eoin, Arran, and Hew. In that instant, I saw my own death, the pressure of the knife against my neck such that I truly believed Niall would draw it across my throat at that moment. I was certain he was about to do just that when Baodan's voice stopped him.

"'Tis not Mitsy ye wish to see dead, brother. Doona take yer hatred of me out on another. No one else need die when 'tis truly me that ye wish to see dead. Release her and ye may run yer sword through me. I willna stop ye."

"No, Baodan, please." The words sent the knife deeper into my neck, but I couldn't remain silent. I couldn't allow him to die for me.

For the first time since entering the room, he looked me in the eyes. The pain and sorrow there sent tears streaming down my face. "Mitsy, lass, I canna lose ye. If I wasna to die now and ye were killed, 'twould not be long before I would follow ye to the grave. The grief of losing ye would kill me."

How could he not see that Niall would kill me anyway? As soon as Baodan was dead, Niall would turn his sword on me. An oath meant nothing to him. "No." My word was only a whisper.

"But ye are stronger than me, lass. Ye have a spirit that canna be starved. Use the rock to return to yer home once I am gone and live a life filled with all the things ye wish for."

Niall said nothing throughout Baodan's speech, only kept his gaze on his brother, his stare dark and unreadable.

Baodan shifted his gaze to Niall. "Let her go, brother. To kill her will serve no purpose. With me gone, McMillan territory will be yers."

Niall's grip on my throat lessened. The idea appealed to him. Too lost in the thralls of his madness, he couldn't see the impossibility of Baodan's words. Niall remained surrounded at every side. Regardless of who died here—me, Baodan, or both of us—Niall would meet his end. Not a soul in the room planned on allowing him to live past sunrise. Baodan knew this, too. Which meant he played his brother. He didn't intend to let Niall kill either one of us.

I startled at the sound of Niall's voice in my ears, and he laughed at my show of nerves. "I will accept yer offer, brother, but I willna run ye through with my sword. If I tried to approach ye, I would be bested, and I will see ye dead." He squeezed the arm around my waist to get my attention and whispered angrily in my ear. "Reach behind ye, lass, and grab the vial tucked beneath the edge of my kilt. Toss it in Baodan's direction."

Poison. My hand trembled as I moved it. I reached for Baodan's death, for I knew he would drink it to save me. As much as I wished to crush the vial in my hand, I knew it would result in my immediate death. "Promise me, you'll let me go as soon as he drinks it. Allow me the chance to say goodbye."

"Fine. Throw it to him now."

Baodan caught it with ease, despite my shaky throw. He didn't wish to think about it, and he smiled as he popped the top. "I love ye more than ye will ever know, lass."

I sobbed as he downed the contents, screaming as he dropped to the floor. I no longer cared about the knife at my throat. Raising my arm, I threw my elbow deep into Niall's ribs and, as the knife fell away, I rushed to Baodan's side.

---

*H*is body shook in convulsions, and his eyes rolled up into his head as I sobbed against him. When he stilled in my arms, Niall laughed ecstatically. Rage exploded within me. I grasped onto the sword that lay to my right and stood to charge him.

He moved quickly when he saw me. Before I could stand, I saw the edge of his sword swinging down upon me. Right before I shut my eyes to await death, I saw a flash of movement out of the corner of my eye.

Screams of agony almost shook the room. In one swoop, Eoghanan fell to the ground in front of me, his body split open from temple to thigh. As he landed, a small glass bottle dropped from his hand and onto the floor, following the trail of his blood.

CHAPTER 43

*I*n the instant Eoghanan hit the ground, I was given the time necessary to stand. I ran toward Niall, thrusting the sword into the center of his chest. The impact of the metal against his ribs reverberated all the way to my bones, and the pain of it forced me to release my grasp on the sword's handle. The jab brought Niall to his knees as he stared down at his bleeding center.

"The vial!" I screamed. "The one Eoghanan dropped. Somebody give it to Baodan now." I couldn't be certain, but unless Eoghanan still carried the poison he stole from Niall, the liquid could be the antidote he had told me about.

Kenna jumped to grab the vial, and I turned my attention to Eoghanan who gasped uncomfortably as blood poured out of him. Mary and Rhona rushed to get bandages. I crouched next to my brother-in-law, gathering his uninjured hand into my own. "Oh, Eoghanan. Why did you do that? It was so stupid. So very, very stupid." The words came between gasps. I could scarcely see him through my tears. He lived, but the light in his eyes dwindled as he continued to bleed.

He moved his hand from my grasp to touch my face. "I told ye I would do anything for either ye or Baodan."

Blood trickled into his mouth, and he coughed as it prohibited his breathing. My hands trembled uncontrollably, but I reached up to clean his mouth, forcing myself to examine the extensiveness of his wounds for the first time.

His head wounds didn't seem deep enough to cause damage. But the gash that extended down his body worried me greatly. Although I was no doctor, I

679

was fairly certain that the blade had missed any vital organs. Still, I could see little hope of survival. His wounds could be closed, but infection would most likely set in. In an area that large, it would kill him quickly. Eoghanan's eyes drifted closed as he lost consciousness. For a brief moment, I tore my gaze away from him and looked up at the dying Niall.

Now collapsed onto his back, he choked on his own blood. My aim was poor enough so that his death was a slow one, and I was glad for it. He lay dying in a room full of people, and not a one paid him any attention. Not even his own mother, who had dropped to her knees on Eoghanan's opposite side.

Mary stepped in front of my line of vision. She called out to Eoin and Arran, instructing them to help her lift Eoghanan. "We will need to wrap the cloth around his whole body. No one will be able to close him up until we have stopped the bleeding," she said.

"Do you know what you're doing?" I asked shakily. Not that it mattered. Mary was doing her best to help, and that's all any of us could do.

"No, lass," she answered. "No one here is a healer. I could be doing him more harm than good for all I know, but 'tis all I can think to do."

I nodded, standing from my crouched position next to Eoghanan. "I know." I turned, unable to bear the thought of the lifeless Baodan who I knew lay behind me.

Instead, Baodan tried to sit up, extending his arm out to me as I ran to him.

"Oh, God. It worked!" I grabbed either side of his face, smothering him in kisses until he reached his hand up to pull me away. "Slow down, lass, I am not leaving ye now. There will be time for that later. Did ye kill him?"

I glanced toward Niall. He no longer moved. As Bri nodded in answer to Baodan's question, I knew. "Yes. He's dead."

"Good. That's my sweet, fiery lass."

The pain of moving roused Eoghanan into consciousness, and his moans caused Baodan to leap to his feet in alarm. "What happened to him?"

"After you fell, Niall ran toward me. Eoghanan jumped in front of him."

"He has saved us both, lass."

"I know." My voice broke again, and Baodan wrapped his arms around me.

"Will he live?" He directed his question to no one in particular, and none knew the answer. I didn't see how Eoghanan could survive his wounds, not with the extent of them. We had nothing to provide protection against infection.

Something hard thumped against my thigh. I glanced up at Baodan, thinking he wished to get my attention. "What was that?"

"What was what?"

"Did you touch me?" I reached down to the spot where I'd felt the touch and gasped at the object within my grasp.

"Are ye injured, lass?"

Wrapping my hand around the object, I pulled out the black stone and held it up for Baodan to see. "The rock. Get something for E-o to float on. We need to send him to Morna."

"Hey. E-o. Can you open your eyes for me? I know you want to sleep, but it's important that you look at me, okay?" My hand lay on his forehead, and I traced the top of his brow with my thumb. Slowly, his eyelids flickered open.

"That is not my name, lass."

I smiled, my faith that he would be fine stronger than ever. Life remained in him, and Morna would heal him. "I know, but…"

He interrupted me before I could say more. "I know. I told ye I would teach ye how to say it when I needed a smile. I am verra much in need of a smile now."

He needed to be on his way, but I couldn't bring myself to deny him. I figured a lifted spirit would heal better than a sad one. "Okay. Teach me."

"Say 'ayo,' then 'wun,' and 'en.'" I tried to repeat him. I thought it sounded pretty good until the left side of his face pulled up into an amused smile. "I knew 'twould make me smile. Wretched job, lass."

"Yeah, well, I'll work on it while you're away."

He blinked his eye to symbolize a nod. "Aye, do. Just where is it that I am going?"

How could I explain time travel to him when I knew how impossible it was to believe until a person had experienced it? "Do you trust me?" I asked, instead.

"Aye. If Baodan does, so do I. I am proud to call ye sister."

"Good. I always wanted a little brother." I winked. He was older than me. Centuries older. "I'm going to leave it to the person I'm sending you to to explain everything. Just know that you'll be taken care of, and you'll be better in no time."

"Then let me be gone, for I doona feel so well at the moment."

"Ok." I bent and kissed him gently on the forehead. "But I think Baodan wants to say something to you first."

Baodan stepped in front of me, taking Eoghanan by the hand. "Blood or not, ye are more a brother to me than Niall ever was. I'm sorry that I went so long not treating ye as such. I hope that when ye return, things will be as they once were. My love will be with ye every moment ye are away."

"And mine with ye."

We stepped back, and Eoin and Arran placed the makeshift raft atop the water, then the stone on Eoghanan's stomach. He drifted gently into the center of the pond and vanished.

The sun rose as Baodan and I entered our bedchamber, but it did not stop us from crawling into bed. Despite the weariness of our bones and the heavy weight of our hearts, a clear feeling of relief spread throughout the castle. Tomorrow was sure to be a better day.

"Is yer neck badly hurt, lass?"

I felt nothing. Compared to Eoghanan's wounds, I had only suffered a scratch. "Not at all." I snuggled into the crook of my husband's arm, reaching for his hand as I smiled up at him. "I don't know if this is the right time, but..."

"What is it, lass? I canna bear any more bad news."

"It's not bad." I pushed his fingers open and placed the palm of his hand against my stomach. "I want us to make a baby right away," I said softly. "Let's not waste any time, okay? I know you're exhausted, but could we get started?"

A slow grin spread wide across his face. "Ye will be the death of me, wife. But it will be a most pleasant way to go."

I smacked him lightly on the chest. "You can't die. I don't plan on raising our child alone."

He laughed, but said nothing, and I thought that I'd rendered him mute with my request. He was cute when speechless.

"You do know how babies are made, right? We'll have to make whoopee again and again until it takes."

"Ah, another one of yer strange words. Aye, I know how to make a bairn, lass. 'Tis only, I'm so happy I doona know what to say."

"Say you think it's a good idea. A great one. Say you want us to have a baby, too." I lifted my face so that my lips touched his.

"Aye," he said quietly. "I want nothing more."

We found solace in each other's arms. As the sun beat down outside, we spent the day wrapped up in one another, our hearts brimming with the happiness that comes from safely holding the one you love most in the world.

685

EPILOGUE

hree Months Later

"*A* man left this for ye in the village."
The messenger gave me a letter, bewilderment etched on his brow. The envelope was entirely modern, from the twenty-first century as opposed to the seventeenth. "Who left it?" Surely, Morna hadn't traveled back herself.

"I doona know. No one seemed to remember, but the man who gave it to me said that it must reach ye at once."

"I see. Thank you." My hands fidgeted on the seal until the man retreated. Then I ripped it open.

I took in the words quickly, then ran to find Baodan to give him the long-awaited news of his brother. I moved so fast that I passed him in the grand entryway, only stopping at the sound of his voice.

"Mitsy, slow down before ye fall and break yer neck. Ye are not graceful enough to run in a dress. Doona dizzy the wee bairn ye are carrying, please."

We had confirmed my pregnancy a few weeks after we sent E-o to Morna. In fact, I felt certain I had conceived on that very day that we put him in the pond with the rock on his belly.

"Look! I told you E-o would be fine, although Morna says his scars will remain. In my book, that's a small price to pay for his life. She hopes that he will be well enough to return home by the time the baby is born and –"

Baodan's eyes widened, stopping me short. As he read Morna's words, he said aloud what I'd been about to say. "She doesn't seem to think he'll be returning home alone."

*C*ontinue reading for a Sneak Peek of ***Morna's Accomplice***.

CHAPTER 1

Mitchell Family Estate – Lake Placid, New York—Present Day

"Pssst…"

Believing he'd heard something, but not sure enough to fully turn his head toward the sound, the corner of Cooper's right brow lifted slightly.

I grinned, making sure not to stick my head out too far past the archway. I didn't want anyone sitting in the outdoor aisles to see me. "Pssst…" I said it once more, waiting for the child to turn his head in my direction so I could wave him toward me.

His bow tie hung crooked and his dirty blonde hair, which I'd gelled down only hours before, now stuck up in every direction, unruly curls descending over his face. He turned his head slowly, deep green eyes widening at the sight of me before the fading sun hit him square on the nose, spreading a soft light across the dash of freckles across his face. He squinted, trying to make me out properly. His little legs fidgeted as he restrained from stepping away from his assigned spot.

Cooper's mouth opened and then closed as I silently waved a finger in front of my lips, pleading with him to stay quiet. Turning the inside of my finger toward me, I extended it out so that I could gesture for him to join me.

It took only a brief moment before his feet found their freedom, and he ran toward me so quickly that I hardly had time to open my arms to him before he sailed into me. I smiled into his collar as he spoke.

"I thought maybe you were Dad!" he said in what I could only assume was his full-hearted effort at a whisper, although it truly ended up sounding more like a breathy squeal. "He bet me five dollars I couldn't stand still until the end of the ceremony, and I been just waitin' for him to try to make me lose."

"That does sound just like him, doesn't it? He's actually waiting for us in the car. How about the three of us get out of here?" I swung him onto my hip, not the least bit worried about smashing any of the lacy mess that covered me head to toe.

"What?" He made no effort to whisper this time.

I quickly took off in the direction of the car before we were noticed. It wouldn't do for anyone to see that the bride and groom, along with their son, were about to bail away from their own wedding. I wanted to be off of the estate property before word got out.

"Shh..." I said nothing else, moving toward our favorite spot by the water. Thankfully, it also happened to be far enough away from the wedding crowd that no one would hear or find us there.

"Are we going to the swing?" Cooper managed a real whisper this time, and the sweetness of it made me lean in to kiss him hard on his cheek. Still young enough not to have total disdain for his mother's affections, he smiled and laid his head against my shoulder.

"Yes, we are. I want to talk to you a minute. Just you and me, before we go join your dad. How'd you know I was taking you to the swing?"

"Don't you member that we always go there when we need *you and me* time at Grandfather's?"

"Of course, I remember. We've just really never discussed it, so I'm surprised you picked up on it."

"Yep. I did."

"I can see that. You're very smart for a four year old." And he was—exceedingly so. If it wasn't for Cooper's small size, most would guess him to be a good two years older.

"Yep, but I'm really four and seven months. That's almost five."

"My, and you're quite sure of yourself, too. That trait comes from your father."

"Yep."

By now, we'd reached what, in my opinion, was the most beautiful part of my parents' grand estate on Lake Placid. Nestled under a wide, broad-leafed tree that stood out among the many pine and spruce trees scattered throughout, hung a large white swing. It was built so that it hung perfectly from one of the tree's largest branches. Large cushions enveloped the floating chair. I collapsed into it, still holding Cooper as we fell back into the softness together.

I tugged playfully on one of his loose curls so he'd look at me. "All right. Enough with the 'yeps.'" He giggled sheepishly at his orneriness. "I want to talk to you about something serious for a minute."

He scooted away from my arm so he could regard me fully and, with all the determination he could muster, pulled the expression on his face into one of sheer seriousness. "I'm ready."

He regarded me sternly so I would get on with whatever it was I wished to discuss with him.

"Ok. What did you think about all of this today?"

His eyebrows scrunched together as if he were thinking very hard about how he should answer. I reached out to squeeze his hand, reassuring him that he could say whatever he wished. "I...I think it's weird."

"How do you mean, Coop? What was weird about it?"

"Well, I know I'm only little, but I been thinkin' about this real hard."

I smiled, no doubt he had done just that. "I'm sure you have."

He glanced up at me beneath thick brown lashes, twirling his little fingers in nervous swirls before continuing. "And...I know that Grandfather thinks that moms and dads should be married, but I like things the way they are now. I heard something..."

He hesitated, gauging my reaction. He had a penchant for eavesdropping, and I could tell he worried I'd get onto him for doing it again. "It's all right. What did you hear?'

"Last night, I heard Grams talking to Aunt Jane and Aunt Lily, and I didn't hear everything, but she said it was wrong of Grandfather to push you into this, Mom. That you and Dad liked each other too much to get married."

It sounded just like my mother. I only wished she'd said it to me and not my sisters. Perhaps I would've decided to call this thing off before the day of the actual wedding. "And what do you think about that?"

Cooper shrugged a little. "I think she's right, Mama. All Grams and Grandfather do is fight, and they're married. So do Aunt Lily and Uncle Jim. I don't want you and Pops to start fighting."

"Pops?" I laughed at the oddity of it. He'd never called Jeffrey 'Pops' once in his life.

"I heard Dad calling Bebop that and I liked it. Thought I would try it out."

"I see." I grinned, messing with his hair. "Well, I agree with you and so does 'Pops.' Your father and I can't get married. It wouldn't be fair of us to do that to this family. But that's why I wanted to talk to you; we *are* still a family. No matter whether me and your dad are married, the three of us are a family. Do you understand that?"

"Yes, Mom." He sighed, clearly believing I had no reason to doubt his understanding. Honestly, I really didn't.

"And one more thing before we join your father. I don't want you to think that because you're little that I think less of what you think. If anything, I value what you think more than anyone else because you are little."

That...and I was slightly afraid he was already smarter than me. But I certainly wasn't going to say something like that to my son. I very much wanted him to think I was the smartest person on Earth for at least another decade.

"Ok, Mom. Can we go find Dad now?"

"Absolutely. Let's get out of here." Lifting Cooper out of the swing, I wrestled with the globs of white lace that gathered around me until I once again stood on two feet. Grabbing his hand, I peeked around the tree to make sure the coast was clear, and we took off, running toward the front of the house where his father waited with our escape vehicle.

"Are we going back to the City?" Cooper's words came out choppy, bouncing with every step of his short stride.

"For a minute we are, but I'll do even better. What's the one place you've always wanted to go?"

In that instant, his little feet stopped moving completely, and I nearly took a tumble with the jolt of his sudden stop.

"No! A plane? Oh Mama, am I *finally* gonna get to go on a plane?"

I laughed. He was four, nearly five truthfully, but still, how long could he really have been waiting? "Yes, you are. You're going to go on a job with me."

We neared the vehicle. Jeffrey must've seen us, for he'd started the car and was awaiting our approach.

"Where are we goin'?"

"Scotland."

"Why?"

"I'll tell you in the car."

"Do you mind taking off your jacket so I can drape it over Coop?" I asked Jeffrey. "He's asleep. Can you hear him snoring?"

"Sweet sound, isn't it?" Jeffrey held his arm out to me so that I would pull on his sleeve while he shrugged out of the tux jacket. Once free of it, I twisted so I could reach into the backseat and drape it over our sleeping son.

"He's the sweetest."

Once I faced the front of the car again, Jeffrey reached over to squeeze my shoulder. "We're getting close. Do you want to call the office to see if he's even there? It's pretty late."

I shook my head, confident that nothing much had changed in Mr. Perdie's routine since I took off work three days before for our wedding. "No, he'll be there. He works so much he wouldn't even come to the wedding, not that there was a wedding to come to, but you know what I mean."

"All right. Are you going to wear that?" He glanced at me, keeping one eye on the road.

"What are you saying? Do you think it's too much?" I laughed, but quickly silenced myself so I wouldn't wake Cooper. "Don't worry. He'll be the only one in the office at this hour, and he'll be so buried up to his elbows in work of some kind that I doubt he'll even take notice of the fact that I'm in a wedding gown. So yes, I am going to wear this. I need to talk to him before we do anything else to make sure it's all right that I start the job early."

For the first time since all of the wedding madness began a few days earlier, I thought about the new job. Mr. Perdie had come into my office literally an hour before I was due to take off for the next two weeks for my wedding.

Apparently, an anonymous Scottish landowner had called Perdie, willing to donate a large sum of money to the magazine under the condition that we would do a lengthy piece on Scotland in an upcoming issue.

The call must have come as quite a shock to my boss. Not only did our readership seem to decline daily but, unbeknownst to the anonymous donor (or perhaps he knew quite well), our small travel magazine neared the brink of death. Only five more issues were guaranteed. The caller's donation would ensure that we could all keep our jobs for at least another five years.

Even more stunning, and the fact that had caused me to spill my sacred cup of coffee, was that the donor requested that *I* do the article. All of it. Writing. Photography. He specifically wanted me to author the piece.

I always worked hard, but being one of the newest photographers at the magazine, I'd never been given an assignment of significant value. I was usually allocated articles like *How To Pack Everything You Need For 10 Days In A Carry-On* and *Best Airport Restaurants*. As of yet, my only photography work had been photos of the inside of a suitcase and airport. Why the man would request that I do the article was beyond me.

After I'd overcome my initial shock, Perdie and I scheduled my trip for right after my honeymoon. But seeing as that would no longer happen, I saw no reason to wait another second. I imagined Mr. Perdie would feel the same, especially since receiving the donor's money was contingent upon my flight information being sent to him directly after its booking.

"Hey...where'd you go?" Jeffrey pulled into the parking garage below my office building and grasped my hand lightly to pull me from my reflective trance. "We're here."

"Sorry, I was just thinking about all of this. Crazy, isn't it?"

The corner of Jeffrey's brow pulled up quizzically, much like Cooper's had done earlier. They were so much alike in behavior and outward appearance that even I often had a hard time believing that they weren't actually biologically related.

"Which part, Grace? The 'you and me' bit, or this work stuff?"

I shrugged a bit, unbuckling and facing him as he slid into a parking spot and stopped the car. "All of it. Everything that seems to be going on." I reached out to grab both his hands. "I'm so sorry, Jeffrey. I can't express to you." I suddenly found myself quite choked up. "What it means...what it means that you've allowed me to pull you into all of this. And I don't just mean now. Always. Our whole lives it seems like I've been dragging you into one mess or another."

He frowned, pulling his hands free so that he could cup both sides of my face. "You dragged me into nothing, Grace. Ever. Your father did, when it came to law school and then joining his practice, but you never did. You're my best friend, and I consider you my closest family. There is nothing in this world that I wouldn't do for you."

"Clearly." I smiled into his palms thinking of the attire we were both wearing now. No matter how platonic our love for one another, he'd been willing to marry me at my father's request. "I love you, too. And gosh—Coop and I, we just couldn't do without you. Are you sure you're fine with me taking him along on the trip?"

Jeffrey released my face and glanced lovingly into the backseat of the car. "Absolutely. I'd come too, but I have one last case I have to finish before I rid myself of your father's firm. Coop will love every minute of it and, since we're going to delay his entry into kindergarten for a year, I have no problem with it."

"Good. Well, I guess I better go talk to my boss. Shouldn't take me long. Be back shortly."

It took me a good minute and a half to swing my feet out of the vehicle and gather the train and fabric that surrounded my legs and ankles. I moved rather self-consciously through the parking garage, although I went unseen. While I had no qualms about Mr. Perdie seeing me in my wedding regalia, I didn't really want anyone else wondering who the nut was roaming around in a gown.

I found my boss in his office, as expected. His glasses sat a bit crooked, and he had a mustard stain on his tie. Looking at him, I worried that he hadn't changed his clothes in the last three days. He was a kind enough man, but just glancing around his office caused a slight rise in my blood pressure. With organizational skills such as his, it was no wonder that the magazine struggled. I couldn't help wondering how many important things fell through the cracks in the black hole of Perdie's office.

"Mr. Perdie?"

He jerked up from his desk so quickly his chair flipped backward onto the floor. "Grace! What in the bletherin' hell are you doing here? I mean, is everything all right? Of course, it mustn't be. You're still in your wedding dress."

He moved toward me quickly, and I instinctively reached out to grasp his hand in reassurance. "Yes, everything's fine. We just called it off, is all. Just drove in from—"

"What do you mean, everything's fine?" the small man asked shrilly, interrupting me. "Didn't you just say you called it off? That's rarely a good thing."

I was utterly shocked to see such concern from him, and it made me believe that perhaps I'd judged him wrongly for many years. "Yes, I promise. Everything is great. We just . . . we couldn't go through with it. Jeffrey and Cooper are waiting in the car, so it was really no tragedy or anything."

He patted my hand in a grandfatherly manner, although still a good many years off from being old enough to be anyone's grandfather. "That's good, Grace. Honestly, I've never really seen it between the two of you. It shocked me when you announced you were to be married."

I squeezed his hand in return, a sudden sensation of closeness growing between me and my quirky boss that I'd never felt before. "Well, Mr. Perdie, I must say I'm rather surprised by you. I never knew you to be so perceptive."

"Ms. Mitchell, perhaps it is you who lacks perception. I can assure you it's not a new quality I have developed. I know most of the time it appears that I can hardly keep my head screwed on, but I do notice almost everything."

I smiled and nodded before continuing on with the reason for my late night office visit. "I'd like to take on the Scotland job now and leave tomorrow, if that's all right. And..." I hesitated. It didn't truly matter whether or not he objected, but I still hoped he would have no problem with Cooper coming along for the trip. "Cooper is coming with me. I hope that won't be a problem."

"Of course you may start right away. As long as you complete the article and do a wonderful job of it, I have no problem with you bringing your son along. I believe we will have more than enough from our benefactor to pay for his flight, as well. I will book the flight for you both right away and will forward you the details when complete. Pack your bags, dear."

I nodded. "Thanks, Mr. Perdie."

As he turned toward his desk, I started to take my leave, but not before I heard his voice, laced with anxiety, follow me down the corridor. "And for the love of all things holy, Grace, do not screw this up. We'll be without our jobs by Christmas without this money."

Continue the story with:

Morna's Accomplice

USA TODAY BESTSELLING AUTHOR
BETHANY CLAIRE
A Sweet, Scottish,
Time-Travel Romance
MORNA'S
ACCOMPLICE
The Magical
Matchmaker's Legacy

BOOKS IN THE MAGICAL MATCHMAKER'S LEGACY

Morna's Spell

Morna's Secret

The Conalls' Magical Yuletide—A Novella

Morna's Magic

Morna's Accomplice

Jeffrey's Only Wish—A Novella

Morna's Rogue

Morna's Ghost

Morna's Vow

The McMillans' Magical Yuletide—A Novella

Morna's Turn

Love Beyond Time
Love Beyond Reason
A Conall Christmas - A Novella
Love Beyond Hope
Love Beyond Measure
In Due Time – A Novella
Love Beyond Compare
Love Beyond Dreams
Love Beyond Belief
A McMillan Christmas - A Novella
Love Beyond Reach
Morna's Magic & Mistletoe - A Novella
Love Beyond Words
Love Beyond Wanting
Love Beyond Destiny

And More To Follow...

LETTER TO READERS

Dear Reader,

I hope you enjoyed this box set. Continue the series with *Morna's Accomplice* where you will find out what happens to Eoghanan, and you will meet one of my favorite characters, Cooper.

As an author, I love feedback from readers. You are the reason that I write, and I love hearing from you. If you would like to connect, there are several ways you can do so. You can reach out to me on Facebook or on Twitter or visit my Pinterest boards. If you want to read excerpts from my books, listen to audiobook samples, learn more about me, and find some cool downloadable files related to the books, visit my website.

The best way to stay in touch is to subscribe to my newsletter. Go to my website (www.bethanyclaire.com) and click the Mailing List link in the header. If you don't hear from me regularly, please check your spam folder or junk mail to make sure my messages aren't ending up there. Please set up your email to allow my messages through to you so you never miss a new book, a chance to win great prizes or a possible appearance in your area.

Finally, if you enjoyed this book, I would appreciate it so much if you would recommend it to your friends and family. And if you would please take time to review it on Goodreads and/or your favorite retailer site, it would be a great help. Reviews can be tough to come by these days, and you, the reader, have the power to make or break a book.

Thank you so much for reading my books. I hope you choose to journey with me through the other books in the series.

All my best,
    Bethany

ABOUT THE AUTHOR

BETHANY CLAIRE is a USA Today bestselling author of swoon-worthy, Scottish romance and time travel novels. Bethany loves to immerse her readers in worlds filled with lush landscapes, hunky Scots, lots of magic, and happy endings.

She has two ornery fur-babies, plays the piano every day, and loves Disney and yoga pants more than any twenty-something really should. She is most creative after a good night's sleep and the perfect cup of tea. When not writing, Bethany travels as much as she possibly can, and she never leaves home without a good book to keep her company.

If you want to read more about Bethany or if you're curious about when her next book will come out, please visit her website at: www.bethanyclaire.com, where you can sign up to receive email notifications about new releases.

Connect with Bethany on social media, visit her website for lots of book extras, or email her:
www.bethanyclaire.com